Cry to Dream Again

IMMORTAL SOULS
VOL. 2

Cry to Dream Again

(The Prequel to *Silent Music*)

Jane Hawking

ALMA BOOKS

ALMA BOOKS LTD
3 Castle Yard
Richmond
Surrey TW10 6TF
United Kingdom
www.almabooks.com

First published by Alma Books Ltd in 2018

© Jane Hawking, 2018

Cover design: Jem Butcher

Jane Hawking asserts her moral right to be identified as the author of this work in accordance with the Copyright, Designs and Patents Act 1988

Printed in Great Britain by CPI Group (UK) Ltd, Croydon CR0 4YY

ISBN: 978-1-84688-437-5

Cry to Dream Again

FOR MY DEAR DAUGHTER LUCY

1

"Chérie, Édouard! Where are you?" Jacqueline's sing-song voice rang out from within the old farmhouse one morning towards the end of the summer holidays of 1937.

"We're here, Maman!" her children called out in reply. "We're outside – in the sun!"

"Ah! So there you are!" their mother said as she appeared in the kitchen doorway. Her son and daughter were sitting at the rickety table under the eaves finishing their breakfast. "Would you like to come out with me for the last time before we leave?" she asked. "Your grandmother says the bread oven won't heat up because there must be a blockage in the flue, so I said we would go down to the village to fetch a loaf from the baker's, then we might call in at the *épicerie*. I know Louise will be pleased to see us, but I must call on Madame de Grandval first; she's very ancient now."

She gave a light laugh and patted the boy on the shoulder. "Mother says we're out of bread because you eat so much, Édouard! Thank goodness we still have a baker here in Trémaincourt; otherwise we would have to go all the way down to Séringy!" She sighed. "I do wish Mother would have the bread delivered, then she wouldn't have to make it herself!"

Rocking from side to side on the metal seat that had seen better days, her teenage son shook his head as he scraped the last traces of the sweet, milky coffee from the sides of his empty bowl. "No, Maman, sorry. I can't come. Grandfather and I are very busy this morning: I'm going to collect the rest of the straw bales, and the horses are already harnessed. Then I have to get started on the ploughing in Long Field. I promised him I'd try to get that done before we leave. He's out there waiting for me."

"*Ah bon*, I understand – well, what about you, Chérie? It's fine now, so let's go soon," Jacqueline asked hopefully, turning to her seventeen-year-old daughter who was always known as Chérie in France because the pronunciation of Shirley, her English name, presented the French palate with too great a challenge, whereas the translation of her brother's name consisted only of a change in spelling from Edward to Édouard with scarcely any alteration in pronunciation. The major difference, however, was that in England no one ever called him Edward, simply Ted.

"Oh, yes, of course I'll come!" Shirley agreed with a ready smile as she folded her napkin and pushed her bowl into the middle of the rusty old table. "I was intending to do some ballet practice, but I'll come with you. I'd love to see Louise. I suppose I'll have to wear my boots if we're going to walk across the fields to see Madame de Grandval?"

"Yes, of course you will! We can come back via the village for the bread, say hello to Louise and then cut through the wood," Jacqueline replied thoughtfully, surveying the remains of a puddle in the middle of the yard. "The ground is still damp from that heavy shower last night, but let's go now before those clouds coming in from the coast arrive." Musing aloud, she added, "And maybe we'll stop at the *château* here in Trémaincourt to see if Madame de la Croix and the family have returned from their holiday. We ought to call on them before we leave."

"Oh, Maman! Do we have to? She's terrifying, and she's so strict! I know she doesn't like me," Shirley protested, reacting with tongue-in-cheek horror. Her mock horror then turned to laughter and, tossing her blond curls, she said, "Oh well, I suppose she won't eat us, but Madame de Grandval is so much gentler and nicer!"

Her mother indignantly took up the defence of Madame de la Croix, saying, "Oh, come on! You are exaggerating, Chérie. She is a formidable lady and you know that's how she behaves to everyone, but she has a heart of gold – it's her manner, that's all."

"Anyhow, at least she won't want me to go inside the *château* in my boots, so that's a relief," said Shirley, comforting herself that for once her less-than-fashionable footwear would work to her advantage, and Jacqueline had to admit that her strong-minded daughter was right. Appearing before Madame de la Croix in wellington boots would not be well received, even if they were necessary for traipsing over the fields.

"All right, then, maybe we'll just call in at the back door to say good morning to Céline, without seeing the Countess," she agreed. Céline, the housekeeper at the *château* in Trémaincourt, was after all a relative, a cousin of Mémé's, Shirley's grandmother, so there was no reason why they should not stop by to see her.

Perhaps, Shirley decided, calling in at the *château* might not be so bad, since there was a chance that, today being a Saturday, Jean-Luc, the eldest son and heir to the title, might be home from Paris. She herself had just visited Paris for the first time, so that trip could provide a useful topic for a conversation that might renew the easy friendship that she and Ted had shared with Jean-Luc and his sister when they were children. In summer they had romped in the fields together, ridden home atop the bales of straw on the cart at harvest time and spread lavish picnics, prepared for them by Céline, on the grass down by the river. There came a time when adolescent shyness began to create a distance between Shirley and Jean-Luc, and this widened as a mutual awareness of the disparity in their backgrounds and their prospects grew. Undeterred, Shirley knew from the stories in her magazines that social differences counted for little where a pretty girl was concerned, and with her blue eyes and blond curls she was confident of being very pretty. After all, Pa was always saying so. "Ah, how's my pretty girl?" was the first question he had always asked when he came home from work in the evening ever since she was quite little.

Nowadays Pa's opinion was confirmed by the wolf whistles that greeted her wherever she went, so she had no doubt that she could easily catch Jean-Luc's eye. Indeed, last summer, whenever the two families had come across each other out on a long walk, she had positively enjoyed holding his gaze, although at that time they had little to talk about and the Countess had cast a very suspicious glare in her direction. She told herself defiantly, when challenged by the older woman's behaviour, that her prospects were not as modest as might have been supposed from her background. Not only was she pretty, she was talented as well. Although people were always telling her that with her looks she ought to be a film star, that was not her major ambition and, despite all its glamour, came second best in her scheme of things. She was determined to become a dancer, a ballerina, and that was the end to which she devoted herself in such waking hours as were not committed to tedious schoolwork.

Jean-Luc was good-looking and faultlessly charming in an old-fashioned way. These qualities he had certainly not inherited from his mother, who made up for her lack of charm and grace in the energetic direction of matters of local concern – to the irritation of the mayor, whose authority she constantly usurped. In the village she was respected and admired, if somewhat feared on account of her forthright manner, whereas her husband, from whom Jean-Luc probably did inherit his dashing looks and wayward charm, was scarcely ever seen in Trémaincourt. "He's so busy in Paris," Madame de la Croix always explained.

7

On the other hand, Madame de Grandval, over in Mont-Saint-Jean, a cousin by marriage of the de la Croix family, was much quieter and kinder, and treated the family with an affectionate courtesy. Her tumble-down *château*, with its profusion of brambles and nettles, would have made such an appropriate setting for the *Sleeping Beauty* that Shirley sometimes imagined that she was Princess Aurora and Madame de Grandval was the good fairy, if somewhat elderly. While her mother chatted with the old lady, she would turn her back on them and indulge this fancy by appearing to study the rusting piece of machinery, left there by some regiment or other after the Great War in gratitude for the hospitality of the *château*, but in fact giving her imagination free rein in this magical place.

Ever since Shirley could remember, and certainly at least once during each of their stays at the family farm in northern France, Maman would insist on taking the track that emerged in the grounds of the *château* at Mont-Saint-Jean, and inevitably they would pass that monolithic piece of pockmarked equipment. "Ah, children," she would say, if both her offspring were with her, "this old tank has been such a big part of my life. I have to come and see it to remind myself how important it was to your father and me." She would indicate a bullet hole in the right-hand flank of the lumbering machine. "Do you see this? There, it's still there! And look, that's the hole made by the bullet that lodged in your poor Pa's hip in the first tank offensive in the Battle of the Somme! Such a coincidence! This is the very tank that he was in!" Shirley and Ted would maintain impassive, bored expressions, as this story held little significance for them.

The first time they heard it from their mother, the tale was lost on them because they were too young to understand, and these days, more than a decade later, talk of the Great War so remote from their own lives failed to interest them. They had heard it all so many times before: how Pa had volunteered to help the war effort when he read an advertisement summoning motorcycle mechanics to an interview in Birmingham. Abandoning his father's workshop, he headed off for the interview and, in no time at all, found himself drafted into a motley company of engineers who, with no military training, were sent off to somewhere in Norfolk to await the arrival of the new secret weapon, the tank. Eventually they went to France in 1916 to join battle on the Somme, but the tanks available fell far short of the numbers required to mount an overwhelming surprise offensive: many ground to a halt in the mud and others were easy targets for the new metal-piercing German bullets. Pa was one of the victims, except that unlike the majority he was not killed, but escaped from the blazing machine and was helped to safety by a handful of straggling infantrymen who, their own forces decimated because the tanks had failed to obliterate the enemy, were hiding in shell craters until dark. Only then was it safe enough for them to make their way back to the British lines, dragging with them any other unfortunates they encountered on the way.

Invalided out of the Heavy Section, Pa was sent home to England to recover, but on his discharge from hospital had been drafted to France again and had initially been posted to a desk job in the regimental HQ in the *château* at Mont-Saint-Jean, where he met and fell in love with Maman. She had trained as a secretary down in Saint-Pierre and learnt some English with old Madame Tisserand, who claimed to have English ancestry, before going to work at the *château* as a secretarial assistant. So intelligent and well respected was she that sometimes she was called upon to act as a courier, taking documents to the Bureau Central des Alliés, the Allied Headquarters in Paris.

No sooner was Pa registered as fully fit than he was sent to supervise the tank workshops down in the valley, but this presented a problem for the young lovers, since he was expected to live in a billet down there, some three miles away. The solution was for Pa and Maman to marry, so that he could move into the farmhouse with her and her parents, and cycle down the hill to work every morning. The commander declared the situation highly irregular, but he agreed to it out of gratitude for Pa's invaluable expertise and Maman's dedication to the cause, and moreover he provided the newly-weds with a sumptuous champagne reception, which took place in the de Grandval *château*. A photo of the wedding party standing on the steps of the house stood on a shelf at the farm, and there was another one on the sideboard at home back in London. A younger Madame de Grandval, together with her husband, since deceased, featured in all the photos. So, although it could hardly be said that they were close friends, it did appear that there had been a mutual understanding and respect, derived from the shared experiences of wartime, between the unpretentious noble lady and unassuming but hard-working little Maman.

Wedded bliss was short-lived for the Anglo-French couple: in the critical months before the tide turned, every able-bodied tank engineer was called back into active service to confront the last-ditch German counteroffensive that threatened the workshops down in the valley and even the local villages and the two *châteaux*. Pa, who was regarded as able-bodied according to the criteria of the moment, was no exception, and once again he found himself in the cramped, stuffy interior of a tank going blindly into battle. In Maman's opinion it was particularly on account of this, his second exposure to the front line, that he had become so badly damaged: he had been injured a second time, in more or less the same place, by a German bullet. Far worse than that was the effect of the numerous tank sorties in which he had been involved, and which had left him listless and depressed, prone to hallucinations and nightmares.

If the double damage to Pa's hip had left him with a permanent limp and much discomfort, even more troubling for the family were the long spells of melancholy into which he would sink periodically. Horrific memories arose to haunt him day and night, causing him to scream out in his sleep or sit motionless and expressionless for hours on end. Maman used to sit with him, patiently soothing his anguish, encouraging him with her bright smile and eventually restoring his good spirits, though her encouragement had never been enough to persuade him to revisit France. Of late, nineteen years after the end of the war, her patience with him seemed to be wearing a little thin, and her reactions to his so-called "black days and nights" had sometimes grown peevish. It was obvious that she longed for her native country and missed her parents, Pépé and Mémé, the children's grandparents.

The maid who came to the door at Mont-Saint-Jean was new and did not recognize Maman. Her manner was brusque, and when Jacqueline asked if Madame de Grandval was at home, she answered sharply that Madame was not well and should not be disturbed. Jacqueline was disappointed, and Shirley was indignant, but there was no arguing with the maid, so mother and daughter had to set off forlornly back to Trémaincourt. "Let's call on Madame de la Croix now, shall we?" Maman suggested. "Though I'm sorry that poker-faced maid would not let us visit Madame de Grandval. I know she would have been pleased to see us and, who knows, we might have been able to cheer her up." Shirley was less than happy about seeing Madame de la Croix, but to humour her mother she agreed.

They took the short cut through the woods to Trémaincourt and found the *château* there closed up. Céline was out, but while they were standing wondering what to do next, old Claude, one of the stable hands, came stumbling out of a barn. After the Great War that *château* had for a couple of years become a hospital for some of the local victims of warfare, one of whom, Claude, his face disfigured and his mind damaged by German shrapnel, was one of those patients. There, in the *château*, he had received treatment, rehabilitation, lodging and, eventually, work, and so had become a permanent inhabitant, living in the cowshed and receiving his food from the kitchen. He managed to impart the information that the house was empty, and Madame and the family were away. Shirley's relief at not having to face Mme de la Croix was tempered by a tinge of disappointment at not seeing Jean-Luc.

2

Before the war, Louise had run the grocer's shop, the *épicerie*, in the village, while her husband Philippe ran the *estaminet*, where, as a rule, women did not enter, and men could relax with a beer or some rather stronger drinks, smoke, read the newspapers and play cards, darts, or *jeu de grenouilles* (frogs' game), or *jeu de marteau* (hammer game), or other such favourites, often to the accompaniment of the accordion played by a local enthusiast. The two establishments were, in fact, the converted front rooms of the couple's house, divided by the entrance. The *épicerie* was on the right of the front door and the *estaminet* on the left.

The arrangement worked very satisfactorily for everyone: women shopped at the *épicerie* for the wide range of basic commodities that they could not concoct for themselves, such as dried raisins and currants, spices, household soaps and sugars, salt and yeast, plus a selection of medicaments, syrups and pastilles, painkillers, cures for insomnia, slimming products and ointments, for which otherwise they would have to make the journey to town. Louise also purveyed a few fabrics, cottons, linens and serge for making and repairing garments for everyday wear.

After all the effort involved in spending too much money, her female customers could spend even more by sitting down with a cup of the coffee or other non-alcoholic beverage that plump, bustling, enterprising Louise started to provide when she became aware of the need for such a service. For male customers, the end wall of the *épicerie* was devoted to minor items of hardware filling the shelves, such as hammers, screwdrivers, nails and screws in boxes, candles and oil lamps, and a couple of forks and spades hanging from hooks for customers in urgent need of such utensils. In those early days, the men would take their purchases and go to join their friends in the *estaminet* away from the feminine chatter.

Then, at the very end of the Great War, Philippe was killed in an accident in the trenches while cleaning guns, leaving Louise with a baby son, Charlot, and the two businesses to run single-handedly. With a strong vein of rustic stoicism, as well as a good head for figures, she stifled her grief and set to work to amalgamate the *épicerie* and the *estaminet* into one enterprise, so that, ever since, the *épicerie* had held the bar, the tobacco, some groceries and other paraphernalia, enabling women to drink not only coffee, but also something more fortifying, possibly a *tricolore*, a coffee laced with a shot of cognac, or other alcoholic refreshment if they wished, while the former *estaminet* preserved its role as a sanctuary for the men to which they could retire with their beer and where they could play their games and read the newspapers. The establishment had recently acquired the added attraction for the villagers of a telephone booth, ensuring more custom and more revenue for Louise.

When Jacqueline and Shirley appeared in the entrance, laden with baguettes from the bakery, Louise abandoned her customers and rushed out from behind the bar to hug and kiss them. "Ah, Jacqueline, they tell me you are leaving soon! How I shall miss you and my little Chérie!" she exclaimed, twiddling one of Shirley's curls in her plump fingers. "You know, my little one, my film star, you are even prettier than when you arrived. It's the fresh country air! My Charlot will miss you so much!"

Charlot, her son, her only child, had always had a soft spot for Shirley, and these days was positively smitten with her, though she tried to avoid him because he, being a chimney sweep, was always soot-blackened whenever she saw him. Added to which poor Charlot was afflicted by a nervous tic that kept his left eyelid in constant motion, and he also had difficulty communicating because of a distortion in the structure of his mouth. Only his doting mother could understand him, so for other people he had to resort to acting out his meaning, particularly because his handwriting, like his speech, was well-nigh unintelligible. He seemed unperturbed by these misfortunes himself, though Shirley found them unavoidably distracting. She bestowed her sweetest smile on Louise, for indeed she was very fond of her, but had no interest at all in Charlot, the apple of his mother's eye. Luckily Charlot was out on this occasion.

Maman and Louise talked nineteen to the dozen for far longer than it took to buy anything. When she was a small child and first came to France for three weeks every summer, Shirley used to while away the time inspecting those shelves that contained everything under the sun, and then to amuse herself she would imagine that the groceries and the fabrics, even the nails and the screws, came down out of their boxes and tins at night to dance together in lines and circles on the counter and the floor. She saw the forks and spades as male dancers leaping across the shop, and thought how exciting it would be if little boys danced as the small items, the trowels, hammers and screwdrivers, while the sweets and the ribbons became little girl dancers in pretty costumes.

This childish fascination had been replaced by a more adult interest in the conversations between her mother and Louise, which previously she had found boring. Peppered with audible exclamations like "Ah, not really? You don't say!" or "Unbelievable!" or "How could she?", it was mostly conducted in a whisper that Shirley had to strain to hear against the chatter of the other customers. It was certainly much more entertaining than any formal interchange with Madame de la Croix could ever have been, because it was nothing more than gossip.

There had always been the traditional disputes between the mayor and the parish priest and sometimes also between the schoolmaster and the priest; there were the long-standing feuds between families in the village that occasionally erupted into bouts of fisticuffs, and, most interestingly, there were the regular surprise appearances of babies who seemed to come unannounced from nowhere. This was not all, for there were also the night-time elopements of people who were not known to have had any previous close contact with each other. Usually, according to Louise, they left messages for their families saying that they were very sorry, though as she pointed out, that really didn't count for much. Of course there were multiple illnesses and accidents to be recounted as well. Shirley would try to piece together what was going on from such snippets of information that she could pick up, and in her mind's eye converted her impressions into a lively fandango of characters, passing each other, jostling each other, weaving in and out of formations, appearing and disappearing, all against a dark, indecisive background.

Today, however, the talk was rather different, for when, after a good ten minutes of chatter, Louise paused to take a sip of coffee, Maman took the lead, announcing casually that she and Shirley had been to Paris for the day. Louise's jaw dropped. "Oh, you lucky girl!" she declared, looking at Shirley and forgetting the rest of her tales. "I've never been there in all my years! You must tell me all about it – when I've served these customers" – and she turned hastily to deal with the queue that had been patiently forming, all the while straining to catch snippets of the whispered conversation. Shirley grasped the opportunity with a childish excitement: there was so much to tell, right from the moment they had left home last Saturday morning. Ted had not been at all keen to join them: a true farmer's boy, as everyone said, he had insisted on staying at home to help his grandfather on the farm.

"I'll take you down to the station in the pony and trap, though, and I'll come and collect you this evening if you tell me which train you'll be on," he offered, as if that was a sure way of putting an end to any further attempts to persuade him to join the excursion.

A sudden beam of light had appeared in sad little Mémé's grey eyes when they urged her to accompany them. Without a doubt she would have loved a trip to Paris, but, after a moment, that light had faded when she brusquely announced that there was too much to do in the house and also in her garden, for she had her winter vegetables to plant and more fruit to gather in the orchard. Anyhow, she asked, what would she be doing with Paris fashions? "Ah, no, Jacqueline, Paris is not for me! I've never been there, it's true, but it's too late for me to be thinking of doing that now!" she muttered. "You two go and enjoy yourselves! I have the washing to do. See, I have the black soap ready here and waiting for me," she announced firmly, pointing to a pile of laundry, "but first I must scrub those sticky marks off the range."

Wiping her hands on her apron, she deliberately turned to the great black range, the source of hot water and the means of cooking the wholesome country fare on which she prided herself. With her back to her daughter and granddaughter, she set to work to subject the already shining surface to a vigorous rubbing with an old cloth. Maman shrugged and made just one further attempt at persuasion – "*Allons, Maman, a trip to Paris would do you good; a change of air would make such a difference!*" – but all in vain, because her mother declared that the air in Paris could not possibly be better than the air in Trémaincourt, so Shirley and her mother went on their own. There was, of course, no point in asking Pépé if he would like to come. Even after the trip, on their return late in the evening, no one had shown any great interest in their day out, so here in the *épicerie* was the chance to savour the excitement of that glorious day once more.

Louise listened, enthralled by Shirley's description of the wide avenues and their tall, elegant buildings, of the networks of little back streets with their small shops, of all the famous sights they had seen and of the gorgeous displays in the department stores. The city was vibrant, alive with its own dynamism. Although Maman said she did not know Paris very well and had only been there once or twice during the War, she expertly led the way down into the Métro at the Gare du Nord, then, a little while later, up and out into sunlit streets where the whole city was on display. It was like an enormous, breathtaking theatrical set with the Seine sparkling in front of them, the cathedral of Notre-Dame to the left rising majestically up out of its island and to the right, across the river, over the tops of the trees, the Eiffel Tower soaring skywards. The whole scene was a glittering interplay of light, colour and motion. Against this backdrop, the smartly dressed people, the traffic, even the river, either came towards Shirley or flowed away from her as she stood transfixed at the centre of that huge stage.

"*Voilà! C'est Paris!*" Maman had exclaimed proudly, spreading her arms in a wide gesture at the beauty of the place, the capital city that seemed to belong to her. In England she switched between French and English, depending on circumstances, but in France she spoke only French and forbade her children to speak English, because, she said, they were half French and ought to speak their second language fluently. Ted certainly would have to learn French properly if he wanted to take over the farm at some future date, but Shirley, aware that French was essential to the ballet, had already embraced her mother's tongue wholeheartedly. Long ago she had realized the advantage that her knowledge of French gave her over her classmates, both in dance lessons and in school, because she could grasp what was required much more quickly and could reply more fluently than anyone else. Here her first sight of Paris left her speechless with delight: ballet was the only language she knew that could do it justice. Paris was, in short, the setting for a glorious ballet in magnificent scenery.

"You see how beautiful it is, Chérie!" Maman breathed in awe when, rooted to the spot, she gazed all around her. "Let's see the sights this morning and then look at the shops this afternoon, shall we?" They hopped on and off buses and the Métro, and took in some of the major attractions, though there was no time to go up the Eiffel Tower or linger for long in Notre-Dame. "I suggest we take a boat down the Seine and eat our lunch on board; that will give us more time," Maman suggested, unusually animated, at about midday.

Although it was hours since they had caught the train that morning, Shirley was neither tired nor hungry, so bewitched was she by this gleaming city that infected her with its vigorous appetite for life. She was determined to return, but not as a tourist with a packed lunch. No, she would come back as a famous dancer; she would stay in the best hotels and travel not by bus or the Métro, but in a chauffeur-driven motorcar, and she would buy the latest fashions in the department stores. Her mother interrupted her reverie as the boat made its way upstream, "Come on, you must eat if you want to go shopping this afternoon!" She handed Shirley a crusty chunk of baguette filled with homemade butter and garlic pâté and a cup of coffee from the thermos flask. "You need a new pair of smart shoes, so let's go and have a look in La Samaritaine; it's a superb department store, and I've been longing to see it since it was remodelled a couple of years ago. You'll love it!"

Three days later, in Louise's café, Maman, glancing at her watch, broke into Shirley's breathless narrative. "Come on, dear, it's midday; Pépé will be waiting for his lunch and you know he can't start without his bread."

"Oh, Maman, let me just tell Louise about La Samaritaine," Shirley pleaded.

"All right, but don't take long. Perhaps I should be setting off," said Maman. She bade Louise goodbye and hurried away, for she knew that her father and son would already be seated at the dining table, and her mother would be serving them the first course. Indeed, all Louise's elderly male customers had long since left the bar and the smoking room, slowly making their way to their homes where they could expect to find the table laid and their dutiful wives waiting to ladle out the soup. The menfolk, husbands and sons, would eat in solitary silence, while the women waited at table, standing behind their husbands' chairs, ready to serve the next course.

Shirley took up the gist of her tale again, telling Louise how right Maman had been about La Samaritaine. Not only was it superb but, as far as she could tell, it had no equal in London for its range of goods, for its magnificent wrought-iron staircase and the views from its top floor. They had lingered over the perfumery and the make-up counters and the silk scarves and the leather handbags, before climbing the flights of stairs to the latest fashions and the lacy lingerie and the fabric department with its rolls of satins, silks, cottons and velvets, then the hats and lastly the shoes. "Since we're here, why don't we buy you a pair of shoes for everyday and also a pair for your cousin Edith's wedding?" Maman had suggested. "You haven't forgotten it, have you? In fact, why don't we find you an outfit for it as well?"

Edith's forthcoming wedding did not merit much mention in Shirley's account. Indeed, she had forgotten all about it until Maman suggested buying clothes for it, so she merely told Louise that there was to be a wedding in Pa's family, without going into details. In Paris it was easy for the French side of her character to assert itself, and her French inner voice told her that she wasn't at all sure that she wanted to go to the wedding. Fat, ungainly Edith, so vulgar and so badly dressed, would doubtless look like a meringue on the day. In any case, she didn't know her at all well. What's more, Edith was older than Shirley by at least five years, so it was unlikely that there would be many other young people to talk to among her guests, apart from Edith's sister Thelma, and she was someone whom Shirley preferred to avoid as much as possible.

"Do I *have* to go?" she had asked plaintively.

"But of course you do! She's your pa's niece. You must be there!" Maman had exclaimed, thereby putting a stop to all protests.

"But aren't you coming? And what about Ted?" Shirley enquired pointedly.

"Oh," replied Maman, "Ted will be camping with the Scouts that weekend, but," she added somewhat vaguely, "I expect I'll probably come too."

"You don't sound very enthusiastic," Shirley answered quickly, scrutinizing her mother with a quizzical eye.

"Well, naturally I'll come to support your father, if he wants me there; but you know I don't understand what those people – your pa's family, I mean – I don't understand what they are saying, and I can't talk to them because they don't understand me, so I'd prefer to stay at home. Anyhow," she added, "I think there may be some special function at the Embassy that day. But we'll see."

The question of whether Maman was going to come or not was frankly unimportant in comparison with the prospect of a new Parisian outfit and matching shoes. They had to be worth an afternoon's discomfort and embarrassment in Birmingham. "All right," Shirley relented, "I'll go with Pa."

Her reward was a divine sea-green dress with a tiered skirt in a light, silky fabric, followed by a small hat like a turban gathered into a green rose which matched the dress perfectly and sat neatly on her head. "Oh, my goodness! That must be so pretty! I'm sure you'll look lovely! I can just imagine how your blond curls will peep out round the edges. I'd love to see it, and I'm sure Charlot would too!" Louise exclaimed with a touch of envy in her voice. "So you also bought shoes?" she continued,

CHAPTER 2

without noticing Shirley's grimace at the mention of Charlot. "Your Maman must have been quite carried away!" She fell silent for a few seconds before observing, "She must have spent a huge amount of money."

"Oh yes, we bought two pairs and you're right: they cost a lot," said Shirley confirming Louise's unspoken calculations. "But you should see them, Louise! One pair is green and shiny with high heels and pointed toes for the wedding, and the other is in smart brown leather with a slight heel and laces for everyday, so, you see, we really have something to show for our trip to Paris!"

"And your mother? What about her? Didn't she want a new outfit for the wedding too?" Louise enquired.

"No, no," Shirley replied, remembering how her mother had taken notes of the dresses that had caught her eye, and had even tried some of them on. "No, she said she had plenty of lovely clothes in her wardrobe, and she would be sure to find something there, or will make something that will do – if she decides to go!" As an afterthought she added, "She hasn't made up her mind whether to come."

"Oh, is that so?" Louise commented, raising one eyebrow.

3

There was a balletic skip in her step, in spite of her wellington boots, when Shirley made her way back up the road to the white-walled, red-roofed farm. Her brother and Pépé were, as expected, already seated at the table, too busy eating to talk, while Mémé and Maman stood between the table and the stove, waiting for the men to finish their meal so that they could then sit down and have their own lunch. The bread had all but been demolished. This traditional, unquestioned segregation at mealtimes annoyed Shirley, who found it difficult to keep her opinions to herself. Mémé worked quite as hard in the house, the dairy, the vegetable garden, the meadow and the orchard and out in the fields as Pépé did, she reasoned, and should be permitted to sit at table with him. Maman, too, deserved better than that, so did she herself, because one day she was going to be famous. This custom was the complete opposite of the way that men, young and old, behaved in the stories she read in her magazines: there, men were unfailingly chivalrous, holding doors open for ladies, pushing in their chairs at table and helping them onto trains and into cars, and would never dream of taking precedence over them. Ted, of course, revelled in the sense of superiority over his older sister that these Gallic mealtimes afforded him. Such behaviour, coupled with the primitive sanitary arrangements and the mud in the farmyard that splashed onto shoes and clothes – not to mention those geese in the meadow – were the rustic aspects of France that Shirley could not endure, and which she refrained from talking about in school. If she ever came to live in France, she would without a doubt have to live in Paris.

She had made no secret of her opinion at home in English, but had simply been advised by her mother that this was the way things were, and always had been, so it would be better to keep quiet for fear of offending her grandparents, especially because Mémé tried so hard to keep everywhere indoors so spotlessly clean, in spite of all the mud outside and the cows in the adjacent barn. In any case, Maman reminded her that, as far as they were concerned, the arrangement was temporary, only for the duration of the holidays.

Maman's calm good sense set Shirley's imagination racing. She envisaged her small, neat mother with her heart-shaped face and deep brown eyes, as a princess who had been captured by wicked sorcerers, a witch and a magician, and trapped in a spooky, remote farm where no one ever spoke and where no music or dancing was allowed, and where she was made to scrub floors, cook meals and wash dishes. Only when a handsome, fair-haired foreign prince, that is to say Pa, came searching for the lost princess, did she escape and fly away with him to a new life. None of this was true, quite the contrary in fact: Mémé was no witch and, though anxious and tearful from time to time, was the sweetest person you could wish to meet, so unlike troublesome Granny Marlow back in London, and Pépé, though taciturn and gruff, was at heart honest and generous. To be fair, neither of them would have subjected their daughter to such a horrendous existence. But still, it made a good story and would make an even better ballet. Undoubtedly the plot owed some of its elements to *Cinderella*.

Despite her subservience, Mémé was not silent for long: waiting at table had given her time for reflection. When her granddaughter appeared in the doorway, pink-faced from her brisk walk home, she observed sadly: "*Ah, te voici!* Here you are, Chérie! I was just thinking, it will be such a long time till we see you all again, and I shall miss you so much!" Then, brightening up, she announced her latest culinary idea. "I think we should kill a goose for your farewell dinner and make a party of it! They're not properly fattened up yet, but there'll be enough to go round. You'll catch one for us, won't you, Édouard?"

"Of course I will," her grandson replied, unperturbed at the prospect. Shirley could not fathom how her brother could bear to go into the meadow, let alone catch one of those honking, hissing creatures. Nevertheless, it would be bound to taste good, especially with some early apples and cider.

The two men left the table together and went out to continue their work in the deluge that Shirley had avoided by running the last fifty yards up the incline to the farm when drops had started to fall out of a leaden sky. Water poured off the roof, held at bay from the walls by the wide overhanging eaves. Although the house was kept dry, the lack of guttering caused a muddy puddle to fill the yard in no time at all.

"There, I said it was going to rain," Maman observed. "What are you going to do this afternoon, Chérie?" she asked as she cleared the table.

"Oh, I don't know, maybe I'll do some *pliés*. I hope there'll be some news about that audition when we get home," Shirley replied with a rueful sigh. She went into the bedroom that she shared with her mother. At least in there, as a special concession to the two of them, the floor was level and boarded, unlike the kitchen with its cold, uneven flagstones.

On the way she paused in the small salon next to the kitchen to look at the strange photo, draped in black gauze, on top of the piano that was never opened. It was such a shame that it was permanently closed, because Ted was a natural pianist. From an early age he had taught himself to play by ear, not here in France, but in England at the home of his other grandparents, Grandpa and Granny Marlow. While interminable, tedious English family gatherings took place around the table in the dining room, he would withdraw to the living room after Sunday lunch and tap out tunes, initially simple and by degrees increasingly complex, on the upright piano. At first the family would listen in amazement, but gradually their attention lapsed and they returned to whatever topic of conversation was uppermost in their thoughts. Maman, who could never quite keep up with the gist and the twists and turns of English gossip – for that was what passed for conversation at these gatherings – would slip away to the living room, quickly followed by Shirley, and together they would play draughts or halma while listening in admiration to Ted's performances of popular songs and dance tunes. Since Grandpa Bill died, visits to the Marlow house were rarer, because Granny complained that she found family parties too tiring, although she really meant that they were too expensive, and whenever they did call on Granny in passing, Ted usually went out to Grandpa Bill's workshop to repair old bikes rather than seat himself at the piano.

Both Shirley and her mother were saddened that this evident talent no longer had an outlet, either in England or in France, but Ted himself did not seem too upset at its untimely end, because, he said, he preferred to spend his time in Trémaincourt out in the fields. Maman had gently remonstrated with her mother several times in an attempt to persuade her to allow the piano to resume its rightful role, but the latter was so distraught at the mere mention of it that the subject had to be dropped. Her reaction was always the same: "Oh, my darling son!" she would cry tearfully. "If I heard that piano being played, I would expect to see him seated there, running his beautiful hands up and down the keyboard!"

Shirley was drawn to the photo standing on the piano, and could not pass it without stopping to peer at the young man in the picture. There were other similar photos that stood on the old sideboard; they, like the piano, were draped in black and showed a very young man in army uniform. He slightly resembled Maman, fine-featured with dark eyes; Maman used to stand solemnly gazing at him, and years ago had whispered to Shirley and Ted that the young man was her older brother Georges, who used to play the piano, but the children should not ask their grandparents about him because he had been killed in the War, at Verdun, and it would be too upsetting for them to be reminded of all that.

This silence had never made sense to Shirley: why stand the photos on the piano if the memory of Georges was too upsetting to talk about? She promised herself that when she grew up she would not brush things under the carpet but would be completely open about everything that mattered to her. It was such a pity, because she sensed that Ted would have liked to play, despite his denials. Although he was obviously talented, he refused to play the sort of beautiful, flowing ballet music she liked to dance to, saying that it was too difficult, and limited himself to popular dance tunes, so she left him alone and did not badger him further.

She pulled her canvas practice shoes out of her suitcase and put them on. Humming one of her many melodies from the ballet, she stretched her arms above her head and bent double to touch the floor before using the ledge of the small, square window for want of a *barre,* though it was not wide enough for her foot to rest on it properly: she felt stiff and clumsy, unable to touch her nose to her knee or extend her leg higher than about forty-five degrees, which was worrying, because her turn-out – the rotation of the leg from the hips to the toes – had evidently worsened through lack of practice. Next, she worked with more success through *pliés, tendus, frappés* and *fouettés*, and then moved away from the window ledge to practise the trickier steps and routines in the centre of the room. For those, she discarded her canvas shoes and donned her satin point shoes, the ones she was particularly proud of. After two and a half weeks with little practice, however, the *pirouettes* did not come easily, and, what's more, her balance *en pointe* was less steady than it should have been. Dispirited, she tried a *petit allegro* of *sautés, échappés* and *relevés,* but quickly ran out of breath. She was annoyed with herself, wondering where all that technique that had enabled her to pass that high-graded exam, the Advanced Two, only weeks before leaving London, had gone.

Even worse than the breathlessness, she discovered that she had been eating too much and had put on a layer of fat around her middle in those idle weeks. That layer would have been imperceptible to anyone other than herself, but she well knew that it was there. It was hardly surprising, because her grandmother's meals were so delicious: her *coq à la bière*, *lapin aux pruneaux*, *carbonnade à la cassonade*, even her *chou farci*, all usually accompanied by that warm bread from her oven, when it worked properly, with fresh salads from her garden, and followed by a rich, creamy dessert or *tarte à la rhubarbe* or *aux poires*, were mouth-watering, the more so because one had to wait for one's turn at the table. That was probably the cause of the problem: watching Ted and Pépé eat gave one such a ravenous appetite.

Why, oh why, she asked herself, had she not done more practice, especially with such a crucial audition coming up in the wake of the Advanced Two? There was no excuse for, apart from the day in Paris, a couple of day excursions by train to a resort on the coast – where they had met their grandfather's gaunt, unsmiling sister Suzanne, and her genial husband François, a fisherman – and frequent trips by bus to the markets in Saint-Pierre and Freslan-la-Tour, there was not a lot else to do, except for taking walks with Maman or giving Mémé a hand in the garden.

On the other hand, it had to be said, the trips to the markets were all so entertaining that they always took longer than expected. There was, of course, the shopping for the more exotic goods that Louise did not stock, such as lemons, oranges and bananas, and Mémé always insisted on buying double quantities of fish for Friday's meals, remarking that Grandfather needed much more fish than meat because he was forever complaining that a single portion of fish was never enough to fill him up. Not only did they linger over lengths of more colourful material for new clothes or curtains than were available in Louise's shop, but they also bought knitting wool and needles for winter cardigans and pullovers, gloves and scarves. Often they would treat themselves to coffee in one of the cafés around the main squares in those small towns, but, come what may, Pépé – and Ted too – would be expecting a cooked meal to be on the table by midday, so there was always a rush to catch the bus back.

Although Mémé baulked at going to Paris, Saint-Pierre and Freslan-la-Tour were within easy reach of home. In one or other of the market towns, she would chat with acquaintances whom she used to meet in the days when she ran a market stall, selling her own produce of vegetables, fruit, eggs and cheese, which she transported to market in a big covered wagon, now rotting and unused down in a corner of the meadow. Sometimes the colour would come back into her faded complexion when she came across old friends from her past, which, Shirley supposed, must have been in the dim and distant days of the nineteenth century.

Mémé admitted that she was glad of the chance to get out and meet people, because winter would soon be drawing in, so she did not expect to be coming to market very often, and then only if the weather were fine and mild. Moreover, after half an hour on the bus on the way home, the walk up the lane from the stop on the main road was quite a struggle for her with full shopping bags. How she regretted no longer using the old wagon pulled by the shire horses, or the little pony and trap, but the pony was too frisky for her to control nowadays.

Shirley delighted in these visits to the markets, even if they took her away from her daily practice. Here the variety of colour and the constant activity were like an open-air ballet, where shoppers holding their wicker baskets under their arms milled across and around the stage, nodding to each other and pausing to exchange news, while stallholders held up their wares with extravagant gestures to attract attention. Leading characters would come to the fore, the blind accordion player, for instance, or a passing troupe of acrobats, or the man selling puppies that everyone wanted to stroke, or the fruit seller juggling oranges and lemons, or the flower seller who would offer the audience bouquet after bouquet of bright summer blooms. Shirley saw herself in the role of the principal dancer, a young girl standing at the side of the stage witnessing the spectacle and finally joining in an extravagant *tarantella* with all the participants.

Mémé was not as lonely at home as might at first appear. She would doze after lunch and then reminisce, either to herself or to a willing audience, about the visitors who used to appear in the afternoons. In days gone by, at least one pedlar or hawker would come to the farm to sell his or her wares every day and, over a cup of coffee, recount news from neighbouring villages. Having packed her precious ballet shoes away, Shirley almost thought that she could detect the unmistakable aroma that used to herald the arrival of old Gilles, one of those travelling salesmen from the past. He walked leaning on his stick beside the little home-made cart that his faithful hound pulled along the country lanes. According to Mémé, they could cover vast distances each day in all weathers, because the cart was well protected by a lid and covered with a tarpaulin. It contained a set of scales and vats of shining dark coffee beans, the aroma of which made the wares so enticing that old Gilles would be sure of a sale in every house along his route. Today would have been no exception. His dripping mackintosh would be hanging up to dry over the stove, and Shirley expected to see him seated in the kitchen, but was always disappointed; instead she had to persuade Mémé to tell her more stories from the past.

Apparently a man with a similar small cart containing a grindstone used to arrive every six months or so to sharpen knives, and with a long rough stone he sharpened shears and scissors as well. Nowadays he came only occasionally, perhaps once a year. Other traders, or *colporteurs* as Mémé called them, brought needles, pins and sewing notions to the door, and the basket weaver came to repair shopping baskets and trugs for use in the garden and orchard, always with an eye to a quick sale if the old items were beyond repair. Mémé said she had hoped that the man who repaired chair seats might come again, because the seats of two of the best chairs were so badly frayed and worn that she feared they might give way, but for some time he had been working only from his market stall and it was too great an effort for her to take chairs down to Freslan-la-Tour or Saint-Pierre. She had not been so keen to receive visits from tinkers, however, because they had a bad reputation and were suspected of setting fire to a barn on a neighbouring farm from where they had been turned away. She clearly enjoyed telling these tales of the motley collection of travelling salesmen, some on foot, some in carts, some on horseback, and if she dozed off in the middle of one of her stories, Shirley would go back to her room and there invent little dances in which she tried to capture the personalities of the tradesmen. The only problem was the lack of music to accompany her choreography.

In the bedroom, after the hundredth repetition of the story of the coffee merchant, she was intending to make up a dance that would incorporate his elegant, sinuous gestures and the exotic nature of his goods, without slavishly copying the Arabian dance in *The Nutcracker* ballet that she and Maman had seen two years earlier, but, in ballet mode once more, her thoughts turned from the distant past to the immediate future. In a few days' time she, Maman and Ted would be on their way back to England, and that letter of such significance, informing her of the date for the longed-for audition with the new, much trumpeted Sadler's Wells Ballet, might already be lying on the mat at home in London, which meant that the audition could be only weeks or even days away.

What would she do if she failed? She could not bear to go back to school, because she was quite certain that she had learnt all she needed to know there. She had scraped through the School Certificate before her seventeenth birthday; her French was excellent; of course she could speak and write English and she knew where to find most of the important countries on the globe. The problem was that she wasn't at all good at maths. Nonetheless, she must have managed to do her sums well enough to pass. What else was there to learn that could possibly be more important than the ballet? And in her heart of hearts she really did want to be a ballerina more than anything else in the world. Musicals were another option, but they would definitely be second best. She worried whether her pa had, in fact, picked up the audition letter off the mat, and hoped he had not lost it.

Poor Pa! There alone in London. Well, he wasn't completely alone because according to his letters, Granny had come to stay with him and keep house, which she had done every summer since Grandfather Bill died. Whenever she remembered that she hadn't given Pa much thought in the weeks they had been away, apart from sending him a postcard from the seaside, Shirley felt a pang of guilt. Once, long ago, she had innocently asked why he didn't come with them on their annual visits to Trémaincourt, only to be shocked at the uncharacteristic vehemence of his response.

Normally, if she asked a question, he would pull her gently towards him and say very seriously, "Now, my pretty little poppet, we shall have to think carefully about this one." And then he would clear his throat, apparently considering his answer extremely carefully, never laughing at her question but making it seem the most important thing he had had to do all day. So, for instance, when she asked, "Why do I have to go to school?" he had made a show of thinking for some time before giving his reply: "Well, first of all, what would you do all day at home while Maman and I are out?" Then, without waiting for an answer to that, he would continue: "In school they have very clever teachers who can teach you a lot about all sorts of interesting things, so that when you grow up you will be able to read all the maps and the signs and travel about, even perhaps go to see your French grandparents on your own. Then you will be able to look after yourself and your money, and make sure that you are given the right amount of change when you buy something – a new dress or shoes, perhaps." He had observed at her slyly out of the corner of his eye. "You would have to do all that, you know, and you would need to be able to read and do sums and write postcards to Maman and me." She accepted his explanation without a murmur and went off to school every day, persuaded that it was the best thing to do.

When, nevertheless, on that one occasion she had asked why he did not come to France, her innocent question did not produce the same beguiling hesitation or smile. Quite the contrary, he put his hands to his head, clutched fistfuls of his sandy hair and all but screamed, "Don't ever ask me that again! I've seen enough of France to last me a lifetime, and I'm never going back there!" Maman came quickly to the rescue and shepherded the two small children away. Then she went back into the living room, closing the door behind her.

With their ears to the door, they could hear her cooing soft words – at first in French and then changing to English. "*Calme-toi, Reggie, mon petit chou, calme-toi!* Don't worry, there's no reason for you to come, if you don't want to. You can stay here if you like or go to Birmingham and spend a few days with Winnie while we're away." Some time later the door opened again, and she ushered the children back into the room. Reggie, their father and her *petit chou*, her little cabbage, had collapsed into an armchair as sweat poured from his brow and his hands trembled. "There, children," Maman said calmly, "go and give your father a hug." Rushing to his side, Shirley scrambled onto his knee and flung her arms around his neck. The memory of that outburst, though long ago, was still so vivid and so frightening that she never repeated the question; indeed she knew the answer to it. For all that, not once did Pa complain at being left in London while his family abandoned him. Strangely too, he never minded when his wife spoke to him or to the children in French, and he was always eager to hear every detail of their visit on their return home.

4

A gale blew from the south-west, whipping up white horses on the heaving waves out at sea as the queue of passengers began to board the ferry for Dover. "Why did it always have to be like this at the end of the summer holidays?" Shirley asked herself, dreading the next three hours on board. The journey out from Dover to Calais earlier in the summer was usually calm and relaxing, preparing the family for the frequently sun-soaked days ahead in the French countryside, far from the pressures of life in the London suburbs, but whenever they returned to England the sea was choppy, the skies grey and, with a few exceptions, everyone was sick. Trying hard to hide her discomfort from her children, Maman would sit in the passenger lounge with her eyes firmly shut for the whole crossing. Edward, on the other hand, who was fortunate to be one of the exceptions, would join a handful of the male passengers pacing up and down the deck, braving the wind, the sea spray and the rain and hanging on to the railings when the ship lurched. He admitted to feeling a little queasy, but usually that wore off when the ship was approaching Dover.

The return Channel crossing invariably made Shirley feel wretchedly sick, a sensation that stayed with her for most of the subsequent train journey to London. Last year, determined not to be overcome by it, she had experimented with a new approach, which, born of desperation, had a ring of foolhardiness about it. Her mother certainly thought so when she announced, "I'm going out on deck; it's too stuffy for me in here."

"You'll be blown overboard!" Maman exclaimed, anxiously surveying her daughter's slight frame.

"No, no, don't worry: I'm not going to walk up and down. I'm just going to get a breath of air, that's all." Maman gave her a headscarf and let her go, too feeble herself to protest further. This method had worked reasonably well last year, so Shirley was inclined to try it again.

While the ship laboriously turned round in Calais harbour before heading out to sea, she did a quick mental survey: the wind was coming up the Channel, so, to be well out of it, she would need to find somewhere to sit on the starboard side of the vessel. She grabbed a handrail and hovered briefly in an entrance where the door was permanently open, flung wide by the boat's heavy list to port. The effort of pulling herself up through the opening was like climbing a steep, slippery rock. Although they were by now out in the open sea, away from the protection of the harbour, it was definitely pleasanter to be on deck, where the angle of the ship pinned her safely to the wall, than in the hot, airless lounge. At least on this side of the listing boat she was not in danger of sliding overboard. Hoping that her brother was safe on the same side, she edged her way along the deck until she came to a slatted wooden bench in a sheltered recess, and here she sat down. The only disadvantage was that she had exchanged the wind for the dirty smoke wafting over her from the ship's funnel, but that was better than exposure to the full force of the storm.

There were no other women on deck, although there were several men, struggling to stand upright as they tried to walk up and down. Among them, she was reassured to see the recognizable shape of her brother, a year younger than her, though much taller, and solidly built like Pa; but there the similarity ended, since Ted had inherited Maman's colouring, while she was fair like her father. Reassured that he was safe, she closed her eyes, thinking to while away the time by creating some sort of dance scenario out of this stormy seascape.

At the ballet school, Miss Patience had for so long encouraged her pupils to make up little dances from everyday scenes that such a pastime had become second nature for Shirley in idle moments everywhere she went. "Now girls," Miss Patience would say, "I don't want to be told what you did on your holidays, I want to see you dance it!" The farm, the markets, the seaside ports, Louise's *épicerie*, all had provided perfect dance scenarios that were beginning to evolve quite naturally into more sophisticated ballets than her early childish attempts, and now she had Paris to add to her repertoire.

The rough sea might also lend itself to some sort of interpretation in dance, if only she could find a storyline for it, but she decided against introducing mermaids for fear of lessening the impact of the storm, though other less fanciful sea creatures, whales and dolphins for example, might be more appropriate. She was just beginning to make some sort of choreographic order out of the chaos of the elements when a well-known voice interrupted her drowsiness. "I say, sis, you do look green!" She opened her eyes to see her brother standing in front of her.

"Oh, thanks, that really does cheer me up!" she laughed. "I'm all right. How about you?"

"Oh, not too bad," he nodded, "not so far to go now."

It was no surprise to see him there, but it was unexpected to hear him speaking English again after three solid weeks of French. "Why have you started speaking English?" she asked.

"Well, why not?" he replied. "We'll soon be in Dover."

"Couldn't we carry on speaking French a bit longer?" she pleaded. "Just till we get to London? Then nobody else will be able to eavesdrop on what we are saying, and we can poke fun at the other passengers! It helps pass the time."

He nodded, remembering that this was a game they often played when on public transport in England. "Yes, I suppose so, if you want to, and I expect Maman will be pleased. It's always hard for her when we leave France, and it'll be a whole year before we come back! You'll be eighteen and I'll be seventeen. We'll be so old! Roll on next year, then I'll be leaving school and can come back here to work on the farm! So let's speak French now if you want to, shall we?"

He was right. She never exactly said so, but Maman would pine for days for her native country and her parents: during that time she would say little and her behaviour would become untypically absent-minded, as if she had retreated into a protective shell where she could continue secret conversations with Mémé and occasionally with Pépé in her own language. Her children had discovered that, at these times, the best way to winkle a response out of her to their questions was to phrase them in French.

The sad truth was that dear Maman had few friends among her English neighbours, even though, with her French manners, she was unfailingly polite and courteous to them whenever she saw them in the street: she was a foreigner and they were suspicious of her. It had been the same at the school gate when she went to collect her children. Other mothers talked among themselves, but they always gave her the cold shoulder, just as their children had tended to ignore Shirley and Edward, calling them names, the favourites being "frog" or "snail" in their early days at primary school.

Shirley's strength of personality quickly overcame this unpleasantness. She shrugged off the name-calling and was blessed with the power to attract other children to her, enchanting them with her bubbly nature and her endless stream of ideas for games and little plays, many of which contained a degree of naughtiness directed against the strait-laced staff, who would feature in the said dramas as trolls and goblins. At first Edward pretended in school that he did not know any French, did not speak the language at all and had never been to France, which was bad for his school reports, but succeeded in making him friends. Eventually he was able to discard this deception because he was well liked for his practical abilities and his lackadaisical attitude to schoolwork, so that no one cared any more. There were no problems in the private schools that they attended later; quite the contrary, their French background was a cause of fascination and admiration.

For Maman, however, it was only at the French Embassy that she met people whom she could talk to easily and comfortably. There, where she was employed as a secretary and translator, she found friends of her own nationality, so naturally she gladly accepted whatever work was offered her and her part-time job was imperceptibly becoming a full-time post. Now that Shirley and Edward were older and could let themselves into the house after school, she often came home just in time to cook supper before Pa's return. She would be cheerful, her cheeks would be flushed and she would simply explain that she and her friends had stayed behind to have a coffee or a glass of wine after work, or that the Ambassador had arranged a brief reception for the staff in honour of one or other of the many saint's days commemorated in France.

In an exhilarated frame of mind after these functions, she would sometimes expansively remark how lucky she was to be living and working in London despite the grime and the fogs. From time to time, she could be heard to wish that her parents would come and stay in her comfortable home. It was only a small semi-detached house, but it was in a pleasant area and had three bedrooms, a garden and a garage. In addition, it was reasonably warm in winter and had a proper bathroom, which could not be said of the farm. Mémé and Pépé never did come, although that was not at all surprising considering how rarely they travelled from home. At most they went once or twice a year to Beauport, which lay south of Boulogne, for the day to visit Pépé's sister Suzanne and her husband, and they relied on Pépé's brother Baptiste to call on them, which he did from time to time. He had fought in Champagne, where he had stayed after the war when he married a girl from Reims.

Ted appeared to be talking to himself in the wind and the rain on deck; in fact he was saying something about wishing that they, or at least he, could go back to France before next summer, because, at last, Pépé was contemplating buying a tractor. "Think how much easier ploughing will be!" he exclaimed. "I can't wait to drive it!" But Shirley was not listening. Her attention was distracted by the approach of two men coming along the deck. One, tall and lean, was middle-aged and rather distinguished in appearance. The other looked to be about her own age, or perhaps a little older, and of similar height to his companion, who was probably his father. Even in such blustery conditions, the younger man was extremely handsome. His hair was wind-blown, but he looked healthy and fresh-faced, not green or sickly.

As they approached, she ostensibly gave Ted her full attention, afraid that if she watched the passers-by she might seem to be staring at them; even so, out of the corner of her eye, she had the distinct impression that the younger man had smiled on passing her. She hoped that once they reached the end of the deck they would turn round and retrace their steps. Maybe if she dropped something, her handkerchief perhaps, the younger man would bend down to pick it up for her and then she would be able to talk to him, if only to thank him and pass the time of day, doubtless remarking what an awful crossing it was. She would go on to say that it was often like that at the end of the holidays and he might ask where she had been. Perhaps a proper conversation might start up between them and they would exchange names and addresses. That was what she hoped would happen, but she couldn't find her handkerchief in her bag and in any case the wind would probably blow it away.

Although her brother was still talking, she had absolutely no inkling of what he was saying until he tapped her on the shoulder to attract her attention: he was commenting that the sea was not so rough now and was asking if she wanted to go inside. "No, I'll stay out here: the air is fresher," she said when she caught his gist.

"Whatever you like, but I think I'll go back to Maman and see how she is," Ted said, and made his way to the door. She watched him go, keeping her eye on the other two men at the same time.

They had come to the end of the deck, where they did indeed turn round, apparently to walk back in her direction, but they reached the door at exactly the same time as Ted and followed him inside. Although Shirley wished that she had gone with her brother, the passing encounter with the young man had given her a brilliant idea for her ballet: the prima ballerina, who would be struggling to survive when the ship she was travelling on rolled onto the rocks in a rough sea, would be rescued by a handsome man who appeared from nowhere, lifted her high and carried her away, whether to dry land or to his distant kingdom, she was not yet sure.

Five minutes later, she decided to join her mother and brother and found the crush in the lounge suffocating. There was no sign of her mother or Ted, and even if they were only half a dozen paces away she would not be able to see them, because she wasn't tall enough to look over the heads of the crowds, pushing and shoving all around her. She stood for a moment debating what to do and where to go, not that there was anywhere to go, because she was hemmed in on all sides. If she allowed herself to be pushed along by the flow, eventually she would most probably meet up with her family in the customs shed, but the big problem was that her passport was in Maman's handbag. She spared a thought too for poor Ted, who would be struggling with her luggage as well as his own and Maman's, and that prompted her to take the initiative. She tapped the man standing in front of her on the arm. "Excuse me, please, I'm sorry to bother you, but could you tell me if you can see a small dark-haired lady wearing a red coat with a tall, dark-haired boy? She is my mother and he is my brother, but I'm not tall enough to see them." The words came out in a rush, in English but with a strong French accent. Only when she had finished speaking did she discover with a beating heart that the person she was addressing was the older of the two men who had walked past her out on deck.

The man turned towards her with a delightful smile. "Of course I'll look for them," he said in the kindliest of manners. "It is a terrible crush in here, isn't it? And I'll ask my son to have a look too." He took a step aside, and Shirley was able to see that the younger man was standing immediately ahead of his father. "Alan," said the father, prodding his son, "this young lady can't find her mother and brother. Can you see a small lady in a red coat with a dark-haired boy?"

When Alan turned round, Shirley saw only the deep pools of his eyes, which made direct contact with her own. She stared into those eyes, and all movement, all thought, all awareness of her surroundings, even of her request, came to a halt as time stood still for an eternity. The ship, the crossing, the wind and rain, the heat and stuffiness, the multitudes, all were forgotten in that meeting of souls. But what seemed to be an eternity could not have been very long in real time because distantly she heard the young man say, "Hold on, let me have a look." He turned away and scanned the throng while she collected herself. "Yes," he said with his back to his father and Shirley, "I think I can see two people answering that description over there."

He turned to his father and Shirley again; in the interval his face had reddened. "What's your name?" he asked shyly. She hesitated between Chérie and Shirley, but opted for the latter. "If you come with me, Shirley," he said, "I'll clear a path through to your family. Here, take my arm so that I don't lose you on the way!" Shirley breathed in deeply. Her legs, usually so strong, were weak beneath her, and she feared she that she was going to faint. She clutched his arm as he steered her through the jostling crowds to where Ted and Maman were standing.

"*Ah, merci, Monsieur!*" Maman exclaimed in relief when she saw them approaching.

"*De rien, Madame, c'est un plaisir!*" the young man replied graciously; he smiled down at Shirley who was still holding on to his arm. She let go in some embarrassment and nodded her thanks. He looked at her and held out his hand.

"*Au revoir,* Shirley," he said. She shook his hand, trying to respond, but the words would not come. She could only gaze into his eyes, longing to ask him whether they might meet again. But of course she did not. He turned on his heel and went back to join his father. Shirley stood spellbound.

"*Oh! Mon Dieu! Qu'il est charmant!*" Maman remarked, her eyes on her daughter who blushed deeply.

The crowds were beginning to drift slowly towards the passenger gangway and dry land. Too self-conscious to permit herself to look back to see whether she could pick out Alan with his father in the queue, Shirley's one and only desperate wish was to see him again. She allowed herself to turn round as they stepped out onto the gangway, but there was no one she recognized in the mass of people behind her. Hoping for a better look at the disembarking passengers, she trailed after Maman and Ted as they marched down onto the quay. Then, as the family walked towards the customs shed beyond the end of the boat, she was overjoyed to see Alan and his father coming down a different gangway, although she was surprised to see them wheeling bicycles. Evidently they had been on a cycling holiday! She could not bring herself to wave and they did not notice her. She wondered where they had been, but trusted that there might be a chance of meeting them again after all. "Come on, Shirley, we'll miss the boat train!" Ted called from some ten yards ahead of her. She quickened her pace to catch up with her mother and brother.

5

They arrived home tired and flustered after the long journey, the rough crossing and the interminable questions posed by the English officer in the customs shed at Dover when he opened their luggage and rummaged through almost all of their purchases. Maman had been ahead of her children in the queue because a burly businessman had pushed in between them. In Maman's suitcase the officer found the eggs, carefully wrapped in cardboard, that she had sent Ted down to the meadow to collect that morning, and a bottle of wine that she had bought for her husband. "Where do these eggs come from?" the officer asked sharply. On hearing that they came from the family farm, he abruptly confiscated them. Young and decisive, he was all too obviously intent on proving himself in his job. "There will be duty payable on this bottle of wine, madam, and I would advise you not to bring contraband goods into this country in future!" he announced, glaring severely at Maman, who shrank under his gaze, before issuing her with a docket for payment that she had to take across the shed to a cashier. The businessman seemed to be carrying minimal luggage; he opened his briefcase, the customs officer looked cursorily inside and waved him through with a smile.

When Shirley moved forward to the head of the queue, the officer brusquely instructed her to open her suitcase, with no hint of a smile or any of the polite niceties that one would be sure to encounter in France. "So you do know, don't you, that there will be duty to pay on these goods?" he enquired as he gingerly lifted the silk dress and the hat out of her case and held them up.

Her instinct told her at once to employ the secret weapon that she had discovered long ago as a small child: she tossed her blond curls very fetchingly, stared the good-looking customs officer straight in the eye and let the tears fall down her cheeks. "Oh, but Maman bought this outfit for me for my cousin's wedding," she sobbed in broken English.

"Ah, just a moment, will you please, miss?" said the customs officer hastily. His cheeks reddening, he tried to avoid Shirley's insistent stare. "Please wait while I check with my superior."

He dashed off and was away for a good fifteen minutes while other passengers in the queue started to grumble, making acerbic remarks in Shirley's direction. "Silly girl! She should have known better," a bulky woman – who was evidently wearing layer upon layer of her own contraband purchases – commented dismissively in a posh voice for all to hear.

"These French, they think they can get away with anything!" an elderly man blustered.

Even her brother, who was standing to one side, sighed in exasperation, saying, "Why do you have to go buying clothes in France? You go to Oxford Street often enough; couldn't you have found something there? At this rate, we'll miss the train." Shirley stepped back from the queue and looked away, on the verge of genuine tears. Further down the line, beyond the bulky posh woman and the elderly man and beyond a good half a dozen other passengers, she was startled to catch a glimpse of Alan, who was craning his neck to see what was going on at the front of the queue. When she caught his eye, he smiled in recognition and waved. That smile and that wave gave her the courage to ignore the insults being bandied about around her, and she returned his smile with a rather coy wave, which annoyed the detractors even more. They all turned round in puzzlement, looking for the recipient of such attention, but Alan had already turned away.

A second or two later, Shirley caught sight of the customs officer returning; she wiped her eyes ostentatiously with her lace handkerchief, one that Mémé had given her as a parting gift, saying, "I don't have much to give you, my little Chérie, but take this old handkerchief. It is rather special; it belonged to my mother. It is made of Valenciennes lace."

"I'm sorry to have kept you waiting, mam'selle," the customs officer's tone was now more conciliatory. My superior says that there might be some duty to pay on these items, but it depends what they're made of." He got out his official notebook again and began to fill in another docket, asking Shirley for her age. On learning that she was seventeen, he appeared even more embarrassed. He turned to Maman, who had just returned from the cashier, and was standing beside her offspring in bewilderment. "My apologies, ma'am, I didn't realize that this, er, this young lady was your daughter. I thought she was much older and was travelling alone." Shirley enjoyed watching his confusion: his face was the colour of a tomato. "Let me see these items," he waved in the general direction of the new outfit. "They're not silk, are they?"

"*Mais non, non,* of course not!" Maman replied in her strongly accented mixture of French and English. "How could I afford silk?"

"Well, then, I think we can let them through, but please remember next time to be careful what you bring back from France." Stepping back to collect his thoughts and recover his composure, he realized that he was being remiss in his duties. "But before I let you all go, I must inspect this other bag," he added as a hurried afterthought. While Shirley folded the dress and put it back in her suitcase, glad that the customs officer had not spotted the green shoes, he turned over her brother's muddy clothes with scarcely a glance and so missed the cheese that Maman had secreted away in that suitcase.

Although Ted kept urging his mother and sister to run to catch the train, Shirley dragged her feet, desperate to find out which direction Alan and his father would take. She hoped against hope that they would be bringing their bikes onto the train and storing them away in the guard's van. In her mind's eye she imagined the father and son walking the length of the train in search of seats and she concocted a plan. If she placed her handbag on the seat next to her, she might manage to reserve that for Alan or for his father, and, even better, if Maman also reserved a seat with her handbag, they might be able to keep two seats.

Ted's fears were justified: the boat train had already left, so there was a long delay before the next one, ample time in fact for Alan and his father to emerge from the customs shed, but there was no sign of them. Beginning to lose heart, Shirley was forced to conclude that they had left the port by some other route and had already headed off by road into the Kent countryside, which meant that it was highly unlikely that she would ever see Alan again. Disappointment, not in any way alleviated by the grey skies and the bleak outlook from the train, was a poor exchange for the joys of life in France.

Not surprisingly, her father was anxious about them, because it was much later than he expected when at last he heard their ring at the door-bell. It took him some time to come to the door and his agitation did not ease with their arrival. That in itself was not so unusual, for he often had bad days, particularly when his war wound played up. Maman, who had been none too pleased at losing the eggs to the customs officer, was annoyed at finding little food in the house and was not very disposed to show her husband much sympathy. "I thought you would be bringing French bread and eggs with you..." Pa said lamely, trying to justify the lack of preparation for the returning travellers.

"Excuses, excuses! How could you, Reggie!" Maman exclaimed irritably. "All we have is cheese and a bottle of rather good wine I brought for a special occasion, and this certainly is not a special occasion! The wretched customs officer confiscated the eggs. They've never done that before, so I don't understand why they should do it now!" Her discontent developed into indignation. "And, Reggie, didn't your mother do any shopping before she left? I left a list for her to take to the grocer's. It's only just up the road! And the greengrocer comes past with his barrow most days. I suppose I'll have to see if there's a tin of something, but it might have to be baked beans." Baked beans and cheese it was for their distinctly unpalatable supper, mitigated by a small tin of French pâté lurking in the cupboard and evidently undiscovered by previous customs officers.

"*Voilà!* I am very, very tired and I am going to bed," Maman declared in annoyance after she had eaten as much of the frugal meal as she could face. What a comedown this was after her mother's delicious meals! How could she bear to stay in England with its dull people and its dreadful food? If only Reggie were a little livelier, it would all be so much more bearable.

"I need to talk to you; please stay down a little longer!" her husband pleaded with her.

"Can't it wait till the morning?" Maman retorted. "Look how tired the children are too!" Ted and Shirley both baulked at being described as children.

With one voice they contradicted their mother: "No, no, we're fine. We'll stay and talk to Pa for a while."

Shirley stared at her father; there was no doubt that something was very wrong. He was tired, not physically in the way that they were tired after their travels, but drained of colour and of spirit. In their absence he had lost more of his fair curls, the curls that she had inherited, and his skin had become flabby and grey. He had scarcely moved from his armchair since opening the front door to them, yet he appeared uncomfortable in it, shifting his increasing weight every couple of minutes to a different position. Though he was not generally renowned for the fluency of his conversational skills, he was even less communicative than usual. Nevertheless, when Ted began to tell him about work on the farm, he brightened up.

That was the weirdest thing: in spite of his insistence that he would never go back to France, Reggie listened eagerly to their news. "The harvest was fairly good, though it did rain on us several times. We've planted winter wheat in the field across the track," Ted was saying, "and I think Pépé is going to sow the field nearer the village with oats next spring."

"That's good, that's good," Pa mused.

"Oh, and I forgot to say, Pépé is thinking of buying a tractor!" Ted exclaimed. At this Pa really did liven up, asking what model of tractor and all manner of technical questions of the sort that Ted and Pépé had discussed many times at great length.

"Well, old chap, you'll have to learn about tractor maintenance then! I dare say I can teach you something about that!" Pa said in evident delight, although he himself admitted that he was unlikely ever to see the tractor himself.

He then turned to his daughter: "So Shirley, did you enjoy yourself?" It was time for Shirley to resume her English identity and abandon her French nickname, Chérie. Shirley, her English name, had been given to her in honour of her paternal grandmother's second name, though she was none too pleased that the name had been appropriated by an American child film star. She wanted that honour to be reserved for herself.

"Yes, Pa, thank you. It was all right. Well, Maman and I went to Paris, and that was wonderful. Maman bought me a dress and a hat and shoes for Edith's wedding; would you like to see them?"

"Go on, then, Shirl," said Pa having recovered something of his old self. "I had forgotten about Edith's wedding. It's in two or three weeks isn't it? Come on; let's have a fashion show, then, if you're not too tired!" Late though it was, Shirley was delighted to don her new clothes, even though the audience consisted only of her brother and her father, and not the officious customs officer, or Alan, that handsome young man who had been such a help to her on the boat. She was sure that she would never forget him or his name and she would look out for him everywhere, in the street, on buses, on the Underground. She had already set her heart on seeing him again.

Pa's reaction was appreciative and surprising. "You look lovely! It does my heart good to see you, Shirl, and to have you back. You too, of course, Ted," he said looking proudly at his son. "You know, I really do enjoy your stories of the farm!" He spoke absent-mindedly to no one in particular, "I sometimes wish I could face going back there. I suppose I have a lot to be grateful for, not least the happy times I spent there with your mother, even if the rest of it was grim. That's where we were married after all – and it's not the fault of France or the French…" Words failed him and a satisfactory conclusion to his sentence eluded him.

Shirley was about to ask whose fault it was when her mother called down the stairs, "Come on, children! It's time for bed!"

Shirley was on the point of heeding her mother's call, but suddenly remembered the all-important letter. "Oh, Pa!" she exclaimed. "How silly of me! How could I have forgotten! The letter about the audition, has it come, do you know?" Her mind had been so focused on her encounter with Alan and the immediate past that all thoughts of the letter had been erased until now.

Pa moved awkwardly in his chair. "Audition? What audition was that?"

"Oh, you know what I mean, the audition with that new ballet company, the Sadler's Wells Ballet; I applied to before we went away," she replied in exasperation at his forgetfulness.

"Ah, that. No, I haven't seen any letters for you, but go and look on the hall table; I expect your granny may have picked up letters off the mat while she was staying here." Shirley went straight out into the hall, but found nothing on the table apart from a vase containing some withered flowers, presumably brought by Granny but not cleared away before she left. Having searched under the table, she took the vase into the kitchen, emptied the water into the sink and threw the dead blooms into the waste bucket, fearing that something had gone wrong. There was no question that her application had not arrived at Sadler's Wells, because it would have been sent off with the others by Miss Patience, who was such a stickler for punctuality, accuracy and detail that there was little risk that she would have overlooked it. What would she do if there were no audition and no place for her in the company? The thought of going back to school was too dreadful for words. She would go and call on Miss Patience first thing the following morning. She put her head round the living room door. "Night, night, Pa, see you in the morning!"

"Was the letter you wanted there?" he asked.

"No, nothing, nothing at all." Disconsolately, she climbed the stairs and fell on her bed, but did not sleep. Anxieties about the audition and images of Alan revolved in her head until eventually they intermingled in her dreams and Alan became the prince who lifted her high above the mass of grey, worrisome creatures writhing about on a stage beneath her.

6

Both Shirley and Ted were surprised to find their father still at home the next morning when they came downstairs for breakfast. Maman had been out to buy bread and other essentials and the milkman had already called, so the cupboard was not as bare as it had been the previous evening. Pa was sitting in his armchair, appearing to have been there all night. Maman shook her head more in frustration than in sympathy. "Your Pa's in great pain; it's his war wound," she said. "He can't go to work."

After the War had finished and he and Maman had moved to England, Pa had become a railway engineer, despite his mental trauma. On the railway he was able to forget about the horrors of war, and trains, which had fascinated him since his childhood, were his lifeblood; he worked on them all day and read about them in magazines at home in the evening. He had only very rarely taken a day off, even when he had flu after the War, or when his wound made him limp badly, so this was undoubtedly one of those awful days that afflicted him from time to time; sometimes they were caused by his nightmares and hallucinations, or at others by his injury; occasionally – and this was probably what was happening now – by both together.

Maman, who only yesterday in France had tried to make light of her sorrow on leaving her parents and her native land, looked like a lost child back in this foreign country. "*Vraiment, je ne sais pas quoi faire,*" she said, reverting to French for comfort. Shirley and Ted did not know what to do either, though at first they were not unduly concerned, for Pa usually recovered quickly and this crisis would be sure to blow over, as others had in the past. "At least you must be off to school, Ted, that's certain; go and get your games kit," said their mother, collecting her thoughts, taking action and giving her son his orders. Ted groaned, ate up his cereal and went out to collect all his school belongings, which had been lying untouched in the cupboard under the stairs for the duration of the holiday.

"Right, I'm off, then," he announced more positively, appearing in the doorway laden with satchel, winter games kit and various other items necessary for the term. "Hooray, only one more year in school for me and then the farm in France!" he exclaimed joyfully to an unreceptive audience. Strangely, no one had mentioned anything about school for Shirley or told her to collect up her satchel, so she remained seated at the table. Her future after the School Certificate had been the subject of some discussion at the end of the summer term. She had made it absolutely plain to her parents that she was not going back to school, but Pa had insisted.

"Look here," he said, "you've done very well in the School Certificate and who knows what you might do if you stay on. Maybe you could become a teacher."

"But, Pa," she had protested, "I don't want to be a teacher. You know I want to be a dancer!"

Maman, who had encouraged her to dance since she was four years old, had taken her every week to Miss Patience's ballet classes, had made costumes and helped with scenery for shows and supported her application for the audition, had intervened, taking her daughter's part, "Reggie, you know she wants to dance and you know how good she is." But Pa, who did not know how good she was, since he had little more than a passing interest in the ballet, only enough for him to sit patiently through the said shows to please his wife and daughter, was purely and irritatingly pragmatic in his reaction.

"She can dance as much as she likes in her free time," he said, "but she must have a proper training also. That's why we've paid for her to have a good education. Remember all those women left penniless as a result of the last war? Well, if it happens again and I reckon with the way things are going, it might, she'll need to be able to earn her own living. Anyhow, you'd think she would be grateful that I want her to have some independence. There aren't many young women who are given that sort of opportunity." After this uncharacteristically long and decisive pronouncement, he sank back into his customary reticence, but Shirley would not let the matter rest.

There had been tears and tantrums, all the more poignant because father and daughter rarely disagreed. For such a mild-mannered man, Shirley had found him unexpectedly dogged. She resented his obstinacy, because she was certain in her heart of hearts that there was a sure future for her in the ballet, and there he was, intent on depriving her of a golden opportunity. Finally, after much argument they had reached a compromise: if she succeeded and was awarded a place at Sadler's Wells, that would be the end of it: she would go back to school only until the dates were fixed for her dancing debut. On the other hand, if she failed the audition she would stay in school at least for the first term of the sixth form, possibly for the whole academic year, until other openings, perhaps a secretarial course, could be found for her. In Shirley's opinion, the sixth form was for girls who were applying to university, so for her it would be a complete waste of time.

Pa had said that he didn't mind paying the fees for one term or longer if he could rely on her to apply herself and make the most of whatever time she spent in her last year at the school. She had therefore come back to England expecting him to announce that the fees were paid and that she should be ready for school the next morning, but at the table after breakfast there was no talk of school. Perhaps in his discomfort, that earlier dispute had slipped Pa's mind, and Maman was apparently too preoccupied with other things to think about it. Edging towards the door, smartly dressed apparently for a special occasion at the Embassy, she said quite sharply to him, "I must be going, I'll be late for work and there will be piles of papers waiting for me, but I'll call at the surgery to ask the doctor to visit you sometime today. You'll be at home to let him in, won't you, Chérie? Your Pa can't even walk to the front door." With that she left.

"Don't you worry, Shirley," Pa said. "If you want to go out, I'm sure I can get to the door, but I'm so slow that the doctor might have gone away by the time I open it. Maybe you should leave it ajar or on the latch and pin a note to it telling him to come in."

"No, no, don't you worry," she replied half-heartedly. "I'll stay until he comes." She carried the breakfast things into the kitchen, where she let the cutlery fall into the sink with a clatter, though she did have sufficient presence of mind to be more careful with the crockery. So I'm to be Cinderella, she thought to herself as she practised some *relevés* at the kitchen sink while doing the washing-up. Self-pity began to gain the upper hand over confusion and annoyance, however much she tried to reserve a modicum of sympathy for her poor Pa, reminding herself that he clearly was not well. "I'm trapped here while Maman goes off to her posh job and Ted goes off to school!" were the thoughts that grumbled at the back of her mind. Given the circumstances, she almost wished she could have gone to school too.

It was an age before the doctor arrived. She used the time to unpack the rest of her suitcase, having taken out the wedding outfit the night before. Then she pulled out her leotard and ballet shoes to practise a few steps *en pointe* in the narrow confines of her bedroom, but nothing seemed right. After doing some warm-ups on the floor, stretching and bending low over her knees, she went out and used the railing on the landing for a *barre*. How quickly the memory of those carefree weeks in France was fading; it was beginning to seem as if they had never happened.

As for that young man, Alan, a hundred years could have passed since their brief meeting on the boat. She closed her eyes in frustration at the dismal turn of events here at home: Pa was indeed very poorly, Maman was impatient with him, the audition letter had not arrived, there was nothing to do, not even school, and she couldn't leave the house. She wondered where Alan was and whether he had returned to his school, or, if he had left school, whether he was at university. Was there any chance that he might be thinking of her as she was thinking of him?

Her exercises were interrupted by a noise on the staircase; she looked over the railing and with alarm saw her pa pulling himself in agony up to the bathroom. She called down to ask if he needed any help. "No, no, I just have to take it slowly, Shirl," he said grimacing, while he dragged himself upwards, slowly, step by step, clutching the banister with all his might. I need to visit the bathroom and then I think I'll have a little lie-down." On reaching the landing, he stopped for breath, leaning against the wall.

"I'll make you a cup of tea and bring it up," Shirley volunteered.

"There's my girl!" he said trying to muster a faint smile. "You are kind to your old Pa!" He wasn't really very old, only in his forties, but he looked an old man, pale and weary, getting heavier and balder by the day and hunched up with the pain in his leg.

Forgetting her own preoccupations, she made tea and sandwiches for his lunch and took the tray up to him. The advantage of his being upstairs was that she had the whole extent of the dining room for her practice, and, with the gateleg table folded against the wall and music playing on the wireless, she began to experiment with a couple of routines based on the scenes at Freslan market. No sooner had she begun to feel more contented than a ring at the doorbell announcing the doctor's arrival interrupted her practice. After a long session upstairs with her father, he gave her a prescription for painkillers and other medications, which he said would help ease the discomfort. "If you could go to the chemist's and fetch these items straight away," he said, "your father would begin to recover quite quickly."

At last Shirley's mood changed and she too began to feel better about the turn of events, for finally she would be able to get out of the house and even call in at Miss Patience's, only a brisk ten-minute walk beyond the chemist's, to find out what had happened to her application. Her father had his head under the bedclothes when she tiptoed upstairs to say goodbye to him, so she did not disturb him, supposing that he was asleep. Taking her ballet shoes with her in case there was any chance of some practice, she ran out of the house and along the road to the chemist's on the corner. The half an hour that the chemist said he would need to assemble the prescription gave her the very opportunity she had hoped for. With her spirits restored at the prospect of entering those hallowed precincts where dance reigned supreme, she let the shop door bang shut behind her and sprinted down the road.

"Shirley!" Miss Patience exclaimed. "We were wondering when you would be back! I hope you've brought lots of ideas from France for us to choreograph!"

"Oh yes, quite a lot," she replied, hastily dismissing all those ballets she had created in her mind's eye in France, "but I've really come about the audition. I haven't heard anything; there's been no reply to my application. Pa said he hasn't seen any letter for me. Have they been in touch with you?"

Miss Patience was baffled. "No, I haven't heard anything, but I sent your application off with the three others and they've already had replies asking them to present themselves at Sadler's Wells a week today."

"But what can have happened to mine? How can I be ready in a week's time?" Shirley asked in dismay.

Miss Patience put a plump arm round her shoulder. "There, there, don't get upset. I'll find out what's gone wrong. I expect it's some administrative error and I'll make sure they give you an audition. I can't let them ignore my star pupil!"

This sensible reaction reassured Shirley, who was about to ask if the dance studio might be free for a while, but Miss Patience anticipated her unspoken request. "The dance studio is empty for at least the next half-hour, maybe longer, so why don't you go in there and practise? You know how to use the gramophone so just find your favourite music, warm up and dance, dance, dance!" That was definitely some consolation.

It was exhilarating to be back in that place where she felt so much at home, and where she was able to give free rein to her longing to dance, but even then she could not entirely rid herself of the fear that the application might have been rejected. Nonetheless, the aptly named Miss Patience inspired confidence: she was that sort of person. Her heart and soul were devoted to the ballet and to the dance school that she had founded when she became too old to dance on the major stages of the world. Rumour even had it that she had toured North America with Diaghilev's company, but she never spoke about herself. She did, from time to time, provide unwitting hints that the rumour may perhaps have been true, saying, "I think this passage requires a little more Russian technique to make it more dramatic!" or, "Maybe we could introduce a more modern extravagance in our gestures here. Imagine you're dancing in a Stravinsky ballet!" Her distinguished past, and the contacts she had made during the course of it, fully explained why she encouraged her pupils to apply to the exciting new company that had opened a couple of years ago in north London.

Maman was already home from work and Ted from school when Shirley came in with the bag of prescriptions. Pa was in the dining room sitting in his armchair and Maman was beside him. Her healthy, tanned complexion had drained to sallow grey, suggesting that she had received a shock. Her coat and handbag were flung over a chair. "What's the matter?" Shirley asked in alarm, tinged with guilt at having delayed her return by much more than the half-hour that the chemist required. "Is Pa worse? Here, I've brought the prescriptions; the chemist needed half an hour to make them up, so I've come pretty much as quickly as I could." This in fact was not far short of the truth. The studio was eventually required for a class, so there had been a limit on Shirley's practice time, although it had definitely taken more than half an hour. Nonetheless, for the sake of an extra ten minutes, it was time well spent, which she didn't think her pa would have denied her, because it had been enough to ease her frustration, calm her anxieties and put her in a better mood.

"No," said Maman, "Pa's hip is not worse, but the news is not good. We'll tell you about it after we've eaten." She went into the kitchen to prepare the evening meal.

Ted tried to enliven the atmosphere at supper by recounting the events of the day in school, peppering his account with jokes which he and his pals had thought riotously funny – for example the arrival of a new master called Mr Baggs, already traduced to "Bags o' money" – but he did not succeed in raising the merest hint of a smile from his parents. Shirley started to tell them that she had managed to call in at the dance studio and that Miss Patience was going to chase up the audition appointment, but when she saw that they were not listening the words dried up in her mouth.

Finally, while they were all still at the table, Maman said curtly, "Children, your pa has something to say to you."

"Couldn't you tell them?" Pa pleaded.

"Why me?" she retorted. "It's your news, not mine. It's not for me to tell them."

Pa cast his eyes down at his empty plate. "Well, I don't suppose it will be too bad," he began inauspiciously. "Dr Forbes came to visit me this afternoon, as you know, Shirley, and after he had inspected this silly old hip of mine…" Here he stopped as if searching for an acceptably humorous way to proceed. "As I was saying, after he had taken a look at this silly old hip of mine, he said that, although he could give me painkillers, aspirin and so on, he couldn't do anything to cure it. It might get a bit better of its own accord, but if I want to be able to walk on it for the rest of my life, I'll have to give up working on the railways. The work puts too much pressure on it, clambering over engines and getting down on my hands and knees to crawl underneath them and so on." He stopped talking, hanging his head to hide his grief.

Shirley reached out and patted his hand. "Why is that so bad, Pa?" she asked. "You can do whatever they do in the station office, can't you? Couldn't you be a stationmaster?"

"I don't think so," he replied gruffly. "I'm an engineer; I would be no good in an office. It's a huge responsibility, dealing with people and all that. And I'm happier with engines."

"Well, there must be something else you could do." Her voice trailed away because at that instant, despite her best intentions, nothing else occurred to her, but she did begin to understand why he had covered his head with the bedclothes when she had gone up to say goodbye that afternoon.

"Reggie," Maman said, "you haven't told them the whole story."

"Give me time," he begged, before continuing with a hesitancy born of reluctance. "You see, children, the fact is that we don't have bags of money; we only have the money I earn and a little more put aside. Of course, there is your mother's money from her job, but I wouldn't want to draw on that. Our savings will last us for a while – perhaps, if I'm lucky, until I find a new job, but if I don't manage to do that, the money will run out."

A leaden silence descended on the room. Ted was the only person who dared ask the all-important question that was hanging in the air. "So what are we going to do?"

Reggie looked helplessly at his wife, hoping that she would say something: she turned away from him with a defiant gesture, which said bluntly, "It's your problem, you deal with it." For all her apparent elfin fragility, Maman could be quite obstinate; she had a way of closing in on herself and passing the buck when she considered certain issues to be too difficult to handle. Shirley often found this sort of attitude very irksome, because she herself preferred a more direct approach, tackling problems head-on. Admittedly this could lead to trouble if other people failed to see the situation from her perspective, or were slow in understanding her point of view because they needed to have it explained to them in fine detail.

Pa shook his head: his sadness was obvious for all to see. "I'm afraid to say," he announced dolefully, "we might have to move house."

True to form, it was the confrontational aspect of Shirley's personality that asserted itself now. "What?" she said aghast. "You don't mean leave here? Leave this house, our home?"

"Yes, Chérie, that is just what he means," Maman confirmed tersely. "He means we will have to leave our lovely house, my lovely house."

Pa kept his eyes on the floor. "I hope it won't come to that, but it depends what happens in the next month or so," he said quietly.

"Where can we go?" Shirley persisted, all too aware that a move might take her away from the dance studio.

"I can't answer that yet," said her father. "Remember, it was only this afternoon that Dr Forbes told me that I have to give up work. I haven't had time to think about it. We shall have to wait and see what turns up." Silence reigned again, broken only when Pa made a desperate attempt at forced optimism. "I haven't tried the medications yet. Let's see what effect they have, shall we? Who knows, I might be better by tomorrow morning!"

Shirley noticed that Ted was keeping very quiet. He was the first to leave the room. He patted his father on the back as he went. "Something will turn up, you'll see," he said comfortingly, though without much conviction. It was obvious why Ted was not too concerned. Only one more year in school, then, after the School Certificate, he would be free to leave for France and take over the farm. Pépé had already promised him that they would work together for a year or two while he gradually worked towards retirement and while Ted mastered all the necessary skills.

7

By the next morning, Reggie's medication had indeed begun to take effect: not only was he less pale and haggard, he was no longer limping in pain. Ted left for school and Maman already had her coat on when her husband announced, "I think I'll go down to the railway yards to see how things are down there."

Maman did not react; it was left to Shirley to protest. "But, Pa, you know what the doctor said. And you know how ill you were yesterday!"

"Yes, yes, I know," Pa said waving her concerns away, "but I need to find out what I can manage to do. And," he added, "I also want to see if there's any other work for me on the railway." Maman shrugged and, turning on her heel, went out; Pa then fetched his jacket and he too left the house. He walked with a jaunty swing, almost a swagger in his step, whistling as he went. Shirley again found herself washing up the breakfast things. She put them in the sink, ran hot water over them and left them to soak while she ran upstairs to collect her ballet shoes and her leotard.

Yet again there had been not so much as a mention of school, so she would be a fool not to make the most of her new-found freedom. With any luck the studio would be unused during the day, so she might be able to dance till mid-afternoon, when the first younger pupils would be arriving at the end of their school day. She was rummaging in her dressing-table drawer for a hairband when the doorbell rang. She ran downstairs expecting to find the postman, or the milkman with his bill. To her annoyance, there was Granny Marlow standing on the doorstep. "Ah, Shirley dear, how nice to see you back! How was France?" she said, pushing her way past her granddaughter into the house. Her remarks and her questions never anticipated a reply: she was not particularly pleased to see Shirley, nor was she at all interested in France; indeed, for her "France" signified foreign, a designation which obviously included Maman, and was not to be trusted. What's more, it was a country about which she had heard far too much earlier in her life when her son had gone there to fight and had returned badly wounded. Nor when she pointedly asked, "Isn't your mother at home?" did she wait for an answer, but carried on, at last coming round to the question for which she did want an answer because it concerned her own property. "Have you seen my scarf, dear? I think I must have left it here. It's the blue silk one your Aunt Winnie gave me for my birthday, so I don't want to lose it."

The scarf was lying over the arm of the chair by the hall table; Shirley had noticed it when she was searching for the audition appointment letter, but had thought nothing of it. Granny pounced on it. "Ah, here it is!" she exclaimed. "I knew I must have left it here." She picked it up, but made no move towards the door. Shirley feared that she had come to stay. "Well, dear," she said, "aren't you going to offer me a cup of tea? Here I am! I've come all this way. By the time I get home, Martha, my new maid, will have gone shopping, and I shall be too tired to make myself a cup of tea. You don't expect me to leave without some refreshment, do you?"

"No, no, come in and sit down and I'll put the kettle on," Shirley replied with ill-concealed resignation. "All this way" indeed! Granny had come on a fifteen-minute bus ride, but, of course, she dramatized everything to a totally unreasonable extent, yet so persuasive was she that one could not ignore even the most trivial of her remarks.

Shirley and her grandmother, whose second name she shared, were too similar for comfort. The younger of the two, Shirley Jeanne, was small and athletic; the elder, Millicent Shirley, was small and wiry. Granny had evidently been blonde in her heyday and her eyes were still bright, though nowadays verging on the beady, and both grandmother and granddaughter had strong, not to say domineering personalities that often clashed when they met. Granny, who had been a shop assistant before her marriage, made "hard work" her motto, but the ballet, which she regarded as frivolous, was not included in that category, so whenever she saw Shirley she repeatedly asked her what she was going to do after leaving school. "There's a lovely new department store opening in our high street, Shirley dear. I know you'd find work there," she had suggested on several occasions over the summer.

Today was no exception. "So you have left school, have you, dear?" Shirley gave the tiniest of nods as she poured the hot water into the teapot, having hastily cleared the breakfast crockery from the sink while her grandmother looked on with a disapproving frown. "Well, dear," she said, "after you've finished washing up the breakfast things, I've news for you." She kept quiet while Shirley slowly dried the dishes and put them away. The longer Granny remained silent, the happier Shirley was. Unable to keep her mouth shut any longer, Granny launched into her news as soon as the kitchen cupboard was closed, the crockery slowly and meticulously stacked inside. "I thought you would like to know that they are still looking for staff at Morley's on the high street; I've told them that my granddaughter will be looking for a job soon and they've said you only have to tell them who you are and they'll be bound to have a place on the staff for you!" she announced triumphantly.

Shirley gave her a blank stare and, muttering "Thank you, Granny", she poured the tea, handed a cup to her grandmother the while asking herself why on earth should she, a rising star, with Advanced Two in ballet and with the School Certificate and excellent French into the bargain, want to be a shop assistant? Much as she liked shops, her preferred view of them was from in front of, not behind the counter.

"Well, come to think of it," Granny persisted in her irritating, nasal whine, "you don't seem to be doing much today here all on your own, so why don't you come back with me and we can go in to Morley's together?" True to form, she did not wait for a reply, but went on, "And we could have a look round and you could buy yourself some new clothes." There was never any question of Granny buying clothes for Shirley, because Granny rarely spent any money on other people, only on herself, but she liked spending other people's money for them.

Although Shirley loved shopping, her granny was not her chosen companion for that pastime, so she had to do some quick thinking. "No, sorry, Granny, that won't work. I have other things to do today. And anyhow I don't need any clothes." She brought out her irresistible punch line with great style, investing every word with a hint of a French accent. "You see, Granny, Maman bought me some lovely clothes in Paris for Edith's wedding. So I'm fine for the moment, thank you!"

The stupefaction on her granny's face was a joy to behold; for once it was some time before the old woman recovered her powers of speech. "Oh, I see, that's nice," she stuttered. "That must have been expensive. I... I look forward to seeing you wearing them at the wedding." Shirley did not rise to this challenge.

Searching for some new topic to alight upon, Granny eventually had to resort to the weather to avoid total defeat. "Well, I think I'll be on my way, dear; the sky looks threatening, and I don't want to be caught in the rain. Thank you for the tea," whereupon she made her way to the door. Only then did she remember a reason to delay her departure even longer. "Oh, there, I nearly forgot! I meant to ask how your father is today. He was so poorly the day before yesterday I was quite worried about leaving him before you people arrived home!"

"He's better, thank you," Shirley replied, and then, to ward off further enquiries, she guardedly provided enough information, she thought, to satisfy her granny's display of anxiety, which was probably no more than curiosity. Above all, Shirley wanted to avoid giving the impression that Maman was in any way at fault, because Granny would seize on the slightest perceived criticism of her daughter-in-law and make huge capital out of it. "The doctor came yesterday and gave him a prescription, which I collected from the chemist's, and today it seems to have done the trick, so he has gone to work as usual," she said as casually as possible.

"So your mother didn't stay at home to look after him then?" came the inevitable barbed interrogation, shooting back at her like a dart at a board.

"It wasn't necessary, because I was at home," Shirley replied curtly, annoyed that after all she had been caught unawares.

"I only ask because I've been thinking about your poor father so much," Granny persevered. "I don't think he should be doing that job on the railway." She paused for effect before announcing, "And I think I might have come up with a solution."

"Game, set and match to Granny," thought Shirley in rueful amazement that such a busybody could always succeed in turning the tables and maintain the upper hand. There was no way that she could dismiss her now. "You had better come back in, Granny, and write a note to Pa if you've something really important so say to him," she said, resigned to enduring her granny's company for the rest of the morning. She seated her at the dining table and furnished her with pen and writing paper.

Granny wrote slowly and deliberately, pausing often to gaze out of the window seemingly deep in thought, but such profound contemplation produced only mindless observations such as "Your grass needs mowing, doesn't it dear?" or "Those branches on your neighbours' ash tree ought to be cut back: look how they're overhanging your garden – I wouldn't put up with that!" Thus engaged, she was content to spend an inordinate amount of time on her task, bringing Shirley to the brink of exasperation. How much longer could she possibly need to write a note? Did it really take that long to say what she had in mind? Shirley was at pains to restrain her curiosity, though the temptation to peer over her shoulder was strong. "There!" Granny announced with a final flourish of her pen. "Can I have an envelope please, dear?" She folded her missive, put it into the envelope and sealed it firmly. "Let's hope that will help your father!" She did not say what "that" was, but propped her letter up on the mantelpiece.

The heavens opened, true to Granny's forecast, and there was no way that Shirley could turn her out into the torrential rain, so she made yet another pot of tea and prepared a batch of tomato sandwiches garnished with a handful of lettuce leaves. "That's so kind of you, dear; I never intended to stay to lunch," Granny exclaimed with disingenuous surprise. Then, an hour later, while Shirley was gently ushering her towards the front door, she searched around for yet another topic of conversation: "Dear me!" she began. "I've forgotten to ask about my dear Edward? My lovely boy! How is he?"

"He's very well, thank you, Granny; I'll tell him you were asking after him. Look, I think the rain has stopped. Perhaps if you leave now, you'll get home before it rains again," Shirley said, grateful for the break in the clouds and a glimpse of blue sky and sunshine.

Only moments after the unwelcome visitor had left in the early afternoon, Shirley grabbed her bag and, setting off at a run in the opposite direction from her grandmother, went out before any other callers could delay her. Turning the corner at the end of the road, a large notice in the newsagent's window caught her eye. She was certain that it had not been there yesterday, when she had passed on her way to the chemist's further down the row of shops. It read: "Part-time assistant wanted, good rates, apply within." Beneath it, a more permanent announcement, faded and curled at the edges, invited prospective paper boys also to apply within. Although she hurried on past the shops, and although she definitely did not see her future standing behind a shop counter, the two notices had awakened her interest and she made a mental note to investigate further on her return.

The dance studio was indeed open, but Miss Patience was not there; according to Stephanie, the austere receptionist, she was away for the day, visiting her elderly mother, and the afternoon's classes were going to be taken by one of her friends, who was already in the studio warming up for her teaching sessions. Shirley tried to conceal her disappointment. "Did Miss Patience leave any message for me?" she asked hopefully.

"Yes, in fact, she did: she said you could use the studio if you came in this morning, but obviously it's too late now, and she said that the matter of the audition is in hand, so could you come back tomorrow?" Having delivered the message, Stephanie returned to the papers on her desk, adding only, in a decidedly offhand manner, "I'm afraid the little studio upstairs is also in use." Shirley was left to make the best she could of such scant comfort. Anger at the delay caused by her granny's visit, irritation at Miss Patience's absence and frustration at the disruption of her plans gave way to a feeling of hopelessness at the growing suspicion that the fulfilment of her ambition to become a ballerina was not going to be as straightforward as she had previously imagined. Certainly she should have practised much more regularly in France, but if only she could gain access to the studio now and in the coming week, she was certain of quickly making up for lost time.

Disconsolately she retraced her steps past the chemist's and found herself outside the newsagent's on the corner. Anything had to be better than going home only to be cooped up in the house again at the mercy of uninvited callers. On impulse she went into the shop. "I've come about the advertisement," she said to Mrs Salvatore, who ran the shop with her Italian husband.

Mrs Salvatore looked up from counting the day's takings at the till. "Ah, it's Shirley, isn't it?" she said in surprise. "Just hold on a moment would you, dear? I'm nearly at the end of my adding up here." Shirley waited, her patience wearing thin as the pace of her existence slowed down once more. Since the end of the summer holidays, and since discovering that she had apparently left or rather been withdrawn from school, her life seemed to have come to a standstill. For someone who was confident of being able to direct the course of events, the discovery that she had no control over such a simple matter as planning her day was alarming.

Previously, the school day followed by an hour or two of ballet had given a predictable and satisfactory framework to her routine, but that framework seemed to have fallen apart. Her life in England appeared to consist of washing up, waiting for the doctor to call, attending to an objectionable old woman and fruitless treks to the dance school to find out whether she had even a chance of a future in the ballet. And now here she was in the newsagent's, waiting again simply to enquire if she might earn some pocket money doing a menial job behind the counter.

She was on the point of turning on her heel and leaving the shop when Mrs Salvatore looked up from her calculations with a disarming smile. "Now then, Shirley," she said, "I'm sorry to keep you waiting, but I was involved in a complicated piece of arithmetic! There, it's done now, so what can I do for you?"

"It's about the advertisement," Shirley said, repeating her request.

"Ah, of course, I'm so sorry," said Mrs Salvatore, apologizing for her memory lapse. "I have to concentrate so hard on those figures, I had quite forgotten. Now let's see, we need an assistant in the shop for a couple of hours or so each day, perhaps more in the run-up to Christmas. To begin with, it would be an hour in the morning and an hour in the afternoon, is that any good for you?" Anything had to be better than her present aimless existence, so Shirley readily agreed, stipulating that she might need to take time off if the hours clashed with her ballet classes; she did not on this occasion mention the audition. Mrs Salvatore raised no objection, so it was decided that she would start the very next day. Shirley was halfway through the door when it occurred to her to ask if the advertisement for paper boys was still valid. "Of course," Mrs Salvatore replied, "we always need paper boys!" Shirley promised to tell her brother about it that very evening.

8

That Ted was already home from school was evident from the pile of bags and the satchel left on the floor inside the front door. Shirley would, in the normal course of events, have scolded him, complaining in her prima-donna style that she could have broken her leg had she tripped over them, but not today. Instead she called out breezily, "Ted, Ted, are you there?"

Ted shouted irritably down from upstairs as if anticipating a scolding, "Yes, I'm here – what is it? I'm washing my hair!"

"I've got something to tell you!" Shirley trilled, still in the same cheerful tone. Her brother came down with a towel draped round his shoulders.

"I thought I'd use the bathroom while everyone else was out. We had rugby today and the mud on the field was worse than in the farmyard in France!" he explained more calmly.

"Yes, fine," Shirley said impatiently, acknowledging her brother's attempts at cleanliness, "but I really have something to tell you, and I think you'll be pleased."

Ted frowned sceptically: he didn't believe that his airy-fairy sister with all her fancy notions about being a ballerina could tell him anything. "All right, go on then. Tell me all about it," he conceded grudgingly.

"Haven't you ever seen the notice in the newsagent's advertising for paper boys?" Shirley asked, excited both at being the purveyor of good tidings and at regaining some measure of control, even if it were only over her brother.

"No, I don't think so – well, that is to say, I haven't looked in that window in a long time, and I don't go past it on the way to school," Ted replied, sceptical of his sister's enthusiasm.

Shirley, satisfied that she had aroused Ted's interest, then embarked upon a breathless explanation saying, "You see, I went in to enquire, and there and then Mrs Salvatore gave me a job as assistant in the shop for a couple of hours a day while I wait to hear about the ballet audition, and she said they are always looking for paper boys. So I thought you might get a job delivering papers before and after school, and then we could both help Pa and Maman by bringing in a bit of extra money – we could, couldn't we?"

It all came out in a rush before Ted had the chance to object. He raised his eyebrows, reluctant to admit too fulsomely that his sister had come up with a good plan. He hardly dared say that he might have trouble getting out of bed early enough in the morning, as that, in the current circumstances, would be regarded as lily-livered in the extreme, and it would be seen as churlish to refuse to help out financially, knowing the household to be in difficulty. "So that's agreed, then?" Shirley said looking at him expectantly. "Shall we tell them about it when they come in?"

"Yes, all right," Ted replied, though he wasn't quite sure either that he knew what he was letting himself in for, or that their contribution would make much difference to the family income.

Maman came home early that evening; she was in a good mood. Habitually, at home alone with her children, she spoke in French. "So, what have you been doing today?" she asked each of them. Ted, who was doing his homework at the dining-room table, laughed. "We played rugby this afternoon, but the field was so muddy we all got bogged down and covered in mud!"

Maman looked him up and down. "You've cleaned yourself up well – I'm amazed!" she teased him. "And you, Chérie?"

"Oh, not much," she replied, "I was going out when Granny arrived and stayed till after lunch."

Maman pursed her lips. "*Mon Dieu!* Poor you! Whatever did she want?" she asked.

"She came to collect a scarf she'd left here. I made her a cup of tea, then she said she wanted to write a note to Pa, so I had to let her sit down at the table with pen and paper, and that took for ever, then it poured with rain, then it was lunchtime and, so what with one thing and another, I thought she was never going to leave! By the time I arrived at the dance studio, it was too late, and anyhow Miss Patience wasn't there. So altogether it was a wasted day!" Shirley scowled, still annoyed at the way her best-laid plans had come to nought. "By the way," she added, "Granny's letter is there on the mantelpiece." She nodded towards the envelope standing propped up behind a small bottle and then gasped. "Oh, no! Gracious! Look! Pa has forgotten to take his pills with him!"

Maman flung up her hands in despair. "How could he be so stupid? How could he have forgotten them? Really, I don't know what to do with him!"

This was perhaps not the best moment for Shirley to enquire whether she was going back to school, but since no suitable occasion had presented itself earlier, since Pa was out and since it was at the forefront of her mind because she had been more or less frustratingly idle for two whole days, she grasped the opportunity. "Maman," she asked, "do you know whether I'm supposed to be going back to school or not?" No sooner were the words out of her mouth than she regretted having asked that particular question at that precise moment.

"But no," her mother tartly replied, revealing not only her puzzlement but also her growing irritation, "didn't your pa tell you? You're not going back to school, because at the end of last term you said you didn't want to, and he thought he might as well save the money for the fees, so he didn't pay them!"

Taken aback by the casual way she had been treated, Shirley flared up in a burst of fury attacking her mother, the messenger of her father's decision. "But we had an agreement that I would go to school at least until the results of the audition were known, and here I am with nothing to do! And neither of you have bothered to tell me anything!"

Ill-concealed anger flared in Maman's reply. "Well, it wasn't my fault. Your father is worried that we shall run out of money if he loses his job, so it seems he took the decision while we were away, because even then he wasn't sure how long he would be able to go on working on the railways. Oh, this family! How can I possibly go on living with you all! Your father is such a misery and never takes responsibility for anything, and you both expect to have everything your own way! What am I to do, trapped in the middle?"

"It's not my fault either!" Ted joined in, declaring indignantly, "I don't cause any trouble!"

"Oh you!" His mother turned on him. "You are just waiting to leave home as soon as you can and while you're here, you don't do anything to help! All you can think about is returning to France."

"That's not fair!" Ted, red in the face, shouted at his mother, before storming out of the room.

It was all very upsetting and confusing, because it was not like Maman to behave in this inflammatory fashion. So calm, capable and uncomplaining, until the past couple of days, she had never been known to turn against her children. Defensively Shirley muttered, "I only asked whether I should be expecting to go back to school."

"I know, Chérie, I know," Maman replied, stifling a sob. "I'm sorry. It was so hard to leave Mémé and Pépé: you probably realize that Mémé is not at all well... and I tried to be positive about coming back here, and then the state your father was in when we arrived was so terrible I didn't know how I could bear it, let alone finding that your granny had not left any food in the house." Shirley had never seen her mother so distraught; she found her tears embarrassing and turned away. She wanted to say something sympathetic and conciliatory, but was still too shocked by Maman's outburst, so instead she stood up and went out of the room, leaving her mother on her own to recover. In the kitchen she found shopping bags full of food, which Maman must have bought on her way home, and started to unpack them.

Resigned to resuming her role of Cinderella, she was beginning to peel some carrots, when she heard the front door opening and voices in the hall. "Now, Reggie," an unfamiliar voice was saying, "here you are, back at home. You'll be all right now, won't you?" The faint reply was inaudible. She opened the kitchen door only to find her father slumped on the chair by the hall table and a large man, Jeff, one of his colleagues, leaning over him. Jeff turned round as the light from the kitchen flooded the dimly lit hall. "Ah, Shirley," he said, "I've brought your pa home because he's in a bad way. He had an accident at work: he slipped on some grease and fell. He's been limping all day and his leg is hurting quite badly. I gather he has some pills here at home. Perhaps you can find them for him." With that Jeff patted Pa on the shoulder and took his leave, saying, "I'll be seeing you, old pal, but take things easy, won't you?"

"You left your pills on the mantelpiece, Pa. I'll fetch them for you and you'd better take them straight away," Shirley said, reassuring him and forgetting how angry she had been with him only minutes earlier. She ran into the dining room, where her mother was reading a French newspaper that she had brought home from the Embassy.

"So your pa's come home, has he?" she asked without moving from her armchair.

"Well, yes, Jeff brought him home because he had a fall and he's rather shaken," Shirley replied.

"That does not surprise me at all," her mother remarked impassively. "I'll go and cook the supper." Shirley grabbed the pills, collected a glass of water from the kitchen and gave them to her father. He was a pathetic sight! Such a change from the younger man who, his self-esteem renewed and restored in mind and body, had strode out of the house that morning, declaring that he was just off to the railway yards to see if he could cope with a day's work. She dreaded the evening ahead.

Pa sat in the hall for half an hour until his pills began to work, and then heaved himself into the dining room, which his wife had vacated some time earlier with only a nod in his direction as she slipped into the kitchen. When she served the evening meal, he tried his best to gloss over the unfortunate events of the day by awkwardly congratulating her on her delicious fried pork with blackcurrants, *porc au cassis*. "Wonderful!" he said. "Wonderful to have my French cook back again!" But she was impervious to his blandishments.

Ted tried to lighten the atmosphere by broaching the plan that his sister had devised that afternoon for earning some money, giving her full credit for the idea. "Shirley and me, we're going to earn some cash to help out!" he announced. "She saw this advertisement for jobs and paper boys in the newsagent's, so I'm going to do the paper rounds and she's going to work there part-time." Then, to Shirley's amazement, he added, "Because you're not letting her go back to school, she thinks she should get a job!" Such support from her brother was unheard of.

Both parents looked up from their plates in astonishment. "Well, I'm glad that someone in this house has shown some initiative!" Maman exclaimed.

Pa nodded. "Yes, well done both of you!" He was pensive for a minute or two, as if trying to recollect something he had forgotten, then tapped his forehead. "Ah, Shirl, I knew there was something I had forgotten! I'm so sorry; I should have told you about your school, Midvale. They wrote to me while you were away, saying that they were forced by lack of funds to amalgamate with another private school – I think it was called River Lodge School, or something like that. It's miles away, a long bus ride, and they're putting the fees up." He paused for breath. "So, since you said you wanted to leave anyhow, I thought there was no point in paying more fees. I'm sorry, I should have told you sooner, but with the pain in my leg it went right out of my mind.

"Oh, I see," Shirley said quietly, totally disarmed by this confession, which painted a very different picture of the situation than her mother's version had done. "I see, Pa. I understand. I was wondering about it. Oh, and by the way, in case I forget to tell you, Granny came over today and she left a letter for you on the mantelpiece. I'll get it for you."

After he had read the letter, Reggie pushed it across the table. "Here, Jacqui," he said to his wife, "have a look at this." She picked up the letter in such a disdainful fashion that one might have thought it was contaminated with some deadly disease, and read it through. She then handed it back to him with a shrug.

"What do you want me to say?" she asked. "Your mother is interfering again!"

"Oh, I don't know. It might be something to bear in mind," he replied in as neutral a tone as he could muster.

Shirley and Ted listened, watching each parent in turn, and then glanced at each other, both of them uncertain whether to say anything or keep quiet. Shirley took the plunge. "Won't you tell us what it's about?" she asked her father.

"Yes, why not?" he replied. "Your Granny says that she is worried about me and my war wound, and she thinks that working on the railways is too much for me. A distant cousin of hers has a business over in south-east London and wants to retire, so she wonders if I – we – would like to take it over."

"What sort of business?" Ted asked.

Pa gave a slight laugh. "Would you believe it? It's a newsagent's!" Maman walked out of the room.

9

Contrary to all expectation, the atmosphere in the household appeared to have returned to normal by the Thursday morning: Ted set out early to begin his paper round, Pa went off to work blithely whistling with his pills in his pocket, Shirley started her job in the newsagent's and, since it was her day off, Jacqueline donned an overall, bound her hair up in an old scarf and set about cleaning the house. Shirley came home at eleven to collect her ballet shoes before yet another visit to the dance school in the hope both of some practice time in the studio and news of Miss Patience or, more precisely, news of her audition. Her first session in the newsagent's had been a success: the work was enjoyable, despite the challenges of the till, and she liked serving newspapers, magazines, sweets and tobacco to customers, many of them on their way to work. They greeted her warmly. "Earning some money for Christmas, are you, Shirley?" some said, while others remarked, "Nice to have you in here, Shirley! It means shorter queues!" In idle moments she wondered if this development, coincidental with Granny's note, was predestined, seemingly preparing her for life in a newsagent's in south-east instead of south-west London. Then she started imagining ballets for all the merchandise, wondering if she could concoct a short dance for the Christmas show, along with the other ones that she had begun to choreograph in France.

At home her mother had a cup of coffee ready for her and was keen to sit down for a chat, in French of course. "It's such a pity that everything went so badly wrong on our return from France," she began, "but I hope that things will be better now."

Not at all sure where this conversation might be leading, Shirley nodded and said, "Yes, it was worrying, wasn't it? Pa was so poorly, but he's much stronger now that he's got his pills. And he's fine today. Let's hope he remembers to take them!"

Maman smiled. "Yes, let's hope so – then we won't have to move house and go and live over some shop in south-east London," she replied. "But,

Chérie, I haven't asked you about your audition! I had other things on my mind. What happened? When is it?"

Astonished by her mother's reference to living over a shop in southeast London, Shirley did not answer at once. "What was that all about? Was it something to do with Granny's letter to Pa?" she asked herself. She had not really believed that they would have to move house if her pa had to change his job, and certainly not that taking over a new business would have such repercussions for the whole family. "Oh, I just don't know," she eventually responded to her mother's questions with a sigh. "There was no letter here waiting for me when we came home and Miss Patience hadn't heard anything when I saw her the day before yesterday. The other girls already have their appointments and yesterday she was away, so I don't know what's going on; I'm hoping she'll be back today."

"I hope so too," Maman agreed. "Time is getting on, isn't it? I expected that you would have heard by now."

Shirley nodded and stood up. "I must be going; I want to find out if there's any news and if I can use the studio."

Such news as awaited her was not encouraging: Miss Patience's mother was critically ill, so she would be away for the foreseeable future. She had left a message for Shirley earlier that morning when she rang from a phone box to say that the usual advanced class would take place on Saturday at eleven, overseen by a Miss Inskip. "Who is she? I don't think I know her. What a funny name for a dance teacher!" Shirley remarked, but her little attempt at humour met with indignation from Stephanie, the receptionist, who snapped:

"She's my cousin and a colleague of Miss Patience's. She was preparing for the juniors' class yesterday afternoon, if you remember. You don't have to come if you don't want to – or if you don't like her name."

Shirley cringed in embarrassment. "Oh, no, no, I didn't mean any disrespect, and yes, please! I do want to come. I'm sure Miss Inskip is a very good teacher!"

Stephanie harrumphed, leaving Shirley in no doubt as to what she thought of her. "Oh, by the way," she had the grace to add, "Miss Patience also said to tell you that she will follow up your audition as soon as she has a moment to spare, and you can use the studio and the small room upstairs as often as you like, if they're not needed for a class."

"I see, thank you, that's fine," Shirley said tersely, trying to hide her exasperation that nothing had yet been done about following up her application.

She danced in the studio, but her heart was not in it, and the moves, which she usually found easy, had mysteriously become extremely difficult. After an hour of struggling to maintain her balance and perfect the simplest of steps, she gave up and went home, comforted by the certainty that Maman would be there. She was there, but she had her coat on and was about to go out. "Chérie! I was not expecting you back so soon! I thought you would be in the dance school all day," she exclaimed in some embarrassment, though she quickly recovered her composure. "I was going to town, but if you prefer I will stay at home and make you some lunch," she added with a certain hesitation; then, even more tentatively, she suggested, "Or, if you like, you could come with me."

Shirley jumped at the chance of lunch in central London. "Let me go and change into something smarter, and so long as I'm back by half-past four for the shop that would be lovely!" She ran upstairs, pulled a dress out of her wardrobe, slipped her feet into her new brown-leather Parisian shoes and joined her mother by the front door in less than ten minutes.

They sat side by side on the train and the earlier disappointment soon evaporated. There was such comfort in discussing her problems with Maman, who today appeared to be so much more relaxed than she had been since their return from France. "I'm sorry to hear about Miss Patience's mother, but I'm sure she will do her best for you," she said. "So, let us not worry about it today. We will have a good lunch and enjoy ourselves." Nevertheless, by the time they reached Waterloo this breeziness had been replaced by a visible tension when Maman, with trembling hand, pulled out her cigarette case. She offered a cigarette to Shirley, who took it because she liked the aura of sophistication that it gave her, and then lit one for herself. "We'll take the Northern Line to Leicester Square," she announced, but almost immediately changed her mind. "No, on second thoughts we'll take the Bakerloo Line to Piccadilly Circus." It made no difference to Shirley; she was happy to be in central London. Undeniably it was not as beautiful as Paris, but it was exciting with all its shops and theatres, its monuments and the river. She loved nothing more than to stand on a bridge, any bridge, and watch the bustling river traffic churning up the muddy waters of the Thames in a carefully choreographed display of manoeuvres. It was a wonder that those craft didn't collide considering how fast some of them went.

"Shall we go down to the river?" she asked hopefully.

Maman didn't answer; indeed she scarcely spoke while they were on the Underground and seemed distracted. At Piccadilly Circus she was trembling so much that Shirley was worried that she might collapse and was about to suggest that they should go home when Maman attempted a faint smile and said, "Oh la la! I am so hungry! Look how my hands are shaking!"

"Well then," Shirley replied in relief at such a simple solution to the problem, "the sooner we find a restaurant around here the better!"

Her mother nodded as she stepped onto the escalator. At the top, Maman insisted inexplicably on taking the exit to Lower Regent Street. "But there aren't many restaurants that I know of there!" Shirley exclaimed. "Why don't we go to Shaftesbury Avenue?"

"No, no, I'm sure we'll find something up here," Maman declared, and proceeded to climb the steps so swiftly that Shirley, who was still investigating the other possible exits from the booking hall, was left behind. When she did emerge into Lower Regent Street, she was astonished to find her mother talking to a well-dressed man; he was quite short, but taller than Maman, with brown curly hair, and by the look of him was French. "Ah, Chérie," said Maman, "this is a surprise! What a coincidence! Let me introduce Monsieur Arnaud Lavasseur: he is my colleague; he also works at the Embassy!"

Shirley proffered her gloved hand, saying *"Enchantée, monsieur"*, but it was impossible for her to return his smile, so convinced was she by the awkwardness of their gestures and their artificial smiles that the encounter between M. Lavasseur and her mother in Lower Regent Street was not the coincidence they would have her believe.

Perhaps discouraged by her frosty expression, M. Lavasseur took his leave hurriedly, saying only *"Au revoir, à demain!"* to Maman and making a small bow in Shirley's direction. Maman was silent for some time after his departure while they walked round Piccadilly Circus and crossed into Shaftesbury Avenue.

Over lunch their conversation was sporadic. Neither was very forthcoming; Shirley because she couldn't think of anything to say that wouldn't sound contrived, and her mother because she was too wrapped up in her own thoughts. It was by no means the joyful occasion that Shirley had anticipated. She glanced down at her watch. "It's half-past two already. I ought to be going if I'm going to get to work in time," she announced.

"Yes, of course," Maman replied, "but if you don't mind, now that I'm here, I'll stay in town a little longer and go up to Oxford Street to look at the shops." It was with a sense of unease that Shirley travelled home. On the way, alone on the train, she turned over the recent strange events, though in fact only one event stood out as being particularly worthy of note and that was the encounter with M. Lavasseur. Shirley was quite sure that there was more to that meeting than met the eye and suspected that it had been prearranged. She was still reflecting on it on the bus and while she walked along the road from the bus stop.

She stopped short of going all the way home and instead of turning the corner went straight to the shop, where Mrs Salvatore was survey-ing a pile of boxes in the middle of the floor. "Shirley!" she exclaimed. "How good of you to come early! You can see how much I need your help! This delivery has just arrived and I have to unpack it and store the contents away before the rush of customers for their evening papers!" There was no more time for reflection as Shirley set to work unpacking the boxes, refilling the shelves and taking the excess goods away to store in the stockroom. There, seated at a desk, she found an elderly man whom she had never previously seen in the shop, though she recalled that he looked vaguely familiar. Possibly she had seen him in church, she thought.

He succeeded in introducing himself as Mr Salvatore, before dissolv-ing into a fit of coughing. "I sit-a here all-a day," he eventually managed to enunciate glumly in a strong Italian accent, "and I deal-a with-a the accounts, but I not-a come in-a the shop-a, my shop-a, because she say the customers not lik-a my cough." Shirley was sorry for the poor man, but indeed his cough was dreadful and there was a spectral air about him, so it was understandable that his presence was not welcome out at the front.

Another surprise awaited her when she went back into the shop, for there stood her mother. "Ah, Chérie!" she began, to Mrs Salvatore's puzzlement, and continued speaking in French. "I want to buy a box of chocolates for your pa from the sweet shop, so I thought I would call in here to see how you are coping and buy a magazine from you!"

It was a pleasure for Shirley to be able to serve her mother, who seemed her old self again, but after she left she had to fend off the barrage of Mrs Salvatore's questions. "So was that your mother? Silly me! I never realized! Of course! I've seen you both in here and at church! Where does she come from? Was that French she was speaking? Why does she call you 'Chérie'?" Shirley answered all these enquiries as briefly as she could, but then had to endure Mrs Salvatore's elaborations on the theme of foreign languages and marriage to a foreigner. "I could never learn Italian," she confessed, "and doubtless you've found out Mr Salvatore's English is not very good, so it's a wonder we manage to talk at all, what with his cough and everything!"

Shirley wondered, but not for long, how this unlikely pair had met. "You see," Mrs Salvatore went on, "I was on my summer holidays in Brighton, and that was where I met Mr Salvatore. He was selling ice cream on the seafront. He swept me off my feet, he did, and I suppose we didn't need much language in those days! It's all different now though." Shirley didn't know whether Mrs Salvatore was going to laugh or cry, but then a customer came in and, after wiping her nose and eyes, she behaved with complete aplomb.

After she had finished serving, she reverted to her rather one-sided conversation. "Does your brother speak French too?" she asked. Shirley's reply that yes, he did, provoked a profound sigh, which proved to be the prelude to another embarrassing outpouring. "Oh how lovely for your parents to have children who speak both languages! That must make such a difference to the way they get on together. We don't have any children, you see, so there's not that connection between us." Mrs Salvatore's voice trailed off and she sniffed into her handkerchief again. "Maybe," she continued, "if we had been able to have children my husband would have taken greater care of his health and wouldn't have smoked so much. He has to work out at the back because I gave him a choice: 'Either, Salvatore,' I said, 'you go to the doctor's or you keep out of the way!'" She became more assertive. "He refused to see the doctor, so there you are: he has to stay out of the shop. I won't have him in here coughing all over the customers! That would be the end of the business!" Without moving, Shirley took a surreptitious peek at her watch. With relief she saw that in less than five minutes her shift would come to an end.

Although she had left the Salvatore establishment behind her, she carried the unfortunate image of the unhappy couple in her mind all evening, unable to decide which partner deserved the most sympathy. Mr Salvatore was in a dire situation, but it was partly of his own making. Had he agreed to seek medical help, his cough might have been cured, and he and his wife would even now be working in harmony, treating their business like the child they hadn't had. Mrs Salvatore was obviously at the end of her tether with worry about his health, tempered by annoyance at his obstinacy, and with exhaustion from running the shop alone. At supper Shirley looked from one to the other of her parents, both of them talkative and happy – quite like old times, in fact – and she took comfort in the thought that after all, in spite of her pa's war wound and his nightmares, and in spite of the mysterious encounter that lunchtime between her mother and Monsieur Lavasseur, hers appeared to be a united and contented family. After dinner, Maman presented Pa with the chocolates she had bought that evening, saying "Here's a little present for you!"

Beaming from ear to ear and passing the box round the table, he exclaimed, "What a treat! How you do spoil me!"

Later, with her hands deep in the washing-up bowl, and without turning to look at her daughter while she spoke, Maman said quietly, "I'm thinking of going to Mass on Sunday. Would you come with me, Chérie?"

"If you want me to," Shirley replied without enthusiasm. Then, after a pause for reflection, enquired, "Will that mean I'll have to go to confession too?"

"Yes, I was intending to go tomorrow evening," her mother replied. "Will you come too? I could meet you on my way home from work."

Shirley's attitude to churchgoing was lukewarm at the best of times, and she knew that her mother was generally not particularly keen either, so if Maman asked for her companionship, it had to be for a good, if unexplained reason. "All right," she agreed, "come and meet me from the shop at about six."

The Catholic Church in the centre of the borough was a forbidding Victorian edifice. Inside, even on a sunny autumn evening, it was even more lugubrious than its outside appearance suggested; its pillars and arches were grey with the smoke that had filtered in through ill-fitting doors and broken windows and the soot from the constant burning of candles. Only the tiny red lamps that glimmered feebly, suspended from the roof above the chancel and in the side chapels, relieved the all-pervasive gloom. Little daylight penetrated the originally garish, though nowadays muted colours of the stained glass. The plaster saints adorning the walls seemed a miserably drab bunch, crying out for a good wash, or so Shirley thought, for she preferred to go inside only when there was a Mass in progress: then at least there was a halo of both electric and candle light reflecting off the silver vessels on the altar, making the gold embroidery on the statue of the Virgin glisten, and illuminating the chancel with a brightness that brought the place alive, like a theatre where the priests and the acolytes, all in their lacy robes, moved in strict, if sometimes pathetically lame dance sequences. No matter that the words they spoke were unintelligible, all being in Latin, the spectacle was engaging, especially when bells rang and incense wafted through the stagnant air.

It had to be said, though, that she preferred going to Mass in France, where the village church was smaller, brighter and cleaner, where the saints were better tended and less dilapidated in appearance. There too the village priest, *monsieur le curé*, was a kind and approachable white-haired old man who knew everyone and who was liked by all. He would come to visit Mémé regularly of an afternoon and would sit quietly talking to her for hours on end. She was always happier after his visits and on the following Sunday would venture down to the village for Mass in the company of her daughter and granddaughter. Then after Mass the whole village would congregate in the church porch in a lively exchange of greetings and news. Here in the London suburbs, the church and the borough were so large that no one seemed to know anyone else and the priests were anonymous figures who flitted in and out of the service and exited by a side door.

That Friday, the day she and her mother were to make their confessions, was not a good day for Shirley: Mrs Salvatore had moaned in the shop and Mr Salvatore had coughed in the distance throughout her two shifts, both of them seeming to regard her as a target for their complaints whether mental or physical. At the dance school there was still no news about her audition and Miss Patience was still conspicuous by her absence. By six o'clock in the evening she was thoroughly annoyed and out of sorts and regretted agreeing to go to the church at all, let alone for confession; she was not in the mood for it.

Walking up the road beside her mother, she longed to be at home sitting in the garden in the last rays of the sun on this fine autumn evening, with a cup of tea at her elbow and a magazine spread open on her lap. She thought too, as she did often, how unfair it was that, as a result of some compromise between their parents years ago, Ted was never required to come to Mass, in England or in France. Ted, like Pa and Granny, was a Congregationalist, and since Pa never went to church, Ted didn't have to either, leaving him free to spend Sunday mornings doing whatever he liked, including being blissfully lazy. Even worse, if he had gone to the Congregational church, apparently he wouldn't have had to go through this business of confession. Shirley was debating whether she might plead the onset of a cold or a headache, but she knew that her mother would not be taken in by that sort of excuse, and in any case, she recalled, she was there to support her. In a defiant mood she entered the church and sat down on a hard pew, while Maman disappeared into a side compartment of one of the wooden cubicles ranged along the wall. She was there a long time, and when at last she emerged, she seemed distressed.

While she waited for her turn, Shirley considered what she might say to the anonymous priest hidden behind a screen. In the past she had admitted to the little lies that she had told, mostly in school, to get out of the trouble which always loomed over her head, but there had also been the stories she had invented with the intention of entertaining the invisible presence, because, she thought, his job must be so boring. These stories probably contained a modicum of truth since they often recounted sins she would have liked to commit, but for which she did not quite have the courage. For example, once she had told him, "Our headmistress is so nasty, I put powdered chalk on her chair and it stuck to her skirt when she sat down, but she couldn't see it!"

Because his face was hidden from her view, she had no notion of the priest's exasperated expression, and was always surprised and not a little annoyed at being quickly dismissed with an absolution and a blessing, saying, "My child, you must say your Ave Marias and pray to Our Lady to help you to behave like a good Christian."

Today was different: she was in no mood to entertain him and anyhow felt herself to be too old to invent such fables, so when she went into the confessional she simply told him of all the frustrations in her own life and of the causes for the irritation that she had experienced in the past four days since the return from France last Monday: irritation against her father, her granny, Miss Patience and Mr and Mrs Salvatore, as well as other untold minor causes of annoyance.

"Let us pray," said the priest with some sympathy in his voice, "that Our Lady, the Mother of God, will help you to find the patience and forbearance to cope with these and other irritations in life, my child. You are beginning to discover a major truth of human existence, and that is that our lives are full of irritations and annoyances, large and small, and how you cope with them is a measure of your strength of character." The disembodied voice cleared its throat, then assumed a gentler tone, speaking, it seemed, from the heart, as though the advice it was imparting was born of its own experience, not gleaned from a seminary discussion or textbook. "You are lucky that you are affected only by these little problems, my child. Many people have far worse to contend with and find their lives blighted in consequence. You must pray that you never encounter greater misfortune than this. Recite your Ave Marias and ask Our Lady to come to your aid." Thus and with a prayer, an absolution and a blessing, he brought the confession to a close.

Shirley left the confessional in an unusually sober and reflective mood. She had always considered, and had been told by Miss Patience and her mother, that she possessed great strength of character on account of the discipline that she devoted to the ballet, and also on account of her determination to succeed in that, her chosen career. How could she possibly need more of that strength, she wondered, and what did the priest mean by talking about "greater misfortune"? She fervently hoped, and her hope was only just short of a prayer, that greater misfortune than all those irritations she had suffered in the past week would never befall her. Indeed, she intended her life to follow the plan that she had devised for it, even to the extent that somewhere along the way she might meet that young man called Alan again, marry him and, after her career in the ballet was over, settle down in a comfortable home with him and a family of beautiful fair-haired, blue-eyed children. Her mother was quiet on the way home and so was she, upset by the disturbance brought to her peace of mind by the priest's depressing predictions.

10

Only Pa's legs were visible, stretching out from underneath his car, when Shirley returned from her ballet class at lunchtime on Saturday. "Hello, Pa!" she called out. "What on Earth are you doing there?"

He eased himself out into the daylight and pulled himself up, first by hanging onto the bumper, then onto one of the headlamps and finally onto the door handle of his precious vehicle. Wiping his hands on an old rag, he declared, "Ah, Shirl, so there you are! You've been out a long time. Been to your dancing, have you?" Shirley laughed at the sight of him; he was so dirty he might have been down a coal mine: his dungarees were covered in oil and his pale skin and hair were flecked with black streaks, yet he was smiling like a small boy who has been playing with his favourite toy.

"Yes, that's right," she answered, "but I did my shift in the paper shop first, and look, I've been paid!" She reached into her pocket and took out a small brown envelope in which coins jingled. "Ted's been paid too, so we're in the money and we can help out!"

"No, certainly not!" Pa replied without a second thought. "You're very kind, but I won't let you do that. You and Ted should save that money for the future. Come on, let's go in and see if lunch is ready." They climbed the steep steps at the back door, Shirley with great speed and agility and her father much more slowly and unsteadily.

Jacqueline was cooking a hot meal in the kitchen. "*Ah, voilà!*" she exclaimed. "So you have come in together! I am just about to serve lunch."

After a somewhat cursory attempt to clean himself up, Pa sat down at the dining table and pulled a letter out of his pocket which he put down beside his place setting but did not read straight away to the family. "That can wait till after I've eaten," he announced, anxious to allay the pangs of hunger. Only after he had consumed his first course did he share its contents with his wife and children. The communication, which had arrived by the morning post, was from Granny: in it she decreed that the three of them – she, Reggie and Shirley – should travel to Cousin

Edith's wedding by car rather than by train, since she would be bringing at least two suitcases plus her hatbox.

After reading the missive aloud, Pa said that he had intended to save money by using his rail pass for the train, but as a result of Granny's command the plans would have to change, so that was why he had decided to give the car a servicing that morning well in advance of the journey to Birmingham. Apart from the cost of running the car instead of free transport on the railways, it wasn't a problem as far as he was concerned, because he loved his car and his leg was well enough to operate the pedals. "So, remind me. When is the wedding?" Shirley enquired.

"End of this month, two weeks today," Pa said, glancing at the calendar pinned to the wall above his head.

"Oh, good!" Ted announced gleefully, "so that *is* the weekend when I'll be away at camp! I was pretty sure it would be." Shirley frowned, went silent and cast her eyes down onto her plate.

"Why, what's the matter?" Maman, who had been quiet until now, asked with a sharpness that was unusual in her, as if any disruption to the plans would not be welcome from her point of view, although she had decided weeks ago that she would not be attending the wedding.

"Well, I had some good news this morning, but it doesn't seem as good now as I thought it was," Shirley replied with a rueful sigh.

Miss Inskip's dance class had been so much better than she had feared. In fact it was quite exciting, and Miss Inskip, who was much younger than expected, proved to be a good teacher, even if she did apply her little cane to various parts of her pupils' anatomies when their postures did not meet with her approval. "Shoulders down!" she commanded, tapping a slouching pupil between the shoulder blades. "Strengthen your core muscles!" she ordered, pointing the stick at another girl's midriff. "Tummies in! Straight legs, no bent knees!" she demanded of the whole class. All these imperious instructions were delivered with a disarming smile, which indicated that, though she meant what she said, her criticisms were in no way ill-tempered. She was poised to lead the class into some routines when her cousin, the receptionist, interrupted the class to summon Shirley to the telephone.

A faint voice straining to make itself heard at the other end, called out, "Shirley, Shirley, is that you? I've some good news for you!" It was Miss Patience. Her "good news" was that after many attempts she had at last managed to get hold of someone in authority at Sadler's Wells and, although no one was prepared to admit to it, clearly there had been a clerical error by which Shirley's name had been omitted from the list of candidates. As a special concession, by no means an admission of guilt, they had offered to give her an audition for the company on the Monday evening in a fortnight's time, squeezing her in at the beginning of a session, at half-past six. "It's not perfect timing, I know," said Miss Patience, "but it was the best I could get out of them. Is that all right for you?"

"Yes, certainly, I think so. I don't see why not," Shirley had replied, thrilled that after an agonizing wait the matter was resolved, and she would after all have the opportunity to demonstrate her prowess as a dancer. It fleetingly crossed her mind that the priest had therefore been wrong yesterday evening at confession when he had warned her of the likelihood of great misfortunes in life. The resolution of the audition episode proved to be a misfortune averted, or so she thought until she sat down to lunch with her family.

Before she had even begun to tell them about Miss Patience's phone call, her news seemed already to have been drowned in a bucket of cold water. Edith's wedding invitation had arrived at the beginning of the summer holidays, so long ago that the precise date had slipped her mind. To discover at this late stage that it was to be on the Saturday prior to the audition, in two weeks' time, came as a shock. Since talking to Miss Patience, she had been counting on spending most of the week preceding the audition, and the whole of that weekend, practising and dancing in the studio. Indeed, Miss Patience had promised her that she could do so. Only then would all her steps, her movements and her routines be as perfect as was humanly possible. Her best-laid plans, along with the news of the audition, had suddenly been thrown into that bucket of cold water by Pa's mention of Edith's nuptials. It was a foregone conclusion that Granny would insist on their driving up to Birmingham on the Friday ready for the wedding the next day, and obviously they would not be returning to London till the Sunday and probably late in the day at that.

Shirley could have wept, but kept her eyes down and chewed slowly on a mouthful of food which she could not swallow. It was not as if she wanted to go to the wedding. In fact, the only reason she had agreed to go was to please her pa and allow Maman to avoid uncomfortable encounters with her English in-laws, who, it had to be said, had never been at all friendly to the French intruder in their midst. Shirley had frequently heard them calling her mother "Froggy" behind her back like the pupils in her primary school, and making snide and crude remarks about living on frogs' legs and snails. There was no doubt that they were jealous of Jacqueline's elegance, which, unbeknown to them, stemmed of course from that natural ability of hers to create the smartest dresses and costumes, based on the latest French fashions, with inexpensive material bought from a shop in Saint-Pierre or from Freslan market.

Indeed, Shirley had watched her mother eyeing up and taking notes in La Samaritaine of the displays of lovely clothes that she had later reproduced on Mémé's sewing machine. It was hardly surprising therefore that her English in-laws envied her neat appearance. They also envied her prowess in the kitchen, which, to their displeasure, was Reggie's favourite topic of conversation. It went without saying that her obvious intelligence and linguistic ability were also causes of their spite, as none of them knew French, and the English that they spoke was intelligible only to the initiated. In short, because they reluctantly recognized in her a superior being, they felt obliged to denigrate her among themselves as a way of maintaining their own self-respect. "She's not one of us. She doesn't belong in our family" was their way of putting it, and this verdict had apparently given them free rein to diminish her and everything about her. The irony was that they were unaware of her humble origins and how she had succeeded in combining her natural gifts with hard work to escape her beloved but limited rustic background.

Jacqueline, with her feline sensibilities, was aware of this thinly veiled hostility and naturally enough avoided contact with Reggie's family, especially his mother, as much as her adherence to the French motto *toujours la politesse*, politeness at all times, would allow. A family wedding was for her the most uncomfortable English occasion, so an important prior engagement at the French Embassy gave her the best excuse for not attending. Shirley understood her mother's unwillingness, not only because of the malicious comments directed against her, which she had previously overheard, but also because she, herself, had also been and still was the target of disapproving stares and innuendoes.

The worst perpetrator of these was Edith's younger sister, fifteen-year-old Thelma, who, being younger and very unsubtle, was more outspoken than the rest of them. She said what the others were thinking when they hid behind an overtly friendly façade. The last time they had met, a couple of years ago, Thelma had remarked in a loud voice, "Ooh, you are skinny, aren't you, Shirley! I wouldn't want to be like that: people would think I was not getting enough to eat, living on all that foreign food like you do!" Exercising considerable self-control, Shirley did not react to this insult, however much she was tempted to do so, because she knew that if she said that it was essential to stay small, slim and light to be a dancer, there would be no end to the jokes perpetrated by her cousin and her companions at her expense. They would sneer at her just because it was crystal-clear that they had no chance of ever attaining the discipline that the ballet demanded, or of ever enjoying the success that it promised to its devotees. Just the idea of large, bulging Thelma being lifted high above a male dancer's head was too grotesque to be contemplated.

Such thoughts raced through Shirley's mind while she frenetically pushed her *crème caramel* around her dessert bowl in smaller and smaller circles, without attempting to scoop up the remaining spoonfuls. It might have been easier if Maman had not appeared so unsympathetic when the question of the wedding had come up. Shirley assumed that because her loyalty to her mother was unquestioning, it was unswervingly reciprocated, so when Maman reacted sharply to her evident dismay at the date of the wedding, she was doubly upset. The last fragments of the dessert were by now whirling in a vortex which would have foretold disaster to an outside observer, but not to her parents, each absorbed in his or her own deliberations or daydreams.

All pent-up emotions of feeling ignored, slighted and cheated by her own parents suddenly erupted in an outburst of temper, and when Shirley lost her temper, the results, as at this very moment, were dramatic. "How could you do this to me?" she shouted. "You haven't listened to me. I had something very important to tell you and you haven't taken any notice! You" – here she turned on her father – "you know I don't want to go to Edith's wedding; you know it will be awful! I'm not going!" Her father looked up from his dessert with a stunned expression. Open-mouthed, he did not reply. "And you" – here she let fly at her mother – "you won't even come to this wretched wedding!" Maman turned away, biting her lip. The vortex in the dessert bowl ceased to turn as the outburst dissolved in a fit of sobbing. Ted hurriedly finished his *crème caramel* and slunk out of the room: he knew that his sister would recover eventually – that is, when she had brought her parents round to her way of thinking.

Although Reggie was still speechless, Jacqueline had sufficient presence of mind to find soothing words, in a confused mixture of both English and French, to calm her daughter down. "But Chérie," she said, "you have not told us what the problem is? How can we *help* you if we don't know what is wrong?"

Shirley wiped her eyes, took a deep breath and launched into an account of the morning's activities, which only a short while ago she had regarded as wonderfully positive. Between her sobs she stammered out the news of the audition, its date and all the complications of going to Birmingham for the whole weekend before that all-important Monday. As her sense of justice slowly returned, she did not think it fair to complain any more than she had already about Pa's dreadful family, and how she resented having to go to the wedding.

He, completely unaware of all the difficulties, stroked his chin pensively, considered the problem and said in consoling tones, "Shirl, I'm sorry about all this. I honestly didn't know that your audition was going to coincide so nearly with the wedding, or that you needed so much rehearsal time." Of course he was right and he was not to blame. There was no way that he, an engineer, could have known how time-consuming the ballet at this level could be. He went on: "I was going to take the Friday off and go up to Birmingham in the morning, but supposing I go to work as usual – well at least until, say, four – and you can do your ballet all day till then and we'll set off for Birmingham in the late afternoon, how would that be?" Shirley nodded at this suggestion.

Furthermore, he then suggested, "And we could come back earlier on the Sunday, say in the afternoon, so that at least you'll get a good night's sleep. And Winnie's house is big enough for you to find a space somewhere for your practising."

Shirley nodded again. "That's kind, Pa," she said, "but what about Granny? She'll make such a fuss if she knows we're coming back early on account of me and my audition; she's bound to tell everyone else, and I don't want them to know, which means I can't even attempt a *plié* or two in Aunt Winnie's house."

"Don't you worry," Pa said reassuringly, "I'll deal with your granny. If I have to work on the Friday, I have to work on the Friday, so that's settled. And as for the Sunday, I'll say that I find driving in the dark too much of a strain these days. And maybe when they're all chattering nineteen to the dozen you can find a quiet corner upstairs."

"Thanks, Pa," she murmured, "perhaps it won't be too bad, but it's not what I had hoped for.

"Don't forget you will be able to wear that lovely outfit we bought in Paris!" Maman reminded her. "You'll be the envy of all the girls and women there," she added with a tiny hint of sarcasm, bringing a smile to Shirley's lips. Maman was on the point of saying something else but was interrupted by a ring at the door, and – because she was seated by the dining-room door – she got up to answer it.

Abandoning her dessert, Shirley smiled at her father in relief and gratitude for his flexibility. The arrangement was not perfect, but was the best that could be achieved in the circumstances and, since he was prepared to take her part to the best of his ability, she could not let him down by persisting in her refusal to go to Birmingham, even though that meant putting up with Granny on the journey there and again on the journey back. Moreover, while they were there, staying in Aunt Winnie's house, she would have to endure Thelma's jibes and her aunt's constant angling for compliments about her house, her garden, her wedding clothes, Edith's dress, Thelma's bridesmaid's dress, the flowers, the reception – in short everything for which Aunt Winnie had any responsibility at all.

Winnie would also whinge about all those things for which she did not have any responsibility and which were not to her liking. Uncle Horace would keep very quiet, as he always did, unless he were called upon to corroborate what Aunt Winnie was saying, in which case he would respond promptly, saying, "Yes, dear, of course, dear," and then carry on his conversation with Pa, who was the only person he ever seemed to talk to, which probably meant that he spoke very infrequently. There was also Edith, who at previous encounters had been far too occupied with her friends to take any notice of Shirley at all, so it was highly unlikely that on this of all occasions she would even acknowledge Shirley's presence.

Maman returned to the dining room and sat down on her chair. She let the paper she was holding in her hand fall to the floor and then buried her head in her arms on the table top. "Maman! What's wrong?" It was Shirley's turn to be solicitous.

Maman raised her head; her face was deathly pale. "Read that telegram," she said, choking back the tears as she gestured to the paper on the floor. Bending down to pick it up, Shirley saw that it was a telegram from Madame de la Croix, conveying in a few words very bad news about dear Mémé, who had fallen critically ill, and urging Maman to leave at once for France. She read it aloud. "*Votre mère est tombée gravement malade. Venez vite. Eugénie de la Croix.*"

Pa came to the other end of the table and put his arms round his wife's shoulders. "Shall I come with you?" he asked. "The car's out. Pack your things and we can go as soon as you're ready."

"No, no, that's all right," she replied, "I don't know how long I shall be away. I'll go on the night train. Could you take me to Victoria station? But," here she stopped to consider her next move, "I need to make a few phone calls, so I will go down the road to the phone box."

She stood up, ready to leave the house, when Shirley – who felt otherwise powerless to help – said, "Poor Mémé! You mustn't worry about us, Maman. I'll keep house and look after Ted and Pa while you're away. Can I make the phone calls for you, telling people that you'll be away from work and so on? All you need do is give me a list of the numbers."

"*Non, ma Chérie,*" her mother answered firmly, "I can do it myself; it won't take long." With that she was gone.

Confronted by this catastrophe, which put her own concerns into the shade, Shirley was overcome with remorse at her earlier display of temper, and wanted nothing more than to compensate her parents for the scene she had made during this most inauspicious of Saturday lunches. It seemed unnecessary now to tell her mother, as she had intended earlier, that she would not be going to Mass the next day, Sunday, because Mrs Salvatore had asked her and Ted to take over the shop that morning so that she and Mr Salvatore might go to church together. At the time it had seemed like a good idea. Shirley had been glad of a good excuse for not going to church: she and Ted would be able to earn more money and, unusually for them, Mr and Mrs Salvatore could go out. "There'll be no hurry to come back. We'll be fine!" Shirley had assured them. Thanking her effusively for being such an obliging employee, Mrs Salvatore had promised them a handsome reward in their next pay packets. Shirley, for her part, had swiftly taken the opportunity to tell her about the audition and how pleased she was at long last to have a date for it. Now she would have to ask for time off for the wedding as well; she assumed that Ted had already told the Salvatores about his camping trip with the Scouts.

11

While she and her brother were manning the paper shop on the Sunday morning, Shirley could not rid her mind of the disturbing sequence of events that previous dreadful day. First of all there had been her elation at Miss Patience's phone call about the audition, then the disheartening information about the conflicting date of Edith's wedding, followed by her shameful explosion of temper when her parents seemed to be ignoring her and disregarding her concerns. After that they had all been thrown into utter confusion by the arrival of the fateful telegram from the Countess. She told herself that she could never have foreseen what was going to happen, but such self-justification was of little consolation. While her father and Ted were clearing the table and doing the washing-up, she, desperate to make amends, had rushed upstairs and pulled suitable skirts, cardigans, dresses and blouses for her mother's forthcoming trip from her wardrobe and chest of drawers, and had spread them out on the bed for her approval. On her return from the phone box, Jacqueline sat down on a chair at the end of the bed, and either nodded or shook her head without saying a word, whereupon Shirley folded each one of the items that she had selected and placed it neatly in the large suitcase, which Pa had brought down from the loft. To her alarm, her mother had also insisted on taking a black costume, shoes, hat and gloves out of her wardrobe, and for these she needed yet another smaller case.

A pervasive silence had reigned throughout the house, both upstairs and down, for no one could think of anything to say that did not sound trite or inappropriate. Shirley had fumbled in her pocket, before breaking the silence and saying, "Maman, look, here are my earnings from the paper shop. They're not French francs obviously, but please would you take them and buy something nice for Mémé?"

Tears streamed down Jacqueline's face as she struggled to speak. "Oh, Chérie, how kind you are! No, I absolutely insist you keep your money, and I promise you I will buy a nice present from you for her

84

– and for Pépé as well." Still weeping, she embraced her daughter in a long, loving hug.

Leaving her mother to finish her packing, Shirley brushed the tears away from her own eyes and went into her bedroom, where she took her writing case out of the bedside cabinet and sat down to write a letter to her ailing grandmother. She wanted Mémé to know how much she loved her, how much she enjoyed staying at the farm and how she longed for next year's summer holidays to begin. She reminded her that Édouard would soon be coming to live in France to work on the farm alongside Pépé, before calling down to her brother to ask him to add a note to her letter, which he did rather awkwardly, though with the best of intentions, reiterating what she had already said. He too offered his earnings to his mother, but yet again she refused to accept them and yet again the tears started to flow.

"I think I will go down to the phone box again and call Madame de la Croix. I should have done that the first time I went," Maman announced, as soon as she had packed the last items and closed her suitcases. "Is there time for me to do that?"

"Yes, plenty of time: we don't need to set out for at least an hour," Pa, who carried every railway timetable in his head, assured her.

"Shall I come with you?" Shirley volunteered, hoping to have just a little while alone with her mother before she left. Perhaps a brief discussion about the audition and how to cope with organizing it would be a helpful distraction for them both. They could also talk about household management on the way, as Shirley was sure that she would need a plan of action in her mother's absence if she were to be running the house and cooking the meals, in addition to practising for the audition and working in the newsagent's. Maman, however, declined her offer: she said that she could do with a breath of fresh air before setting out on a difficult and tiring journey and needed to collect her thoughts; so, if Shirley didn't mind, she would go alone.

She was out so long that the family began to worry about her, both on account of her distressed state and because they feared that she would miss the train. They were shocked when at last she slipped silently into the house: her eyes were very red and swollen, while the rest of her face was ashen pale, but she seemed calmer and told them the upshot of her call to France without weeping, without even a sob. "Eventually they put me through to Madame de la Croix," she said almost impassively.

"Apparently Mémé is very ill and not expected to live much longer." She paused, then continued, "I knew she was not well, but I didn't realize how ill she was when we were there. She would not admit it and of course she refused to see a doctor, although I tried to persuade her." Her resolve began to crumble, and she reached into her pocket for her handkerchief, able only to add, "So if it's all right with you, I would like to set out straight away."

Pa hustled the family into the car and put the luggage in the boot. He and Ted made a great effort on the journey to Victoria to cheer up the passengers in the back by pointing out the variety of craft on the Thames as they crossed the river, the trees beginning to change colour and other similar diversions, but their efforts fell on deaf ears. At Victoria Station Pa went to book his wife's ticket, which was easily done as there were still sleeping compartments available in the middle carriages, where Maman said she preferred to be, though there was a problem when it came to deciding on a return date. Jacqueline said that she could not possibly say when she might be coming back. Pa turned away crestfallen, but he kept his feelings to himself and simply ordered an open return.

With her ticket in her hand, she was about to make straight for the platform, despite having plenty of time to spare, as Reggie had told her. He took charge, and steered her in the other direction towards the station hotel for some refreshment, which in other circumstances might well have been a special treat, but on this occasion lacked any inkling of pleasure. All Jacqueline would consume was a single cup of coffee, while Ted, of course, was ready for the next meal and Pa decided that he was hungry as well, so the two of them ordered omelettes. Shirley, who had not eaten much at lunchtime, rather envied her father and brother, but could not bring herself to order anything other than a toasted teacake. Maman had already drunk her coffee when the food order arrived. Her mind elsewhere, she declared, "The train is sure to be ready, so I think I will board it now and settle into my sleeper." She stood up, at first without noticing that her husband, Ted and Shirley were still eating, and then sat down again until her family had finished.

The procession to the train was funereal. Pa carried Jacqueline's suitcases on board while she hugged her children briefly. "Please don't wait for the train to leave. That would make matters worse," she pleaded as she turned, mounted the steps and followed Pa into her compartment without waving goodbye.

He emerged a moment or two later, downhearted and pensive, all his earlier attempts at joviality having evaporated. "I suppose we have to do what she says and leave," he said, glancing hopefully into the open carriage door, but as there was no one there with whom to exchange a few fond words of parting, he said, "Well, let's be off, then!" and led the way around cases and boxes and laden trolleys strewn all over the platform, back to the ticket barrier. As they gave up their platform tickets, Shirley, who in the recent past would have observed the bustling crowds for inspiration for a ballet, perhaps entitled *Departures*, but now in busy public places always kept an eye open in the hope of spotting Alan, was shocked to see a recognizable figure, who was not Alan, running in the opposite direction carrying a small suitcase. She was sure that it was the man who had been standing waiting for Maman in Lower Regent Street. What was his name? She racked her brains trying to recall it. "Ah, yes, it was Lavasseur, Monsieur Arnaud Lavasseur," she remembered. What was he doing here? She turned to see where he was going and could have sworn that he climbed into a carriage next to or near the one that Maman was travelling in.

On the way home she sat quietly in the back of the car by herself, casting her mind over all the misfortunes that had befallen her and her family that day and trying unsuccessfully to put them into some sort of order. As if all that were not enough, there was now the mystery of M. Lavasseur's appearance, if indeed that passenger hurrying along the platform really was him. The sight of him augured ill – of that she was certain – though her sixth sense stopped her drawing Pa or Ted's attention to him. Reluctantly, she admitted to herself that today's events had shown that there was some truth in the priest's advice at confession after all, since the past few hours had seen misfortune piled on misfortune, each far greater than her minor irritations recounted to him in the confessional.

At home, she pulled herself together and searched in the cupboard and the larder for food. Although they had eaten omelettes at the station, Pa and Ted hinted apologetically that the emotional disturbances had left them feeling very hungry again, and she herself was feeling a little light-headed, so she rustled up a passable supper with some bread, ham and salad and a tin of peaches, which they ate at the table, uncomfortably aware of Maman's empty place. Pa yawned as he put down his spoon. "Well, Ted," he said, "you and me, we've got to look lively. We can't expect Shirl to wait on us hand and foot: if she prepares the food, we had better clear the table and do the washing-up."

Resigned to a new regime, Ted agreed, while Pa, seemingly strangely enlivened and vociferous, proposed a modus vivendi for the foreseeable future. "I was thinking on the way home how we might organize ourselves while your mother is away. We can send the linen to the laundry and wash our clothes ourselves. I'll give you some housekeeping money, Shirl, if you could do the food shopping up the road, and I'll buy the bulky things at the weekends. I suppose we could make a cleaning rota and do that at weekends too. What do you think?"

"Sounds more or less all right to me," Shirley conceded. "I can shop at the butcher's and the greengrocer's after I've done my shift at the Salvatores' in the morning, and leave the bags with them to collect on my way back from ballet, so that should work out all right. Oh, and there's a baker's right by the dance studio, so I can get the bread too. The only thing is the cleaning: I don't want to spend the weekend cleaning the house."

"No, nor do I," Ted said with a grimace. "I've an early start for the paper round on Saturdays and Sundays, just like any weekday, as you know, then I have to do my homework and there's football on Saturday afternoons and Scouts on Friday evenings, so I don't have much spare time."

"Ah," said Pa, whose carefully thought-out plan had not met with wholehearted agreement, "we'll have to see about that, but at least for the moment we have a plan. So, come on, Ted, let's start on the washing-up, and you, Shirl, you are looking very tired. Why don't you go and have a nice hot bath and then go to bed?" Shirley was only too pleased to take up her father's suggestion and escape to the bathroom. Although she had baulked at his ideas about the housework, it was a nice surprise that he had thought not only to take the initiative so soon in sorting out the household arrangements to tide them over until Maman's return, but also to make sure that the tasks were fairly allotted, so that she would not be overwhelmed by the chores and would not find her ballet curtailed.

However, the next morning, as she arranged yet another bundle of Sunday papers on the counter, she rather wished that she had not been so hasty in agreeing to Mrs Salvatore's request to take charge of the shop until lunchtime, for this was precisely the sort of rare occasion when she herself would have found solace in going to church. She went over to a shelf to tidy some magazines that customers had thumbed through and then left higgledy-piggledy. "Oh, look at this mess!" she exclaimed to Ted, who had just finished serving a customer. "Some people just come in here to read the magazines without buying anything!

"You know," she went on, changing the subject, "I honestly would have liked to go to church this morning. It was stupid of me to agree to look after the shop."

No sooner had she spoken than she wished she had kept her thoughts to herself. Ted would be bound to poke fun at her as he always did. He could be relied upon to pounce on any excuse to tease his older sister to distraction, thus venting his frustration at being the younger sibling. More than ever now that he was growing up, he grasped any opportunity to assert himself and offset the insult dealt to his burgeoning masculine pride by his inferior position in the family. Shirley, on the other hand, had never felt any sentimental attachment to him, for he had arrived while she was still a baby herself, so, if anything, rather than experiencing a small girl's maternal affection for a newborn infant, she had resented his sudden and intrusive appearance on a scene which she was accustomed to regard as her domain.

Today she was amazed to find that her fears were unjustified. Ted did not ridicule her; instead he took a deep breath and said quietly, "Yes, I know how you feel. I wouldn't want to go to your church, of course, but I do wish I could be out in the fields on the farm with the horses and the plough, or driving that new tractor that Pépé was talking about. It's only there that I can think in peace and sort out my worries." His voice tailed off. "I do like working here, though," he added more cheerfully, "and that's funny when you think how different this place is from the farm! I suppose it's because there's always something new here every day, with all the papers and magazines coming in, and there's lots to do and people to talk to."

Taken aback by her brother's reaction, Shirley wondered if she had caught him off guard, so that he had briefly forgotten that he was talking to her, his big sister. But no, he picked up his more serious thread again, saying, "You see, I assumed Mémé and Pépé would always be there, so it's a shock to discover that they might not be. Maybe the farm won't always be there either. Anyhow, it wouldn't be the same without them. And it's strange without Maman; I hope Pa won't have one of his turns while she's away. Then what on earth would we do?"

Shirley had never heard Ted talk like this, and had never credited him with any worries because he constantly gave the impression of having life under control. His remarks had come as a revelation, suggesting a thoughtful, mature young man rather than the hare-brained, inconsiderate youth she had considered him to be. "Oh, Ted," she exclaimed, "I'm so glad to hear you talking like that! We both think the same way after all. And, I suppose, if we both think the same way, we'll manage somehow."

"Yes, of course we will," he replied. "All you have to do is just let me know what I can do. I know you've got a lot on with this ballet business, so just say if you need help." Shirley dropped the magazines she was carrying and went over to her brother to give him a sisterly peck on the cheek. "Oh, and look, there's not much to do here now that the early-morning rush is over, so why don't you go to Mass? I can cope perfectly well on my own," he said thoughtfully.

The running of the household proceeded harmoniously for the next week: a cooked meal, of sorts, was on the table in the evening from Monday to Friday and high tea at the weekend; the laundry collected dirty linen and brought it back washed and ironed; and Mrs Salvatore, on hearing about the crisis in the family, sent in an Italian relative of her husband's to do the cleaning on a Wednesday morning. Her costs were so reasonable that Pa decided that she should wash their clothes in the old washtub on Thursdays as well. Ted and Shirley offered to pay for these services, but Pa wouldn't hear of it. "As long as I'm in work, there's no problem," he insisted. "If one of these days I can't work that will be a different matter, but for the time being we are fine." He was fairly buoyant, confident that his wife would be home again within a matter of days, and in any case, unlike the long summer holidays when his entire family was away, he had his son and daughter with him for company and support.

Apart from the disruption to her normal routine caused by the shopping and the cooking, and her work in the shop, Shirley was able to attend her classes, still taken by Miss Inskip, and dance whenever there was space for her in the studio, and thus from day to day she noticed an improvement in her figure, her confidence, her flexibility of movement and above all her technique, which only weeks earlier before the summer holidays had reached such a high level of competence. She had recovered the rotation in her hips, her turnout, and could raise her legs high. She had actually started to look forward to the audition, thinking that the trip to Birmingham for her cousin's wedding was not going to be the great hindrance that she had at first thought.

One evening Ted made a suggestion out of the blue: "Look, sis, I've been thinking, when did you say this audition of yours was going to be, and where is it?" he asked.

"Sadler's Wells, Rosebery Avenue, Monday week at half-past six," she answered, perplexed by his question. "Why do you ask?"

He shrugged. "That's north London, Islington, isn't it? And it'll be getting dark by the time you come out, won't it?"

"Yes, maybe," she replied; she had not thought of that.

"Well, I don't think it's safe for you," Ted went on. "So I'm coming with you. I can get out of games on that Monday afternoon and we'll go together."

"That's kind," she replied, "but I'm sure it's not necessary."

"No arguments," he insisted, "that's settled." Discreetly, Ted did not reveal that his offer was prompted by his anxious father. Nevertheless, Shirley was convinced that their mother would have returned by then and was counting on her to accompany her to Sadler's Wells. All the same, it was reassuring to have Ted's offer in hand.

12

Shirley's cautious optimism was encouraged by the arrival of a telegram from Maman saying that she had arrived safely and that Mémé seemed to be making a good recovery in hospital in Saint-Pierre. This news lifted the dark cloud of anxiety hanging over them by a fraction: Pa's brow became less furrowed and Ted started teasing Shirley again, but more gently and sensitively. She decided that she preferred Ted in this, a modified version of his old mode, for the reformed Ted that she had witnessed over the past week since Maman's hasty departure had been far too serious and prematurely old, although she was grateful to discover that she could confide in him. It would be easy to keep the household going for a few more days, even another week or two, in the almost certain knowledge that Maman would be returning before very long – not that she had said so in her telegram, but it was implied in the tone of her message.

The wedding in Birmingham, coming up the following weekend, was an inconvenience, but even that could be a pleasant change, if the weather were good, especially for Pa, who had not been on holiday and had not seen his sister for some time. Most significantly of all, the prospect of the audition on the Monday after their return from Birmingham, next Monday in fact, was no longer shrouded in anxiety, because she had been able to spend all her free time in the studio stretching her limbs, correcting her posture, revising her steps and exercises and rehearsing her dance sequences until once again they had all become second nature to her. Miss Inskip had given her much useful advice, together with a helpful demonstration of some very difficult manoeuvres, and rumour had it that Miss Patience would be back before the end of the week, having installed her aged mother in an old people's home in the vicinity. So not only was the storm cloud lifting, it was dispersing, revealing detectable patches of hopeful blue sky through the white wisps of the lingering haze of uncertainty.

Shirley and Ted had reviewed the latter's camping gear on the Wednesday evening to see whether it was all clean for his weekend in the great outdoors with the school Scout troop. Now, on Thursday morning, any remaining odours of unwashed socks and neglected items of Scout uniform were being dealt with by Mr Salvatore's niece Francesca in order to have everything stowed away in Ted's rucksack for him to take to school the next day, ready for departure in the early evening.

As for herself, Shirley had started to pack her own luggage for the wedding and could not resist trying on her Parisian outfit; she turned to survey it from all angles in the full-length mirror that her parents had given her for her last birthday. It was so pretty that she found herself wishing that Alan could see her wearing it. The more she thought about him – which she did often – the more she felt she knew him, but three weeks had passed since their return from France, and even though that brief meeting on the ferry was engraved on her memory, she was beginning to fear that their fleeting acquaintance would for ever be her one and only memory of him, however much she wished she could conjure him up and make him appear suddenly before her, whether out in the street or on the Underground or at a railway station, just as he had on the ferry. Sadly she reminded herself that the magic of fairy stories and many ballet plots did not extend to real life, and chance encounters were no more than tantalizing visions of a future that might have been. She dropped a couple of items into her suitcase and went downstairs to check that all was well with Francesca and give her the week's earnings. On the way down, she glanced at the hall clock and was horrified to see that it was about to chime midday. A whole hour had passed, had been wasted, since her shift had ended, a whole hour in which she could have been warming up, stretching at the *barre* and doing her exercises.

Francesca was hard at work scrubbing a couple of khaki Scout shirts, a collection of odd socks and a pair of gabardine trousers. She was a lively, plump little soul, always singing, but happily not given to talking because she spoke no English. She applied herself to the cleaning and the washing as if there were nothing else she would rather be doing, and last week had been effusive in her gratitude for the coins that Pa had left for her when Shirley slipped them into her hand. "*Grazie, molte grazie, signorina Shirley,*" she had said with a broad smile. Again this week, as Shirley counted out her money on the draining board, Francesca responded with the same engaging smile and demonstrative expressions of gratitude, which were quite disproportionate to the wages she was receiving. But today Shirley was impatient to rush off to the dance studio, so cut Francesca's gibberish short by gesturing first to Ted's uniform in the sink and then out to the washing line.

Annoyed with herself for wasting time, she ran upstairs again to change into her leotard and grab her ballet shoes. While she was in her room, the doorbell rang. Her heart sank. She loitered on the landing with an awful premonition, as if she could see through the fanlight of the front door. If she didn't answer the door, perhaps the irksome caller would go away, but that was a vain hope, because Francesca was already on her way down the hall to open it. From above Shirley heard a well-known voice exclaim in surprise, "Ah, good morning!" in answer to Francesca's "*Buongiorno, signora!*" After some hesitation, the voice then asked, "Is my granddaughter at home?"

Recognizing the resemblance between Shirley and her grandmother, Francesca called up the stairs, "*Signorina Shirley! Signorina Shirley! Ecco tua nonna! Che bello!*" There was no way that Shirley could leave Francesca to cope with her grandmother; in any case, Mrs Marlow had by now stepped into the hall, so she was obliged to go downstairs to greet her.

She glanced up as Shirley slowly descended the stairs, with no sign of a welcome on her pursed lips. "Oh, there you are, dear!" Granny said. Then, indicating Francesca, asked, "Who is this person? What is she doing here? I haven't met her before, have I?"

"No, Francesca comes to clean and wash for us," Shirley replied, cautiously adding, "while my mother is away in France. My grandmother is very ill, you see."

This was almost more news than Granny could take on board. Her brow furrowed. "No one told me! But then, of course, you don't have a telephone here, do you?" she said indignantly, before embarking upon a whole list of exclamations, questions and critical insinuations, such as: "How are you managing? And what about your father? How is he? Oh dear, I am surprised you didn't think to let me know: I could have come over to help! I don't suppose he is eating properly, is he? Who's doing the cooking?"

Shirley answered this torrent with an exasperated, single, all-embracing retort: "We're fine, thank you, Granny."

Then the visitor, looking Francesca up and down, asked suspiciously, "Where does she come from?" Francesca bobbed up and down as if curtsying to Granny, her round face wreathed in smiles.

Shirley managed to give Francesca a friendly nod at the same time as issuing her grandmother with a curt response: "She is Italian and very hard-working." Then, going on the attack – and determined to take up her side of the interrogation before the visitor installed herself too comfortably – she asked brusquely, "What can I do for you, Granny? I am just going out." She followed this with a quick explanation, using the first incontrovertible excuse that came into her head, while grabbing her jacket from the coat peg above her grandmother's head. "I have to buy food for Pa's supper."

"I see," came the reply. "I thought I would call in, hoping we could have a chat over a cup of coffee," Granny peered hopefully into the kitchen. "I was wondering if your pa had bought a wedding present for Edith and Jim, and I thought you and I could go shopping to Morley's to look for something suitable, and perhaps see if they have a job for you after a bite of lunch." She peeped through the crack in the dining-room door, searching for signs on the table that a "bite of lunch" might be in preparation, but her hopes were dashed. The table was bare, without a cloth, plates or cutlery.

Shirley suddenly realized that in the turmoil of the past three weeks Pa had not even thought about a wedding present for Edith and Jim, and nor had she. How was she going to escape from this predicament? She searched for inspiration, which thankfully was not long in coming. "That's really kind of you, Granny, but you see, I have to do our packing, and I have to get Ted's things ready for Scout camp, so I just don't have the time to come out with you, I'm afraid." She could see that her opponent was preparing to pounce with a counter-attack, probably to the effect that these mundane things could be easily dealt with in the evening, so jumped in speedily, saying, "But I'm sure Pa would be delighted if you could buy something nice for us to take, and I know he will pay you for it tomorrow afternoon at four o'clock."

Crossing her fingers behind her back, she hoped that her granny would accept this stratagem, and that she wouldn't buy anything terribly expensive that Pa could not afford. Knowing what to expect by way of response, she then gestured towards Francesca and said with feigned goodwill, "I'm sure Francesca would make you a cup of coffee, Granny, if you want to sit down for a while before you leave."

Deflated, her grandmother cast a dubious eye over Francesca and said, "No, dear, thank you, dear. I think I will be going too; I have such a lot to do today. Warn your father, will you please, that my wedding present to Edith is a china tea service which is packed in a large box, so he will have to make room for that in the car as well as my two suitcases." Reluctantly she made her way towards the door. Anxious to see her grandmother off the premises before her own departure, Shirley adopted a steely, determined glare to ward off any more temporizing with trumped-up ideas. This time she proved to be a match for her grandmother, who huffily declared, "I'll see you and your father tomorrow afternoon, then. I'll be ready by four." With that she strode away without a backward glance, in a clear show of annoyance at her granddaughter's inhospitality. Shirley gave a wry chuckle, picked up her bag and set off as always in the opposite direction, which took her away from her granny's route.

Miss Patience was in the studio office eating a sandwich. "I was so sorry to hear about your mother," Shirley began after their warm exchange of greetings. "How is she now?"

"Oh, Shirley, you are so kind!" Miss Patience exclaimed. "You are the only one of my pupils to have enquired after my mother. It must be something to do with your French background! But thank you, she is doing well and will soon be out of hospital. Now," she went on, "I gather from Miss Inskip that you've been working very hard and are well prepared for next Monday, so why don't you show me what you can do?" Shirley was about to start her routine at the *barre* when Miss Patience interrupted her. "By the way," she said, "we've had some good news today. You know Violet, don't you?" Shirley nodded. "Well, she had her audition two weeks ago and we've heard that she's been accepted by Sadler's Wells! Isn't that good?"

Shirley tried to look pleased for Violet and hide the sudden attack of envy that gnawed at her insides. "Yes, yes," she replied falteringly, "she must be very pleased." She began her routine, but the news of Violet's success had taken the wind out of her balletic sails: she could not glide across the floor in *posé* turns; she could not *pirouette*; she certainly could not manage a *grand jeté*, leaping high in the air with her legs apart in the splits, for she suspected that Sadler's Wells were very unlikely to accept two dancers from the same school.

"What's wrong, Shirley?" Miss Patience asked, deeply concerned by such a dramatic change of attitude.

Shirley had to make up a quick excuse. "I'm not feeling very well today," she said feebly. "I think I'll go home."

She swiftly changed her shoes and made for the door, heedless of Miss Patience, who was calling after her, "You will come back tomorrow, won't you?"

Fighting back the tears, Shirley ran all the way home; then, once she had slammed the front door, she leapt up the stairs and flung herself down on her bed, where she sobbed until the coverlet was soaked. It was so unfair: Violet was not as good a dancer as she was, although she, too, was small, but had the advantage of neat dark hair pulled back in a bun. If Violet had "stolen" the place, she would never forgive her. Nor would she forgive herself for making such a mess of the practice session today. Perhaps life as a dancer was going to be too challenging for her, emotionally as well as physically. Exhausted by the turmoil, she fell asleep. She woke with a start half an hour later and glanced at her watch. At least she had not forgotten her shift in the newsagent's. She washed her face, changed her clothes and went off to work.

This was one of Mrs Salvatore's expansive days and, to Shirley's aggravation, she would not stop chattering. "So is Francesca a help to you?" she wanted to know.

"Yes, thank you, she's wonderful!" Shirley assured her. Not content with that, Mrs Salvatore gabbled on and on about Francesca's past in Italy, where she had grown up in Mr Salvatore's family because her own family was already too large for her parents to cope with her, the new baby. When Mr Salvatore moved to England, he had decided to bring her too, planning to give her work in the house and the shop, but Francesca simply could not learn English however hard she tried, so although she could run the home for Mr and Mrs Salvatore, she was hopeless in the shop. The best that she could do was to deliver papers, but that was a struggle for her as she did not ride a bike. Nowadays, she delivered the papers only if Ted or any other of the paper boys were away, and outside the home she had to take on menial jobs to earn her keep. By all accounts she was delighted to be working for such lovely people as Shirley's family. Mrs Salvatore called out to her husband for corroboration of her story. He emerged from his den at the back to repeat in his broken English everything his wife had said. It was some consolation that he was looking much healthier and happier, which explained why he had been summoned to the front after his long exile in the back room. According to his wife, after going to the Mass, he had at last gone to see his doctor, who had prescribed medication for his cough, which, miraculously, had now cleared up.

Delighted by his own recovery, Mr Salvatore was overwhelming in his appreciation. "Thank-a you, thank-a you, Shirlia," he said, shaking her hand, "Francesca very pleased-a to work-a for you. You very nice-a *famiglia*." Mr Salvatore's gratitude could only partially alleviate Shirley's distress, and she was glad to reach the end of her shift. Out in the street on her own, without having to keep up a smiling appearance, the depths of dejection reclaimed her; she no longer wept, but walked along the road in an unseeing daze.

Ted was already at home and opened the door to her on hearing her key in the lock. "What are you doing here?" she asked, startled to see him home so soon. "What about your paper round?"

"Oh, didn't I tell you? I'm having time off from that this evening and over the weekend because I've too much to do. I can't be doing with that long name either, so from now on I shall call them Mr and Mrs S.," he blurted out in irritation at having to explain his movements. Shirley agreed that Salvatore was rather a mouthful, but that they must be careful not to use the initial when talking to the couple.

Ted nodded impatiently. "Good, Mrs S. said that was fine – my taking the evening off, I mean. I must let her know on Monday, though, whether I shall be doing the evening then. If Maman still isn't back, you do remember I promised to come to Sadler's Wells with you?" At the mention of Sadler's Wells, Shirley burst into tears, then tried to suppress them, fearing that Ted would make fun of her. He did no such thing. Instead, the maturing side of his nature came to the fore and, as his impatience subsided, he placed a comforting hand on her arm. "Shirl, don't cry!" he said. "Come and sit down; I'll make a cup of tea and you can tell me what is wrong."

She allowed herself to be led into the sitting room, where she sat down in the large, softly padded armchair where Pa usually settled his bulky frame, and where as a small child she had often sat on his knee while he read her a story. There was comfort simply in sitting in this chair. She leant back and closed her eyes until Ted reappeared with a tea tray. "Now tell me all about it," he said, as if he were speaking to a small child. As she began to explain her distress, it struck her that it was all rather silly, and Ted, after he had listened to her tale of woe, more or less said so, though not in mocking or critical terms. "Look here," he said, "what difference does it make? If a dancer is good, I would have thought that it doesn't matter where she comes from! If a school has a reputation for producing talented pupils, they are probably going to give dancers from that school preference over someone who comes from a school they haven't heard off." He spoke admirable sense, giving her a perspective on the situation that she hadn't thought of.

She nodded. "I suppose you might be right. Thank you, Ted." She gave him a wan smile and added, "Yes, I should be very glad if you would come to Sadler's Wells with me."

13

"See you this afternoon, Shirl! Enjoy yourself, Ted!" Pa called out as he left for work.

Having finished the morning paper round, Ted was heaving his rucksack onto his back. "I'm off, then," he said to his sister, "have a good weekend!" With a cheeky grin he added, "I don't envy you! But at least they say the weather should be fine. Let's hope so, for all of us!" As he made for the door, he tentatively asked, "You are going to your dance school this morning, aren't you? I'm sure everything will be all right for you on Monday."

"Yes, yes, I think so too, thanks to you!" she replied, and added, "We'll see you on Sunday evening then. Don't forget your key in case you arrive home before we do!" He produced it from his inside pocket, where it was tied to the buttonhole in the pocket flap with a piece of string. Standing on the doorstep, Shirley watched him as he trudged off towards the bus stop, and waved to his back. Never had she felt so close or so grateful to her brother. His words, so wise for his age, had transformed her perspective on the present circumstances and enabled her to view not only the audition next Monday, but also the weekend, with a certain amount of equanimity. She picked up her ballet bag from where she had flung it down in the hall the previous evening, and followed in Ted's footsteps out through the still-open door.

After her stint at the paper shop, she did not go home for a coffee as usual, for fear of finding her grandmother on the doorstep, but went straight to ballet, where the wrinkles on Miss Patience's face faded visibly as she walked through the door. "Shirley! I'm so glad to see you! I was quite worried about you yesterday afternoon! Are you all right now?"

"Yes, I'm fine," Shirley reassured her. "It was just one of those things, you know. Better that problem yesterday than on Monday."

"Of course," her teacher agreed. "Well, if you are feeling better, let's take up where we left off. Go and warm up while I look through this morning's post and then we will go right through the programme, beginning of course with the set routines. We must make sure that everything is firmly fixed in your brain."

The session went well; Miss Patience's reaction was one of fulsome praise, with the addition of a couple of helpful suggestions here and there, and Shirley was pleased. Her dancing seemed to have taken on a new dimension since yesterday. Perhaps, she thought, she needed that jolt to challenge her to aim for a higher level, both of awareness and of ability. "Beautiful! Beautiful!" Miss Patience exclaimed, clapping as Shirley whirled *en pointe* in tightly controlled *posé* turns across the floor and then leapt back in a *grand jeté passé développé*. And so it went on throughout the session. "Amazing! Quite amazing! I've never seen you execute that so well!" Miss Patience said, applauding her *double rond de jambe en l'air sauté* at the end of it. "Especially considering what a wretched time you were having yesterday." Eventually she said, "Look, I think you should leave it there. You're on tip-top form and we don't want to overdo it. Go to the wedding in Birmingham. Have a nice time, and then come back here refreshed on Monday morning for a run-through before going off to Islington."

Although she would have preferred to dance until the last minute – that is, until she had to go home to dress for the journey – Shirley obeyed her teacher. She still had some packing to do and felt in need of lunch, if only a boiled egg on toast. She ate, sitting out at the table in the garden in the autumn sun and reading a magazine left over from last week and given to her by Mrs Salvatore. It was a treat to have time to be lazy, but in less than two minutes of perusing the magazine, her thoughts unexpectedly turned to Alan, that extraordinary, unforgettable young man she had met on the ferry, and whose presence had begun to haunt all her waking moments. Absence was certainly making her heart grow fonder by the day and she dared to wonder if it might be having the same effect on him. She invented madcap schemes for trying to find him: an advertisement in the paper perhaps, or an announcement on the wireless asking Alan to get in touch with Shirley, even going down to Dover to find out where the roads from the port led to. These were crazy ideas, but, for lack of anything else, they were the best she could think of at present. It never occurred to her to doubt that Alan would want to see her again; indeed, he might at this very moment be searching for her. The flame that had leapt between them in that stuffy, crowded lounge on the ferry, and the thrill she had experienced when she took his arm, were both very real sensations that could only pass between two people who felt the same intense attraction to each other. This was an indisputable truth that she had learnt from the stories in her magazines.

There had, of course, been boys in her life before: with her looks that was inevitable. Boys were drawn to her like moths round a candle. They were the boys whom she had met on the bus on the way to and from school or at the ballroom-dancing classes she attended on Tuesday evenings, but none of them had been at all special. The ones who were funny and entertaining tended to be too short, too fat, spotty or simply plain ugly, and those who at first sight seemed outwardly attractive were often dull-witted or too serious for comfort. They passed for friends, but none of them had aroused or could ever arouse the sort of powerful, instant reaction that she had felt on meeting Alan. He, and only he, was the person for whom she was destined – of that she was certain.

In a flash, she saw how it would have to be if that meeting on the boat were not simply to be a fading glimpse of things that might have been, but, instead, the harbinger of a real and beautiful future. It would be up to her to realize her ambitions beyond her wildest hopes, and become a truly famous ballerina. Then Alan would inevitably read about her; he would see her photo in the newspapers, hear about her on the wireless, even perhaps he might come to the theatre where she was performing. Her imagination ran riot as, in her mind's eye she saw him standing waiting for her outside the stage door with a bouquet of red roses in his hand. That glowing image of him was intoxicating, but all too soon her rational self took charge and brushed away the delightful excesses produced by such flights of fancy, sharply reminding her that the fulfilment of all her fantasies – for in truth that was what they were – depended on the results of Monday's audition at Sadler's Wells. Far from being daunted, her determination was reinforced by such a huge challenge. She closed her eyes and let the magazine slip from her lap. It was all decided: she could dream again.

The roar of a motorbike interrupted her pleasure at the caress of the warm sun on her fair skin. The noise came closer, then stopped. Seconds later, the doorbell rang. Reluctantly she rose to her feet and went round to the side of the house, where she found the motorbike parked in the driveway. At the front door there stood a man in uniform. "Telegram for you, miss," he said, handing her an envelope. "Please sign here, would you?" She took the pen he held out to her and scrawled her name on a sheet of paper. She turned the envelope over and over, not wanting to open it, for she had a premonition that it was bringing news that she would rather not read. She took it into the garden and resumed her seat by the table before plucking up the courage to read the telegram. There was no doubt that it was from her mother, to whom they – she, her father and Ted – had all written several times without receiving any reply. The most recent communication that had come from Maman was the reassuring telegram she had sent the week after her arrival in France.

Shirley unfolded the small single sheet of paper. "*Mémé est décédée*," it said. "*Crise cardiaque. Funérailles demain à 14h*. Maman" And that was all. The earlier good news had been erased by this huge bolt from the clear blue sky, falling to earth like a meteorite and obliterating the sunniest of September days. Shirley sat motionless, unable and unwilling to digest the news that Mémé, her dear French grandmother, was no more, that she had died of a heart attack. It was of no help to be told that her funeral was tomorrow, as it was absolutely impossible for the family – that is to say, for her two grandchildren, and her son-in-law as well – to be present at the village church in northern France. The irony of having to attend that dreadful wedding on the very same day as the funeral did not escape her, and she buried her head in her hands.

A couple of minutes later, a gentle tap on the shoulder startled her. "What is it, Shirl?" her father asked. He must have come home early and seen her sitting out in the garden. She handed him the telegram. "Oh, no!" he cried. "I thought your Mémé was getting better! What a terrible shock!" He sat down heavily at the table on the chair next to his daughter and put his arm round her shoulders. "She was such a kind person and so good to me. The world needs more people like her. We all loved her, didn't we?" That was as much as he was capable of saying, and probably that was enough. They sat quietly for the next half-hour, not speaking, only reflecting.

"Would you prefer to stay here rather than go to Birmingham?" Pa asked after a while, adding: "I really wouldn't mind, myself; I'm not too keen to go. We could even catch the boat train and arrive in France in time, all being well." His offer was appealing and generous, considering that he had not seen his own family for a long time, not only his sister but also his younger brother Paul, who lived in Newcastle and was also going to be at the wedding. Even more surprisingly, without so much as a second thought, he was actually offering to go to France for the first time in almost twenty years, as if the offer he had made to his wife when she had left precipitately had been germinating in his mind and had blossomed into an eagerness to return to the country which he had formerly loved so well.

Shirley pondered his suggestion, almost convinced that it might be a possibility. "Mm, that would be nice," she said, but soon realized very reluctantly why staying at home was not an option. "But what about Granny?" she asked.

"Oh, dear! Yes, of course, you're right!" her father exclaimed. "She'd never forgive us if we didn't take her. I'm sorry. It looks as if we haven't any choice. Can you bear it?"

Shirley nodded. "Yes," she said, "but let's have tea first to give me time to try to get over the shock, and then we had better set out, otherwise we'll be late for Granny."

When father and daughter arrived an hour later than planned, Mrs Marlow was not best pleased to see them. "Where have you been?" she asked sharply. "It's nearly five o'clock and I've been sitting here with my coat on since four! If only you had a telephone! You said four, didn't you, Shirley?"

"Yes," Granny, "I'm sorry—"

Shirley began to apologize, before her father intervened: "It's not Shirley's fault, Mother," he said tersely, "we've had some bad news."

"Oh, what was that?" his mother demanded, unaccustomed to the slightest hint of disrespect from her eldest son.

"We've just heard that my mother-in-law has died and that the funeral is tomorrow." His mother fell silent while she considered how best to react. Sympathy was not her strong point and words of condolence were conspicuous by their absence from her vocabulary. Any faint hope that she might volunteer to travel by train, or indeed hire a taxi, which she could well afford, so that her son and granddaughter could catch the boat train, for which there was still time, and arrive in France for the funeral, was dashed before it was even contemplated.

"Well, that's a shame, but I gather it was not altogether unexpected," she remarked with an utter lack of emotion. "But we must get on the road if we're to arrive by dinner time. Winnie is expecting us, you know. My luggage is over there." She pointed to a pile of suitcases blocking the hall.

"Oh and by the way," she added swiftly, "you owe me for the sets of bed linen I bought for you to take as a wedding present. I haven't wrapped them up so you can see what I've bought. They're there on top of the box with the tea service in it. Perhaps you might like to settle up before we set out?" Tight-lipped, she looked her son straight in the eye. "Shirley suggested I should buy them as you had forgotten to buy anything," she added accusingly.

"How much do I owe you?" Reggie asked with ill-concealed irritation, and then blanched on hearing the cost. "They are of course top quality, the best that Morley's could provide," his mother assured him. "Look how pretty they are – they'll last Edith a lifetime."

He glanced at the sheets and pillowcases. "Yes, thank you very much," he said without any display of enthusiasm. Shirley inspected them cursorily: they were pretty and certainly had an extravagant appearance; one set was white with a gold embroidered border, the other had a similar green edge. How fortunate it was that she had thought of buying some wrapping paper, ribbon and a card at the stationer's next to the paper shop that morning! She had the distinct impression that her granny had deliberately omitted to add those items to the purchase.

"I'll wrap them up now," Shirley said. "It won't take a minute."

"Right," said Pa, "I'll write you a cheque, Mother, and then I'll pack the car while Shirley wraps the present."

It seemed that the whole of London was trying to escape to the country that fine, warm Friday afternoon. The suburban roads were blocked with traffic in all directions, and even when the built-up area was behind them it was barely crawling along. Unlike the traffic, Mrs Marlow's mindless tirades were unstoppable. Shirley was thankful to be squeezed in the back of the car alongside her grandmother's suitcases and boxes, which had multiplied from the original two to several. Her own luggage, together with her father's and their wedding present, was stowed away in the boot.

She sat in a sombre, trance-like state, carried away to another country, to France, where Maman and Pépé would be holding a wake, sitting beside Mémé's open coffin and greeting all their friends from the village as they came to pay their respects. How she wished that she could be with them and share in their grief. As it was, she had no choice but to sit in the car on a long, slow journey to a wedding that she did not want to attend, and listen to her grandmother's spiteful remarks. She tried to close her ears to the invective that the old woman was relentlessly aiming in her father's direction. "I still don't see why it took you so long to come!" she complained. "It wasn't as if you could do anything about the death and that funeral over there. And there I was, wondering where on earth you could be! It would have been better if you'd put all that to one side and forgotten about it for the weekend. I really do think you should get a telephone."

This observation was followed by only the briefest of pauses, only time for her to draw breath before continuing, "When Billy died – that was on a Saturday, if you remember – there was nothing I could do after the funeral directors had come to take him away, so I went away to Brighton with my friends Joan and Angus – you remember them, don't you? – for the weekend as we had planned. It did me the world of good to get away after all those weeks of waiting for Billy to give up the ghost."

Her son, normally so phlegmatic, was by now fuming helplessly while trying to follow the road and avoid the other traffic, since not only were his mother's remarks untimely and insensitive in the present circumstances, but she was also making no bones about how little she cared for her husband, and this caused him great pain. Reggie owed the happiest memories of his childhood to his father, in spite of the repressive regime his mother exerted over the household. From him he had learnt all that he knew about engineering and the mechanics of every imaginable type of motor, large and small, and it was his father who had spared no expense to obtain the best treatment for him when he was brought back to England, so badly damaged after the War. Shirley closed her eyes as well as her ears and not long afterwards she heard her father say, "I think we should be quiet. I see in the rear mirror that Shirley has shut her eyes. Poor child, she's very upset, and that's made her tired. I expect she wants to have a little sleep." Shirley heard her granny sniff as if to say, "I don't believe it!" but she too fell quiet and, before long, loud snores issued from the front passenger seat.

14

"My goodness! They must have huge electricity bills!" Granny exclaimed when she woke up with a start as the car drew to a halt. Light streamed from all the windows of the mansion on the outskirts of Birmingham that Uncle Horace had inherited from his grandfather, the founder of the meat-pie business on which the Rayner family fortune was based.

"I expect they'll have their hands full, organizing a wedding," Reggie responded laconically, unwilling to speculate how much poor Horace had to spend on utility bills, if indeed he had any money left to pay them after his womenfolk had frittered away his earnings on anything and everything that took their fancy. He helped his mother out of the car then lifted out the luggage. When at last Shirley was able to climb out and stretch her cramped limbs, her grandmother was already standing on the step waiting for the door to be opened. Shirley was not inclined to join her, but stood waiting by the car for her father to finish unloading.

At length the door was opened by Uncle Horace. "Ah, Mrs Marlow," he said, with a perceptible aversion in his tone. "Do come in." Then, looking over his mother-in-law's head, he saw Reggie out in the driveway and abandoned the old woman, leaving her to find her own way into the house. "Reggie, my dear chap, how good to see you! Let me help you with all that luggage. I suppose it mostly belongs to *her*." He pointed in the direction of the front door through which the least welcome of his guests had disappeared.

"How did you guess?" was Reggie's sardonic reply.

Catching sight of his niece by marriage standing in the twilight on the other side of the car, Horace exclaimed, "And here's Shirley! It's so nice of you both to come!" This was by far the warmest reception that they were likely to receive, so they were happy to stand out in the driveway exchanging news.

To prevent any misunderstanding, Pa grasped the opportunity to explain that he and Shirley might find it difficult to be the life and soul of the party because of the recent death of his mother-in-law. At this Uncle Horace hugged Shirley, saying, "I'm so sorry for you and for your mother too. How hard it must be for her!" His sympathy brought tears to Shirley's eyes for the first time since receiving the telegram that afternoon. In the intervening hours she had been too stunned to weep, and now she had difficulty holding back the tears, although she knew that it was essential to do so to avoid the inevitable disapproving stares that otherwise she would encounter on entering the house.

There was plenty of time to dry her eyes, however, since Uncle Horace did not seem at all inclined to go indoors. Her father then asked, "What about you, Horace, how are things here?"

"Don't' even begin to ask!" was Uncle Horace's resigned reply. "It's all hell let loose in there!"

"Oh, really? Surely it can't be as bad as that?" Pa said mystified.

"Yes, it most certainly is!" Uncle Horace replied, snorting loudly. "Thelma's fallen ill – the flu or something – and she's the only brides-maid! You wouldn't believe the fuss. You'd think that Edith could manage without a bridesmaid, but oh no, not according to my missus! There's got to be a bridesmaid to wear the dress and the shoes and carry the flowers that are already paid for. If I were you I'd go and stay in a hotel, if only there were one around here!"

Light streamed from the open door through which Granny had passed, and sounds, wailing and shouting, which gave some credence to Uncle Horace's account, also came streaming out. "Perhaps we should just come and say 'hello' and then try and find somewhere to eat," Pa suggested. He was tired after the journey and was in need of sustenance rather than confrontation.

"There's not much hereabouts; we'd have to go into Birmingham to find a restaurant" was Uncle Horace's discouraging assessment of the eating possibilities. He went on, "Winnie was preparing something for supper an hour or so ago, cold meats and salad and suchlike, when Thelma came in complaining of a fever and a headache. I suppose the food is still there in the kitchen. If you feel like braving the wailing banshee in the hall, we could go and have a look in the larder." They walked in trepidation towards the front door.

The caterwauling died down when they came into the circular entrance hall, and Reggie went over to his distraught sister, who was seated on a bench, to give her a fraternal pat on the back and a peck on the cheek where her make-up had run in streams of red, orange, blue and black. "Oh, Reggie, you don't know what it's been like!" she cried, blowing her nose noisily and wiping her eyes ostentatiously. "I've worked so hard these weeks and months for this wedding, and then, only just now, Thelma comes in and says she has to go to bed and feels too ill to be a bridesmaid! And I've spent a fortune on her outfit! And as for Horace" – here she glared at her cowering husband – "all he can say is if Thelma's ill that's unfortunate, but these things happen! How can he be so unfeeling! Why doesn't he go and give that girl an aspirin and tell her she's got to get up, come down and lend me a hand for a change? And look, there's Mother, just bossing me about as usual!" She pointed accusingly at her mother, who, standing arms akimbo in the centre of the circle and fixing her daughter with an icy stare, had clearly been telling her to pull herself together and not make such a fuss. It was equally clear that this was not the first time in her life by any means that Aunt Winnie had been subjected to Granny's withering scorn.

Hiding behind her father, Shirley could almost have pitied Edith, the bride, had she been able to feel any warmth towards her. Ebullient, garrulous Edith was at a loss for words. And there was poor Uncle Horace hovering in the doorway, not daring to enter his own house! Momentarily she found it hard not to burst out laughing at the ludicrous scene, worthy of a pantomime, but then suddenly her inner laughter was abruptly suppressed by the sad, contrasting image of her mother and grandfather sitting beside Mémé's open coffin so far away in France: yet again she wished she were there with them and not here with these dreadful relatives of her father's. "Thank goodness Alan cannot see them!" she thought. How would she ever be able to bring herself to introduce them to him? Would she have to invite them all to her own wedding? Since no one had noticed her in the hullabaloo, she was tempted to run out of the house and make her own way back to London. Only the thought of leaving her pa behind, coupled with the fact that she didn't have enough money in her purse, restrained her.

"Well," Granny announced firmly, "I came expecting dinner to be on the table. I haven't eaten since lunchtime. Reggie and Shirley were an hour late coming for me so I didn't even have my tea at home. We stopped for a cup of tea on the way and that was all. Aren't you going to offer us something to eat?"

Edith jumped to attention and found her tongue. "Oh, yes, of course, Granny," she said, "there's food in the kitchen. Follow me!" The party trooped into the kitchen, leaving Winnie snivelling on the bench in the hall. On the table a cold collation of ham, pies, sausages, all provided by the family firm, lay ready for the guests to help themselves.

"Humph," said Granny, "I don't approve of having to serve myself in the kitchen; I like my food to be brought to me at the dining table."

"You go and sit down over there, then, Granny," said Edith, waving towards the veranda, where tables bearing lighted candles were laid with silver cutlery and crystal glasses. Shirley, thankful to be relived of that demanding person's care, warmed to Edith as she attended dutifully to their grandmother's every wish and whim.

Uncle Horace had crept into the kitchen and collected a plate of food to take up to Thelma. He reappeared still carrying the laden plate, saying, "Thelma really isn't well. She now says she's feeling sick and can't eat anything. I think we ought to call a doctor."

"Rubbish," said Granny, "a good night's sleep and she'll be fine by the morning."

Aunt Winnie, who had at last come in from the hall, where she was no longer the centre of attention, started dabbing her eyes again. "What a waste! That lovely dress!" she said between her sobs.

Then she noticed Shirley. "Oh, Shirley, I didn't see you lurking there. I didn't even know you'd come! So I see your mother isn't here then?"

"No, I'm afraid not," Shirley replied, regretting that her pa's warning to Uncle Horace had evidently not been conveyed, and wondering how best to explain her mother's absence.

She could have saved herself the trouble, because, as quick as lightening, her grandmother provided her own version of the situation. "Oh, she's off in France," she said airily, "something to do with her mother dying, I think."

To her credit, Aunt Winnie registered surprise and said, "Oh, I am sorry to hear that!" Shirley reckoned, uncharitably, that she probably meant that she was sorry that Jacqueline was not there to be the butt of her sarcastic remarks.

Having served her grandmother, Edith came over to Shirley and was eyeing her up and down. "You know, Shirley," she said to the astonishment of the assembled company, "you could be my bridesmaid tomorrow!"

"Don't be stupid, Edith!" Aunt Winnie, fully recovered and in possession of her biting tongue again, reprimanded her daughter. "Shirley looks like an urchin off the streets: she's far too thin and short to wear that lovely dress of Thelma's, and we couldn't have it adjusted in time!"

"Well, that doesn't matter!" Edith retorted. "Maybe there's something else she could wear, and at least she could carry Thelma's posy. What do you think, Shirley?"

Shirley was as astounded as anyone else and took a little while to reply. "Why, yes, if you would like that," she said uncertainly, not at all sure whether she herself would like it."

"What were you going to wear anyhow?" Edith persisted, but her mother intervened before Shirley could reply.

"Whatever she wears it won't be anything like Thelma's peach satin and her headdress, and the shoes will be too big for her, so just forget it."

"No, Mother." Edith, having recovered her usual style, asserted herself. "I want to see what Shirley has brought with her. She always has nice clothes. Come on, Shirley, let's have something to eat. Help yourself and then I'll take you up to your room so you can show me what you've brought."

The cousins sat together at the table, making only fitful conversation during the meal because they had never exchanged more than a few words in passing before: Edith, older by five years, had never shown any interest in Shirley and, for her part, Shirley had found previous visits to Birmingham to be boring and unwelcome distractions from the ballet, as well as the cause of much discomfort caused by the hostility directed towards her mother. The general atmosphere had improved by the end of the meal, when the company dispersed into the various ground-floor reception rooms: Horace and Reggie disappeared into Horace's study for a quiet smoke, while Granny and Aunt Winnie settled themselves comfortably in the lounge, having temporarily made up their differences. Edith led the way upstairs, picking up Shirley's suitcase in the hall as she went. "I'm afraid we're on the top floor," she said as they climbed the stairs. "My parents, Granny and your father are on the first floor, and the three of us – you, me and Thelma – are on the top floor. Uncle Paul's not coming till tomorrow, so we all fit in nicely. You won't mind sharing the bathroom with me and Thelma, will you?"

"No, no, that's fine," Shirley replied uneasily, sensing that the arrangement was not fine, though unsure why. She was at least quite pleased to be able to avoid outspoken Thelma, who, in her opinion, was the most obnoxious member of the family and whose vicious tongue had in the past caused her much distress.

Edith took her into a large, luxurious bedroom and put the suitcase down on the bed. "This is for you, Shirley. Now do show me what you're going to wear tomorrow." Having glanced round the room in admiration tinged with envy, Shirley opened her case and carefully pulled out the Parisian dress, hat and shoes. "Ooh, my goodness!" Edith exclaimed. "That's beautiful! It's real silk, isn't it?" Shirley smiled, neither confirming nor denying Edith's supposition. "And look! Shoes to match! What a lovely colour! I do like that pale green! It's so much nicer than that awful peachy satin Mother chose for Thelma. And it will go perfectly with the posy! Where did you get it?"

Shirley nonchalantly replied, "Maman bought it for me." She paused for effect. "We bought it in Paris just a few weeks ago, especially for your wedding."

Edith gasped. With her wholehearted approval of the Parisian outfit, she rose in her cousin's esteem. "You'll make a gorgeous bridesmaid! Are you going to try it on, Shirley? Shall we go down and show the others? My, they will be surprised!" she continued enthusiastically, but the sight of the dress and the sudden memory it evoked of the day in Paris with Maman had dampened Shirley's enthusiasm.

"No, if you don't mind, I'd prefer not to parade around in it today." She stifled a sob.

Edith was perplexed at first, then exclaimed gently, "Oh, of course! I'm so sorry to hear about your French grandmother. It's so good of you to come here, because I'm sure you'd rather be in France." Her sympathy astounded Shirley, even more so when she heard Edith's next remark: "How awful for you to have to come here with that old baggage instead of being with your mother. Maman, isn't that what you call her?" Shirley nodded sadly, but broke into a smile on realizing that by "that old baggage" Edith meant their shared grandmother.

That candid reference laid the foundations of a bond between the two cousins that began to grow steadily stronger with each of Edith's pronouncements. "Ooh, Shirley," she said, "how I wish I'd had a kind grandma like yours, but my dad's mother died before I was born." It was a telling comment on that's family's inner workings that Edith referred to her father affectionately and casually as "Dad" and to her other parent as "Mother", the disparity indicating a certain distance and coolness. "And now just look what we're left with, you and me!" Edith was saying. "Only that nasty old woman downstairs who only ever thinks of herself and hasn't a good word to say about anyone, least of all me! What's more," she added, "my mother's terrified of her, always has been since she was little. That's probably why she's in such a state and is so difficult. You saw what she was like when you arrived, didn't you?"

Edith proved to be a surprisingly fertile fount of information, and what she had to say was a revelation to Shirley, who had previously put all her father's female relations in the same category, regarding each and every one of them as mean, vindictive and selfish. It dawned on her that the strained relations between Maman and Edith's family were possibly in large part due to tales and untruths that her grandmother had spread liberally around on her visits to Birmingham. She decided to put her theory to the test and quizzed Edith: "I bet Granny says some pretty horrid things about us, doesn't she?"

Edith considered her response carefully. "Mm, well," she replied, "the funny thing is she doesn't quite know how to handle you and your mother because you're French and are always so smartly dressed. She doesn't understand what you are talking about when you talk among yourselves and you don't fit into her cosy scheme of things where she can boss the rest of us about as she likes. She suspects that you come from an aristocratic family with a lot of land, and that scares her!"

Shirley laughed out loud at such a preposterous suggestion, but said nothing to disabuse her cousin of their grandmother's delusion. Instead she asked, "Why do you think she's like that?"

"Ooh, now you're asking!" Edith exclaimed. "Mother says she thinks it's because when Granny was young she fell in love with someone and was not allowed to marry him. Whether it was because her parents thought he was not good enough for her, or the other way round, Mother doesn't know, but she thinks, or rather Auntie Bess – you wouldn't remember her because she died before you were born – Auntie Bess, Granny's aunt, once told her that they eloped and were caught and never allowed to see each other again!"

Shirley stood open-mouthed in amazement. "Goodness!" was all she could say. Then she frowned. "But what about Grandfather Bill?" she asked. "Where did he come into it?"

"Oh, I suppose after that Granny's parents made sure to arrange her marriage for her and settled on Grandfather Bill. He had a hard time of it though, because obviously she didn't love him and made his life a misery."

"Poor man!" Shirley whispered, trying to recall her scant memories of Grandfather Bill, though a very distant recollection reminded her that her father had loved him deeply and had been inconsolable when he died.

"Yes, poor man!" Edith echoed. "But I suppose, when you think about it, "Granny must have been very unhappy, so perhaps it's 'poor her' as well."

"Maybe," Shirley mused, "but really she doesn't have to go on taking it out on everybody else."

"True," Edith agreed.

Overwhelmed by so much unsolicited family history, Shirley changed the subject: "Won't you show me your wedding dress?" she begged her cousin, who until now had not volunteered to divulge her big secret.

Edith hesitated shyly, "Well, it was going to be a surprise, but since you're my bridesmaid now, why not?" She led the way into the next room, an even more luxurious bedroom, where a superb gown hung from the wardrobe door.

Shirley was mesmerized: this was a glorious creation in a creamy-white lace with a matching veil, stylish in its understatement, not the white meringue that she had expected. Just as Edith had admired her Parisian outfit, she cooed her admiration, carefully fingering the delicate lace. "It's very beautiful!"

"Ooh, you like it do you?" Edith asked in surprise. "I wasn't at all sure about it myself. I fancied something with flounces in white organza myself, but they persuaded me that this would be more fashionable.

"So, who were they?" Shirley enquired, expecting that Edith's friends had had some influence in the choice. If so, they were good friends indeed.

Rather sheepishly Edith admitted, "I have to say it was Granny's choice. She came with Mother and me when we went looking for wedding-dress patterns in the summer and she saw this one and insisted on it, so Mother bought it. She also insisted on the lace and she came with us to the dressmaker and gave her plenty of instructions. I think she could have made it herself if she'd chosen to."

"Well, fancy that!" Shirley exclaimed, but then, as reluctant as Edith to give her granny any credit whatsoever, she added, "I think you made the right choice, because you must have had the final say. You'll look lovely in it tomorrow."

"Well, if you say so, Shirley, it must be all right!" was Edith's relieved conclusion.

"I'm sure your husband will love it!" Shirley said, now wanting whole-heartedly to give Edith her encouragement.

Surprisingly, she was enjoying talking to this cousin who previously had been a stranger. It was a pleasure to discover someone from such a different background with whom she appeared to have so much in common. "Do tell me about your fiancé. What's he like?" she asked.

The two girls sat down on the bed and Edith shrugged. "Oh, he's all right, I suppose," she said. "We met one evening when I went with the girls down to the City Ballroom, not that I can dance very well of course, but he can." She gazed at her wedding dress. "He works in the car industry in Coventry, so that's where we're buying a house. Mother doesn't like him, but that's to be expected. My dad says he's a good chap and gets on well with him. He's not what you might call good-looking, but then I'm no picture book, am I? Not like you, Shirley, you're so pretty, you should be a film star."

Shirley gesticulated with a modest wave of the hand. "No, no," she said, "I've no wish to be a film star," but she didn't admit where her ambition lay.

Deftly she turned the conversation back to Edith: "So what do you do, Edith?"

"Me? Oh, I'm doing my nursing training," Edith said, then she corrected herself: "Well, actually, I'd like to be doing my nursing training, but at the moment I'm a ward orderly, have been these last five years, though whether I shall keep it up when I'm married remains to be seen. All those night shifts! I don't think Jim will be very happy if I go out as soon as he comes home in the evening. More likely we'll start a family quite soon. I'm twenty-two already, you know." She paused, "Anyhow, to tell the truth, I can't wait to get out of this house! Not on account of my dad, but Mother and Thelma – not to mention Granny when she comes to stay – drive me crazy! I need a home of my own, a husband and a family!" How different, Shirley thought, from her own hopes for the future. Edith's lack of enthusiasm for Jim contrasted strongly with her passion for Alan, and Edith's lukewarm approach to her career was hugely removed from Shirley's obsession with the ballet. Nevertheless, there was a kindred spirit between the two cousins that bridged the gap and enabled them to feel not only comfortable, but also safe and trusting in each other's company.

"Let's go down and tell Mother that the bridesmaid problem is solved!" Edith suggested. "I'll just call in on Thelma on the way. Do you want to come and say 'hello' to her?" Shirley did not want to call in on Thelma, but had no choice. "Look, Thel, Shirley's here and she's going to be the bridesmaid tomorrow! So you don't have to worry about that. And she says the wedding dress will be fine!" Edith called out cheerily to the recumbent figure on the bed in the room next to Shirley's.

"Go away!" came the muffled command from under the bedclothes, so they tiptoed away downstairs. There no one took much notice of them. Winnie and Granny nodded without showing much interest when Edith announced that Shirley had a very pretty dress that was perfect for the occasion and was definitely going to be her bridesmaid, and Horace and Reggie, still in the study, were deep in conversation.

"I think I'll be going to bed," Edith said. "The hairdresser's coming at nine in the morning. Would you like her to do your hair as well, Shirley?"

"Yes, please!" Shirley replied. "In that case, I think I'll be going to bed too."

15

The wedding ceremony took place a couple of miles away in a plain red-brick Congregational church which contrasted markedly with the gloomy, ornate building with which Shirley was familiar in London. As she followed Edith up the aisle, she was impressed by the unpretentious openness of it all and liked its straightforward approach to religion: here there were no forbidding confessionals, like little prison cells, along the walls, nor were there bells and incense, added to which the priest was not wearing a lacy gown. It was less dramatic certainly, less appropriate for a theatrical setting, but friendlier and more comfortable. The simple service was followed by a sumptuous reception in a splendid hotel out in the country.

Although no expense had been spared, the truth was inescapable that the considerable financial outlay was not for Edith's benefit but for that of Winnie's friends: a crowd of brash women, bedecked with vulgar, expensive jewellery, and their loud-mouthed husbands, who seemed to have little in common with Uncle Horace. He, for the most part stood behind his wife, trying to muster a smile and nodding politely as the guests filed past. Jim's parents received short shrift from the bride's mother, who shook their hands haughtily while muttering "pleased to meet you", but Uncle Horace, making up for his wife's social shortcomings, gave them a warmer greeting, saying what a good husband Jim would undoubtedly be for Edith. The rest of Jim's family merited very little attention from Mrs Horace Rayner. As for Jim himself, certainly he was a rather weedy specimen with little in his appearance to recommend him, but he did have a firm handshake and a kindly light in his soft brown eyes which matched Edith's exactly.

After the dinner, Uncle Horace succeeded in enunciating an appropriate sentence or two by way of a speech, thanking his "dear Edith" for being a dutiful and loving daughter, and recommending her to Jim's care in the sure anticipation that he would be an excellent husband. Jim was surprisingly articulate when he spoke, praising his lovely bride for her warmth and enthusiasm, and thanking the beautiful bridesmaid who had stepped into the role at the last minute on account of Thelma's unfortunate illness. He asked for a special round of applause for Shirley, who basked in the limelight and the effusive praise that was being showered upon her. In one fleeting moment of sadness she wished that her mother could have been there to witness the success of the Parisian outfit, which had been much admired.

However, her granny – who had not uttered so much as one word of congratulations to the bride or the bridesmaid on their appearance and, when they descended the staircase dressed in their finery that morning, had deliberately turned away – now lost no time in broadcasting loudly to anyone in earshot the fact that Shirley's dress, with its matching hat and shoes, came from Paris, bought only in the last month, and was made of silk, while it was she who had chosen the design and material of Edith's gown and veil. Anyone listening to her might erroneously have thought that she had paid for everything. The best man, for his part, clearly had expected something different from this rather smart affair that Jim, his best friend, had let him in for, so had had to tone down his speech and delete any show of ribaldry, which left him with very little to say except that Jim was a good chap and a great pal and always had been. He too asked the guests to raise their glasses to the bridesmaid.

A band struck up, playing dance music which made Shirley's feet tap under the table. The best man asked her to dance, as was proper, but only once, as he was already married and thereafter had to dance with his wife. There was a scarcity of eligible bachelors, and those there were spent the evening propping up the bar. Aunt Winnie kept a gimlet eye on that area and every so often drew a sharp breath, observing, "That looks like another double whisky he's serving over there. Really, Horace," she said, "you should have put a limit on the drinks at the bar so that those boys would have to pay up when they've exhausted their allowance."

"No dear, I couldn't do that," Uncle Horace remonstrated mildly. "I wouldn't want to appear mean today of all days." Aunt Winnie was about to make a caustic comment, but he took the wind out of her sails by adding, "And you wouldn't want me to, would you?"

Otherwise, Aunt Winnie glowed with self-satisfaction: "Oh, look, Horace!" she commanded. "I told you those dahlias I chose would match my dress perfectly. And they do, don't they?"

Uncle Horace turned his attention to a huge bowl of flaming-red dahlias in the centre of the room and nodded wearily, "Yes, dear, quite striking!"

"I knew this was the right colour for an autumn wedding!" Aunt Winnie declared triumphantly, straightening the pleats in her dress and patting her hat, now on a chair by her side. "Of course, Edith's dress is perfect as well, but Shirley is in quite the wrong colour! I would never have allowed her to wear green if I'd had any say in the matter. Such a pity Thelma couldn't wear her lovely peach satin!"

Pa, who was sitting between his brother Paul and his mother, had been engrossed in animated conversation with Paul, avoiding their mother, who vented whatever carping criticisms she could think of on Paul's long suffering wife, Madge. Eventually the latter must have given her husband a secret signal indicating that she had had enough, as he got to his feet, saying "Well, I think it's time for a dance with my wife; we don't have much of a chance for that these days!"

Pa, now alone with his mother, immediately stood up also and called to Shirley across the table, "What about a dance, Shirl?" She leapt to her feet, grateful that at last she could take to the dance floor. "I don't think I'll be much good. I haven't danced for years and this old hip won't let me move very easily, but let's see how we get on, shall we?" He whirled his daughter onto the floor and together they glided effortlessly through waltzes, quicksteps and foxtrots while Jim made a gallant effort to push Edith round the floor.

"You know, Shirl," Pa said when they sat down for a break, well away from Granny, "this does my heart good. I haven't danced like this in years. What a pity your mother isn't here – she'd love it too!"

"I didn't know you could dance, Pa!" Shirley exclaimed.

"Oh, yes, yes, your mother and I used to go out to the Palace Ballroom if my leg wasn't giving me too much trouble, and we'd enjoy ourselves so much! Do you remember old Mrs Watson from next door? She used to come and look after you and Ted while we danced the night away."

"I do faintly remember her, but I expect I was usually asleep," Shirley answered.

"It's not your sort of dancing, of course, though you are good at it," Pa went on, revelling in nostalgia, "but it's such a nice way to spend an evening out."

"Why don't you do it nowadays?" Shirley enquired.

"Once your mother started working at the Embassy we stopped because she was too tired at the end of the day, so that was that." There was wistfulness in Pa's voice, but Shirley's eyes shone with delight at the discovery of a hidden aspect of her parents' past, a joyous aspect, so unlike the endless sad stories of the Great War.

"But you dance so well! Just like Fred Astaire! Maybe you should take it up again," she suggested.

"Perhaps, when your mother comes home," said Pa doubtfully.

At nine o'clock the band paused for refreshment and the bridal couple appeared, smartly dressed in their going-away clothes. Edith, wearing a wide-brimmed hat which accentuated her generous proportions, came over to Shirley. "You've been wonderful, Shirley! Thank you so much," she said, "I feel I've gained a lovely friend as well as a cousin in you. You looked so beautiful in your dress and that pretty little cloche hat. The posy was just right, wasn't it? Do come and see us soon, won't you?"

Touched by such kindness, Shirley promised Edith and Jim that she most certainly would visit them. After their departure in a flurry of confetti, she was surprised to find herself at the centre of an admiring group of Edith's friends. "Edith told us you're her cousin!" they chorused. "You're so pretty! Won't you come and sit with us?" She went over to their table and sat for a while chatting. Most of them, like Edith, worked at the hospital.

Some were nurses, some ward orderlies, but the one Shirley liked the best was Elsie, who said that she was coming to the end of her training in midwifery. She was small and quiet with large eyes that shone from behind horn-rimmed glasses. "I love babies!" she declared. "But I don't suppose I shall have any myself. I'm twenty-three already and I don't even have a boyfriend! So, I shall just have to look after other people's babies and resign myself to being a maiden aunt." Although her voice trailed away sadly, Elsie suddenly smiled brightly, as if deliberately castigating herself for casting a gloom over the celebrations, but Shirley, who, in her ignorance, hadn't the slightest clue what she was talking about, tried to reassure her that she would be bound to have a baby one day. Despite her best intentions, Shirley was aware that her words rang false, and there ensued an awkward silence.

The band struck up again, giving Shirley the opportunity to move away from an uncomfortable situation; she made her excuses, saying that she couldn't possibly leave her pa at the mercy of her grandmother any longer. Her concern for her father was only a half-truth, though a genuine and adequate one which was readily understood by Elsie and Edith's other friends, who let her go with what appeared to be a knowing wink. The other half of the truth was that she yearned to take to the dance floor again and imagine herself to be Ginger Rogers dancing in that gorgeous swansdown dress in *Top Hat*. Her able partner would be not Fred Astaire or her pa, but Alan. On the dance floor, she closed her eyes and imagined that she was dancing in his arms.

It was after midnight when they arrived back at the Rayner mansion. Mrs Appleton, Winnie's cleaning lady, who had been called in to keep an eye on Thelma, greeted them wringing her hands anxiously in the hall. "Oh, Mrs Rayner," she said, "Thelma's not at all well. She keeps being sick and I've had to change her sheets I don't know how many times. And she has such a fever!" Uncle Horace ran upstairs, but Aunt Winnie took no notice and went into the kitchen.

"We'll leave Horace to deal with Thelma," she said, her speech slurred by an excess of alcohol. "What about a nice cup of tea, Reggie?"

"No, thanks," said Pa. "I'll just have a glass of water; what about you, Shirl?"

"Oh, same for me, please, then I think I'll go to bed," Shirley replied. She took her glass and went up the two flights of stairs. Now that Edith had gone, the house seemed empty without her large presence, her rich Brummie accent and her carefree attitude. To think that only yesterday Edith had represented an unknown, possibly hostile quantity and today had become the closest of friends, far closer in fact than any of Shirley's contemporaries, either at school or at ballet! As far as school friends were concerned, she had a scant amount of time for meeting them outside the classroom, and as for any friendships in the ballet class, they were always overshadowed by a wariness born of the competitive spirit so prevalent in that milieu.

She lay in a bath scented with Edith's bath salts, casting her mind back over the day with pleasure. Indeed, with the exception of Aunt Winnie and Granny, who were probably still downstairs congratulating themselves on the success of the day, and then, in a drunken stupor, quarrelling over who had been responsible for that success, it had been so much more enjoyable than she could ever have imagined. The photographer had taken many photos of her, both outside the church and at the reception, specifically asking her to pose for him, rather than snapping her indiscriminately as he had the rest of the guests. He had promised to send her the proofs, and she hoped that they would not be long in coming, since she was impatient to see them. Absorbed in these and other happy memories of the day, she lay back luxuriating in the warm water, taking care not to wet her hair, for the hairdresser had styled it so nicely that morning that with any luck it would still be fine for the audition, until she remembered that her pretty curls would have to be swept back and pinned up on Monday, because a neat hairstyle was an essential requirement of the ballet.

Her thoughts were lazily turning to Monday when her sybaritic drowsiness was interrupted by a loud banging on the bathroom door and a voice shouting, "Quick, quick, let me in! I'm going to be sick!" She leapt out of the bath and grabbed a towel, wrapping it round herself before opening the door. Thelma pushed past her, making a dash for the lavatory pan, into which she retched up the contents of her stomach. Shirley ran into her room, put on her dressing gown and dashed down the two floors in search of Uncle Horace, who was nowhere to be seen. She could hear the raised voices of Aunt Winnie and Granny in the sitting room, engaged in a loud argument about the merits of the wedding cake that Granny had been responsible for ordering and paying for.

"Come now, Mother," Aunt Winnie was expostulating, "I don't know what you were thinking of, ordering a wedding cake with blue icing! You don't have blue icing on a wedding cake! I told you that the colours were cream and peach."

"Well! I like that!" Granny exclaimed. "The flowers at the reception weren't cream and peach: they were red, and you were wearing red!"

"That's different," Winnie said, dismissing this unwelcome objection but without silencing her mother.

"Anyhow it was only the piping that was blue," Granny protested, "and it was very pretty! I don't know why you are complaining. It was expensive enough! Anyhow, the top layer will be all ready for their first baby's christening."

"Only if it's a boy!" Aunt Winnie retorted curtly. Evidently Uncle Horace was not in that room: he knew better than to stand in the line of fire.

Shirley ran upstairs again to the first floor and tapped on her father's bedroom door. He opened it, dressed in his pyjamas. "Shirl, what's the matter?" he exclaimed. She blurted out a rapid account of the crisis in which she had unwittingly become involved, whereupon he knocked loudly on the door of the neighbouring bedroom to rouse his brother-in-law, who came out rubbing his eyes.

"What's going on?" he yawned, but, as soon as he heard that Thelma had been sick, he ran up to the top floor and went into her room, where she lay complaining that she could not move her head.

"She is ill, you know, Pa," Shirley said seriously, "I think we ought to leave."

"Yes, you're right there," her pa agreed. "We'll go in the morning."

She snatched the opportunity to jog his memory in case he had forgotten her all-important engagement. "You do remember, Pa, don't you, that my audition's on Monday and I can't afford to go down with a bad tummy upset or flu just now? That would be a disaster."

"Yes, of course," he replied. "Look, why don't we swap rooms? You sleep in my room and I'll go upstairs, then you won't have to use the same bathroom as Thelma." Shirley accepted his offer gratefully, trusting that he would not suffer as a result.

It was not as easy to leave early the next day as they had anticipated, because Aunt Winnie would not hear of their going before lunch. "You can't leave!" she exclaimed crossly. "Not now that I've done all that cooking! Horace, tell them they must stay for lunch!"

Horace tried reasoning with her, saying, "I think, dear, they must do what they want." But that was totally ineffective. It was Granny's turn to voice her opinion.

"I certainly don't want to leave before lunch. I don't see Winnie all that often and we still have a great deal to say to each other, don't we, dear?" One might have expected that her mother's intervention would have produced a contrary reaction in Aunt Winnie, but it did not.

Instead of saying, "Oh, yes, you must be going straight away!" she agreed with her mother. "Mother and I have to put Edith's wedding dress away and I need her advice for that. We'll do it this morning and then have lunch," she asserted firmly, brooking no opposition.

"In that case," Pa said equally firmly, "we'll go for a ride and maybe a walk this morning and come back in time for lunch. Come on, Shirl, let's go out." Shirley followed him out of the house, after witnessing his and Uncle Horace's failed attempts to assert themselves. "We'll go over to Weatheroak and have a walk there," Pa said as he started the engine. "The country's lovely in those parts and the fresh air will help blow away any germs."

Lunch was no more ready to be served when they returned from their walk than before they went out. Aunt Winnie and Granny were still upstairs in Edith's room debating whether to store her wedding dress on a hanger in the wardrobe or fold it away in a large box. Sensing Reggie's displeasure, Uncle Horace rummaged about in the pantry and emerged with the remains of Friday's supper. "I've been trying to cool Thelma down with wet towels; her head is burning. I'm going to ring the doctor this afternoon; I should have done so sooner but there's been no time. And up there," he pointed upstairs, "they're so involved with whatever they're doing they've forgotten about lunch," he said apologetically as he laid the kitchen table with crockery and cutlery.

He had just begun to carve some slices of ham when Aunt Winnie burst into the kitchen. "Horace! What do you think you're doing?" she exploded. "Horace, don't you remember! I put the lamb in a slow oven after breakfast, and now all it needs is another half-an-hour while Mother and I do the vegetables! Put all that away! We'll eat in the dining room."

"No, Winnie, don't bother about the lamb," Pa said, the exasperation audible in his tone. "I said we should be leaving after breakfast, and now look: it's one o'clock, and we can't wait any longer." He didn't actually say that his sister was to blame, but the implication was clear. "We'll just have a bite of that delicious ham that Horace has put on the table and then we'll be off."

Granny had by now come into the kitchen. "What's all this?" she asked, eagerly scenting disagreement.

"Granny," Shirley chipped in quickly with a clinching argument, "we have to be going. At this rate Edward will be home from Scout camp before us and he'll be very tired. We can't have him sitting there on the doorstep waiting." Although she knew that Ted had his key about his person, she also knew that he was Granny's favourite grandchild, so her little white lie had a magical effect.

"Oh, of course! My darling boy! We mustn't forget about him," said Granny, "if I could just have a cup of tea and a sandwich, I'll be ready to leave in ten minutes."

Aunt Winnie started to whine: "Mother, not you too! You can't leave me with all this food. And the dining room's so beautiful; we've had it decorated especially for this weekend!"

Her whining fell on deaf ears. "Sorry, dear," said Granny, "but you should have finished cooking the lamb sooner!"

"Thank goodness for that!" Granny remarked as they pulled out of the driveway. "I thought we would never get away. Winnie is so disorganized! She always was. I should have been quite happy to leave after breakfast, but she wouldn't let me go; she said she wanted to take me round the garden, though to tell the truth there are more flowers in my garden than hers. And hers is so huge, all trees and bushes, you know. Very uninteresting! Then she said she wanted to show me the new colour scheme she's planning for Edith's bedroom, which is going to be the guest room now that Edith is married. I can tell you I was dying for a cup of coffee! So by the time you came back we had only just begun to fold Edith's wedding dress away. Such a lovely dress with all that cream lace! Just like my own!" She rattled on in a similar vein for the next half-hour until she fell asleep and slept all the way to London.

16

Images of Thelma vomiting on a bare stage surrounded by a *corps de ballet*, consisting of Granny, Aunt Winnie and Edith, Jim and Uncle Horace, *en pointe* and wearing ridiculous hats, while she and her pa drove past waving at them, all swirled in a vortex through Shirley's dreams that Sunday night. After long periods of wakefulness between the nightmares, she had sunk into a sleep so deep that at daybreak her father had to shake her to rouse her. "Shirl!" he called in her ear. "I've brought you a cup of tea; you'll miss your shift if you don't rise and shine now!" Bleary-eyed she resisted the temptation to pull the eider-down over her head and ignore him. "Ted's done his paper round and has gone to school already," he announced. "He promised he'd be back here at half-past three to accompany you to your audition. I'm off too. You've had a long sleep so you should be fine. Good luck!" He sounded as though he was talking through a megaphone, and with that he was gone, leaving Shirley helpless and isolated. What a way to begin one of the most important days of her life!

Alone in the house with no one to encourage her, a cold sensation of despair crept over her. How much easier it would be to stay at home in bed! She forced herself to sit up to drink her tea and tentatively put one foot out of bed and then the other; she stood up and stretched up to the ceiling and down to her toes. Out on the landing she used the railing at the top of the stairs as a *barre* on which she rested one leg and bent over it to touch her knee with her nose, only to find that, just as she had feared, sitting in the car for that long journey home from Birmingham had left her lower back stiff and inflexible. Today of all days she would need a longer warm-up. Nevertheless, downstairs it was a pleasant surprise to find that Pa had left her breakfast on the table, and this allowed more time for her stretching exercises on the dining-room floor before she set out for the shop.

Mrs Salvatore was overwhelmed with customers that morning. "Ah, Shirley!" she exclaimed. "Goodness, am I pleased to see you! It's all these magazines: I can't keep up with them! There are so many more women customers these days!" She indicated a rapidly diminishing pile of *Woman*, the new magazine that had come out that month. "I wasn't sure that you would be in today since I know it's your audition this evening, but I am so relieved you've come! You must tell me about the wedding later during our break." Shirley worked alongside Mrs S. until the crowd dispersed and, to her surprise, Mr S. appeared from the back room bearing a tray with two cups of richly aromatic Italian coffee on it.

"Meessa Shirlia! I am so glad-a to see you." He set the tray down and prepared to take over running the shop. Shirley stared at him in amazement, hardly able to believe that this was the same poor little man who had sat all day every day in the stockroom out at the back coughing miserably. The cough had vanished and he was transformed, having taken on a new lease of life.

"Well, that's good, now we can have a little talk. Come with me," Mrs S. said, moving towards the back room. Shirley was puzzled by this unusual turn of events but, carefully carrying her cup to avoid spilling the precious brew, followed Mrs S., while Mr S. stationed himself at the till.

"Tell me about the wedding: how did it go?" Mrs S. enquired.

"Much better than expected, I suppose, in the circumstances," Shirley replied casually, giving only a brief account of the best aspects of the weekend, omitting any mention of Aunt Winnie, Granny and Thelma, but lingering longer on the sad contents of Maman's telegram that had cast such a dark shadow over the weekend.

Mrs S. duly expressed her condolences. "I am really so sorry!" she exclaimed. "I know how difficult it is for the family when a foreign relative dies." She paused for a moment's contemplation on what she saw as a strong point of contact with Shirley's family; then, with a sigh, she whispered, "It's not easy, is it?" Shirley was by now regretting having talked about her grandmother's death and funeral in France, so she sniffed on the verge of tears and nodded vigorously. "Oh, dear, I didn't mean to upset you," said Mrs S. patting her arm, before launching into the real reason for her mysterious subterfuge.

"Mr Salvatore brought us coffee and I asked you to come out here because we wanted you to know how happy we are to have you helping us, Shirley dear," she began. "You – and your brother, of course – have been so kind and hard-working. What's more, having you young people here these past weeks has truly enlivened Mr Salvatore." Shirley smiled modestly and was about to say that she and Ted needed no thanks: their pay packets were sufficiently generous and they enjoyed the work so much that no more thanks were needed, but Mrs S. was not to be deflected from her purpose. "Because this is a special day for you," she continued, "we would like to give you a little present to bring you luck." She opened a drawer and took out a small package wrapped in tissue paper and tied with a pink ribbon, which she then handed to Shirley. "This comes with our love," she said rather shyly. "It belonged to Mr Salvatore's mother and we don't have anyone else to give it to, so please don't be embarrassed."

Shirley was unprepared for this turn of events and wondered if she should refuse to accept the gift, but on second thoughts she realized that the offer was a very genuine token of gratitude and that the Salvatores might be very hurt if she appeared to reject their friendly gesture. "That's very kind of you!" she said. "Can I open it now?"

"Yes, please do!" Mrs S. urged her. Inside the pink wrapping was a small box. Carefully she opened it and gasped at the sight of its sparkling contents.

"But it's a diamond!" she stammered. "A diamond pendant!" There it lay on its blue velvet cushion, a diamond pendant on a silver chain!

"That's right," said Mrs S. casually, as if the gemstone was of no matter. "It is small, but it is a real diamond on a white-gold – not silver – chain, and it will look very pretty round your neck. Shall I help you with the clasp?"

"Oh, yes please!" said Shirley, overcome with amazement.

As she walked along the road to the dance studio for her last practice before the audition, Shirley, her feet barely touching the ground, could not believe what had just happened. It was all such an extraordinary contrast to those nightmares and to the ludicrous scenarios of the past couple of days which had held absolutely no inspiration for a ballet in them at all. How was it, she wondered, that people she scarcely knew could be so kind, generous and thoughtful, yet her own close relatives – by whom she particularly meant her granny and Aunt Winnie – were so selfish, bitter and unpleasant? She had never owned any jewellery before, let alone a diamond! How cheap it made Aunt Winnie and her friends look with all their bangles and brooches and necklaces! She knew that her granny had a large sapphire ring locked away somewhere that she could no longer wear because her arthritic fingers were too swollen for it, though whether she had any diamonds as large as this one she doubted. Maman had one or two nice rings; one of them was her engagement ring, but those diamonds on either side of the emerald were tiny by comparison. She raised her hand to her neck to make sure that the precious gemstone was still there. Reassured, she glided into the ballet school as if dancing in a dream.

Miss Patience was sitting at her desk working on timetables. At first she simply glanced up, but then, taking another look at her pupil, asked anxiously, "Shirley! Whatever is the matter? You look as if you've seen a ghost!"

Shirley laughed, "No, don't worry, I've just had a shock – well, a surprise, really." She showed Miss Patience the pendant and told her the unlikely story of how she had come by it.

"That's lovely!" Miss Patience remarked. "How kind of those people! They must think very highly of you!"

Shirley shrugged, "I don't know why; I haven't done anything special for them, only my work."

Miss Patience was deep in thought. "I... I don't want to spoil your pleasure or upset you, but you do realize that you won't be able to wear your pendant for the audition, don't you?"

Shirley's jaw dropped in disappointment. "Why not?" she asked.

Miss Patience, always the believer in the empirical approach, replied, "Well, try it now while you practise, but I'm sure you'll find that the chain will get in the way. It will swing about your neck when you turn and *pirouette*, and the diamond will end up round the back, getting caught in your hair most probably. I think you should take it off before you go to Sadler's Wells and leave it in a safe place."

"I see," Shirley said pensively, "but I'll try it now, because I don't want to take it off until I'm safely back home.

Of course, Miss Patience was right, so Shirley had to be grateful to her for her unwelcome advice. The pendant did indeed react badly to the movement of the dance. It swayed, swung and – bouncing on its white-gold chain – was a distracting nuisance. "Don't worry," said Miss Patience, "even if you're not wearing it for the audition, I'm sure it will still bring you good luck – not that you need it – because it comes with so much goodwill." In spite of the pendant, both Miss Patience and Shirley herself were pleased with her performance. "The weekend away has done you no harm at all. Your dancing is the best I've ever seen, from you or from any other pupil in this school!" was Miss Patience's proud verdict, and at the end of the long session she held out a sheet of paper. "Now," she said, "here are directions for finding Sadler's Wells. Go home, take off the pendant, put it somewhere safe in its box, have something to eat, then have a rest. Come and tell me all about the audition tomorrow!" Shirley did as she was told, though she did call in on the Salvatores on her way home to thank them once again.

She was having a bath when Ted arrived as promised at half-past three. Earlier, while the house was quiet, she had carefully placed all her essential items: her leotard and ballet skirt, her point shoes and a sponge bag with brush, comb, some spare kirby grips and a powder compact in a small case so as to be ready to leave after Ted had had his tea. After turning it over several times to inspect it from every angle, she gently placed the diamond pendant in its box in the top drawer of her dressing table, where it lay hidden by her underwear. Although she couldn't wear it, the mere certainty that it was hers and that it would be there waiting for her in her top drawer boosted her self-confidence. "Shirl! I'm ready! We ought to be going!" Ted called up the stairs. He was scrutinizing a map spread on the hall table. "I've found Sadler's Wells on the map. I think we want to take the Northern Line to the Angel: it's only five minutes' walk from there to Rosebery Avenue. We just need to make sure we're on the right branch of the Northern Line, so come on, let's go!"

Ted knew exactly where to go and which trains and Underground lines to take. Without him there would have been little chance of finding the theatre, though, once there, Miss Patience's written directions sent them to the stage door, where the keeper, a bent old man with white hair, opened the door and checked Shirley's name on a list. "Now, miss," he said, leaning heavily on his walking stick, "I'm going to take you to the dressing rooms, and this young man..." he surveyed Ted uncertainly. "And may I ask, who *is* this young man?" he enquired.

"He's my brother Ted: he came with me so I wouldn't get lost," Shirley explained. At this the old man gave a nod of approval and said:

"Nice to meet you, Ted. My name's Tom and, sir, if you don't mind waiting here, I'll see what I can do for you."

The doorkeeper turned to Shirley, saying, "You're very lucky today, you know, miss. The decorators are in, painting the main studio, so the auditions are taking place in the theatre. That doesn't happen very often,

I can tell you." Whatever nervous tensions Shirley might have been experiencing were immediately dispelled by this bizarre situation: absurdly, here in the new home of English ballet, the door had been opened by a poor old man who could hardly walk, and she was going to dance on the stage! It was difficult to control the urge to laugh outright at such a comic situation, although it did enable her to view the forthcoming ordeal more lightly.

"Now, miss, if you would kindly follow me," the old man said as he set off along corridor; Shirley gave her brother a peck on the cheek and then caught her guide up in no time. After a few paces he abruptly turned off, and Shirley found herself in the wings, looking out onto the stage where the curtain was down. She gasped in awe. "Put your ballet shoes on and I'll wait just two minutes while you try out the surface of the stage. We are rather late already, so I can't let you have longer, I'm afraid," the old man said. She felt the smooth surface under her feet and, in her day clothes, tried out a few moves across the stage, *glissades* and *chassés*, and found to her joy that it was like no other surface that she had ever danced on. She checked it for uneven or sticky patches, but there were none. "Right, miss, it's time for you to change now," the old man said, beckoning her to come off the stage. He knocked on a door further down the corridor, and ushered her in, saying, "You can change in here and get yourself ready for your turn, and, if you wish, you can then go straight along the passage to the small studio at the end to do your warm-ups."

Tom smiled encouragingly and Shirley warmed to him. "Remind me, what name shall I give to Madam?" he asked. Shirley was nonplussed. Who was this "Madam"? Presuming that she was someone important connected with the theatre, she gave her name without question, and went into the dressing room, which was full of girls changing into leotards, scraping their hair back into tight buns, plucking their eyebrows and powdering their faces, preening themselves in front of mirrors and generally admiring themselves, but not talking to each other. They turned as one to look at Shirley, then, without a word, but with a slight sneer, returned to their preparations.

She put her bag down on a long table and, taking her courage in both hands, whispered to a girl who was standing next to her, "Can you tell me who is 'Madam'?" The girl turned towards her in haughty astonishment.

"Do you really not know?" she asked loudly, exaggerating her surprise.

"No," said Shirley, "I haven't been backstage here before."

"Madam is Miss Ninette de Valois, the founder of the company! Fancy not knowing that!" The girl had dropped her lipstick in her disgust at the ignorance of this candidate who clearly had no hope of succeeding; she picked it up and resumed the painstaking painting of her lips.

Dispirited, Shirley opened her case and began to change as quickly as she could, anxious to leave the dressing room before any other of the candidates administered further blows to her morale. The problem was that her curls, styled by the Birmingham hairdresser for the wedding, were still prettily framing her face and refused to be scraped into a chignon. The best she could do was to pin them smoothly and tightly back, anchoring them behind her ears. The effect was not exactly prepossessing, because her hair was so blond that her head appeared bald, or at least her hair thin, in the bright lights around the mirror, unlike the other girls whose dark hair set off the neat shape of their heads and faces to perfection. She panicked at the loss of time and hastened out into the corridor. Then, as if by magic, a picture of her diamond came into her mind, safe at home in her top drawer. Instantly she felt more positive and ready for a fight, because this was what it was going to be: a fight to prove herself better than any of the others, just as they would be fighting to prove themselves better than her.

There were more girls already in the studio, all absorbed in their own exercises and routines. A clock on the wall gave the time at a quarter past six. Perfect timing, thought Shirley, though she could not imagine how long it would take for the judges to watch each of the crowd of girls in the dressing room and these others already in the studio. Perhaps they had all been asked to come for half-past six, in which case her audition, which she had been given to expect would be the first, might not take place for ages and poor Ted would have to wait around. She stretched for the fourth time that day, tried a few *pliés*, *entrechats*, leaps and *pirouettes*, then sketched in an outline of her routine.

She felt sufficiently well warmed up, the early-morning stiffness being but a distant memory, and was wondering what more to do to fill the time when the door opened and a young woman called her name: "Shirley Marlow! Are you here?"

With a thumping heart, she replied, "Yes."

"Please follow me," the girl said with a heart-warming smile. "You do know who Madam is, don't you?" she asked as they went down a corridor.

"Yes, she's Ninette de Valois, the founder of the company, isn't she?" Shirley answered, almost grateful for her earlier humiliation.

"That's right," the girl said. "It's just that some people who come here have no idea who she is at all and that can lead to embarrassment. If you have to talk to her, you must address her as 'Madam'. Take care not to call her 'Madame', which is what French girls tend to do, but you aren't French, are you?" Shirley shook her head. "I will take you into the wings," the girl went on. "Madam will call your name, and then you must go straight onto the stage and curtsy. She will then instruct you how to begin."

"Right, thanks." Shirley nodded as she tried to digest the information, which, though simple, seemed overwhelming.

"When you've finished," the girl continued, "curtsy again, leave the stage, go back to the dressing room and, when you're ready, show yourself out. The judges won't say anything to you. Well, if you're really good and lucky they might say 'thank you'."

Shirley suddenly thought of poor Ted. "What about my brother? He came with me; he brought me here and is at the stage door."

"Ah," said the girl, "don't worry: old Tom will look after him until your audition is over."

Shirley waited in the wings, where a draught chilled the muscles of her arms and legs. Rubbing them vigorously to keep them warm diverted her attention from any lurking feelings of stage fright and enabled her to think clearly. From where she stood, the panel of judges, which presumably included Madam, were outside her field of vision, but she could see the full extent of the empty stage which, now that the curtain was up, seemed much larger than any that she had ever known. She used the time to calculate her moves across and round it to be able to take advantage of all the available space. "Miss Marlow!" a disembodied voice called from the auditorium. She breathed deeply, assumed an erect posture with strong core muscles, lowered her shoulders and raised her head, before running delicately out to make a low curtsy to the audience, which consisted only of the judges immediately at her feet. A woman, probably about Maman's age, with a decidedly waspish expression, stared at her from the front row without a vestige of a smile, but the two men, one on either side of her, applauded and smiled encouragingly.

"Miss Marlow," the woman said, "first of all, we shall give you a set of movements that we would like you to demonstrate, then you will dance through the routines on your schedule, and finally the pianist will play a piece of music to which you will listen once; there will be a pause and then he will then play it again for your freestyle dance on your chosen theme of..." here she turned over a sheet of paper, "ah, yes, woodland life."

Shirley's confidence grew, for not only had she practised every possible movement, step, turn, *pirouette* and *grand jeté*, until both Miss Patience and Miss Inskip were satisfied with the minutest of details, and rehearsed passages for the routine either to accompaniments played by the pianist at her dance school, or to a variety of records on the school gramophone, until she knew it by heart, but she had also, while in France, composed little sequences based on her walks with Maman through the woods at the *château*. They had stayed in her mind, and in idle moments, at home or in the studio, she had tried out steps and movements, again experimenting with suitable recordings on the school's gramophone, so the possibilities for the dance were not completely unfamiliar. She was confidently impatient to begin. This was going to be fine, because it would all be second nature to her.

It was indeed fine. Having executed all the sequences and the set routines, her heart leapt at the opening bars of the familiar piano score, an excerpt from the music by Schumann, entitled *Woodland Scenes*, which Miss Patience used in classes and which she had hoped might be chosen for her set piece. The rhythm, the dynamics and the melody were second nature to her, and its very familiarity gave her confidence for her final demonstration. She illustrated the music with every movement appropriate to the lives of small woodland creatures and then, with the leap of a squirrel launching itself from treetop to treetop, she sprang in a *grand jeté en l'air sauté* from upstage to centre stage, spun in a quick *pirouette* and sank to the floor in a profound bow with her right leg curled under her and her left leg extended behind. She stood up and curtsied.

The two men on the panel applauded, as did Madam. "Thank you, Miss Marlow," she said. "I think you come from Nora Patience's dance studio, don't you?"

"Yes, Madam," Shirley said, startled to hear Miss Patience's Christian name and also, now that it was over, awestruck by the whole experience of dancing on the stage at Sadler's Wells, not to mention of being applauded and addressed by such august personages as Madam and her fellow judges.

"Please give her my greetings and apologies for the delay in dealing with your application. That was why we called you in first this evening."

"Yes, Madam, of course, I will. Thank you!" Shirley whispered, scarcely able to pronounce even those few words. She curtsied again and left the stage.

She was glad to find that there was no one in the dressing room: all those other girls were probably in the practice studio, awaiting their turns, maybe even wondering what had become of her whom they so obviously despised. She changed quickly, gathered up her belongings and went out to meet Ted, who was standing in the doorway, waiting for her with Tom, the doorkeeper. "Shirley! You were magnificent!" Ted exclaimed. "I had no idea that you could dance like that! I'm no expert, but I would say your performance was stupendous! And I'm sure the jury thought so too."

Old Tom was beaming too. "Yes, miss," he said, "don't tell anyone, because I'd lose my job – no one is allowed to watch the auditions, you see – but I took your brother up to the gods at the top of the theatre, where it was so dark no one could see us. He's right, you were. I'm sure they will take you on! I'll look forward to seeing you again soon!"

Although she was inebriated with her success, Shirley succeeded in maintaining a modest façade. "I hope you're both right," she sighed. "I loved it, and this is where I want to be more than anything else!"

Her eyes continued to sparkle as her brother guided her down to the Underground and onto the train. "Ted," she said, thoughtfully, "it was lovely to have you there. Thank you so much for coming with me. I do just wish Maman could have been there too." She did not say so, but she thought how wonderful it would have been if Alan also could have seen her dancing on that stage, in that theatre, on that day.

"Never mind," Ted reassured her. "I've no doubt Maman will see you dance there many, many times! And if you don't do so yourself, I shall tell her how wonderful you were!" His eyes shone with pride at his sister's achievements. Because they were so close in age and he had become so much bigger than her, he had begun to treat her even more like a little sister and had of late grown much more caring and protective. "Anyhow we can tell Pa all about it this evening," he continued. "Do you know? I think dancing is for you what farming is for me. Strange that, isn't it?"

With a sudden change of expression, he added, "It sounds as if Pépé will need me more than ever now that dear Mémé has died, and I can't stop thinking about her. It must have been awful for you having to go through that wedding knowing that her funeral had taken place in France just the day before. How I wish I didn't have to stay in school for the whole year! I have had enough of it. They don't teach me the things I want to know!" His eyes were red and watery.

Shirley took his arm. "I know how you feel," she said. "France seems so far away at times like these, and poor Maman is there all on her own, trying to help Pépé and organize everything for him. It must be so hard for her. But I'm sure Pépé will be all right; he'll be out working in the fields and will be lost in his own thoughts, as he always is. Then from August next year he'll have you there with him. The house won't be the same though without Mémé cooking and cleaning, scrubbing her stove and working on the farm as well."

17

They were both tired by the time they reached home, and so were glad to find that their father, slaving in the kitchen, was stretching his limited cookery skills as far as omelettes for supper, even though he was struggling with his concoction. "Well, how did it go?" he asked, anxiously turning to the cookery book which was open on the side. His culinary achievement, which could hardly be described as a mouth-watering success, fell out of the frying pan in burnt pieces as he tried to turn it onto a plate.

"It was wonderful!" Ted said before Shirley could open her mouth. "Shirl was amazing. I had no idea she could dance like that! You should have seen her, Pa! Those leaps across the stage!"

"Oh, I'm so glad to hear that!" Pa replied, though without any great display of interest, because he was still intent on scraping the remains from the side of the pan. "I was quite worried about you this morning, Shirl," he added. "I was afraid yesterday's journey had been too tiring for you."

"It went very well!" Shirley announced, still glowing in the certainty that she had given of her best and that, to judge from Madam's reaction, her best had been well received. Otherwise why would Madam have applauded and spoken to her at the end of her performance? "I've had such a good day, Pa. There's so much to tell."

"I'm sorry about these omelettes – they don't look very appetizing – but come and sit down and tell me all about it," he rejoined, handing each of them a cold plate bearing a burnt offering and a smidgen of salad, before ushering them into the dining room.

"So, come on then, I want to know all about the audition," he urged his daughter while doing his best to give his full attention to a dance form which, in truth, held little appeal for him. Despite the bullet holes in his hip, ballroom dancing was different, because it was at the basis of one of his favourite social events, where couples danced together with delightfully romantic overtones, but, ignorant as he was of the strict discipline and dedication involved, ballet brought out the puritan in him, rendering him distinctly uncomfortable at the sight of all those nearly bare bodies prancing about the stage, winding themselves around each other, often caught up in a very close embrace.

Whether he intended it or not, it also brought the philistine side of his character to the fore, because his down-to-earth nature prevented him from giving himself over to its fantasy world and enjoying the ethereal music and unlikely scenarios which he considered good only for fairy tales. In short, he found it impossible to suspend his disbelief: on the one occasion when Jacqueline had taken him to a performance of the Ballets Russes, he occupied himself by wondering how the scenery was put together and shifted so smartly out of the way without falling apart, and how the lighting had been set up, this being the only way he could rescue himself from total boredom and preserve at least a pretence of appreciating the performance. He was glad that it was his daughter, not his son, who was passionate about ballet, and he could understand why it appealed to her. She was after all the delicate if spirited little fairy for whom it was entirely appropriate.

The detailed if chaotic accounts that he received from her and from her brother of everything that had happened at Sadler's Wells put him partially in the picture, even if they left him a touch confused as to both the timescale and the order of the proceedings. "I couldn't have coped without Ted," was Shirley's opening gambit. "I've been there with Maman, but I would never have found it on my own! Ted knew exactly where to go, so we arrived on time and he was a great support all the way through. It was nearly dark by the time we left, and I tell you I wouldn't have liked to be wandering those streets alone."

"Oh, come on!" Ted joked. "I tell you, Pa, no robber or anyone else would want to meet her out in the street at night in Islington. You should see those high kicks of hers and the speed with which she whirled across the stage. She'd knock them all out and leave them panting for breath!"

Their father laughed. "That's good! Do you know? I almost wish I could have been there!"

"Yes, I wish you could have, and Maman too!" Shirley said wistfully, though Ted disagreed.

"If they'd been there, I probably wouldn't have come," he observed, "and I wouldn't have missed it for worlds! Anyhow," he continued in a flush of enthusiasm, "I was so lucky: normally you can't watch an audition, but the nice old doorkeeper took me right up to the top of the theatre, out of the way, and we watched from there."

His voice trailed off when he saw the anxious look on Shirley's face. "Oh, I shouldn't have said that! You mustn't tell anyone, Pa, because it's strictly forbidden for anyone other than the judges to watch the auditions; the old man might lose his job if it gets about. And, Pa, you should have been there to see that woman in the front row talking to Shirley! The old doorman told me she never talks to anyone! I didn't catch what she was saying. What did she say anyhow?" he asked his sister.

"Oh, that was the funny thing," Shirley replied. "She seems to be a friend of Miss Patience's; she called her 'Nora', can you believe it? And she asked me to give Miss Patience – or Nora, as she called her – her greetings! I must do that tomorrow."

Her father listened attentively and tried to ask sensible questions, which revealed that he had no concept of how an audition was conducted. "Was there scenery for your dances?" he asked, endeavouring to show the informed interest of someone who had once been to a ballet performance.

Shirley corrected him gently. "No, Pa, I was dancing on a bare stage with not even a backdrop. They don't have scenery for auditions."

"Ah," he said, "I see." Then he asked: "Was there an orchestra for you to dance to?"

"No, Pa, they don't provide orchestras for auditions! There was just a pianist. That's all," she replied patiently.

He reflected for a moment before his next question: "So, um, did you dance with the other girls or on your own?"

By now Ted was guffawing at his father's ignorance. "Pa," he said as if talking to a visitor from another planet, "she was the first to dance, and of course she danced alone! That's what it's all about: selecting the best dancers one by one!"

The reminiscences round the supper table went on until Pa glanced at the clock on the mantelpiece and said, "Ted, if you don't go to bed soon, you won't be up in time for your paper round in the morning!"

"Oh, goodness!" Shirley exclaimed. "I've forgotten something really important, Pa. Wait a moment, will you? I have something to show you!" She left the table and ran upstairs. She reappeared very soon afterwards carrying a small blue box. "You won't believe this, Pa, but look what Mrs Salvatore gave me this morning to wish me good luck!" She opened the box and placed it in front of her father, whose mouth fell open at the sight of the diamond pendant on its blue velvet cushion.

"Mrs Salvatore gave it to you? You don't mean it?" he asked incredulously.

"Yes, I do! She said how grateful she and Mr Salvatore were to me and Ted for – well, I suppose you might say – transforming their lives. They're both so much happier since we have been working for them!" she announced jubilantly.

"But Shirl," Pa said, "that's a diamond! You've only been there a few weeks and they scarcely know you. How could you have made such a difference?" Shirley bristled, sensing that this exchange was in danger of becoming an interrogation. Instead of admiring the diamond and saying, "That's beautiful! How kind of them! You lucky girl!" as she had expected, her father, to judge from his doubtful expression, appeared to be on the point of dousing her earlier elation with an icy shower.

Casting her mind back over the conversation with Mrs S. that morning, she answered his question with sullen defiance: "Mrs S. said how happy she and Mr S. were to have us helping, that we were kind and hard-working, that Mr S. was much livelier now and, and..." – she tried to recall Mrs S.'s exact words – "that this was a special day, so she wanted me to have this present to bring me good luck. And it has certainly done that, even though I wasn't wearing it! Miss Patience told me not to, because it would get in the way."

Pa stroked his chin, considering the best way to convey the blow he was about to deliver. "I'm very sorry, Shirl," he said gruffly, "but I think you must take it back to the Salvatores in the morning."

A fleeting silence descended on the room as Shirley's temper mounted. "No, I won't! Why should I?" she burst out, red in the face with indignation.

Pa, keeping very cool, said, "Even I can see that it must be very valuable, a diamond as big as that. Do you know how much diamonds cost?" Shirley shook her head. "No, nor do I," he said, "but I do know that I could never afford anything like that. It's very kind of Mr and Mrs Salvatore, but I suspect they ought to be leaving it to a member of their family."

"No, no, you don't understand!" Shirley cried in exasperation. "It belonged to Mr S.'s mother; Mrs S. said so. I don't know where it came from before that, but they say they haven't anyone else to give it to, and

I shouldn't be embarrassed about accepting it. I'm just sorry that there isn't anything for Ted."

"Maybe," said Pa, "but she was wrong to say they haven't anyone to give it to. What about Francesca?" Shirley, who was about to flare up again, stopped short: she had not given Francesca, who was most definitely a part of Mr Salvatore's family, a moment's thought, and perhaps there were many more relatives, all over London and even all over England, let alone the ones back in Italy. If Francesca was Mr S.'s niece, she probably had a mother or a father and maybe she had brothers and sisters too.

She sighed. "Well, whatever you say, I'm not taking it back," she declared. "If you want it to go back to the Salvatores, you must take it yourself. I'm going to bed!" With that she stormed out of the room.

Ted, who had witnessed the scene in silence, bade his father goodnight and followed her. "Calm down, Shirl," he said when he found her sitting on the landing, rubbing her eyes with clenched fists. "What does it matter? You've had that diamond for today and it has brought you a lot of luck, even if you weren't wearing it. I don't imagine you'll need that much luck ever again."

"It's just," she sobbed, "that it's beautiful and I don't have many beautiful things. And I believed Mrs Salvatore because she said they *really* wanted me to have it. Out of gratitude, I suppose. Why does Pa always put such a dampener on the nice things?"

"I think perhaps I understand what he's thinking," Ted replied. "You know what these foreign families are like – not only foreign families come to that. I don't know that ours is much better – well, that's to say on Pa's side – but I bet you the Salvatores' relatives will be expecting that diamond to be passed on to them, and they might be very angry if they discover it has been given away. And if they find that you've got it, supposing they come searching for it? They might burgle the house and beat us all up!" His imagination was running away with him, so he paused to collect his thoughts. "Cheer up," he said to his sister, who was still snivelling, "I'll go down again and talk to Pa, and we'll see what we can come up with. Maybe we can find a solution. Anyhow we won't do anything in a hurry."

Shirley stayed on the landing, listening to the voices down below, but she was unable to make out what they were saying. Possibly there was some truth in what Ted had said: she did not want to be beaten up, nor did she want her father and brother to suffer. As for Maman, she would never survive being attacked. Maman! How they all missed her! Pa had been so strong and well in her absence that one could almost forget the terrible traumatizing events from his past that always lurked in the background. Maman had been away for so long and so much had happened in that time! Where was she now? Perhaps she was busy helping her father adjust to life without Mémé. He would need someone to look after him and cook his meals. More tears trickled down her cheeks when the image of dear Mémé floated across her mind, shut away from the sunlight in the family tomb down in the graveyard of the church in Trémaincourt. This was followed by a horrible question that sneaked uninvited into her thoughts and made her tremble: was that Monsieur Arnaud Lavasseur in the area? She had disliked him from the moment she set eyes on him, and she certainly did not trust him.

Drying her eyes, she resolved to write to Maman to tell her about the audition; if she wrote at once she would be able to post the letter in the morning on her way to the paper shop. Granny was right about one thing: it was such a nuisance that Pa refused have a telephone installed, for it would make life so much easier, especially at the moment with Maman far away in France, and there was so much to tell her. With a phone in the house she would be able to ring Louise, who would ask Maman to come to the *estaminet* at a certain time to receive the call, and then they could talk without having to write letters, even if calls were very expensive.

It was unlikely that Pa would ever change his mind. He said that he loved old-fashioned engineering and that meant trains and cars, not these new-fangled devices that were going to become the bane of everyone's life. "Mark my words," he declared, "in fifty years' time, let alone a hundred, these new inventions will be driving everyone crazy." Her anger had now subsided, and although a dejected weariness was taking hold of her, tempting her to fling herself down onto her soft bed, she put the pendant box on the dressing table and reached for her writing case on the shelf above it.

The letter took at least half an hour to write because first she told her mother at length about the diamond pendant and how surprised she had been to receive it from the Salvatores as a sort of good-luck charm. She went over to the dressing table and picked it up, turning it in the light, to remind herself how large, how dazzling and how multi-hued it was, before putting it carefully back in its box and placing it down among the muddle of hairpins, powder, combs and brushes on the dressing table. She didn't want to go downstairs to fetch her dictionary, so describing it in French at that time of night and at the end of such a demanding day was a challenge, until she decided that *éclatant* and *brillant* were the two best words to do it justice.

After that, she concentrated on every aspect of the audition, from Ted's help on the journeys, through a description of the dressing rooms, the stage and the other girls, to her performance and Madam's personal address to her at the end of it, including the discovery that Miss Patience's name was Nora, all of which meant that the wedding in Birmingham received scant coverage. Indeed, apart from recounting how beautiful the green silk dress, hat and shoes were and how perfectly suitable they turned out to be when Edith asked her to be the one and only bridesmaid, the wedding was only mentioned by way of an aside in which she reassured her mother that the journeys had not been too exhausting either for her or for her pa, and that he was well and had not suffered any of his attacks while she had been away in France.

She did not bother to mention Thelma's illness nor the unpleasant circumstances associated with it, as that was merely an insignificant detail, and anyhow Thelma was bound to have recovered by now. She paused in her writing to speculate where Edith might have gone on honeymoon. Somebody had said the Lake District, though Uncle Horace was sure that he had heard north Wales mentioned. As Edith, unlike Thelma, was so friendly, she decided that she certainly would like to see her again one day. Perhaps Edith would come to one of her performances.

By this time, both Pa and Ted had long gone to bed. She had heard their voices wishing each other goodnight. "We'll talk more about this tomorrow," she heard her pa say. Having finished the letter, signing it off with kisses – *"mille bisous, chère Maman"* – she folded it, placed it in an envelope and sealed it, ready for the post in the morning. Then she changed into her nightdress and fell into bed, grateful for the soft embrace of the feather mattress that moulded itself around her tired limbs. She stretched her legs to the end of the bed and yawned. What a strange day it had been, she pondered, so full of excitement and apparent success, and yet, aside from the pleasure of writing the letter to Maman, how unpredictably it had ended. Whatever Pa might say, she was definitely not going to give the diamond back to the Salvatores. That was a preposterous idea. How upset and offended they would be!

18

Mrs Salvatore met Shirley with a broad smile and open arms, in itself a sufficient indication that Pa had not gone into the shop that morning to tell her that his daughter could not accept the diamond. According to Ted, their father had set off for work early and might well have forgotten about it altogether. Shirley had not seen him, because she was too busy upstairs admiring her treasure, which she had retrieved from her top drawer, unable to resist the temptation to look at it once more before going to work. "You know how forgetful he is" was Ted's parting comment. Indeed Pa could be rather absent-minded, especially if he were preoccupied with an engineering problem, so Shirley hoped that that was the end of the matter. She took the precaution of thanking Mrs Salvatore again for the gift of the diamond pendant, in case she too had lapses of memory and might have forgotten giving it to her the day before, which in the circumstances was unlikely.

Indeed, Mrs S. was anxious to know whether the diamond pendant had brought the good luck that she had promised, and to this awkward question Shirley had to find a speedy yet truthful response while avoiding telling Mrs S that she had not been able to wear it for the audition. "Yes, thank you! It certainly brought me luck!" she exclaimed. "I don't want to boast, but I don't think I could have danced better!"

"There, I told you so!" Mrs S. declared with a note of triumph as she flicked a feather duster over the shelves of magazines. Mindful of her father's misgivings, Shirley then made a point of going into Mr S.'s office, for this was what he now called the drab little room at the back, to thank him, in case he was not aware that she was now the proud owner of his mother's magnificent jewel.

"Of-a course-a, Shirley-a!" he said, beaming from ear to ear. "We want-a you to have-a the neck-a-lace. It-a no use-a to us." Shirley hugged him, and his normally pallid complexion turned a bright, healthy red.

"Your-a brother-a said-a you-a were amazing," he went on.

"I said so, didn't I? I'm not at all surprised," Mrs S. announced from the doorway. She said that Ted had been bursting with pride when he had come for the papers that morning, and had told them every detail of his sister's performance on the stage. For someone who had never been to a ballet, he had waxed so lyrical about her movements, steps and choreography that Mrs S. was able to repeat a word-for-word description of nearly everything that he had witnessed and she had done. It was Shirley's turn to blush at the fulsome recitation. "Your brother was full of admiration!" Mrs S. continued. "He said you leapt and spun on your toes as if you had danced on that stage for years." Shirley edged towards the door, because by this time her shift had come to an end and she was in a hurry to see Miss Patience. "Remember! I can't wait to see you on the stage!" Mrs Salvatore said.

"Well, that is, if they offer me a place," said Shirley with a modicum of caution.

"Oh, they'll be sure to do that," Mrs S. asserted. "Just keep wearing the diamond!"

For a split second Shirley froze, as it occurred to her to wonder where she had left the precious gemstone. That fuss with Pa last night had been so upsetting that she was not conscious of what she was doing and was still confused by mixed emotions of the elation of the audition and the disappointment of her father's reaction to the pendant all coming together. She knew that she had taken the pendant upstairs with her – lest Pa chose to confiscate it – and thought she had put it away in her drawer but wasn't sure. Racking her brains, she then recollected putting it on the dressing table, which was not the best place for it, but she reckoned it ought to be safe enough there. The house was occupied at present, since Francesca had arrived to do the cleaning and wash Ted's camping gear that morning, so the priceless gift was bound to be secure from burglars and she would put it away as soon as she returned home.

Ten minutes later, Miss Patience drank in every word of Shirley's report, which had gained a breathless immediacy from her sprint down the road to the studio. At last she had the opportunity to recount the significant technicalities of her dancing – the *grandes pirouettes*, the *fouettés en tournant*, the *sautés en pointe*, not to mention the *grands jetés en l'air* – which she had wanted to keep for Miss Patience's ears and which no one else would have appreciated. What's more she rather cheekily relished the prospect of conveying the extraordinary news that

Madam had enquired after her by name, Nora Patience! Doubtless she was the only person in the school who knew their teacher's Christian name. The rumours that Miss Patience had actually danced in the Ballets Russes might well be correct, though her appearance suggested that she was rather older than Madam and had probably danced in that company some years earlier. "And do you know?" Shirley concluded her account with a saucy grin. "Madam, as they call her, asked after you by name! 'Please give my greetings to Nora Patience,' she said!"

"That's nice of her. Her name's really Edris," Miss Patience observed drily, as she turned to pick up the receiver of the phone that was ringing on her desk. "I don't know why she had to change it. I thought it was a pretty name, Irish you know."

While she stood by the desk waiting for the call to finish, Shirley watched the expression on Miss Patience's face change from one of mild disapproval at Madam's invented name to astonishment. At first she briskly announced: "The South London Academy of Dance. Can I help you?" Then there was a very brief pause, as the unidentified caller must have asked if he or she were talking to Miss Patience, who said, "Yes, speaking." The person at the other end, scarcely stopping to draw breath, launched into a long diatribe that had her reaching for her pen and a piece of paper on which to write down all the information that was being flung at her. "I see, I see," she muttered from time to time. "Yes, I think that would be possible," she ventured, looking up at Shirley, who took this gesture as a hint that her time could be better spent at the *barre* in the studio. As she turned to go through the double doors, she heard Nora Patience say, "I am so glad to have had a word with you again after all these years. I have followed your achievements with admiration. Thank you so much for ringing! I'll tell her straight away. I know she will be delighted."

Shirley's ears pricked up at this. Since she was the only other person in the studio that phone call must have been about her, unless Miss Patience was expecting someone else to arrive very soon. Rather than appear to be eavesdropping, she carried on through the doors to the *barre* only to hear Miss Patience's footsteps behind her. "Shirley, Shirley, come back!" she called. "I've news for you! That was Madam" – she emphasized the "dam" – "on the phone! She is so keen to offer you a place that she herself rang me! Something she would never do otherwise, and certainly she didn't do that when Violet was awarded a place. I suppose it might be partly because she knows me from days gone by and my name had come to the fore when I rang to find out what had become of your application, but mainly, I suspect, because she doesn't want to lose you to another company! There will of course be a formal letter in confirmation. You will accept, won't you?"

Shirley sank onto the nearest stool. "Yes, of course I will!" she tried to say, but, overcome with dizziness, had to put her head down between her knees to recover from the shock. The after-effects persisted for some time, leaving her legs trembling beneath her and her head giddy, all of which made dancing difficult, though that was a small price to pay for such unbelievably good news.

"It's hardly surprising that you're overcome," said Miss Patience, bringing her a glass of water. "I am too. I haven't spoken to Edris in years and my knees are knocking! I think we probably ought to have something to eat. Let me take you out to that new restaurant on the other side of the bridge for lunch. How would you like that? I'll ring Stephanie to ask her to come and hold the fort: she's due to come in soon, so that won't matter." Although in other circumstances lunch with Nora Patience would have been a delightful treat, Shirley had no appetite for food. She pecked at the plate of salad that was placed in front of her, wishing that she could go home and digest the news rather than the food.

Miss Patience, however, attacked her food with relish, until she remembered that she had more to say about the telephone call; she put down her knife and fork and looked across the table at Shirley. "There's something more I have to tell you, if you're feeling stronger," she said, lowering her voice, "and this is secret, so you mustn't tell anyone, but Madam said that she is expecting you'll soon become a principal dancer in the company, and will be taking the major roles." Shirley's eyes widened in disbelief as Miss Patience went on, forgetting in her excitement that what she was about to say was still supposed to be confidential information. "You must have danced so well yesterday! I was as certain as I could be that you would be offered a place, but to think that you are going to become a prima ballerina – and so quickly! You'll be in there with that Margot Fonteyn. You know, don't you, that she very soon became a principal, and she's only about your age or maybe a bit younger. I am thrilled for you, Shirley, and I trust you are too!"

"Yes, of course," Shirley replied with some hesitation, "it's rather a lot to take in at present; I need time to adjust. I expect I'll get used to the idea!"

"I understand," Miss Patience said, nodding sagely, "I felt the same when they told me that I had been accepted by Diaghilev for the Ballets Russes. It quite took my breath away and I needed some time to recover. There are more details, but they can wait for another day or until the official letter arrives. There's no great hurry."

Shirley veered the conversation away from the ballet and her success towards Miss Patience's mother, both out of courtesy and because she simply could not face any more discussion about the dance and her future in it. The sensational news she had already received was as much as she could absorb at present, and although she would have hated Miss Patience to think her feeble or even blasé, her earlier excitement had been supplanted by a notion surging in the depths of her mind which she was impatient to consider in private. Encouraging and generous though Miss Patience was, her conversation was generally monothematic, devoted to her profession unless she was steered in another direction, except where her mother's health was concerned.

Over coffee, Shirley listened with one ear to all the trials and tribulations endured by Mrs Patience in hospital after her stroke and now living with her daughter in the care of nurses, and made the appropriately sympathetic noises. As they finished their coffee, Miss Patience looked at her watch. "Ah, two o'clock," she said. "I ought to pop home and see how my mother is before the start of the afternoon classes. She is rather confused by all the changes in her life. Are your legs less wobbly now?" she then enquired of Shirley, who assured her that her legs, and her head as well, had benefited from a break and some refreshment. "Well then, I suggest you go back to the studio and do some gentle practice. If the large studio is occupied, you can go upstairs and do some *barre* work," she suggested.

"Yes, that's a good idea," Shirley agreed as they parted company.

Only when she was alone was she free to appreciate the full significance of what was happening. At last, she said to herself as she strolled over the bridge to the studio, she was sure that she *was* going to be famous, and that was what was needed for everything else to fall into place! She was actually going to fulfil her ambition of becoming prima ballerina with her name in lights. Most importantly, that would make it possible for Alan, her Prince Charming, to find her! She couldn't be sure from their meeting on the ship whether or not he knew her name, but she had absolutely no doubt that he was searching for her just as she was searching for him. She realized to her joy that consequently not only was her future in the dance assured but also a lifetime's happiness.

She debated with herself whether this good luck might be the effect of the diamond. Was that possible? She had been persuaded to think so yesterday, and today the temptation was there to think so again, however improbable and superstitious it might seem. It certainly contradicted the miserably depressing advice that the priest had given her in the confessional some weeks ago. She told no one in the dance school her news, not even Violet, the other girl who had been offered a place at Sadler's Wells, but went straight upstairs to the small studio where she knew she would be alone, undisturbed by the arrival of other pupils and their chatter. She stretched at the *barre* and practised some *pointe* work, perfecting her stance, confident that in so doing she was investing in that longed-for future.

Intent on telling Mrs S. the astounding news, she came out of the studio an hour later to hear a voice hailing her from the opposite side of the road and recognized Frank, one of the boys whom she used to meet on the way to school and with whom she sometimes used to go ballroom dancing on Saturday evenings. He wasn't very good-looking, though he was pleasant. "Hey, Shirley," he called, "wait a minute! Let me cross over!" She wasn't particularly keen to see him and would have preferred to let her mind roam free, indulging her romantic notions; nonetheless she waited for him to cross the road.

"Nice to see you, Frank," she said half-heartedly.

"You look as if you're wandering in a dream!" he exclaimed, and then asked: "Where have you been all this time? Have you left school? All your school friends are missing you, and your brother said he didn't know whether you'd left or not."

"Yes, I have left," she replied, without proffering any further details.

"Why don't you come ballroom dancing with us any more?" he asked eagerly. "It's not the same without you. You're so good at it," he smiled, as if he were expecting that this would lead to a friendly chat.

"I've had so many other things to do," she said, conscious that he would not be satisfied with such an empty excuse – he was after all an intelligent boy. She was aware too that the times she had flirted with him, which were several, probably entitled him to a better explanation; nevertheless she was extremely reluctant to admit any casual friend into her private dreams or allow him to bring her down to boring reality from the cloud on which she was floating. "I've had to keep house for Ted and my father because my mother is away. My grandmother died, you see," she said, trusting that those few words would be sufficient to draw the conversation to a close, but her hopes were misplaced.

"Oh, I am sorry!" he said with feeling. "I know what that's like. My Grandma died in the summer and we miss her so much. Do you have time for a cup of tea in that café over there? We could talk about these things and help each other get over them."

"No, I'm afraid I don't have time. I've my job to go to," Shirley said brusquely, cutting short his invitation, but regretting that on the spur of the moment she had told him about her job, because he naturally asked where it was and what it was. "Sorry, no time today. See you again soon! I'll be late if I don't go now," she called back over her shoulder as she set off at a run, leaving Frank standing forlornly on the pavement.

"Shirley, Shirley, you're early. Are you all right?" Mrs Salvatore asked in surprise as her assistant ran into the shop. Shirley glanced out of the door. There were only a handful of people in the street and she was fairly sure that Frank hadn't followed her, since he still had a long walk to his house from the bus stop. Although she was annoyed that his interference had interrupted her thoughts and brought her back to the everyday reality from which she had briefly escaped, she made an effort to recapture her earlier excitement for Mrs S.'s benefit and said, "Yes, even better than this morning! I've come in early to tell you the good news! They've awarded me a place at Sadler's Wells!" She refrained from giving Mrs S. too much information, not only for fear of appearing boastful, but also because she might find herself inadvertently giving away those associated thoughts that she did not want to share with anyone else. When Ted called in at the shop for the papers for his evening round, Shirley was too busy to talk to him. There was no opportunity to tell him her news and she had to content herself with a quick wave.

She returned to her deeply personal reflections while she dealt with her customers rather more mechanically than they were used to. Her encounter with Frank, nice though he was, had persuaded her, if she needed persuading, that there was and would ever be, only one man, Alan, in her life – apart that is from her pa and Ted, and perhaps at a distance Pépé. She vowed that she would no longer flirt with the boys; she would not have boyfriends; she would not dance with anyone other than her father, unless it happened to be required in performance on the stage, and she would dedicate herself entirely to the pursuit of the two goals she had set herself: ballet and the search for Alan. As for her school friends, it was a pity not to see them, because she had been popular and she liked many of them: they had played tennis together in summer and taken trips into town in winter. She doubted, though, that she would have any time to spend with them once she had enrolled at Sadler's Wells. They, like everyone else, would have to come to the theatre if they wanted to see her.

19

Head held high, Shirley walked through the door of the shop at the end of her shift as if she were about to step onto a stage, but a strong gust of wind blew her off course as soon as she put a foot outside. The gust was followed by large globular drops of rain falling one by one noisily onto the pavement from a leaden sky. Though her instinctive reaction was to step back into the shop for shelter, a glimpse of the louring clouds told her that she might be there for the whole evening, so she decided to chance it and make a dash for home. The distance was short, only five minutes at walking pace, so, if she ran, she would soon be there. This proved to be wishful thinking, because in less than no time the rain began to fall more heavily and a flash of lightning shot through the encroaching blackness. Distant thunder rumbled in the west, where the setting sun was almost obliterated, its jaundiced rays streaking out from under the clouds, giving everything they illuminated a sickly, sinister aspect. Running up the path she fumbled for her key, but her fingers were so cold that she had to struggle to insert it into the lock. "Here, let me do that," said a well-known voice behind her. Drenched from head to foot, Ted had flung his bike against the fence and reached to take the key from her hand. They stumbled into the house, one after the other, treading on the afternoon post that had accumulated on the mat.

"Phew!" Shirley exclaimed. "I'm glad to be home! Look at you! You're soaked! You'd better go and change, maybe have a bath even."

"It came down so heavily; I cycled as fast as I could," he said. Then, surveying her, he said, "You're pretty wet yourself; don't catch cold. At least put some dry clothes on." He went up to the bathroom while she put the kettle on and then she too went upstairs, intending to change out of her wet clothes.

On entering her bedroom, she was distracted from the cold and the wet by the sight of the diamond glistening there on her dressing table even in that gloomy light. Bewildered, she stood in the doorway shivering. The diamond was there where she had thought she had left it that morning, so her anxiety on that score had been unjustified. But why was the box open, the diamond on display for all to see? She thought she had closed it, indeed she was nearly – but not entirely – sure that it was shut when she had placed it down in among her hairbrush, comb and other odds and ends. The glittering jewel drew her cautiously over to the dressing table, where all her other bits and pieces were just as she had left them, higgledy-piggledy, gathering dust. She looked around the room: it was neat and tidy, and the carpet had been vacuumed. She turned back the sheets on her bed: the linen had been changed. Puzzled, she began to take off her wet clothes and pulled some dry ones out of her chest of drawers, which she noticed had been dusted and polished. Only then, as the lightning flashed and the thunder roared outside, did she begin to fathom the mystery. Her knees faltered beneath her for the second time that day and she had to sit down on her bed.

How stupid she had been! Stupid to have left the diamond on her dressing table, stupid to have thought that it was safe there from burglars – above all, stupid not to have realized that it would attract Francesca's attention! And who was Francesca? Why, she was Mr Salvatore's niece! Without a doubt she would have known about the existence of the diamond that had belonged to her grandmother, Mr S.'s mother, and perhaps she had been hoping, expecting, to inherit it from Mr S., since he had no children of his own. To find that it – or one so remarkably like it – was on Shirley's dressing table must have given her a shock. The fact that Francesca, to all intents friendly and hard-working, could not speak English did not mean that she was a dimwit or could not speak volubly in her own language. Probably she was right now telling all her relatives, apart from the Salvatores, that the precious family heirloom had been given away to that Shirley Marlow who had only recently begun to work in the newsagent's. Maybe she was even telling them that "Signorina Shirley" had stolen it and they were concocting plans to retrieve it: maybe they would threaten her or Pa or Ted out in the street or burgle the house and murder them all. She felt sick with worry. What was she going to do? If she told Pa, he would want her to take the diamond back to the Salvatores, as he had insisted last night; if she told Ted, he would say that she had to tell Pa.

Still shivering and weak at the knees, she took a closer look, not at the diamond, but at its case. She peered at the inside of the lid and managed to make out a few of the gold letters imprinted on the worn

CRY TO DREAM AGAIN

satin lining discoloured with age: "Carlo Rocca Gioielleria Genova". She was not sure whereabouts in Italy the Salvatores were from, but there was no doubting that the diamond pendant had originated in a place called Genova in Italy and was not English in origin, which meant that the mere sight of the inscription would have been enough to confirm Francesca's suspicions. On an impulse she closed the lid and shoved the case deep into the top drawer. Today was Tuesday and Francesca would be coming on Thursday, but at least that gave her a few hours to think up a plan. She did not need those few hours, because a flash of inspiration told her what to do. She would wear the pendant, even hiding it under a blouse or a sweater to make it invisible, though that wouldn't be easy in the dance studio. The question remained: had she left the box open or had Francesca opened it? Was it a threat? Was it a subtle hint that she, Francesca, knew where the diamond was? There was no way that Shirley could guess at Francesca's thoughts. Tired of speculating, she went downstairs.

"Shirl, you are blue with cold!" Ted exclaimed at the sorry sight of her. "You make the tea and I'll light the fire." He ran out, dodging the pelting rain, to fetch wood and coal from the shed. While the thunder rumbled ever closer and the lightning flashed, Shirley poured the tea, trying to pull herself together. "It has turned cold with this rain, hasn't it?" Ted remarked, as he crumpled up paper and laid kindling on top of it. "I'll get this fire going and that'll warm you up." Shirley smiled wanly. Who would have thought even a couple of months ago that she would be so grateful to this brother of hers? Since Maman's departure for France, he had become a good friend.

"If I weren't so cold, I would tell you my good news," she said.

"Won't telling it warm you up?" he asked. "Go on, give it a try!"

"All right, then," she replied, and told him about the offer of a place at Sadler's Wells.

"Gosh, that's quick! Well done! They must want to have you!" he whooped. "But I should think they were afraid that if they didn't jump in with their offer you might go somewhere else."

"I don't exactly know where," she said, "although, come to think of it, there are a couple of other new companies starting up, but I don't know what they're like." She was drawing breath before telling him about Madam's prediction that she would soon become a principal in the company, when he butted in with a welcome offer:

154

"Why don't I cook the supper tonight while you sit there warming yourself by the fire. I see you've bought sausages and I know there's a tin of baked beans. Sausages and baked beans are well within my range. We cook them with baked potatoes all the time at camp." Shirley was happy to oblige him, and happy to keep the rest of her news for Pa. With any luck, that might distract him from the diamond. She would be happy to be distracted from it herself.

A tantalizing smell of sausage, onion and baking potatoes wafted from the kitchen, where Ted was applying all his camping skills to his one recipe. The thunder crashed overhead only seconds after each flash of lightning. "Glad I'm not out in this!" Ted shouted from the kitchen.

"Yes, but what about poor Pa?" Shirley shouted back. "I wonder where he is?" Her question was answered by the sound of a key turning in the lock. "Ah, here he is!" She ran out into the hall as the door opened and a soaking, writhing figure flung itself onto the hall carpet.

Shrinking back, she stood dumbfounded as the figure advanced crawling on all fours along the hall, shouting, "It's the guns! It's the guns! They're firing again!" Ted emerged from the kitchen to see what the rumpus was about and stopped abruptly halfway down the hall.

"Oh, no!" he cried. "He's having one of his attacks!" Shirley, convinced that by telling Maman that Pa was well she had tempted Providence, burst into tears. Ted kept calm. He lifted his shaking father onto his feet, eased him out of his wet raincoat, and led him into the dining room, where he settled him in an armchair by the fire; he promptly drew the curtains on the raging tempest outside that had evidently caused his father's panic.

"Shirl," he asked, "can you go and finish the supper? The sausages are nearly ready and I'll look after Pa." He went over to the sideboard and took out a bottle and a small glass. "Bring me some sugar and a spoon too, will you? Oh and some hot, but not boiling water from the kettle," he called. Shirley hastily did as he requested. He mixed a spoonful of sugar in the bottom of a glass with a little hot water and poured in a shot of brandy. "Now, Pa," he said, "sip this and you will soon feel better." Their father's eyes were bulging with fright as he turned his head towards Ted.

"Who are you?" he asked. "Where's Jacqueline?"

"She's out. She'll be back soon," Ted reassured him quietly. "I'm the new doctor. I've come to help you get over the shock, so just sip a few spoonfuls of this medicine and let me put some cotton wool in your ears to dull the noise." He beckoned to Shirley to fetch some cotton wool from the bathroom cupboard while he fed his father spoonfuls of brandy and sugar. He then rolled the cotton wool into small balls that he stuffed into his father's ears.

Reggie relaxed a little. "The guns are going away, aren't they?" he asked, still shaking.

"Yes, yes, I think so; they may be noisy a bit longer, but you're feeling better now aren't you?"

"Are we safe?" Pa asked dreamily.

"Yes, we're a long way from the front line here," Ted replied, holding his hand. "Nurse!" he called. "Can you fetch a blanket, please?"

"Certainly, doctor," said Shirley. She ran to the hall cupboard and brought a tartan picnic rug, which she draped over her father's knees and tucked around his chest. He was already drowsy and drifting into sleep.

"How did you know about giving him brandy?" she asked her brother as they sat down to eat. She was full of admiration for his performance, so unlike hers of the day before, yet nonetheless so convincing.

"Oh, that's nothing," Ted said modestly. "I've seen Maman do that. It usually calms him down. That's why she used to keep us out of the room when we were little if he had a bad turn: she didn't want us to know about the brandy. But once I came in as she was taking the bottle out of the sideboard, so instead of slamming the door shut she showed me what to do."

"You are amazing!" Shirley exclaimed, echoing his compliment to her of the previous evening. "You should be a doctor."

"No, no, that's not for me! You know I'm a farmer's boy and I'd rather be feeding people than mending them" was his final comment. They ate their supper, discussing in low voices what their next move should be, while their father dozed by the fire.

None of their various plans had to be put into effect. The storm passed over and their father woke up. "What am I doing here?" he asked in surprise. His features were still hollow and his skin grey, but he seemed cheerful.

"You weren't well when you came home, but Ted looked after you, and now you are better, so come and have some supper. Ted cooked it," Shirley said, indicating his plate of food that she had just brought to the table. "Then," she continued, "I'll tell you my news."

"Yes, that smells good!" he said appreciatively, referring to his supper. "Maybe just a dab of mustard would help, if you don't mind, Shirl."

"Of course," she said, and mixed some mustard once she had found the tin at the back of the cupboard. While her pa ate she did the washing-up, anticipating his pleasure at her success. There was much to be proud of that day, she reminded herself, if one could overlook the worry about the diamond. She pushed it to the back of her mind.

Shirley was still washing all the plates, dishes, cutlery and pots and pans, which after her brother's culinary efforts needed a great deal of scrubbing, when she heard her father leave the table and hobble straight into the front room, where he turned on the wireless. She listened from the kitchen doorway and could hear him muttering, "I must catch the news; there have been speeches today by that nasty little man in Germany, that Hitler, with his Italian pal Mussolini. They're up to no good and they spell trouble; I don't know why somebody doesn't get rid of both of them." Pa was right: a month after making his *Lebensraum* speech, suggesting that Germany should expand to the east to accommodate her large population, Hitler, together with Mussolini, was trying to cover his tracks by claiming that the speech had been wilfully misinterpreted by the rest of the world and that their intentions were peaceful. "Hmph," said Pa, talking loudly to himself in the sitting room, "if you believe that, you'll believe anything! If you ask me, Hitler's got his eye on colonies in Africa and is going to take a leaf out of Mussolini's book now that Abyssinia's in Italian hands."

Like her mother, Shirley often found Pa's obsession with world events inexplicable, frustrating and even irritating. Despite his traumatic memories of the Great War and the appalling psychotic effect those experiences had produced on his mind, he still avidly soaked up all the news connected with present conflicts, as for instance the Japanese invasion of China, or the Spanish Civil War, especially in the wake of the horrors of Guernica, or with growing conflicts nearer home which he knew were threatening to explode into something bigger. This awful fascination compelled him to listen to the wireless every night and every Friday to go to the cinema to see the Pathé newsreels, which reported to packed audiences the visual images of what he had heard on the wireless during the week.

Maman refused to accompany him to these showings; she said she would rather enjoy the present and not know what was coming next, but he said that it was important to be prepared for the worst so that if the world stumbled into warfare, like the last time, he would not be caught unawares. Sometimes he prevailed upon Shirley or Ted to go with him, but they too would have preferred to be elsewhere, though Shirley had been fascinated by the scandal of the abdication of Edward VIII and had enjoyed the coverage of the new king's coronation. It was a pageant such as she had never seen and could be made into a wonderful ballet. She said as much to Ted, but he took little notice of her as his thoughts were still on the Teutonic threat. The Germans lost the last war, he reasoned, so why should anyone be afraid of them now? Ted's convictions in that respect were stronger than Shirley's. "It's all bluff," he said, "they wouldn't dare, not again." Nevertheless Shirley, who had plenty of time to read the newspapers at work, was at heart worried by the endless reports streaming daily out of Germany, reports of concentration camps being set up for enemies of the state, of attacks on Jewish people, of claims to more land outside Germany's borders.

Reggie was so exhausted after listening to the news that he decided that it was time for bed. "It's been a long day," he said, "and something odd happened, but I can't quite remember what it was. Has there been a thunderstorm round here?"

"Yes, Pa," Shirley replied as she shepherded him to the bottom of the stairs, "it was huge." She shouted up to Ted, who was doing his homework in his room, to tell him that their father was on his way upstairs. This was enough warning for Ted to come out of his room and keep watch, because Pa was often unsteady after one of his attacks. On checking that the front door was locked, Shirley noticed the pile of post on the mat and bent down to pick it up. She and Ted had rushed into the house to escape the storm and had overlooked it; then in the crisis with Pa it had been crumpled and crawled over. Now it was damp and stained and some of the writing was illegible. Mostly it consisted of bills, but there was one letter that had a Birmingham postmark. It was unlikely to be a thank-you letter from Edith, since she would still be on her honeymoon, so perhaps it was from Aunt Winnie, though why she should be writing, Shirley could not begin to guess. "Oh well, she can wait," she thought, "tomorrow is time enough for that." She put it down on the hall table, turned out the lights and went up to bed.

20

There were two batches of post for Reggie to open the next evening: that day's and the mud-streaked handful that had been overlooked from the previous evening. Shirley had enjoyed a blissfully uneventful day: she had not worn the diamond pendant, because she reckoned that it would be safe in her drawer until Thursday, the day of Francesca's next visit, when she would wear it discreetly tucked inside her jumper and she would allay Miss Patience's disapproval by telling her that Mrs S. had asked to see her wearing it. Nora Patience had set her some exercises, which she said might be helpful in preparation for her forthcoming entry to Sadler's Wells, and had then left her to work on those.

Pa came home in a receptive mood, saying, "Did you say that you had some good news yesterday, Shirl? I'm very sorry, but I forgot all about it, so is it too late to tell me today over supper?" His face wrinkled in the most disarming smile and, considering the unfortunate circumstances of the storm on the previous evening, it was not hard to forgive him his lapse of memory. He was delighted to hear of her triumph, though in recounting the details of it she had difficulty mustering that intoxicating excitement, disbelief and anticipation that had coursed through her when the news had first come from Sadler's Wells – over the telephone, delivered by Madam to Miss Patience herself. Nor was there any point in telling Pa of Madam's predictions for her, because they would not mean anything to him.

"So, when will you be starting work there?" he asked, as if this were any old job that she had been offered.

"I don't know yet; I'll have to wait for the formal letter to come through. I expect they'll be doing a Christmas production and I hope I'll be part of that, so I expect it will be soon."

"Very exciting, very exciting," he murmured, "but I wish your mother were here to share it all. Is there a letter from her, do you know, Ted?"

"I don't think so," Ted replied, reaching over from the supper table to the sideboard, from where he picked up the pile of post.

"Oh dear! What's happened here?" Reggie asked as he saw the grubby marks on the envelopes.

"Some of those are today's and some yesterday's. We didn't get round to opening them last night, what with the storm and everything," Ted said with gentle tact.

Having finished his supper, his father looked through the pile. "Um, I can't see anything from your mother," he remarked sadly, "and it looks as if they're mostly bills. But here's a letter. I can't read the writing. It's been wiped out, but the postmark says it's from Birmingham. Must be from my sister. Perhaps it's some sort of thank you. That can wait till later."

As usual, he took himself off into the living room to listen to the accounts of the latest atrocities that had been committed around the world. After the news, he was not as tired as he had been on the previous evening, so sat down in the dining room to peruse the post. "Good Lord!" both Ted and Shirley who were in the kitchen, heard him exclaim; then he sighed a long sigh and said, "Oh, dear!" before calling them to join him. "I'm afraid this is bad news. Winnie writes to tell me that Thelma is in hospital with infantile paralysis and is very ill. She can't move her right arm or her right leg and is having difficulty breathing."

Shirley and Ted looked at each other in shock: they had both heard of infantile paralysis and were well aware that it was a dreadful disease that could be deadly. Indeed, throughout their childhood they had been expressly forbidden by their protective parents from going into certain shops and stores and, above all, from swimming in the municipal pool. They were allowed to swim only in the sea, and if they wanted something from one of those shops, something that everyone else in school had, they had to ask their parents to buy it for them. The notion that Shirley had been exposed to the disease by her own family – or rather Pa's family, for she did not really like to include Winnie and Thelma among her close relatives – was too terrible to contemplate.

"But I slept in a room on the same floor as Thelma and had to share the bathroom with her! And she charged into the bathroom while I was having a bath and she was violently sick!" Shirley cried out, as terrified alarm spread across her face.

"I know, but let's try and be calm about it," Pa said, though his hands were shaking and his face was ashen. "Let's see what else Winnie has to say."

"Oh, her! She's useless! She should have taken more care of Thelma last weekend, but all she could think about was herself. She should have called the doctor as Uncle Horace kept saying, but she wouldn't listen!" Shirley burst out. Her alarm had quickly changed to fury, and she stood up, stamped her foot and banged furiously on the table as if that piece of solid furniture were the cause of all the trouble.

"Calm down, calm down, Shirl, while I read the rest of the letter," Pa pleaded and then read the letter aloud. "Our doctor says Shirley will be in quarantine and should see your doctor as soon as possible. I've telephoned Mother, who says that Edward can go and stay with her as long as necessary."

"Not likely!" Ted exclaimed. "I wouldn't go and stay with her for anything!"

"Now, now, Ted," Pa remonstrated with his son, "we have to be sensible about this." Both children looked to their pa to resolve the situation, and the silence in the dining room was heavy with anxiety as he tried to decide on the best course.

At last he said, "There's nothing we can do tonight, so I suggest that tomorrow we carry on as usual and Shirley must go to the doctor's. Then we shall really know how serious the situation is and what to do for the best. How does that sound to you?" Ted and Shirley nodded their approval, glad of the reprieve from immediate action. For Shirley the one silver lining of this particular cloud was that it had completely diverted Pa's attention from the diamond pendant, if indeed after his crisis last night he still remembered it; she doubted that he would ever ask about it again.

She was in no great hurry to go to the surgery in the morning. As usual, she went to work, wearing her diamond under a new pink jumper that Mémé had knitted for her during the summer holidays. "This is for those chilly autumn days," her French grandmother had said, "and when you wear it, you can think of me." Thinking of Mémé these days was much more painful than had been her intention when she issued that request. Fearing that it might make her sad all day, Shirley was undecided whether to wear the jumper or not, but a quick review of her collection persuaded her that this was the only one that would do the pendant justice. What's more, it was only right that the jumper should be the one to have the honour of being worn with the diamond. She was conscious of the cold stone lying close to her chest under the warm wool, and only when the shop had emptied of customers did she pull the gem out by its chain for Mrs S. to see.

The pink jumper set the translucent gem off nicely and Mrs S. was duly ecstatic at the sight of it: she called her husband out of his office to admire the combined effect. "I'm sorry I haven't worn it to show you sooner, but I've had other things to think about," Shirley said.

"We know that, Shirley dear – don't apologize," Mrs S. laughed. "But do be careful. I don't think you should wear it all the time and not in the shop. There might be all sorts of wicked people about just waiting to get their hands on it!" Shirley did not like to say that that was precisely why she was wearing it and that she had a good idea who those people might be; in fact one of them was at that moment hoovering the carpets at home. Shirley had given Francesca her money, nodded graciously to her and left the house without a word. She hoped that her disdain would be a clear and sufficient indication to Francesca that her interference had not gone unnoticed, and with any luck also that any further designs that she might be hatching would be severely dealt with, although, of course, she did not know how or by whom. Mr S. emerged from the backroom, grinning from ear to ear and muttering, "*Bellissima, bellissima!*" Then he disappeared into his office again to brew a celebratory cup of rich Italian coffee.

Shirley was grateful for the coffee: the shop had been very busy from the moment she arrived and the work had been tiring, yet at all costs she did not want to go home for a drink before her dance session for fear of finding her granny waiting on the doorstep. In the studio she was glad to discover that Miss Patience was having a morning off, so then there was no need for her to conceal the pendant, though it did keep getting in the way and swinging round her neck. Finally she had to resort to her original plan and pin it inside the high-necked ballet top that she had deliberately selected to hide the jewel while she danced. Thus she had nearly completed her exercises and routines when she heard Miss Patience's voice out in reception. Deciding that she had worked hard enough for one morning, she changed quickly back into the pink jumper and hastily put on her coat.

"Ah, Shirley!" Miss Patience said. "I hoped I might just catch you! I've had another call from Madam. She asks if you could go over to the Wells next week – I think she said on Wednesday – so you could find out more about what's needed and join in one of their training sessions.

The letters haven't been sent out yet, but she wants you to begin as soon as possible!"

"I'd love that! That's excellent news!" Shirley replied. "My Pa was asking when I would be starting, but I couldn't tell him, because I didn't know."

"Right, I'll ring them and say you are happy to begin and will go over there next Wednesday, shall I?"

"Yes please!" was Shirley's response.

"Oh, and may I come too?" Miss Patience enquired shyly. "I would love to see the Wells and meet Edris again." Shirley was only too pleased to agree.

So thrilled was she by this unexpected turn of events and by the success of her ruse to protect her diamond that she turned right on coming out of the studio and headed for home. It was not until she reached the newsagent's that she remembered that she was supposed to be going to the doctor's. She was tempted to carry on, but her conscience told her that Pa would not be pleased, so she turned round and, retracing her steps past the studio, she walked to the surgery, which was not much more than an outbuilding of an old red-brick house set back from the road in a large garden. In the usual course of events there was a hubbub of patients coming and going in the driveway, a few bicycles leaning on the fence and a collection of prams parked by the door. Today there was no sign of life and nothing in the driveway – no patients, no bikes, no prams. She went up to the door and tried the handle: it was locked. She then noticed a small piece of paper pinned high on the door frame. She stood on tiptoe to read it: "Surgery unavoidably closed today. In case of emergency, please go to Dr Kinnaird." The address given for this Dr Kinnaird was miles away, so Shirley gave up and went home to make herself some lunch.

Her first thought, however, was to put the diamond away where its fascinating radiance would be hidden from the world. Her legs were aching as she climbed the stairs and having placed the diamond in its box at the bottom of the top drawer, which showed no signs of disturbance, she lay down and went to sleep. Perhaps, she told herself on waking, she had been unjust to Francesca, who may have peeped inside the box on Tuesday out of curiosity without malicious intent. Everyday life would certainly be easier if Francesca were trustworthy.

By the time she made herself a bite to eat, it was already late, with the result that her afternoon practice time in the studio was much curtailed, but, refreshed from her heavy doze, she concentrated on mastering many more new steps at high speed until the schoolchildren began to arrive for their lessons. On reaching the newsagent's, she felt unaccountably tired again, but ascribed that to the effort she had put into dancing and to the earlier longish walk to the surgery. After her stint in the shop she longed to go home, have a cup of tea and, unusually for her, put her feet up. She was asleep in Pa's armchair when Ted came home and was still asleep when their father arrived an hour later. "All the excitement catching up with you, Shirl?" was his reaction.

"Yes, I suppose so," she replied. "I must start cooking the supper."

Pa's first question once they had settled themselves at the table was not about the diamond. He did not say, "Have you taken the diamond back to Mr and Mrs Salvatore?" Instead he enquired, "Did you go to the doctor's today, Shirl?"

She was happy that she could answer truthfully, "Yes, I went, but the surgery was closed, all locked up with a notice on the door saying: "Surgery unavoidably closed today."

"That's odd: I've never known Dr Forbes to abandon his post," Pa commented. Then he asked: "Was that all?"

"Oh, it also said, 'In an emergency please go to Dr Kinnaird' and gave his address. But that's miles away, so I didn't go there."

"Well, make sure you go back tomorrow, won't you?"

"Yes, if you say so, Pa," Shirley answered with some reluctance.

"Promise me that you will." Pa insisted.

"I promise," she conceded. She did not fulfil her promise first thing in the morning, but left it until the end of the working and dancing day.

Dr Forbes was a sympathetic man with a kindly manner, so it was always a pleasure to see him whenever he came to the house, as he had often when she and Ted were little and had succumbed to measles, or chickenpox or mumps, and nowadays, on his visits to Pa, he always had time to stop for a chat that was not necessarily limited to medical matters. He shared Pa's passion for trains and model railways, he admired Shirley's ambition to be a ballerina and he had not only travelled in France but had served in the Medical Corps in the Great War. Given all his positive attributes, Shirley could not explain to herself why she so vehemently detested going to visit his surgery. It was not as if the surgery were particularly clinical. It was in fact a rather chaotic tumbledown sort of building where the patients sat on rickety chairs in the waiting room, and where the room to which Dr Forbes summoned them was more like a study with a large desk at which he sat. There were very few items to suggest any medical involvement at all, apart from the examination couch hidden by a curtain in the corner.

By the time Shirley arrived, darkness had fallen, and she rather hoped that the surgery would already be closed. She could always tell her pa that she had been delayed by the customers in the shop. There was, however, a light on in the waiting room, where ahead of her in the queue four or five patients were blowing their noses with early colds. She calculated that she would not be seen for at least an hour, so she picked up a magazine which she found she had already read in the shop, sat down and waited patiently, regretting that she had left her visit so late after all, because Pa and Ted would be home soon and would be hungry for their supper. If only she could stand up and practise some exercises, then the time would not be wasted! She contemplated abandoning the visit, but knew that Pa would be very displeased if she went home again saying that she hadn't seen the doctor.

An hour later, at seven fifteen, Dr Forbes put his head round the waiting-room door. "Ah, who have we left?" he asked with a weary smile. Then he saw her sitting in the corner and exclaimed, "Shirley Marlow! Come in! What can I do for you?" He showed her into his room and enquired how her father was coping and whether the pills he had prescribed were working.

"Yes, thank you, he's doing quite well, but we did have something of a crisis the other evening with that thunderstorm. He thought he was back on the front line and went quite berserk."

"Oh dear! How did you manage?" Dr Forbes asked with a deep concern, which made Shirley realize that he thought that she had come to the surgery to talk about Pa. She hedged the question because she wasn't sure that Dr Forbes would approve of Maman's recipe of brandy, sugar and hot water and simply replied: "My brother calmed him down." After this she knew she would have to take the plunge.

"Actually," she said, launching into her report without having thought out clearly what to say, "Pa wanted me to come and see you, because last weekend we were staying with his family in Birmingham and my cousin fell ill. We've now had a letter saying she has gone down with infantile paralysis and she was in the bedroom next to me and we were sharing a bathroom."

Dr Forbes's expression had changed from one of friendly greeting to one of grave anxiety. "Can you tell me how ill your cousin was then and how ill she is now?" he asked.

"She was moaning in bed about not being able to move her head and she was sick in the bathroom while I was in there. She's in hospital now and is paralysed down one side and can't breathe easily," Shirley said, telling the doctor everything she knew while he scribbled notes on a pad.

"So when was this?" he asked, and when she said that it was last Friday that she and her pa had gone to Birmingham, he noted down "six days" on his pad. "I think I'd better examine you, Shirley," he said, gesturing to the couch. "Please loosen your clothing and lie down over there, will you?" He felt round her neck, listened to her heart, tapped her knees with a little hammer and took her temperature. "Are you feeling off-colour?" he asked.

"No," said Shirley; she thought she was fine.

"I gather you're intending to be a ballerina, isn't that right?" he continued.

"Yes!" she replied, excited that at last the interview was turning to a subject in her own sphere.

"Have you done much ballet this week?" he asked.

"Oh, every day! I've been to an audition at Sadler's Wells and they've offered me a place!" she told him, thinking that this latter would prove how fit she was.

"Well, then," he said, unimpressed by her achievement, "my advice to you is to take it easy for the next few days. Don't dance any more this week and with any luck you'll be in the clear by about Monday or Tuesday. You are in fact in quarantine for infantile paralysis and must keep away from all public places. Stay at home; don't go out further than your own back garden – or perhaps for a ride in the car – but keep away from public places and other people. You must ask your father to ring me if you start feeling poorly."

Shirley was flabbergasted. "What about my job?" she asked. "I work in the newsagent's every morning and afternoon. What am I going to do about that?"

The answer was straightforward. "You'll have to send them a message saying you're not well and won't be able to work for the next few days. Don't say you're in quarantine for infantile paralysis: I don't want a public-health scare on my hands." Then he added, "Look, I'll write a letter for you to take to your father. It will say virtually the same as I've told you, then he'll know what to expect." Crestfallen, she stood up and straightened her clothing, thinking that perhaps she had been wrong to like Dr Forbes, when he plied her with more questions. "What about your brother? Did he go to Birmingham too?"

"No," Shirley replied, "he went to camp." Dr Forbes drew in a deep breath and scribbled even faster on the letter he was writing to Pa.

"Now, Shirley," he said as he handed it to her, "take this letter home to your father, give it to him straight away and let's hope our precautions are unnecessary!"

21

"Ah, Shirley, been to the doctor's have you?" Reggie asked by way of a greeting that evening.

"Yes, it took rather a long time," she explained, handing him the doctor's letter.

"Ted and I thought that was what had happened," he said, pointing towards the kitchen. "He's putting a few bits and pieces together for supper." He puzzled over the contents of the letter. "Dr Forbes is a very nice man," he remarked with a sigh, "but how anyone is supposed to read his writing, I don't know."

Shirley looked over his shoulder. "He says that there are certain things you ought to know, Pa," she said, trying to be helpful. "He says that the incubation period for infantile paralysis is five to ten day. He told me I would be in the clear by Monday or Tuesday at the latest, and that's really important, because I've been asked to go back to Sadler's Wells on Wednesday."

"I see, I see," said her father; in his forehead the fine lines were becoming more pronounced as he read further on. "He does say that you will be in quarantine for the best part of the next week and" – here he paused to adjust his spectacles – "and so will Edward – that is, until we can be sure that you haven't passed any germs on to him." He took a deep breath before continuing, "He says that this comes in three forms, depending on the patient: one is very virulent and dangerous, one is much milder and doesn't necessarily leave any lasting damage, and the third, well, people often don't know they've had it, but they can pass it on to others."

Shirley began to panic. Supposing she caught the first type, the virulent dangerous type, what would that mean? "Now, Shirl," Pa said as he turned the page and peered at the illegible scrawl trying to make sense of it, "Dr Forbes says here that you must tell me the moment you begin to feel unwell. If you have a headache or a stiff neck, if you feel very tired or if you think you've got flu or a temperature, or if you can't move an arm or a leg. Oh, and if you feel sick. Do you feel any of those symptoms?"

"No, I don't think so," Shirley replied, checking the state of her head, limbs and neck. She was not aware of any unusual sensations in her lithe, supple body, though just hearing the list of possible manifestations of the disease was sufficient to make her feel faint and queasy

Ted brought an assortment of ham, cold sausages left over from earlier in the week, mashed potato and salad to the table. "I'm sorry, old chap," Pa said, indicating the doctor's letter, "but you are going to have to stay with Granny for the next week or so, and you won't be able to go to school. This illness of Thelma's is serious, and you are in quarantine until we know whether Shirley has caught it."

Ted's features froze, turned to stone in an image of appalled horror. "I can't go and stay with her, Pa! I'd rather go to school! She'll drive me round the bend. And what am I supposed to do all day if I can't go to school?"

"Whatever happens, I'm going to get the car out and take you over there after supper," Pa decreed firmly. "And if you're wondering what to do with yourself, I suggest you have a look in your granny's garage: there are plenty of old bikes in there that need repairing. If you do them up, maybe she will let you sell them and you can make a bit of money."

Ted's resistance was appeased for a couple of minutes, but the mention of money had brought a further objection to mind. "What happens to my job at the Salvatores' then? And Shirley's for that matter? You know how dependent they are on us!"

Their father had no answer to these questions; all he could say was: "I'll write the Salvatores a note now, telling them that Shirley is in quarantine and so are you – I don't have to say what for – and we'll put it in their letter box on our way." Then, for the first time since Shirley had given him the letter, he gave a glimmer of a smile. "Who knows, maybe I could help them out at the weekend, if they'd have me."

They ate without the usual banter between father and children across the table, as each of them was absorbed in his or her own thoughts: Pa was worrying about both his children, Shirley was consumed with anxiety for her health and her future, and Ted, though he hated the prospect of staying with his granny, was, in his heart of hearts, glad of an excuse not to go to school, and was even gladder of the opportunity to make some money. Bicycle repairs were easily within his range of skills, for had farming in France not been his top priority he doubtless would have become an engineer like his father.

"What's more, you know," Shirley ventured, "you can play Granny's piano to your heart's content."

"Mm, perhaps, I suppose so," Ted replied. "I'm terribly out of practice, but I would quite like to take it up again."

Thus appeased, he responded positively when his father announced that it was time for him to pack his rucksack, adding, "Don't forget your toothbrush! We must be going if we're to arrive before your granny goes to bed. I'll stop at the phone box to let her know we're coming, and we can put the note through the Salvatores' door at the same time."

Then Reggie settled down with pen and paper to compose the note, couched in suitably vague and reassuring terms, to the newsagents, telling them only that Shirley had been in contact with an infection, so both she and Ted were in quarantine and would not be able to work for the next week or so, but that he would be happy to help out at the weekend if they would have him.

The menfolk went out in a hurry, leaving Shirley alone in the house. She sat down on the living-room floor to lengthen her spine and extend her hamstrings. There was no detectable weakness in her limbs, either in her legs, splayed wide and straight on the floor in front of her, or in her arms, raised high above her shoulders and then brought down low over her toes. As she leant forward, she wondered what the chances were of her catching Thelma's horrible disease, and if she did, how serious the effects might be. There was little comfort in knowing that there were three ways in which the disease could affect people and that it wasn't necessarily fatal. If her worst fears were realized and she was unable to dance ever again, it might be better to be struck down with the fatal form. She shuddered at the thought. What would happen to her place at Sadler's Wells? Would it matter if next Wednesday's visit were postponed? Worst of all, how would she ever meet Alan again if her dancing career came to nothing? And if that career, so full of promise, were killed off just as it was about to blossom, and all dreams of a future with him was nothing more than a vain hope without any basis in reality, she might as well be dead already. Painful questions raced through her mind until, tired out by trying to find answers for them when as yet there were none, she decided to go to bed, but not before she had written a letter to Miss Patience for her pa to deliver, telling her that, although she would be in quarantine for the next four or five days, she was sure of being able to go to Sadler's Wells the following Wednesday. She left the note on the dining table with a message for Pa asking him to deliver it on his way to work.

Her intention of having a lazy morning in bed was frustrated much earlier than she would have chosen by her father. "Shirl," he called out, his voice loud in her ear, "I've brought you a cup of tea. I've seen your letter for Miss Patience and I want to know how you are before I go to work."

"I'm fine, Pa," she replied sleepily, "but what about you? Have you taken your pills?"

"Bless me! I forgot!" he exclaimed. "It's just as well you asked!" By now Shirley was sitting up in bed, relieved to discover that she felt no worse than usual early in the morning. In fact she was surprised by how bright and breezy she was.

"So what am I going to do all day, Pa?" she asked.

"Oh, I'm sure you'll find something. I must be off. Bye!" Pa called over his shoulder from the landing. From the bottom of the stairs he called out again. "I'll do the shopping on the way home, so don't you worry about that."

She drank her tea and lay back, wondering how to fill the day which stretched out before her in a prospect of interminable tedium. As her own bookcase was full of books that she had already read, she went into her parents' room to search along Maman's shelves for anything interesting in French; she picked out *Madame Bovary*, which to her surprise absorbed her so deeply that an hour fled by before she realized that, with the house to herself, she could practise and dance to the wireless in the front room. This would have been fine, had not her parents recently invested in a new carpet, which, with its thick pile, was hopeless for dancing. Nonetheless, it was much warmer and more comfortable than the floor of the studio for seated warm-up exercises. The hall, though narrow, was long enough for her *grand allegro* of big jumps and leaps, of *posé* turns and *grand jetés*, especially when she managed to extend its length into the kitchen by moving the table out of the way, giving her a clear run from the front door to the back.

Halfway through her exercises, a ring at the doorbell interrupted her concentration. She crept on all fours to the window sill and peeped over the ledge. There, standing on the step sheltering from the rain under a large umbrella, was a small hunched figure with its back to her. Even from behind, that figure, normally so upright and straight-backed, was recognizable, though it lacked its customary decisive air. Perhaps it was the rain and the drop in temperatures that had caused the old woman to shrivel and turn in on herself for warmth. Shirley's better nature took hold of her. She switched off the wireless and, before answering the bell, pulled on the skirt that she always kept by her for just such an eventuality.

She opened the door to find that her grandmother presented such a woebegone picture of dejection that she took pity on her at once. "Granny!" she exclaimed. "What's wrong? Do come in out of the rain!" Her first thoughts were for her brother, wondering in consternation whether something terrible had happened to him in the short time he had been staying at their grandmother's. She shepherded her into the dining room and threw a match onto the fire that Pa had laid before going to work.

"Oh, Shirley, dear," the old woman snivelled, "you'll never guess what's happened. It's too frightful!"

"No, Granny, I can't guess, but tell me: is Edward all right?"

"Yes, yes, dear, he's fine. I've left him mending bicycles in the shed."

"Oh, thank Goodness!" Shirley exclaimed. "What's the matter then?"

Granny blew her nose. "It's Thelma, dear: she died last night!"

Shirley's legs gave way beneath her and she slumped to the floor at her grandmother's feet in a markedly ungraceful pose. Her Granny sat stock-still, then leant over and with a tentative gesture stroked her hair. "It's terrible news, isn't it? They – Winnie and Horace, I mean – never even suspected it could be infantile paralysis, because she didn't have any paralysis in her limbs. They thought it must be a bad case of flu. Then the diagnosis was a shock, but they were sure that she would make a full recovery and she wouldn't be affected for life. But it went to her lungs and she couldn't breathe. So she suffocated." She snivelled, "I knew it would be a shock for you, Shirley dear! She was such a lovely girl! You will miss her, won't you?"

At this last remark, Shirley bridled and edged away out of reach, nipping those unprecedented first shoots of bonding between grandmother and granddaughter in the bud. It was typical of Granny that, having never given much thought to other people, she had such a poor grasp of human relationships and personalities. Naturally Shirley was very sorry that Thelma had died of infantile paralysis and said as much. That was most definitely not a fate she would have wished on her worst enemy, but to suggest that she would actually *miss* Thelma was wide of the mark. Indeed, she hardly knew her, and what little she did know did not dispose her to like her or regard her either as a close friend or a cherished relative, for there was certainly no love lost between the cousins.

"I didn't know what to do," Granny kept on moaning. "Winnie rang this morning. I would have phoned you but, as you don't have a phone, I thought I ought to come over and tell you and your pa, because, you see, I shall have to go to Birmingham straight away. Poor Winnie will need me there. And of course I shall have to stay for the funeral. So I don't know what to do about Edward. He says he'll manage on his own – with Martha, my maid there – but he's rather young to be left in charge of my house." Shirley was not at all bothered about her grandmother's house. As far as she was concerned, Ted would look after it perfectly well. The news of Thelma's death from infantile paralysis, the very illness for which she was in quarantine, was quite enough to absorb her totally. What's more, Thelma's illness must have fallen into the severe category which paralysed the lungs, and that was the category to which she herself had been exposed last weekend in Birmingham.

Still trembling, she stood up. "You stay there by the fire, Granny," she said. "I'll make us a cup of coffee."

"You see, dear, I don't know what to do!" Granny kept on repeating. For once, the decisive and inflexible matriarch was caught on the horns of a dilemma. "Winnie needs me, of that I have no doubt, but what can I do about Edward?"

Shirley's practical nature came to the fore. "When is the funeral, Granny?" she asked, anxious to put a stop to these mawkish outpourings.

"It's next Thursday afternoon, dear," Granny replied.

"Well, there you are!" Shirley exclaimed. "There's no problem! By next Wednesday I shall be out of quarantine and Edward can come home, so you can go to Birmingham." As Shirley saw it, that aspect of the dilemma was solved; in fact it was no dilemma at all. She was also quite certain that, whatever importance her granny attached to her presence in Birmingham, Aunt Winnie was better off without her; she might even feel grateful to her London relatives for detaining her mother.

"I shall have to talk to Winnie about it. I'll ring her tonight," Mrs Marlow senior mumbled. "But certainly that would solve the problem. Of course I love having Edward to stay. He is my favourite grandson and he is always so cheerful! It does me good having someone so young and lively in the house. Martha is all right, but she is so dull! But Edward, the way he plays the piano has to be heard to be believed!" Edward might well be her favourite grandson, but there was no doubt that Thelma, headstrong and self-centred, had been Granny's favourite granddaughter.

Shirley contemplated her next move. If there was one thing worse than being in the house on her own, it was having her granny there all day with her, but in present circumstances she could hardly show her the door and send her out into the pouring rain. She made a jug of coffee and took a cup to her visitor, who was still seated, immobile, in the dining room. "Here's something to warm you up, Granny, but would you like a rug over your knees?" she said, summoning the most solicitous tone in her repertoire.

"No, thank you!" her granny retorted with a lively touch of indignation. "I'm not that old, you know, dear!" she replied briskly. "I've not reached the stage of life of needing a rug over my knees!" She sipped her coffee, grimaced and asked rhetorically: "Of course, I suppose you can't come out with me, can you?" Shirley shook her head, unwilling to rehearse the list of restrictions on her movements. "Well, that's a pity, because Morley's have opened a food hall and they have a delicious, rich dark coffee in there. If we'd gone out together, you could have bought a pound of it and then you wouldn't have to drink this awful stuff from that bottle. It really is only good for flavouring cakes and so on."

"Oh, this is fine for me," Shirley replied mildly, thankful that there was no chance of a trip to Morley's, where doubtless Granny would have secured a job for her in an instant as a shop assistant in the fabric department.

Moreover, the re-emergence of her granny's acerbic tongue was sufficient reassurance that the emotional crisis occasioned by Thelma's untimely death was passing and that her grandmother was resuming control: therefore she, herself, could with justification adopt her usual defiant attitude. "What will you be doing this afternoon, Granny?" she asked innocently.

"Gracious me!" Granny exclaimed. "With this dreadful news about poor dear Thelma, I had completely forgotten that today is my bridge afternoon! Let me see, what's the time? Ah, half-past eleven." She considered for a second or two. "If I could have a bite of lunch with you, dear, I could then go straight on to bridge; it's only about ten minutes from here and that would be so much easier for me."

Mischievously, Shirley gazed into the distance as if deep in thought. "I'm afraid the grocer hasn't delivered this week's order yet, and I don't suppose the greengrocer will come by with his barrow in this weather. I could open a tin of baked beans and we could have them on toast. There are a couple of slices from the end of a loaf in the bread bin. How would that suit you?"

Granny was horrified at the suggestion. "Oh no, dear! Isn't there anything else?"

"No, I'm afraid not, and you see I can't go out because, as you know, I'm officially in quarantine, but if you would like to go up the road, there's the grocer's and the baker's on the parade. I'm sure you would find some ham and a loaf of fresh bread. And oh, there's the greengrocer's shop for some salad and tomatoes. Wouldn't that be nice? And look, it has stopped raining! I do believe the sun is coming out!" Mrs Marlow had no choice but to do as Shirley suggested, and consequently she set out for her bridge match after a good lunch of fresh ingredients. As she was leaving, she mentioned the cost of the goods – the ham, the bread and the salads – that she had bought, but Shirley simply said, "I'm sorry, Granny, I don't have any money. Pa hasn't given me any and I haven't been to work."

Exhausted both by her visitor's presence and by the shocking news that she had brought, Shirley slowly went upstairs wondering what it would be like if she couldn't climb the stairs at all. She intended to lie down and read *Madame Bovary* to take her mind off the news and its implications, but as soon as her head touched the pillow, she fell into a deep sleep. It was already dark when she awoke to the sound of rain pattering on the window panes. In the light of the street lamp outside her window she could see the droplets trickling down the glass: some shot straight down onto the window sill, but others wandered on the way and took longer to reach their target. They would make a good subject for a ballet, she thought to herself, remembering that she had once heard a piece of music called the 'Raindrop'.

Suddenly these creative musings were interrupted by a voice inside her, which said, "You might never dance again if you fall ill!" While the rain poured down outside, the tears ran down her cheeks until she heard her father's key turning in the lock downstairs and the front door opening. Quickly she turned on her bedside light and wiped her eyes; as she heard him mounting the stairs, she opened her book and was making a pretence of reading when he came into her room. "Oh, Shirl," he said with alarm written all over his face, "are you all right? I was surprised to find the house in darkness when I came in just now."

"Yes, Pa, I'm all right, though I'm shocked to hear from Granny, who came round this morning, that Thelma has died."

He sat down heavily on the bed and buried his face in his hands.

The two sat in silence until eventually he raised his head and said, "I've bought us some chops for supper; I'll go down and start cooking them. You stay here."

"No, Pa," Shirley said firmly, "I'm coming down too and I'll cook the supper. I need something to do."

"I understand," he said.

They ate their meal attempting to avoid all reference to Thelma's death, though it was without much success that Pa tried to summon a forced jollity. "I called in at the newsagent's, and they'd be pleased to have me helping out tomorrow morning. You must tell me what I'll have to do!" he announced.

"Of course," Shirley said glumly, hoping against hope that her father had forgotten about the diamond, as indeed she had in the turmoil of the past twenty-four hours. To lose that precious jewel at this precise moment would really compound her misery, for it might prove to be her only salvation if, as her pa had suggested, it could be very valuable. Perhaps it would bring her good fortune even in the present circumstances.

22

Reggie returned from his shift at the shop in high spirits that Saturday morning, thus partially helping to dispel the gloom that had enveloped Shirley ever since she woke up. Her dreams had been troubled by a disturbing vision of a princess limping along in as much haste as she could muster, in flight from a black-clad figure who, brandishing a long stick, was quickly gaining on her helpless victim. The evil witch had already succeeded in casting a spell over the prince and had turned him into a smoking block of charred wood, which she had hurled to the bottom of a great lake. The nightmare was so terrifying that at first, on regaining consciousness, Shirley was reluctant to open her eyes in case the dreadful scene was still being played out in her own bedroom, but finally she courageously peeped out from under her eyelids. Light entered the room through the homely, flowery curtains, and all was quiet apart from the distant hum of traffic on the main road and the sound of the milkman's cart, its bottles rattling and its horse's hooves clattering on the tarmac. Though these mundane extraneous noises offered her a comforting return to normality, the apparitions had left her shattered even before the day had begun, unable as yet to embrace the reassuring familiarity of the real world.

Slowly she raised herself up in the bed and was grateful to discover that her pa had left a cup of tea on her bedside table. Although it was cold, the refreshment revived her briefly, but after drinking it she sank back into her pillows, trying to rid her mind of those frightening images. While doubtless, she reasoned, they were the effects of the news of Thelma's death and of its implications for her, it also seemed that they carried a message for the future and were making horrific predictions that were more ghastly than she could comprehend. She told herself that she had two options: one was to stay in bed being miserable with her head under the covers, and the other was to get up and behave sensibly. Having decided on the latter course, she forced herself to get out of bed; she stretched, dressed and went downstairs to busy herself in the kitchen. It was just as well that she had made the effort, because only minutes later her pa came home; his exaggerated pleasure on finding her up and about was an indication of the depth of his concern for her. "Shirl, I didn't wake you, because I was afraid you might not be feeling well, so I'm really happy to see you down here!"

She tried to laugh, but laughter dried in her throat. "Not to worry, Reggie," she said. "I'm collecting up a few things for lunch."

Pa's delight in his unexpected Saturday job was infectious. His animation had loosened his tongue, not usually given to long or enthusiastic pronouncements. "I can't tell you how surprised I am myself," he declared. "I thought this stint in the Salvatores' shop was simply a way of helping them out in your absence. I never thought it could be so interesting! You wouldn't believe the numbers of people who came in and said, 'Reggie! How nice to see you! What are you doing here?' Well, of course, I didn't tell them why I was there, but as soon as it calmed down I did stop for a chat with some of them. Old Herb for instance; I hadn't seen him for ages. Do you remember him? He said he's coming up to retirement. How time passes! And then when there was only a dribble of customers, mostly for cigarettes and baccy, as the papers had all gone by then, I had time to look through some of the magazines. Oh, and by the way, I saw an advertisement for Brighton and that made me wonder whether a little trip might be a good idea for tomorrow. What do you think?"

"Oh, yes, please!" Shirley replied, her eyes lighting up. "I'd love that!" A breath of sea air was exactly what she needed. "But what about the quarantine?" she asked, afraid that her pa's good intentions might still come to nought.

"No, don't worry," he said. "I thought of that and I rang Dr Forbes from the telephone box. He said it would be fine and probably the best thing for you, provided we keep away from other people. So we'll take a picnic to eat out in the country somewhere nice and we'll sit or walk along the beach well out of the way of the public." Having excelled himself with all this strategic planning, Pa broached yet another idea. "And because I shall have to fill the car with petrol this afternoon, I thought we might call on Ted – and your granny if she's there – to see how he's getting on. You'll have to stay in the car, of course, but Dr Forbes said you could talk to Ted through the open window."

"Oh, lovely!" Shirley replied, her enthusiasm at seeing her brother muted only by the prospect of encountering her grandparent again.

The effort of formulating and presenting all these ideas in one fell swoop after his morning's work proved too much for Pa, so after lunch he had to settle himself into his armchair for his forty winks while Shirley checked the cupboards for the ingredients for a picnic and then filled a thermos flask. If they were going to take lunch with them the next day, they might as well take at least a thermos and some biscuits that afternoon, and perhaps they could find somewhere out in the open away from people and traffic where they could walk. Richmond Park would be glorious, she thought, on this warm autumn day now that the overnight rain had ceased. She filled the picnic basket and fetched a rug; then, while waiting for her pa to wake up, she practised some of her exercises. Her muscles responded without complaint when she stretched her legs and her arms, then she donned her point shoes to practise *tendus, frappés, fouettés and développés*, followed by *sautés, échappés* and *relevés*, concluding as always with some *pirouettes* on the hard lino floor of the hall. The ease with which she accomplished her routines and her excitement at the projected excursions revived her spirits until all memories of the horrible nightmare and all thoughts of Thelma's untimely death were at least temporarily put to rest.

Ted was repairing an old bike out in the front driveway of Granny Marlow's house. He looked up in astonishment, which soon changed to his characteristic broad smile, as the car turned in at the gate. From the passenger seat, Shirley waved and smiled, at the same time surveying the large detached house with a rueful eye. In her opinion, and in her mother's opinion, that house was far too big for one little elderly person: she had often wondered why her granny did not offer to exchange it for their house, small and too cramped for four adults but ideal for a single person on her own. Their house was much more convenient, much easier to run, close to shops and to all connections into central London.

There would be inconveniences in living in Granny's house, of course, because there they would be deprived of all the advantages of situation that they now enjoyed, but the great attraction of it for Shirley was its vast hall with its wooden floor, which would be an ideal practice area if not a dance studio. The reason that Granny had never suggested – never even thought probably – of swapping houses was obvious: she was too mean. Shirley crossed her fingers, fervently hoping that she was out. She had seen quite enough of her for one week and, as the memory of her visit the previous day flashed through her mind, she could not help but recall Thelma's death from the horrible disease for which she herself was now in quarantine.

Abandoning the bike, Ted ran towards the car. "What a surprise!" he said. "I didn't know you were coming!"

"No, nor did we till this afternoon!" Pa replied, now even more animated on being reunited with his son.

"She hasn't gone to Birmingham yet, but she's out, I'm glad to say, and Martha, the maid, is having the weekend off." Ted informed them with a smirk and a gesture towards the house.

Pa did not comment, but through the open car window Shirley exclaimed, "Oh, that's a relief!"

"You're right there!" Ted exclaimed. "Otherwise I wouldn't be working out here. I'd have to stay in the garage because she doesn't want the neighbours to see all these old bikes out in her driveway! That was all right yesterday because it was wet, but I don't want to be shut up inside today!"

"So where's she gone?" Pa asked.

"Oh, I think she said she was going to Richmond Park with some friends who've got a car," Ted replied. At first Shirley was disappointed, for she had been looking forward to walking across that huge park with its magnificent views. However, Pa soon quelled her disappointment with a better idea:

"That's funny! Shirley had suggested going to Richmond Park, but we don't need to do that now. If Mother's out we can stay here in the garden and have our picnic," he said, "and we can spend the afternoon with you, Ted. Let's take the basket into the garden then." He turned to Shirley: "And if you keep well away from Ted, I think you could come too, Shirl."

She kept a safe distance from her brother as they walked across the manicured lawns – a testimony to the work of a team of gardeners – and, in response to their questions, Ted recounted his experiences of the past forty-plus hours since his father had deposited him at his grandmother's. "It's not too bad really," he said with a shrug. "She's always grumbling about something or other of course, but she's out most of the time with her friends." He guffawed. "And what do you think of this? She says I'm much too thin. She reckons I don't get enough to eat at home! Can you believe it? So she cooks enormous meals with lots of puddings: rice puddings, steamed puddings, tapioca puddings, the lot; if it goes on like this I shall blow up like a balloon!"

Father and son sat down on the garden seat while Shirley spread the rug on the lawn; she lay down on it and gazed up at the blue sky. This was better than walking in the park because it was more restful, and they could all be together. She listened drowsily as Pa and Ted discussed gearing and hubs, tyre sizes and chains, and then talked about the newsagent's. "I could do that job if I ever have to give up the railways" was the last remark she heard. It seemed only seconds later that she was woken with a start by a familiar voice calling loudly in her ear. "Teatime, Shirl!" Pa placed a cup down beside her. "Just a few more minutes and we must be going," he said.

"Why, what's the time?" Shirley asked with a frown. It had been warm in the sun when she had lain down, though now there was a chill in the air and the sun had disappeared behind the trees at the end of the long lawn. "Ted says your granny will be back about six and it's now half-past five," Pa replied. He was clearly anxious to be going.

As they cleared away all traces of their presence, Ted cautiously murmured to his father, "Pa, watch out! I suspect Granny will want you to drive her to Birmingham next week."

"Thanks for the warning," Pa replied. "I suppose I ought to go, if only to keep poor Horace company."

"By the way, is there any news of Maman?" Ted enquired as they were loading the picnic basket, the rug and other bits and pieces into the car.

"Why, bless me, yes! So sorry, I forgot to tell you! There was a letter on the mat this morning as I went off to the shop. It's here in my pocket." Pa pulled a crumpled blue envelope out of his pocket. "She says, well, it's all in French so why don't you read it for yourselves?" Ted scanned the letter before relaying its contents to Shirley who was standing on the other side of the car, within earshot but well out of reach.

"Good!" he exclaimed. "She's coming home soon, but she doesn't say when! Everything is settled: Pépé is more himself now, and she thinks it will be all right to leave him."

"At last! Some good news!" Shirley sighed.

"We won't be seeing you tomorrow, old boy," Pa said as he patted Ted on the back. "We're going to Brighton for the day. It's a pity we can't take you in the car with us, but that's not allowed at the moment."

Ted laughed. "What a coincidence! Don't apologize, Pa! I'm going to Brighton too – with Granny and her pals! She said they were too old to catch infantile paralysis and weren't worried about it. It's nice of them to invite me, but I'll be sure to look out for you. I bet I'll be in need of a change of company!" They made tentative arrangements to meet somewhere beyond the West Pier away from the crowds in the early afternoon. "I'll be there," Ted shouted optimistically as his father and sister drove away, already involved in a long discussion of plans for the morrow.

"Let's try to get away early," Pa suggested, "before the crowds. I think there is another thermos in the cupboard, so we could put coffee for the morning in one and tea for the afternoon in the other. I bought some groceries this morning so we can make plenty of sandwiches and take some apples." They then realized that they had not fixed a precise time for meeting Ted, but comforted themselves with the expectation that he would be sure to find them or they him.

"I'll make a batch of egg sandwiches and another of fish paste and cucumber; Ted likes those. I know there are several jars of fish paste in the cupboard because I saw them this morning," Shirley volunteered. Then as an afterthought, she said, "And I think I'll make a cake this evening; we haven't had any cake since Maman left. I'm so excited that she's coming home, Pa – she's been away for so long!"

"Wait a moment," said Pa as he searched for a gentle way to issue a word of warning. "I think I had better make the sandwiches and you can tell me how to make the cake. We don't want to take any chances, you know, even though you seem to be perfectly well."

"Ah, yes," Shirley replied, her excitement abruptly dimmed by this reminder of the medical restrictions.

She tried to cheer herself up with reminiscences about Brighton. "I do love Brighton, except for the pebbles on the beach, Pa, don't you? We've had some lovely holidays there, haven't we? That's where you taught Ted and me to swim, do you remember? And I loved those shows on the pier!" Keeping his eyes on the road, Pa nodded at her chatter. He was glad that she seemed fit and excited about travelling. Brighton had been his favourite holiday resort ever since his early childhood. Everyone was happy there: his mother because it was fashionable, his father because the air was relaxing by day and there was no shortage of pubs to entertain him in the evening, and he and his sister simply because they were on holiday. Once, he recalled, they had tried the east coast, but that had proved to be far too cold, so his mother had insisted on going to Brighton for another holiday immediately afterwards to recover from Clacton, or wherever it was that had irritated her so much, and when she was irritated they all knew about it, so their father had had to comply with her wishes, just as everyone had done ever since.

23

Shirley's fond attachment to Brighton, which had been the setting for many happy family holidays during her very early childhood, had given way before the excitement of holidays in France as soon as she and Ted were old enough to undertake the journey each summer. Even then, there were still the occasional day trips and weekends to Brighton, either at Easter, with the exhilarating promise of more visits over the summer, or during the autumn as a final, almost desperate, attempt to soak up the fading rays of sunlight and breathe in lungfuls of salty sea air before the onset of the dreary, dirty London winter. Sometimes Shirley saw those excursions as a challenge to winter itself, daring it to remain at bay, to refrain from blighting their lives with its freezing temperatures, its black nights and its coughs, colds and outbreaks of flu.

The forthcoming trip she regarded even more defiantly, not just as a challenge to the dark season but also to the lurking threat of serious illness, or worse. However, the day dawned unseasonably warm for the time of year and the sun shone strongly from a clear sky, encouraging her to forget about the change of season, and to ignore those fears that in quiet, solitary moments forced themselves inescapably into her mind. Determined not to let any anxieties spoil such a special day, she dressed in light summery clothes and took a sunhat out of her wardrobe. "I say, that's a bit optimistic! You'll catch cold like that!" Pa remarked in surprise at the sight of her standing in the kitchen doorway prettily dressed as for high summer. Do at least take a coat with you."

"I won't need it. It looks as if it's going to be a lovely day!" she retorted.

"Maybe it does at present, but you're forgetting that this is October, and the weather on the coast can change without warning."

The road to Brighton was packed with slow-moving traffic, delaying their schedule so much that by the time they turned off into a country lane, intending to have a cup of coffee from the flask, it was already lunchtime, so they opened their packs of sandwiches, spread the rug on the verge and ate the picnic looking out over the South Downs. Shirley was enthralled by the view over bare expanses of hilltop, contrasting with valleys where villages nestled comfortably around church towers, their houses and golden trees huddling together against the breeze blowing in from the coast; the wind brought a chill with it, making her reach for the coat that she had reluctantly thrown into the car and pull it round her shoulders. Nonetheless, in no way did the wind cast a chill over her irrepressible vivacity, which had bounced back in abundance, for she had slept well without nightmares, and was convinced that the afternoon spent in the fresh air of her grandmother's garden the previous day had blown away whatever malaise she might have been contracting or indeed was already suffering. She had chatted all the way from home – about her hopes for the day, her memories of happy days in Brighton, her excitement at her mother's imminent return and her preparations for Wednesday's initiation at Sadler's Wells.

But as she gazed out over the Downs, her intuition told her that Alan lived somewhere in this lovely part of southern England. The intuition grew into a firm conviction that he lived in one of those houses in the hamlet that lay immediately beneath their picnic spot. She wanted to follow the steep path down to it, to walk along its main street, look at its houses and go into its church. The village was so small, she was sure that somebody would recognize her description of him and be able to tell her where he lived.

"What about a little walk?" she asked her pa hopefully.

He looked at his watch. "I don't think so, Shirl; it would be nice, but we're late already and Ted might be waiting for us. We'll come here another time, but we must be getting on the road now." Somewhat petulantly, Shirley helped him pack the picnic things in the boot and resumed her seat. She sat in silence and her father did not notice her mood, because the volume of traffic required him to keep his eyes and his concentration firmly on the road ahead, quietly rattled now and then when some madcap driver pulled out from behind to overtake in the face of oncoming cars.

On the outskirts of Brighton, Pa relaxed and began to voice his thoughts out loud, wondering where Ted might be and whether he was already waiting for them on a bench down by the West Pier. "I expect he'll be having lunch somewhere posh with your granny and her friends," he speculated. Shirley did not comment on this piece of wishful thinking. First and foremost, Ted was supposed to be in quarantine, which meant not eating in restaurants, and secondly she could not imagine anything that Ted would hate more than having lunch with Granny and her friends; besides, it was highly unlikely that Granny would pay for Ted's meal, and he probably didn't have enough money to pay for it himself, despite his earnings from bicycle repairs in the past week and his paper rounds in the week previous to that. Doubtless if they met Granny, she would ask Pa to reimburse her for the food she had bought for her own lunch when she had called on Friday.

Clouds on the horizon greeted their arrival at the seaside. The traffic in Brighton was even worse than it had been on the main road from London and everywhere was crowded with day trippers. "I don't know how they could have got here before us!" Pa complained indignantly. "We left home early enough!"

"I expect some of them came by train," said Shirley coolly. "They all want to make the most of the sun, like us," she added, but then she looked at the clouds. "I'm not sure that we're going to see much sun. those clouds are approaching fast over there." She gestured out to sea.

Reggie was becoming more and more gloomy, and a touch impatient, as the clouds advanced rapidly while the car edged along at a snail's pace. "If only we could move faster and find a parking place, then we could at least see a bit of sun before those clouds come right overhead," he muttered.

Shirley was rather glad that they couldn't move faster, because as well as allowing her to glimpse all those sights that she had enjoyed so much in the past, the leaden pace gave her the chance to scan the crowds for the unmistakable tall figure with its handsome face and wavy hair that had so firmly imprinted itself on her mind during the last Channel crossing. While her father grumbled about the traffic, she pointed out the landmarks, without mentioning the real cause for her scrutiny. "Look, Pa, there's the Pavilion and there are the Lanes! Oh, I wish I could get out and go for a wander round there!" At last they turned onto the front, and she exclaimed excitedly, "Oh, look there's the Palace Pier. Wouldn't it be nice to go to a show! We did last time we came, do you remember? With all those dancers in brightly coloured costumes!"

Her father refrained from reminding her that the theatre was out of the question; he simply said, "Let's hope the traffic will begin to move faster along the front."

When eventually they began to advance towards the West Pier, Pa asked, "Keep an eye out for Ted, will you?" And as he pulled into a space just beyond the pier, there, sitting on a bench right by their parking place was Ted. He was gazing out to sea and seemed out of sorts.

Shirley opened her window. "Ted! Hello!" she called. "We're here!" He turned round but didn't seem particularly pleased to see them.

"Hello!" was all he said.

"Are you all right, old chap?" Pa asked, as he awkwardly heaved himself out of the car.

"Well, not too bad," Ted replied, "but I have been sitting here for an awfully long time."

"We had a terrible journey, a lot of traffic, but it's only half-past one. We thought you'd be having lunch," Pa explained.

"Oh, ha, ha!" was Ted's bitter response. "I haven't had any lunch. Granny and her pals stopped at the Grand Hotel and, as they went in, she said to me, 'Ted, you won't be wanting to eat in here with us old cronies. Anyhow, I dare say you ought to keep away from public places, so you go and buy something from one of those stalls, and come back here at half-past four.' And off she went. I wouldn't have minded, but I don't have any money and I'm starving."

"That's too bad!" Shirley exclaimed angrily. "If we'd known, we'd have saved some of our sandwiches for you."

Instead of venting his irritation against his mother to no purpose, Pa came up with a practical suggestion. "Of course, I keep forgetting; you'll have to stay by the car, Ted, because of the quarantine, but I'll go and find a tea shop, even perhaps here on the pier, and ask for a drink and a plate of sandwiches for you." He thought for a second or two. "But I think you ought to stay inside the car, Shirl, while there are so many people about and you're the one most affected," he said apologetically.

"Yes, I suppose so," she sighed, disheartened by the constant reminders of her enforced isolation.

Although Shirley would have preferred to stand outside with her brother, breathing in the sea air, she sympathized with the undeniable urgency of his hunger pangs. The fact that she was doomed to stay in the car proved a blessing in disguise, for no sooner had she cocooned herself comfortably in the front seat, and her father had gone to look for a café, than the heavens opened and the rain poured down. Ted hurled himself onto the back seat of the car, and Shirley's hopes of encountering Alan in Brighton were quickly washed away in the deluge that beat against the windows and whipped up white horses on the mounting waves which previously had been little more than ripples.

As the windscreen and the windows quickly steamed up, blotting the outside world from view, she cautiously asked her brother if he really ought to be sitting so close to her and breathing in the same air. He wound his window down and, facing and, therefore, breathing outwards, he replied, "Well, what *am* I supposed to do? Stand outside in the rain and catch pneumonia?" It was useless to argue with him, so she occupied herself in wiping a patch of glass clear on the off-chance that if Alan were to come along the front, she would recognize his gait and his posture from the unforgettable image of him striding with his father along the deck of the ferry in that howling gale over a month ago, but the front was deserted. In any case, had he appeared, what could she have done? She could scarcely have got out of the car, stood in his path and said, "Hello, do you remember me? We met on the ferry, but I can't shake hands because I'm in quarantine for infantile paralysis." For the same reason she could not have invited him to take shelter in the car with her and Ted. Neither she nor her brother spoke, each absorbed in a sullen silence.

Finally their father returned, soaked from head to toe, jubilantly bearing sandwiches and a mug of tea, which Ted wolfed down. Then he was ready, he said, for a long walk on the promenade or a stroll on the beach, perhaps going down to the sea for a paddle since the rain had stopped. "Shirley could come with us, couldn't she, Pa?" he suggested, his usual good spirits restored. "There's no one else around."

"Oh, I'd like a paddle!" Shirley fairly shouted, brightening up with the discovery that the day had not come to an untimely end. The sky was less threatening, though the clouds overhead were still grey, and the sun put in only an occasional watery appearance, never aspiring to radiate the warmth of the early morning again.

"Yes, I'm sure that would be fine. I'll get a towel and an umbrella from the boot," their father agreed, as his son and daughter set off towards the steps down to the shore.

The steps were slippery; Shirley was only halfway down when she lost her foothold and slid to the bottom, landing on the hard, wet walkway three or four yards from the beach. "Oh, my back and my leg!" she screamed. Though Ted raced down to her, she had the presence of mind to shoo him away.

"No, Ted, you mustn't touch me, remember? I'll wait for Pa to come. I'll be all right in a moment. Those steps were so slippery I missed my footing." Ted hurried back up the steps to call his father, who came as fast as his war wound would allow. "Don't run, Pa," an ashen-faced Shirley called from her resting place on the paving. "You'll fall too: those steps are lethal." Slowly and methodically she untangled her left leg from where it lay bent under her body and, grimacing with pain, eased herself up onto the cold, damp bottom step.

Above all, it was important to appear normal to avoid frightening her family, especially her pa. "Don't try to lift me. I'll sit here for a bit and then work my way up on my behind." Her father and brother watched her efforts anxiously.

At the top, her pa held out his arm to her and asked, "Can you stand on that leg? How's your back?"

With a deeply furrowed brow she grasped his outstretched hand and gingerly pulled herself upright, straightening out her leg as she did so. "The leg's only bruised, I think," she groaned, "though that was quite a wrench. I can stand on it, so it's not broken." Putting a hand in the small of her back, she said, "It hurts a lot here, but I expect I'll recover." Leaning on her father, she slowly and painfully made her way back to the car. Uppermost in her mind was the appointment at Sadler's Wells: she had to be well enough for that on Wednesday next.

Pa wore that uncertain air which he often did when he was missing Maman and needed her guidance to resolve a tricky situation. Shirley and Ted exchanged glances, realizing that together they would have to direct operations. "I think the best thing for you two to do would be to go home," Ted announced, much to his sister's relief. "I'll stay around here until I have to meet Granny."

"Yes, I was going to suggest that but didn't want to spoil the day," Pa replied hesitantly.

"I certainly would like to go home," Shirley declared. "Standing up is frightfully painful and I can't walk very far."

"Right," said Pa, empowered by his children's decisiveness, "let's make a move then. Shirl, if you can ease yourself into the passenger seat, I'll pad cushions round you to try and make you comfortable. And Ted, here's some money so you could safely go off and enjoy yourself on one or other of the piers until half-past four, because it looks like most of the trippers have gone home. Don't be late for your granny, will you!"

Shirley spent the journey back to London in the front seat in dire discomfort. She would have liked to stretch out in the back, but it would have been agony to stoop to climb in and stretch out at one end of the journey, and to sit up to climb out at the other. Added to which, Pa had to drive unbelievably slowly yet again because of the volume of traffic returning early to London. He kept glancing anxiously at his daughter, asking, "How are you, Shirl? Just as well I can't drive faster. I wouldn't want to jolt you."

"No, Pa, that's all right, thank you," she replied with a touch of exasperation. The faster the journey, the easier it would have been for her, even with a few bumps on the way.

Her father was pensive. "I've been wondering what to do," he said eventually. "We'll have to put you to bed first of all as soon as we get home; I don't think we could find a doctor at this time on a Sunday, but there are aspirins in the cupboard and I think there's some sort of embrocation that your mother brought from France a couple of years ago. You could try rubbing that in. Or maybe you could even take one of my pills. They are for pain, after all." He fell silent while he considered the next move. "Then, in the morning, I'll call on Dr Forbes and ask him to visit you."

"But supposing I can't get downstairs to open the door to him?" Shirley asked.

"Oh, I've thought of that already. I'll take the spare key to him so he can let himself in. What do you think of that?" he asked, pleased with his solution to multiple problems.

Shirley nodded. "Yes, I suppose that would be best," she agreed.

There was nothing more that she could say without upsetting her pa. If only there was someone she could talk to, someone in whom she could confide how downcast and disheartened she was! So much had gone wrong just in the past ten days. First of all Mémé had died and Maman had had to go to France; then there had been the unavoidable contact with Thelma's germs in Birmingham, and Thelma's horrible death; and today that fall down the steps, spoiling their, particularly her hopes for a lovely day out at the seaside, where she had anticipated being free and invigorated, able to roam out in the open, unconstrained by the rules and regulations of quarantine and able to breathe the life-giving air. Powerless to resist the onslaught of so many negative considerations, she gave a little sob.

Her father heard it and said, "Come on, old girl, tell me what's wrong!"

"Everything, Pa, everything's going wrong: the quarantine, Thelma dying, our day out ruined by that silly fall down the steps. And Maman's not here with us! What's going to happen next?"

"Now, now, Shirl, this has been a very hard time, that's true, and they do say that troubles never come singly. Life's like that: it's not a bed of roses you know."

Shirley scowled: that was not what she wanted to hear. Pa was sounding like the priest in the confessional. He had come to the end of his homily and, in the silence that lay between them, was obviously trying hard to think of encouraging things to say. "But it will get better, you'll see. Maman will be home soon and then she'll set us back on course." His belief in Jacqueline's power to change fate was touchingly naive, yet Shirley knew he was clutching at straws because, although it would be a wonderful comfort to have Maman back, there was little that she could do to change the situation. "Anyhow," Pa continued after a long pause, "it's not so bad you know. You were thrilled, only this past week, that your audition at – where was it? Sadler's Wales? – was such a success."

Shirley had to smile. Trust Pa to get it wrong! "I think you mean Sadler's Wells, Pa," she said correcting him.

"Oh, is that what it is?" he exclaimed, laughing. "I was puzzled; I couldn't for the life of me think what Wales had to do with a ballet company in north London, or how you and Ted managed to go there and come back in one afternoon!"

Yes, thought Shirley, it was true: the audition had been a resounding triumph, and even if she had sprained her back and her ankle, perhaps Madam would keep the place open for her. Prompted by talk of the audition, her thoughts turned abruptly to the diamond. How was it that in all the troubles of the past couple of days she had completely forgotten about it? The problem was of course that she couldn't wear it, either for dancing or at home, where Pa would be bound to see it, and it certainly hadn't brought her much luck since the audition. She promised herself that she would have another look at it as soon as her leg and her back would allow her to negotiate the short distance from her bed to her dressing table.

24

The battle to climb the stairs that evening, combined with the painkilling concoction of pills administered by her father, plunged Shirley into such a sound sleep that she did not hear him when, in the throes of the worst nightmare in weeks, he shouted out loud, often screaming in terror, during the long hours of darkness. In fact, she did not wake until a tap on her bedroom door roused her; from the other side the doctor was calling quietly, "Miss Marlow, Miss Marlow, are you there?" Dr Forbes then came into the room and drew back the curtains. "Now, young lady, what have you been doing? Your father came to see me this morning and said you'd had a nasty fall, so I've come straight away to have a look at your leg and your back to see if you need to go to hospital. I can come later with my car after my surgery and take you there." Shirley herself had not had time to consider the state of her back or her leg, but once fully conscious, she sensed that all was not well and not only in those parts of her anatomy that had suffered from the fall: she also had a splitting headache and a very stiff neck.

"I think my back must be quite badly bruised," she complained. "I can't move my neck and my head hurts so much. I can't sit up, and I feel rather sick!"

"Oh, is that so? Well, take your time; you're not properly awake yet," said Dr Forbes sympathetically, but also with ill-concealed anxiety. "I'll take a look at your leg while you are coming round."

Shirley was shocked to find on trying to move her left leg – the one that had been injured in the fall the previous day – that it was locked in an excruciatingly tight spasm. "That's odd," she cried. "I must have broken it after all: it won't move, and it hurts so badly!"

"Ah, is that so? Well, then, I think the sooner we get you into hospital the better," Dr Forbes remarked with no trace of his usual breezy tone. "Let's see, you don't have a telephone here, do you? No, of course you don't. I'll dash back to the surgery to order an ambulance and then

I'll come back as soon as I can. I'll ring your father at his work; he's given me the number. Will you be all right? Do you need to go to the bathroom?"

"No, I don't think so," was all Shirley could say before he left. She reached out for the tea that Pa had put down on her bedside table, but sipping it and swallowing it with a bad back and a stiff neck demanded too much effort, so she sank back into the pillows, whimpering in pain, unable to make sense of what was happening to her. Yesterday, she recalled, she had had a bad fall, but there was some other element in this situation that she could not grasp. She dozed off into such a deep slumber that she was scarcely conscious of being lifted and carried downstairs by the ambulance men, and only vaguely did she hear a distant voice which must have belonged to Dr Forbes, telling them to lift her carefully because she had damaged her coccyx. She did not hear the doors of the ambulance banging shut, nor the clanging of its bell as it set off.

When next she opened her eyes, she found herself lying in a bed, apparently in hospital, surrounded by people, some dressed in white coats and others in blue uniforms. She herself was wearing a stiff white gown, but there were no covers on the bed and the people were gazing down at her. She heard someone say, "Her back is badly bruised, but it will recover." They turned their attention to her leg and prodded it and poked it. "Hm, not so good," someone said. Then one of the nurses exclaimed, "Look, she's opening her eyes!" As one they moved from her leg to the head of the bed.

"How are you feeling, Miss Marlow?" one of the white-coated men, evidently a doctor, asked.

She groaned, "I don't know," she answered quite truthfully, because she really couldn't say which was worse, the pain in her head, the ache in her back, the stiffness in her neck or the mounting nausea in her stomach, let alone the spasm in her leg. At last she summoned sufficient energy to describe her symptoms, adding, "but I *do* need to go to the bathroom!" Whereupon there was a flurry of activity round the bed; the doctors disappeared and two different nurses appeared carrying some strange pieces of equipment. "Why am I here?" Shirley asked one of them. "I haven't broken anything in that fall, have I?"

"What *are* you talking about?" the younger nurse asked frowning. "You're not in here for a fall: you've got infantile paralysis and we have to decide what to do about your paralysed leg!"

"Shh!" said the other nurse. "You're not supposed to say that!" But it was too late. Shirley had heard the diagnosis, so brusquely delivered, all too clearly. Not that it made much difference whether she heard it from a nurse or from a doctor; either way it was equally harrowing. Although she closed her eyes again to shut out the awful truth, that truth was already inside her, gnawing away at every corner of her mind, swiftly devouring all her hopes and her dreams.

Infantile paralysis – that was the disease that had killed Thelma; it was the disease that left so many children lame. You saw them often, wearing those ugly callipers, limping along behind their families, trying to keep up with their brothers and sisters. None of them ever had the slightest hope of becoming a dancer, let alone a prima ballerina on the stage of Sadler's Wells. It was goodbye to *Swan Lake* and the *Sleeping Beauty*, goodbye to *Giselle*, goodbye to *The Rite of Spring*, *Petrushka* and *The Firebird*, and goodbye even to *Coppélia*, playing the part of the clumsy wooden doll made by Dr Coppélius.

Saying goodbye to the ballet spelt the end of the cherished plan for giving Alan the chance of finding her again, if, as she believed, even from those few moments together on the ferry, he was as attracted to her as she was to him. She wanted to bury her face in the pillow, but the stiffness in her neck would not allow her to turn her head, so she lay in the hospital bed looking up at the blank white ceiling with hot tears streaming down her burning cheeks. Worn out by so much pain and misery, she drifted into sleep.

Another bustle of activity aroused her from her slumbers. A nurse was noisily drawing back the curtains around her bed. "It's visiting time," she called out sharply. "You'll want to see your parents, won't you?" Nodding was impossible, so she tried to summon a smile. Thank goodness! There would be so much comfort in having Pa by her side: he would tell her what was going on, since no one else in this hospital seemed inclined to give her any information, and when they did it was either delivered in a sharp, unfeeling manner or, as with the diagnosis, it was given to her by mistake.

"When will the visitors arrive?" she croaked to the nurse who was propping up her pillow.

"Arrive? No, they won't exactly arrive," she replied. "You'll be able to see them through the glass screen over there." She pointed across the ward to the wall opposite, which was solid painted brick in the lower part but glazed in the top half, though the window did not look out onto the outside world, only onto a wall.

"What do you mean?" Shirley asked.

"There's a corridor on the other side of that window," the nurse answered testily, as if she did not have time for such elementary explanations. "The visitors walk along the corridor and look through the window. When you see your parents you can wave to them."

She turned on her heel about to walk away, but Shirley would not let her go so easily. "Why are my parents going to be shut behind that glass?" she demanded. "That's stupid! I live in the same house as my parents and my pa and I have been together all the time." To clarify the circumstances, she quickly added, "My mother has been away because my grandmother died!" Although it was quite unreal and uncomfortable to be talking about darling Maman and dear Mémé in cold English terms, Shirley sensed, even in her reduced state, that it was important to avoid confusion and make sure that the nurse fully understood what she was saying.

"Oh, yes, I understand that," said the nurse impatiently, "but you must understand that we have to do all we can to avoid spreading the infection. If your parents come in here, they might pick something up from you or from someone else, and then pass it on to without knowing. And, what's even more important, they might bring in germs, like a bad cold or flu, from outside and that could be deadly for some of these children, even possibly for you." With that she raised her eyebrows and walked off.

The all-enveloping sense of loneliness and despair was overwhelming. What Shirley wanted more than anything was to have her pa near her, to be able to talk to him, to be comforted by his presence, to find out what he knew about this horrendous situation. Maman would not be there, of course, as she was still in France, but maybe she would come back soon and maybe he would have news of her. To see him from behind a glass screen would be almost worse than not seeing him at all. The frustration would be so cruel, the emotion of it made her even more bilious than before, though, as far as she could see, there was no way of summoning a nurse. Anyhow she was sure that no one would come as it was plain that the nurse who had just gone out was unlikely to come back in a hurry.

On the wall opposite, above the glass panelling, there hung a large black-and-white clock, its hands pointing to ten to six. Even such minimal mechanical contact with reality and life outside this prison offered a crumb of comfort. On the assumption that visiting would start at six, Shirley awkwardly reached out to the right, searching with her hand for a bedside table in the hope of finding her brush and comb. There was a table, possibly even a cupboard underneath it, but no brush or comb. She called out to a passing nurse, "Could you please see if my brush and comb are in the cupboard? I need to have my hair brushed before visiting time, and," she added, "I'm feeling rather sick."

The nurse gave a callous laugh and said, "There's nothing there. Your parents will bring your things, but I'll get you a bowl." With that she too walked off, and, contrary to Shirley's expectations, she did come back bringing a bowl, which she put down on the far side of the table without a word. Twisting to the right with extreme and painful difficulty, Shirley saw that the bowl was out of her reach.

"Oh, so helpful!" she said to herself. "How can I be sick into the bowl if I can't even reach it, let alone sit up?"

Having twisted so far to one side, she was startled to find another bed beside hers beyond the table. In that bed there was a girl who was probably slightly younger than herself. She was sitting up reading a magazine. When Shirley turned towards her, she gave her a nervous smile. "Do you want your bowl?" she asked. "If I fold up my magazine and reach out, I might manage to push it nearer to you." Shirley was grateful for such consideration from a fellow sufferer when the staff showed so little. The girl looked away while Shirley used her bowl, but then, with the same shy smile, turned back to her and said, "It's horrible when you first come in here, isn't it? But you'll get used to it, and they do make you better. Look at me! I'm getting better, though I didn't have it really badly, and they say I can go into rehabilitation in a day or two." Although Shirley would have liked to reply to this friendly overture, her only thought was for her father, and so anxious was she not to miss him that she used up all her strength in keeping her eyes fixed on the glass screen.

A line of melancholy adults began to shuffle along the corridor behind the screen, their faces lighting up with sad recognition as they waved to their offspring in the long row of beds and mouthed messages through the glass. Some tried half-heartedly to cheer the dismal scene by pulling funny faces and other such antics, but never to much avail. Were the participants on both sides of the window not so fraught with anxiety, it could have been developed into a wonderful mime, even a ballet, Shirley thought fleetingly as she envisaged this scene of bed-bound children and anxious parents on stage, desperately, comically, tragically, trying to communicate through a glass panel. It was a situation that contained many an opportunity for invention and elaboration. The corridor was filling up with visitors, and she started to worry that there would be no room for her father, fearing that she would not be able to see him squeezed in, as he was bound to be, behind the throng of other parents.

However, there was one space opposite her bed and it was just large enough for him, so it was with indignation that she saw two figures move into that gap. That was not fair! Why were they taking the place that should be earmarked for her father? Then those two people began to wave and blow kisses to *her*. The overpowering joy when she recognized them sent a tingling through her body from head to toe, even through her paralysed leg. One of them was indeed her pa and the other was Maman! The initial joy gave way to despondency that there would be no opportunity to talk to Maman, to hug her or to weep on her shoulder. Like her fellow patients in the other beds, she stretched out her arms imploringly towards the glass screen.

Pa produced letters from his inside pocket and held them out as if trying to pass them to his daughter; Maman showed her a smart new sponge bag, presumably from France, and opened it to reveal all those personal items that had not travelled with Shirley to the hospital. At least now she would be able to brush her hair. Shirley watched them, uncertain how to respond so that they would understand her delight tempered with sadness, until an idea struck her; she was annoyed that such an obvious idea hadn't come to her sooner.

Despite the griping pain in her back, the hot, throbbing ache in her head and the burden of her lifeless leg, she eased herself up on the pillow and began gesturing to her parents, using the mime language of ballet. She beckoned them towards her and folded her arms across her chest to signify her love for them. She reached out to them opening both hands, begging them to come to her; then she folded her arms on her chest again and hung her head down over them in a gesture of sadness. Not only the eyes of her own parents but the eyes of all the other parents were staring at her, transfixed by her performance, and, as it drew to a close, they clapped their hands together behind the glass. The sound of the applause penetrated the partition and drew the attention of the duty nurse, who came with pursed lips to check up on her charges. At the sight of her, all the visitors waved hastily and filed out in a well-ordered line, as if they were schoolchildren afraid of a caning.

Shirley sank back and kept her eyes closed while the same duty nurse did the round of the ward. The effort had exhausted her; her throat had become very sore, although she had not said a word, and her face felt as if it were on fire, yet the rest of her body was icily cold. She scarcely noticed the nurse stopping by her table and placing packages, a letter and her new sponge bag down onto it, nor, only minutes later, the team of doctors and nurses, armed with equipment and medications, hurriedly assembling around her and drawing the curtains shut. A thermometer was pushed between her closed lips while a band was pulled tight around her arm and pumped up. Next a wooden stick was forced to the back of her throat, making her retch, and someone placed the bowl under her chin. "One hundred and five, mm," a woman remarked, and someone else replied:

"Fetch a drip quickly and some cold compresses." Shirley lost consciousness. The letter and the packages on the bedside table remained unopened, together with the new sponge bag from France.

25

A pale light invaded the small room through the slats in and around the edges of the venetian blind which covered the single window: they were not the rays of a golden autumnal sun that reflected off the white walls and ceiling, but a chill, grey pall which spread itself evenly, like a layer of varnish, over the sparse furnishings and the linoleum floor. Shirley rubbed her eyes, wondering how she had come to be in this setting. Everything that revealed itself to her uncomprehending gaze was clinical, harsh and cold; she was definitely not in her own bedroom at home – that much was obvious – so was she, she asked herself, still in that horrendous nightmare into which she had slipped yesterday or the day before or whenever it was, maybe even weeks ago? In the nightmare tight-lipped nurses had come to and fro past the bed where she, with a bursting head and a paralysed leg, had lain immobilized, unable to do anything to help herself. She felt that she was being pinned down in some sort of iron box. Here in this room an unreal, inhuman quality still prevailed.

At least she was alive. She turned her head from side to side: the room was bare apart from a chair and a bedside table where there stood a glass and a jug of water through which the grey light from outside gleamed malevolently. On the other side of the bed was a tall metal pole, and hanging on it was a rubber bag from which a long tube led directly into her right hand. Beyond this piece of apparatus there was a wide-open door, allowing a glimpse into a dark corridor. She raised her hand and was surprised to see a bandage wrapped over the place where the end of the tube entered it. Although the bandage was bloodstained, it didn't hurt much. There was only a slight tingle when she moved her hand, but there was indeed something very peculiar about this situation, quite apart from the room itself, and it took her a little while to discover exactly what it was.

Still turning her head from left to right and from right to left, she then recalled that in the nightmare her neck had been so rigid that she had not been able to move it at all. Now she was able to turn it fairly easily, which implied that the former stiffness must have been a figment of her imagination. Or was it? There remained however a great deal to explain: for example, what was that rubber bag doing up there on the pole? Or the tube in her hand? Or, most importantly, what was she doing alone in this place, with its white walls, in a hard bed with crackly sheets? Satisfied that her neck was mobile again, if indeed it had ever been immobile, and forgetting the tube in her hand, she flung her arms above her head and stretched. Although the tube was long enough to stay attached, the needle in her hand jerked beneath its dressing, making her wince in pain. Then she was shocked to find that she could stretch only one leg while the other lay motionless, as if detached from her body. It would not move, however hard she tried to force it into action. She let out a scream. "Help, help!" she called. "I can't move my leg!"

A bevy of women, all wearing that same blue uniform which had featured in the bad dream, came crowding into the room. They were clearly not dancers, because their movements were too clumsy. Anyhow the portly lady in a white uniform with medals on her chest, who came in with them, walked with none of the grace and agility that Miss Patience always displayed, despite her well-built proportions. The portly lady waddled round the bed and, without a word to Shirley, picked up her free hand. She took one of the medals off her chest and looked at it keenly while she held the hand at the wrist. "Good! Good!" she announced. "Her pulse is getting back to normal. She's recovering. She's over the delirium, I reckon, though we shall have to wait for the doctor's round to know for sure."

Shirley was dumbfounded: what was this woman talking about? "It's my leg!" she wailed. "Not my hand! My leg won't move!"

"Let's not worry about that for the moment," the woman said curtly. "The important thing is that you are recovering and are over the fever. You've been delirious, you know, and you've kept us in a state of high alert, young lady! Thank goodness you can breathe again!" She removed the bedclothes and lifted Shirley's left leg. "I see, I see," she said, pondering the heavy, lifeless leg. "Well, you're a lucky girl: you're in the right place, the very best place in fact." Without more ado, she let the leg fall back onto the mattress, pulled the sheet and blanket over the patient and, like a mother duck followed by her ducklings, waddled out of the room while the younger nurses dutifully filed out in line behind her.

Although the intrusion left Shirley scarcely any the wiser, her mind gradually cleared itself of the mists that had befuddled it when first she had blearily opened her eyes. At last her senses began to function fully and her reason to assert itself, arguing that, because her left leg was as motionless in real life as it had been in the supposed nightmare, it was entirely possible that all those other horrible things had happened too, but had disappeared before she woke up. The leg, which perhaps would recover, might be the only remaining sign of something very wrong, like all those other nasty symptoms.

She checked the facts as best she could: for instance, although her leg would not move, she could turn her neck, which was no longer rigid; the nausea and sickness had been disgusting but had evidently passed. In addition, the pain in her head, which had ached so agonizingly, had gone and there was only a slight bruising on her back. Apparently she must also have had trouble breathing, but that now seemed to be all right. She took a deep breath to prove to herself that her lungs worked. There was no mystery about her bruised back, because it, and for that matter her leg, had suffered in the fall at Brighton, which she remembered only too well.

It was puzzling though: her back had been so badly hurt it was unbelievable that it could have mended in only a day or two. This raised the question of how long she had been lying in the delirium that the senior nurse had referred to. She had no idea what day of the week it was or whether the all-important Wednesday had come and gone. Had anyone thought to contact Sadler's Wells to tell them that she was injured and could not attend? Injured! That was the very word she had been searching for; it enabled her to formulate the all-important question: were her symptoms injuries from the fall, or were they symptoms of infantile paralysis, as the young nurse who had spoken out of turn, whether in the nightmare or in reality, had said?

The story did not end with her symptoms, present and past, though, because it was not simply her health that had been so severely compromised: there were also the bewildering circumstances of that weird room with beds down one side and a glass wall on the other. She recalled that visitors had come to view her and the other young people in their beds from behind the glass screen. It was after that sublime moment when Maman had seemed to appear beside Pa that everything had gone black. Casting her mind back over what little she remembered of those minutes, it was difficult to decide whether Maman actually had been there in flesh and blood, or whether her appearance was simply that of an unsubstantial wraith conjured up by her own fevered brain.

On the other hand, the evidence was beginning to point to the reality not the fantasy of the whole sequence of events; that is to say, she truly was in hospital suffering from infantile paralysis. Dreadful though that was, Maman's return was the best get-well present she could possibly hope for. She longed to see her again, but without the impediment of a glass panel between them. Would her parents be allowed to visit her in this room away from all those other people? She hoped so. There would be so much to tell her, so much to recount: the disastrous trip to Birmingham, the audition at Sadler's Wells in front of Madam and Ted's support that evening, Granny's disturbing visit, the unfortunate day out in Brighton, Thelma – the name made her shudder – and so many other details which escaped her memory.

Running through her mental diary of the past weeks, a wave of depression engulfed her. Birmingham evoked only disturbing images of Thelma, bringing with it omens of death and disease. As for the audition, it was no longer a source of excitement and pride, but a sad reminder of her best hopes, which, if her leg did not recover, were already dashed for ever. The memory of the trip to Brighton brought back a vision of the beautiful view over the South Downs and the idyllic small village where, she was convinced, Alan lived. That vision, which had aroused such expectation in her, had become all the more poignant since she would have to steel herself to erase both it and him from her thoughts. That was easier said than done, because his image had become a constant fixture in her everyday life, and a source of encouragement and hope for the future. All that was left was the fairly humdrum account of life behind the counter in the newsagent's, which in any case had begun before Maman's departure.

However, there was still plenty to tell because, uneventful though it was, she had enjoyed the constantly changing cast of busy customers, and if Mr and Mrs Salvatore were to be believed, she was good at it. Maybe she would be able to take it up again if all other avenues were closed to her. With the flickering ray of hope offered by her job and the Salvatores, there came yet another associated recollection jostling for position in her thoughts. Of course! Mention of the Salvatores had aroused the memory of the diamond pendant. Was it still in her drawer where she had left it? She had intended to take it out before she went to bed after the Brighton excursion, but the pain from the fall made it impossible to walk that far, or even reach out as far as her dressing table that night.

There was no way she could ask Pa to fetch it, because he would hand it straight back to the Salvatores and might well be annoyed that she had not done so herself; nor could she ask Maman without going into a lot of explanation about her subterfuge and disobedience, and then Pa would be sure to hear about it. She would just have to hope that Francesca had not found it, for that smiling, curtsying, apparently ignorant person certainly was aware that the Salvatores had given it to her. The pendant had not brought the good luck that she had been promised, or if it had, it had promptly taken it away again, leaving her much worse off than before.

Confusion, bewilderment, anxiety, uncertainty and frustration – these comprised the range of unruly reactions that assaulted Shirley while, there in her hospital bed, she attempted with half-closed eyes to put them into some sort of order. A dark shadow crossed her field of vision and came to a halt beside her, blocking what little remained of the daylight seeping through the blind. She could scarcely be bothered to open her eyes, but did so just in case it might be Pa. Standing by her bed was a tall, elegant man who was definitely not her pa. She let out a gasp of surprise and then closed her eyes again. "I'm sorry to have startled you," the man said. "I'm Neil Harper, the senior consultant here. Sister told me that you were feeling better, so I've come to see how you are."

"How stupid of me!" Shirley thought. How could I have mistaken him for Alan! Trembling from the shock, she was also tongue-tied. He was a nice man, certainly, and handsome too, but was probably about her father's age – that is to say, much older than Alan.

She tried to pull herself together and remember all the questions she wanted to ask of a senior doctor, for this was her opportunity to find out the truth of what was happening. "In case you're wondering," he said with a smile, "I have seen you before, only you haven't seen me, because you were very ill at the time. Sister has given me your notes from her visit this afternoon, so I don't need to take your pulse or your temperature, but I do need to look at your leg. But first," here he stopped to pull up the one and only chair, "let me answer any questions you may have." Shirley decided that it was easy to warm to this handsome doctor, despite his age, so she began to relax in his company. The mere sight of him was enough to make her feel better. He was so different from the other members of the medical team, who treated her impersonally like an object for examination rather than a human being.

"Yes, I do have questions, quite a lot of them actually," she answered promptly. "I want to know where I am; I suppose I'm in hospital, but I don't know which one, or whether I'm here because of the fall I had… or some illness, and I don't know how long I've been here or how much longer I shall be here… and what's going to happen to my leg. Will I ever dance again? Oh, and where are my parents; can they come to visit me?"

"Well, that's a long list, but let me take one question at a time," he replied. "You are still in the same hospital, but we had to move you into a room on your own because you were in a delirium and critically ill, and we had to put you in an iron lung to help you breathe. We are not sure whether the high fever was a symptom of infantile paralysis or whether that was caused by another entirely different infection. However, I do know that you had a bad fall and I've been wanting to ask you if you can remember whether you really did slip on those wet steps in Brighton, as it says here in your notes, or whether your left leg gave way beneath you. Was it particularly weak that day?"

Shirley nodded, deep in thought, realizing that this was a moment of truth. "Yes, I said I'd slipped, but that's not what happened. I felt my leg give way, it went limp quite suddenly, as I was about halfway down those steps, and then I tumbled onto the hard surface at the bottom. I didn't want to upset my father or my brother because I was in quarantine for infantile paralysis, so I invented the story about slipping – and the steps were slippery. You see, my cousin died of infantile paralysis last week, or whenever it was – I don't remember exactly."

"Yes, I know: I've seen it in your notes," he said, "and in fact you've had it too, and quite badly, but the good news is that you are definitely much better now. You've been in here for some time, delirious for much of it, which, as I said before, is why you're in a room on your own. I think the illness had already begun before you went to Brighton, so you are now coming out on the other side, which is very good news!"

Shirley's first thought was for Ted. "But if I already had it when we went to Brighton, what about my brother? He was there too. Will he catch it?"

"No, I don't think so," came the reassuring response. "Your father has told me all about that trip and about how careful you all were. We've examined your brother, so I'm fully expecting that he'll be fine. Anyhow he's out of quarantine."

The information was coming so thick and fast that Shirley would have liked to ask the doctor to slow down in order to be able to take it all in, even to allow herself time to enjoy the relief of knowing that Ted would not fall ill, and that she herself had not been hallucinating. If she had been in her right mind all along, then she *had* seen Maman in the queue of visitors behind the glass! Above all she *had* survived, whereas Thelma had had not been so lucky.

The consultant was still talking, unaware that her attention had wandered. She forced her concentration back onto what he was saying, reproaching herself for frittering away this golden opportunity. "As for your other questions," he was saying, "you are in one of the best specialist hospitals in the country for treating infantile paralysis, and we are not so very far from your home. What's more, we are lucky to have a special visitor from Australia here this year: her name is Sister Kenny and she has devised her own method for treating the paralysis. In fact, she is setting up a clinic here in this very hospital. She will be coming to see you soon to work on your leg, so there's every hope that by the time you leave us, you will be able to walk without crutches and will not need a brace or a calliper. And finally I expect that your parents will be able to visit you in three or four days' time when you go into rehabilitation."

He stood up to inspect Shirley's leg. She, in a very small voice, plucked up the courage to enquire, "So I'm not going to die, but will I ever dance again?"

He stopped in his tracks, as if the second question had caught him off guard. "No, I can assure you that you are not going to die!" he said with a laugh, but then asked rather more cautiously, "What sort of dancing?"

"Well, ballet – I have a place at Sadler's Wells, and I am supposed to be starting training, or I *was* supposed to be starting on Wednesday – well, I don't know which Wednesday that was – to become a prima ballerina… perhaps it was last week…" her words drifted away.

Neil Harper was unprepared for this development and could only stammer an unprepared remark or two in response. "Um, we shall have to see what we can do in Rehabilitation; we'll do our best!" was the sum total of his reply. He glanced quickly at the leg, moved it around a bit, saying, "Mm, mm, good, good," and then rather hurriedly left the room, calling "Goodnight!" over his shoulder as he went out.

26

After all the confusion and distress of the illness, both on the ward, where the nurses appeared to have instructions not to smile or treat the young patients with anything approaching human kindness, and in the colourless, separate room where Shirley found herself isolated and lonely, Sister Kenny's clinic came as a huge relief. The word "rehabilitation" was encouraging, because it meant that the illness had run its course, that she was still in the land of the living and that like the other patients she was no longer infectious so was permitted to receive visitors. Bright paintings and colourful decorations adorned the walls of the Rehabilitation Wing, where the patients were not confined to bed by day and, when not being physically "rehabilitated", were allowed to associate with each other, sitting at a table at mealtimes, playing board games, drawing or painting and chatting in the groups that formed naturally: groups of children and groups of teenage girls and boys, each of whom sought out company among his or her peer group to discuss and compare their shared experiences of the previous weeks. The best part of it was that at last parents and siblings were allowed to visit.

Maman's first visit was magical, the more so for being so long awaited. Mother and daughter hugged each other while the tears rolling down their faces took the place of words to express the grief and unhappiness of all those many weeks of their separation. That their encounter was wordless did not matter, because Maman promised to return the next day, and she did. She was there in the front of the queue for entry every afternoon in that first week, and was the last to leave in the early evening. Once their tears had dried, she sat with her arm around her daughter's shoulders asking questions and listening attentively to the lengthy account of the multitude of troubles that had occurred during her absence. Shirley wanted these to be as brief as possible, but through her sobs her mother kept repeating, "*Ma pauvre petite Chérie, ma pauvre petite!* My poor little one!"

Shirley, who was forcing herself at the insistence of Sister Kenny and the other members of her staff to concentrate on retrieving her willpower by thinking only positive thoughts, could not help being increasingly irritated by these constant reminders of troubles that, once they had been rehearsed for her mother's benefit, she would henceforth much rather forget. The worst of the illness was over, she kept telling herself; she was thankful to be alive, despite losing the use of one leg, and was resolved to try hard to make the best of whatever future awaited her.

Suppressing her profound despair at all the golden opportunities of which she had had a tantalizing glimpse but which were now to be denied her, was the hardest possible challenge. It was inevitable that she often found herself sinking to the depths of self-pitying hopelessness, but, over and above that, the pity of others, even of her own family, was unwelcome and undermined her efforts. All that was needed was a sympathetic initial acknowledgment of her misfortune. She would have much preferred to hear about France and the farm and her friends there, albeit without ignoring the sadness that had occasioned her mother's return to her native country.

Unaccountably, Maman was not inclined to talk much about France – apparently there was nothing new to convey – nor did she dwell on her own recent sorrows: the pain of her mother's death, the organization of her funeral, the wake with all the messages of condolence, the visits from well-wishers, the funeral itself – with the cortège led by the black-plumed horses pulling the hearse as it snaked its way down to the village church. Nor did she tell her daughter about the numerous and complex legal entanglements she had had to sort out, and all the arrangements she had subsequently made to keep the farmhouse running and in good order to enable her father to continue living there alone in the place he loved best.

All she said was: "We must be grateful that Mémé did not suffer for very long. She'd had a hard life and thankfully she passed away in peace." Here tears came into her eyes, but she persevered. "And as for Pépé, well, you know *him*: he seems to be carrying on much as usual, but her death really affected him deeply and he refuses to talk about it, although a stranger might think he'd hardly noticed that Mémé had gone." She paused and turned to the window to hide the moisture in her eyes, before resuming more brightly: "But he did say how much he is looking forward to having Edward working on the farm, and he does hope that you will both go and stay for the summer. And of course you will be well enough by then!"

Shirley was struck by this latest turn in the conversation. What did Maman mean by saying "you" and not "we"? "Won't you be coming with us, Maman?" she asked.

"Oh, I expect so," her mother replied, gazing out of the window at nothing in particular.

It was only on about the third day, once the emotion of the reunion had started to subside, that Shirley began to sense a deeper degree of unease in her mother's behaviour, as though something greater even than mourning for her dearly loved mother and anxiety about her daughter had extinguished her customarily optimistic and sunny nature, as though the inner spring that had given her the energy to do her part in the Great War, marry an English husband who had been so badly damaged by it and bring up a family in a none-too-welcoming foreign atmosphere, had finally snapped. "And how was your father while I was away?" she tentatively enquired of Shirley.

"Mostly he was fine," Shirley replied, keeping quiet about Pa's panic attack on the evening of the thunderstorm. "In fact, he coped well, and was quite cheerful. He looked after me very well when I started to fall ill." Then, after a brief reflective pause, she added, "Of course he missed you, Maman, and was so much looking forward to your return. He kept saying he couldn't wait for you to come home."

"Ah, I see," Maman replied absent-mindedly. Shirley tried to recall if previously she had ever seen her mother in this distracted state. Eventually, after the latter had gone home, she recalled that day with Maman in central London where she had introduced her to that man M. Lavasseur, who had obviously been deliberately waiting in Lower Regent Street. She cringed to think that he might in some way be connected with Maman's apathy and preoccupation.

Pa came to visit in the evenings. He would arrive looking tired and drawn, but his happiness at witnessing his daughter's recovery from the illness, if not yet from the paralysis, soon overcame his own weariness. "It does my heart good to see you sitting there and chatting away with not a care in the world," he said on his first visit, although in Shirley's estimation this was a considerable exaggeration of her present state. A couple of days later, he announced, "There are so many people who want to come and see you, Shirl, including Ted, of course. Oh, and that Miss

Patience, your dance teacher, but the powers that be say that they don't want you to be overwhelmed by visitors just yet, so it's just your mother and me to start with, and then Ted will be coming next week. By the way, they've given him a clean bill of health and he's completely out of even the longest possible quarantine! What's more, I'm allowing him to drive the car so that he can come whenever he wants to! I know he hasn't passed his test yet, but he is a better driver than me, so I don't suppose he or my precious Lanchester will come to any harm." He gave a broad smile, having delivered the good news, but then had nothing more to say, and his smile quickly reverted to the dejected air that he wore every evening on arrival at the hospital from work. Oddly enough, except as a passing reference, he did not once speak of Maman, whose return he had so eagerly awaited and upon which he had placed so much hope.

On those first occasions there were long periods of awkward silence between father and daughter that lasted until Shirley decided that she, the patient convalescing from a serious illness, would have to do the talking in an effort to animate what was in danger of becoming a tedious and uncomfortable daily chore. She tried asking questions. Had they been out to Richmond Park? she enquired, thinking that that was one subject that would be certain to awake her father's interest.

No, he said, there hadn't been time.

Had he been to his model railway club lately? was her next question. No, he hadn't, because the season was over and it had closed down for the winter. How was the garden; what was in flower? she asked. Not much, only a few chrysanthemums, he replied, reminding her that it was late November and winter had already come in with a vengeance, bringing sharp frosts and icy mornings. The garden was dank and brown with fallen leaves and dead stalks. She vaguely remembered having heard the bangs and the whizzing of fireworks as she lay in the white room; she had opened her eyes and was wondering what the noise was about when flashes of coloured light penetrated the half-closed blinds and she had realized that it must be Guy Fawkes Night. She searched around for more topics, and asked about his work, at which he buried his head in his hands. This was answer enough.

Visiting time became easier and livelier when, one evening about a week later, Ted appeared with his father, though on their arrival Shirley was immersed in the copy of *Madame Bovary* that her mother had brought her from home and did not notice her brother until he was standing in front of her. She was at that moment debating whether to sympathize with Emma on account of her stultifying existence with the boring and inept but good-natured Charles Bovary, or criticize her for her wilfulness, her ambition and her deception of her husband, though she wasn't exactly sure what was going on with the other men in Emma Bovary's life. "Hey, sis! It's me!" Ted called out, waving his hand in her face. She glanced up in brief incomprehension and a touch of annoyance at being dragged out of nineteenth-century France, but quickly returned to twentieth-century England when she saw her brother.

Reggie, who had come with Ted to show him the way, discreetly took himself off to an armchair on the other side of the room. Brother and sister were truly thrilled to be with each other again and talked non-stop. "It's been such a long time, Ted!" Shirley cried, and he nodded as words failed him.

"Well, you're getting better, so you'll soon be home and you can boss me about as much as you like. I won't mind!" he stuttered as soon as he found his tongue. "So, tell me what are they doing to you here?" he asked, uncertain whether to enquire how his sister was or how she was feeling. Having followed every twist and turn, every crisis and deterioration in her critical illness through his father's daily reports, he was surprised at her decisive answer:

"Well, to tell the truth, here in rehab it's not bad at all." But her expression darkened when she continued: "The illness was ghastly, although I don't remember very much about it because they tell me I was very ill and they put me in an iron lung to keep me breathing, and it was horrible on the ward with all those stiff, strait-laced women who treated us like parcels. It's different here. Sister Kenny is lovely. She is so nice. She calls me 'Shirley', instead of 'Miss Marlow', unlike all the others back there." She gestured in the direction of the ward. "And when I told her I was a dancer, she said I might not be a prima ballerina, but she reckons I might one day manage to dance in the *corps de ballet*! Can you believe it? Or, failing that, I'll be able to teach, so you see she's totally convinced about the treatment she's invented.

She says the last thing you should do with a paralysed leg," here she unselfconsciously tapped her left leg, "is to strap it in an iron calliper. I can't tell you how relieved I was to hear that! 'How can anyone walk with irons strapped round their legs, let alone dance?' she says. So we all have to do our exercises morning and afternoon and she makes me try to put this leg on the ground and use it. At first I had to hop along between bars to strengthen all my muscles because they were weak after being in bed so long; then she held my left leg down so that it had to stay on the floor and she made me stand on it; then I had to take a couple of steps using it, and today I thought I felt a muscle twitching!" Shirley smiled, and that gleeful smile helped encourage her brother to smile too. Previously the tale she told had been so upsetting he had had to keep his eyes on his hands to avoid showing how deeply affected he was by it.

"Sister Kenny says that being a dancer helps a lot," Shirley went on, taking up the thread again, "and the more careful exercises I do, the better. It's just like doing ballet warm-ups, though with one leg missing, or that's how it feels at present. Sister Kenny says I'm lucky to have both my legs the same length. Apparently some people come out of this illness with one leg shorter than the other. Can you imagine?" There was a lull while Shirley drew breath. "If you like, I'll show you what I can do?" she offered.

"OK," Ted agreed rather nervously; he was not sure that he wanted to be responsible for this fragile creature with a will of steel.

"If you'd give me a hand to stand up," Shirley entreated, "and then stand on my left with your hand under my elbow, I'll show you. Maybe we'll aim for those chairs over there near where Pa is sitting." She nodded to a couple of empty chairs under the window near where their father was dozing. Slowly, with halting steps, they made their way across the room. "There! What did you think of that?" she asked when they made it as far as the chairs. "Though, of course," she added, "you haven't seen how bad it was a couple of weeks ago, so you can't really appreciate how far I've come." Ted found it hard to reply, because at the forefront of his mind he held the image of the agile, featherweight little dancer who had given such a staggering performance on the stage at Sadler's Wells some weeks earlier and was now reduced to hobbling at a snail's pace across a hospital lounge.

"That's very good. You're doing so well," he said, lying through his teeth.

"I can't believe how exhausting all this exercise is!" Shirley exclaimed. "Let's sit down on these chairs for a bit, shall we?" Ted helped her lower herself onto one of the seats and then sat down beside her. "Oh, Ted, silly me! I've forgotten my blanket! I'm so sorry. Could you please fetch it for me? I've left it on the chair over there," she begged him. Ted was about to reply that it was no trouble at all, since the chair was within easy reach, but he stopped himself in time in case that sounded dismissive of all the superhuman effort that she had put into crossing the room, so he quickly got to his feet, bounded over to the group of chairs where they had been sitting and picked up the blanket, which he wrapped round his sister's knees. "Sister Kenny says we must keep warm," she said. "It's part of her treatment. She puts hot-water bottles and warm compresses on the paralysed muscles – to wake them up, she says. It's very comfortable and I do think it's beginning to work."

Sensing that an encouraging comment was required of him, Ted remarked, "I dare say you'll be back in the shop quite soon, Shirl. The Salvatores have asked after you every day, and they've sent you a pile of magazines. I've brought some of them with me." He pulled four magazines out of his pockets. "Did their get-well card arrive?" he asked.

"Yes, not only a card but flowers as well," Shirley replied. "They are so kind. Please thank them for me and tell them how much I'm looking forward to being back."

With self-imposed restraint, she added: "Oh, and if you should go anywhere near the studio, please would you thank Miss Patience for her get-well card and her letter and tell her that I shall call and see her one day." She did not say, as she might have in other circumstances, "Tell her that I can't wait to be back in the studio!" or "I can't wait to dance again!" Instead she kept her mind on her correspondence. "And if you see Granny, please thank her for her card and the box of soap. That was certainly a surprise!"

"Yes, I thought so too," Ted said, "but, you know, she was very worried about you. I suppose if you are very worried about someone, then you realize that they do mean a lot to you."

Shirley considered these words of wisdom. Then turning to look Ted full in the face and leaning towards him, with her hand shielding her mouth, she asked him in a whisper, "Do you know if there's something wrong at home, Ted? Maman and Pa have been acting so strangely since they've been visiting me here, I couldn't help but notice. They never come together, except, I remember, when Maman came home. At first I thought that was deliberate – so I wouldn't be left alone – but I'm not so sure, because they hardly mention each other."

Ted raised an eyebrow. "I was hoping you wouldn't ask that," he said, also whispering for fear of waking their father, "but since you asked, I suppose I ought to tell you so that it's not too great a shock when you're discharged. The truth is the atmosphere at home is terrible, and I don't know why – well, only partly. You see, the trouble started when Francesca left."

Shirley flinched. "Why did she leave?" she asked, interrupting Ted's narrative.

"Oh," he said, "I don't know, but it must have been at least four weeks ago, or longer; I think it was soon after you fell ill. She came once then never again. The Salvatores said they hadn't seen or heard from her, and didn't know where she was until the cousin who she had gone to live with in Battersea told them a few days later that she had gone back to Italy; and so she had, apparently, taking all her belongings with her. The cousin said she was afraid of catching infantile paralysis. And of course the Salvatores were shocked at that, because they didn't know that that was what you were suffering from, so Pa and I had to try very hard to assure them that you hadn't brought the germs into the shop." They weren't too pleased, but they're all right now, because no one else has fallen ill.

Shirley wrinkled her nose as if she had smelt a bad odour. The nose wrinkling had nothing to do with a bad odour or with the Salvatores' anxiety about infantile paralysis, but arose from a strong suspicion of what Francesca had taken with her in her belongings; nevertheless, there was no point in worrying about that now, especially because that diamond pendant had brought only trouble. She was almost glad if it had gone.

"The problem was," Ted continued, "that without you and Francesca, Pa and me, well, we weren't too good at housekeeping and washing and that sort of thing, so it all began to pile up, and when Maman came home a couple of weeks later, she was furious with us, mainly with Pa, because she said he ought to have known better. I've never known her make such a fuss. I offered to help with the clearing-up and the cleaning, but she wouldn't hear of it, although she keeps saying she's *au bout du rouleau*, which I think means she's at the end of her tether. She just kept on blaming Pa, and then he started having nightmares again, and she said he was making her too tired to do her work properly at the Embassy. And poor Pa, because he was so flustered and tired, he forgot to take his pills and his hip got worse, so either he was groaning in pain, or he was hallucinating. In the end, I went to call the doctor. He's a good chap; he came to visit straight away and told Pa he had come on the off-chance, just to check that all was well, which I thought was very good of him – and he gave him some new pills, so the situation is improving a bit, but, as you probably can see, Pa is exhausted. I've heard him say that this time he certainly is going to have to look for a new job."

"I'm glad you've told me," Shirley said. "I knew something was wrong, but I still don't understand why Maman is so emotional. I know dear Mémé's death affected her deeply, and I've been critically ill, but usually Maman would be the best, the most level-headed person; instead she seems so depressed and weepy. I don't understand why and sometimes I wish she wouldn't come visiting, because all she seems to do is to sit there crying. And Pa too, he's pretty miserable." She thought it best not to tell Ted her suspicions about M. Lavasseur in case her imagination was running away with her from reading too much *Madame Bovary*.

27

Although Ted constantly urged his sister to stay put in the hospital for as long as possible, she was naturally impatient to escape from the four walls which had imprisoned her since early October. She assumed that he meant that the longer she could benefit from Sister Kenny's treatment the better, though in fact that was not entirely what he intended. He occasionally touched on the worsening situation at home, but without elaborating in detail, because that would have involved telling the whole unpalatable truth – which was that their parents not only scarcely ever spoke to each other, but neither did they see each other very much. Maman went out to work early every day and arrived home so late in the evening that often they did not eat until after nine o'clock, and then the meals, which were no longer elegantly served at the table but put onto plates in the kitchen, consisted not of *gigot de sept heures* or *marmite dieppoise*, delicious but economical recipes, but, as often as not, of sausage and mash or omelette and chips, of which Ted had had his fill while he and his father had been cooking for themselves. It was, he said, the sort of food you expected at Scout camp but not at home.

Maman's explanation for the gastronomic lapses was that she visited Shirley on her way home from work every day, so did not have time to concoct elaborate meals, and since the importance of that was indisputable, Ted and his father had to accept her reasoning without complaining about the food. After supper Maman would go straight to bed in anticipation of a disturbed night, while Pa stayed downstairs to listen to the nine-o'clock news, which, with its talk of mounting Fascist and Nazi oppression throughout Europe and war in the Far East, only added to his anxieties. On Saturdays Maman would go out, saying that she was off to the hospital, which she probably was, but she stayed out all day, and on Sundays she stayed in bed until lunchtime before going to visit Shirley in the afternoon. She never went to confession or to Mass.

For Ted, therefore, life at home might have seemed much as it had been during Maman's absence in France, though nowadays he and his father did make concerted efforts to keep the house clean and do their own washing in the tub on Saturday mornings. The main difference was that, during Maman's absence, he and his father, and Shirley before she fell ill, had lived in peaceful harmony. That blend of fellow feeling and team spirit had evaporated and had been replaced by a poisonous brew of silence and hostility. On Christmas morning, before the hospital had opened its doors to visitors, Ted had been party to a scene during which Pa had showered Maman with presents, but she had ignored them and given him nothing in return. Then she had put her coat on and had walked out. Ted was so shaken that he too had gone out, leaving Pa to cook dinner for only the two of them. He took the car and drove round to the hospital, but walked in the grounds to calm down before going in to the Rehabilitation Wing. At all costs he wanted to spare Shirley any suspicion of the growing friction he had witnessed earlier that morning, on Christmas Day of all days, for fear that it might have a detrimental effect on her improving health. He spent as much of the festive morning with her as he could, passing on many presents and messages, before reluctantly returning home for dinner in dread of what he was going to find.

After Ted's departure, Shirley opened her cards and presents, scrutinizing each and every one of them. Her pleasure at receiving so many good wishes and messages was all the greater because she was already anticipating being able to thank most of her well-wishers in person. The Salvatores, who said they were looking forward to seeing her back in the shop as soon as she was fit enough, had sent a large, tinselled card, resplendent with a rubicund Father Christmas riding his sleigh high above trees and rooftops; there were also cards from many members of her dance class, as well as a few from the school friends she had not seen since last summer. Two or three boys, Frank among them, had sent little notes guardedly wishing her well, as if they felt obliged to do so perhaps from parental prompting, but no longer thinking her worth pursuing and wanting to distance themselves from her as politely as possible. These she put straight in the waste-paper basket.

Miss Patience, who had come to visit only a couple of days earlier and had stayed for well over an hour, had left a Christmas card and some talcum powder. On that occasion Shirley had been grateful for her discreet avoidance of any mention of the dance studio, although she sensed that there was something more that her teacher was on the verge of confiding, but for which she could not quite pluck up the courage or find the right opportunity. Shirley well knew that it had something to do with Sadler's Wells. Instead they concentrated on Shirley's miraculous recovery and the beneficial effects of her regular exercises, without any reference to the ballet. Nora Patience was so full of praise for her ability to walk on both feet that one might have thought that to be the greatest physical achievement imaginable. Nevertheless, after an embarrassing hiatus, she let her irritation subside because clearly Miss Patience's remarks were well intentioned. The weather, from which, in hospital, Shirley was shut off, provided a useful, if pointless, change of topic, and then they found a sure subject for lengthy conjecture in Miss Patience's mother. "I don't know how much longer she will be able to stay at home with me, or even how much longer she will live," Miss Patience remarked sadly. "Her heart is so weak, I'm afraid it might stop in the night."

Shirley nodded with understanding. "Yes, of course," she said, "that's what happened to my French grandmother."

The conversation turned to France, where Miss Patience had lived when she was a young dancer. She described Paris vividly as she remembered it from before the Great War, and inevitably the ballet crept into her account, but not in any upsetting way, since this was a topic that Shirley had always wanted to raise with her. At last, little by little, she enticed her teacher and mentor to describe the notorious first performance of *The Rite of Spring* in Paris in May 1913. Although, out of modesty, Nora Patience never referred to her own part, rumour had it that she had danced in that performance and, as her account proceeded, it became more and more obvious that she had in fact been involved in some significant but undefined role.

Then, carried away by the power of her own recollections, she began to talk openly about her days in the Ballets Russes, describing the wealth of artistic innovation in the dance forms, the music, the costumes and the sets. Shirley listened avidly as she went on to describe many of the illustrious personages associated with creating that famous unity of dance, music and design that had typified the performances: Diaghilev, Stravinsky, Nijinsky, Cocteau, Picasso and Joan Miró, as well as innumerable other distinguished artists. Her imagination fired by these descriptions, Shirley was transported into that extravagant world and was none too pleased to have the magic spell broken by the arrival of Sister Kenny.

Like a ship in full sail, Sister Kenny blew into the day room where they were sitting that afternoon. She did this sometimes to check whether her patients were usefully employed in near-normal activities, sitting in chairs, playing games or browsing among the bookshelves, or whether they had gone to laze on their beds, which was strongly discouraged. Her appearance was as startling as though a character from the pantomime had strayed into the world of the ballet. As always, to brighten up the atmosphere, she arrived wearing a huge floral hat, which never failed to raise a giggle from even the most despondent of her patients because she, a massive figure, looked so ridiculous given both her dimensions and the time of year. She strode into the room bellowing a cheerful "Good afternoon, one and all!" Miss Patience, who appeared quite diminutive in comparison, flinched at the sight of the terrifying spectacle bearing down on her, but when she saw Shirley's wry grin, she too mustered a nervous smile.

"This is Sister Kenny, Miss Patience," Shirley said quickly.

"Ah, yes," said Miss Patience standing up to shake hands. "How do you do, Sister? Shirley has been telling me all about your miraculous treatment and how beneficial it seems to be for her."

Sister Kenny shook Miss Patience's proffered hand vigorously. "Yes, yes I know who you are. You're the dance teacher, aren't you? That's just beaut! Well, I think Shirl ought to show you what she can do. See, she's walking with a stick already. Let's go into the clinic."

She led the way into her practice area, which resembled a small gymnasium rather than a hospital clinic, and indicated the tools of her trade as she went. "See here, on this table we wrap the paralysed limbs in hot, damp towels to bring them back to life before we set to work on the exercises. We then manipulate the muscles, but that has to be very gently done at first because we don't want to cause any damage: if it's a leg for instance, like in Shirl's case, we massage the foot, the ankle and on up the calf to the thigh. We flex and point the foot and bend the leg at the knee while the patient lies back on the bed. Then we take our young patients – they're usually children and young adults – over to those parallel bars, where we encourage them to make their way along, first of all letting their arms and the good leg take the weight and then gradually putting the lazy foot down to the floor. It's really important not to take it too fast. Sooner or later the message gets through and the muscles in the paralysed leg start to respond again. See, I don't think the problem is with the nerves to the muscles, I think it's in the muscles themselves. They've been put out of action by the illness and they have to be made to get going again." She turned to her patient. "Shirl," she said, "why don't you demonstrate what you can do for your dance teacher? Come and lie down for a bit while I heat the water for the towels and then I'll wrap them round your leg."

Sister Kenny was right. The muscles loosened up and life came back into that leg under her large, firm hands, which ran smoothly and soothingly up and down, releasing the tensions which, without treatment, would have led to wasting, callipers and permanent disability. At the parallel bars Shirley threw down her stick and, holding the bars to steady herself, walked on both feet the length of the apparatus. "I think she'll dance again one day," Sister Kenny declared.

Nora Patience chose her words carefully in reply: "It's a remarkable treatment you have devised here, Sister. I think we could well use the hot towels and the massage to good effect in the dance studio, and who knows what Shirley might do one day! Anything is possible."

That Christmas Day, after Ted had gone home, Shirley arranged her cards on her table and, happily recalling Miss Patience's visit, put the talc in her drawer. Then she turned to her other presents. In amazement she unwrapped a large package that bore Granny Marlow's handwriting: she had assumed, wrongly it seemed, that the box of luxury soap was as much attention as she would receive from that quarter. Inside the parcel she found a stylish, soft, emerald-green cardigan and jumper and a matching pleated skirt. The accompanying card read: "You will find it cold when you come out of hospital, Shirley dear, and will probably need these. If they do not fit, you can return them to Morley's. Your loving Granny." Shirley could not resist a rueful smile. Granny was determined to get her into Morley's even if it meant buying her expensive clothes that might have to be returned. There was even a gift of a pretty silver bracelet from Uncle Paul and Aunt Madge and their sons; it gleamed a pure white against the green wool of the cardigan.

With instructions to open it after his departure, Ted had left a small parcel which contained a pretty brooch that must have cost a large share of his paper-round earnings; Shirley was touched, wishing that she had opened it earlier in his presence, but, quite apart from obeying his instructions, she had at the time been distracted by the tension writ large across his face. One had only to look at him to see that he was not enjoying Christmas. She had wondered why, suspecting that there had been more trouble at home. He had already told her that Pa was having frequent night terrors again and that Maman was not coping very well, but this morning his expression gave an unmistakable hint that something more serious had occurred. Over dinner Shirley tried to join in the communal jollity, pulling crackers and wearing paper hats, but in the anticipation of a difficult afternoon visit, or series of separate visits from her parents, her mind was elsewhere. If they were going to disturb the calm atmosphere here in the hospital, which had become not only her prison but her sanctuary as well, she wished that they would stay away. If they did come, either together or alone, she hoped that Ted would be there too.

On her way back from the refectory to the day room, she stopped to admire the baubles and lights on the Christmas tree and was gazing at them forlornly when she heard footsteps approaching from behind and a hand tapped her on the shoulder. "A penny for them, Shirl," her father said. She spun round as fast as her left leg would allow, and saw him standing there, hand in hand with Maman. Ted stood a step or two behind their parents, wearing a triumphant grin. There followed emotional outbursts of "Merry Christmas!" and "*Joyeux Noël!*" as Shirley embraced each parent in turn and then gave Ted a peck on the cheek.

"Well done! Thank you!" she whispered in his ear. Speculation as to how genuine the parental show of unity really was would be a fruitless exercise, Shirley surmised, so she entered into the spirit of the festivities, the while suppressing her suspicions that the united front was contrived at Ted's insistence.

The spirit wobbled when she showed her mother the presents she had already received, among them Granny Marlow's skirt and twinset. Maman's face fell when she saw it. "If you open my present to you now, I will take it back to the shop after the holiday," she insisted. Shirley untied the package and was dismayed to find inside exactly the same combination of skirt, jumper and cardigan in red.

"Oh, Maman, but it's a lovely outfit!" she stammered. "And such a wonderful, warm colour!" In truth, although scarlet suited her well, she preferred Granny's emerald green, which was so much more flattering.

Maman picked up the clothes, petulantly declaring, "I will take these back; you can't have two of the same sets of clothes; it is not often that your grandmother and I have the same idea!"

"No, no, please don't," Shirley cried. Pa's face clouded over and he turned away. The display of marital unity, it seemed, was little more than a façade, designed to placate Ted and delude Shirley into thinking that she could expect an unchanging home life on her discharge.

28

The patient was determined to walk unaided, without a stick though still limping, to the car on her discharge from hospital on her eighteenth birthday in mid-February 1938, but a heavy overnight fall of drifting snow, which almost put paid to her departure altogether, thwarted her plans. Sister Kenny was very much against her leaving, not only on account of the treacherous conditions underfoot, but also because of the extreme cold, both of which, she warned, might undermine or even reverse the beneficial effects of the treatment. Shirley, for her part, was silently convinced that she was the only person who could bring her warring parents together, and argued that Sister Kenny, coming as she did from the Australian bush, in all probability had never seen snow so was not used to it, whereas for anyone who had lived all their life in England, it was what was to be expected in winter, simply a mere inconvenience.

Remarkably for her, Sister Kenny conceded that she had met her match and let her go, but only with the proviso that she should be wrapped in blankets and hot-water bottles, and be pushed to the car in a wheelchair, which did not please the convalescent patient in the slightest. She was expecting to make a triumphant exit, surrounded by admiring staff and watched from the windows by her fellow sufferers, whom she was leaving behind. Thus her discharge from the hospital where she had spent the best part of four months was marked neither by celebration nor ceremony. Instead, with Pa and Ted as the sole onlookers, the porter tried to push her out of the main entrance to the waiting car as quickly as possible, but he had to slow down when the wheelchair skidded on a patch of ice beneath the snow and, lurching forward, almost tipped the occupant out onto the cold, white carpet beneath its wheels.

The chill in the air as she emerged from the entrance out into the grey daylight cut through the frail young patient like a finely sharpened blade of steel. She pulled her winter coat close about her and stuffed her gloveless hands into her pockets, trying to recall the last time she had consciously been out in the open air and remembered that it was in

Brighton, a lifetime ago. A lifetime was the only adequate description of the days and weeks and months spent in hospital, because, in the interim between Brighton and the present day, so much had changed so dramatically that her life would never be the same again. Everything that had happened before Brighton was now irrelevant. All those hopes, all those ambitions, all those plans that she had fondly hatched and cherished, never expecting that they would be so summarily dashed by one tiny, invisible microbe, were nothing more than stardust, as ephemeral as the snowflakes falling from the sky. The big question, for which there was simply no answer, was why? Why did this happen to me?

What would she do next, apart from, perhaps, returning to the newsagent's if and when her leg grew stronger? Was that to be the ultimate goal of her existence? Would she always lead a life of dependence on her parents, at home with no freedom of movement, always regarded with pitying glances as a sad case, a poor girl who had been struck down in her prime after showing so much promise and having the world at her feet? She shuddered. Ted noticed and, assuming that she was feeling the cold, asked. "Are you warm enough, Shirl? We'll soon be home." At first she pretended that she had not heard, but when he repeated his question, she replied with grim fortitude:

"Only a little. I'll be all right." For a split second she contemplated going back into the warmth of the Rehabilitation Wing, all too aware that in her obstinacy she had already denied herself that option. She had decided to go home and she was now on her way, whether, when faced with the true nature of that decision, she wanted to or not.

By the time they reached the car, parked less than fifteen yards away, she was shivering from head to foot. The porter lifted her into the front seat, shaking his head as he did so. "I hope you've brought some blankets, sir," he said to Pa. "I have to return these and the hot-water bottles as well to Sister. She keeps a close eye on equipment, you know, and I'll be in trouble if she finds they're missing."

Reggie rummaged around in the boot and brought out the worn, old tartan blanket that had served as a beach mat in warmer seasons and as a picnic rug on the journey to Brighton. Sand fell onto the snow as he shook it out. "There's this," he said doubtfully. "We haven't very far to go; it should keep her warm until we get home." With the car doors wide open, Shirley was by now blue with cold, and the tartan rug afforded her no comfort whatsoever: quite the opposite in fact, because the rug was as cold as she was, having rarely been taken out of the boot of the car. Pa and Ted tried to raise her spirits with encouraging but rather obvious remarks like, "At last you're out of hospital!" or "We'll soon warm you up at home, Shirl!", which did not have the required effect. Her teeth were chattering so violently that, even had she wanted to, they would not have let her join in the show of misplaced optimism.

"Shall I drive?" Ted asked hopefully.

"No, no, the roads are too hazardous," Pa replied. "We don't want any accidents." Ted climbed into the back seat, their father into the driver's seat beside Shirley, and finally both doors were closed, although Pa insisted on keeping his window open, because otherwise, he said, the windscreen would steam up. There was no heating in the car, and he drove at a snail's pace, probably with some justification because a few abandoned vehicles that had slewed off the road onto the verge or into trees came dimly into view. "You know, Ted," said Pa as he edged with extreme caution along the tracks in the snow made by other motorists, "I think we ought to be able to fix up some sort of heating in this car. After all, the engine has to be cooled, so why couldn't we direct the heat from it into the car?"

"Yes, good idea," Ted agreed, "but we can't do that today. A pity we didn't think of it sooner."

With her blood freezing to icicles in her veins, Shirley was past caring, but when she became aware of tension building up in her left leg she hoped and prayed that this journey – which seemed to go on for ever through areas unrecognizable on account of the mask of snow disguising all otherwise familiar buildings – would swiftly come to an end. From the back of the car, Ted tried to distinguish local landmarks. "Oh, look," he called out cheerfully, "there's the bus station! We'll soon be home! We've got such a lovely surprise waiting for you, Shirl!" At that moment "a lovely surprise" was for Shirley the last straw. Above all she longed to fall into her own soft feather bed and snuggle down, surrounded by numerous hot-water bottles under a pile of blankets and the eiderdown, perhaps with a hot cup of tea and a piece of cake on her bedside table. The mere mention of "a lovely surprise" annoyed her, and it was only because she was so listless that any show of temper remained silent.

To her relief the house was blissfully quiet when, dragging her left leg behind her and leaning on her stick, she slowly climbed the doorstep. "I'm just like Pa," she thought. He followed her into the house, also walking with a pronounced limp. All was quiet indoors until Maman came out of the front room, flinging wide the door. Then a shout of "Happy Birthday! Welcome home, Shirley!" rang out from inside the room. Appalled at this, she wanted to run away as fast as her legs would carry her – which they would not. She allowed her mother to kiss her on both cheeks and then peered into the room.

What she saw was worse than a nightmare. The lounge was packed full of people, all smiling and raising their glasses to her. She recognized many faces: Granny was there, naturally, and so were the Salvatores. There were also neighbours from the road and other shopkeepers from the Parade. Ruefully Shirley reflected that, since it was a Thursday, early closing day, all these people were free to come. Miss Patience stood smiling in one corner next to Dr and Mrs Forbes, and not far from her was a group of girls from the dance school, among them Violet, who doubtless was bragging about her place at Sadler's Wells. Above their heads, with the tiniest surprising surge of pleasure, she saw her cousin Edith and Uncle Horace. "Come on, Shirley, don't be shy! You're home now!" someone called out.

She ventured hesitantly into the room with as much joy as if she were mounting a scaffold; both her legs were on the point of giving way when someone pulled up a chair. "You must be so tired after the journey," a disembodied voice observed. "And what terrible weather for your discharge!" The Salvatores planted themselves in front of her. "*La povera ragazza! Mia povera ragazza! Buon compleanno! Buon compleanno!*" Mr S. kept exclaiming as tears rolled down his cheeks.

Ever practical, Mrs S. nudged him out of the way. "He's Italian, dear," she explained, "and he's very fond of you, that why he's so emotional. We must be getting back to the shop; we closed it so that we could come to see you, but all you have to do, when you're ready, is drop by and we'll be delighted to have you back! Happy Birthday!" Shirley nodded weakly. Clearly everyone was trying to be kind, but their reactions and their expressions spoke louder than words. With sharpened sensitivity, she could tell that they were all sorry for her and could only see the physical disability, which was all the more pronounced on account of the weather and the temperature. At least the mass of their bodies had contributed to the warmth in the room, which the coals in the grate were singularly failing to do, as if they felt as weak and unenthusiastic as she was.

The ballet girls in a tight group glanced in her direction, uncertain whether to talk to her or not, in case with her leg she might have lost her tongue. Ted, who had been watching them from behind Shirley's chair, was quick off the mark and went over to greet them. They preened themselves at having the company of such a good-looking boy, and were eventually prevailed upon to approach his sister, who treated them, especially Violet, with disdain. However, one girl, Cynthia, stood a little aside from the rest, and only when they had stuttered their hasty "goodbyes" and "get well soons" did she sit down at Shirley's feet. "I'm sorry about them," she said. "They haven't a brain cell between them. But it's wonderful to see you again. It must be rather a shock to come home and find all these people in your house. I'd love to know about your treatment, because you are walking amazingly well, so much better than I expected. And if there is anything I can do for you, just let me know."

This friendly overture from someone who had never been more than a passing acquaintance encouraged Shirley to overcome her reluctance to talk about the ballet and to ask Cynthia about her dancing. "Well, you see," Cynthia replied sadly, "I didn't get through the audition at the Wells. It was horrible. Madam as they call her, evidently didn't like me – I don't know why – and she tore my dancing to shreds. She talked all through my session to the two men sitting on either side of her." She turned away, still shamed by the humiliation that she had endured.

"Oh, I'm sorry – that's awful!" Shirley exclaimed. "I'm shocked to hear that." Then, to her surprise, she heard herself saying, "It makes me quite glad I'm not going there after all."

"Yes, I suppose I have to be glad I found out in time," Cynthia said seriously. "I expect I'll find work in a show or something. That might be more fun, and then," she hesitated, searching for the right words, "and then, when you're back on stage, maybe we can dance together in the same shows!"

As her frozen limbs thawed out in the comfortable temperature of the sitting room and the unexpected pleasure of Cynthia's company restored her battered self-esteem, Shirley recovered something of her natural effervescence and began to participate in the gathering that on first sight had so much upset and annoyed her. In her armchair she tested her left leg and was relieved to discover that the tension caused by the icy temperatures was relaxing: she could point her toes, flex her foot and bend her leg at the knee. "Look everyone!" she cried out. "My leg and my foot are moving! It must have been the cold that froze them solid!"

Startled by this announcement, the remaining guests stopped talking and turned to look; then they all applauded. "Well done! Shirley!" they called, cheered that they no longer had to talk in hushed, embarrassed voices at this party that had earlier seemed so ill-timed. Dr Forbes patted his patient on the back and congratulated her on her extraordinary recovery. "I never expected to see you as fit as this ever again, Shirley," he said, "and here you are obviously well and truly on the road to good health."

He and his wife took their leave, followed soon afterwards by Nora Patience. "Shirley," she said as she made for the door, "I have a couple of letters for you in this envelope. I have replied to the important one so there's no need for you to do anything about that. I'm sure you'll be glad to see it." She slipped the envelope down the side of the armchair. "Read them when you have a quiet moment," she said as she left.

Next it was Granny Marlow's turn to come over to her granddaughter. "My dear," she said, "I'm so glad to see that you are wearing my skirt and twinset! I must say it suits you. I thought it would and I was right. And I hope it's warm enough for you. I can still take it back to Morley's, you know, and maybe you would come with me!"

Shirley smiled. "It's lovely, Granny, and nice and warm. That was so kind of you!" She trusted that her mother, who was not in the room, had not heard this exchange. Presumably she was in the kitchen pouring more cups of tea.

Then Edith, who had not been in the room either, came in carrying a tea tray laden with the cups and more birthday cake. Given Maman's mistrust of her husband's family, it was unbelievable that she could have let Edith help her out in the kitchen. Having distributed the cups, Edith came to join the crowd standing round Shirley's armchair. She gave her cousin a bear hug and, sobbing, said, "Oh, I'm so glad you're better, Shirl, I was so worried about you! Father and I came down specially to see you. Jim's at work – he couldn't come, but we're staying the night at Granny's so I can come and see you again tomorrow when there aren't so many people here." She whispered in Shirley's ear: "Don't be upset if Father doesn't say very much to you. He's still in mourning for Thelma. Mother sends her love. She's too distraught to come out of the house, let alone go on a journey."

Still taking refuge in the kitchen, Maman was busy preparing a festive dinner that initially had been intended for her close family but, after Edith's kind offer of help, had generously been extended to her in-laws, including her mother-in-law. Thanks to Jacqueline's superlative mastery of French cuisine and a bottle of excellent wine that Reggie had kept stored in the cupboard under the stairs, the evening proceeded almost without incident.

It was unfortunate that Granny, unused to alcohol in any quantity, was carried away under its influence and made a few ill-timed remarks, just as she had at the time of Edith's wedding. Whether she would have made them without the alcohol no one knew, but charitably they ascribed them to the effects of the wine. At the beginning of the meal, she turned to Shirley and declared, "Let's drink to the health and the birthday of my favourite granddaughter!" Shirley blushed in embarrassment and made a mental note to assure Edith the next day that she was nothing of the sort, for until only recently it had been clear that their granny had not thought highly of her at all. Towards the end of the meal, by which time the company had relaxed into good-natured banter, Granny raised her glass again and said for all to hear, "Here's to our Shirley. We are so glad to have her back. Thank goodness she was luckier than my dear Thelma!" No one spoke, except to repeat a phrase that had been uttered umpteen times already that afternoon: "Yes, welcome home Shirley!" Edith kept her eyes down, firmly fixed on the floor at her feet, while her father turned pale, bit his lip and blinked.

Pa said loudly, "Come on, Mother, I think it's time you were going home."

Edith was the first to stand up. "I'm so tired; it's been a long day for us and Shirl must be exhausted" she announced. She shepherded her father and grandmother towards the door, stopping only to stoop to Shirley's level and mutter. "Don't worry about her. You know she talks nonsense and changes her mind as often as she changes her clothes. I'll see you tomorrow."

All through dinner, tiredness had been squeezing its iron grip on Shirley, and no sooner had the guests departed than she said, "I can't keep awake any longer. I must go to bed!" Maman left the washing-up in the sink and Ted abandoned his homework to help her mount the stairs, which she took one by one, imitating the great effort that her father had to make every night. Maman preceded her and Ted followed behind in a slow procession. When, at the end of a long and challenging day, she flopped down onto her own soft mattress, she closed her eyes and fell asleep, dead to the world, thankful to be alive and at home.

Her mother woke her the next morning. "Chérie, Chérie," she whispered, shaking her gently. "It is half-past eleven and your cousin will be here soon. Let me help you dress." Although Shirley was reluctant to leave the warmth of the bed, she found to her joy that when she stretched out from top to toe both her legs responded.

"No, Maman," she said, "I'm fine; don't worry, I can do it myself!"

"If you are really sure," her mother replied. "I'll leave as soon as your cousin and her father arrive. I need to go to work for just a little while. I promised your cousin that I would prepare some lunch, and she will serve it when they come. I never knew what a nice girl she is. I will be back before they leave."

Though encouraged by Maman's warming towards Edith, Shirley was most put out to discover that on this, her first full day at home, her mother should even consider going to work. She had imagined that they would spend the day together in the sort of close mother-and-daughter companionship that they had enjoyed of old when they used to talk freely all day about everything and nothing. For a part-time employee Maman seemed to spend an excessive amount of time at the Embassy, more now than she had before her trip to France. Her explanation was that she had to make up for time lost while she was away, but that did not fool Shirley, because she remembered that her mother had visited her, on the other side of the glass panel, when she first fell ill, and that was a long time ago.

On the other hand, the separation had been so long and so traumatic on so many counts that possibly the mother-daughter relationship would never be the same again. Although physically at present she was more dependent on her parents than she had ever been since babyhood, and although the black pit of despair was never far away, Shirley had grown in self-assurance: she knew her own mind and was inclined to keep her own counsel, where previously she would have had no qualms about seeking her mother's advice or opinion on a particular course of action, so this morning she did not protest but simply let her mother go. It helped of course that Edith was coming for lunch.

Over lunch the two young women studiously avoided any mention of Thelma in front of Uncle Horace, but when he took himself off to the sitting room for forty winks before embarking on the long drive back to Birmingham through the snow, Edith turned to Shirley with tears in her eyes and said, "Shirley, I'm so glad you've come through this awful illness! There were times when I wished I'd had it instead of you. After all you caught it in our house at my wedding, and I was never going to be a ballerina, was I?"

Shirley shrugged. "It wasn't your fault, Edith," she said. "And anyhow it has taught me one lesson, and that is that you can't plan your own future. You simply don't know what's going to happen." She sighed and magnanimously enquired, "How's your mother?"

Edith shook her head. "She's in a dreadful state, quite incapable," she said, "but the worst of it is that Father is having to bear her grief as well as his own, and you can see what that's doing to him." Indeed Uncle Horace was little more than a shrunken shadow of his former self and appeared to have lost the power of speech. He communicated only through nods and shakes of the head, seemingly too weary to open his mouth. "Thank goodness I've got my Jim," Edith went on. "Without him I don't know how I would have survived."

29

That her parents were unable to keep the deception of unity and harmony going for very long after her return from the hospital did not come as a surprise to Shirley, although it was a disappointment. It would have been so much nicer if the joy of her return home on her birthday had been the cause of a genuine effort to re-establish the old atmosphere of family solidarity and dependability, but the situation had deteriorated so badly that there was little hope of that happening, now or in the future. At night Pa emitted ghoulish screams which echoed through the house as the old terrors took hold of him again, and Maman frequently had recourse to the sofa in search of a couple of hours of solitude, if not sleep, before the new day dawned. She rose early and went out of the house scarcely bothering to acknowledge her children, let alone her husband. There was no question but that Maman was under huge strain and deserved a great deal of sympathy, yet her attitude discouraged any commiseration. Ted particularly felt alienated from her. "I don't understand her," he grumbled. "It's poor Pa we should be feeling sorry for, and she just doesn't seem to care."

"That's not fair!" Shirley retorted. "It's very hard for Maman too. Don't forget that it's only a few months since her mother died." Anyhow Ted was a fine one to talk; after all he would be leaving for France in five months' time and would be well out of the way of these domestic wrangles. His sister was more circumspect, because she could see the situation from all angles and pitied both her parents. Moreover, she had an uneasy intimation that Ted's forthcoming departure, her illness and its effects and Pa's hallucinations and his increasing disability were all manifestations of the same fundamental malaise that was inevitably pointing to a major disruption in their lives.

To make matters worse, as her leg grew in strength, Pa's deteriorated. "It's the old war wound again," he observed, stating the obvious and gritting his teeth against the pain. Although he needed stronger pills, as his current ones were no longer effective, he refused to call Dr Forbes. Shirley could not understand why until one morning, while dusting the furniture in the dining room in her mother's absence, she came across a bill propped up on the mantelpiece behind the clock. It was from Dr Forbes outlining the cost of treatment provided to the household over the past six months. She was shocked by what she read, because it had not occurred to her that there could be so many huge expenses associated with her own illness or with Pa's wound and his hallucinations. Dr Forbes had always appeared to be simply an old friend of the family who came to offer his services without charge in a very relaxed manner. The figures on the bill abruptly put paid to that impression.

Of course that bill might explain a great deal about the present circumstances. For instance, worry about the bills was most certainly weighing heavily on Pa's precarious state of mind and increasing his anxieties. Poor Maman too! How wrong they had been to suspect her of abandoning her family, because it was most likely that she was taking on more work to supplement the family income. Shirley was ashamed of her earlier resentment towards and suspicion of her mother, wishing that she herself were strong enough to take up her job again, or even go out into the world and find full-time work, to help pay the mounting bills, which was what she and Ted had intended to do last autumn when Pa had been very depressed and had talked about moving house to some business over in south-east London.

There was, however, a certain awkwardness in going back to work for the Salvatores after the various problems associated with the diamond, which in the flurry of her return home and the birthday party, together with the resulting tiredness, had again slipped Shirley's mind. She had not searched it out since coming out of hospital. Who knows, it might no longer be there at the bottom of her stocking drawer. It was Maman who brought the subject up the following day. She was as good as her promise and appeared early in the afternoon, shortly before Edith and Uncle Horace left. "So, *ma Chérie*, what is all this about a diamond that you were given?" she asked as she sat down with a cup of coffee when the visitors had gone. "You wrote to me about it, you remember?"

"Yes, that's right," Shirley replied, pulling a not-so-pretty face. "I was so excited at the time. I had never seen anything so beautiful, all bright and shining, reflecting all the colours of the rainbow. It was just before the audition at Sadler's Wells and Mrs Salvatore promised me it would bring me luck – which I suppose it did, because the audition went well and I was offered a place, but after that it all went wrong and I wish I had never been given it. At first I was so pleased with it I told Pa that evening. He wasn't pleased at all. He insisted that I should take it back to the Salvatores because it was obviously a very valuable heirloom, and they should give it to someone in their own family. Ted even said they might come searching for it and beat us all up."

"So did you give the diamond back to the Salvatores?" Maman enquired gently.

"No," Shirley admitted in embarrassment, "you see I wanted to keep it just for a little while and then I fell ill."

"So where is it now?" her mother asked without casting any aspersions on her daughter's duplicity.

"It's in my bedroom, or at least it should be." She explained her worries about Francesca. "Ah, well," said Maman, "before we accuse anyone of scheming, even in our hearts, let's go and see. Come on, the exercise will do you good."

They climbed the stairs – still a slow undertaking – and went into Shirley's bedroom. "You sit down on the bed. Shall I have a look for it?" Maman suggested, calmly taking control of the situation, as she always had in the past whenever there was a crisis. She went over to the chest of drawers, opened one of the small top drawers, plunged her hands into the muddle of underwear and stockings, and eventually pulled out the small box. "Is this it?" she asked as she gave the box to her daughter. "It wasn't easy to find in that chaos!" she added. Shirley opened the box, and there inside was the diamond in its pendant setting. "So it's there after all, is it?" Maman said, smiling. Shirley was humbled by the discovery and very ashamed of suspecting Francesca of having designs on it. "It is certainly very beautiful, isn't it?" Jacqueline said. "I propose taking the pendant with me when I go to work on Monday, if you don't mind, because there is a jeweller near the Embassy and I can ask him to value it for the insurance, and don't worry: your father will not know anything about it."

A couple of weeks later, when the snow had melted and bright-yellow and deep-purple crocuses were heralding the arrival of spring, Shirley was contemplating a short unaccompanied walk when Maman arrived home earlier than usual. "I took time off work to go to the jeweller's," she explained, "because he said he would have the pendant back from the valuation by now. Here it is, but I'm afraid it's not good news. The diamond and the pendant are much less valuable than you were led to believe! When I saw it for the first time, I thought it was artificially bright for a real diamond, and the valuation has confirmed that. It is simply a rhinestone in a silver setting. Anyhow, we don't need to tell your pa about it, do we? Or if we do, we can tell him that it's just an ordinary piece of jewellery of no great value." She gave Shirley the box to put away in her drawer. "It is quite nice," she said, "you can wear it when you go out to dances with your friends and you won't have to worry about losing it."

Shirley was surprised and dismayed, but suppressed her disappointment that the sparkling jewel was not a diamond at all and decided that Maman, as usual, was right. After a pause, she announced brightly, "I'll tell you something."

"So what is that?" Maman asked frowning.

"I'm actually quite glad it's a fake," Shirley replied. "It didn't bring me the good luck that Mrs Salvatore promised, or if it did, it brought it and then took it away again and a whole lot of very bad luck has followed on from that. Anyway, it's much better not having to lie to Pa; I can tell *him* it's not what the Salvatores thought it was, but I could pretend to *them* that it is the real thing. I'd still feel a bit uncomfortable about it though, but never mind. Let's hope I'll be able to find a proper full-time job soon. I was thinking of going for a little walk. Would you like to come too? If so, I'll be down in a minute."

While Jacqueline went downstairs to put her coat and hat on, Shirley opened her stocking drawer once again and pulled out the box. The pendant lay in its worn setting, but the more she looked at the bright, shiny object and took it into the palm of her hand, the more she began to have her doubts about it. It was certainly the same size and shape as the gemstone she had entrusted to her mother, but unaccountably it did seem brighter and whiter, just as Maman had said. Moreover, it did not give off that fascinating multi-hued sparkle; nor did the colour of the otherwise identical setting and chain seem to resemble the one she remembered very precisely. The metal seemed harsher, greyer than the piece of jewellery she had given her mother to take to the valuer.

"Could the valuer have tricked Maman?" She wondered. Here was a puzzle she had no way of solving. Should she tell Maman her suspicions? If she did, Maman would feel very guilty and upset at taking the pendant away in the first place, and she would not know what to do either, except perhaps to go to the police. The other possibility was that Francesca had in fact taken it while Shirley was in hospital and then made off to Italy with it in her luggage, substituting a fake. Shirley decided that it would be simpler to wear the pendant and chain and forget about the mystery, even if that incurred losing a valuable asset to which she, in any case, did not feel entitled, so she attached it round her neck and went out for a walk.

Despite her earlier intention of going out alone, Shirley was pleased to have her mother's company. They set out up the road with hesitant steps, but as they approached the corner, Shirley's pace quickened until she fairly ran into the newsagent's on the Parade. The welcome for her there was ecstatic. "And you're wearing the diamond!" Mrs S. exclaimed. "You see, it has brought you good luck!" Shirley let this comment pass with a nod of the head, fingering the pendant with a smile as if in demonstration of her gratitude. Coming out of his office to see what all the fuss was about, Mr S. appeared in the doorway.

"Meessa Shirlia, Meessa Shirlia! You come-a back to work-a for us!" he exclaimed. Maman assured them that Shirley would do so as soon as she was strong enough, but, she insisted, not before then. Amid excuses for not staying longer on account of Shirley's health, they beat a hasty retreat from the excesses of the paper shop.

"How do you feel now?" her mother asked once they were outside.

"All the better for being out of doors!" Shirley replied happily. "I've been shut up inside for too long."

"Do you think you could walk as far as the ballet school? Would you like that?" Maman suggested.

After some hesitation, she replied eagerly, "Yes, I think I would!"

Their pace slowed after a quarter of a mile or so as the strain began to assert itself again in Shirley's leg, but then as one they both stopped in their tracks altogether. "What is that? Can you see it?" Maman asked, pointing to a white board attached to a fence a hundred yards or so further on.

Shirley squinted. "It looks like a 'For Sale' sign," she said. "I do believe it's on that little bit of fence outside the dance school!"

"Surely not!" Maman said, echoing her daughter's disbelief. As they came closer, there was patently no doubt about it. The ballet school, or at least the house, was up for sale.

"Oh, no!" Shirley cried out in despair. "It can't be closing down!" She almost leapt up the steps up to the front door and turned the handle. The door opened. All was quiet inside. She went as far as the reception desk, where Stephanie, the secretary, apparently the only person in the building, was organizing papers on her desk.

She looked up. "Ah, Shirley," she said impassively, "we haven't seen you in a long time. Are you all right?"

Taken aback by this chilly welcome, Shirley replied meekly, "Yes, I'm all right, thank you."

There followed an awkward hiatus during which nobody said anything, and the secretary returned to her task. Maman, indignant at such discourtesy, broke the silence. "You must be aware," she said curtly to the bowed head on the other side of the counter, "that my daughter has been very ill. This is the first time she has been out and she wanted to come and see her dance school and meet dear Miss Patience."

Stephanie looked up again, surprised at being taken to task. "Yes, I see. I'm sorry," she said, though it was not clear what she saw, nor what she was apologizing about. "Perhaps you did not know that Miss Patience has left and the school is closing down." Shirley's left leg folded under her in much the way that it had when she had slid down the steps onto the beach in Brighton; had her mother not been standing right beside her, she would have fallen to the floor.

She leant heavily on Maman's arm as they left the house without a word. "I can't believe that Miss Patience didn't tell me! I would have thought I'd be the first to know!" Shirley cried as they staggered back home in the dying light.

"I am surprised too, but maybe there's more to it than we know," said Maman. In shock they speculated as to the causes of this sudden development without coming to any plausible conclusion. "I expect," said Maman, "that she didn't want to upset you, so perhaps that was why she kept quiet about it. I'm sure she will get in touch and explain what has happened." Shirley could not accept any of Maman's excuses on Miss Patience's behalf. She became more and more agitated as she dwelt upon the injustice that someone she admired and respected could treat her in such an offhand manner. By the time they reached home, her agitation had grown into a fiery rage, and there was little that Maman could do to calm her down. "Chérie," she said as she began to prepare the supper, "I think you should lie down on the sofa for a little while. I'm sure Miss Patience did not expect you to go to the dance school today. She is a good, kind lady. She probably wanted to tell you the news herself. Maybe she will write you a letter." In exasperation Shirley stormed out

wishes for a full and speedy recovery and tell her that she will always be welcome here, either as a dancer when she is well enough, or in any other capacity behind the scenes or at front of house. I hope that you will continue to give her the benefit of your excellent tuition and guidance.
Yours most sincerely,
Ninette de Valois

Madam had signed off with her own signature. At the bottom of the page Miss Patience had written a note to Shirley to the effect that there was no need for her to acknowledge the letter as she had already done so.

In her excitement Shirley dashed back into the kitchen. "Maman!" she yelled. "It's from Madam, saying that I can go back to Sadler's Wells when I am well enough!"

"*Voilà!* That is excellent news!" said Maman, turning round from stirring a sauce in a pan on the stove. "But you said there were two letters in the envelope. What about the other one?" Shirley went off to fetch the other letter and soon returned with it.

"This one is from Miss Patience herself," she said, scratching her head as if she did not know how to interpret the contents. Shall I read it to you?" Maman signalled her approval with a wave of her free hand. "So, here goes," said Shirley, "she says:

"Dear Shirley,
"I enclose a letter that may surprise you as much as it surprised me. There is no need to acknowledge it, as I have already done that, or return it to me, as it concerns you alone. I am sorry I did not send it to you earlier, but I thought that at the height of your illness you might find it upsetting. I hope you will regard it as very good news and will one day be able to take up Madam's kind offer. You clearly made a great impression on her.

"I have some news of my own, which I should like to share with you, my prize pupil. Much as I love my work, I feel that I have reached the age when retirement beckons, not because I am tired of teaching ballet, but because I find the administration too wearisome and dispiriting. So I have decided to close the school and sell the house. There is another development in my life that has contributed to this decision, namely that I am to be married to an old friend. He has a large house on the south coast and is able to accommodate

of the kitchen, limped into the sitting room and closed the door. She sat down heavily in one of the armchairs.

"How many more doors will close in my face?" she asked herself angrily. It was bad enough to have to contend still with the after-effects of infantile paralysis, but the end of her beloved dance school, where she had spent so many idyllic hours and where she had secretly in her heart of hearts clung on to the hope that she would find the encouragement and the means to achieve a total recovery and a resumption of her career prospects, was an unbearable blow. She felt cheated, cheated by everyone around her, cheated by that stupid diamond, cheated by fate, cheated by life and cheated by Miss Patience, cheated even by her parents who individually were their normal sensible selves, but who, together, had not a civil word to say to one another.

She wanted to tear something apart and dug her fingers into the upholstery, ready to rip out the filling, but stopped when her right hand touched something stuffed down between the heavy velveteen cushions and the side of the chair. Pulling it out, she found that it was an envelope, not just a discarded empty envelope, but a sealed envelope with a thick letter inside. She looked at it more closely. It was addressed to her, in Miss Patience's hand.

She summoned all her energy and agility to stand up quickly and, taking the envelope with her, went into the kitchen. "Maman! You won't believe this! It's a letter from Miss Patience. I remember now. She gave it to me at my birthday party, or rather, I think she slipped it down the side of the armchair and I forgot all about it!"

"*Voilà!*" was Maman's laconic reply, as if to say, "I told you so."

"Go and read it and tell me what it says." Shirley returned to the sitting room, sat down slowly and opened the envelope, which contained not one but two letters. First she read the one headed "Sadler's Wells Ballet Company": it was a typed letter, addressed to Miss Patience and bore the date 25th October 1937.

Dear Nora,

I write to tell you how sad I am to hear of the illness of your pupil Shirley Marlow. She proved to be an exceptionally talented dancer when she came to the Wells for an audition, so much so that I was intending to appoint her to the status of principal dancer in the company after a suitable period of initiation. Please give Miss Marlow our very best my mother as well. I expect to be moving in March. I hope you will come and visit us there.

"*Meanwhile do your exercises and get well as fast as you can without overdoing it.*

"*Your admiring teacher,*
Nora Patience

"Oh dear, there's no home address for me to write to, only the ballet school, and that may be closed if I send a reply there. Miss Patience will be wondering why I didn't write sooner!" Shirley lamented.

"Don't worry," said Maman, as she spooned a cream sauce over a platter of delicately cooked meat, "I'll call in on my way to work and ask that secretary for the address and then you will be able to stay in touch. Give Ted a shout, will you, *ma Chérie*? The supper is ready and we should eat it while it is hot. Your father can have his when he comes in."

No sooner were the words out of her mouth than there was a rumpus at the front door. Shirley looked round to see her father hurling himself in through the opening. "Help! They're chasing me!" he shouted, slamming the door behind him. Maman stood stock-still, not batting an eyelid; Shirley moved towards her father, but Ted came charging down the stairs and took his father by the arm.

"Come on, Pa," he said, "you need a little sit-down." He led him into the lounge and urgently called out over his shoulder, "Somebody bring some brandy please!" Maman did not move. Her face was a study in sullen disdain.

"Shall I get the brandy and sugar?" Shirley asked. Maman simply raised one eyebrow.

30

It came as no surprise to Shirley the next morning to find her father seated alone at the breakfast table. There was no sign of her mother. Pa was reading a newspaper that Ted must have brought in after his paper round before going to school. Sometimes, if there was a spare copy, Mrs Salvatore would give it to him to bring home. This always involved an element of surprise: one day it might be *The Times*, another the *Daily Mirror*, but Pa was usually quite happy with either as, whichever it was, it was free. Today, despite the free paper, he did not look at all happy: in fact he looked downright miserable. His skin was sallow and drawn, while the bags under his eyes spoke of yet another sleepless night caused by the panic attacks, compounded by the persistent pain in his wound, which had woken the whole household, and possibly the neighbours as well. He had pulled a chair close to where he was sitting, and on this he was resting his leg.

Shirley grieved at the sight of him, particularly when she remembered how well he had coped with Maman's absence in France and what a tower of strength he had been during the whole long period of her own illness. She recalled that, as Ted had told her, he had driven the twelve or so miles to the hospital every day after work to visit her, often, apparently, in the early days while she was unconscious, from behind one of those glass panels. Later, he would sit silently in the waiting room waiting to hear news of her condition from the nurses or from the consultant, Mr Harper, who were caring for her in the white room.

As her condition improved and he was allowed to visit her, he had brought her magazines and flowers, chocolates and fruit. He never had much to say for himself, and although he tried to make conversation, he would run out of words unless he happened to be talking about his model-railway club, or his car or some famous engine that had come into the yard at work for repairs. He rarely talked about the news, though his brow furrowed whenever he did happen to mention events in Spain or Germany. She, on the other hand, tried to fill the gaps in their conversation with lively accounts of the day's happenings in the hospital, not that there was much to tell on that score since very rarely did anything of interest occur, until, that is, she found herself on the rehabilitation ward being rehabilitated by Sister Kenny. Then indeed there was plenty to tell, because Sister Kenny's expansive Australian personality had brought a whiff of the bush and the outback, the South Pacific and above all, the sun, into the wintry atmosphere of a drab south London hospital, where death lurked in the wings ready to grab a young patient and whisk him or her away.

Today, the sight of her father looking so wretched at the breakfast table filled her with pity for him. "Is there anything I can do for you, Pa?" she asked, desperate to be able to help him.

"No, I'm afraid I don't think there is, Shirl," he replied sadly, "unless you can wave a magic wand over this leg of mine as that Australian woman seems to have done for yours. Oh, and rid me of the shell shock too, so that I can stop waking your mother with my rantings and ravings."

Shirley considered for a while, then cautiously enquired, "I wonder, what do you think it is that brings these attacks on?"

"Oh, I know that well enough," he replied. "It's my work. Don't misunderstand me: I love the trains, but when I have to climb down to inspect them from underneath, I don't know why, but I get the jitters and I go hot and cold all over, and it's getting worse. I can't think of any alternative, though, and here I am off work again!"

"Yes, I understand," Shirley said thoughtfully. "Couldn't you get another job?" she asked.

"I wish I could, but what can I do?" he replied.

She took a deep breath before launching into an idea that had suddenly occurred to her. "Do you remember how much you liked working in the newsagent's when you took over my shift? I wonder if we couldn't find a similar job for you. It would be less stressful than working on the railways." He did not reject the idea; instead his face brightened gradually as he turned it over.

"Mm," he said, "I think you might have something there, Shirl. You're right: I did enjoy doing your shift. I haven't given it much thought lately because I've been too busy, and the Salvatores said they could cope until your return, which I suppose will happen quite soon." Shirley nodded. Indeed, she was contemplating an experimental return to her part-time job, as her leg grew stronger by the day and did not appear to have suffered unduly from the walk the previous afternoon.

Pa stood up briskly. "I'm going to back the car out of the garage and go over to your granny's," he announced. "Do you want to come? I'll stop at the call box on the way to find out if she's at home." Shirley was perplexed as much by her father's sudden change of mood, from pained lethargy to ready enthusiasm, as by his suggestion of visiting his mother. She was far less enthusiastic about calling on her granny than he was, but there was no time to ask the reason for his abrupt decision, because he was already on his way to the garage and shortly afterwards she heard the sound of the cranking of the starter motor. Curious to find out what he was planning, she grabbed her coat and went out to the waiting car. "Hop in," he said. "I had a bit of trouble getting her started, but now she's rearing to go."

"Won't you tell me what all the hurry is about?" Shirley asked after settling her left leg into a comfortable position. "I don't expect you'll remember," Pa began to explain, "but when you came back from France in September I was having a rather bad time. Mother suggested that I might be interested in buying a business over in south-east London from some relatives of hers who were thinking of retiring. At the time, although I mentioned it to you all one evening, I didn't really take it seriously, and anyhow I felt better as soon as I started taking Dr Forbes's pills, so I didn't give it any more thought till now. The truth is that the pills are losing their power and Dr Forbes says he doesn't have anything else to offer me, so I need to find another occupation. What's more, the business is a newsagent's and, since helping out up the road, I learnt a lot from the Salvatores and I grew to like working there. I reckon I could manage a business like that and, when you suggested it, I thought it might suit you too. Well, that is until you're fit enough to go back to your dancing. So this morning we are going over to your granny's to find out if she knows whether the business is still up for sale. 'Striking while the iron's hot' you might say!"

Shirley was impressed at her father's speed of action, even more at his speed of thought. She was also grateful that he had included her in his calculations, especially now that the dance school was closing down and Miss Patience was moving away, although of course he did not know that. The news, which the previous afternoon had come as such a body blow, today assumed a different perspective, because the closure of the dance school freed her to move away without regret. Her only misgiving was on her mother's account. "I think it's a good idea," she said encouragingly, "and I'd love to work in that sort of business for the time being, but what about Maman? I do know she doesn't want to move from here for anything in the world; this may be second best to France for her, but she loves her house and it's very convenient for her."

"Yes, I don't know how she'll take it," Pa said with some hesitation, "but let's do a little research first before we cross too many bridges, shall we?"

Granny Marlow was not particularly pleased to see them. "My friends are coming to tea this afternoon," she complained when she opened the door to them, "but you'd better come in. Not for long, mind; I have a great deal of preparation to do before four o'clock."

"But, Mother," Pa protested, "it's only ten o'clock in the morning!"

"That's as may be," she retorted, "but I have to make cakes and put out the best china! It may need dusting first!"

With tongue in cheek, Shirley came to her father's rescue. "We won't stay long, Granny, but Pa has something to ask you. If we could have a cup of coffee, I'll get out the china for your tea party while you have a chat."

Granny quashed Shirley's suggestion outright. "No, no, certainly not! I can't have you handling my best china: you'd be sure to break something! I'll do it after you've gone. Oh! I suppose I'll have to make a pot of coffee. But you'll have to sit in the kitchen and we'll talk there while I start my baking." Shirley turned away, trying to hide a life-enhancing grin.

Pa sat down by the table in the spacious kitchen and, while Shirley creamed butter and sugar for the first of her grandmother's sponge cakes, he told his mother the reason for their visit. "I've no idea what Archie's doing," she said tartly. "It's rather late to be asking about his business. I told you he was intending to sell up months ago."

"If you had his address, then I could get in touch with him myself," Pa replied, trying to appease her wrath. With a vexed sigh, his mother opened a drawer in the kitchen table, from which she pulled out a tattered address book.

"Look him up in there," she instructed, and ring him up yourself. I'm too busy to be dealing with this today." Pa was unusually quick off the mark. He took the address book out into the hall and, having located Archie's number, dialled it immediately, before his mother realized that he was using her telephone.

He came back a little while later in an aura of triumph, both at having been able to use her phone and at the success of the call. "Thank you,

Mother," he said, putting the address book back in the drawer. "Archie says he hasn't sold his business yet and we would be welcome to go over there and see it later this morning!"

His mother gave him a horrified stare when she looked up from her mixing bowl. "Oh, really!" she said crossly. "I didn't say you could use *my* phone, and not for such a long call. You must have been on the phone for ten minutes at least! I meant you to ring from a phone box. As I'm always saying, you should have a phone installed in your own home, and then you wouldn't be taking advantage of poor old people like me!"

"We must be off," Pa declared, unrepentant and downing the remains of his coffee. Come on, Shirl, let's be going!"

Shirley jumped to her feet. "There you are, Granny," she said. "I've creamed the mixture for you. Add the eggs and the flour and you'll have one sponge all ready to go in the oven. Thanks for the coffee. I must be going with Pa. Don't bother to see us out. Goodbye!" They made a dash for the door, climbed into the car and drove off before Mrs Marlow could remonstrate further. On the way across south London, neither of them referred to the less than friendly reception given to them by their close relative; instead they congratulated themselves not only on account of its highly satisfactory outcome, but also on their own extraordinary prowess in making such a quick getaway.

"I didn't know I could run like that any more," Pa remarked, pleased at his own sudden spurt of athleticism.

"No, nor did I!" Shirley exclaimed. "My poor leg is so much better!"

Granny's cousin Archie lived above his shop, which was about a hundred yards from a suburban railway station. The building, at the end of a terrace, had little to recommend it aesthetically, presenting an intimidating, grimy façade to the road. At the back it overlooked the railway line and at the front the busy thoroughfare. Shirley was discouraged since, as she said to herself, Maman most certainly would not approve of it. There was not a tree in sight.

Pa, on the other hand, was in his element: he had not seen Archie for years and they immediately struck up a relaxed conversation reminiscing about old times and catching up on family news. Archie gave them a tour of the property, which was pleasanter inside than out, and he and his wife Eileen invited Shirley and her father to stay for lunch. "It's a nice area; we've made many friends here," she said reassuringly, "and with the station so close you can get into central London in no time at all."

"As for the business," Archie said, "you'd have no trouble, Reggie. It sounds from what you say that you know a lot about it already, and I'd be happy to help out to start with. We're not moving far away, only down the road and round the corner, so I could guide you through the takeover period and I'd be happy to come and to help out if you need me." It seemed as if it was all settled once Pa and Archie had agreed on a purchase price, which would certainly be covered by the sale of the family home. Although Shirley herself had first mooted the idea, she was alarmed to find that her father was so readily agreeing to a monumental upheaval in their lives, the more so because she was aware that she was viewing the situation through her mother's eyes and, as such, was not pleased with what she saw.

It was obvious that both Archie and Eileen, both of them undemanding and unsophisticated, were quietly satisfied with their way of life. They showed off their property with pride for, indeed, they had created a successful business to judge from the constant flow of customers for newspapers, magazines and tobacco, and had made a comfortable flat out of the two upper floors. If Shirley had been hoping that the long flights of stairs would deter her father, she was disappointed, for he bounded up the steep flights like a two year old, eagerly admiring everything he saw, particularly the view. "Look at this, Shirl!" he exclaimed. "This is perfect! I can sit up here all evening and watch the trains go by!" He pointed across a yard down below, which was so small as to be almost invisible from the upper floors, to the gleaming railway lines beyond. Shirley credited her father with the best of intentions, aware that in purchasing the business he was attempting to provide her with a future, but dreaded her mother's reactions.

Maman, a country girl whose notion of city life had been formed by trips to Paris and work at the French Embassy in central London, would never agree to a property with the roar of traffic at the front and the roar of trains at the back all day and all night. It was even worse if you considered what she would be leaving: her neat, stylish semi-detached house with its pretty garden that she loved so much, in a tree-lined road where a passing car was the exception rather than the rule. She would pine for her flowers at all times of year. There would be nowhere to sit outside on a fine day, and the seasons would be registered not by new growth in spring, fragrant blooms in summer, harvests and the glory of changing colours in autumn, but by the angle of the sun glinting on the railway lines. As for Ted, he would be well out of it, for it was the exact opposite of what he wanted from life.

Shirley was silent on the journey home, though her father was ebullient and would not stop talking about his plans. His mind was made up: he would hand in his notice on the railways, sell the house and buy the business. It was the obvious solution to his present troubles. He was certain that there would be plenty of money to spare to redecorate the flat and render it attractive to his wife. He seemed so determined and so certain that Shirley worried that he might not even tell Maman about his project until it was too late. "You will tell Maman, won't you, Pa?" she urged him, unable to keep quiet any longer.

"All in good time, all in good time," he replied unconvincingly.

"But you can't leave it until the house is sold!" she exclaimed indignantly.

"We'll see," was his only answer.

The question did not arise as soon as Shirley would have liked, because Maman was so animated that evening that Pa had no opportunity even to begin to propose his plans. "I am making us a special dinner," she announced cheerfully, "and then I have good news to tell you!" Ted, who was drawn to the kitchen by the rich aromas emanating from within, regaled his mother and his sister with a vivid account of a rugby match in which he had scored three tries against a rival school that afternoon.

"Now that's something I shall miss!" he declared.

"You can find a rugby club in France; I am sure of that," Maman said, "though I remember that some years ago our team was banned from the international competition because of violence on the pitch, but I expect that is over now." Pa had gone into the sitting room to listen to the news on the wireless and did not emerge until Maman called out, "*À table, à table!*" She served Pa's favourite dish of *rognons à la moutarde* – sautéed kidneys with mustard. Then, after dinner, she stood up and said, "I have an announcement to make!" Reggie, Shirley and Ted all held their breath in trepidation at what sort of announcement this might be and opened their mouths wide while she spoke. "I have been asked by the Embassy," she went on, "to go to America, to Washington, for a month!" Ted whistled through his teeth, while Shirley and her father sat in stunned silence.

31

The summer sun shone into the bedroom around the edges of the closed shutters, creating a rectangular halo of bright golden light, disturbing Shirley's fitful early-morning sleep in which she was drowsily weighing up all the events and the changes of the past month. It was not a deep sleep, because she had already been woken by the chugging of the tractor when someone, probably her grandfather or maybe Ted, backed it out of the cart shed up by the gate. This disturbance was followed by the clanking of a piece of farm machinery, mostly likely the new reaper-binder which Pépé had proudly shown Ted and Pa on their arrival in France two weeks ago. Shirley had not shown much interest in these acquisitions, though she had been struck by the change in his appearance.

On their previous visit to Trémaincourt, before Mémé's death last September and, for that matter, for as long as she could remember, Pépé's expression had always verged on the dour side, with his features set in an impassive frown, and his communication skills almost non-existent. Since last summer, he had become surprisingly relaxed, cheerful and talkative. Indeed, in an unprecedented show of enthusiasm on the arrival of his grandchildren and their father, he had hugged his granddaughter and addressed her personally instead of simply acknowledging her presence with a nod. "*Et voilà, ma petite Chérie! Comment vas-tu?*" he had said, as if these were words he had been formulating at the back of his mind for about eighteen years but which had never succeeded in reaching his vocal chords. The change was unquestionably due in part to the new tractor and reaper-binder, the first of which, he had informed them, had halved the time spent ploughing, and the second of which was going to reduce not only the time spent harvesting, but also the cost, because he hoped he would have to employ fewer labourers out in the fields.

This was not the whole story. Pépé had, according to Maman's account, at first sat motionless for hours on end, unable to come to terms with Mémé's loss. So distraught was he that Maman was afraid that he might waste away and soon go to join his wife in the graveyard. However, she had had the bright idea of asking her mother's cousin Céline, who had retired from her work at the *château*, to cook meals for him and attend to the daily chores. He had raised no objections because he already knew Céline and accepted her intervention as an easy solution to the problem of running his home. What nobody had anticipated was the sudden and dramatic transformation that she was to bring about.

Not only did Céline do all those things on a daily basis that had previously been Mémé's domain, such as tending the vegetable plot, milking the cows, making butter and cheese, cooking mouth-watering dishes and cleaning till everything in the house shone, but she also in no time at all left her widow's cottage on the estate and moved into the farmhouse with Pépé. She could have been a younger reincarnated version of Mémé, so similar was she to her deceased cousin, except that she seemed to be endlessly happy, filling the house with laughter, even over the most contentious matters. "You know, Chérie, I told your grandfather," she announced with evident satisfaction, "that, if he wanted me to cook his meals, he would have to allow me to sit at the table and eat them with him. I was not going to stand and serve him, like your poor dear grandmother did. Oh, no! I did that for my Gabriel, God bless his soul, but never again! This is the twentieth century and times are changing!" Céline's word was law, and clearly Pépé had decided not to argue with her for fear of losing her.

Shirley enjoyed the company of this lively lady of indeterminate age, whose forceful opinions were expressed with such joyful eloquence that no one, least of all Pépé, who always wore a broad smile on his weather-beaten face, ever thought of gainsaying her. Moreover, because she was so like Mémé in appearance, her presence was comforting rather than obtrusive or irksome. So at mealtimes they all sat together: Shirley, Ted and their father with their grandfather and his housekeeper. The most remarkable difference from the visits of their early childhood, especially at mealtimes, was that Pa was with them while Maman and Mémé were not.

The sale of the house and the consequent purchase of the newsagent's over in south-east London had left Pa with some spare cash, most of which he spent on renovating the shop and the flat above it. He had inherited an employee, a young lady called Tilly, from Cousin Archie, the former owner, and Tilly proved to be such a reliable and knowledgeable asset that he felt quite confident about leaving the business in her hands with help from Cousin Archie for three weeks in the low season, the silly season in terms of news, while he took a well-earned holiday with his son and daughter. Often he had remarked with nostalgia how much he loved France and how he hankered to return to that country which had given him so much, but he could not face the challenge because of those wartime experiences that had damaged him in body and in soul and still haunted him with a terrible threatening power.

Nonetheless, once he had given up his job working with the huge, dark, menacing engines on the railways, day and night, winter and summer, his shell shock and night terrors abated and he began seriously to consider a trip to Trémaincourt. The clinching argument which overcame all other considerations was that he wanted to spend as much time as possible with his son, who had left school that summer, and who, for all he knew, might be spending the rest of his life across the Channel, settling in and working the farm. If that were to be the case, he would have to reconcile himself to visiting his old haunts again, however traumatic some of the memories associated with them were.

Reggie even briefly considered travelling by car, but decided that, given all the other costs he was facing, that was too expensive a luxury. Anyhow, he dreaded some accident befalling his precious motorcar while it was being heaved onto a ship by a crane, for he had heard of cars being dropped into the sea or onto the docks as they were being swung high overhead. He took the journey calmly and, once on shore across the Channel, he found himself in a new country in the process of shaking off its war wounds. He himself could do no less, he decided, especially since the small corner of that country that he knew so well welcomed him as a returning hero, one of its own.

The fact that his wife had not come with them was still a puzzle and a source of disappointment whenever he had time to stop and think about her absence, but, even so, he was sure that she would return to London at more or less the same time as his daughter and himself. He truly expected that her visit to America to work in the French Embassy in Washington was, as she had promised, or at least given him to believe, only a temporary measure, although she had now been away for more than six weeks, when she had originally told them that she was going for a month. He had summoned sufficient generosity of spirit to be glad that she had been given the opportunity to stretch her wings, though in his heart of hearts there lurked the unspoken fear that stretching her wings might mean her taking flight altogether.

That fear had risen uncomfortably close to the surface when she did not return in time to join in the annual visit to her home and her father in France and was reinforced by the uneasy awareness that he and life in England had long demanded much more of her than she had imagined when she married him. Indeed, she had given her best for a long time, for all the years of their marriage and the upbringing of their children. He also knew, but accepted only with reluctance, that she had nobly suppressed her longing for her native country and had made light of the none-too-friendly treatment she had received from her English relatives, the while creating a happy home life and caring for a husband broken by the horrors of war

He vowed to himself that he would try to make life easier and pleasanter for her on her return, but at present there was little or no time to think about the uncertain state of his marriage. No sooner had he, Shirley and Ted arrived at the farm than his father-in-law had set him to work to repair the new tractor, which, since the day of its purchase six months ago, as well as delighting him with the promise of its efficiency, had been infuriating him with its constant teething troubles. The repair was urgent as the corn was ripe and ready to harvest, and, as far as Pépé, who was not given to religious pronouncements, was concerned, the appearance of his son-in-law with his engineering skills was a gift from God. The work on the tractor was for Reggie a joyous distraction from his preoccupations, and from his other project, which was to find an old car or van, probably hidden away in a barn somewhere in the vicinity where it would probably be providing comfortable housing for hens and their chicks.

For some weeks, ever since he had given up his job on the railways, he had been harbouring the idea of doing up an old banger for Ted to allow him some freedom of movement from the confines of the isolated farmhouse. That was not the only reason, however, because Reggie believed that such a project would help him overcome the withdrawal symptoms from the loss of his beloved engines. Once the tractor began to run smoothly, the next priority was harvesting and attending to the reaper-binder, so the plans for Ted's transport – and incidentally his own personal therapy – were still on the waiting list, but his watchful eye had one or two possibilities in view. At the *château* at Mont-Saint-Jean, for instance, there was just such a vehicle draped in wisps of straw at the back of the cow barn. Chickens ran in and out of it through gaping doors that hung by no more than one rusty hinge. No matter, he was fairly certain that the engine was intact and that a couple of weeks' work at most would put it to rights. He had spotted another similar vehicle down in the valley, but he anticipated that the car over in Mont-Saint-Jean would be more easily acquired, given the good relations between his family and Madame de Grandval.

Madame had been delighted to see him and his children, and had given a small party in his honour at which she had opened champagne to celebrate his return after so long, twenty years in fact, since the end of the War. The *château* was just as he remembered it from the days when it had been the headquarters of the Tank Regiment and Jacqueline had worked there. Of course it also brought back memories of that glorious day of their wedding. Such happy memories stood in sharp contrast to the searing recollections evoked by the old tank that stood rusting in the grounds on the very spot where it had been left by the regiment. Although on the one hand it brought back a certain nostalgia for that period of intense camaraderie, loyalty and patriotism, on the other he winced in very real pain when he saw the hole made by the bullet that had pierced his leg, and with a shudder recalled how close the guns had sounded when the Germans had made their final push in 1918, only to be repulsed by the concerted Allied attack. Above all he remembered all those brave companions and friends whose bodies lay buried under French soil. He worried that these images might reawaken his shell shock, but the warmth of the champagne reception that he and his family received from Madame de Grandval – as welcoming and as charming a lady as ever, despite her advancing years – effectively cast those frightening thoughts aside.

Many villagers from Trémaincourt, as well as Mont-Saint-Jean, came to the reception, and naturally enough they all asked about Jacqueline. Their reaction was one of admiration at the success of a local girl: they shook Pa's hand warmly and expressed their congratulations on her posting to the United States. None of them enquired when she would be returning to Europe, although one or two did ask if Reggie had considered joining her there. At this he shook his head and said that wouldn't be possible, because he had his new business to run and had been able to come to France only because he had a reliable team of staff. Little did Reggie know that Céline had already primed the locals by telling them that Jacqueline had gone to work only temporarily in America, at the French Embassy in Washington, DC, and would be returning to England in the autumn.

Paying lip service to this version of her mother's absence, Shirley decided that it was by far the simplest way to account for the trip to America, although she was less sanguine than her father about her mother's departure. Nevertheless, she was careful not to disturb his seemingly optimistic interpretation. "It's a great opportunity for her," he had remarked with a philosophical air, and a semblance of maintaining a purely pragmatic attitude, despite niggling anxieties. "She won't be away for long, and when she comes back we will have the new business up and running; this trip couldn't have come at a better time. She deserves a change of air and will be spared all the trouble of moving." The audience nodded in perplexed agreement.

Shirley, however, remembered only too well her mother's horrified reaction when for the first time Pa drove her over to see the shop and the flat in south-east London where he was proposing to live for the rest of his working life. "*Non, non!* How could he expect me to live there in that dreadful place? And there's all that traffic going past at the front and all the trains at the back!" she had declared to her daughter on their return home. "The air is putrid, foggy all the time. We shall die of asphyxiation there!" She spread her arms wide as if embracing her neat suburban house and its pretty garden. "Doesn't he understand that this is my house? This is where I live and have lived since it was new – here with the garden and the trees. If I have to live in this country at all, I want to stay here!" She broke out in sobs and buried her face in her hands.

Hugging her mother, Shirley had tried to comfort her by stammering half-heartedly that Pa needed a different job because working on the railways in among those monstrous steaming, smoking beasts was contributing to his poor mental health, and he had been presented with something that he was well able to do and something that he enjoyed. She added that perhaps they would not be living for ever in south-east London, because maybe when Pa had grown accustomed to the business and had made a success of it, they would be able to move out of London altogether, but that argument cut no ice. "I don't want to move out of London altogether!" was Maman's immediate retort. "I want to stay here in our lovely house and it's so easy for me to get to the Embassy from here; it would take me all day from over there." She gestured disconsolately in the vague direction of south-east London.

It was in the week after Maman had made her excited announcement about her impending trip to Washington that Pa took her and Ted to view the property. Shirley was fairly certain that the sight of their new home, which had left Maman so wretched and in such a state of despair, had finally clinched her decision to go to America, because when she left in a car sent by the French Embassy to take her to the airport, she gave them not one backward glance. Unbeknown to her husband, she had packed very nearly her whole wardrobe: summer clothes, winter clothes, smart clothes, work clothes, everyday clothes and all the accessories to go with each outfit. After her departure, Shirley had opened her wardrobe to find it pretty much bare, but thought better of sharing that information with her father.

As for Ted, once he had overcome his astonishment at such sudden decisions from both his mother and his father, he had made no comment on either matter except to observe drily to each parent in turn, "If that's what you want, I'm sure it will suit you very well, but you don't need my opinion because you know I won't be here: I'll be in France, remember? Though I expect I'll come back from time to time." And that was the sum total of everything he had to say on all subjects.

Shirley too was initially deeply shocked both at her father's project and by her mother's plans. Her first impressions of the run-down building and the shabby accommodation had not been at all favourable, yet she understood why her father wanted to make this move, even though so far he had not found a garage for his beloved Lanchester and was going to have to park it on the broad pavement in front of the shop. She felt herself to be somewhat responsible for this momentous upheaval in their lives because she had all but encouraged her father in the undertaking.

The truth that Maman preferred to disregard was that those dreadful panic attacks that Shirley and Ted had witnessed, while she was away in France at Mémé's funeral, were most definitely provoked by Pa's job: in spite of the railway being so close to his heart, that job was damaging his health by perpetuating the shell shock from the Great War that could still be so easily aroused when he was under stress. Both children had often, in his absence, discussed what could be done to improve his situation, and each of them had independently come to the conclusion that a job like working in the Salvatores' shop might be just the thing for him, if such a job could be found. He himself had hinted as much when he had taken Shirley's place during her illness.

Since an opportunity had presented itself, Shirley did not want to discourage him, though she sympathized with her mother's point of view. The two factors that more or less coincided – that is, Maman's departure for Washington and her resistance to the move, not to mention her suspected friendship with M. Lavasseur – gave Shirley a genuine cause to fear that she might not return to Europe, and that disturbed her profoundly, but at the same time, she trusted that Maman would not leave her family altogether. She would simply not do anything like that; it was not in her nature.

For her own part, she reasoned that although there were already encouraging signs that she might eventually recover the use of her left leg sufficiently to become a dancer, if not a prima ballerina, her recovery from infantile paralysis was progressing slowly, so she would need to find a secure but physically undemanding job for the time being. Dr Forbes had said as much when he had tapped her knee and pulled the muscles about a bit a couple of weeks ago on her final visit to him before the move. "Be patient a little longer, keep up your exercises," he had advised, "and I think you will find that the flexibility and agility will return." When she had asked how long it would be before she would be fully mobile again, he had said that he would be surprised if her leg were not as good as new in a year's time, but that he couldn't promise anything. With this in mind, she regarded Pa's new venture as a temporary but fortunate situation, because she would be able to earn some money in a fairly agreeable occupation, effectively working at home for as long as was necessary. There was no doubt that her father would need her help, because Tilly was expecting a baby and in six months' time would have to give up work, at least until her baby was old enough to be left with its grandmother.

Although the accommodation was not perfect, it had potential: there were sufficient rooms upstairs and they were large with high ceilings. The room earmarked for Shirley, she was pleased to find, had space for practice exercises, even for a short *barre* along one wall. The redecorations, which were completed just before they came away, had transformed the place so that, had she seen the renovated property, even Maman might have been impressed. True, there was no garden, but as far as

Shirley was concerned that was an advantage, for she was not interested in gardens and, even with Tilly's help in the shop, she and Pa would be far too busy to tend a lawn and flower beds; without Tilly's help they would be hard pressed simply to keep the business going. The great advantage, of course, was that they would be out of Granny Marlow's reach, although the necessary business telephone line meant that she could always get in touch with them. She was unlikely to come over to visit unless Pa collected her and took her home again, because the journey involved changing trains or buses several times.

Having the railway so close at hand suited Shirley very well since that particular suburban line would take her to where she would, when her leg was better, want to go. Unlike her mother, whose destination was Kensington and Belgravia, she was happy so long as she could change to the Northern Line, either at Waterloo or London Bridge, for central London or even the Angel, Islington, since she still cherished the secret longing that one day, perhaps not so distant after all, she might return to Sadler's Wells. If she could dance at Sadler's Wells, instead of little-known provincial theatres, she could always remain hopeful that Alan might be in the audience.

Depressing though the past year had been, the hope sprang eternal that they would meet again, even perhaps on the ferry on the return crossing to Dover. If that proved a false hope, there was in a month's time, exactly a year after Edith's fateful wedding, another opportunity on the occasion of Nora Patience's marriage. Shirley had scarcely been able to believe her eyes when she read the invitation to the wedding in a small village, scarcely more than a hamlet a few miles north of Brighton. She had looked on the map and was fairly certain that that village was the very one she had seen when she and Pa had picnicked on the way to Brighton the previous autumn, the day before the onset of infantile paralysis. She had had a sixth sense at the time and that sense had grown that that was the village where Alan and his family lived: the drawback was that she would rather not meet Alan again while she walked with a limp.

Jean-Luc and his mother had been at Madame de Grandval's for the party in Pa's honour. His mother had perfunctorily kissed Shirley on both cheeks, saying, "I was so sorry to hear of your illness, but I am glad to see that you have made a good recovery," and then turned away to talk to someone else. As for Jean-Luc, he conspicuously did little to conceal his reluctance to greet her. That this ungallant behaviour was prompted by her slight limp was obvious, although Shirley did not care, for she no longer found him attractive. In fact, she wondered why she had ever thought him handsome and charming, because he compared so unfavourably with Alan. Jean-Luc was conceited and ill-mannered, too much influenced by Parisian sophistication, she decided, while Alan was handsome, kind and helpful. She was almost one hundred per cent sure that he would not reject her on account of the limp; nonetheless she did not want to take any chances so decided to keep away from central London, where she expected that she might one day come across him, until she could walk with grace and ease.

32

The clanking farm machinery had gone out of earshot into the fields, leaving Shirley daydreaming, still in bed. Her repose was interrupted by Céline calling from the kitchen, "Chérie, Chérie, are you there? Could you come and give me a hand, please?" Shirley pulled her working clothes on hurriedly and ran into the kitchen. She passed the piano and the photo of her uncle, neither of which were draped in black any more. When, soon after their arrival, Ted had tentatively opened the lid and played a few bars of a popular tune, no one had scolded him. "Ah, Édouard!" Céline exclaimed, clapping her hands in delight. "So you can play! We can sing round the piano in the evening! You would like that, wouldn't you, Daniel?" she said turning to Pépé.

Shirley could not remember Mémé ever addressing her husband by name, let alone asking him if he would like a sing-song in the evening. Nodding benevolently, Pépé had replied, "Yes, why not?" Thereafter Ted had played the piano every evening after the day's work out in the fields was done, and a pleasant sense of contentment fell upon the well-fed inhabitants who sat round the piano humming and singing with a glass of wine in their hands.

Céline was hard at work cutting long slits into a baguette on the huge kitchen table. "Ah," she said, "look what a beautiful day it is! Your grandfather has been so worried about the harvest with all that rain we had last week, so today he has already been out to check that the sun is strong enough to dry out the dampness, and he reckons that by the time they get those machines going the corn will be ready to cut. It's certainly ripe enough for harvesting, and he wants to get it in as soon as he can. He's going to start up the hill on Long Field because he thinks that will be drier than the others; it drains better, you see. Let's hope we don't have any more rain."

Outside, supervised by his grandfather, Ted was gingerly sharpening the blades of the reaper-binder with a file. Once or twice he stopped abruptly and licked a finger. "Oh, look, the poor boy has cut himself again!" Céline exclaimed. "Your grandfather was not sure he should try that task yet but he insisted. Quick! Take a sticking plaster out to him, will you, dear?" She handed Shirley a strip of plaster cut from a roll. Shirley ran quickly out into the yard to attend to her brother, but fortunately the cuts were nothing more than minor scratches, though Pépé was sternly warning Ted how careful he had to be, because that particular job would have to be repeated on each day of the harvest.

As soon as Shirley had patched up Ted's wounds, he, his father and his grandfather drove off in their chugging, clanking vehicles to the fields and she went back into the kitchen, where Céline pointed to a bowl of milky coffee and a plateful of fresh bread ready and waiting on a side table. "Your breakfast is there waiting for you, Chérie," she said, "and as soon as you've drunk up your coffee and eaten your bread, I would like you to help me with this picnic for the workers, if you please. There are just as many of them this year after all, even though your grandfather has his tractor and that other thing, so it will not be any easier for us than it was last year when I came to help your poor dear grandmother – do you remember?"

"Oh, yes, I remember," replied Shirley sadly, recalling how tired poor Mémé had been, even though she and Maman, as well as Céline, had helped to prepare the harvest picnic. Mémé had never complained, so no one had realized how ill she was until it was too late to call the doctor.

"So, what can I do to help?" Shirley asked Céline.

"Well, if I cut the baguettes, you can spread the pâté inside them, and we will fill them with tomatoes and lettuce." A bowl of home-made chicken-liver pâté stood on the table and alongside it were two bowls, one full of lettuce and the other of tomatoes, both from the garden.

"Mémé worked very hard, didn't she?" Shirley observed, looking to Céline for her agreement.

"Yes, dear, she certainly did, like all countrywomen, but she more so than the rest of us. I think her work was the only thing that kept her going after your uncle died in the war. She was such a happy, lively person before that." Céline pulled out a handkerchief and wiped her eyes. "Georges was killed such a long way from home! They never saw him again and were never really sure where he was buried."

Because Shirley had never known her uncle, except from his photo on the piano, she had absolutely no memory of her grandmother being a happy, lively person. Indeed, it was difficult to imagine her as such, for the Mémé she had always known had been quiet and gentle but mournful and rarely smiling. "Your grandfather was the same, absolutely shattered by his son's death, and could scarcely speak as a result of it," Céline went on. "But it was a strange thing, you know. It was as if the two of them had a pact that he wouldn't speak and she wouldn't enjoy life at all after the Great War. But then after she died, it seemed as if he was all at once freed from that pact and he began to be like his old self, never exactly bubbling with life, but warm and friendly, much as he is now." The two of them carried on in silence. Shirley went on pasting and filling baguettes until Céline looked at the clock on the wall and exclaimed, "*Mon Dieu!* The men will be waiting for their coffee! We'll have to hurry!"

The harvest was the aspect of farm life that Shirley loved the most. At this time of year it was easy to overcome her aversion to the discomforts and inconveniences, the mud and the smells. She put the baguettes to one side and went out to the pump in the yard to fill a pan for the coffee, which Céline placed on the hot stove. While it was heating, Shirley returned to the job in hand, listening as she did so to Céline's irrepressible chatter. "Can you believe it?" she said, as she counted out the requisite number of tin mugs and put them in a basket. "Benjamin came up from the village this morning and said that his wife gave birth last night, not to the one baby they were expecting, but to three! And what's more, three girls, so he is not the happiest of men this morning. Says he wants to get out of the house and stay out in the fields working. I'll have to get my knitting needles out and find some pink wool!"

Still busy with bread, pâté, tomatoes and lettuce, Shirley laughed, but her laughter died at the news that three girls were viewed as a disaster, whereas the birth of three boys would have been greeted with delight and endless celebrations. She pulled a face and carried on with her work. "Chérie, that's excellent!" Céline commented, eyeing the pile of baguettes, each wrapped in a red cloth. "I think we have nearly enough there. Let's put them all in the baskets and they will be ready to take up to the fields at lunchtime. Now it's time to take the coffee out. Can you carry this big jug and the basket with the mugs? I'll take these two others with the sugar." They negotiated the puddle in the yard, left by the previous week's rain, and turned out of the gate onto the track which led up to the cornfields about half a kilometre away.

The cornfields spread before them in waves like a sea of gold, swaying in the breeze and glistening in the sunlight. Shirley drew in a deep breath of contentment, standing still in silent wonder at the beauty of the scene. Trees in the distance divided the earth from the sky, which cast its azure veil, stretching out in all directions as far as the eye could see, extending its reach high over their heads and beyond. To the west the sky was brilliantly clear, not a cloud in sight, an indication that there would be no more rain coming from the coast for the time being. *"Allons, ma petite!* The coffee will be cold by the time we get up to Long Field!" Céline called, beckoning her with a shake of her head. Shirley followed her along the track between open fields on both sides: to the right were cornfields, to the left the shiny dark-green leaves of sugar beet. She mused on what a glorious backdrop that scene would make for a ballet.

She vaguely recalled a scene she had seen in a book in school in which there were pictures of medieval harvesters scything a large field, rhythmically working their way up to the top in staggered lines to avoid colliding with each other. Her ballet would be about the harvest and would feature a young girl taking refreshments to the harvesters. At the top of the field, where they paused for breath and a drink, there would appear among their number a tall young man with finely chiselled features who stood out from the rest and attracted her attention; she, the principal ballerina, could feel his eyes settling on her as she put the jug down on a stone slab in the corner of the field. He would come over to her and she would hand him a mug of beer, which he drank quickly, never taking his eyes off her. Drawn to each other, they would perform a *pas de deux* in the middle of the cut corn…

The ballet was taking shape nicely in her mind's eye, but then she and Céline, who was panting under the weight of her provisions, turned a corner into Long Field and the plans for the show were abruptly cut short. They breathed in the sweet, fresh fragrance of the cut corn, but the rows of reapers scything their way up through the glowing corn had disappeared into the past, the same past to which the poor old horses had been consigned since Pépé had bought his new tractor. He was driving it round the field in ever-decreasing rectangles, while Reggie, sitting behind him on the reaper-binder, was trying to control the cumbersome machine which had a habit of straying out of line.

Ted, together with Benjamin, the father of the newborn triplets, and the other labourers, was gathering up the bound sheaves, which they collected into groups of twelve and stood upright in "*moyettes*" as Pépé called them, or "shocks" according to Ted in farming parlance, or "stooks" in Pa's more recognizable terminology. To Shirley they simply looked like yellow wigwams. There was, however, no tall, handsome young man, only the band of workers. She was not disappointed; rather she was delighted to have found the inspiration for a new ballet. It could be completed anywhere at any time, even back in England in the winter. What was important was that she had begun to imagine choreographic sequences again, for the first time since she had reached out, nearly a year ago, with balletic gestures to the parents huddled behind the glass screen at visiting time in the hospital ward. That memory sent shivers down her spine.

The men drank their coffee in silence and returned to their labours. Ted was allowed to take a turn at driving the tractor, which at first, with barely concealed excitement, he did slowly, since intense concentration was essential to keep the lines straight while his father continued his efforts to keep the harvesting mechanism on course. Nonetheless, the reaper-binder held up progress because it broke down often and adjustments had to be made to it.

Mesmerized by the whole slow process, Shirley asked Céline how long it would take to harvest the entire crop. "I don't know, dear, because the machines are new. Did you know that they were bought with your grandmother's savings? In my opinion she should have spent them on herself, but apparently she left your grandfather a nice little windfall – well, that is to say, I found it in a bag under their bed when I was cleaning one day and there was a note in the bag addressed to your grandfather. I don't know precisely what the note said, but I expect it told him that the money was for him. So you see, your grandfather was able to buy the reaper-binder as well as the tractor. Anyhow, I'm no expert on harvesting, but they will be out late tonight, that's for sure. They'll probably have to use torches to finish it off," she said, coming to the end of her lengthy explanation. "Your grandfather wants to finish this field because it's the largest, and then make a start on the Short Field, the one down there at the end of the orchard, if there's time before it's too dark." She gestured along the track down towards the house. "Then, of course, there's that new field over towards Mont-Saint-Jean, the one he acquired earlier this year, also bought with your dear grandmother's money. He said that, with Edward's help, he could manage more land. That seemed sensible to me. Of course that new field is the only one he really owns; the rest belong to the *château*, but he's the tenant farmer. And when he's finished all that there will still be the smaller fields to do."

She bent down to pack the baskets with the empty jugs and mugs. "Come on, we had better go home and collect the lunch and then, don't forget, we have to prepare the supper and I shall need your help for that! The men will not have much time to eat so we must have it ready for them." Leaving her creative ideas aside, Shirley accompanied her back to the house, where they hastily packed up the lunch of baguettes and salads, apples and freshly made lemonade. Céline added several bottles of beer to the baskets, and then they went out again carrying the heavy loads up to the fields.

This was the essence of their working day, every day for several days: it consisted of trudging to and fro to the fields with drinks and food. As soon as one delivery was consumed they returned to the house for the next batch. During the lunch break, while the men rested in the shade under the tall trees at the edge of the field, the two women prepared more baskets of cool drinks and biscuits for the afternoon, and also placed a large earthenware pot full of meat, potatoes and vegetables, which had been marinating since the morning, in the stove for the supper. Traditionally, this was then served on a long trestle table out in the yard. Much of the yard was still damp from the recent thunderstorms, but near the house there was sufficient dry ground for the table. Céline mopped her brow in the heat of the kitchen, but otherwise worked quickly, so much faster than poor Mémé had ever succeeded in doing.

Pépé was beginning to show his age, in spite of his resolute determination to carry on until the end, and could be seen nodding off from time to time over the supper table. Pa dealt with him quite firmly that first evening. "Daniel," he said, "I can see you are tired, so I will drive the tractor tonight and Ted can sit on the reaper-binder." Pépé protested, as was to be expected because he was very taken with his new toys, notwithstanding the setbacks and the breakdowns of the various pieces of machinery. Pa assumed an authoritarian tone, unfamiliar to his children but which doubtless was a remnant of his professional past as a railway engineer, and would hear none of Pépé's objections. "You were asleep at the table, old fellow, so I don't want to be anywhere near if you insist on driving that tractor of yours. It's a powerful machine!" Pépé was silenced.

The skies kept clear, enabling the harvesters to work late into the evening after supper. Shirley was amazed at her father's skill when, even in the twilight, he drove in neater lines than Pépé had achieved, and also he drove faster, so that the labourers had to run to keep up with him. Ted steered the reaper-binder as best he could, while the labourers had the tricky task of holding their torches in one hand and gathering up the bound sheaves with the other as darkness fell. Eventually, when there was only a small patch left standing in the middle of the field, Pa decided that it was time to stop.

Pépé was well satisfied. "We can easily scythe that tomorrow before we start on the new field," he remarked in gruff satisfaction at a good day's work, with some sixty per cent of the corn cut and gathered, bound and collected up in stooks. The next day they all finished off the remaining square with scythes and then, using the tractor and reaper-binder again, began work in the New Field, which was how it would be known henceforth. The smaller patches of arable land that belonged to Pépé, not under tenure from the *château*, were left for the men of the family to harvest later after the jobbing labourers had been temporarily dismissed. They would be needed again, he told them, for bringing in the stooks ready for the arrival of the threshing machine, the use of which was rented out to the local community and shared among the farmers.

During the lull in activity while they waited for their turn with the threshing machine, Reggie went to check over the old car he had seen at the *château* in Mont-Saint-Jean. He would have preferred it to be a van, he said, but since Madame de Grandval had said he was welcome to take it away as she had no use for it and doubted anyone else would want it, he jumped at the opportunity. So once he and Ted, with some help from Pépé and his tractor and trailer, had succeeded in bringing the old vehicle out of retirement, they spent their time out in the yard, first of all taking the car to pieces, sanding and greasing every part, and then putting it back together again. Shirley and Céline did their best to clean up the interior, which in itself turned out to be every bit as arduous a task as renovating the engine, because not only had hens nested inside but pigeons and mice had also made it their home, tearing the upholstery and ripping out the filling, as well as leaving more obvious signs of their presence. When Pa put petrol in the tank and cranked the starter motor, a cheer greeted the engine as it coughed and spluttered its way back to life.

33

Repainting the vehicle was postponed when Pépé insisted that it was time to bring in the stooks, because he had received word that three days hence it would be his turn to use the threshing machine and there was no time to waste. As much of the cut corn as possible would have to be brought into the barn, but not too soon in case it spontaneously combusted – as had happened in a farm near Séringy with disastrous results a year ago – and the rest would have to be brought in on the day the threshing machine came to the farm. All hands were needed, including Shirley's and Céline's, and the work was hard and exhausting. By the middle of that Saturday morning Shirley's back was breaking, her left leg hurt badly and limped more than it had done for months, her hands were sore and scratched and the nape of her neck was scorched by the sun, but she could not allow herself to complain, for Céline, who was more than three times her age, was stoically and rhythmically gathering up the stooks and flinging them up onto the cart.

After the mid-morning break, Shirley suggested to Ted that they might change places for a while: stacking the stooks on the cart looked so much easier than collecting them up on the pitchfork and lifting them into the air. "Oh, all right, if you like," he said, "but you have to put them the right way round for stacking into the barn and then feeding into the thresher when it comes." Shirley clambered up on to the top of the growing load, but found it hard to stay upright; the corn slithered and gave way beneath her feet, and catching each bundle from the pitchfork and putting it in its proper place was much harder than it looked, so eventually she offered to go and fetch the lunch, an offer that was gratefully accepted.

The best part of it was riding home at the end of the day high on the cart on top of the bed of cut corn. Even as a small child, when she had played in the fields while the others worked, she had loved that, riding high like a queen above her subjects and waving to neighbours and strangers as she went. By the end of the long day, when they had filled the barn with the cut corn from Long Field and New Field, Pépé decided to leave Short Field and the smaller patches for the day of the threshing. "We'll need more workers," he said, "but I have never liked to fill the barn too full; it's too dangerous."

The approach of the huge threshing machine, as it was drawn up the lane and round the corner by a large tractor, was heralded by the sort of terrifying thudding that would signal the arrival of an invading giant in hobnailed boots. Seconds later the tractor slowly negotiated the turn into the farmyard and everyone scattered to make room for the lumbering machine, which in no time at all, once it was installed outside the barn, was connected up to the tractor motor by a belt. A pipe for discharging the straw was put into position well away from the house and a sack to receive the grain attached to another pipe. Then the tractor engine was started up and the mechanism began to stir into motion. Ted, Ben and Reggie shovelled sheaves of corn onto the conveyor belt, which sent them into jaws of the machine to be disgorged either as straw or into the sacks as grain. Dust and chaff blew everywhere, filling noses and ears and sticking to eyelashes and beards. The noise was deafening.

Pépé was out on his tractor in the fields away from all the turmoil, gathering up the remaining stooks with a crowd of helpers and bringing them as quickly as possible to the farmyard, where they were gobbled up by the thresher, disgorging the grain and the straw, as fast as Ted and his companion workers could load them onto the conveyor belt. Still there came more and more cartloads of corn, so that it was nearly dark by the time the work was finished and a huge line of grain sacks, piled one on top of the other, lay under the eaves awaiting the massive lorry which would take them to the mill. The mountain of straw almost filled the yard, leaving barely enough space for the trestle tables and benches that Céline and Shirley had brought out of a shed.

Blowing in the evening breeze, chaff and dust kept settling on the white cloths, to Céline's annoyance, though Shirley tried to pacify her by saying that that had always been a problem, but Mémé had thought little of it. "No matter, it will provide a bit of extra nourishment if it blows on to the food," she had remarked philosophically, but Céline liked everything to be perfect. Despite being a country girl born and bred, she had never lived on an arable farm, although she had helped out at many a harvest, so this experience was relatively new to her. Her husband's family had kept a herd of cows and a smallholding, which meant that she was a dab hand at milking, churning butter and cheesemaking, and could easily tend a vegetable plot and orchard, keep hens, ducks and geese and, as a result of her work at the *château*, was used to cooking meals for large numbers of guests. She was not yet used, however, to the inconveniences of living on a working farm and was fast becoming flustered, although Shirley, who had been present at these occasions for as long as she could remember, tried hard to help – and even direct her.

There was a round of applause as the last sheaf went into the thresher. Then the workers turned their backs on it and thankfully slumped onto the chairs grouped around the table. They quenched their thirst from the plentiful jugs of beer and cider put at their disposal before demolishing the first course of *œufs à la russe*. All that day, and for a couple of days past, Céline had been simmering numerous chickens in red wine in preparation for the harvest supper. As the yard had dried out, she had confidently invited the whole village to the feast, though most of the farming community were regretfully too busy with their own harvests, which was probably just as well, as there would not have been room for everyone. Madame de Grandval declined the invitation as she herself was hosting a harvest supper, but Madame de la Croix had accepted with pleasure, although as usual her husband did not come. "He's very busy in Paris," she said, repeating her normal formulaic apology for his absence. She arrived early, on foot, bringing her son Jean-Luc and Hélène, her daughter, with her.

Shirley politely shook hands with Jean-Luc and allowed him to kiss her on both cheeks, but then edged away. She was quite sure that not only did she no longer find him attractive or at all desirable, but began to regard him as odious, particularly when she remembered how disdainfully he had treated her – undoubtedly on account of her limping left leg – at the party given by Madame de Grandval. In addition, by comparison with the muscular, tanned farmworkers, Jean-Luc did not appear to advantage, but looked pale and weedy. She was uncomfortable in his presence, although for his part he seemed unaccountably drawn to her by comparison with his earlier behaviour; out of the corner of her eye she was aware that he was following her whenever she circulated among the guests or went into the kitchen to fetch more food. To her annoyance, he seated himself next to her at the long table and attempted to strike up a conversation, but as Benjamin was sitting on the other side of her, she turned to him and plied him with questions about his tiny daughters.

Unfortunately his replies tended towards the monosyllabic and finally dried up altogether, so Shirley was forced to take notice of Jean-Luc.

He was heaping the sort of praise on her that she would much rather have heard from other lips. "How lovely you have become, Chérie! I was so concerned for you when we met at Madame de Grandval's and so sorry to have missed you last summer!" Shirley did not believe a word of it. Suspicious of his motives, she was anxious not to find herself alone in his presence. He shifted on his chair and leant in her direction. "I want to talk to you, Chérie," he drawled. She pretended not to hear and looked to her father for help, but he was engrossed in conversation with Madame de la Croix; Ted was talking and laughing with Hélène, Jean-Luc's sister, and Céline was not at the table.

"Oh, Céline must have gone into the kitchen!" Shirley exclaimed. "I must go and help her." She stood up hastily and in doing so knocked over her glass: wine spilt over the tablecloth. Calling out "I'll bring a cloth", she ran off.

When she burst into the kitchen, Céline was leaning over the oven bringing out one *tarte Tatin* after the other. She placed them in rows on the table, muttering, "Now for the cream."

"I'll get it!" Shirley blurted out, startling Céline as she dashed past her to the pantry.

"Oh, you surprised me!" Céline said, holding her hand to her heart. "What are you doing indoors? I can manage this perfectly well on my own. Out you go and enjoy yourself!"

Should she take Céline into her confidence? Shirley asked herself, and then, lulled into a sense of security by Céline's similarity to her grandmother, she launched into a tirade that took the older woman by surprise. "No, I am not enjoying myself and I won't go out there again; not that is, if I have to sit anywhere near Jean-Luc. He's horrible and I don't like him." Her eyes flashed in anger.

In astonishment Céline dropped the oven cloth she was holding. "What do you mean, Chérie?" she asked. "He's a lovely young man! I should know: I brought him up from a baby and I always thought of him as the child I didn't have. So I don't know what you are talking about, and I don't understand you! I remember when he was only a little boy he used to say to me, 'Céline, I am going to marry Chérie one day; she is so beautiful!'"

Shirley bit her tongue and realized that she had to find some excuse to explain her anger without making any concessions. "I don't believe that," she said. "He ignored me at the party at Madame de Grandval's, doubtless because of my limp, and now he thinks he can make advances to me!"

"Oh, that!" Céline retorted. "He told me after that party that he was shocked and sorry to see how much you had suffered and didn't know what to say. So I suppose he is wanting to make amends."

Céline was as hurt and angry as Shirley was agitated and indignant, but clearly there would be no sympathy forthcoming from Céline, who was not Mémé, her grandmother, despite the resemblance between them. Shirley saw that her spur-of-the-moment decision to involve Céline, expecting that she could depend on her to give her the same sort of sympathy as Mémé might have done, was a mistake. She apologized hastily and explained, "I just don't like the way he keeps coming closer and putting his arm over the back of my chair."

Céline did not understand. "Oh, Chérie, you are so English! What's wrong with that if he likes you?" she asked. "You should think yourself lucky: there are plenty of girls round here who would be delighted to receive Jean-Luc's attentions – and from what I gather, you did once too. What a catch he would be for you!"

Shirley sighed. "I'm sorry. I shouldn't have said what I did. I am sure he is a very nice young man. I expect I have had too much wine. I spilt some and came in to fetch a cloth."

"Hmm," said Céline, turning her back as Shirley went out into the yard again. Jean-Luc's place was empty and there was no sign of him in the yard. She mopped up the spilt wine and was standing in the doorway, on the point of going to sit near her father when she heard the slamming of a car door out on the track and a familiar and welcome figure came round the corner of the barn.

Louise was short of breath, as though she had run all the way from the *estaminet*, and sat down heavily on the chair that Jean-Luc had vacated. "Sorry we're late," she said, addressing the whole assembly. "We've come as fast as we could, but it was difficult to shut up shop early." Then she added with a touch of pride, "Some of our customers are reluctant to leave, you know." She looked to her son, who had haltingly followed her into the yard, to corroborate this little advertisement for her business. "That's right, isn't it, Charlot?" He nodded. In fact, he had brought his mother in his chimney sweep's van, which he used less often these days because he was more comfortably employed in helping her with her business.

"Harvest time is always a busy time for us too," Louise went on. "There are so many small items that people need when they're out in the fields. I can't tell you how many sticking plasters we have sold today; so many people have been getting their skin torn and scratched out in the fields, and you wouldn't believe how many cuts from those reaper blades I've had to patch up! They are very dangerous, those things! And that's not all," she continued, "the new Bakelite mugs are flying off the shelves. People don't want tin mugs any more; the Bakelite ones are so much more colourful." With a satisfied air she folded her arms and settled comfortably into a seat. Shirley went straight back to the kitchen to collect a tray of food for Louise and Charlot. Céline, who was preparing to light gas lamps around the yard, ignored her.

"Chérie! So you are here! I didn't see you before!" Louise exclaimed. "Is this anyone's place?" she asked. "Can I sit here?"

"Yes, that's all right, stay where you are," Shirley reassured her. "Jean-Luc was sitting there, but he seems to have gone home; perhaps he wasn't feeling very well."

"That's odd," Louise remarked, frowning. "We saw him, didn't we, Charlot? He was running in the direction of the *château* as we came up the road. We wondered why he was in such a hurry." Yet again Charlot confirmed his mother's account by vigorously nodding his head. Shirley found herself warming to Charlot, whom previously she, like most other people, had always regarded with distaste. Her own recent illness and persistent limp gave her a far greater insight into the young man's suffering, because, in addition to his other woes, he too limped slightly. She smiled at him, and in return he gave her the most ravishing heartfelt smile, as if to say, "I'm so glad you've noticed me at last! That's all I've ever wanted!"

Louise watched this exchange and used it to bring up a subject that she had not broached on Shirley's shopping visits to the *estaminet*. "You see, Chérie, Charlot knows how you have suffered this past year with your leg. We were so sorry to hear about your illness. That's what Charlot had, you know, infantile paralysis, but it was when he was a baby and there wasn't the treatment for him then. I suppose we are lucky that he's alive." She sighed, and Shirley felt ashamed that she had treated Charlot so badly in the past. She smiled at him again and vowed that she and Ted would be his friends. "Of course," Louise was saying, "he's done very well, all things considered. He's made a success of his chimney sweeping, though it wasn't easy for him, and now that he's working in the *estaminet* with me he's really happy. He still does some chimneys, though. He comes here to your grandfather's, and he goes to the *château* – that's a big job – and some other houses in the village."

"That's good!" Shirley exclaimed in pleasure at Charlot's success and relief that she was talking to Louise and not Jean-Luc.

At that moment Madame de la Croix looked up and noticed that her son was missing from the table, where trays of cheese and salad vied for space with the empty bottles and plates. Shirley could see what was coming so dived into the kitchen to fetch the dessert, leaving Louise to answer Madame's inevitable question: "Where is Jean-Luc?" she asked.

"I think he's not well," Louise answered, to the best of her knowledge. "We saw him running back down the road to the *château*."

"In that case maybe I should go home and see what's wrong," Madame said, rising to her feet. She cast a quizzical glance at Shirley, who was bringing large bowls of crème caramel out to the table. "Have you seen Jean-Luc, Chérie?" she asked.

"Just briefly," Shirley replied, "but I've had to help Céline with the serving, so I didn't have much time to talk to him."

"Ah, well, come and see us at the *château* before you leave, won't you?" Madame said tartly. "Then you and he will have time to talk."

"Thank you, Madame," Shirley replied, colouring noticeably with irritation rather than pleasure.

"Are you coming, Hélène?" Madame asked, turning to her daughter.

"I'll come later, Maman. I'm sure Édouard will see me home, won't you, Édouard?"

"Of course!" Ted quickly replied. "And, Madame, I could take you in my car, if you wish? It hasn't been painted yet, but it goes!" Madame de la Croix shook her head dismissively. Having thus declined Ted's invitation, she sharply summoned her daughter, who had no choice but to follow her, and did the rounds of the guests with her usual charm and aplomb, shaking them by the hand or kissing them on both cheeks, as appropriate. She gave Shirley a quick peck on both cheeks without a word and then, turning her back on the gathering, set off at a brisk pace. Hélène hovering slightly behind her, turned round to wave shyly to Ted and Shirley.

Louise watched her go; she leant towards Shirley, who had sat down again. "Be careful," she said in a hushed tone, "Madame is a gracious and generous lady, but she does not allow herself to be crossed, and that son of hers is the apple of her eye, although we all know that he is a grave disappointment to her. Rather like his father, really." She paused. "I don't suppose you know," she went on in a whisper, "but I'm sure that she is intending that Jean-Luc should marry you. Conveniently, he's been crazy about you since he was a little boy and, although such a marriage would most definitively not have been what Madame initially wanted for him, she now sees it as his salvation, because he would stand to inherit your grandfather's farm and incorporate the land into the estate of the *château*."

Shirley was aghast. "But she can't do that! It will belong to Maman when Pépé dies and then to Ted and me!" she exploded. Fortunately the rest of the company were either so engrossed in their own lively conversations or so inebriated that they did not notice her outburst.

Louise put a finger to her lips and a hand on Shirley's arm. "Not so loud," she whispered, "I think, even so, she, or Jean-Luc probably, could do that when the leasehold runs out on the land. The house and stables belong to your grandfather, but basically the land, or most of it, belongs to the *château*."

"How do you know?" Shirley asked, desperate to ascertain whether this dreadful information was founded on fact or only speculation. "Well, you know my Charlot, don't you?"

"Yes, of course, but what has he got to do with it?" Shirley asked impatiently.

"And you also know that people think he is an idiot, poor boy, on account of his handicaps?" Shirley tried to indicate gently that that was the case without implying that she herself had ever been party to such an opinion. "Well, my Charlot is not nearly as stupid as people think. Whether he is working in the *estaminet* or out sweeping chimneys, he listens and he observes and he remembers, so that often, at the end of the day when he comes home, he will tell me in his own way what he has seen and heard.

"Earlier this summer, it must have been in June or July," Louise said, "Charlot was sweeping the chimneys at the *château*. They are so big that sometimes he has to take a ladder, crawl inside them and climb up to be able to reach the sootiest places. And of course in an old house like that the chimneys join up, so that you can start on the ground floor but then find that you are at a junction where a first-floor chimney meets the one coming up from the ground floor. Sound carries and if there are people talking in the rooms you can hear what they are saying, but they don't necessarily know that you are there.

"Well, on that particular day, Charlot had climbed up the drawing-room chimney to where it was joined by a flue from a bedroom. He stopped for breath on a little platform and could hear Madame talking into the telephone in her boudoir. As a rule he would whistle or sing or make some sort of noise to let people know that he was there; he was about to do that when he heard your name mentioned. Madame was saying, 'Frédéric (that's her husband, though you won't remember ever seeing him), I want to talk to you about that pretty little girl, Daniel's granddaughter Chérie, or whatever her English name is.' Frédéric must have asked why on earth he was phoning her to talk about Chérie, and she replied, 'Listen, I think she may be the answer to our problems. You see the boy is a darling, so handsome and charming, but all he thinks about is enjoying himself. Frankly he's a good-for-nothing, and if we don't marry him off soon he'll have frittered away all his inheritance.' Then her husband must have made some comment to the effect that he didn't see what Chérie had to do with it, and she replied that she had a plan, which was that Jean-Luc should marry that pretty little girl, although of course she was far beneath him in birth, but the marriage would bring all those tenanted lands back under the control of the *château* when Daniel died. Monsieur de la Croix must have made some objection to the effect that he didn't think it possible because it would be illegal to claim back those lands, but Madame would hear none of it. 'Oh, don't worry about that!" she exclaimed, 'We have enough friends with influence in high places to sort that out for us!' Then Monsieur must have said, 'But you can't force people to marry these days.' 'Don't worry about that either,' Madame reassured him, 'the silly boy dotes on her, always has, and would marry her at the first opportunity, even though she walks with a limp. She had infantile paralysis last year.' A pause followed in which she must have been listening to what her husband was saying, because she then said, 'No, no she's not infectious any more.'

"Charlot was furious," Louise said, "and had to be extra-careful not to make any noise in the chimney, so he sat there for ages until Madame left the room. Then he clambered over to another part of the house and swept a bit more before descending and emerging down his ladder into the drawing room. He collected it up with his brooms and came straight home to tell me what he had heard. I have been waiting for a moment to tell you about it, but every time you have come into the *estaminet* we have been too busy to have a chat. And of course it's all so much more difficult because your Maman is not here this summer. When is she coming back, by the way?"

Shirley was horrified by the tale she had just heard and was quite unable to answer any questions about her mother's whereabouts or plans. She thanked Louise – and Charlot, who had listened as his mother spoke and nodded from time to time. She felt weak with the callousness of all she had heard and wanted nothing more than to go and lie down. Small wonder, she said to herself, that Madame had left the party in such a haughty fashion, or that Céline, who had been so closely involved with life at the *château* for so long, should have been so annoyed, though she doubted very much whether Céline was party to the full extent of Madame's machinations. There was no one, apart from Louise, whom she could talk to about this appalling state of affairs. She would have to lie low, avoid running into Madame or Jean-Luc out in the fields or in the village, and count the days until the return to England. As for Ted and Hélène, any hint of romance between them would be nipped in the bud: that much was certain. Hélène was doubtless destined for a loftier future; marriage to Ted would not aid Madame's plans to regain Pépé's land for Jean-Luc.

Keeping Ted away from the *château* proved difficult in those final days of the summer holiday, despite Shirley's various stratagems, as for instance, her suggestion that he might drive her down to the market in Freslan-la-Tour. His answer to that was that, while the weather was fine and the air still, he and Pa had to get on with the business of painting his car. Once the rains began, creating droplets on the surface, or the wind blew, carrying dust onto the sticky paint, it would be impossible to achieve the perfect finish to which he aspired. That the task was necessary was indisputable, but Ted's reply put his sister in the awkward position of being obliged to go out alone, leaving him to his own devices, quite contrary to her intentions.

Céline saw no reason to go to the market as she had everything she needed within arm's length and, she said, if she needed something, there were always the travelling salesmen who called regularly. In any case, Céline had ceased to be good company since a different side of her personality had revealed itself. After the evening of the harvest supper she had been polite towards Shirley, but the warm displays of affection had suddenly been replaced by a frosty indifference, as if she had been personally slighted by such strongly expressed dislike of Jean-Luc. Shirley regretted this acrid divergence of opinion, but was not going to marry Jean-Luc just to please Céline. On the other hand, she decided not to tell her what she had heard from Louise about the de la Croix plans, because she knew that Céline had recently decided that the *estaminet* was a den of iniquity. "Hmm, I don't go there any more," Céline had remarked curtly when Shirley had asked early in the holiday if she would like to go there for a coffee.

Undoubtedly this was the result of much idle speculation about Céline and Pépé in that establishment of late: apparently, according to Louise, someone had indiscreetly, in full view of all the other customers, asked Céline while she was shopping there, when she and Daniel might be going to marry. "Imagine! The cheek of it!" Céline had exclaimed with righteous indignation. "If I went about telling what I know about the people in this village, I could write a book!" In consequence, she had not crossed the threshold of the *estaminet* since. Naturally enough, she now regarded Louise as the queen of village gossip and any tale told by her as outright slander.

Anyhow, confiding in Céline would involve incriminating Charlot, which Shirley wanted to avoid at all costs because of her changed opinion of him from one of childish dislike to one of adult sympathy and respect. Were his story of listening from inside chimneys to be widely broadcast, it would doubtless lose him all the remaining customers for his chimney-sweeping business, and might even rebound on the *estaminet* as well. So Shirley caught the bus at the end of the lane to go to the market alone that morning and later walked to the *estaminet* for a chat with Louise by a long and circuitous route to avoid the *château*.

Although it reminded her of many visits over the years that she had made with Maman and Mémé, particularly of the one last year, the market did not lift her spirits as she had expected. The atmosphere was disappointingly different: it seemed duller and more muted, and the colourful spectacle of last summer's market with its acrobats and the blind accordion player had faded. The sky was overcast, the flower stall was not there, nor was the man with his puppies, and the man juggling oranges and lemons to an admiring crowd had retreated to the back of his stall, where he busied himself rearranging his wares. The other stalls and stallholders were there unchanged but appeared mundane and uninteresting. Without Maman and Mémé there were no acquaintances with whom to pass the time of day, leaving her with a sense of isolation, a mere observer of a scene in which she played no part. The result was that here in Freslan-la-Tour, even more than at the farm, she realized with an acute pang of sorrow how much she missed dear Mémé, and mourned her loss more keenly. On the other hand, as regards her mother, there grew in her a prickly, uncontrollably angry reaction to her mother's departure to America, leaving her husband and her children deprived, for such a long time, of her company, which previously had had such a constant unifying effect on the family. Had Maman been present, the incident with Céline over Jean-Luc would certainly never have happened and, somehow or other, Maman would have found a way of dealing with the problem.

There was nothing in Freslan-la-Tour to inspire a new ballet. What's more, Shirley was disturbed to discover that several old men were ogling her. She was not flattered as she might well have been had they been young and handsome. Nor was there any point in going into a café on her own, for then she would have been even more conspicuous, but she did feel the need to buy something to justify her excursion. Although she baulked at buying fish, which she would have to carry home on the bus, she eventually settled on some haddock and a bag of oranges as a treat for Céline and Pépé, since obviously neither haddock nor oranges were grown on the farm. Unfortunately, her attempt at a practical peace offering was not well received. Céline turned her nose up at it, remarking, "We do eat fish, you know, but we prefer the freshwater fish that your grandfather sometimes catches down in the river at weekends." She sniffed, wrinkling up her nose at the smell. "I suppose I can do something with that haddock. I hope it keeps fresh for tomorrow, because I have already prepared today's meals." She put the oranges in a fruit bowl, muttering, "Well, of course, we do have a lot of lovely plums in the orchard."

Predictably, Ted was not in the yard when Shirley returned, nor was his car. He drove in as she was laying the table for lunch, and clearly had not lifted a paintbrush or opened a pot of paint all morning. There could be no doubt as to where he had gone. Provocatively, his sister asked how the painting was going. Ted's reply was perfectly plausible in that he said he had had to go down to the *estaminet* for a new brush and some white spirit. He did not say where else he had been. As far as she was concerned, Shirley did not care whether he had been to the *château* or not, but she did care that he stood to be very hurt if the growing relationship with Hélène were discovered and banned by Madame de la Croix. That such a marriage did not figure in her plans for her daughter was obvious for anyone to see, except, it appeared, for Ted.

After lunch she again took the long route down to the *estaminet*, where Louise lost no time in telling her that Édouard had indeed come in that morning to buy some bits and pieces for his car. "What a delightful young man he is, your brother!" she exclaimed, before turning her attention to one of her customers. Louise was so busy that there was little chance of a conversation with her, but at least in the comfortably familiar surroundings of the *estaminet* Shirley felt more at ease about buying herself a coffee than she had in Freslan-la-Tour.

"Pa and I will be going back to England in two days' time, so maybe I should say 'goodbye' now," she said, as she drained the last drops from her cup.

"Oh, so soon?" Louise asked. "How time flies! We haven't had time for a proper chat. Won't you come down here again tomorrow? I did so much want to know about your mother and what she is doing in the United States. I don't suppose Édouard will tell me very much. That's men for you!" Shirley was thankful that Édouard could be relied upon not to tell Louise anything and was glad, too, that she herself would no longer be there to answer Louise's penetrating questions. She made a mental note to stay away from the *estaminet* as well as the *château* over the next couple of days and concentrate instead on her project.

The one consolation of the Jean-Luc business was that, unlike Freslan-la-Tour, it provided the budding choreographer with new material for her ballet. She had decided that the girl out in the fields had come from a poor background in the village, but no one knew who her mysterious, handsome labourer was. He said simply that his name was Alain. Their romance progressed rapidly and happily, as if they were destined for each other. Each evening they met on the village green, where all the young people assembled, and danced in a group with the villagers who of course formed the *corps de ballet* while the two lovers again danced a *pas de deux* as the principals. One evening, however, the villagers scattered swiftly on the arrival of the lord of the manor, an ugly, dark-haired, arrogant young man who set his sights on the girl and insisted on dancing with her, much to her disgust. Shirley was aware that she was doing Jean-Luc an injustice because he was not ugly, though he certainly was dark-haired and arrogant, but that was immaterial. In the ballet, a villain had to look like an out-and-out scoundrel for the audience to be able to recognize him. The heroine's handsome lover tried to pull her away, but the lord of the manor flung down his glove, challenging his rival to a duel the next morning.

Shirley was aware that her plot was becoming more and more reminiscent of *Giselle*, but encountered a problem when she could not decide which of the two rivals was going to die in the duel. If the handsome boy killed the lord of the manor, he would be arrested and condemned, in which case the girl would without a doubt seize a dagger and kill herself, but if the lord of the manor killed the hero, he, because of his position, would escape punishment and would be free to marry the girl, who would still seize a dagger and kill herself. It was all rather complicated and was fast becoming a tragedy, which was not what she had intended that day out in the fields when the sun shone and the idea had first come to her.

Clouds had rolled in from the coast since then and the skies were grey, which may have explained the difference in tone and the threat of impending tragedy, but another element had come into play here: it seemed as if the characters had taken on a life of their own and were developing a storyline beyond her control. This had never happened before, never in all the years of devising ballets for Miss Patience's annual ballet shows, and it was unnerving, so she decided to abandon the plot for the time being and devise the dances, the steps and the movements for the *corps de ballet* and for the principals, which proved to be an absorbing way of passing the remaining two days of the holiday when rain fell in heavy autumnal showers over the region.

Not once did Shirley fail to ask Céline if there was anything she could do to help her in the kitchen, but the answer was always the same: a brusque "*Non merci, Chérie*", which was both upsetting and liberating; upsetting because it showed that Céline was still angry with her, but liberating because it gave her the freedom to do as she liked. Therefore, while Céline prepared the meals or went out to milk the cows, Shirley repaired to her room and either practised some movements or conjured up dance sequences. Although the limp was still there, her leg no longer ached and had become much stronger than even a month ago, probably from all her hard work out in the fields, allowing her to straighten it like a rod as she stretched it out when doing her exercises on the floor. Eventually it appeared to be almost as straight and strong as the right leg. The muscles twitched and her hamstrings pulled, but she took no notice of them in her pleasure at the renewal of her strength and flexibility. She reckoned that the time had come to search out another dance school on her return home to England.

Ted had parked his car in the cart shed out of the rain before joining Pépé and his father in the barn to help store the harvest machinery away and service the tractor ready for the seasonal task of ploughing. Pa grinned when Pépé announced, "Reggie, without you and your knowledge of engines, this would have cost me a lot of money, even though I haven't had this tractor a year yet and it's supposed to be under guarantee. I must say, if I'd known how much expense and trouble it would cause me, I might have kept the carthorses…" He said no more, because he knew in his heart of hearts that, although he loved his horses, put out to grass in a meadow adjoining the farm, the tractor exerted an irresistible fascination over him. With this new-fangled piece of machinery and the reaper-binder establishing him in the forefront of modern technology, he somehow felt proud, reinvigorated and rejuvenated.

Reggie answered good-naturedly, "It's my pleasure, Daniel; all sorts of engines are my business – or that's to say, they were – so any time you need me, let me know!" Nevertheless, it was unlikely that Daniel would have to summon him, because he had been at pains to teach Ted how to service the tractor and what to do if a problem arose. Once, some time ago, he had hoped that his son might study engineering, but Ted was above all a practical young man who, in spite of his engineering skills, first and foremost wanted to be a farmer. The engineering prowess that he had most definitely inherited from his father, and which he had already put to good use with bicycles, cars and motorbikes, would serve him well in looking after the tractor and farm machinery.

Shirley noted with some satisfaction that Ted would be unlikely to go to the *château*, since he had put his car away and was fully occupied with his work. While Céline dozed in an armchair in the kitchen, she spent the early part of the afternoon sitting at the table in her room planning her balletic enterprise. She had not resolved the question of the ending – that is, which of the two rival lovers would win the duel and survive – but since the characters seemed to have taken over, she left them to sort out the plot, and was happily engaged in working out the details of the dance and the music instead. Thus she was occupied for the whole afternoon.

In the distance, through the thick medieval walls, she could just make out the hum of voices in the yard and assumed that the three men were discussing their usual topics of farming, animals and machinery. It was only when she emerged from her room to fetch a coffee from the kitchen that she noticed that Ted's car was not in the cart shed across the yard. Her heart sank, for she knew perfectly well where he had gone. "Where's Ted?" she asked Céline.

"He's taken his car for a drive in the rain!" she replied. "He asked me if I wanted to go with him, but it's too wet outside for me. I have to go out in it quite enough as it is, so when there's no need, I prefer to stay indoors. I think he said he might call in at the *château*." She added in a caustic tone: "He, at least, appreciates that lovely family." In Shirley's opinion Céline was deluded, while she herself was dismayed that her brother was pursuing his relationship with Hélène, nice girl though she was.

Naturally Ted had had girlfriends in the past, just as Shirley herself had had boyfriends, but they had mostly been the intense though fleeting experiments of adolescence, little more than part of the learning process in which attraction was based on physical attributes rather than a combination of mutual chemistry and shared interests, ambitions and opinions. They may, at the time, have felt like passionate romances that would continue for ever, but they were not destined to last and usually came to an abrupt and painful end. Ted and Hélène's relationship, young though they were, was undeniably different. The ease with which they had conversed at the harvest supper was completely natural, for there was no hint of flirting in their behaviour and the light in their eyes spoke of a deep and serious attraction that went beyond the purely physical. Hélène's reluctance to leave that evening, and Ted's to let her go, spoke of a burgeoning interdependence. It reminded Shirley all too cruelly of her encounter with Alan a year ago.

Céline was already serving the supper and Pa was serving the wine when Ted arrived home. His face glowed in the lamplight. "So sorry I'm late," he apologized to Céline, whose attitude towards him was markedly different from her attitude towards Shirley.

"Don't you worry," she said, enveloping him in a warm smile. "I decided to serve dinner because this gammon will dry out if we leave it any longer." Ted sat down at the table next to Shirley, who did not ask him directly where he had been, although she could not see his face which, forever open and honest, was always the indicator of his feelings.

She asked simply, "Have you had a good time?"

"Oh, yes!" he replied. "The car goes like a bird. Thanks so much, Pépé and Pa, for helping to get it going! It will really be useful and," he said turning to Céline, "I can take you out for rides, even down to Saint-Pierre, if you like."

"Oh! That would be good!" she replied. "So much quicker than going in the pony and trap or waiting for the bus. So, have you been to Saint-Pierre this afternoon?"

"Well, er, yes," Ted replied with a certain indecision, "it was quiet there this afternoon, but I have brought some *pâtisserie* for us all for dessert!" He placed a neatly wrapped parcel on the table and opened it to reveal five chocolate éclairs to a chorus of grateful exclamations.

Then, rather quickly, also revealing some uncertainty about what he was going to say, he announced, "I see that there's a new film coming out next week. It's called *The Baker's Wife*, by a director called Pagnol. I don't know if you have heard of him?" He looked around the table, but only Shirley nodded. He went on, "It's supposed to be very funny. I thought I might go and see it." Hesitantly, he invited Pépé and Céline to accompany him. Pépé, who never went anywhere if he could help it, predictably replied in the negative.

"No, no, my lad, I'll stay in and clean the guns. The shooting season starts next weekend, remember?"

Suspense was evident in Ted's gestures as he waited for Céline's response. "No, Édouard, I'll stay with your grandfather, but why don't you take a friend? What about Hélène?" Although her view of Ted's face was only partial, Shirley could almost feel the heat coming from his reddening cheeks, and she knew what that blushing implied.

"That's an idea. Maybe I'll ask her," Ted said slowly, and then gazed intently at his plate. Shirley knew that she was outnumbered. Once she had left, Céline would do all in her power to promote the romance, because for her an alliance with the gentry would fulfil her wildest dreams, and Pépé, dear simple man that he was, would be sure not to have any opinion on the matter that did not coincide with Céline's. He would definitely not intervene but would smile, nod and just say "Good, good".

As for Pa, he would not understand, so it was pointless to try to talk to him about matters of the heart. In any case, he had other things on his mind. While he and Shirley waited for the train to Calais at the station in Saint-Pierre, he took Ted aside. He was not very practised at speaking in a whisper, and Shirley's ears were sharp enough to hear every word. "You will take care, my boy, won't you?" he said. "Remember the talk we had before we came to France?" Ted nodded. "I want you to keep a close eye on the news; I know that's difficult here with no radio and we have been rather out of touch over these past weeks. I suppose we ought to have gone to Saint-Pierre to see the newsreels at the cinema." He paused and bit his lip. "The situation was pretty bad before we left home, and I don't expect it's any better now, so do go down to Louise's and read the newspapers when you have a chance." He delved into his pocket and pulled out some notes and some coins. "Look, here are some francs. I won't be needing them, so take them and have a beer from time to time on me."

Then he returned to the subject that was troubling him. "The French say they are arming and Chamberlain has promised to come to the rescue if France and Belgium are attacked, but I don't want you involved in any fighting. Make sure you get out before the Germans come in!"

Ted shrugged. "Don't worry, Pa, I can take care of myself, and they aren't likely to come here anyhow. And what about Pépé and Céline? I can't leave them, can I?" Ted may well have been thinking of Pépé and Céline, but he was even more likely to have been thinking of Hélène as well.

Pa, unaware of the undercurrents, sighed at his son's obtuseness. "Ted, you don't understand. Wherever they go the Germans are rounding up anyone they regard as undesirable. Look what's happened to the Jews in Austria! Pépé and Céline will be fine, because they are French citizens with French identity papers, but you are not. You are English, with a British passport, and that could well mean they will just take you out and shoot you, or at best ship you off to some internment camp hundreds of miles away. But frankly I don't believe they would bother with taking you prisoner."

Ted pulled a face and said, "All right!" unconvincingly.

Pa then remembered something else. "Oh, and by the way, I've written down the number of our telephone in the new place for you. You may have to order a call in advance, but you should be able to phone us from the *estaminet*." The same idea had occurred to Shirley, so she was glad to hear her father mentioning it. The train was pulling into Saint-Pierre Station when Pa turned to his son one last time. "And, one more thing, you will make sure you get a gas mask when they distribute them here, won't you?"

"Yes, Pa," said Ted in bored exasperation.

"Ah, good," Pa replied. "I know your mother will ask about it when she comes home. Maybe in Washington they know more about what's going on than we do – let's hope so."

35

In London late that Saturday afternoon, the returning travellers found the shop apparently in good order, ready for them to assume control. All was clean and tidy, the shelves were well stocked and, according to Tilly and Cousin Archie, the business was ticking over nicely. Their faces gleaming with pleasure and excitement at the prospect of the new venture, Reggie and Shirley both congratulated Tilly and Cousin Archie on their careful management, but then the latter, rather too nervously for their liking, sounded a note of caution. "Of course," he said in anticipation of Reggie's request to see the books, "we don't expect high takings at this time of year. Most of our regular customers are away either at the seaside or, if they can't afford that, picking hops in Kent, so there's not a lot of demand for newspapers and baccy at present. Anyhow, it's the silly season for the papers and there are only a certain number of sightings of that Loch Ness monster that people want to read about."

Reggie's optimism swung swiftly from cheerful expectation to dismay, although his cousin went on hastily to explain that people were still making their usual purchases, but elsewhere. They would be back, he insisted, and then they would slip into their normal routines. "You wait," he said, "the queue will be out of the door by next week!" Reggie sincerely hoped that he was right. The columns in the accounting books somehow did not look nearly as healthy as they had when Archie had shown them to him before he bought the business, and he began to wonder whether he had made an ass of himself. After all, he did not know his cousin very well and it was only on his mother's recommendation that he had come to view the property. Perhaps he had seen it through rose-tinted spectacles and agreed to it too quickly, because it offered him the chance of remedying his own personal situation.

Archie shifted from foot to foot, sensing Reggie's displeasure. "Trust me, old chap," he said, "I do know what I am talking about. Tilly here and me, we've been working hard, haven't we Tilly?"

"Oh, yes," agreed Tilly, "it's just a bit quieter than usual at the moment. People have gone away for a final fling before they have to settle down for another winter."

Reggie sighed. "Ah, I see," he said, before assuming a brisker tone and asking to be reminded of the arrangements for the following morning, when the paper boys' bags would have to be loaded with the Sunday papers; at least he hoped they would have to be loaded.

"Well, there you are!" Archie exclaimed. "The orders for the Sunday papers are already up from last month, so some people are back and settling into their routine. We always sell at least as many papers on Sundays and more magazines than on weekdays, because the customers like to relax and catch up on what they've missed."

With that Reggie had to be satisfied. Shirley, who was watching this exchange, feared that this, her father's early disappointment, might colour his whole attitude and plummet him into the dark pit of despair from which he had so recently escaped. She decided to butt in to head off any further bad news. "I'm sure it will be all right, Pa. Don't forget we've had a long journey and we're both tired. Let's ask Cousin Archie if he would be kind enough to come back tomorrow while you recover, and gradually see what has to be done, then we can take over with Tilly's help on Monday." It was generally agreed that this was a good idea. Puzzled that such an insubstantial blonde, who looked more like a film star than a practical working girl, could make such a sensible suggestion, Cousin Archie gave Shirley a cheerful appreciative glance indicating that she had already risen considerably in his esteem.

After the departure of the two assistants, Reggie closed up the shop and locked the door. He looked anxiously at his daughter as he considered what to say next. "I do hope this is going to be all right, Shirl," he said wearily. "I hope I haven't taken on a dud here."

"It will be fine, Pa," she reassured him. "You and I and Tilly will make a go of it. And of course there's Cousin Archie: I like him and I think you'll find he will be only too willing to help out. You'll see. But come on, let's go upstairs. We've only just arrived and we haven't even taken our coats off! Can you manage the stairs, do you think? Tilly said she's done some shopping for us so we can at least make ourselves toast and an omelette." She picked up her suitcase and went ahead. The stairs were steep, but no steeper than they had been in their former home, and both she and her father were stronger and fitter after three weeks in the French countryside.

It was strange to be coming into somewhere new and untried, somewhere that smelt of paint and plaster, and not, as the key turned in the lock of the door of the flat, into the friendly, familiar hall leading straight through to the kitchen of their old house. It was then that Shirley realized that this had definitely been the right decision, because she and Pa would have been so lonely in that house without either Ted or Maman: they had left Ted behind in France and there was no sign of Maman's expected return. In their former home she would have been so conspicuous by her absence, but here she had not carved out a place for herself. Who knows, thought Shirley, maybe she never will, but then she quickly put this unwelcome idea to the back of her mind. "You know, Pa," she said, "you and I would feel so miserable in our old home without Ted, and Maman is away, so she wouldn't be there either. It would be full of ghosts and memories, but here we can start again, just you and me, and we'll be fine!" Pa smiled at this novel perspective on the situation. "You may be right, Shirl," he said. "Right that is until your mother comes home. You usually are." They feasted on omelette and toast and then made up the beds in their respective rooms before settling down for the night.

Shirley had difficulty in sleeping. Her bedroom, as they all did, overlooked the railway, along which trains passed all night, some slow and shunting, others fast, rattling and whistling. Pa no doubt was dreaming that he was in heaven, but not so Shirley, for whom the contrast with the silence of Trémaincourt was overwhelming. Switching on the light, she looked at her watch: it was half-past two. Convinced that she would never enjoy a good night's sleep again, she got out of bed and searched for her sponge bag, turning over the contents of her suitcase. At the bottom of the bag, under combs and her nail scissors, face powder and hairpins, she found a ball of cotton wool which she tore into small pieces and stuffed into her ears. She climbed back into bed and fell asleep straight away, though not before she had wondered how her mother would cope with so much nocturnal disturbance – if, that is, she ever came back to them. The future, in regard to the unity of the family, did not look rosy.

Pa was up and dressed, ready to start work, when his daughter appeared in the kitchen next morning. "How did you sleep, Shirl?" he asked, though the answer was staring him in the face.

"Not very well. It's very noisy, isn't it?"

"Oh is it?" he replied. "Can't say that I noticed anything myself, although I did stand watching the trains for a bit when I woke up at six. You'll soon get used to it." Shirley did not reply, for she never took kindly to being told that she would soon get used to something, whatever it might be. The same unsympathetic remark had been made by someone, she did not remember whom, when she first crossed the Channel on a rough sea, and again when she first went to school, and of course when she first tried to walk after the paralysis. With most of these discomforts she had had no choice and had eventually become used to them, but she did not like being told so, because it always sounded so sanctimonious. How could anyone else really know what would suit her, what she could cope with, what she would or would not get used to? No one else could feel quite as she felt, know how hot or cold, how painful or uncomfortable, or how loud or quiet an experience might be for her. She toyed with the piece of toast that her father put in front of her, drank her tea and yawned. "You go back to bed," Pa suggested more helpfully this time. "I'm off to work to meet the paper boys as they come in for their rounds. We won't need Archie today after all." He laughed. "To think that work is only downstairs!"

Shirley nodded, "Yes, that is something new, isn't it, Pa? I'll be down as soon as I'm dressed."

The morning passed very agreeably, although, not unlike the year before on their return from France, their diet consisted only of bread, eggs and tomatoes, redeemed by some delicious and particularly smelly cheese, all of which Shirley had smuggled in from France, defying the customs officers to search her suitcase. Despite the pervasive odour, none of them had dared to look in the suitcase of the small but glamorous young person with such a queenly presence. Otherwise the crossing had been disappointing. The sea was calm, but it rained hard all the way, so the passengers sat inside where it was hot and stuffy with little room to move around. Shirley scanned the drowsy heads for Alan and his father with no luck. There was no sign of them even when, braving the constant downpour, she went out on deck. "You're not going out there, are you?" her father had asked in horror. "You'll get soaked!"

"It's too hot in here," she complained, "and I can't breathe." In fact, there was no one out of doors on either side of the ship. She went to the doorway on the port side and peered out along the deck and then did the same on the other side. The cliffs of Dover were just about visible through a mist of rain, but nothing else. She was disappointed but took heart from the prospect of Miss Patience's wedding in that little hamlet north of Brighton in three weeks' time.

To his own surprise as much as anyone else's, Pa was in his element meeting the paper boys downstairs in the shop and excitedly reviewing all aspects of his business. It helped of course that Cousin Archie and Tilly really had taken good care of it during his absence, and on the whole there was nothing with which he could find fault. He was pleased, on closer inspection, that the books appeared to be in a rather healthier state than when he had glanced at them after Archie's warning shots the previous evening. Henceforth, the plan was that he and Shirley would be running the shop on Sundays, while Tilly took a well-deserved rest, and Cousin Archie would gradually fade into retirement.

However, as Shirley had anticipated, Cousin Archie seemed reluctant to take a back seat. "It's all right for the missus," he grumbled. "She's got her house and garden, not to mention her sewing, to keep her occupied and there's plenty she can do in the kitchen, but there's nothing there for me. My life is here in this shop. So I'd be happy to come in and work whenever you want me to, Reggie."

"That's good of you, Archie," Pa replied, "but I'm not sure we can keep two members of staff on the payroll as well as Shirley and me. Shirley needs a job, as I told you before, and this is now my main source of income. I need it to supplement my pension, which isn't that great." He paused to let his words sink in.

"Don't worry about that," Cousin Archie responded with alacrity. "You don't have to pay me, well, not very much. You see, I'd die of boredom at home all day with the missus. You'd be doing me a good turn, and anyhow, when Tilly stops work, then you'll need someone to take over from her."

"Yes, I do see," Pa replied, "and I'm very grateful for your offer, Archie, but it's early days yet. Give me time to think about it, will you?"

Archie seemed satisfied. Shirley was grateful for his offer of help, because at the end of the stay in France she had begun to worry whether she would be able to reconcile herself to being involved in the shop full-time, all day every day, into a distant future. That would be but a poor, blank prospect compared with the golden future that she had once planned for herself. It would be fine as a stopgap, but once Pa was well established, she was determined not to abandon all her ambitions. As she stretched out over her left leg, which was becoming even straighter, stronger and more flexible, her confidence grew that she really might be able to return to dancing sooner than she had expected, and if not dancing on the stage at Sadler's Wells, then possibly in another company or in a musical or, failing that, she was prepared to work in a theatre in any capacity whatsoever: front of house, backstage, even selling programmes or ice cream, until a better opportunity presented itself. The difficulty was that she did not know how or when to mention this proposed change to her father. Nevertheless, on this particular Sunday morning, having just witnessed his reluctance to keep Cousin Archie on the books, she was persuaded that she would have to bring the matter up sooner rather than later; otherwise she might find herself trapped behind the counter for ever.

Pa was in an ebullient mood at lunchtime after closing the shop door. The morning had gone so much better than he had dared hope, especially given his earlier disappointment, and nothing could dampen his enthusiasm. Shirley therefore decided that the moment of truth had come. "Pa," she said with some hesitation, "I need to talk to you about my role in the shop."

"Oh, why is that?" he asked, looking up from his meagre lunch.

"Well…" she said, and was about to embark on this rather delicate matter when the phone rang.

Pa reached out to the sideboard to pick up the receiver. "Hello, hello!" he shouted into the mouthpiece. Despite being annoyed at this interruption to her carefully prepared speech, Shirley grinned both at her father's excitement on hearing the instrument ring, which was quite extraordinary for one who had resisted its use for so long, and at his clumsy handling of it.

The caller evidently thought so too, because after listening to a harangue from the other end for a minute or two, he lowered his voice and said, "Oh, I'm sorry, Mother, I didn't mean to deafen you. I thought I would have to speak loudly into this phone as it's an extension from the one in the shop." Granny Marlow was evidently not amused but continued to berate her son about various matters for the next ten minutes. Shirley caught the gist of the conversation from his response. "Yes, Mother," he said into the phone, "we had a very good time in France and I'm sure we sent you a postcard. I expect the post is rather slow. Maybe it will arrive in a day or two." A couple of minutes later, he said, "I'm afraid we didn't have time to write letters because we were so busy with the harvest." There followed a pause during which he reached out for the day's paper; turning the pages with his free hand, he read an article or two while his mother prattled on. "Yes, yes," he said at last, "Shirley was needed too. She worked very hard helping us. It was a case of all hands on deck." There was another pause. "Yes," he said, "Shirley's here. We're having lunch at present, but I'm sure she would like to speak to you."

Shirley groaned and went over to the phone. "Hello, Granny," she said pleasantly, only to be met by Granny's whinging voice:

"At last you have a telephone! Almost everyone I know has had one for at least ten years!" Shirley ignored this biting and untrue comment, and then, without allowing her grandmother to gain the upper hand and scarcely stopping for breath herself, launched into a full description of the harvest in France, followed by a description of the journey home, followed by a lengthy description of the shop. At the end of all this there was a long silence, before Granny curtly said, "I am glad to hear that you and your father are both well and so very busy, although I should have liked to hear more about Edward, my darling boy..."

"Ah, he's fine; he's doing what he wants to do most of all," Shirley informed her. She then added somewhat gratuitously, "I don't expect he'll ever come back to this country. He's so happy in France!" This was not the news that Granny Marlow wanted to hear. The click of her tongue at the other end of the line was audible.

"I see. Come over and visit me soon, won't you? We could go to Morley's together. Goodbye!" Granny said and called off.

Father and daughter exchanged glances as if to say, "What a nuisance!" But, if anything, Pa's glance said more than that. It also implied: "Now you understand why I've never wanted to have a telephone before!" Shirley raised her eyebrows and sat down again at the table. Pa had been eating his lunch while she was on the phone, and she wanted to catch him before he went down to the shop to count the morning's takings. "I was about to say, Pa," she began, "that I think you should consider keeping Cousin Archie on part-time if he is so keen to work."

"Why is that?" he asked in surprise. "With you, me and Tilly we are fully staffed as it is, and I don't think we could afford anyone else on the payroll."

"Well," Shirley said, trying to sound as diplomatic as possible, "Tilly won't be with us for much longer and who knows what she will do after having her baby."

There was silence while Pa stroked his chin thoughtfully. "Yes, that's right," he said eventually, "but by then you and I will be well used to running the business, so we probably won't need her."

"No, it's not quite like that," Shirley said cautiously, "you see, Pa, my leg really is getting better and I do want to dance again. Maybe I'll be able to get a job in a theatre somewhere. I should be happy to help out in the shop just like I did at the Salvatores', but I don't see myself working behind the counter for ever."

"But Shirl," Pa protested, "I bought this business for you! I wanted you to be able to work and have some money of your own in partnership with me when it seemed that you would never dance again!"

"I realize that, Pa," she replied, "but if the opportunity to dance presents itself after all, I want to be able to grab it with both hands!" Her blood was rising as she saw that she was going to have to fight to get her own way. Her father was growing more and more irritated by the minute and was not prepared to give in so quickly.

"All I can say," he retorted, "is that I am very disappointed in you, Shirl. Ted's left us and gone off to France, but I did hope that you would stay and help me make a success of this business."

"I am doing that, and I shall do that, Pa, but you must understand that for me dancing comes first!" With that she collected up the plates and flounced out into the kitchen.

Tempers cooled later in the day. Reggie spent the afternoon doing his accounts and then listened to the wireless while Shirley shut herself in her room and practised her exercises. She emerged at dinner time and found a tin of previously unnoticed tuna among Tilly's shopping. Mixing this with salad cream, she put it and the remaining bread and salad on the table. Pa was quiet, even glum, as he sat down. Finally he took a deep breath and said, "I do understand how you feel, Shirley, and I will ask Archie to help out as necessary until we see how things work out. If you should change your mind about this dancing of yours, then let me know."

"Thank you, Pa," Shirley replied, glad to have won the battle but saddened to see her father so downcast. "Don't worry: I shall be pleased to help out for the foreseeable future. I only wanted to warn you that my plans may change."

"That's fine, fine," he said. "But, um, tell me, is there any post for me? We forgot to look for it yesterday evening and there wasn't time this morning."

Shirley went over to the sideboard on which Tilly had neatly stacked a pile of mail. "In all the excitement, I had completely forgotten about this!" she exclaimed. She brought the pile to the table and sorted the envelopes. "Here are two for you – oh, and another one," she said, handing her father three brown envelopes. "Those look like bills. But there are two letters for me!" She scrutinized the two white envelopes before opening them.

Pa opened the bills while she read her letters. "Oh, this is from Miss Patience!" She says there will be a car to pick me up at Brighton Station to take me to her wedding! I say, listen to this! She has sent the address of a dance school a couple of streets away from here! She says it's owned by someone she used to dance with. This other one," she said, opening the second letter, "ah, it's from Cynthia. She says she is going to the wedding too and can we go together?"

"Is that all?" Pa asked despondently. "No more letters? Nothing from your mother?"

A grimace replaced Shirley's flush of happiness at the two letters she had received as she replied, "No, I don't think so; I'm afraid not."

A letter did come from Maman, but not until ten days later. In it she said that she hoped that Reggie and Shirley were well and that the shop was proving to be a success. She was sure that they must be very busy so hoped that they would not mind if she stayed longer in the United States. She did not say how long, and the letter was handwritten on official writing paper bearing only the address of the French Embassy in Washington, DC. Pa slumped in his armchair on reading it and stayed there for the whole afternoon, leaving Shirley, Tilly and Archie to run the shop. Shirley made up the excuse that her father had not been well at lunchtime and was taking the afternoon off. She too was profoundly upset but tried not to show it, because for the time being the family business had suddenly become her responsibility.

During the rest of the day, her dismay turned to annoyance and then to anger. "How could her mother do this to them?" she wondered. How could she leave her husband and daughter in such a sly, devious manner? Her anger grew with the sense of betrayal until she wanted to throw anything she could lay her hands on across the shop. With difficulty she contained herself until after closing time when she went out into the yard and threw stones down onto the railway line. The letter had as good as said that, for all her excuses and fine words, Maman would not be coming back, and that only confirmed what she already suspected in her heart of hearts, although she had clung to the hope that her mother would reappear and take up her rightful place in their lives.

Her father was in the same position in his armchair when she went upstairs; he had not moved since lunchtime and appeared to have sunk into a slough of despond at the news. He had fallen so far from the castles in the air that he had been constructing over the past few weeks that the positive gloss he had put on his wife's absence was now unsustainable, based on nothing but his own fantasies, and those castles had finally vanished into thin air. Shirley was sorry for herself and even sorrier for him, for she knew how optimistic he had tried to be and how hard he had tried to block out his niggling suspicions that the trip to Washington was more than just a work-related visit, if indeed it had ever been that.

This was almost worse than if Maman had died, because it implied that she did not love her family any more, if indeed she ever had. Why, Shirley wondered, had she chosen this particular moment to disappear across the Atlantic? Was it because, as certainly seemed likely, she hated the thought of moving? With discussion and compromise that problem could perhaps have been resolved. Maybe Pa could have waited until the Salvatores retired and packed their bags to go back to Italy. Then, even if they had to sell the house to buy the business, they would still be in the same area and would have a small, sunny garden out at the back of the shop.

Or was there more to it than that? Could it be that she had deliberately chosen the timing of her trip to coincide with Ted's departure for France? Was he, as Shirley had sometimes idly speculated, her favourite child? Had she decided that, once he had left home, probably for good, there was no point in her staying in England? The suspicion that after all these years perhaps her mother did not care very much about her was too terrible to contemplate. Might it be in some way her fault? She cast through her mind and could not find any instance of real or violent disagreements with her. Perhaps it was just something that happened; maybe mothers naturally preferred their sons. She fought back the tears as she reflected on all these possibilities, unable to come to any specific conclusion, because Maman, who held the key to the situation, was thousands of miles away and had given them no personal contact details at all.

Shirley's vivid imagination plunged her into a desperate state, caught between anger and sorrow, tinged with a touch of guilt that perhaps in the past she had been unduly selfish; that, despite all the encouragement Maman had given her, she had not helped her mother enough in the home, that she had not make enough effort to encourage her to integrate into English society... The list went on and on. She went into the kitchen to cook the meat and vegetables that she had slipped out to buy earlier in the hope that her father would be inclined to eat them.

There was no question now: she would not be able to take up a career in dancing for a long time, if ever, because her main priority would be caring for her father and trying to protect him against any more blows. At least there was one thing that she could do: she could write letters, one to the French Embassy in Washington and one to her brother to ask him if he had heard from their mother. She toyed with the idea of telephoning Louise, since, with the telephone there on the sideboard, a call to France, booked in advance and rather costly, had become a perfectly feasible option, but no sooner had she contemplated that than she dismissed it for fear that Louise would spread gossip round the village. Perhaps Céline was right and Louise was the queen of village gossip.

36

The storm that had been threatening for so long on the horizon, but which he had deliberately ignored, engulfed Reggie as he succumbed to the harsh truth that his wife had left him. He did not put up a fight or run away; on the contrary, he sat silently in his old armchair for days, immersing himself in the newspapers of which he had a plentiful supply, or listening grim-faced to the wireless, which told daily of more atrocities committed both in Spain and in Germany. However fierce the effects of the storm on his mental well-being, he said little, except to remark from time to time, "There's trouble on the way; anyone can see that, except, it seems, our own Prime Minister. He won't get much out of Hitler, if anything at all, at that Munich conference, that's for sure. That madman and his cronies are hell-bent on conquering everyone everywhere." As such remarks were purely rhetorical, Shirley did not reply, but simply went to sit on the arm of his chair and pat his hand. For two weeks he spoke scarcely at all and never mentioned his errant wife, except that at night his cries and moans were audible throughout the flat, leading Shirley to fear a recurrence of the shell shock which had appeared to subside after his retirement from the railway.

One evening Shirley came upstairs to find that he had turned her mother's photograph to the wall and, referring to another on the sideboard he said, "Take that picture away, will you, Shirl, please." Shirley removed it to her own room, where she put it on the dressing table. It was the companion photo to the one of Georges that stood on the piano at Trémaincourt and showed her mother as a young girl with long, thick brown hair. The subject stared out of the frame with an intent gaze and a hint of a nervous smile. "Please come home, Maman! Don't leave us!" Shirley sobbed in French. The subject of the photo went on smiling blandly, unmoved by her sobs.

There was no time to investigate the ballet school that Miss Patience had suggested and that was apparently only a few streets along the road; there was scarcely time for practice, as Shirley found herself in charge both of the home and the shop. She plunged into the business, opening the premises in the early morning and closing again at night, every night, before turning her attention to the housekeeping. As a rule she would sneak out after the morning rush to buy food and other essentials from the row of shops in which the newsagent's stood.

Fortunately Cousin Archie was only too pleased to take on the accounting and the ordering, and he stayed behind every evening on weekdays to do the stocktaking. "I never thought I'd be quite as busy as this," he observed, rubbing his hands in glee. "Poor Reggie, it's his old war wound playing up, is it? Oh, he did suffer badly!" he remarked, shaking his head, but carried on without waiting for an answer. "Just as well I was allowed to stay on, wasn't it? It's put a stop to my missus ranting about her plans for going on holiday, I'm glad to say. Thought she would like to go up to Scotland, she did. I ask you, who would want to spend all that money going somewhere else when you can be so comfortable at home?" Shirley was warming to this distant cousin of her father's and found herself grinning at some of his comments. Above all, she was so very glad that he had stayed on and not gone up to Scotland, because his help was invaluable. It would have been impossible for her and Tilly to manage without him.

She made a point every evening at supper time of telling her father every detail of the events of the day, rather in the style of a balletic scenario. At first he took no notice, but after a few days he began to listen to her account because her mimicry of some of the characters who came in to buy tobacco or newspapers was so compelling. She told him about the man they called "the Major", with his broad handlebar moustache, which unfailingly he twirled before beginning a sentence. A conversation with him went something like this, she told her father: the Major would come into the shop, would twirl his moustache and only then would he greet the shopkeepers, one of whom would politely wish him good day and ask how he was. There would follow more twirling of the moustache, which she imitated by point her finger tips to her cheeks, while he considered his answer, which inevitably would be "Top hole, top hole, old boy!". "Old boy" could just as well refer to Tilly or herself as to Cousin Archie. Then there would be an exchange about the weather or the news, which would take twice as long as necessary because of all the twirling of the moustache.

There was also the lad with the ginger hair which stood straight up on the top of his head seemingly in a permanent state of shock, and there was the lady, always dressed in black, who came in every day, come rain or shine, with her umbrella fully open. Tilly said it was useless to ask her to close it or to point out that it wasn't raining, because she didn't speak English. She would indicate what she wanted to buy by pointing the open brolly, and proffering the correct money with no words being exchanged. The most unwelcome customer, at least in Tilly's opinion, was Jonas the gardener, who worked in the municipal gardens: whatever the weather, to her exasperation, he always came in covered in mud. "As sure as night follows day," she said, for no sooner had she washed the floor, morning or afternoon, than he would be certain to come in for his tobacco.

Little by little, with similar character studies, always accompanied by the appropriate gestures, Shirley succeeded in arousing her father's interest, until after lunch one afternoon he heaved himself out of his armchair and said, "I think I'll go and see what's happening in the shop, Shirl." He clambered down the stairs and stayed there for the rest of the day, coping with the Major, the foreign lady with the umbrella and with Jonas the muddy gardener.

His daughter grasped the opportunity to take the afternoon off. At first she retired to her room for a practice session, and then, because her father had not reappeared, collecting up her leotard and her ballet shoes, and putting Miss Patience's letter in her handbag, she made her escape. The trouble was that she had no idea where to find the ballet school. Although it would have been sensible to ask Cousin Archie or Tilly where it was, she did not like to interrupt the proceedings in the shop and possibly distract her father from whatever it was that had absorbed his attention, so instead she opened the door of the neighbouring shop, a sweet shop, and went in.

Compared with the bustle of activity in the newsagent's next door, the sweet shop, where one might have expected to find hordes of children, was morbidly silent. Not a single customer had ventured into the dim interior, lit by only one dingy lamp standing on the counter. Dark, dusty shelves were lined with sweet jars in which the contents appeared to have congealed and lost their original colour, while the faded boxes of chocolates in the glass-fronted counter must have been there since the Twenties, if not longer.

Since there was no one in attendance, Shirley was about to beat a hasty retreat from the dreary scene, when an elderly woman, bent double, came hobbling out of a room behind the shop. For a moment Shirley imagined that she had encountered the witch from *Hansel and Gretel*, and edged nervously towards the door. "Well," said the white-haired woman sharply, "what do you want?" Shirley was on the point of making a feeble excuse, but then decided at least to ask for the directions, though she certainly was not going to buy anything.

"I was wondering if you could tell me where I could find the Belinsky School of Dance, please? I'm new here and don't know my way around. This letter says it's in Castle Road."

The old woman bluntly replied, "My shop is for the purchase of sweets. I do not dispense information."

"I see. I'm sorry to have troubled you," Shirley said pleasantly and backed away closer to the door.

"Where are you from?" the woman enquired, her curiosity now aroused.

"I live next door. My father has bought the newsagent's," Shirley answered, although on second thoughts she wished that she too had said that she did not give out information.

"Ah," said the old woman triumphantly, "well then, please can you go and tell your father, and that girl and the old man who work there, not to make so much noise. I can hear them through the wall downstairs all day and upstairs all evening." She tapped on the dividing wall through which the dull murmur from the newsagent's was barely audible.

Shirley was not aware that she and her father had made any noise at all upstairs, until it occurred to her that it must be the sound of Pa's wireless that penetrated the wall into the adjoining flat; certainly not the sound of any jollifications or sustained conversation into the middle of the night, because there had been none. She apologized and promised to convey the complaint to the supposed revellers next door, though in fact she had no intention of doing any such thing. To her surprise the woman became almost civil, at least to the extent of giving her the information she needed. "Turn left out of here and go along the road for about half a mile; on the bend, where the main road veers off to the right, you turn left into Castle Road which winds round and backs onto the railway line. The dance school is on the left less than a hundred yards further on."

"Thank you," Shirley said as she fairly raced for the door, anxious to be out of the dank, musty smell and into the comparatively fresh, smoky atmosphere which emanated from the railway station a quarter of a mile or so away.

With a certain amount of scepticism, she followed the instructions and was surprised to find that they proved to be remarkably accurate, as Castle Road and the Belinsky School of Dance were indeed exactly where she had been told to find them. The school was housed in a large grey double-fronted Victorian house, reached by a flight of steps. She tentatively pushed open the heavy door, with its inset glass panel depicting red and green flowers on long thin stalks, and peeped inside.

In the hall a group of girls were clustered around a reception desk, busily talking to a middle-aged secretary. This was a familiar sight from which Shirley took courage, though, annoyingly, anxiety had taken hold of her, making her left leg limp slightly. The girls turned to stare as she walked up to the desk, while the secretary averted her eyes, pretending to be otherwise engaged. Shirley was so furious that defiant energy coursed throughout her whole body, even into her left leg. "I have a letter from my teacher, Miss Patience, who was a colleague of the dance teacher here," she announced imperiously to all and sundry, though to no one in particular. The girls shrank away and the secretary looked up from her desk.

"I think you mean Madame," the secretary said pointedly. "Please take a seat while I tell Madame that you are here. What name shall I give?"

"Shirley Marlow," she replied curtly, "and please say that I was recommended by Miss Nora Patience."

Shirley was not prepared to take a seat; she had not come here to be treated like an invalid. She would stand until this Madame, whoever she was, appeared. "Why did these women call themselves 'Madame'?" she wondered. She suspected that Madame probably thought herself more important than she actually was. Dear Miss Patience had no such pretensions. How she longed to be once more back in her school! Alas, that was a vain hope, because not only had she and her pa moved away, but Miss Patience's academy no longer existed. It had closed for good a long time ago.

The sound of voices reached her ears and from somewhere in the distance she detected instructions being given in French. The secretary reappeared after a longish interval to ask if Shirley would return on Thursday, as Madame was busy at present. Shirley reflected. Thursday was early closing, and she did not yet know how the evening papers were dispensed on that day, but that did not deter her and she agreed to meet

Madame on Thursday at four o'clock. "And can you tell me, please," she politely enquired of the secretary, "what is Madame's name?"

"Madame Belinskaya," the secretary replied in a tone that suggested that Shirley should have known that before entering the premises. "And by the way," the secretary added superciliously, "you do know, I suppose, that Madame speaks only Russian and French?" Shirley did not reply. She simply raised one eyebrow and left the building. Once outside, she allowed herself a moment of pleasure, confident that both Madame and her insolent secretary were going to have a surprise.

She marched briskly home to the shop in a good mood, despite the obstacles she had encountered. At least she had achieved something, she told herself, even if she had not succeeded in meeting Madame Belinskaya. Despite her misgivings, she was not going to allow this Madame to intimidate her, because there was no way that Madame Belinskaya could be as terrifying as Madam at Sadler's Wells. She would walk into the building on Thursday afternoon with her head held high and her left leg fully functional. If she had to speak French, so much the better: though others might be deterred by that particular challenge, she would be perfectly at ease. She was looking forward to recounting the afternoon's events to her father at supper time in the hope that they might cheer him up and encourage him to emerge further from his doom-laden despondency.

To her surprise she discovered that he was still hard at work in the shop, giving the paper boys their instructions for their evening rounds. Cousin Archie was doing the books and Tilly was serving behind the counter, sitting on a high stool. Evidently Shirley had not been much missed. "Come on in, Shirley," Cousin Archie exclaimed. "We wondered where you were. Had to make our own tea, we did!"

"I'm sorry about that—" Shirley began to apologize when he interrupted her.

"Don't you worry about that, my dear young lady. I'm just teasing," he said, chuckling. "Everything's under control here and your father is glad to be back at work. Aren't you, Reg?" he said, asking for his cousin's confirmation.

"Oh, by the way," she said, changing the subject, "will you need me on Thursday afternoon? It's early closing day, isn't it? But there's something I have to do." Before Reg could reply, Cousin Archie jumped in with the fervent assertion that Shirley could do what she liked, go wherever she liked, because he would take charge of the evening papers on Thursday, which indeed was early-closing day. Reggie turned round, somewhat irritated.

"No, Archie, you don't need to be here. I can see to the papers on Thursday evening."

"Oh, and something else," Shirley intervened before the disagreement became an argument, "what can you tell me about that old woman next door in the sweet shop?"

"Why on earth did you go in there, Shirley?" Tilly exclaimed in astonishment.

"It was only to ask for directions," Shirley explained. "I didn't want to disturb you as you were all so busy."

"Don't go in there again," Tilly warned her. "She's completely crazy and never sells any sweets. The children are terrified of her: they think she's a witch." She shrugged and softened her tone. "She's a poor old thing really. Her husband died in the Boer War and her son died in the Great War. She kept the shop going for a time, but when she got too old she let it all go to pieces, and it's been like that for years."

"That's right," Cousin Archie chipped in, never one to be left out of a chat, "the shop is a memorial really. A museum piece. The missus tried to help her, but she wouldn't be helped, so we had to leave her to her own devices. The strange thing is that she opens it up every morning and closes it every evening, although she never sells anything and never buys in new stock. I suppose she must have a war widow's pension and that keeps her going." He added knowingly, "O' course, it's not like where you come from round here. There are some funny people about."

Shirley did not have to be told about the funny people, for she had met plenty of them already, but she did pass on the message about the noise from the shop. There were times when Cousin Archie's confidence that he had a solution for everything could be irritating, but this was not one of them. "That's a coincidence," he said. "Your father and I were just discussing where we might put up some more shelves for magazines, so we'll cover the dividing wall with them and then she won't hear a thing." Although she had sworn that she would take no notice of the complaints from next door, the sorry tale of the old woman's losses had moved Shirley more than she expected and, having already resolved the one problem of the noise from the shop, she tactfully suggested, when her pa switched his wireless on that evening, that he might move it away from the wall, thus solving the other.

At the root of her sympathy for the old woman next door lay the memory of her French grandparents' inconsolable sadness at the loss of their son. A shiver ran through her as a shocking notion struck her: how dreadful it would be, she thought, if Ted were killed in a war. After all, Pa had only just survived the Great War. She panicked as it also occurred to her that if Alan – by now reduced to little more than a fleeting image, which disproportionately still gave her great hope for her future – were killed in a war, she would never know. Trying to erase such thoughts, she set about cooking supper, but the troublesome ideas were not so easily suppressed and kept recurring, so that they were still worrying her when she pulled the covers over her head later that night.

By Thursday afternoon she had other less distressing and more immediate things to think about and, leaving her father to watch the trains from a chair, which he had pulled close to the window in his bedroom, she presented herself at the Belinsky School of Dance in good time for her appointment with Madame Belinskaya. She had spent all her spare time practising until her limbs ached and her head spun, though there was not enough space in her room to try out some *grands jetés*, for which she needed a studio. If only Madame Belinskaya would simply let her use a studio to practise her routines and variations, even if she would not admit her as a pupil, that would be better than nothing.

When she told her father about her plans, he had approved them, somewhat to her surprise, although she doubted that he had really grasped what she was saying. Typically of his changed state of mind since acknowledging the end of his marriage, all he said was: "That's fine, Shirl," thus clearing her conscience on the subject once and for all. It was obvious that the shop was well managed whether she were there or not, and that her father had gradually emerged from the edge of the frightening pit of depression, even though he usually spoke only in gruff monosyllables, and that the business was, as Cousin Archie had predicted, so profitable that there was plenty of money to pay the boss and his staff. Moreover, even though Tilly would soon be reducing her hours, Shirley had quietly achieved her goal of working only part-time, mainly because, despite the agreement that Cousin Archie would work only when he was needed, he succeeded in making himself indispensable most of the time, to which, luckily, Pa raised no objections.

As she climbed the steps to the front door of the Belinsky School of Dance, Shirley checked every part of her body and raised herself up as tall as she possibly could. With head held high, shoulders lowered and certain that her left leg was performing well, she opened the door for the second time. The secretary pretended that she did not recognize the visitor. "What is your name? Do you have an appointment?" she demanded. Shirley reckoned that two could play at this charade.

"Oh, yes," she said, "you must remember: I came in on Tuesday afternoon and asked to speak to Madame Belinskaya."

"Ah," replied the secretary rather shamefacedly, "it's Miss Marlow, isn't it? Do take a seat while I go and check if Madame will see you."

On this occasion Shirley did take a seat and surveyed the hall, which was grander, smarter and better appointed than the rather scruffy entrance to Miss Patience's dance school. A huge vase of autumn roses stood on a table in front of a mirror on one cream wall, while opposite, an array of framed photographs of dancers performing *arabesques en pointe*, *grand jetés* and *posé* turns, advertised the success of the enterprise. She went over to the display and was scrutinizing the photos when the secretary returned and announced tersely. "Madame suggested I might show you round; she is busy at the moment, but will be with you soon. Follow me, please."

She turned on her heel and led the way up a long flight of stairs, at the top of which she briefly indicated the bathroom and changing facilities on one side of the house and a small but well-appointed and well-lit studio on the other. "As soon as they arrive," she explained, "individual students register with me and then come up here to change into their shoes and leotards and store their clothes away in a locker." She waved in the direction of the cloakroom. "Beginners' classes take place up here as well," she said, "the studios on the ground floor are for advanced classes and practice sessions."

Shirley was impressed, though she avoided appearing to be so. "I see, I see" was all she said. The studios on the ground floor with their pink walls and huge mirrors were impressive.

"I expect you will want to sit down, won't you?" the secretary said, unusually solicitous, when they came downstairs.

"No, no, that's all right, thank you; I'd prefer to take a good look at those photos," Shirley replied casually.

Some five minutes later, an electric bell rang on the desk. The secretary went to the rear of the house and came back saying, "Madame would like to see you now, Miss Barlow."

"Marlow," Shirley corrected her and followed her to an office at the bottom of four steps at the end of the hallway. A slight woman as straight as a ramrod and with greying hair pulled up in a chignon stood behind a large desk. There was not a trace of a smile on her severe features as she said, "*Bonjour, mademoiselle*," and held out a hand which Shirley shook as she returned the greeting in French. The interview continued in French until Madame appeared to have run out of questions, or perhaps she had run out of vocabulary in which to formulate them, because her French was not as fluent or as idiomatic as Shirley's, and she spoke with a thick accent which Shirley supposed to be Russian. In any case her questions were fairly superficial, mostly about her full name, date of birth, address and school achievements and hardly concerned the ballet, except for a passing reference to Shirley's previous dance school. Nor was there more than a scant mention of her past experience or of the ballets and shows that she had not only danced in but had also choreographed. Madame only wrinkled her nose at the mention of Nora Patience. Even so, Shirley found it hard to conceal her pleasure at finding that she had gained the upper hand in French, although she was perturbed at the cursory nature of the interview, as if Madame did not take her seriously. At last the woman announced that it was time for some practical tests.

She led the way to one of the rather grand studios on the ground floor, placed a record on the turntable of a gramophone, which did not revolve when she turned it on. "Mees Smit, Mees Smit, come 'ere at once!" she called out.

In no time the secretary, presumably Miss Smith, was at her side. "Yes, Madame, what is it?"

"Vat ees eet, Mees Smeet? I weel tell you! Zee gramophone ees not vorking!"

"Ah, I am so sorry, Madame. I will wind it up straight away. I thought I had done it earlier!" Madame scowled while Shirley enjoyed "Mees Smeet's" discomfort. Madame reverted to French when the secretary had gone out.

"Now, I want you to do *pliés*, *tendus* and *grands battements* at the *barre*, and then the beating steps of the *batterie* and the *entrechats* in

303

the centre; later I will instruct you what to do next, but do you have a routine to show me?"

Shirley nodded. "*Mais oui, Madame. Bien sûr!*" This was all familiar territory to her; she had been through it so many times that she was certain of being able to acquit herself well.

After those exercises, Madame, as impervious as ever, standing absolutely still, said, "Now I want you to do some *grandes rondes de jambe*, as I call out the positions, followed by *développés* and *arabesques* and then some *pirouettes*. She changed the record on the turntable to an *adagio* and wound up the gramophone herself. Shirley performed exactly as requested, whereupon Madame allowed herself the merest glimmer of a smile. "Now finally," she said as she changed the record again, "some *grands jetés* across the studio!" This was the move that Shirley had not been able to practise at home or in France for lack of space. She took up her position in one corner of the studio and listened to four bars of music before launching into the runs and the leaps.

Madame permitted herself another faint smile after the performance. "So I have seen what you can do. You are a better dancer than I expected. However, in those *grands jetés* your left leg was limp and bent," she said abruptly. With that she turned on her heel and was about to leave the room, but Shirley was quicker off the mark and leapt into the doorway barring her exit. She was livid.

"*Non, Madame!*" she shouted, glaring at the ballet mistress who shrank visibly before her eyes. "I could see from the moment I walked into your office that you were determined to find fault with me. Your questions were so basic and so inadequate for a dancer of my experience! You have dismissed me without even having the courtesy to ask why I have a slight limp: I can tell that my limping left leg has given you the perfect excuse for refusing to give me a chance here in this school of yours!"

Madame Belinskaya took a step backwards away from the inferno of Shirley's fury. Her expression changed from one of haughty superiority to meek astonishment. It appeared that Shirley had burst the bubble of her overpowering self-esteem, which had obviously held all her pupils and her staff in thrall for a long time. Her features softened, as did her voice. "So, tell me," she said, "what is your experience of the ballet?"

"In a nutshell," Shirley replied, still defiant, "I started dancing when I was five years old, and a year ago I won a place at Sadler's Wells to train as a principal dancer under Madame Ninette de Valois – that is to say, 'Madam'." She stressed the name, spelling it out in monosyllables to impress its importance on this trumped-up Madame, but a sob came into her voice all the same. The most famous name in English ballet did indeed have the desired effect, producing a gasp of amazement from Madame Belinskaya.

"*Oh, la, la!*" she said in some confusion. "Then why are you not at Sadler's Wells now?"

"I'll tell you why," Shirley replied, in as caustic a fashion as possible, "the reason I am not at the Wells is because a year ago I fell critically ill with infantile paralysis and my left leg was totally paralysed. I've worked extremely hard to get it moving again, and I think it's now ready to learn to dance again. I didn't necessarily want to come here for lessons or to join a class, only to ask if I might come to practise in an empty studio. I know my *grands jetés* need improvement, and that's because we don't have space for them at home. As you did not give me any chance to explain this in your so-called interview, I want you to understand it now before I leave!" As if to put a definitive full stop to her tirade, she stamped her right foot, then executed a perfect *grand jeté* across the room.

"I understand; I am sorry," Madame stammered. "I did not know…" Unable to cope with embarrassment, she stared out of the window. "I do understand now that you have told me your story, and I understand, because a similar thing happened to me once, a long time ago. You see, I was a young principal dancer in the Imperial Ballet in St Petersburg, and I lived for the ballet, nothing else. But then one winter I had a bad fall on the ice on the River Neva and broke both my ankles. Recovery was very slow, and although I was taken back into the *corps de ballet* at the Mariinsky Theatre, which the Soviets now call the Kirov of course, I knew that I would never dance the principal roles again. Later, during the Revolution, I escaped to Paris, but the problem was that there was nothing for me to do there, because I couldn't dance for other reasons, and there were already so many ballet teachers in that city; so that's why I finally came to London and set up my own school here." Her voice quavered. "Of course you can come here, Miss Marlow. You can use any studio that is free, and I personally would be glad to teach you if you would like that. Let's hope that one day you will be able to resume your career in the theatre! Oh, and please do give my regards to Nora Patience. I did not know her very well, but she was an excellent dancer. She danced with the Ballets Russes, I remember…"

Wearing her green silk dress with her blond curls peeping out from under her hat, Shirley cut a striking, if diminutive, figure as she stood in Waterloo Station waiting for her friend Cynthia on the morning of Miss Patience's wedding. Dressing up for the wedding had distracted her from the reports in the newspapers about the Prime Minister's return from his meeting in Munich with Adolf Hitler, and the agreement he believed he had concluded with the German Chancellor. Pa's attention had been glued to the wireless the night before and he had shaken his head frequently at the talk of "peace in our time". "Mark my words," he said sombrely, "that agreement is not worth the paper it is written on. In no time at all, Hitler will tear it up. I tell you all those crowds cheering Chamberlain as he arrived home will soon have the smile wiped from their faces."

The subject had provoked a lively discussion in the shop early the next morning. Pa stuck with a gloomy tenacity to his prediction, which upset Tilly particularly. "I think Mr Chamberlain is right," she declared tearfully. "I don't want my baby to be born into a war like I was!" Cousin Archie remarked sagely that Reg was probably right, but the agreement did give the country a much needed breathing space and time to rearm.

"Those sandbags out in the streets and the gasmasks won't help us much if our forces don't have the proper arms," he concluded. The customers joined in with a variety of opinions, some of which branded the Prime Minister a fool who had had the wool pulled over his eyes.

The gathering in the shop was becoming heated when Shirley left it to attend to her appearance. Donning her dress, combing her hair and powdering her nose, the while surveying herself in her dressing-table mirror, she put ominous current affairs out of her head. There was nothing that she could do to influence world events, she reasoned, so she might as well enjoy herself. Her enjoyment was tempered with regret that Maman was not there to help her make the final adjustments to her hat or flatten the collar of her dress, but once again, like last year, her mother was absent from her preparations for a wedding at which she would wear the green Parisian outfit. Shirley's efforts were well rewarded, however, and attracted admiring gazes from the male passers-by on Waterloo Station, though the women either looked away, pretending that they had not seen her, or raised their eyebrows in envious disdain. She enjoyed provoking reactions because that was what one was supposed to do on the stage, and Waterloo Station was as good a stage as any other for practising the art.

Smartly but demurely dressed in a navy-blue coat and hat, Cynthia was the perfect foil to her glamorous companion. "Oh, Shirley, you do look gorgeous! What a lovely dress!" she exclaimed generously as she approached, arms outstretched. Revelling in the compliment, though doing her best to appear modest, Shirley confessed that the clothes were not new but had been bought for her cousin's wedding a year ago, at which she had been a bridesmaid. She was uncomfortable at the memory of that wedding with its disastrous consequences. Nevertheless, that did not prevent her from showing off the outfit that she had worn for it. It was not so much that she wanted to stand out at this wedding, which, considering the age of the principal participants, would probably be a quiet affair; rather she had in her mind, both at the back and at the forefront, the vision of that little village nestling in the South Downs just north of Brighton that she had identified on the map as Hambley and about which she had had the uncanny and inescapable sensation that it was Alan's home. If there were even the tiniest chance that she might come across him there, she wanted to be sure of looking her best. There was therefore a powerful undercurrent to the day's excursion that held a much greater significance than the wedding of her former teacher.

As the two girls boarded the train, Cynthia glanced back along the platform towards the ticket barrier. "I'm terribly sorry," she said, "but Violet begged to be allowed to join us on the journey. I hope you don't mind. I know you don't like her very much, but I didn't feel I could say no, as we are all going to the same place and the same wedding."

Shirley was not overly concerned and graciously accepted Cynthia's apology. "Oh, don't worry about that," she said. "At the time I was upset that she had been offered a place at Sadler's Wells before I had even had an audition, but really, it doesn't matter now. It wasn't her fault, and anyhow it will be interesting to find out how she's getting on."

The practice sessions in Madame Belinskaya's studio and the private, though free lessons that Madame gave her were fast restoring her self-confidence and feeding her ambition. Secretly she was anticipating the opportunity to show Violet that she was back in business and, who knows, might even reappear at the Wells one day. Leaning out of the compartment window, Cynthia waved to a small person running along the platform and shouted, "Come on, Violet, you'll miss the train!" Shirley looked out too, although she scarcely recognized Violet, who threw herself into the train, pursued by the piercing shriek of the guard's whistle.

"Oh," she gasped, "I didn't think I was going to make it! I overslept this morning." She sank into a seat and closed her eyes. She was very pale and very thin, dressed in what appeared to be the first items that came to hand when she had jumped out of bed: a pink cotton skirt, a crumpled white blouse, white socks and shoes. "Oh, dear, do I look a wreck?" she enquired nervously when she saw Shirley sitting opposite her.

"No, no you're fine," Cynthia said kindly though untruthfully.

Violet was near to tears. "I did so much want to dress up and have a lovely day with you two," she said plaintively, "but Madam insisted on having one of her sessions after last night's performance, telling us where we went wrong, of course, so that we didn't get away from the theatre until after midnight, and I was so tired I didn't have time to get out my clothes for today: I simply collapsed into bed and slept." Her eyes moistened as she sniffed into her handkerchief. "Oh, it's so hard there! You've no idea. I don't know how much longer I can cope with it, but I don't know how to get out of it either."

The remnants of Shirley's antagonism melted before this pathetic sight. Since the three girls had the compartment to themselves, she opened her handbag and pulled out a hairbrush and her make-up. "You can borrow my make-up, if you like," she offered, holding her powder and lipstick out to Violet, "and I've brought my brush and comb, but I haven't got any hairpins because my hair is too short to need them. Do you have any, Cynthia?" With Shirley's brush and comb and Cynthia's pins, they dressed Violet's hair, and then with Shirley's make-up brushed some colour into her cheeks until she appeared at least half-ready for a wedding.

"Miss Patience is sending a driver for us, so maybe we could ask him to wait for half an hour or so – we're in very good time," Cynthia said wondering aloud, "then we could quickly find a dress shop and buy you a nice dress, Violet. How much money have you brought with you?"

Violet delved into a scruffy handbag and pulled out her purse. "Not much, I'm afraid; I haven't been paid for ages. Could I borrow a pound or so from you?"

"Yes, of course. Here, I think I've got at least one pound in my purse," Cynthia said. Then she asked, "What about you, Shirley?"

"Well, yes, I've brought my earnings from the shop, so I have plenty of money," Shirley replied loftily. "Have as much as you like." She was pleased to be able to appear more affluent than a dancer from the Sadler's Wells *corps de ballet*.

The driver, sent by the bride to Brighton Station, was not bothered at being expected to wait while the girls went on a shopping spree. "There's plenty of time," he said, "the wedding is not till three o'clock and it's only half-past twelve now, so you three can go off and spend all your money if you like. I've been booked to look after you for this wedding all day, and I won't have anything to do if we arrive too soon, so just go and enjoy yourselves! And you can leave whatever you buy in the boot of my car. It'll be quite safe there! I'll park on the front. That's where you'll find me." Violet was thrilled, and so was Shirley, because she already feared that she had not dressed appropriately for the weather.

"It was so warm in London!" she exclaimed shivering, momentarily recalling her last, unfortunate visit to Brighton. "And down here by the sea there's a chilly breeze. I think I need to buy a jacket, or at least a stole."

"Well, it is the first of October today, so you can't be surprised at that. We should count ourselves lucky the sun is shining," Cynthia remarked. "But come along, you two; we'd better look sharp if we are going to do all this shopping and still arrive at the wedding on time!"

Brighton was not short of dress shops. It took Shirley no time at all to find and buy a smart but warm cream jacket, while Violet could not decide whether to choose a red skirt and blouse with long sleeves that were hanging on the end-of-season reduced rack or a similar outfit in turquoise. "I think the turquoise is more stylish," Shirley observed curtly in ill-disguised exasperation at the length of time that Violet was taking to make up her mind. She realized too late that this time could have been better spent strolling round the village where the wedding was to take place and memorizing each and every detail of every house, every garden and every inhabitant in case any of them were related to or connected with Alan. She had made her purchase, powdered her nose in the ladies' room and wanted to be setting off.

After an age, Violet finally chose the turquoise. Then she looked at her feet and wailed, "But I can't wear these shoes with this lovely costume! They don't match."

"Oh yes you can!" Shirley retorted firmly. "They have a small heel and they are quite smart; all you need is a pair of stockings and they will look fine!" So it was decided: Violet was marched off to ladies' underwear without more shilly-shallying.

The driver was asleep in the car when they found him parked on the Front. He was impressed by the transformation in Violet's appearance. "Seen your fairy godmother, have you, dear?" he asked with a wink at the other two girls, as he placed a paper bag containing Violet's old clothes in the boot of the car. Half an hour and we'll be there!" He drove at such a leisurely pace that it seemed they might never arrive. Shirley grew more and more impatient by the minute and kept looking at her watch. It was a quarter to three when they pulled up outside an old church in the hamlet. "There you are, ladies. How about that for perfect timing?" he announced proudly.

His timing was perfect if all that one wanted to do was to go straight into the church and find a seat in a pew to await the arrival of the bride. There was no plausible excuse that Shirley could find for delaying, so, with the utmost reluctance and many a backward glance, she followed Violet and Cynthia into the church. The rest of the village was hidden from view behind walls, fences and hedges overhung by large trees. Disgruntled, she sat down in a pew beside Cynthia, who kept up a whispered commentary: "What a pretty church!", "What beautiful flowers!", "Quite a lot of people, aren't there?" She paused to survey the guests as they came into the church. "Oh! That must be Miss Patience's mother! Oh, so she's still alive!" she whispered as a very old lady advanced slowly down the aisle leaning on the arm of a nurse. Then she sat up tall, craning her neck to see over the heads of the wedding guests to the occupants of the front pew. "I suppose those are Miss Patience's relatives," she surmised. "Oh, I say! There's a handsome man sitting there at the end of the pew. I hope I meet him!" Shirley raised herself up and caught a glance of a handsome young man, but he had dark curly hair and was not Alan. The disappointment made her even more irritated with Cynthia's whispered remarks, so she closed her eyes and pretended not to hear, and Cynthia addressed her observations to Violet instead.

At that moment the organist struck up the wedding march. The congregation stood up and all eyes turned to the back of the church, where Nora Patience was making her entry on the arm of an elderly gentleman. Shirley had a good view, since she was at the end of the pew. At first she assumed that the elderly gentleman must be Miss Patience's father, but that was before she remembered that Mr Patience had died many years ago, leaving his daughter solely responsible for her mother, so perhaps the gentleman was an uncle. Dressed in a warm, though not garish shade of yellow with a cream veil and carrying a bouquet of cream carnations, chrysanthemums and roses, the bride looked lovely in a modest, middle-aged sort of way. Her face was set in a broad, happy smile, which she bestowed on all her well-wishers, including Shirley, whose mood improved in the warmth of that smile. As the wedding party progressed up the aisle, she expected to see a middle-aged man step out of his pew on the other side of the church, but that front pew was occupied only by ladies. She was perplexed and then more than a little shocked when she realized that the gentleman who had accompanied Miss Patience to the altar was neither her father nor her uncle, but the groom himself. He was at least as old as Pépé, perhaps older, because Pépé was much weathered by being out of doors in all seasons and in all weathers.

She had never been to a wedding where an old man had married a lady in late middle age, and found it extraordinary. When she talked to Cynthia about it later, Cynthia said, "Well, you told me that you expected your grandfather would probably marry his housekeeper one day, so what's the difference?" The difference was that Céline was already part of the family, so it was natural that she should look after Pépé and that they should marry without there being any romantic connotations. Even so, the prospect of such marriages made Shirley uncomfortable. In her opinion, weddings were for beautiful young couples, heroes and heroines, with their lives to be lived happily ever after ahead of them.

She trusted that her pa would never do anything so stupid if in fact Maman had really left him, though that was a matter still open to question. Some days, mostly on fine sunny days, Shirley was sure that her mother would return; on chilly grey days she was less certain. Pa never spoke about Maman, though his night terrors had quietened down again, so she discreetly and deliberately avoided mentioning her, difficult though that was. It would have been so much easier if, with the innocence of early childhood, she could have openly wondered aloud what her mother was doing and where she was, rather than obeying the guarded expectations of early adulthood, which required her to pretend that Maman did not exist any more.

The couple were now standing in front of a tubby, rather jolly clergyman who was saying how delighted he was to be officiating at his brother's marriage and how grateful he was to the vicar of the parish – whose name Shirley did not catch because she was too involved with her own thoughts – for allowing the wedding to take place in his very special and ancient church. This last pronouncement was not lost on Shirley, however: in fact the closest she had been to anything like this church was the village church in Trémaincourt, which also was medieval, but was decorated with garish plaster saints and faded artificial flowers. This English country church was appealing in its musty odour, its bare walls and its uncluttered simplicity. Although it was small, it gave the impression of light and soaring spaciousness. Like the tower outside, the pillars seemed to reach upwards to the vaulted roof and the heavens beyond.

The church was certainly ancient and so unlike the dark Victorian Catholic church in London that her mother had attended, with its grimy walls and windows, its tiny red lamps and expressionless images. Although she had tried hard when she was little, she had not experienced any intimations of sanctity in that place where the priests in their elaborate robes performed their ritualistic ballet in the circle of light by the altar. In contrast, a year ago Thelma's wedding had taken place in a plain red-brick non-conformist church in Birmingham where exactly the opposite problem prevailed, for that church was totally devoid of any hint of ceremony and everything seemed bare and bald. This was different, and she wondered if all Church of England churches were like this, or only the ones in small villages out in the country. If they were, then she hoped that one day she would be married in a church like this.

After the photography outside the church, the taxi driver ushered the girls into his car. As he started the engine and drew away, he remarked, "Lovely wedding, wasn't it?"

"Oh, yes, beautiful!" Cynthia and Violet chorused, but Shirley was too preoccupied to join in. She had noticed a car that had just pulled up outside a large house in the lane that led to the church. The taxi slowed to pass the parked car, giving Shirley ample opportunity to see the driver. She was sure that the man who was getting out was Alan's father. The frisson of surprise took her breath away and made her head spin. How she wished that she could stop the taxi, get out, run along the lane to the car and, if necessary, follow the man up to the house, but frustratingly there was nothing she could do. Instead she sat in the taxi, feeling light-headed and paralysed both in movement and in speech.

She tried to shut out the driver's chatter; he was waxing lyrical about the elderly bridegroom, who apparently was a well-known doctor in Brighton. "Such a good doctor and a kind man!" he exclaimed. "My wife wouldn't be here today if it wasn't for him! She gave herself an electric shock a month ago when she was doing the ironing: the flex had worn thin and she touched an exposed wire." He blew out his cheeks before continuing, "Dr Ellison came immediately, he did, and gave her first aid and brought her back to life!" Nodding as if to stress his approval of the doctor, he went on, "I said to him, 'Doctor, if you ever need a car, all you have to do is let me know and it'll be my pleasure to be there!' So that's why I'm ferrying you young ladies about today."

Had her mind not been elsewhere, Shirley might have been humbled by this account of the virtues of the bridegroom. As it was, she was plunged into a vortex of confusion. On the one hand, her brain swam with jubilation that her intuition had been proved correct, and she was sure, really sure, that Alan did indeed live in Hambley; on the other, the further away from the village they drove, the further her anguish and desperation sucked her helplessly downwards, until she felt herself to be drowning in turmoil. She stared out of the window, wretchedly impervious to all that was happening around her.

It was not until later, not until after the pleasant reception and the delicious meal in a hotel in Brighton, at which she had hardly been able to concentrate on anything that was being said, or speak two sensible words to anyone, let alone the middle-aged people on the same table, that the truth dawned that the information she had so surprisingly acquired was of little use. What could she do with it? Write to a person addressed as "Alan's father, or even Alan himself, somewhere near the church in Hambley"? That would be completely idiotic. She sank into a corner of the railway carriage on the journey home and closed her eyes to avoid having to talk to Violet and Cynthia. "Are you all right, Shirley? You do look pale," Cynthia, ever caring, enquired.

"No, actually, I'm not feeling very well. Too much excitement, I expect. Maybe I ate something that didn't agree with me." She realized that this was a gloss on the truth that she would have to perpetuate because she had forgotten to tell Miss Patience, now Mrs Ellison, that she was having lessons with Madame Belinskaya, who had impressed upon her how much she wanted her to convey her congratulations and best wishes to her former colleague.

In a reversal of the roles, Violet, who had been so miserable on the journey to Brighton, had become the life and soul of the group. "That young man I sat next to, he was gorgeous!" she exclaimed. "He said what a lovely dress I was wearing and how well it suited me! When I said I was a dancer, he said he would like to come and see me on stage!" Cynthia, who had had designs on the handsome, dark-haired young man herself, kept quiet while Violet babbled on all the way to Waterloo. The girls parted company at the ticket barrier, where Violet expressed her undying thanks to Cynthia and Shirley, promised to repay them their money as soon as she received her monthly salary and invited them to a performance at Sadler's Wells. Cynthia, whose career in the dance had advanced as far as selling programmes for a musical show, said that she would love to come if she could have time off from her job, and Shirley nodded her grateful approval, saying that she would have to check her diary. This partial but non-committal acceptance of Violet's kind invitation would give her the chance to decide in private whether she could face going to the Wells to watch Violet dance.

The lights were still on in the flat above the shop when Shirley arrived home. She was tired and her left leg was giving her trouble as she dragged it up the stairs. Her father was sitting in his armchair, thumbing through his model-railway magazines. "Pa, there was no need to wait up for me!" she said indignantly as she came through the door.

"No, I'm not waiting up for you, because it's not that late, but I thought it would be nice to hear how the day went, that's all," he replied. "So, come on, tell me all about it. Did you have a good time?"

Shirley pouted. "Oh, it was all right," she said grudgingly.

"That doesn't sound very enthusiastic, and you were looking forward to it so much," her father remarked. "What went wrong?"

"I don't know really; it's just that I found it rather odd, you know, old people getting married and behaving as if they were young." She sat down and took off her hat, which she put on a side table.

"Oh, I say, that's rather hard, isn't it?" her father exclaimed. "Do you mean to say that older people shouldn't enjoy life?"

"No, it's not quite like that. I don't know what it is, but it seemed weird to me that they were behaving as if they were in their twenties."

"Oh, my Shirl," her father sighed, "you live in such a dream world: you want everyone to be young and beautiful, and you only allow young people to fall in love. Like those ballets you are thinking up all the time. What a miserable place that would be for anyone older than, say, thirty-five! Life's not like that, you know, and young people don't stay young for ever. They grow old, as you will, but life goes on and they have to make the best of growing old and enjoy themselves as and when they can. Come on, I'll make you a hot drink, then maybe you'll cheer up." In that long speech Pa had voiced all his thoughts on the subject, so he withdrew to make some cocoa.

When he reappeared, carrying two cups, he asked, "Anyhow, what about that lovely dish you gave them for a wedding present? Weren't they pleased with it?"

"Oh, that," Shirley said remembering the beautiful Lalique dish that she had bought with ten shillings from her first pay packet and an equal contribution from her father a couple of weeks or so ago. She had seen it in a shop in Bond Street on one of her infrequent visits to central London to meet Cynthia and had marched into the shop to buy it on impulse. Its swirling pattern of translucent milky-blue glass was so exquisite she had wanted to keep it for herself but, had resisted the urge. Now, although she rather wished that she had not been so generous, she was happy to have shown Miss Patience, or rather Mrs Ellison, her appreciation of all her tuition, kindness and encouragement over many a long year.

"I'm sure they must have been pleased with that," Pa commented.

"Yes, I expect so," she said. "I left it in its box on a table where they were collecting all the presents, so I don't know whether they liked it or not."

38

Shirley slept badly that night. A strange ballet of conflicting figures kept revolving in her head till daybreak. In the dream Miss Patience was dancing a *pas de deux* with the clergyman, her brother-in-law, in the red-brick church in Birmingham, while the elderly Dr Ellison was engaged in a duel with Alan's father out in the lane in Hambley. They were fighting over the ownership of a car in which Violet was sitting dressed in her old clothes, when another familiar figure appeared on the scene: it was Alan. He went over to the car, opened the door, sat down in the driving seat and then drove off with Violet beside him. At this point Shirley awoke trembling. She sat up, but was so dizzy she had to fall back onto her pillows. On the second attempt, which she took much more slowly, she managed to sit up and, in one move, swing her legs round so that her feet touched the floor. Gingerly she stood up and made her way to the bathroom. Although she moved without difficulty, she was convinced that there was no sensation in her left leg. In a panic, she screamed, "Pa! Pa!"

Deaf to her cries, her father was busy sorting the Sunday papers in the shop, which was closed off by a door from the staircase leading to the living quarters. Only when the morning's business was completed did he come up to the flat where he found his daughter lying on the sofa, shivering. "Shirl! What is the matter?" he cried in horror.

"I don't know, Pa, but I think my leg is paralysed again," she answered in an ethereally faint voice that seemed to come from a long way off.

"No, surely not!" he exclaimed. "You were limping a bit last night when you came home, but that was only because you were so tired. Come on; let's see what's going on here. But first of all, have you had anything to eat?"

"No, not yet" was all she could stammer.

"Well, then," Pa said as he disappeared into the kitchen, "I'm going to fry some eggs, toast some bread and make a pot of tea." That Shirley felt weak was no surprise, because she had eaten so little the previous day. Lunchtime, when otherwise she and Cynthia might have gone to a restaurant in Brighton, was taken up with fitting Violet out with suitable new clothes, and at the wedding banquet after the church service she could scarcely eat anything at all because her whole being was mercilessly agitated by the recent sighting, as she thought, of Alan's father in the village of Hambley.

Pa's lavish, though late breakfast helped restore a little of her strength, but not her composure. Even though she could stand and could walk, she still insisted that her left leg was paralysed and that probably her right leg was showing symptoms of paralysis too. Her father was mystified, because what he saw told a different story. There was no doubt in his mind that his daughter was overwrought: indeed he suspected that something had gone wrong the previous day, though he could not tell – and nor could he ask – what it was. He was fairly certain, however, that she was not falling victim to infantile paralysis again. He scratched his head, searching for a solution. "Shirl, I think you should go back to bed while I try to decide what to do. I can see that you are not very well and maybe I should try to find a doctor. The problem is that it is Sunday, and as we don't yet have a doctor here…" He paused in midsentence and scratched his head again before picking up the thread of his thoughts. "It might be best to wait till tomorrow, and then I'll take the morning off and drive you over to Dr Forbes. He knows you well and knows what you went through last year, so it seems to me that he would be the best person to consult. Off you go. I'll put the kettle on for a hot-water bottle." Shirley obeyed her father meekly, only too glad to take to her bed.

The leafy streets of south-west London seemed, on the following morning, to belong to another world, so different were they from the smoky, noisy surroundings into which Shirley and her father had moved a mere couple of months earlier. The contrast was not lost on Reggie, who became even more subdued than usual, as they drove along the clean, well-kept roads lined with modern houses on the way to the doctor's surgery. His daughter also fell silent and wished that they had not come at all, particularly when they passed the former site of Miss Patience's ballet school, which had been cleared away to make room for a block of luxury flats. She would have liked to call in on the Salvatores, who had been so kind to her, but that would have taken her and her father much too close to their old home for comfort, and probably for the well-being of them both; inevitably it would have brought back so many memories and might have reawakened Pa's night terrors, which had once more subsided. Such a visit would undoubtedly also have aroused some resentment, not unlike her mother's, at the move which Pa in his quiet and undemanding, though determined way had forced upon them. As it was, Shirley was shaken by the reminder of how pleasant their way of life used to be.

Dr Forbes was pleased, though surprised, to see them. He greeted them heartily. "You look well, Reggie," he said. "I would say that your change of lifestyle is suiting you."

Rather sheepishly Pa nodded his agreement, but hastened to add, "It's not me, but this young lady I rang your wife about. She was so poorly yesterday I was very worried about her." Shirley followed the doctor into his room, where he gave her a thorough examination.

"I'd say you probably have a slight chill, Shirley," he said after he had taken her temperature, "but that doesn't account for your father being so worried. Is there anything more that I ought to know?"

Shirley hardly knew where to begin: what to tell the doctor and what not to tell him. "I was afraid," she began hesitantly, "that I was going down with infantile paralysis again yesterday. Both my legs seemed numb, though Pa said I was walking perfectly normally."

Dr Forbes was scanning through Shirley's notes. "Of course," he said, "it is almost exactly a year since you fell ill. You are slightly under the weather, and perhaps the memory of that illness is giving you phantom symptoms, that is to say, your left leg is imagining that it is still para-lysed and the other one is reacting in sympathy with it. The body can do funny things, you know, especially if it's under stress." He gave her a searching look. "Would you say that you are under stress?" he asked.

Shirley considered his question and, at length, having decided what she was prepared to talk about, confided in him that deep down she regretted the move, although she knew that it was for the best, and she also told him about Maman's absence, which by the day was becoming more permanent. "Mm," was Dr Forbes's reaction, "your father looks so well I had no idea that the move was not right for the whole family, and I certainly didn't realize that your mother had gone away. What about your brother?" Shirley told him not only how happy Ted was to be in France but how much she missed him. Everything she said was real and true and brought tears – which in any case were very near the surface today – to her eyes, though in truth she knew that none of those subjects was behind the state of near collapse that she had experienced the day before, because she had already nearly adapted and almost learnt to live with each one of the situations that she had just recounted.

Yesterday's malaise was another matter altogether, and one that she was not prepared to divulge. Indeed her embarrassment at recounting it would undoubtedly have increased her distress. Dr Forbes sat back in his revolving chair, which he twisted round, turning from side to side. "It sounds to me as if you have all had a great deal to cope with," he said pensively, leaning across his desk. "I'm sure your father thought he was doing his best for everyone when he decided to change his job, because, after all, as things were, he was becoming so incapacitated that sooner or later his health would have given way altogether, and then he would not have been able to provide for you. Have you considered writing to your mother and asking when she is coming home?"

"The problem is," Shirley explained, "she hasn't given us a private address, and if we write to the American Embassy in Washington the letters might be opened by anyone."

"Yes, I can see that that must be very disturbing for all of you. I suppose that you, as well as missing your mother, have had to step into her shoes and keep house for your father? Have you had to give up all your own interests as well?" he enquired.

Shirley nodded. "Yes, that's right, I have," she replied.

"Is there anything more?" the doctor persisted. Shirley's indecision gave her away, but Dr Forbes let it pass. "My diagnosis," he said, "is nervous exhaustion, exacerbated by a chill. I shall prescribe a tonic for you and I shall tell your father that you must take it easy for at least three weeks." He invited Reggie into his room to tell him the diagnosis and the treatment. "By the way," he asked, "simply as a matter of interest associated with some research I am doing, is there anyone in your generation in the family who is particularly highly strung?"

"Yes, there most certainly is," Pa replied immediately. "It's my sister, Winnie!"

"Nervous exhaustion" was not an expression that was familiar either to Shirley or to her father, though it definitely had a ring of plausibility about it, and that, together with the "phantom symptoms", appeared to be an adequate description of her condition. She was glad that the doctor had taken it seriously and could put a name to it, because she had feared that she might be accused of imagining or inventing the symptoms. On the other hand, she was appalled to hear that she shared a condition with her aunt and dreaded turning out like Winnie. The stupid woman did not have one sensible thought in her head.

Pa, despite instantly identifying his sister as being highly strung, was less understanding of the doctor's diagnosis of nervous exhaustion, and no sooner were they out of the surgery than he made a suggestion which proved that he had little notion of what Dr Forbes actually meant. "What say we go to call on your granny, Shirl, after we've collected your prescription? That would be killing two birds with one stone, and we wouldn't have to make a special journey to pay her a visit sometime in the near future." Shirley closed her eyes: the visit to the doctor had worn her out, and she wanted nothing more than to go home and rest as he had instructed. She could appreciate the logic of Pa's suggestion and said so, but nevertheless, her granny was the last person she wanted to meet.

"All right," she conceded, "but only if we don't stay very long."

Granny Marlow answered the door herself, though only after she had called out from the inside, asking who was there. "I wasn't expecting you," was her first comment on opening the door. "Why didn't you telephone me before setting out? Then I could have told you whether it was convenient."

"We hoped you might be pleased to see us," Pa replied. "I brought Shirley over to see Dr. Forbes and we thought we might call in."

"I hope she's not infectious," Granny said, edging back into the house and pulling the door to until there was just a thin opening through which she eyed her granddaughter up and down.

"No, no, don't worry," Pa reassured her. "The doctor says it's nervous exhaustion, so she's not infectious."

"Nervous exhaustion? What's that?" Granny asked. "I've never heard of that. One of these newfangled medical terms, is it?" Shirley was thoroughly put out by this wrangling on the doorstep, which she found offensive, and decided that it was time to say so.

"Well, Granny," she intervened, "I didn't want to come here; I said so to Pa. The doctor told me to go home and rest and that's what I think I should do!"

Her grandmother's tone changed. "It's all right, dear. No need to get uppity," she retorted. "You are welcome to come in, but Martha is away for a few days, so I have to be sure that I can manage on my own, and

I should not be able to do that if I fell ill as a result of your visit." She opened the door wide. "In fact," she said, "I'm quite glad to see you. I have matters to discuss with you. Now do you think you could make us some coffee, dear?"

Pa shifted uneasily from foot to foot. "Do you think you could do that, Shirl?" he asked anxiously.

With a bad grace that she made no effort to conceal, Shirley sighed. "Oh, I suppose so," she said, and went into the kitchen. The one consolation was that she and her father would be able to drink Granny's best coffee.

She made a large pot and searched for the best biscuits, which she put on a tray with milk and sugar. She could hear voices, or rather Granny's voice, coming from the living room, which suggested that the discussion had become one of those harangues for which Granny was famous. As she walked across the hall, the topic became clear. "I remember from seeing your flat when Archie lived there that you have plenty of space, enough to put up Paul's boys at Christmas, particularly as my darling Edward is in France..." The harangue tailed off as Shirley came into the room.

"What is this all about?" Shirley asked, her suspicions aroused.

"Oh, your granny is saying that my brother and his family are coming for Christmas, and she is asking if we could have the boys to stay."

"Yes, dear," Granny concurred, "I thought how nice it would be for you to get to know your cousins better, and I don't have room for them all here."

Shirley nearly dropped the tray. She was about to remonstrate: "Rubbish, Granny, you have seven bedrooms here! And they are small boys! We can't possibly have them staying with us. The shop will be very busy right up to closing time on Christmas Eve." However, a better idea occurred to her, and she said quite calmly, "I'm pretty sure that Edward will be coming home for Christmas and we only have three bedrooms you know – mine and Pa's on the first floor and Edward's up on the top floor." Pa looked surprised and, from his face, Shirley could see that he was on the point of interrupting, and he would probably say, "Oh, is that so? I didn't know that Ted was coming home for Christmas," so Shirley quickly added, "He doesn't know for sure, but he is intending to." Granny was silenced.

Pa was quiet, even by his standards, as he drove home. When eventually he spoke, it was to ask in injured tones, "I didn't know that Ted was coming home for Christmas. Has he written to you separately?" Shirley drew in a deep breath, although she had already prepared her answer, because she had anticipated this question from the moment she had said that Ted would be coming home.

"No, he hasn't. The only letters from him have been the ones he sends us both each week. But I suppose it was wishful thinking on my part and, if he should want to come home, where would he sleep if Uncle Paul's boys have taken over his bedroom?" This reply in Shirley's opinion was more digestible for her father than the one she was inclined to give which was, "It's not fair! Granny has all that space and all those bedrooms and yet she expects us to accommodate her guests!" To be fair, Granny and those boys were not the best of companions, because the young rascals, scarcely in their teens, were pranksters and their grandmother provided them with an irresistible target for practising their jokes. It was not so long ago since she had discovered that, minutes before the end of their stay in the summer, they had snipped off all the flowers in her herbaceous border just below the surface of the soil, and then pressed the soil back into position to make it look as if they were still growing.

However, Pa was not satisfied with Shirley's excuse. "I'm not sure you should have said that," he remarked mildly, "untruths, even half-truths, have a way of catching up with you, you know."

Shirley, pushed to the end of her tether, flared up, "Well, what did you want me to say then? That we would love to have them to stay, that the shop will run itself, that we will cook for them, look after them and take them out sightseeing? Really Pa, you expect far too much of me! I am keeping house for us both already, as well as helping out in the shop, and I don't want to be doing this for the rest of my life! How can you expect me to? Granny has a huge house, she doesn't work, she has lots of money *and* she has maid!" Jolted out of his apparent complacency by this outburst, her father said no more. Shirley went straight upstairs to bed on their return home and he disappeared into the shop for the rest of the working day.

Only at supper time did father and daughter meet again. After a long afternoon nap she was feeling better. The memory of seeing Alan's father still persisted in her mind, but she felt calmer about it and had begun to regard it in part as a bonus which increased her fund of knowledge about Alan, minimal though that was, and slightly raised her chances of meeting him again. After all, Miss Patience, or Mrs Ellison as she now was, probably had close contacts with Hambley, where she and Dr Ellison had chosen to hold their wedding, so if all else failed she would write to Mrs Ellison to ask if she knew the family. On the other hand, the more she recalled about that chance sighting, the more it worried her; the car she had seen was very smart, large and new, and the house outside which it was parked was lovely, double-fronted and set in a beautiful, well-tended garden. All of which confirmed what she already suspected: Alan came from a well-heeled, possibly aristocratic background, to which she, though well educated, could neither aspire nor compete. Granny's wealth, which Maman always delighted in describing as bourgeois, did not count in these circumstances, because what Alan would see would be the shop where she and her father worked, in a run-down, grimy part of London, and their home, which was a three-bedroom flat, surrounded by roads and railway lines. Anyhow, even supposing Alan were to visit Granny's mansion, much larger, more comfortable and set in gardens that could almost qualify as grounds, he couldn't avoid meeting Granny, who by her very presence would damn Shirley's chances for ever.

Reggie came lumbering up the stairs with a full shopping bag. "Here, Shirl," he said, "I've been out to do some shopping for us. I'll cook while you sit by the fire, and then I have something to tell you." Pa's attempt at cooking potatoes, cabbage and pork chops, though little more than passable, was greeted with genuine gratitude by his daughter. During the course of the meal he told her how grateful he was to her for supporting him in the move and for her help in setting up the new business. He was sorry for the strain he had placed on her shoulders and hoped she would approve of his plan for the future. She listened attentively.

"As you are aware," he said, "Tilly is leaving us – or, that is, the shop – at the end of next week, but her baby is not due for another two months and she needs to go on earning money, so I've asked her if she would be prepared to do some shopping for us and a little light cleaning every day for a couple of hours, if it's not too much for her. What do you think of that?" Shirley beamed at him.

39

After ten days of rest, if not necessarily in bed, Shirley was ready to take up the reins again. Her first port of call was Madame Belinskaya's studio, where she was welcomed with open arms. "Chérie!" Madame exclaimed, "We have missed you so much! Come and tell me what has happened to you!" Madame encouraged her to do no more than some gentle exercises before dismissing her with instructions to go home for more rest and come back two days later. Even the tight-lipped secretary mustered a vestige of a smile.

In the shop, Cousin Archie fussed over her like an old woman. "Come and sit down, young lady – we don't want you falling ill again, do we?" he said. Tilly, despite the encumbrance of her pregnancy, was pleased to be earning some money and found the household chores demanded of her to be well within her robust capability.

Given how quickly Shirley had recovered, she was afraid that she might be viewed as a fraud, yet no one even so much as hinted at such an unfair interpretation of her phantom symptoms, but she herself knew that in part they resulted from her confusion on seeing Alan's father in that same village where her sixth sense had told her that he lived. "Nervous exhaustion" was without question the perfect description of her condition. Dr Forbes said as much when her father drove her over to his surgery three weeks later for a check-up. His assessment caused her to reflect in quiet moments about herself and her future. She was shocked at how strong and how physical her reaction had been at that chance near-encounter in Hambley, although secretly she had hoped that something of the sort might happen. Without a doubt she certainly could not go through that again without it having disastrous consequences for her health. What would it be like if she were to catch a glimpse of Alan himself? Her obsession with him, she told herself, was nothing but ridiculous fantasy. After all, what did she know about him except for his name and his good looks? She was stupid to set so much store by a chance meeting with someone she would never see again, and, if she did, she would in all likelihood make a terrible fool of herself.

This honest appraisal convinced her that the search for him had become a crazy obsession and an unhealthy one at that and it had to come to an end, otherwise she would go mad. If only she *could* put him out of her mind! She knew it would not be easy, but she was determined to try. In any case, even if they were to meet and he to propose marriage, the drudgery of domesticity was no longer her main ambition in life, not that it had ever been so, except in a fairy tale, happy-ever-after sort of scenario. Her present circumstances, in which she had become her father's housekeeper, persuasively demonstrated, especially with the threat of Christmas looming, that slaving over the hot stove was not for her.

Despite her resolution, erasing Alan from her every thought was a painful and arduous process that demanded immense and constant concentration, because the memory of him and the desire for him had so deeply insinuated themselves into her whole being. The only other activity that required equal intensity of application was the ballet, so it was therefore a happy coincidence that Madame Belinskaya had begun to plan her school's Christmas show. When she asked Shirley if she could contribute any ideas for ballets, the answer was an unequivocal and firm "Yes", and Madame found herself deluged with notes, all carefully and clearly drawn up, in the wad of exercise books, prepared over long periods both in England and in France. If past experience was anything to go by, Shirley steeled herself for total involvement in the production in the knowledge that while her brain and her body were so fully engaged there would be little opportunity for any unwholesome images to intrude.

The theme that Madame had chosen for this year's show was "The Seasons". She intended it to begin with an excerpt from the Stravinsky ballet *The Rite of Spring*, to be performed by the younger members of the school. Shirley was appalled. "No, Madame," she exclaimed, "you can't have the little ones performing that! It's much too aggressive and angular for them. Anyhow, what about the human sacrifice at the end? They can't dance that!" Madame Belinskaya sat down heavily, as if she had been knocked over; then she stared at Shirley in silent surprise. Evidently no one other than Shirley had ever crossed her before and certainly had not queried her ideas.

"Yes, yes, of course, you're right," she said at last. "I don't know what I was thinking about. What can you suggest, Chérie?"

Shirley rose to the occasion. "Oh, I would think we should put on a very pretty and gentle opener to please the little ones and their parents. The girls could represent the first signs of spring, dancing as snowdrops, aconites and crocuses peeping out of the dark, cold ground to a lyrical but simple score, while the boys – we do have a couple of boys, don't we? – could be the warmer spring breezes or perhaps small animals emerging from their burrows."

"I like that," Madame conceded. "It's a good plan. I'll find some music for it and you can choreograph it."

An adaptation of Shirley's plans for a ballet about harvesting presented Madame with the ideal representation of summer, while for autumn she was delighted with the interlude that Shirley had devised the previous year depicting the market at Freslan-la-Tour with its fruit-laden stalls and flower sellers, complete with the blind accordion player and the acrobats. "We could certainly use some music from *Petrushka* for that," Madame announced with satisfaction. "You can listen to the records on the gramophone here down in the basement." The show was to conclude with an excerpt from *The Nutcracker* to represent winter. Enlivened and ecstatic at her unexpected immersion in all aspects of the ballet again, Shirley threw herself into preparations for the show. Between adapting the choreography to the music for *Petrushka* and dancing a principal role in the afternoon rehearsals, not to mention her morning shift in the shop, her day was so well filled that there was no time for even the slightest hint of Alan's name, let alone image, to creep into her brain. With a satisfied sigh of relief, she considered herself fully cured, both of him and of infantile paralysis.

Sometimes in the evening, usually on a Friday, Pa would go down to the pub with Cousin Archie and his pals; there they would sit putting the world to rights over a couple of beers. However gloomy the subject of their discussions, which generally veered towards the growing might of the Führer and whatever outlandish solutions they were able to invent for impeding his advance, Pa was always cheered by spending time with his peers, many of whom had been through similar trials in the Great War, and who understood his way of thinking. As was his custom, however, while Shirley cleared away whatever Tilly had prepared for supper, he stayed at home and sat, as ever, with his ear close to the wireless, as if without his undivided attention to the news the world would fall apart. When Shirley laughingly made this observation, he was not amused, but launched into a tirade, the like of which was unusual for him but which had become more frequent since the return of Neville Chamberlain from Germany at the end of September.

"The world *is* falling apart, Shirl," he ranted. "What did I tell you when our unelected prime minister came home flapping that piece of paper? I said Hitler wouldn't take any notice of it. And look what's happened: he invaded Czechoslovakia straight away, and all the others are following on in his footsteps, carving up that country to suit themselves. Who is to blame? We are – because of that policy of appeasement!" He paused for breath in the midst of his heated diatribe. "And now he's turning his attention to the Jews, poor things. Haven't you heard what's happened in Germany? All their businesses have been attacked and they've been beaten up and murdered, and the population, even mothers with their children, came out to watch as if it was some sort of entertainment." Shirley stood arms akimbo respectfully listening to his tirade. "I ask you! *'Kristallnacht'* they call it. And they say it's to maintain their racial purity or some such non-sense!" He shook his head in incredulous sorrow. "It's not as if it's only in Europe either. There are those Japs invading China too." He paused again for breath, before concluding with a gruff word of warning. "You ought to take more interest in the news, Shirl; someday it will affect you, you know."

"Oh, I haven't got time for all that, Pa. I'm too busy with the Christmas show; I shouldn't even be standing here talking to you now," she replied blithely, and took herself off to her room, where her notes and papers awaited her, spread out on the open gateleg table that she used as a desk.

Sitting at her desk, her concentration kept lapsing, because at the end of the day, naturally enough, her mind was too tired to be able to focus, so that more than once she found herself wondering about Alan and the longing for him crept stealthily back into her mind. She tried to persuade herself that nothing was to be gained by dwelling on him, but her brain was always at the ready with a tempting response. "How wonderful it would be if he came to your Christmas show," it whispered, "and then he would see you dancing, and he would see your name on the programme as principal choreographer as well as principal ballerina!" This temptation to indulge in a little bout of fancy was so hard to resist that often of an evening she sat idly at her table, pen in hand, doodling, rather than achieving any sensible work. This was both annoying and pleasing at one and the same time: annoying because her resolve proved to be so easily undermined, yet pleasing because she sensed that an element of fantasy was essential to her creative instincts. Without dreams and fantasy, life was so much drearier and duller. With them came all sorts of inspiration and ideas; they opened the door to colour, emotion, promise and excitement. The problem was to find a balance between the two.

To distract herself on one particular evening when inspiration for more choreography had dried up, she began to write a letter to her brother with the uneasy sense that there was more to Pa's warnings than she had cared to admit. Sandbags, which had become a familiar sight all over London, and those ugly gasmasks with their scary protrusions lurking in cupboards must have some purpose. Or at least somebody somewhere must have thought that they had a purpose. As a diversion from these thoughts, she imagined what it must be like in France on the farm with winter approaching but away from all such anxieties. She began her letter – "Dear Ted" – and then debated whether to write in English or in French. Having decided to use whichever language was more appropriate for the subject in hand, she launched into a positive and cheerful description in English of life in south-east London, which she judged was not so bad after all. She described her work for the Christmas show, in French, as that was the language of the ballet, and went on, in that language, to ask about Ted's life on the farm.

She remembered to ask if there was any remote chance that he might come home for Christmas, though this was hardly more than a rhetorical question, because she already guessed what the answer would be. Wistfully she imagined the parties in the village, at the *estaminet* and possibly over at Madame de Grandval's *château*, if not at the *château* in Trémaincourt, all of which would keep him in France as close as possible to Hélène. She also enquired if he had received any letters from Maman. Pa had not once mentioned her since her last letter, the one that had arrived soon after the summer holidays. Nothing had been heard of her since. Pa seemed to have made up his mind that she would not be coming back, and that the best way to cope with that was to forget about her. Shirley's letter came to an end with a flourish of *bisous* – kisses – to Pépé, in which Céline was grudgingly but diplomatically included.

No sooner had she slipped her letter to Ted into the box the next morning, hoping to catch the early post, than one arrived from the United States. Incredibly it was from Maman. Pa peered at the envelope then handed it to her over the breakfast table. "Here, Shirl," he said, "I'd like you to read this and let me know if there's anything in it for me." With trembling hand, she opened the blue envelope and pulled out the single sheet of paper. There was little of interest in the letter. Maman's main reason for writing, she said, was her concern for the worsening state of affairs in Europe, and she was anxious to know how her family were. She had been horrified to read about the sandbags – and the piles of grit by the roadsides waiting to be shovelled into pillowcases or whatever suitable bags people could lay their hands on. She asked if Shirley and her father had been given gas masks and if they knew whether Ted had one in France. Apart from casually, even guiltily confessing that she was enjoying America, her letter mostly consisted of a list of questions, presumably meant to convey her extreme concern for her family.

Not until the end did she casually mention that, although she had hoped to be home for Christmas, there were some new appointments coming up in the Embassy in Washington as a consequence of which she could not afford to leave her post. In any case, she said, the Christmas holiday was very short because the Americans also had their Thanksgiving celebrations at which they ate roast turkey and all the trimmings, and these would be taking place in a week's time, at the end of November, only a month before Christmas in fact. She did not say why the new appointments mattered to her so much. Yet again the only address that she gave was the official one of the Embassy. Long ago she had told Shirley that all letters were opened by the clerks, who then distributed them to their destined recipients.

"Anything of interest?" Pa enquired warily, as if he could not allow himself to show too much enthusiasm because he was trying desperately to forget the love of his life.

"Not much," she answered. "She's worried about us and she says she won't be coming home for Christmas because the holiday there is too short. You can see it if you like." She held out the letter to her father.

"No," he said, "that's all right. I don't need to see it."

"I think I ought to write a note to the embassy in Washington, don't you?" Shirley said. "To let her know that we and Ted are fine."

"If you think so," he replied, then abruptly changed the subject.

"I'm wondering what I can do, Shirl," he said, "they're appealing for people to join the Territorials, and obviously I can't do that, so I'm hard pressed to know what I can do to help." Shirley tried to appear sympathetic to her father's patriotic sense of duty, although she considered that he had by far excelled himself in that respect nearly a quarter of a century ago.

"We could help shovel that grit out on the street into bags," she suggested. "We don't have any spare pillowcases, but there are a five or so empty coal sacks in the shed in the yard; maybe we could use those, if Cousin Archie doesn't need them. I expect he forgot to take them when he moved out."

"Right, we'll do it at the weekend," Pa agreed, his self-respect restored. He finished his lunch and, with head held high, went to open the shop and take in the bundles of newspapers.

After lunch, Shirley penned a short note to her mother and addressed it to the French embassy in Washington, DC, before going out to ballet. She did not take her gas mask with her, despite the official advice to all citizens to take their masks wherever they went. She held that device in horror and from the outset had vowed never to use it: the goggles and the nosepiece, which looked more suited to underwater equipment, were scarily hideous, while the smell of new rubber, which she had encountered for the first time when she and her father went to the local school to be fitted, made her queasy. Apparently the government were preparing for a poison-gas attack but, as war had not yet been declared, that seemed a remote threat. In any case, more people were being suffocated by putting their heads in the gas oven to test their masks or by breathing in the exhaust from their cars than had yet been killed in an enemy attack. Even when one Saturday afternoon she went into central London to meet Cynthia for tea and a chat, she left it behind, regarding it as cumbersome and unnecessary.

Certainly in the West End the preparations for war seemed more advanced than in the suburbs: mountains of proper sandbags stood in neatly symmetrical piles outside Tube stations and important buildings, as if wrapping them in warm clothing for winter. The effect was weird and unnerving. The prospect of war raised all sorts of questions and issues, particularly, as Pa had said, because a future war, unlike the last one, would not be limited to confined geographical areas, like for instance northern and eastern France and Belgium and so on. It would be widespread, carried abroad by aeroplanes. How could she and her pa possibly hope to protect their premises? There was no way that they could fill enough sandbags to cover that building which, when all was said and done, was uncomfortably close to a railway line, with the station only two minutes away. As she dropped the letter to her mother into the pillar box, it occurred to her that Maman would be out of harm's way in the United States. No fully laden aircraft could cross the Atlantic and drop bombs on the cities there, so she knew exactly what she was doing by staying there. On the other hand, what would war mean for Ted, dear, darling Ted? He was in that part of France, not so far from Trémaincourt, that had been so close to the front line in the Great War that the guns were audible, and it was highly probable that if war with Germany were to come, northern France would be on the front line again, if not invaded.

In the run-up to Christmas, London was packed with shoppers all seemingly oblivious of the threat of war, despite the sandbags: the shop windows were adorned with decorations, the streets with lights and bands of musicians and carol-singers added to the surreal atmosphere. In cafés and restaurants there was not a table to be had, but fortunately Cynthia had arrived in good time at the Lyons Corner House at Marble Arch and had queued until a table became vacant, which was precisely when Shirley appeared.

Cynthia, usually so quiet, restrained and sensible, was bubbling with excitement that afternoon, which helped keep Shirley's many worrisome preoccupations at bay. She, an understudy, had been called in to perform at the Royal Variety Performance at the Coliseum in the presence of the King and Queen. "Can you believe it?" she exclaimed. "I had to dance with the John Tiller girls! Mind you, I had seen their routines, so I knew what to expect, and I can still do my high kicks. Oh, it was such fun!" Cynthia's unaccustomed gaiety was so intoxicating and infectious that Shirley had no option but to share in her delight, despite the fleeting twinges of envy that overcame her when first she heard of her success. Her conscience overcame the envy and would not let her deny her friend her moment of glory. In any case, the recollection that she herself was not just dancing but choreographing a show as well, albeit not as glamorous and not at the Coliseum, helped quell the surge of jealous indignation. "The Queen smiled and waved at us all!" Cynthia said laughing. "And I am quite sure that for a split second she smiled at me!" Her laughter was self-deprecatory, as if she could not believe her own good fortune. By this stage, Shirley's congratulations to her companion, who hitherto had not had much luck, were fulsome and genuine.

As they stood up, about to part company, Cynthia exclaimed, "Oh dear, I nearly forgot! Violet asked me to invite you out to tea somewhere special; not a Lyons Corner House like this, but maybe Fortnum's if you would like that. She says she has the money to pay us back and wants to give us a treat by way of a thank you for helping her on that day in Brighton." While Shirley was naturally glad that her loan was to be repaid, she was unnerved by the casual reminder of that day in Brighton.

"Yes, that would be nice," she replied half-heartedly, "but I'm choreographing and dancing in a show for Madame Belinskaya so I'm not sure when I will be able to manage it." Shirley's unexpected indifference to Violet's invitation jogged Cynthia's memory, reminding her how upset Shirley had suddenly become as they drove away from the church after Miss Patience's wedding.

"Let Violet or me know when you are free – there's no hurry," she said gently.

Then, sitting down again, she said, lowering her voice to a whisper, "Oh, I forgot to say that Violet is completely crazy about that young man, one of Miss Pa… oops, I mean Mrs Ellison's relatives. Do you remember? I quite fancied him when I saw him from behind, tall and dark-haired, but when he turned round I didn't like his face – well, not very much. But poor Violet is just mad about him. Whether he is about her I don't know, but I'm worried that she might get into trouble, if you know what I mean."

Shirley frowned and said, "No, I don't think I do. What do you mean?"

"I mean," said Cynthia, "that if she's not careful, she might have a baby!"

"Golly!" Shirley exclaimed. "How do you work that out?"

"Didn't you do biology in school? Your grandfather has a farm, doesn't he?" Cynthia asked, embarrassed by Shirley's ignorance.

"No to your first question, and yes to the second," Shirley replied. "That is, I know what the animals get up to on the farm, but I'm not sure what goes on between human beings." Cynthia took a deep breath and gave Shirley a brief whispered biology lesson in human procreation. Shirley listened gravely, her eyes popping out of her head, and then said, "Oh, so that's what happens! Thanks for that, Cynthia. I don't have anyone I can ask; Maman is away and I certainly can't ask Pa."

"Mother says it's a warning sign if you desperately want to be with a boy and can't get him out of your head," Cynthia went on. "Of course," she said, "Mother is being very Victorian. I don't suppose it really is that bad."

On the way home on the train, Shirley pondered the details of Cynthia's brief lecture. She was not altogether ignorant, because she had suspected as much from watching the animals on the farm, but had been mystified as to how their activities could be translated to human beings. Now she had the answer to a question that had been puzzling her since reading *Madame Bovary*, and that answer was that she had suddenly discovered precisely what had taken place between Emma Bovary and her admirers. Cynthia had said that her mother had cautioned her to be careful of getting too involved with a man because, unless he proposed marriage, an unwanted pregnancy was all too likely to happen, which of course was what Cynthia had meant when talking about Violet.

Suddenly it dawned on Shirley that her obsession with Alan could have led to the same conclusion if she had been more forceful and determined in pursuing him, if indeed she had jumped out of the car in Hambley and spoken to his father. That could have opened the floodgates for a passionate affair that might not have led to marriage and domestic drudgery, but, worse than that, to an illegitimate baby. She was eternally grateful to Cynthia, who had just saved her from a terrible fate. She had no wish ever to have a baby, let alone an illegitimate one. Edith had produced a baby boy a couple of months ago and had written to say how lovely he was, but that he cried all night and she and Jim were exhausted. A crying baby would be the end of ballet, the end of freedom and the end of her independence. Obviously she had taken the right decision in banning thoughts of Alan from her mind, and that decision was reinforced by her newly acquired understanding of the likely dreadful consequences.

After the afternoon with Cynthia, Shirley threw herself heart and soul into the ballet as never before, doubling her commitment, to the extent that she did little else in her waking hours, except to complete her morning shift in the shop. At night she fell asleep as soon as her head touched the pillow and did not stir till the early morning. Her efforts were well rewarded with an astoundingly successful show, which was reported in the local newspaper with her picture on the front page. Her father shelved his reluctance to attend such spectacles and brought Cousin Archie and his wife; Tilly came with her husband and her mother, as did many of the regular customers who had seen the posters in the shop window and in the neighbouring area. The greatest surprise was Granny Marlow's appearance, wrapped in a sleek fur coat, in the front row sitting next to Archie's wife, Eileen. "Of course I had to come when my cousin told me about this," she informed the bemused people sitting nearby. "And look, that's my granddaughter there on the stage! And what's more, she has created the whole show!"

Granny enjoyed the reflected glory, though she took care not to shower too much adulation on her granddaughter after the performance. "Yes, very nice, very nice," she remarked, "but I must be on my way. It's late and my taxi will be waiting for me. In this weather I don't go out very often." As an afterthought, she enquired, "By the way, is Edward coming home for Christmas?"

Shirley thought better of compounding the half-truth that she had already told with yet another, so she simply said, "No, Granny, I'm afraid not. We had a letter from him this week, and he says he is staying in France."

"Oh, that's all right then," Granny announced, apparently unconcerned by her favourite grandson's absence. "You see, your Uncle Paul is coming with his family and so are Winnie and Horace. They are bringing Edith and the baby in their car – and James as well of course," she explained, demoting Edith's husband to a passing reference, doubtless to show what she thought of him. She went on, as a glimmer of pride emanated from her worn cheeks, "I am a great-grandmother now you know. So, I was wondering how we would all fit round the table – that is, if Edward came too. You will come on Christmas Day, won't you?"

"Thank you – that would be nice, wouldn't it, Pa? That is, if the weather permits," Shirley replied dispassionately, thankful that the question of accommodating Uncle Paul's family appeared to have been forgotten.

Christmas at Granny's was a lavish occasion, catered for by the army of staff Martha had been commissioned to engage. Shirley had looked forward to seeing Edith again, but she and Jim were completely absorbed in their baby son, who was a happy little boy, endlessly smiling at all and sundry until something went wrong and then he howled. Above all, he was indignant at being laid down in his carrycot in the lounge when his parents deemed it time for a sleep. Then he hollered until someone picked him up and took him back to join the party in the dining room. "Would you like to hold him, Shirley?" Edith asked, passing the small bundle of life over to her cousin, so there was no way that Shirley could avoid dandling her new relative on her knee. All those present were amazed at her competence as she swayed back and forth to a dance rhythm that seemed to delight the child. "Shirl! Who would have thought it!" they exclaimed. "You're a born mother!"

Lulled into a comfortable and benevolent feeling of achievement, she was actually enjoying holding the baby until his tummy began to emit explosive gurgles and, turning red in the face, he squeaked in discomfort. In alarm she was about to hand him back to his father, who was sitting beside her, but, alas, it was too late and the results of the explosions were already leaking through his nappy onto her skirt, the green one that Granny had given her last Christmas. "Oh no!" she cried. Jim quickly relieved her of the messy infant, but no one, even the dry-cleaner when the shops opened again, could remove the stains or the smell from her lovely skirt.

She tried not to make a fuss, because Edith was so apologetic and obviously mortified. It was bad enough that Aunt Winnie kept harping on about the incident for the rest of the afternoon, making all sorts of preposterous suggestions, doubtless with the best of intentions. "You could borrow one of my skirts, Shirley dear," she said.

"That's kind, but I shall be all right," Shirley replied, knowing full well that Aunt Winnie's skirts would be at least ten sizes too big.

"Or you could wrap a towel round yourself" came the next suggestion.

"No, I expect we shall be going soon, so there's really no need" was Shirley's answer to that.

"Why don't we wash it out and hang it by the fire to dry? I'm sure it will be all right if we do it straight away," Aunt Winnie persisted.

"No really, please don't bother; I think the colour will come out if we do that, and it will shrink," Shirley said in a polite attempt to remain civil, though inside she was seething. Across the table, Pa was enjoying himself with his brother and Uncle Horace, and on the floor the three young cousins were building a mechanical contraption that one of them had been given for Christmas. She was trapped for the rest of the afternoon and into the evening, when she would much rather have been at home trying out the wonderful Christmas present her father had bought her, but which she had had no chance of enjoying before setting out for her grandmother's. Her decree had been issued, loud and clear, that they were to arrive not simply in time for Christmas dinner, but in time for church, and woe betide anyone who thought that attendance at church on Christmas Day was optional, so the present lay untried and untested.

40

The New Year celebrations in the pub were much more satisfactory than Christmas at Granny Marlow's, not that there were many young people of Shirley's age present, but Tilly's baby had not emerged so was not causing any trouble yet, and Shirley could be confident that her red skirt – last year's Christmas present from Maman – was, unlike the green one from Granny, safe. It was warm in the pub, where all sounds were deadened by the deep snow outside. The revellers too were on the whole fairly quiet, mostly being middle-aged or older. They sat drinking and chatting about curious events that had taken place in recent months, not least the unfortunate dramatization of *The War of the Worlds* on radio in the United States. Some young chap, Orson Welles by name, had interrupted the regular broadcasts to tell the listening public that the Martians had landed! Chaos ensued in the eastern states with terrified listeners trying to escape in all directions. It seemed funny now, though Shirley was afraid for her mother, who though she had proved herself clever, wise and brave in the Great War, also had a sensitive and nervous side when taken by surprise. If she had been caught up in the scare, she would have been very frightened.

Drinks in hands, the party gathered round the piano for a sing-song, after which they all formed in the largest circle that the cramped space would permit, held hands and sang 'Auld Lang Syne' to welcome in the New Year. When the pub closed, they trudged through the snow to Cousin Archie's house round the corner to prolong the jollifications. Although there was some discussion about the recent announcement of the distribution of air-raid shelters – focusing on what they would be like and what they would be made of – the international scene for once was left untouched, as if there was a tacit understanding that no one should spoil the evening by speculating on what might lie ahead.

The 1st of January 1939, a Sunday, was an even quieter day than usual for New Year's Day. There were no bundles of papers to be distributed among the paper boys, so Pa availed himself of the opportunity to have a rest. On the other hand, though the shop was closed, as was the ballet school, Shirley had no desire to rest. Over the past year she had done enough of that to last her a lifetime, and she had been given a very exciting new device to which she devoted herself day in and day out to fill the time until the ballet school opened again. She closed the flaps of the gateleg table in her bedroom and pushed it into a corner. Then she heaved onto it a sizeable wooden box, which since Christmas had stood on the floor. Having raised the lid, she placed a black disc onto the turntable, wound up a handle in the side of the box, replaced a needle in the arm and then lowered it onto the record. Music poured forth from the loudspeaker while she danced and danced to her heart's content.

The gramophone was her father's Christmas present to her. "Happy Christmas, Shirl," he had said, beaming and struggling under the weight of a large parcel. "I wanted you to have this not just as a Christmas present, but to show you how grateful I am to you for all the help you've given me over the past months. Setting up this new business and moving house and so on…" Panting from the effort, he had to put the parcel down on the dining table.

Shirley's surprise and delight knew no bounds when she opened the box. "Pa!" she exclaimed, giving him a hug. "I dreamt of having my own gramophone, but never thought I would! It's wonderful. Now I can work at home instead of planning ballets in the basement at Madame's." Breathless with excitement at the endless possibilities of this amazing present, she cried out, "I can dance whenever I want to without having to wait for music on the wireless!" She twirled around in a neat pirouette and tripped lightly across the room.

Regard for rhythm had always been uppermost in Shirley's mind, because only the ticking metronome in her head, constantly keeping time, enabled her to practise her routines at home without musical accompaniment when there was no music playing on the wireless. Ballet was the most highly disciplined activity imaginable, and it required intense concentration, since there was so much more to remember than simply carrying out the strenuous physical exercises: one had to maintain the correct positions and postures, not to mention balance, at the same time as performing the steps and the routines all in the right order; but these requirements, once mastered, were not sufficient in themselves if the vital magic ingredients – emotion, interpretation and expression – were lacking: they were the means through which the dancer made contact with the audience, and without them he or she might as well be a gymnast with no emotion to convey and no story to tell.

However accurate her technical prowess, Shirley had long been aware that the latter was the area where her dancing fell short of perfection; Miss Patience had refrained from saying as much, because doubtless she, like Shirley herself, had hoped that this lack would be made good during her training at Sadler's Wells. Although she possessed a strong visual sense and a good memory for all the physical demands of the ballet, she realized that henceforth she would need to take much greater note of the emotional content of the music and try to absorb its ebbs and flows, its passion and its despair, in order to develop her sensitivity to its demands and its direction. Her father's exceptionally generous present would allow her to attend much more closely to the melodies in order to gain a more intimate understanding of their range of feeling, which was something that she would be able to do at length at home, instead of in the dance studio. Through that understanding she intended to enrich her wordless storytelling with those intangible, elusive qualities of expression and interpretation.

Mastery of technique was all very well for the *corps de ballet*, but once again she had begun to harbour the secret desire, the ambition, the compelling urge to become a prima ballerina. It was not as if she were a stranger to emotion, for if in the past year she had had enough enforced rest to last a lifetime, so had she experienced enough feeling: a blossoming passion for Alan, the elusive stranger, sorrow at Mémé's passing, shock at Thelma's infantile paralysis and death, fear at the diagnosis of her own illness and lameness, worry at Maman's absence and separation from Ted, let alone the prospect of war, all turbulent, searing, disturbing and bewildering.

The collection of records which her pa had given her with the gramophone turned out to be a disappointment, because most of them were either of music for ballroom dancing or of songs from the shows. These had been the rather unsatisfactory accompaniment to her dancing since Christmas, but now, on New Year's Day, she pulled out a record hitherto unnoticed at the bottom of the pile and found to her surprise that it was a medley of music from *Swan Lake*. She was irritated that she had not noticed it before, but the reason for that was that there were not many distinguishing features on the uniform brown-cardboard record covers. *Swan Lake* was the record that she carefully placed on her newly acquired turntable on the morning of New Year's Day 1939.

The sounds of the overture to Act Two ringing out from the machine sharply brought back memories of the shivers of excitement and foreboding tingling up and down her spine at the opening of a performance that she had seen with her mother at Sadler's Wells some four or five years earlier. The same music now transported her in its broad sweep to a fantasy world of misty lakes, royal courts, enchantments, villains and of course its doomed hero and heroine. It was classical ballet as she had never heard it before – except in the theatre – at its greatest and most powerful. Unbelievably, here it was playing in her bedroom! The music compelled her not just to listen but also to dance. She took the needle off the record while she donned her *pointe* shoes and her leotard, and then devoted the rest of that day and many days thereafter – as well as many gramophone needles – to the pursuit of the mercurial dream that had so cruelly been cast down and all but destroyed by infantile paralysis.

At the beginning of the new term, Madame Belinskaya's school opened again. Madame was still effusive in praise for the Christmas show, which she said had raised the profile of her school so much that it was flooded with applicants for places. There would have to be two classes a week for each age group, because there were too many pupils to fit into one class. Space was not a problem, since the house had three floors, with two main studios, as well as smaller ones, on each level, some of which had until now been unused; the trouble was, according to Madame, that there was such a shortage of teachers because classical ballet was still relatively new in Britain. Marie Rambert and Ninette de Valois had pioneered the style of British ballet through the work of their two companies, but they had not as yet been able to produce teachers as well as performers.

Madame regarded Shirley intently at the beginning of the new term. "*Ma Chérie*," she said at length, "how would you like to become a teacher and teach here? I know you have your work in your father's shop in the mornings, but maybe you would be interested in working here for me in the afternoons? Would you like to take one or two classes a couple of times a week? You could still have your lessons and your practice time, and, of course, you would be paid." Shirley was astounded; she had never expected her efforts for the Christmas show to reap such a stupendous reward. In fact, while mapping out her future plans during the Christmas holiday, she had reached the conclusion that it was still too early for her to reapply to Sadler's Wells. If she were to dance there again, she would have to go in at the top of her form, and to do that she had to take time to exploit the all-important discovery of the power of music through her gramophone.

There was absolutely no question of whether or not she would accept Madame's invitation, and did so with alacrity, already anxious to begin planning her classes. It was agreed that she would take two classes in succession four days a week: on Mondays and Thursdays she would teach two classes of small children brought by their mothers after lunch, before the older children came out of school. On Tuesdays and Fridays she would be teaching two classes of ten- to twelve-year-olds later in the afternoon. She was uncertain as to why she had agreed to teach the little ones, considering her aversion to babies, but found their keenness infectious: wearing their dancing pumps gave them a profound sense of their own importance, and each and every one of them, no matter what her shape or size, declared with absolute certainty that she was going to be a ballerina. The classes for the older children were, to her surprise, more difficult to teach and the pupils less amenable. Some of the girls evidently had talent, but others did not, causing Shirley to wonder why they came. Tactfully she asked one of the stragglers if she liked ballet. "I don't know, miss," the girl said. "I've never seen one. I do it because my mother wants me to."

Some of these less enthusiastic pupils were becoming obstreperous, so to prevent the situation becoming critical, Shirley sought Madame's opinion and asked her permission to adjust her teaching methods by continuing with the normal procedure of using the first half of the lesson to teach and practise technique, and the second to teach dance routines, but with one important difference: this was that the dance should be performed in costume, of which there were plentiful supplies in the school's extensive wardrobe down in the cellar.

This suggestion met with Madame's immediate approval, although it created more work for Shirley in that she not only had to plan a new dance for each week and base it on some suitable music, but also dig out suitable costumes from the damp, dusty basement. She brought out costumes for kings and queens, princes and princesses, frogs and fish, cats and dogs, lions and tigers, and blew the dust off them. She took them home to wash and also took plenty of records with her for her evening listening while she did the ironing. Her pupils responded with unprecedented enthusiasm, and her classes became the most sought-after in the school, often attracting audiences who crept in from other classes and sat silently round the edge of the studio.

In the middle of the term two dark-haired, dark-eyed sisters, Hanna and Sara, joined one of those classes. They came with a cousin whose mother explained that they had been sent to England on the Kindertransport from Berlin by her brother and his wife. Teaching them could have been difficult since they spoke no English, but in fact the language barrier was not a problem because they were keen, and ballet proved to be intelligible universally. They copied the movements of the other girls and, when a difficulty arose, their cousin translated instructions for them in an unknown tongue that apparently they shared. Aged twelve and thirteen they learnt quickly, with an eagerness that was touching, especially when their pale faces lit up with pleasure on mastering new steps or a new sequence. Shirley warmed to these sad children and patiently gave them extra attention in the hope that, like her, they would find in the dance an escape from their troubled lives. She told her father about them on the evening of their first class. He shook his head as he remarked, "I doubt they will ever see their parents again, poor little things, nor will any of the children who are coming over. Be kind to them, won't you, Shirl?"

Shirley was in her element as her dormant talent for teaching emerged. The three-year-olds responded well and the ten- to twelve-year-olds revealed hidden talents once their interest had been aroused. She was also proud to be earning money, a sum from each of her jobs in the two establishments sufficient to amount to a proper salary. She had mastered the running of the shop so that, were Cousin Archie or her father to fall ill after Tilly's departure, there would be no difficulty in keeping the business going, and at Madame's she had already become a respected and inspiring teacher for her very small and her rather larger charges. Sometimes she dared to think that it wouldn't matter if she never danced on the professional stage because she was so happy in her present occupations. Or that was what she thought until she met Violet and Cynthia on the afternoon of her birthday in February in Fortnum's.

She and Cynthia met in Oxford Street at Cynthia's request, because she needed help in choosing a new lightweight coat in Selfridges for spring. As far as Shirley was concerned, this seemed as good a way to spend a birthday as any. "Don't you think it's rather chilly for trying on spring clothes? You won't be wearing them in these arctic temperatures," she taunted Cynthia.

"Well, you might think so, but I want to spend my earnings from the Royal Variety Performance and I want something new and smart ahead of the season. You can try things on if you like, but you don't have to buy anything." Shirley was tempted, and before long the two girls had tried on every coat in the store before Cynthia settled on a reasonably priced pale yellow item and a silk hat, while Shirley's eye was drawn by a coat in a heavenly turquoise blue and a matching feather hat. On the one hand there were as yet no occasions for which the coat and hat would be appropriate; on the other, she saw no reason to resist temptation, because Pa had given her a handsome cheque for her birthday, and she had earned so much money since Christmas that she reckoned that her savings account could perfectly well finance a treat for herself. Well-satisfied with their purchases, they took a shortcut to Piccadilly via Bond Street and, having scanned the tearoom for Violet, seated themselves at a table.

Cynthia pulled a small parcel out of her bag and handed it to Shirley. "Happy birthday!" she said with an enigmatic smile. "You'll laugh when you see this!"

Bemused, Shirley opened the parcel gingerly and pulled out a silky scarf in the same blue as the coat that she had just bought. She exclaimed, "It's lovely! How did you know I was going to buy a coat and hat in this colour? It's an exact match! Thank you so much!"

"I didn't know!" Cynthia said, shaking her head. "Isn't that extraordinary? I bought it weeks ago!" They were laughing over the coincidence when a ghostly pale figure in an ill-fitting coat, flustered and panting, approached their table. Yet again Shirley did not recognize Violet, nor for that matter did Cynthia. They both tried to hide their surprise. "Violet! There you are! How nice to see you! We sat down but haven't ordered anything yet!" Cynthia said, quickly taking the lead.

"Yes," Shirley chipped in, "we were wondering about these gorgeous cream cakes! What do you think?" Violet's pallor turned a sickly shade of yellow at the mention of cream cakes.

"Lovely to see you both," she said haltingly with a shadow of a smile. "Do have whatever you like – this is on me, remember? But I think I'll just stick to a cup of tea for the moment. Oh Shirley, now I remember: it's your birthday today, isn't it? Well, happy birthday, I'm sorry I haven't brought you a present." She more or less collapsed onto a chair. In doing so, the panels of her coat opened, revealing a round bulge. Shirley was staggered: transfixed by Violet's tummy, she was lost for words.

Cynthia had to call her to attention, saying, "Now Shirley, what did you say you were going to have?"

"Oh, um, I think I'll just have a sandwich, thank you; don't worry, the tea will be a lovely birthday present, Violet," she replied with a heavy heart, because those cream cakes looked delicious and the shopping expedition had given her a craving for something sweet, preferably a birthday treat for want of a birthday cake.

It was hard to know what to say next. Conversation stalled until Cynthia brightly asked, "Tell us about the Wells, Violet."

"Ah," said Violet as if she had been stung by a large wasp, "there's not much to tell, except that I've lost my job."

Cynthia and Shirley gasped in unison. "No! Surely not! Why?" they both exclaimed, although each of them already knew why.

"You can see why, can't you?" Violet replied curtly. "I'm sure you can see that I am expecting."

"Hm, I did wonder," Shirley mumbled.

As if to play for time, Cynthia coughed unconvincingly, took a gulp of her tea and then, with a detectable insincerity, said, "How lovely! You must be pleased." There was a pause, then she said, "What about your parents? Is this their first grandchild?"

Stony-faced, Violet ignored Cynthia. "I've been thrown out of the Wells so there's a space in the *corps de ballet*, Shirley," she said, "and they are short of dancers, so I thought perhaps you might be interested. You're quite well now, aren't you? And you're dancing again. Are you interested, do you think?"

Shirley did not answer straight away but sat wide-eyed in surprise while she considered what to say. After a brief pause, she neatly sidestepped the question, which in any case did not admit of an easy answer. "It's so kind of you to think of me, Violet," she said politely, while Cynthia sat silently watching her. "Can I have time to think about it, please? You see, I have so much on at the moment." In the past, only eighteen months ago, she would have jumped at such an offer. Today at the tea table in Fortnum's, though flattered and genuinely grateful, she was not sure that she wanted to dance in the *corps de ballet* at Sadler's Wells after all.

Her hesitancy was justified when Violet went on to say, "Honestly, I'm glad to be leaving; you wouldn't believe how difficult it is, dancing there, especially now that girl is taking all the best parts. You must have heard of her, Peggy something or other, do you know her? She's changed her name, of course, into something foreign-sounding and fancy. Well, they think she's the cat's whiskers and she's getting every principal part, so the others have been demoted into minor roles. Mind you, you should see her mother! If my mother was as pushy as that, I would have been top of the bill ages ago." She stopped, drew breath and then added, "My mother's just a snob, that's all. Oh, I must have another fag!" Whereupon she pulled out her cigarette case and lit up. Casually, she flicked the ash over the white tablecloth.

"So when is the baby due?" Cynthia asked, anxious to revert to the original subject.

"Oh, some time in the summer," Violet said airily, adding with a malicious grin, "and don't worry: I *am* getting married. My parents have seen to that. They were furious at first, but now they've calmed down and Mother insists we should get married soon before I get too big and it's very obvious. My father was livid and he had quite a set-to with Henry's parents until they and Henry agreed to the wedding. Henry wasn't too pleased at first, but as it's all his fault he'll just have to put up with it." She shrugged her shoulders as if to say she couldn't care less about Henry's opinion. It was Shirley's turn to venture a cautious question.

"Henry? Have we met Henry? You'll have to remind me who he is."

"Yes, of course, you've met him!" Violet snapped. "Don't you remember Miss Patience's wedding?" Shirley remembered it all too well, but chose to look blank. "Henry is Mrs Ellison's great-nephew; he was sitting at the front of the church, remember? Tall and dark. He and I were introduced at the reception; you might say he swept me off my feet." She giggled. "He said he was bored to tears and was so delighted to meet someone… um… so pretty and alluring. We became close friends immediately. Love at first sight, you might say, though that's not quite how it's turned out." She wiped her nose, then her eyes, while both Shirley and Cynthia staunchly resisted the temptation to tell her what a fool she had been. To tell that home truth would be preaching to the converted.

"Oh, by the way," Violet continued, "as we're talking about the wedding, I wondered if you two would like to be my bridesmaids? Mother says it's got to be a proper wedding, so that even if people suspect what's happening, it will all look perfectly natural. You will be bridesmaids, won't you?" Both Shirley and Cynthia were stunned into silence. They glanced at each other in a look that spoke a million words. Neither of them had any wish to be involved in Violet's wedding at all, let alone as bridesmaids, but neither of them could find a plausible excuse.

Shirley began by saying, "It's very nice of you to ask me, Violet; it rather depends when the wedding is. I might be going to visit my brother in France, you see." This excuse rang hollow, because everyone knew that Shirley went to France in August.

Cynthia's excuse was just as flimsy when she said, "I'm not sure when my next job might be coming up, so it could be difficult."

"What is the date of the wedding?" Shirley enquired cautiously.

"The fifth of March in Watford. My parents decided it had to be Watford as nobody knows us there. In fact, I don't think I've ever been there," Violet shot back brusquely.

"Ah," said Shirley, then, when a lightning flash of inspiration reminded her that she and Cynthia had just bought new spring outfits that would be perfect for a wedding, she suggested, "well, as I'm not absolutely sure what I shall be doing then, and nor is Cynthia, why don't we say we should love to come to the wedding but not as bridesmaids?" To her surprise, Violet did not appear at all disappointed.

"Yes, that would be fine," she said, standing up rather hastily and abandoning her cup of tea. "Sorry, girls, all of a sudden I don't feel at all well," she said. "I must be going!" She ran off without paying the bill.

"Oh dear!" Cynthia exclaimed as she watched Violet run through the store to the exit. "Poor thing! I expect she's feeling sick. That was unfortunate." She turned back to Shirley with a welcome suggestion: "But look, it's your birthday, so let's start again and have some of those cream cakes? The treat's on me. Oh and by the way, you were thinking of our purchases when you said we would go to the wedding as guests, not bridesmaids, weren't you? Well done! Our new coats will be just right. That was a narrow escape, though; I wondered how we were going to get out of it!"

"Yes, I don't mind going as a guest – because we can leave when we've had enough – but not as a bridesmaid. We'd have to help with the organization and sit through all the photos and stay till the bridal couple leave. I suspect it will be a nightmare; and I hope the weather will have warmed up a bit by then, otherwise I shall freeze in that new coat" was Shirley's pessimistic assessment of the forthcoming event.

Cynthia agreed, saying, "And I don't want to find myself in the middle of a shouting match. Violet is used to having her own way, and so, I gather, are her parents. Anyhow, on a brighter note, maybe Mr and Mrs Ellison will come. It would be so nice to see them."

"Yes, of course," Shirley said, nodding pensively. She would of course be delighted to see her old friend and teacher again, but even the slightest reference to that earlier wedding outside Brighton brought back painful memories. The thought of Brighton also brought back the memory of having to dress Violet for the occasion. Today Violet hadn't even paid for the tea to which she had invited Shirley and Cynthia, let alone refunding the money for the outfit that Shirley had bought her. "Never mind," Shirley magnanimously said to herself, "we did buy her clothes in the sale and she did suggest I should apply for her place at the Wells."

For days afterwards, Shirley considered Violet's suggestion about applying to the Wells, changing her mind every time the subject came up, which was often. One day, with a thrill of optimism, she found herself all in favour of submitting an application; the next she would tell herself that she was quite happy as she had a good mixture of practical, down-to earth employment, earning good money in the shop, and creative activity, also earning money in the ballet studio, where she was not only teacher and dancer but choreographer as well. Choreography was almost certainly the way forward, because when she was too old to dance, she would still be deeply, passionately involved in the theatre as a choreographer. Madame was giving her the best training imaginable both in the dance and in choreography, and she doubted that it could be bettered even at the Wells. Perhaps one day she would still dance as a principal but, failing that, she would become a famous choreographer. She was certain of one thing, which was that she did not want to dance in any *corps de ballet*. Madame was of the same opinion when Shirley broached the topic to her. "*Ma Chérie*," she said, "why turn over the apple wagon when it is running so smoothly?"

In addition, of course, there was the appalling situation in which Violet now found herself. This, it seemed, really was the living proof of the consequences of unbridled passion, the sort of passion that she herself had most definitely felt for Alan. Most shocking was the revelation that Violet and Henry – with a baby on the way – were going to have to marry even though the earlier passion between them had obviously faded away, blossoming in a burst of colour like autumn flowers, and then dying, leaving little more than withered stalks blackened in the first frosts of winter. It was strange that such a scenario never featured in the ballet. There lovers pined for each other and strove to overcome the obstacles in their path, sometimes successfully leading to the sumptuous wedding pageant of the final act, sometimes ending in tragedy. Whatever the ending, the dance was driven throughout by passion. Never in all the ballets with which she was familiar did it lead to the birth of an unwanted baby and the prospect of a loveless marriage extending into an unhappy and uncertain future.

As expected, that wedding was a nightmare. Shirley had agreed to go because simply being a guest was so much less demanding an option than being a bridesmaid. Moreover, she still felt a certain warmth towards Violet for kindly suggesting that she might apply for her place in the Wells' *corps de ballet*. Although she had decided not to take it up because she was so well settled in her routine for the present and aspired to greater things in the future, Violet's suggestion implied a touching concern and a genuine respect for her talent. Cynthia accepted the invitation to the wedding because, as she said, it was always a useful experience to see how people behaved – or misbehaved – at weddings and what was expected, in preparation for the day probably in the distant future, when she might tread the path to the altar. After some discussion, they decided that Violet could be counted among their close friends, so the least they could do was to support her, because she was clearly in trouble.

The only good thing to be said about Violet's wedding day was that the weather offered a respite from the freezing conditions that had dogged the country since mid-December, allowing Shirley and Cynthia to wear their new spring clothes; these gave a festive air to an occasion that otherwise was decidedly dark and mournful. Violet's mother, grandmother and aunts all wore black fur coats and broad-brimmed black hats, which, though undeniably smart, stylish and expensive, befitted a funeral rather than a wedding. The hats hid their faces, which was probably an advantage since their expressions were unremittingly haughty and contemptuous. The women in Henry's family, who had been smartly dressed at Miss Patience's wedding, were also wrapped in furs, but theirs were neither new nor smart: not uniformly black, they were mostly fox, and moth-eaten fox fur at that. Violet's family seemed to be making some sort of statement by their superior mode of dress, while Henry's were expressing their views by not bothering at all.

Shirley and Cynthia grinned at each other as they took their places in the church, craning their necks to search for Mrs Ellison, who, to their disappointment, was not there. Violet arrived dressed in a voluminous creation of frothy white drapery, designed no doubt to hide her bulge, over which she carried a huge bouquet of cream flowers and trailing ferns. A small girl in pink followed her up the aisle and relieved her of the bouquet, but only when she had turned her back on the congregation at the chancel steps. Henry stepped out unsmiling to meet his unsmiling bride. In fact, no one smiled except Cynthia and Shirley, who made a bet with each other to see which of them could raise the greatest number of smiles. The going was tough. One could have been forgiven for thinking that there had been an announcement forbidding any show of joy or pleasure, or, perhaps as Shirley suspected, a witch had cast a spell over the gathering, turning all their features to stone. Even the organist seemed to be affected by the general air of gloom, for never had the wedding marches, whether by Wagner or Mendelssohn, sounded so lugubrious.

As soon as the service was over, Violet and Henry hurried out of the church, almost running for the door, apparently intent on escaping from the small congregation as fast as possible. At the reception in a rather drab local hotel, they separated to opposite sides of the room, Violet remaining with her family, Henry with his. The two parties snatched furtive, suspicious glances at each other, each side determined not to mingle with the opposition. Shirley and Cynthia joined Violet, whose only reaction was "Thank goodness that's over! At least the baby will have a father!" Violet introduced them to her parents and her relatives, but no amount of gushing compliments would bring the slightest hint of a smile to their impassive faces.

After these unproductive introductions, Cynthia and Shirley were left standing on their own in the middle of the room while Violet's relatives conferred among themselves in a tight-knit huddle, so the girls drifted over to Henry's family. The not-so-handsome bridegroom gave them the glad eye, which they found most disconcerting, while his parents regarded the two prettily dressed girls with puzzlement, doubtless wondering if they had come to the wrong wedding. It was left to Shirley to introduce herself, which she did to blank faces. As they did not respond, she quickly followed her introduction with an inspired question. "I gather you are related to Mrs Ellison?" she cheerfully enquired of Henry's mother, a plump, kindly lady whom she vaguely remembered from that earlier wedding in Hambley.

"Oh, yes! Dear Nora! Such a shame she and her husband weren't able to come today. She's my husband's cousin!" she exclaimed with a beaming smile which lit her sad features. "How do you know her?" she asked.

Not to be outdone in the smiling competition, Cynthia butted in, "She was our ballet teacher in London before she married Mr Ellison. We miss her so much!"

Henry's mother was still wreathed in smiles. "Well I never; you must have been at her wedding near Brighton?"

"Yes, and so was Violet," said Cynthia, gesturing towards the bride on the other side of the room, whereupon the smile faded from Henry's mother's face.

"Ah, of course," she said. There was an awkward pause, then she announced, "Do excuse me, I must have a word with Susan over there." She pointed to a corpulent, red-faced person who was making the best of a bad situation by holding out her glass, always empty, in the path of each passing wine waiter, and walked away. Henry's father had little to say for himself and proffered no smiles. The wedding breakfast was a buffet-style meal from which it was easy for Cynthia and Shirley to escape unobserved.

"I won the bet!" Shirley announced without much satisfaction.

Violet's baby, a boy, arrived in July. Taking a romper as a gift, Shirley went to visit the new arrival in August just before leaving for France. She found Violet living in abject conditions in a one-room flat in Camden Town. The baby appeared to be well cared for, despite the dingy surroundings: the stained, peeling wallpaper, the damp patches in the ceiling and the pervasive smell of cigarette smoke. Violet seemed unconcerned: "Look how sweet he is! He will look lovely in your romper – what a pretty blue!" she exclaimed, holding the infant out to Shirley for her inspection. Shirley tried hard to admire the baby, but kept her hands firmly by her side, lest she should inadvertently find herself holding him.

"Are you all right here?" she asked Violet, trying to hide her horror at the dismal circumstances to which Violet had been reduced.

"Oh, it's better than it looks," Violet said. "We're fine, aren't we, Harry? Quite comfortable actually." She tickled the baby under the chin. "Will you have a cup of tea, Shirley?" she asked, and went to fill a kettle from the sink-cum-washbasin in the corner beside an antiquated double bed. She placed it on a single gas ring on the floor next to the chimney piece.

"No thanks; I just popped in to see little Harry and now I must be off. I have to pack, you see." As an afterthought, she enquired, "How's Henry?"

"Oh, he's fine, I don't see much of him, actually; he's out most of the time, but that suits me fine. At least he gives me some money each week," Violet replied nonchalantly.

41

That fateful summer of 1939 Shirley and her father were again in France. Convinced that there would be an announcement sometime soon of the outbreak of war, Reggie had insisted on buying a wireless for the farm, in spite of Pépé's protests that Louise had one of those machines – *un poste de TSF*, she called it – and would keep them informed of any adverse developments. Since the Munich Crisis, Pa had constantly worried so much about his only son that during the past year he had written letter after letter urging him to return to England. Ted's reaction had been stubbornly unconcerned and unchanging. "Don't worry about me" was the basic message behind all his replies. "All is quiet here, and anyhow, even with Benjamin's help, Pépé would not be able to manage without me."

Therefore, for the second time since the Great War, Reggie was obliged to cross the sea to France, not on this occasion with a view to taking a holiday on the farm, but with the firm purpose of bringing Ted home to England. To his surprise he found that all was remarkably calm across the Channel, as if there were no perceptible threat from the east and as if for the farming community the cycle of the seasons, with its accompanying demands, far outweighed the importance of any political machinations. Indeed, Pépé – who had not personally been involved in the Great War because of his age and the safe distance of the farm from the front line, but who had lost his only son in it, and most certainly had witnessed its dreadful effects in Arras and the surrounding area – had in his advanced years suppressed all recollections of that terrible conflict and its consequences for the population. Strangely, in the present circumstances, he showed little concern, even when Pa tuned in the wireless and the reports about rearmament and conscription came over loud and clear. Ted used these to his own advantage. "There, you see," he said with a note of triumph, "if all the French workforce from all over the country is being called up, they will need people like me to work the land. Otherwise what are people going to eat?"

Unconvinced by his son's optimism, Pa continued to despair of Ted's obtuseness, to the extent that Shirley had to take her brother aside to warn him that his attitude was damaging their father's health. "Look, Ted," she said, "Pa's so worried about you, it wouldn't surprise me if he falls back into his old ways and starts hallucinating again. You can see how tired and haggard he is every morning for lack of sleep, and that's because he lies awake worrying about *you*. At least tell him that you'll take the first ferry home if the situation gets any worse." Ted listened to his sister to keep her happy, though deep down he thought her bossy, and he had not taken any notice of his father at all.

"All right," he conceded, "but it won't be until the last minute." Fortunately this was not the way he put it to Reggie. "I'll come home the moment we hear that the Germans are going to invade," he promised, and his father had to be content with that. At least his anxiety dropped from an astronomical level to one which allowed him to participate in the harvest as he had the previous year, to enjoy the outdoor life associated with all aspects of farming and to lend his expertise whenever the tractor gave trouble, as it still did frequently, to Pépé's great annoyance.

"Sometimes I wish I still had my old horses in harness," he remarked with a nostalgic nod in the direction of the calmer, quieter past that he fondly remembered. On these occasions Reggie had to point out to him that the past was not as golden as his memory led him to believe, and that the harvest was much more easily and quickly gathered in with the help of modern machinery, enabling the farm to produce greater yields. Pépé was not convinced; he puffed on his pipe, gazing into the distance as if conjuring up the image of how things used to be, conveniently forgetting the upheavals of the battles being enacted, relatively speaking, on his doorstep.

Yet again Shirley played her part in the harvest, helping Céline to prepare the meals and the picnics that she carried up to the fields. Céline had resumed her warm, friendly attitude, apparently having laid aside her anger over Shirley's rejection of Jean-Luc's attentions, possibly because the family at the *château* were not in evidence. Apparently none of them had been seen for some time. Shirley did not wish to bring up the subject again, but found it strange that the *château* was so completely closed up, the shutters blotting out the windows like heavy eyelids, and the outer doors barred. She asked Ted what he knew, but he shrugged away her question with a mumbled reply while avoiding his sister's gaze.

"Oh, they've gone off to the Côte d'Azur, I think," he muttered, then went swiftly out to milk the cows. That too was odd, considering how strongly attracted to each other Ted and Hélène had been last year. The absence of the de la Croix family was particularly conspicuous at the harvest supper, but as the rain began to fall no sooner than the last sack of grain had been safely stowed in the barn, catering for the smaller numbers in the farm kitchen made Céline's task lighter.

Louise was a much more fruitful source of information about the de la Croix family, though Shirley was careful not to ply her with questions when she was busy with a shop full of customers. She judged her moment to enquire casually where they had gone. Louise lowered her voice, even though the bar of the *estaminet* was almost empty that afternoon. "You haven't heard, then?" Louise asked, scrutinizing Shirley with a frown, possibly wondering how much she knew and how much she should tell her.

"Nothing, except that Ted says he thinks they have gone to the Côte d'Azur."

"Hmm," Louise answered with a grimace, "if you believe that, you'll believe anything. I think myself that they've gone abroad. To South America, to get out of the way of this war that's supposed to be coming, if you ask me, though some do say they've gone to their house down in the Midi."

Shirley's reflective silence spurred Louise irresistibly into divulging more information. "According to my Charlot, there were all sorts of comings and goings before they left, a frenzy of activity, you might say. The house is not just closed up, it's shut down; they've put dust sheets over all the furniture as if they won't be coming back for a long time and they've taken the horses to stables over in Mestres." She put some takings in the till and slammed the drawer. "If you want to know more, *ma petite*, you should ask your brother to show you his arm." She turned to serve a customer who had just come to the bar, leaving Shirley both mystified and alarmed.

She found Ted in the cowshed. She stood in the doorway watching him while, oblivious to his sister's presence, he milked the cows, talking to them gently as the warm liquid splashed noisily into the pail. He had his sleeves rolled up; there, clearly visible on his left arm above the elbow was a large purple scar. She waited silently until he had finished milking and then said, "Hello, Ted," as if she had just that minute rounded the corner. He unrolled his sleeve quickly down to his wrists, but not quickly enough. "I say!" Shirley exclaimed. "What's that on your arm?"

Sheepishly, he replied, "Oh, nothing. I just walked into a sharp edge, that's all."

"Sharp edge, what sharp edge was that?" Shirley demanded.

He looked around, searching for a sharp edge to corroborate his story, but there was none. "Well I don't exactly remember," he stammered. "You know how it is when you're busy: you feel the pain, but you don't necessarily remember what it was that you crashed into."

"Ted, do you expect me to believe that?" she asked. "I think there's more to it, isn't there?" She adopted a pleading tone. "And you must tell me what it is."

Ted put down the pails of milk. "I suppose you've been talking to Louise?" he asked, eyeing her warily.

"Yes, I have, but she didn't tell me what happened. She said I must ask you."

"I see," he replied. "You had better come into the barn. We'll sit down over there on those straw bales. And we'll talk in English." He gestured across the barn to where a pile of bales were stacked against the wall, ready for use during the winter.

"So tell me what happened," Shirley said quietly. Ted buried his face in his hands, revealing a rare glimpse into a vulnerable streak in that apparently capable, cheerful young man's armour. All of a sudden he seemed like a tiny chick that had lost its mother. When finally he looked up, there were tears in his eyes.

"I don't understand it," he said, "but you know how close Hélène and I were last summer?" Shirley nodded. "Well," he went on, "it seems that the de la Croix were quite happy for Jean-Luc to chase after you, but they didn't want me and Hélène to become close and maybe one day get married, which was what we were planning to do." Shirley feared she knew what was coming next.

"So did you and Jean-Luc have a fight?" she asked.

"Not exactly, though you could put it like that," he replied. "I was working out in the fields down by the road one morning in the autumn, not so very long after you and Pa had gone back to London, when Jean-Luc came past with his dogs. He stopped when he saw me. He kept watching me and suddenly he turned bright red with rage. I was very scared: I thought he was going to let the dogs loose on me, but he didn't do that. All he said was: 'Peasant, keep away from my sister!' I was too shocked for words, but I kept my head and didn't say anything.

"He stomped off, leaving me to wonder what on earth was happening and what I should do. I couldn't give Hélène up, and I'm certain that she didn't intend to give me up either. I went home, thinking I might write to you and Pa, but then I realized that there was nothing you could do and it would only worry Pa. When Céline asked what was wrong, I just said I had a headache, but later on I decided to tell her. She thought about it for a long time, then she said, 'They used to be such nice people, *mon petit*, but they have their plans and it seems you don't fit into them, though your sister could have done very nicely for herself if she had married Jean-Luc, but perhaps it is just as well that she didn't. I've heard it said that they are panicking because their money is running out and they need to find a rich husband for Hélène and grab more land for Jean-Luc to farm. He used to be such a lovely boy when he was little; I don't know what has gone wrong with him. I expect it's that Parisian set he's involved in. The only thing that you can do for your own safety and Hélène's is to give her up.'"

Ted fell silent and buried his head in his hands again. Shirley heard him sobbing quietly to himself, so she turned away to avoid embarrassing him and to give him time to compose himself. Eventually she asked gently, "Have you seen Hélène again since then?"

He shook his head. "No," he said, "Céline made some enquiries in the village and found out that she had been sent away to a finishing school in Switzerland, but nobody knew where. Céline also went to the *château* in the hope of finding out more, but the reception she got there was decidedly frosty. I was sure that Hélène was not allowed to write to me, and if I did find out where she was, my letters would certainly be torn up before they reached her. Louise tried to help, because of course the news was all round the village once I had told Céline. Louise suggested I should write to Hélène, if we could find out where she was, and she would put my letter in an envelope folded into a letter from her, which she would send to a cousin in Dijon and ask her to forward it.

"As chance would have it, Charlot had to go into the *château* to clear one of the chimneys, which was smoking, and since none of the family was at home, he had a good look round. He came across a letter on a table in Madame's study: it was from Hélène, who pleaded to be able to come home. He memorized the address, because you know he has a phenomenal memory, and he wrote it down for Louise when he got home. So we could put Louise's plan into action. Louise is so clever. She didn't give her address here in Trémaincourt. Instead she sent the package to her cousin, who then forwarded it in a fresh envelope with her own address on the back, and when a reply came from Hélène, the cousin forwarded it to Louise here.

"The plan worked beautifully. Hélène wrote to say how unhappy she had been at being dragged away without even being allowed to say goodbye to me, and how miserable she was at not being able to write. She said she simply could not eat anything, she couldn't sleep and of course she couldn't do whatever work they are supposed to do in those places. Those few short weeks when we could write to each other every day were wonderful! But that only lasted until the school discovered what was going on. They probably wondered why Hélène seemed so happy and had begun to eat again. That was just before Christmas, and after that there were no more letters and I very much doubt that any of mine reached Hélène."

"So did Hélène come home for Christmas?" Shirley enquired.

"No, they all went away; Louise reckoned they had gone to their flat in Paris, so I didn't see Hélène at all. To tell the truth, I rather wished I'd come home to England, because it was so quiet here with only Pépé and Céline." He avoided his sister's gaze and stared intently at the floor of the barn.

"But you haven't told me what happened to your arm," Shirley persisted, certain that there was more to come.

"I haven't got to that yet," said Ted. "After Christmas, Jean-Luc and his mother came back to Trémaincourt; they opened up the house and all seemed quite normal. They even gave a party for the village in January, apologizing that it was late because they had been delayed in Paris. I thought it best to keep out of the way so didn't go, although Céline and Pépé did. They were given drinks and food, but Madame ignored them completely once she had shaken hands with them and kissed them on both cheeks and all that; and Jean-Luc deliberately turned his back on them. Everyone noticed. I heard about it from Louise, not of course from Pépé or Céline.

"Then one Sunday in January, Pépé and I went out with the shoot. We were surprised to find that there were not many local people there, but Jean-Luc had brought a crowd of friends. They didn't know what they were doing and just larked about. It was pretty dangerous really. We had bagged a few birds and a hare or two and were about to give up and go home when Jean-Luc asked me to help him reload his gun because, he said, it wasn't working properly. I should have known better. Like a fool, I held the gun while he checked it and reloaded it. I saw him turn it slightly towards me and, before I realized what was happening, he had cocked it and was about to pull the trigger. I ducked out of the way, but my left arm was still in his line of fire…"

"That's attempted murder!" Shirley exclaimed.

"Yes, I thought so too, and so did Pépé. Come to that, so did the half a dozen or so chaps from the village who were there and had seen what happened," Ted continued, picking up the thread of his tale. "But Jean-Luc apologized profusely for what he called '*un accident*', and all his friends backed him up. They fetched their posh cars and drove me to hospital in Saint-Pierre. I fainted on the way, and when I came round I was in a hospital bed with my arm all bandaged. It has taken a very long time to heal. Pépé wanted to call the police, but he was laughed down by Jean-Luc's pals, so nothing could ever be done about it. You see they outnumbered us and they are much more powerful. I couldn't write to tell you what had happened, because Pa would have come over on the first ferry to take me to England and I didn't want that. My life is here, come what may."

"Maybe it is, maybe it isn't," Shirley said. Ted's account of his injury horrified her, but she wisely did not commit herself to any more controversial point of view that might deter her brother from confiding in her in future. "But what happened to you is shocking," she went on, "and I don't see how you can stay here."

"Don't worry," Ted replied. "Jean-Luc left immediately after the so-called accident and hasn't been seen since. His mother came once just briefly to apologize for the accident. '*Mon cher*,' she said, 'there's no doubt about it; poor Jean-Luc, he is mortified; he would never have hurt you!' She made it sound as if Jean-Luc was the one who was injured, not me; she brought some peaches and paid the hospital bill by way of sufficient compensation and an end to the matter. Afterwards she shut herself away in the *château* and scarcely ever came out, until a couple of months ago when she packed up and left for good."

He sighed. "The trouble is I have no idea where Hélène is or what she's doing. I haven't heard from her since before Christmas, so I suppose that's that." He pulled out a muddy handkerchief and wiped his nose and eyes.

Shirley put her arm round his shoulders. "If you ask me, you're well out of it, and so am I," she said grimly. "Just imagine what a terrible time you and Hélène would have had of it if you and she had run away together. She might have been taken back into the bosom of the family eventually, but only if she left you. They would never have allowed you into their drawing room, you may be sure of that. Just imagine, too, what a terrible time I would have had of it if I had agreed to marry Jean-Luc! What a bully he is! My life would have been a misery with him. No doubt he would have discarded me like an old rag once he had got what he wanted out of the match." She was both furious and confused.

"If only we could ask Maman what to do!" she cried, bursting into tears. "She always used to solve hopeless situations!" Without warning, before even she herself knew it, Shirley's anger turned against her mother, as if she were responsible for this and every other disaster that had befallen her family. "What can she be thinking of, leaving us and Pa like this? What a treacherous, disloyal thing to do! Who would have believed she could be capable of doing that!" She quivered with rage, venting her fury against the mother who had abandoned her husband and children without so much as a word. She sounded like a small child whose favourite toy had been taken away from her.

Ted kept quiet to avoid adding fuel to the flames until it was his turn to comfort his sister. Eventually, when Shirley's anger had run its course, he put his hand, his right hand, on her shoulder and asked, "Have you heard from her lately?"

"No, she sent Christmas presents, lovely, expensive things from Washington: silk stockings for me and a smart shirt for Pa, which he refuses to wear. Then in February she wrote saying that she had become Head of Information or something like that, in the Embassy. She wrote before Christmas saying that she couldn't come home because they were busy with sifting applications for a new job, but she didn't say that she was one of the applicants! Since then she's only sent a few postcards from places like New York and the Niagara Falls, but she never gives us any news. I don't really think she's coming back." Her anger exhausted, it was her turn to wipe her eyes and bury her head in here hands. "What about you?" she asked.

"Yes, I've had much the same sort of thing, but I suppose I was so upset over Hélène and the de la Croix affair that I didn't really give it much attention," Ted replied. "I will say one thing though: I do remember that she said that she thought she was well placed in the Embassy in Washington to find out what was happening in Europe."

"I can't imagine how," Shirley retorted sharply. "I would have thought she would be better placed here. Anyhow, doesn't she even mention us when she writes to you?"

"Oh, once she said she was pleased you and Pa were well settled in the new business and she hoped we were all well."

"I can't believe that she cares so little about us," Shirley sobbed.

"Mm, that's hard," Ted agreed, "but calm down, sis, we have each other, and Pa, and Pépé and Céline. Over there she hasn't got anybody, and she was very good to us when we were little, and don't you remember how patient she was with Pa? All those broken nights and the shouting and the screaming? I thought she was a saint to put up with all that."

"Maybe you're right," Shirley conceded, though privately she was convinced that her mother was not alone in Washington but was enjoying life with Monsieur Lavasseur.

That night she lay awake. First and foremost she was worried about Ted. Hélène's disappearance had hit him very hard. If ever proof of the old maxim that true love never runs smooth were needed, their relationship was a prime example, but then, she reasoned, so was her love for Alan, still ever-present in her mind and not as easily ignored as she might have wished. Even now she often caught herself scanning crowds, particularly on the ferry, hoping against hope that he might appear out of nowhere, just as he had in that storm two years ago. And if perfect matches like hers with Alan, and Ted's with Hélène, were doomed to failure, what chance had other less fortunate couples? Though Pa and Maman might well have been made for each other when they were young, the after-effects of the Great War and other unhappy circumstances had conspired against them over the years, till the silken thread of marital bliss that had held them together, once stretched to its limits, had finally snapped. Her thoughts turned to another couple, Violet and Henry: there was no hope that their marriage was going to bring either of them happiness, despite, or perhaps because of their baby. Judging by the atmosphere on their wedding day, that was a foregone conclusion for which one did not need a crystal ball. That the truth was worse than any foregone conclusion Shirley had seen for herself on her visit to Violet and her tiny offspring only a month ago.

42

Although Shirley had reconciled herself to the impossibility of ever intervening in Violet's sorry state of affairs, she was determined where her brother was concerned to find a way either of saving him from a doomed relationship which already had nearly cost him his life, or, alternatively, of encouraging that relationship and helping the star-crossed young lovers overcome all the obstacles in their path. The problem was that it was not at all obvious where that way might lie. Lying awake far into the night, she turned over various ideas in her mind, knowing full well that in the cool light of day they would appear nonsensical.

For instance, she briefly considered making up the quarrel with the de la Croix family and more or less offering herself to Jean-Luc, because deep down she suspected that her rejection of him had been at the root of all Ted's troubles, and she knew that with a toss of her blond head and a provocative pose or two she would be able win him over. This idea she discarded at once; it sent a shiver of disgust down her spine, knowing full well that it was impossible for her to go through with it; it would be tantamount to marrying her brother's attempted murderer, someone whom she now detested. Next, she wondered if there was any point in sending Céline as a sort of ambassador to the *château* to build bridges and gently reactivate the old friendship without committing her to any sort of relationship with Jean-Luc, but dear innocent Céline had already tried and was no match for the machinations of Madame de la Croix, and anyhow the *château* was closed up and there was no one at home.

Then she contemplated taking a train down to Switzerland, to the address that Charlot had discovered, to find out if Hélène still attended the finishing school, and if she did, well, what then? Day was dawning when at last the first sane, if less dramatic notion came into her mind. She would in the final days of the holiday build up her own relationship with her brother in the hope that he would henceforth take her fully into his confidence, trusting her with all his thoughts, his hopes and fears, his anxieties and his despair, so that through regular correspondence, even from a distance, she would be able to judge the situation and know when to intervene, even crossing the Channel if necessary to keep him out of harm's way. For her part, any hope of success would mean taking her brother into her own confidence.

There was an opportunity to put her plan into effect that very afternoon when she found Ted sitting on his three-legged stool in the barn, milking the cows. Shirley reckoned that they were not likely to be overheard in there, not that there was anyone to listen to their conversation since Céline was baking in the kitchen and Pépé and Pa were out ploughing in the straw from the harvest. In any case the siblings spoke in English when they did not want to be overheard. Ted was remarkably receptive to his sister's ideas, which she prefaced with an account of her own obsession for Alan, for obsession was what she had come to believe that it had been. First she reminded Ted of that rough return crossing two years previously and asked him if he remembered meeting Alan. "I don't think I met him exactly," he said. "I remember a tall chap bringing you through the crowds to find Maman and me, but I don't really remember what he looked like, though I did wonder if he was a friend of yours."

It was enough for Shirley that Ted retained at least that indistinct memory, so she went on to relate how she had relentlessly searched for Alan among the crowds and the passers-by in central London without success, how she had dreamt of him, how she longed to be famous so that he would recognize her face, if not her name, on posters, how infantile paralysis had destroyed all her hopes and finally how the effects of that glimpse of his father in Hambley after Miss Patience's wedding had brought her to her senses and made her realize that the obsession had taken over her life to a ridiculous degree.

Ted listened intently, almost appearing to understand the damaging potential of such an obsessive relationship. When she reached the end of her narrative, it was his turn to comfort her, for tears were rolling down her cheeks. "You poor thing," he said gently. "I had no idea."

"No, of course you didn't," Shirley replied, "because there was no one I thought I could tell, but now I feel so much better having told you. Do you see how important it is just to have someone you can talk to, without having to bottle it all up?"

Ted nodded. "Yes," he said, "though the problem for me is that there isn't always anyone at hand to talk to. Céline was very kind and tried to find out what was going on at the *château,* but she's too old to understand what it's like. She said, 'Don't worry, *mon petit*: it will pass.' I needed someone nearer my own age with a similar experience."

"Well there are plenty of people who fit that description, and you have someone of nearly your own age," Shirley reassured him, "and that someone is me! Shall we write to each other much more regularly? A problem shared is a problem halved, you know."

A cloud lifted from Ted's face as he said, "Yes, why not?"

Ted's growing willingness to communicate on personal matters was reassuring. In his relative isolation he gave the impression that it was a relief to discover someone who would listen and respond sensibly and sympathetically to his woes. Although he considered himself more than half French and had become very fluent in the language, he did not have a peer group of friends in the village in the way that he had had in England during his school years. He had not expected to receive such support and companionship from his sister, who previously had been so engrossed in her own world, and whose reactions he feared might have been caustic and sarcastic.

If, as a schoolboy, he had cast her into the role of the bossy elder sister who had also in the recent past assumed the role of their absent mother, he was now beginning to see her in a different light. Her revelations about her own love life opened a window not only into her life, but also into her personality and her way of thinking that he had fleetingly glimpsed when together they had tried to cope with their father's shell shock, when he accompanied her to Sadler's Wells for her audition and when she was convalescing in hospital and at home, but which had faded again when she had resumed her old routine of dashing off to the dance studio at every opportunity. He discovered to his surprise that she was much more sensitive, sensible and caring than he had expected.

The bond between the siblings was cemented by the announcement of the outbreak of war. They listened to it in French at five in the afternoon, having already tuned into the English announcement by Chamberlain that morning. On each occasion they clustered with their father, their grandfather and Céline around the wireless that Reggie had insisted on buying to keep the farm in touch with current events, and on each occasion he had difficulty in controlling his anger. In the morning, on hearing the English declaration of war, he cried out, "That lunatic, Hitler! He invaded Czechoslovakia, then he annexed Austria and two days ago he invaded Poland, and he won't budge! He's making a mockery of us all! What next?" By the afternoon Pa's anger had assumed a despairing tone. "So here we go! It's the Great War all over again," he sighed, digging his upper teeth into his lower lip, "more young men being sent off to war, never to return." Pépé stared resolutely into the middle distance without responding. Céline stood up and bustled about in the kitchen, while Shirley and Ted sat in silence, trying to digest the news and wondering what the future held for them.

"Well, Ted," Pa said grimly, "there are no two ways about it; you must come home with us."

To this Ted put up a spirited resistance: "No, Pa, I'm not moving from here till we know more clearly what this means. Maybe Hitler will leave us in peace. He seems to have his sights elsewhere at the moment. But I promise you I'll come home if he looks like coming this way. It's not as if he can do that overnight, is it? Anyhow, it'll take the Boche a long time to get this far west."

"I wouldn't be too sure of that," his father retorted swiftly. "It will be different this time for all of us. They have planes now, remember."

"So do we," Ted said, "but I promise I'll take the first ferry when there's trouble brewing here."

"And what happens if the ferries are not running and you're called up here, or interned or shot?" Pa persisted, not easily convinced by Ted's assurances.

"I don't think I'll be called up at present," Ted replied, looking meaningfully at his sister while stroking his left arm. She understood what he meant. "Anyhow, I could be called up as soon as I step foot in Dover, so it makes no odds, does it?" He avoided his father's references to being interned or shot.

Ted took Shirley aside after this exchange. "I couldn't explain to Pa, Shirl, but I think I ought to tell you that, before you and Pa arrived, I went down to the recruiting office in Saint-Pierre to sign up. I didn't want to be called a sissy, so I went to volunteer, but they wouldn't have me, not because I was English – that didn't seem to matter at all – but because of this arm." He gently rubbed his left arm above the elbow. "They sent me for a medical check-up and the doctor said he couldn't pass me as fully fit, or fit enough, until it has healed. He told me to come home and work the land because the crops will be needed. I feel bad about it because so many other boys have joined the army. At least the people round here know about my arm and that so-called accident, so they don't tease me." He sighed. "Anyhow, now you know. But don't tell Pa, because he will wonder what really happened. I told him that I had an accident on the farm and that the arm is healing up."

"All right," Shirley promised, "but you must be careful."

Reggie decided not to leave immediately, because Sunday the third of September fell on a bank-holiday weekend in England, which he thought meant that the ferries would be crammed with returning holidaymakers, anxious to cross the Channel at the earliest opportunity, and on the other side the roads would be impassable. Instead, he spent the following day readying all the vehicles on the farm, including Ted's car, for a long period without spare parts or maintenance. Shirley, meanwhile, shopped for all the necessary supplies, from soaps and knitting wool to scrubbing brushes and coffee, which could not be bought from Louise.

When eventually father and daughter left early in the morning on 5th September, intending to catch the ferry from Calais to Dover, it was with heavy hearts. Ted drove his father and sister to the station, but did not come onto the platform to see them off. He made the excuse that the cows needed milking, but his sister sensed a deeper reason: the station would be crowded with departing troops who would jeer at him, an apparently fit young man in civilian clothes, and they would mouth insults. The trains were still running, though there was pandemonium on the platform as frightened families tried to flee pell-mell south, or west towards the coast, despite there being no sign of air raids. Travelling east in the opposite direction, masses of troops were filling the trains to capacity for the journey to the Maginot Line of fortifications built against German invasion. Travelling north to Calais, the passengers were mostly British, hoping against hope that the ferries were still running.

If there was chaos at the stations, in the port of Calais there was bedlam. Two days after the declaration of war, there still remained a great influx of frightened travellers desperately wanting to leave France urgently. Announcements in French blaring out over loudspeakers at the port bludgeoned the long, fearful queues, wilting as they stood in the baking sun, with snippets of increasingly depressing information. First of all they were told that the port of Dover had been closed to civilian traffic, so that passenger ferries could no longer be directed there. Next they were informed that the passenger ships in the docks at Dover had already been commandeered as troop carriers and would not be sailing to Calais to pick up them up. Finally they were advised that the only alternative on offer was to travel to Folkestone, where the port was still open, but that, because the harbour was smaller than at Dover, there were fewer ships operating.

Shirley and her father sat down on their leather suitcases, resigned to an interminable wait. Around them British families did the same, the parents despairing as they tried to control their truculent children. Listening to the grumbles of the waiting masses, Shirley realized that many of these families did not understand the announcements which at best were indistinct and unintelligible to foreigners, so she passed the time by walking up and down the line translating for the disgruntled homeward-bound hordes. Naturally she allowed herself the hope that Alan and his father might be among the crowds, so she persevered to the far end of the line. Eventually she forgot that vain hope when it gave way to the satisfaction of finding that her efforts were appreciated.

The many people she spoke to smiled wearily in gratitude that someone had been kind enough to think of translating the information, however dispiriting. Knowing what to expect, they said, meant that they could plan how to cope with the delay. Some unwrapped their picnics and began to munch their sandwiches, releasing mouth-watering aromas of pâté and garlic; others went to join the queue at a nearby chip stall for a final indulgence in one of the culinary delights of northern France, while yet more went in search of the lamentably basic facilities attached to the customs shed.

At about six o'clock in the evening, a port employee came down the line checking tickets and organizing the bedraggled passengers into groups. Those who already had tickets for Folkestone were given priority, as were families with babies, and were allowed to board the first ferries to arrive. Those still left on shore, whose tickets had been issued for travel to Dover, were less fortunate: they had to wait until long after all passengers for Folkestone had embarked and their ships departed. Shirley and her father were in this group, destined to wait for a minimum of another five hours until those same boats returned.

By the time the last passengers boarded the ferries, the sun had set and a cool breeze blew up the Channel, but the only place to sit was on deck out of the squalor left inside by the earlier travellers. Again sitting on their suitcases, Reggie and Shirley made the best of their situation by constantly reminding each other how lucky they were to be on the ferry at all, how welcome the breeze was after the heat of the day and, although the boat was destined for Folkestone, whereas the Lanchester had been left parked in Dover, the bus fare for the ten miles along the coast to Dover was a small extra price to pay for being almost in sight of home. "Just as well we didn't take the car across the Channel," Pa remarked. "We wouldn't have been able to bring it home!"

Retrieving the car, however, was easier said than done, because when they arrived in Folkestone the buses had ceased to run and they were told that in their absence the port of Dover was not only closed to civilian traffic, but had been declared a militarized zone since the outbreak of war. In his anxiety for Shirley's well-being, Reggie put a brave face on the expense and took a taxi into Folkestone to a run-down hotel, recommended by the taxi driver, where they spent the night, before catching an early bus to Dover the next morning.

"You can get off by the military outpost on the road, sir," the bus driver declared, "but I can't drive into the port itself. You'll 'ave to talk to the military to find out whether you left your car in the militarized zone, though I doubt that you'll 'ave much luck there. They don't say so, but I reckon they're gonna launch an attack."

"Hmm," said Pa, "a good thing too. I always thought we should have attacked the Nazis long ago and caught them unawares. Not that that will help me get my car back." As the bus drew up at the stop near the port on the way into Dover, a young guard appeared at the driver's window.

"You can't go any further," he said, "the port's now out of bounds."

"I know that, but this gent's parked his car somewhere round 'ere; he doesn't know if 'e left it in the militarized zone," the bus driver explained, adding, "and he's had to come back to Folkestone from France. Wha's more, his daughter 'as been suffering from that paralysis thing, so help 'im out, young chap, if you would."

Reluctant to resort to any regressive step, Shirley, having powdered her nose and reapplied her lipstick, nevertheless made a convincing show of letting her father carry her down off the bus and, when he set her down on the pavement, leant fetchingly against him, balancing on one leg. "Ah, I see," the young guard said, hurrying off and calling back over his shoulder, "I'll call one of my superiors." He returned half an hour or so later driving a staff car. "I've been told to take you round the streets until we find your car, sir," he announced to Reggie. "This is a special dispensation because, er, because..." Tongue-tied, he gazed at Shirley until he remembered what he was supposed to be saying. "And, um, he asked me to tell you, in case you don't already know, that the blackout came into force last Sunday, so if you have a long journey and are driving in the dark you have to cover your headlamps." Shirley gave the young man a ravishing smile before settling into the back of the staff car.

Cousin Archie and Tilly, already at work in the shop, were amazed to see them. "We thought you might be stranded in France for the whole of this war!" Archie exclaimed. "How on earth did you manage to get back here?" Tilly, who had a tendency to panic, was greatly relieved to see Shirley alive and well but, since her baby was old enough to be left with her mother, was reluctant to give up her temporary job, both because she liked it and because of the contribution it made to the family income. She had been coming to help out in the mornings while the boss was abroad and, even though the boss and his daughter had returned, kept finding odd little tasks to perform to delay her departure.

"I'll just clear up this mess," she said, indicating a pile of old newspapers in the corner.

"No, no, leave them, please, Tilly," Reggie decreed. "I want to catch up on the news and find out what I've missed while we've been away."

"Ha, ha! Don't you know we're at war, old boy! That can't have escaped you over there!" Cousin Archie exclaimed.

"No, no of course, not," Pa replied irritably, "but I do like to read the editorials and the commentaries."

"Oh, well, please yourself, but, for myself, I've heard quite enough about it already," Tilly said. "I wish we could go somewhere far away where this war won't ever reach us," she cried. "Maybe it's all peaceful where you've been, but we've had a taste of it already, haven't we, Mr Archie?"

"Well, it wasn't really war, more of a false alarm, you might say: we'd only just heard the Prime Minister's announcement, but it fairly terrified everyone, didn't it, Tilly?" he replied, before explaining that, after the declaration of war, the sirens had gone off and they all had braced themselves for a German attack. The "attack" proved to be nothing more than an English plane practising manoeuvres, and that had set the sirens off.

"It was terrifying," Tilly moaned. "If that's what war's going to be like, I don't want to be here, and I don't want my baby to be here either!"

Archie tactfully veered the subject in a more useful direction. "You won't have seen the shelters, Reggie, but every house is having a shelter delivered. Ours is coming today, and I was thinking, you don't have room for a shelter here out in the yard, so if the sirens sound, you and Shirley must run round the corner to us; then you'll be safe."

"Oh, thanks, but I'm not worried," Reggie replied casually. "We might not have anywhere for an Anderson because we can't dig up the concrete, but we do have a cellar and we can reinforce that. We can go down there. Better than being in the trenches."

Shirley was appalled. "No, Pa," she said shivering, "I'm not going down in that cellar. It gives me the creeps, all dark and dirty with the coal heap and the damp down there. Anyhow, supposing the house falls down on top of the cellar, how are we going to get out?"

Pa thought for a moment before conceding defeat. "Perhaps you're right, Shirl. Thanks Archie, we'll come to you if we need to, but I don't suppose anything is going to happen here. Not, that is, if we get in first and send our planes over to bomb those Germans before they know what's coming, and I think that's what's going to happen. Dover is already a militarized zone, ready for attack rather than defence." Cousin Archie looked on in admiration of Reggie's advanced knowledge of the situation.

"Well," he said, concluding the discussion, "let's hope they've taken your advice on board, but our shelter is there for you to use whenever you need it." Shirley was grateful for the invitation, if such it could be called, particularly in view of her father's apparent indifference.

Although she tried to apply herself to her morning job in the shop, her mind was not on her work, and since Tilly showed no signs of leaving, she made the excuse that she needed to buy some essentials in case the shops ran out of food. "I should buy as much as you can," Archie observed knowingly. "My missus is stocking up because they say there's going to be rationing." Heeding his advice, Shirley made a mental note to buy twice as many items, especially of tinned goods, as there were on her list. She stood for a moment on the threshold. Across the road the fence leading up to the station was covered in posters exhorting passers-by not to go out without their gas masks. She disregarded this message, then glanced up the road to the station itself; it was hidden by a barricade of sandbags, rendering it unrecognizable. An eerie quietness prevailed in all directions, even the traffic was muted. She turned her back on the station and set off down the road, calling in at the shops, where everything seemed quite normal; then she took the side turning which led to Madame Belinskaya's. The road was blocked outside the ballet school by a large lorry, from which workmen were heaving curved sheets of corrugated iron. She stood watching from a distance until the men had carried the metal sheets round to the rear of the building, and then went into the house by the front door.

Madame Belinskaya was standing in the hallway, banging her fist on the reception desk, behind which the secretary sat impassively working at her typewriter. "It ees too much," Madame shrieked in English. "My life 'as been war, revolution and war, nothing but violence all ze time! And now they want to dig up my beautiful garden, my 'aven of tranquillity, my paradise, to put that 'orrible piece of metal in the ground!" When this diatribe came to an end, she turned round to find Shirley standing beside her. "Ah, *ma Chérie*, so you have come home from France!" she exclaimed with a sudden change of mood, a change of language into French and a welcoming smile, though at the thought of France she applied her handkerchief to her eyes. Without warning she then marched, tall, stately and erect, into one of the ground-floor studios. Shirley followed her across the large room to the window overlooking the garden. "You see! Just look out there. What a mess!" Madame declared angrily. "And all because of those greedy Germans! Can you believe that a whole nation would go to war on its neighbours for the second – no, the third – time in a century?" she shouted, slipping back into her earlier furious frame of mind.

Shirley had no answer, not that one was expected. There was nothing that she could say to comfort her justified anger. She herself was shocked at the sight of the lovely garden being churned up to accommodate the bomb shelter and, for the first time, was scared at the prospect of war. She was struck by the prospect of the chaos it was going to bring, chaos to her life, chaos to the lives of countless people, chaos that would have repercussions from which she and her father would not be immune. She resolved there and then to participate in the war effort, rather than to stand on the sidelines as an observer. She did not try to comfort Madame Belinskaya with empty words, for that would have been a futile exercise given her teacher's strength of character and opinions. Instead, she curtly remarked, "I think that shelter may well be needed, Madame, especially if we have the school full of pupils. At least we can herd them to safety."

Madame nodded, "Yes, *ma Chérie*, you are right, as always. Again we will all have to do our best." Shirley took refuge in one of the studios, where she started to practise with vigour all those exercises, the beating steps of the *batterie*, the *entrechats*, the *sissonnes fermées* and *ouvertes*, and all their variations, which in France had been overlooked. After half an hour of exercising her limbs, she felt more in touch with her real self, because only when immersed in the ballet, whether it were a dance, a sequence of steps or simply practising *pliés*, did she find her true centre, that inner sense of well-being that enabled her to cast aside all her anxieties, all her worries about war, about Ted, about her pa and Maman, and about herself, her present and her future.

43

Tilly came to work again the next day, saying, "Ma says it's fine. She loves having Albert for the morning, so I can come back to work and here I am!" Pa appeared uneasy at this unexpected arrangement, fearful no doubt of the cost to the business, but Tilly's presence allowed Shirley to grasp the opportunity that she had been hoping for all night. In the wakeful moments of a fitful sleep, she had decided how to support the war effort, though she feared that she might be needed in the shop in the morning and would not be able to slip away to enlist. In the afternoon she was to resume her ballet classes, which had to take priority over all else, so the morning was her only chance of registering for volunteer work. She could see that her pa was shifting from foot to foot, a sure sign of embarrassment, as if he were on the point of saying something discouraging, which he had probably been rehearsing ever since Tilly had appeared, to the effect that the business could not support four employees and that she had been invited back to fill in only for the length of his absence abroad.

Before he could open his mouth, Shirley raced for the door, saying, "It's so kind of you to come in today, Tilly. I need to go out now, so I'll leave you to it!" Pa stood speechless and Tilly grinned as Shirley shot out of the shop.

To her annoyance, there was already a queue at the enquiries desk at the council offices. Nonetheless, if this were what doing one's duty entailed, she would have to put up with it, especially because there was no one present to field complaints. As the queue gradually shortened, she saw that people were coming away from the desk carrying papers and forms to fill in, which suggested that they were all on the same mission as herself. However, on approaching the front of the queue, she was bemused to hear the man ahead of her ask about the Anderson shelters and why his hadn't arrived. The receptionist apologized, said that there must have been a mistake and gave him a sheaf of papers with instructions to fill in the forms and send them off. He was not impressed, despite her apology. "Hmph, all very well, but supposing there's an air raid before then?" he remonstrated.

The receptionist, having acquitted herself of all that was required for that particular caller, ignored him and turned her attention to Shirley, whose brief question was briskly answered. "Oh," said the receptionist, in obvious irritation at this time-wasting request, "didn't you see the sign outside the door? It points to the entrance round the corner: that's where you go to enrol."

Shirley was angry with herself for having missed the sign and wasted so much time. As she came out of the main entrance, she searched for it, only to find a small notice stuck on the door, which she in her enthusiastic haste had not seen: it was handwritten in pencil. She marched round the corner, where another even longer queue stretched out of the side entrance. This time she took the precaution of asking the person in front of her what she was waiting for. "We can't find our gas masks, and anyhow the children's heads have grown since they were issued, so we've come to ask for replacements," the woman replied, before launching into a tirade against the government for distributing the gas masks much too soon. "What a stupid thing to do! They weren't needed then, though it looks as if they will be now!" she complained. Shirley did not stay to listen to her grumbles, but bypassed the line, incurring frosty looks and muttered protests about queue-jumpers. Inside the door was an arrow pointing to the left to a door marked "gas masks", while on the right, with only a few people waiting outside, was the office she was looking for.

At lunchtime, her pa, who did not usually enquire about her movements, asked with a hint of exasperation, "So, where were you this morning, Shirl? I was expecting you'd be at work in the shop so I wouldn't have to pay Tilly another morning's wages. I can't keep her on and pay her as well as you, even though business is brisk at present."

Shirley's hackles rose. "I was trying to do my duty! Not that anyone else around here is! And I was doing the shopping because there's nothing left in the cupboard or the larder," she retorted sharply, "and if you don't want to pay me, that's fine!"

They ate in silence. After he had finished his baked beans on toast, Pa said grumpily, "I only wanted to know if you were coming back to work in the shop, that's all. Anyhow, you haven't told me where you went."

Shirley heaved a sigh. "Yes," she said, "of course I want to work in the shop, but today there was something more important that I had to do. I went to volunteer for the ARP!"

Pa was startled and his attitude changed. "Air Raid Precautions? Good for you!" he exclaimed, whistling between his teeth. "I thought of doing that myself, but I haven't had the time yet to go down to the council offices."

Shirley recounted the frustrations of her morning, warning her father how to avoid them. She then showed him the explanatory papers and forms, and told him to the best of her knowledge what was involved. "I have to do a training course, and then they'll give me a uniform and a helmet. As far as I can tell, you have to keep a lookout for enemy planes and set the sirens off if you see one, and you have to send people into the shelters and make sure they've got their gas masks with them. I was told off because I went out without mine. And if bombs fall, you have to assess the damage and call the emergency services, administer first aid and maybe lift people out of bombed buildings. Oh, there are lots of other things, but I expect I shall learn all that. I've signed on for two evenings a week to start with, but there are plenty of spaces, so you could apply, Pa."

She laughed, remembering the young man who had taken her details; he had surveyed her up and down and enquired, "Aren't you rather young for this type of work? Are you strong enough for it, do you think?"

"I'll be twenty next birthday," she had answered, "so I think I'm quite old enough, older than some of those young soldiers who've gone off to war, and of course I'm strong enough: I'm a dancer!" His cheeks had reddened, and he turned away to shuffle the papers on his desk.

"The clerk said there weren't many women on their team," she continued, taking up the thread of her account for her father, "and he was surprised I had applied. I said I had to. You see, Pa, I can't spend the whole of this war teaching little girls to dance. I have to play a part in it. Oh, and by the way, we must put up blackout curtains everywhere; that's one of the things we have to check. We were supposed to have done that last week, so we're lucky they haven't come knocking on the door. Look, they gave me *Public Information Leaflet No. 2*. It says that 'popular discipline will be required for the regulations to be enforced': that will be one of our jobs. What's more – and you won't like this

– you're going to have to install something to stop light escaping as customers open and close the shop door in the evening."

"Ah, right, but good girl! I'm proud of you, and I'll go and enlist tomorrow, if you'll take my place in the shop. We'll see about those blackout curtains tomorrow afternoon." Pa replied, shedding a smile of pride at his daughter's patriotism and initiative.

Shirley spent that afternoon in the dance school, where Madame Belinskaya had calmed down since her anger the previous day at the installation of the air-raid shelter. "I have known worse in my life," she said mournfully, gazing out onto the mound where once her lawn had been, "and I suppose it's my fate to be pursued by trouble." She stopped to reconsider the troubles she had known. "But remember, *ma Chérie*, troubles make you into a much stronger person with a much deeper understanding of what life is about. And they make you appreciate the present day and all that is good in it, without waiting for a better day in the future, because that better day might never come."

Such words of wisdom would have been somewhat indigestible to a young person such as Shirley had she not already encountered troubles in her life. They transported her back to that session with the old priest in the confessional; he had said much the same, and although at the time she had been tempted to laugh at him, the events in her life since then had increasingly and depressingly begun to prove him right. While she applied herself to her own practice and to teaching her class with her customary vigour, she could not erase the sense of foreboding contained in those words.

"We should have put up blackout curtains much sooner, Pa," she upbraided her father that evening. He switched on a small table lamp, directing its beam away from the window, and turned off the main light before drawing the flimsy curtains across the double window.

"I haven't needed to turn the light on in the shop yet, and I do my accounts as you know in the back room, where nobody can see, so I think we're all right."

"No, that's not the point," she reacted angrily. "It's not so much a question of whether the neighbours and passers-by on the ground can see us but whether some German bomber comes over and sees our light and drops his bombs on us. We are a sitting target with that light on!"

"Now, now," he countered, "there haven't been any German bombers yet and we haven't had time to put up the blackout curtains, that's obvious. Archie says Eileen will run them up for us; she has plenty of material, she's making quite a little business out of it apparently, and should be able to do them quickly, so it will only be a couple more days. She's going to make a heavy black curtain to cover the doorway so the customers can sneak out of the shop without letting out much light as they go. They'll only have to push it aside slightly. I thought we might put up a stand with a box for the money on the pavement for the evening papers, so people don't have to come into the shop so often, though that will be bad for our other sales and it might be difficult in winter. I think we should start selling torches and batteries; there's going to be a great demand for them." He sat back in his armchair, mulling over his plans for a minute or two before turning the wireless on for the nine-o'clock news, at which he rubbed his hands in glee. "There, you see! I said attack was the best form of defence, and that's just what the French are doing! They are invading Germany! They're crossing into the Saar!" He was jubilant.

In contrast to her father's reaction, Shirley's mounting agitation was not quietened by the news from France, or the information that Cousin Archie's wife was probably even now in the process of making blackout curtains, so she took herself upstairs into her room, where by torchlight she wound up her gramophone and one by one placed her favourite records on the turntable. She did not dance, but sat on the floor listening to the music. She felt numbed physically and mentally. Like the gramophone when it needed winding up, it seemed that the pace of life was slowing down in the weird silence and darkness that reigned over the whole city; it was like being caught in a black snowstorm where all sounds were deadened and the way ahead was obscured in a pall of smoke. Her own life was slowing down too: yesterday's eagerness for joining the ARP had subsided into a dull inertia at the sobering awareness that this was not play-acting, nor was it the stage set for a ballet: it was a scenario for deprivation and desolation, death and destruction.

All that she had known and loved had gradually been disappearing in the past two years until there was little left of her earlier life, yet again she reviewed the losses in her life: Mémé had died, Maman had left, Ted was in a precarious situation in France, she and her father had had to leave their home because of the shell shock he had suffered in the Great War, and as a result of infantile paralysis all her earlier personal hopes had died. Yet despite this sense that all life had come to a standstill, there lurked the intimation that something momentous was going to happen, but whether it was for the good or the bad, she had no idea.

She stood up and, dragging her left leg slightly, went over to her chest of drawers to search for clean handkerchiefs. She plunged her hand to the bottom of her top drawer, where her fingers came into contact with a small battered box: it was the blue box from Genoa that contained the false pendant. She pulled it out and opened it. The fake gemstone in its tarnished setting glistened malevolently in the torchlight, like an evil eye. "White gold, not silver," Mrs Salvatore had said. What rubbish! Possibly the pendant and chain were not even made of silver, but some inferior metal that had now blackened. She would never wear it and was about to throw it in the bin but, on impulse, for reasons she could never explain, thought better of it and pushed the box back into its place beneath a pile of underwear in the depths of the drawer.

The pendant had at least brought to mind that old couple, the Salvatores, over in south-west London. After her last visit to Dr Forbes for a check-up, she had braved a return to the tranquil borough of her childhood. While her pa had gone over to visit his mother, she had taken the bus over to the area she knew so well, and was forcibly struck by the dire contrast between her present and her former circumstances. She got off the bus at the end of the road where formerly she and her family had lived and gazed impassively at the neat row of clean semi-detached houses. There, a hundred yards along the road on the right, was her old home, shaded by the tree set into the pavement in front of it. She dared not approach it closer for fear of bringing on another of those attacks of "nervous exhaustion" and a corresponding episode of phantom paralysis in her left leg, but stood staring at it while the tears trickled down her cheeks.

The Salvatores, of course, were thrilled to see her when, after drying her tears, she pushed open the door of their shop, and they were impatient to tell her that they were retiring from the business and moving back to Italy. "You see, Shirley, our lives have been so dull since you and your brother left," Mrs S. declared sadly. "We couldn't find anyone to take your place here in the shop; you were always so cheerful and reliable. We have missed you so much. Mr Salvatore has never been the same since you left. As for the paper boys, after your brother went off to live in France, they have been a disaster, not turning up for work, delivering the papers to the wrong addresses... I could go on telling you all about them till kingdom come. So I said to Mr Salvatore, I said, 'Mr Salvatore, it's time we retired. We'll go and live in Italy.' It will be good for his health, and I'll be glad not to have to light the fire and bring in the coal in the winter.

"That winter last year was terrible and it was all too much for me, because he," here she raised her thumb in Mr S.'s direction, "was not well enough to help. Oh, and by the way, Francesca sends you her love and hopes to see you again someday." Shirley smirked at the mention of Francesca, whom she never wanted to see again, but managed to express her sympathy and understanding to the Salvatores for the trials and tribulations of life for an elderly couple in the British winter, and wish them well for their return to Italy. With some awkwardness and diffidence she thanked them yet again for the "wonderful gift of the diamond" and said how sorry she was not to be wearing it that day.

As soon as she had sat down in the car for the return journey, her exasperation burst out. "Pa! Can you believe it? They are going to retire, so presumably they are going to sell the business. If only they had thought of offering it to you! Then Maman could have kept the house and wouldn't have gone gallivanting off to Washington! And we would all be together just as we used to be!" The British winter might have been too much for Mrs S., but her failure even to consider offering to sell the shop to Pa was too much for Shirley, who was very angry with the Salvatores, husband and wife. In her estimation they had caused a great deal of trouble, not least by introducing Francesca and that diamond pendant into the Marlow household. Her agitation was not helped by her emotional reaction to the sight of her old home.

"Calm down, Shirl," Pa said. "Mr and Mrs Salvatore weren't to know that I wanted to go into the newsagent's business. I never mentioned it to them, and anyhow I would never have been able to afford to buy their shop and keep our house," he reasoned. Then, in confirmation of her own suspicions, he went on, "It would have been beyond my means, and living above a shop so close to her old home might have been worse for your mother than moving away altogether, so I don't hold any grudge against them and nor should you."

Clutching the steering wheel, he put his foot down on the accelerator and exclaimed, "I say, what happened to that diamond pendant? I completely forgot about it. Did you give it back to them?" Shirley had been careful not to refer to the pendant when complaining about the

Salvatores, so was surprised when her father brought up the subject out of the blue. A truthful answer came readily, because she was quite sure that he had forgotten the time sequence relating to the gift of the diamond.

"Oh, Maman took it to be valued and was told that it was worthless, no more valuable than the sort of thing you can buy in Woolworths. So, somewhere along the line the Salvatores must have been duped."

"Do you know," Pa remarked after a thoughtful pause, "I'm quite glad about that, because I didn't think it was right for you to have it, and they must have relatives who would have wanted it for themselves. Who knows, perhaps they had stolen it long ago." Shirley agreed that that was quite possible.

Remembering the Salvatores and their funny ways helped lull Shirley into sleep that night, despite her earlier irritation with them. They had been kind and well meaning and, as Pa said, it was not their fault that they had not sold him their business. Italy was without a doubt the best place for them. She imagined it as a magical land where the sun always shone, the sea was blue like the sky and oranges grew on the trees, though to judge by the Salvatores' relatives, she was not sure that the people were always happy. They would, however, escape the war, because Mussolini had announced that Italy would be neutral.

She awoke refreshed from her dreams of blue sea and sky. Hazily recalling that she had promised to run the shop in the morning, she dressed quickly and ran downstairs. A long queue of customers had formed, stretching up the road almost as far as the station, all anxious for news and wanting to buy almost everything in the shop. Pa had not been able to go to the ARP recruiting office and Tilly was busy serving behind the counter. "Come and take over from Tilly, Shirl!" Pa called out as soon as she came through the door. "She needs to go into the stockroom for more cigarettes, and I have to open those bundles of *The Times* and the *Daily Mirror*." Business was certainly brisk, because news of the French invasion of the Saar was on everybody's lips and everybody wanted to read about it in detail. Optimism and celebration were in the air in the belief that in the wake of the French invasion, certain victory over the Germans could not be long in coming.

Staggering under a heavy bundle of blackout curtains, Cousin Archie pushed past the waiting customers and, easing himself through the doorway, he placed his parcel down on the counter. "Phew! Thank goodness I didn't have to bring those any further. I would have had a heart attack!"

he said panting. "And to think they probably won't be needed after all! Maybe I'll go down as the only casualty in Britain! Well, I'm a small price to pay for victory!" The customers laughed with him.

"We'll miss you, Archie! We'll put up a plaque to you right here, saying you won the war for us!" There was laughter all round. Although Pa had been jubilant the previous evening, he was more cautious now.

"I think there's still a long way to go," he said, casting a chill over the atmosphere. "I'm going down to the office to sign up for the ARP when I've finished serving, because I don't think it's over yet."

Someone in the queue called out, "Archie, you'll have to take your poor old boss down to the pub tonight and buy him a drink to cheer him up!"

Everyone laughed, but Pa held his own. "It's not over yet, you wait and see," he said.

The Air Raid Precautions training courses took place in the hall of the local primary school at weekends, which meant that Tilly's help was required in the shop alongside Cousin Archie on Saturday and Sunday mornings while Shirley and her father attended their classes. Shirley had to return home for her gas mask, which she had forgotten, so her father arrived at the school several minutes before her. On his arrival he was treated with deference as an old soldier from the Great War. "Pleased to have you with us, sir," the instructor greeted him with a slight bow, which was almost reverential. "I gather you were in the Heavy Brigade and were wounded twice! It's very good of you to be prepared to go back into battle again."

"Oh, well," Reggie replied with a modest laugh, "the Great War was a long time ago, and this is hardly the same as being cooped up in a tank and bombarded by enemy bullets!"

However when Shirley came into the hall the same instructor surveyed her, whistled between his teeth and then barked, "You're late, miss! You'll have to be more punctual and reliable or I'll have you thrown out!"

"That's my daughter," Pa remarked quietly behind the instructor's back, whereupon the latter turned round, his face colouring and said:

"Oh, I'm sorry, sir, I did not realize…" Shirley joined her father, put her arm through his and enjoyed the instructor's discomfort.

The session began with an introductory talk outlining the history and the role of the ARP wardens. The participants were told that, as long ago as 1935, the then Prime Minister Stanley Baldwin had suggested that plans should be developed for the protection of the population of each local authority in the event of an attack. The Air Raid Wardens' Service was formed in 1937, leading to an influx of volunteers. The instructor apologized for not yet having uniforms for the new volunteers, but he expected that these would be issued eventually. For the time being, they would have to wear their own clothes, with an eye to practicality, and would be provided with an armband, a helmet with a large "W" on the front and wellington boots. The duties of the wardens would initially involve making sure that everyone carried his or her gas mask when out of doors, and enforcing the blackout by touring their areas and checking that all lights, which might indicate a built-up area to an enemy aircraft, were invisible. If they were not, it would be the duty of the warden to call at the offending property and firmly tell the occupants to put the light out or cover it. Failure to comply would incur a visit from the police. An addition to the blackout aspect of the work was the protection of members of the public who had difficulty finding their way in the dark. Many people had become lost, tripped over, fallen under cars and buses or even wandered into rivers and canals. With a small torch focused on the pavement, but not shining up in the air, a warden could point the way and lead pedestrians out of danger.

The instructor said that, when the war, in his words, "took off", the wardens would be required to watch for enemy aircraft and sound the sirens. They would then have to usher people to safety in the shelters but remain outside themselves until they had checked their areas. During a bombing raid they would also be required to visit the shelters in turn to see if the people were in need of help. A further duty, according to the instructor, would involve assessing the damage, administering first aid, calling the emergency services and extinguishing fires. Rather hastily he glossed over other requirements, such as collecting up scattered body parts and attempting to reunite family members. The object of the training course, he said, was to prepare each volunteer to perform his or her duties to the best of his or her abilities in the service of the country, and they would begin by looking at some ways of re-enforcing the blackout while avoiding accidents.

Shirley listened attentively, carefully noting all the information. She was excited and impatient to start on the practical elements immediately, but after his talk the instructor asked for questions from the floor, some of which were sensible, but many were inane, and then he invited the group to stop for a cup of tea and meet the other wardens in their sector. In Shirley's opinion this was a waste of time, although her father did not think so. She was particularly annoyed when a burly young man of about her own age approached them. "Hello! How are you getting on?" he asked both father and daughter, although Shirley was aware that his eyes were on her.

"Fine, thank you," her pa replied. "My daughter and I want to do our bit for the war effort and I expect you do too," he went on.

"Yes, we all have to do what we can, don't we?" the young chap replied. "I'd really like to be a soldier, you know," he said with some pride, "conscripted to go to France and all that, but I'm in a reserved occupation so they won't let me go."

"Oh, what's that?" Pa asked.

"I work on the railways, a signalman, so they say I'm just as important here as if I went to fight." After this exchange, there was, of course, nothing that Shirley could do to drag her father away from the signalman, who introduced himself as Bert.

"What a nice young chap! I've invited him to come round some time," Pa announced at the end of the day. "I think he took a shine to you, Shirl; it would be good for you to have some friends round here and get out a bit, to the cinema or something, before this war really flares up, as no doubt it will."

Shirley was irritated. "I'm sure you both have plenty to talk about, Pa, but I don't think he's quite my type." The image of Alan rose before her. How could she possibly exchange the image of that elegant, handsome man for podgy Bert with his grimy fingernails and greasy hair? She had not thought about Alan for quite a while, but since the memory of him had resurfaced, she wondered with a pang of anxiety whether he had been posted to France in the British Expeditionary Force, whose movements Pa followed with such dedication every night on the news and every day in the papers, as well as once a week at the cinema.

44

There were no air raids, no fires to extinguish and no casualties to treat on dry land during the months of that autumn of 1939. Although Shirley's nights for ARP duties were Mondays and Wednesdays, and Reggie's Tuesdays and Thursdays, he insisted on accompanying her on her patrols after the unpleasant experiences she had been subjected to in certain quarters of their area of south-east London. On her first sortie, full of patriotic zeal, she had come across several houses with all their lights on, and their doors wide open, but whenever she called on the inhabitants to put out the lights, as she had been instructed, abuse and defiance rained down on her. "Miss Goody-Goody, we've not had any air raids here, so why should we bother?" was the general tenor of the reception meted out to her.

Accustomed to having her own way, and unused to being on the receiving end of such hostile reactions, she was seething by the time she reached home and let fly. "I felt like yelling, 'You should be doing your duty! Think of all those soldiers putting their lives at risk for you!'" she told her pa. "But I didn't, because by then they had closed their doors, so they wouldn't have heard anyhow. But they didn't close their curtains. You could have seen their lights a mile off!" She slammed her helmet down on the table and slunk off to her room, her fervour dampened by such a lack of public spirit and such scant regard for public safety.

"Do you think they are German sympathizers, Pa? Should I report them?" she asked later, still fuming from the experience.

Her father shrugged. "I shouldn't think so: they're just stupid." When, during the following week, he accompanied her and gruffly threatened to inform the police of the infringements, the attitude was less confrontational and the lights went out promptly. A week or two later, Shirley insisted on hurrying round the neighbourhood on her own, determined to manage without her father's help. She made a mental note of cases of non-compliance with the law, before devoting herself to helping the elderly and infirm cross the road in the dark with the use of a little torch, which with its beam covered in grey tissue paper, directed a dim light onto the ground at their feet. Pa informed the police of the houses that had broken the rules for the blackout, and the next morning he put in an order for a supply of the small torches that were permitted by the regulations. They sold well, as did the batteries for them.

Often of a morning, after a visit by the police to various offending properties, Reggie would hear indignant raised voices among the customers in the shop, complaining that some invisible ARP warden had been snooping about and had called the police, who had arrived in the middle of the night, and had issued warnings that the offenders could end up in court or in jail. Reggie would keep his head down without comment, while Shirley slipped out to the rear of the shop, an area that served all sorts of functions. There either her father or Archie did the accounts; there they made the tea and kept biscuits, and used the basic and antiquated bathroom facilities. To her amusement, Shirley realized that there were complaints about the ARP wardens every day of the week and at the weekends, not simply on the mornings after her round or her father's, so she became inured to them. Indeed, she rather enjoyed listening on a weekday morning to grumbles about the nocturnal visits by the police, knowing that either she or her father might have instigated them, and she secretly hoped that the complainants would in fact end up in court or in jail one day on account of their irresponsibility. "It would serve them right!" she said to herself.

Inevitably, during the course of her duties during the autumn she occasionally came across Bert, whom she had met on the training course and whose beat adjoined hers, but she was never as delighted to meet him as he was to see her. "I'll come on your rounds with you, if you like, and afterwards I'll do my own," he volunteered one very dark night when there was no moon and not even a reassuring hint of light peeping out through chinks or holes in curtains. Walking along the side roads was a scary, not to say dangerous pursuit, like walking into a black fog out of which an unlit vehicle might loom suddenly, the only warning of its approach being the low hum of the engine. On the first occasion she was glad of Bert's company, but was put out that he took her consent to mean that she was pleased to see him every night. He seemed to contrive to arrive just as she was setting out, which made her suspect that he had been watching her movements. They talked as they walked, though they had little in common. In Shirley's opinion

Bert and her father would have been better companions. However, it did transpire that Bert was keen on the pictures, so they spent the time comparing notes on films they had seen. Shirley was a frequent visitor to the cinema; indeed, in the past year, always with her father, she had seen many films, among them *The Hound of the Baskervilles*, *Goodbye, Mr Chips* and *The Wizard of Oz*. Bert had seen the same films, so they were not short of conversation.

Then, later that autumn, he offered to take her to the cinema. This seemed quite natural in view of their shared interest and was an invitation that she saw no reason to refuse, especially since the film, *Wuthering Heights*, was one that she was keen to see and had missed on its first showing. Before she had had time to think, she found herself saying eagerly, "Oh, yes, please! I so wanted to see that! I missed it the first time round." Then, on more cautious reflection, she asked, "But what about tickets? They are hard to come by, so they say."

"Oh, that's no problem!" Bert replied. "I have them here in my wallet." He patted his inside pocket. Shirley frowned. Why had he bought the tickets before asking her? That was presumptuous indeed! But she thought better of protesting, simply asking how he had come by them. "A friend of mine works in the cinema – he's a projectionist – and he let me have them. They'll be in the back row, but you don't mind that, do you?" Shirley wasn't sure. The shared cinematographic interest did not mean that she regarded Bert as any more than a casual acquaintance: she certainly was not harbouring any romantic feelings towards him, which, as she understood it, was implied by having seats in the back row.

Her father was pleased that Bert had invited her to go to the cinema. "I'm so glad! You need to have some friends round here, Shirl! I like Bert: he's a nice chap."

Shirley was by no means as enthusiastic as her pa, and was even less so when she discovered that Bert's idea of a visit to the pictures with a girl for whom he had bought a ticket was that he could run his hands where and whenever he liked all over her. She was angry, the more so because in her efforts to fend him off she missed half the film. As it drew to a close with the ghosts of Heathcliff and Cathy walking hand in hand beneath Peniston Crag, he tried to kiss her. "Get off!" she spat in a loud whisper. "I didn't say you could do that. You're not my boy-friend!" Shocked and insulted by his behaviour and frustrated at having missed most of a film that she had truly been longing to see, she refused to let him walk her home in the pitch-black night. She escaped from the cinema with the lightning speed and agility of a practised ballerina, having succeeded in knocking off his glasses as she pushed past him on her way out of the back row.

Without embarrassing her father by telling him exactly what had happened, Shirley made it quite plain that she was never going out with Bert again. Reggie was startled. "But I thought you liked him!" he exclaimed.

"No, Pa, it was you who liked him because he works on the railways, not me," she retorted, "and I don't want him to come on my rounds with me either!"

"Well," said her father mildly, "I don't know how we can stop him."

"Oh, I do!" Shirley retorted. "We'll swap days, you and me, then you can walk the beat with Bert on Mondays and Wednesdays and I'll go on my own on Tuesdays and Thursdays!" She was adamant, leaving Reggie with no choice but to agree to the change of plan.

"I suppose I'll have to ring the control office and tell them about it," he said, mulling over her demand, "but if that's what you want, that's fine by me, except I'll come with you on nights when there's no moon. Otherwise I shall worry about you, because this war's hotting up and who knows what will happen next."

He was in a reflective mood and began to review the current situation aloud yet again, shaking his head as he did so. "Those German submarines have already sunk too many of our ships out in the Atlantic, not to mention the *Royal Oak* in Scapa Flow. I've just heard on the news that they are laying magnetic mines that attach themselves to the hulls of ships. And as for that monster battleship down there in the South Atlantic, it's wreaking havoc! I bet you it won't be long before they start sending their planes over here."

"Yes, yes, Pa, I know all that; that's why I'm an ARP warden, remember?" she reminded him impatiently. Given that she was doing her duty, she preferred at other times to overlook the fact that there was a war on. Thereafter, despite her protests, Reggie accompanied his daughter when the moon was out of sight, allowing her to go out alone only if there was some light, be it only a glimmer of starlight, in the sky. On such occasions, Shirley persuaded her father to stay at home and rest. She reckoned that going out alone in the dark was a small price to pay for being spared Bert's attentions. Their paths rarely crossed, except on training days, but that was not a problem as her father always attended them too.

After her sterling efforts to obliterate Alan from her thoughts, Shirley surprised herself by fancying that he was walking alongside her as she went out on her night watch. It may have been her outburst at Bert's impertinence when she had told him firmly that he was not her boyfriend that had reawakened her dreams of Alan, not that he could be called her boyfriend, though she certainly wished that he were. Even as an imaginary boyfriend, he was an infinitely preferable companion who would never cause her any embarrassment: of that there was no doubt. Indeed, walking along the back roads in the light of the moon, his imagined presence was a delightful comfort, bringing an aura of magical romance to her duties, which were becoming rather tedious. "Where was he now?" she wondered, wishing that she could cast a spell that would bring him to her. All her earlier attempts to forget him were thrown to the four winds as she wholeheartedly embraced his memory, knowing in her heart of hearts that she would never find anyone else to match him and at the same time consigning the likes of Bert to oblivion.

Mentally she chatted to the unseen presence while she walked, telling him that for the first time in months she had begun to plan a new ballet, set against the background of war, in which two young lovers, who had been separated by the conflict, would meet by chance and portray their passion in dance. Try as she might, a suitably happy ending would not materialize. These plans, though disturbing in their refusal to admit of the conclusion that she wanted, together with her imaginary chats with Alan, provided an absorbing way of coping with the boredom of those long, dark, chilly nights spent watching for aircraft, scouring the neighbourhood for lights and pushing leaflet after leaflet through letter boxes.

The local branch of the ARP had decided to reproduce the messages on the posters, which formed part of the government's safety campaign, and to distribute them to the populace. Variously these advised people to count to fifteen before going out into the streets to allow their eyes time to adjust, not to step out of moving vehicles, whether buses or trains, to make sure that the train had actually reached the station before getting out and that the open door was on the platform side. It was understandable that the blackout was unpopular, given that in such a short time there were already more than four thousand fatalities. "I doubt that German bombs would have killed so many victims," Cousin Archie observed sagely one day when the subject came up for discussion in the shop.

In addition, the weather was not kind to the wardens: it appeared to be fighting a war of its own between cold air coming down from the Arctic and milder weather from the Atlantic. Shirley shivered in the freezing temperatures, which began in early December and would continue with only the occasional break until February; only then did the Atlantic weather win the battle. As Christmas approached, she always felt cold, despite wearing her warmest clothes with mittens and socks, and under her helmet a woolly hat that Mémé had knitted for her, and also keeping up a brisk march round her area, sometimes slipping on the frozen pavements. With increasing regularity she allowed herself to call in briefly at Madame Belinskaya's for a warming cup of cocoa and five minutes in front of a roaring fire to thaw her hands and feet, before resuming her duties. It was on these occasions that she discussed her plans for the new ballet with Madame, who was impressed by her pupil's resilience and determination.

"My only reservation, *ma petite*, is that in wartime people might prefer something happier. But you are quite right, why don't we put on a show?" she said. "And let's start work on it now before those Nazis begin to drop their bombs on us." The phoney war had given Madame the chance to adapt to the changing circumstances and come to terms with the ugly protrusion in her lawn, which in any case was buried under a heap of snow. "Let's have something colourful, like a series of scenes from a Mediterranean country, Spain or Italy for instance. That would please the audience in these dark, drab times!" she suggested, and Shirley agreed. Together of an evening they put their minds to work on a new show, until Shirley became aware that her visits were growing longer and longer, and that if she were caught sheltering indoors anywhere other than in a designated ARP post, of which the shop was one at the other end of her route, she could be in trouble. Cheered at the luxury of having even a brief refuge at the furthest point from home, she set out again.

ARP work, apart from the cold and the many inconveniences, held one particular drawback, which was that Shirley, after being out of doors from dusk until the end of her shift at midnight, slept long and soundly until well into the next day. From the point of view of her ballet teaching and practice sessions, that was not a problem, because she was wide awake by the afternoon, but it did entail loss of earnings from her work in the shop, since on both Tuesday and Thursday mornings Tilly had to take her place. Although he was anxious that his daughter should not suffer as a result of her devotion to duty, her father was hard-pressed to pay her as well as Tilly for those mornings when she was still asleep, until a solution to his financial problems arrived in the form of many devices which, as well as the small torches, were designed to help people cope with the blackout. He ordered a huge quantity of white armbands and luminous goods, such as badges and pin-on flowers, so that pedestrians could be seen in the dark, plus luminous sticky tape and a collection of walking sticks with a tiny light at the end. All these items flew off the shelves, enabling Reggie to pay Shirley a modest allowance so that she was not out of pocket.

He was in a jovial mood as Christmas drew closer, because he now clung to the hope of victory in the Battle of the River Plate and the scuttling of the pride of the German fleet, the battleship *Admiral Graf Spee*, given that the French attack, upon which he had previously pinned his hopes, had not yielded results. He therefore decided to give a small party for his staff in celebration and asked Shirley for her approval. She was all in favour of showing appreciation to Tilly and Cousin Archie and their nearest and dearest, that is to say, Eileen, Archie's wife, and Tilly's mother, so she readily agreed to help with the arrangements with the proviso that Bert should not be invited. On the other hand, she included on her guest list Mrs Fothergill, the sad elderly lady from the ghostly sweet shop next door, whom she called on from time to time to deliver the newspaper and collect her payment. A search in the attic uncovered decorations from the previous year, and a simple menu of boiled beef in beer with onions and carrots, which she had watched Céline preparing in France, followed by tinned apricots and tinned cream, was much appreciated, even by Tilly's baby, who relished a dish of mashed potato with beery gravy. Tilly mopped her eyes, "Oh I wish my Fred could see him!" she cried, referring to her husband who had been called up long ago and sent to France.

Pa was pouring glasses of beer and Shirley was making a pot of tea for the ladies when the phone rang. Thinking that it might be Ted on the line, she succumbed to its compelling ring. As usual her heart sank on hearing her granny's voice. "Shirley, dear, it's such a long time since I saw you – not since you came over with your father after you'd been to the doctor's – and it's such a long time since we last spoke, so I decided to ring you with my news!"

Shirley sighed in exasperation. "Granny, I haven't come with Pa to see you because I'm always busy here and we have visitors at present. I'll ask Pa to ring you tomorrow," she said curtly.

"Oh, but I wanted to let you know that I won't be here for Christmas, so you'll have to make other arrangements!" Granny said, the indignation mounting in her voice.

"Well, thank you for letting us know, but I'm making tea for our guests, so perhaps I could call you back later."

"Guests, did you say? Who are they?" Granny harped on.

Shirley opted for what she supposed to be the least contentious reply. "Cousin Archie and Eileen," she said.

"Really? Well, in that case, I'll have a word with Archibald then."

Shirley called Archie to the phone. "Sorry, it's my granny, and she wants a word with you," she whispered.

Taking the phone, he raised his eyes to heaven and sighed. "Hello, Cousin Millicent, it's Archibald here," he said, holding the phone slightly away from his ear. He was rooted to the spot for about half an hour, with no chance of escape or saying anything other than "I see" or "Yes, of course" or simply, as he grew wearier and wearier, "Um". Shirley first brought him a chair, then a glass of beer and then a cup of tea. Finally they heard Archie saying into the mouthpiece, all in one breath, "Don't worry, Millicent, I'll tell Reggie your news, but I'm afraid he's rather busy at the moment, so I expect he'll ring you tomorrow or perhaps he'll come and see you. Bye!"

He put the phone down smartly and brought his chair back to the table. "She can bend your ear, that one, can't she?" he remarked, before downing another beer in one go. "She wants you to know, Reggie, that she's decided to sell up and move to Birmingham to live with your sister!" Shirley sniggered out loud, while her father strained his face muscles in an obvious effort to remain serious.

"She told me," Shirley said, "that she's going away for Christmas, so we can't go to hers. Perhaps that means she's leaving straight away."

"No, no," Archie intervened, "she's going to Birmingham for Christmas so she can choose which room she'll have in Winnie's house, and then she's moving some time in the spring or early summer, by which time they will have redecorated the room for her."

"I hope Horace knows what he's letting himself in for, though I don't suppose he's had much choice in the matter," Pa remarked.

There followed a long silence until quiet, industrious Eileen ventured to speak. "It would be lovely if you would like to join to us for Christmas.

I mean all of you," she said timidly, glancing round the table at those present.

"Yes, yes, we would like that!" Archie chimed in fulsomely. The invitation was gratefully and readily accepted by all, including poor little Mrs Fothergill from next door, on whose lips there appeared a glimmer of a smile.

Parcels began to arrive from the United States containing carefully and elaborately wrapped packages addressed to Shirley and her father. Shirley opened the boxes and placed the presents under the small Christmas tree that her pa had bought from the greengrocer's along the road. A card and a letter accompanied one of the parcels. It seemed that Maman was so far out of touch with her husband and daughter that she had run out of appropriate things to say to them. She had no idea of the realities of their lives in wartime south-east London, partly because she had visited the premises only that once when she had taken an instant dislike to them, and partly because Shirley only ever wrote to her in response to a letter that she had received, and then imparted merely the bare bones of news. For instance, she had written that Ted was still working on the farm, though she had not mentioned his gunshot wound; that she herself worked in the shop in the mornings and, now that her left leg was so much better, danced in the afternoons; and that Pa was well with no signs of a recurrence of his wartime traumas or of the pain from the bullet wound in his hip, in spite of the outbreak of yet another war and in spite of all his hard work. She considered it discreet to refrain from any reference to their ARP duties in the interests of national security, or that Ted was in France, which Maman knew anyhow, in case her letter on its long voyage fell into the wrong hands.

Maman had little to say except that the war in Europe had increased her workload hugely, that she missed her family and would love to hear more news of them, and that she hoped they were all safe and well. Pa never wrote to her, and showed no interest whatsoever in reading her letters. Although she was still angry with her mother, Shirley began to feel a tinge of sympathy for her in her distant isolation, because she was pretty sure that Pépé had never written a letter in his life and was not about to start writing to his daughter. What's more, she knew that Céline was not a fluent correspondent and that, if Ted wrote at all, his letters were bound to be brief and matter-of-fact.

However, in spite of her lovely presents, which contained beautiful clothes, make-up and silk stockings, and Pa's that contained a box of cigars and chocolates in a colourful box that looked as if it had been embroidered, Shirley was not inclined to share any further information about her experiences with her absent mother, who gave no indication at all as to whether she might ever return to them. There was, it seemed, a definite lack of candour on both sides of the Atlantic.

As for Ted, his promises to share the details of his emotional life with his sister did not amount to much. He wrote short notes fairly often, but his accounts of problems with the health of one of the cows and yet more repairs to the tractor did not reveal the desired information about his state of mind, his love life or his safety. He did at least let his sister know that his arm was healing well – nearly a year after the "accident" – but that the authorities still maintained that he was not fit enough to join up. She sensed his frustration at his own inactivity, particularly because with the freezing weather there was little useful work to be done on the farm, apart from cutting hedges, mending fences and replacing rotting posts. Nevertheless he always included a little note from Céline which was not much more informative than his letters. She said that Ted was well and working hard, as was Pépé, despite the dreadful weather. Mysteriously, she once added that there were things happening in the village and so was glad that she was not living down there. Pépé, of course, never even added his name to Céline's notes. The letters generally contained so little information that clearly the censor did not bother with them.

The uncertainty worried Shirley and her father, with whom she shared her letters from Ted because there was absolutely nothing in them that could be considered confidential. One evening just before Christmas, her pa said, "I think we should try telephoning to find out what's going on."

"That will cost a lot," Shirley warned him, but he shrugged that off.

"Nothing is too expensive where Ted is concerned," he declared. "Do you have Louise's number? Perhaps you had better ring, as your French and your hearing are better than mine."

One Saturday evening Shirley tried calling Louise. It took ages for a line to be put through. "This may take some time. The lines to France are not very good at the moment; there seems to be a lot of interference," the operator said when she asked to be connected. Shirley persisted until, on her fifth attempt, she heard a distant phone ringing. A male voice that she did not recognize answered, speaking loudly with a strange accent. Clearly and loudly over the crackling airwaves Shirley asked for Louise.

"Wait, please!" the male voice commanded rather than requested, and eventually Louise came to the phone.

"Ah, Chérie, it is so nice to hear you!" she exclaimed. "How are you?" After the exchange of pleasantries, Shirley asked if she had seen Édouard lately. Louise hesitated. "No, not much," she replied. "He doesn't come here very often, though Charlot has seen him. He's fine." Then she lowered her voice. "I can't talk, Chérie, we have some strange visitors here at present, so I must say *au revoir* at once."

"Wish Ted and Céline and Pépé a Happy Christmas from Pa and me, won't you?" Shirley asked, but Louise had put the phone down and that was the end of the call. Shirley was puzzled. Her father, standing beside her, watching her quizzically, was expecting an account of the conversation. "Ted's fine, Pa," she said, "but Louise was very busy, so she couldn't talk for long."

"Well, didn't you ask her if Ted could come to the phone at some prearranged time so that we could talk to him?" he demanded.

"No, sorry, I forgot, and the *estaminet* was full of customers – I could hear them talking very loudly in the background – so she had to go and serve at the bar."

45

Reggie mopped his brow while he listened to the nine-o'clock news early in the January of 1940. "I'm beginning to lose track of what's happening in this war. I don't understand it at all. It's bad enough the Germans invading all and sundry, but why do the Russians have to go on the attack too? What is the world coming to? Look at the poor Finns, battling to push the Red Army back to where it came from!" he huffed, despairingly reviewing the perilous state of affairs throughout Europe. "How I wish that bomb in Munich in November had wiped Hitler out! Mind you, I'm glad we weren't taken in by that flimsy offer of peace he made. That would have been another of his charades! At least I suppose we have to be glad that the Spanish War is over. Those poor Spaniards, so much for their attempts at democracy! They've ended up with that Fascist Franco. I can't see that there's much to choose between them, the Fascists and the Nazis, I mean. They both go around torturing and murdering." Wearied by his own depressing assessment of current events, he retired to his armchair.

Shirley listened intermittently: she was more concerned with the prospect of rationing. At the end of December, it was announced that meat and sugar were to be rationed, so she had bought as much sugar and as many tins of meat as she could carry and had sent her father out to buy more, but there was little that anyone without a cold store could do to prepare for the rationing of butter, ham and bacon that had just come into force. They would have to eat margarine when their supply of butter ran out, but ham and bacon were staples of their diet, and as she thumbed through the ration books, which had arrived late in 1939 and were now duly registered with the butcher and the grocer down the road, she could not see how she would be able to stretch the meagre rations to provide decent meals for both of them.

A quarter of a pound of butter, a quarter of a pound of bacon and three quarters of sugar a week per person did not sound very much, especially considering Pa's healthy appetite and his way of spooning the sugar liberally over his cornflakes at breakfast. He would not like corned beef or spam, that was certain, even if the corned beef were combined in a hash, as was suggested in one of the recipes in a magazine she had read in the shop. On the other hand, she herself was not particularly keen on bacon, because she did not like fat, so he could have her share of that. The unfairness of the system lay in the fact that people who could afford to eat in restaurants and workers who ate in canteens would not have to hand over their ration books, whereas she and Pa, by the very nature of the business, always had to eat at home, using up their precious rations, and that irked her.

There was one consolation though. Christmas at Cousin Archie's was a lavish affair at which Eileen had served a large goose. Shirley had offered to help prepare the feast in the kitchen and had admired the goose as Eileen, struggling under its weight, lifted it out of the oven. "Well, dear, I have to confess," she said, choosing her words carefully, "I am so grateful to you and your pa. You have done me – and Archie, of course – such a good turn by letting him keep his old job in the shop. I don't know what I would have done with him moping about here at home if you hadn't had any use for him. He would forever be wanting me to make him cups of tea, but, as it is, thanks to you, I can do my sewing and look after my garden and have my friends round without his constant interruptions. You see, that business is his lifeblood."

"Don't worry about that, Eileen," she reassured her elderly relative, "Cousin Archie is a great asset to the shop. Just think, if it weren't for him, we wouldn't be able to go on holiday, Pa would never be able to take a day off and I wouldn't be able to do my dancing. Tilly, of course, is a great help too, but she wouldn't be able to run the business, it would be too much for her."

"Don't tell anyone I've said this, will you? I wouldn't want Archie to think I didn't want him here at home," Eileen confided nervously.

"My lips are sealed," Shirley assured her, in surprise that this shy, painfully thin little person should be so anxious to protect her exceedingly self-confident husband from an obvious truth.

"Oh, and I meant to say," Eileen continued, "don't worry about the rationing, not the meat rationing anyhow. My brother has a farm in Surrey and he's going to keep us provided with ham and pork, and eggs and the occasional chicken too, I shouldn't be surprised. The goose comes from there, you see. There'll be far too much for the two of us, so I'll be glad to share it with you and your father. It's the least I can do." Wondering whether Eileen would remember her promise, because she recalled that Cousin Archie had been known to complain about his wife's forgetfulness, especially when he came down one day to find that she had left the iron on all night, Shirley decided that it would be better not to rely on her, and tried to work out how far she could eke out the weekly rations and what best to do with them.

Her father was right: there was no shortage of bad news, which made the problem of rationing appear almost trivial. The Soviets had advanced in Finland, both a Union-Castle liner and a destroyer had been sunk and the accounts of Nazi atrocities were horrendous. Fortunately, there then came enough good news to raise Reggie's spirits. He listened jubilantly to reports of the arrival of a squadron of the Canadian Air Force, and the rescue of three hundred British prisoners of war trapped in a German tanker in Norway, as well as the pledge of planes and airmen from Australia. Thus clinging on to a sense of perspective, he did not protest at his diminutive daily portions.

He and Cousin Archie took one Friday in February off to go into the City to join the cheering crowds on the return of the victorious sailors who had sealed the fate of the *Admiral Graf Spee*, while Shirley and Tilly ran the shop together. Apart from Christmas Day, Reggie had taken very little time off of late, so that missing one afternoon's ballet did not upset his daughter unduly, despite the frenzy of preparations for the new show, which was taking shape nicely, and was coming up in March.

Although neither she nor Madame knew much about Spain, apart from the dreadful reports over the past three years of the Spanish Civil War, they looked for pictures of that country in happier times, read Washington Irving's *Tales of the Alhambra* and searched out suitable records of Spanish-style music from the collection in the basement. The mothers of the cast set to work to make colourful costumes with whatever scraps of material they could lay their hands on, while their daughters attempted to mimic flamenco dancers in the style of the ballet. Bizet's *Carmen* provided a plentiful source of dramatic music, as did Ravel's *Boléro* and his *Rhapsodie espagnole*. Manuel de Falla's music for his own ballets added a truly authentic flavour to the repertoire, with excerpts from *Love, the Magician*. Shirley was in her element as she both choreographed the entertainment and danced in it, but was disturbed by Madame's unusually intense scrutiny of her practice sessions. She feared that a barrage of criticism was about to hit her.

After one long Friday afternoon of challenging sequences, Madame hesitated before speaking. This in itself was unnerving, because it was very uncharacteristic of someone who as a rule was so forthright. Never before had Madame found it so awkward to voice her opinions. "I don't know how to put this, Chérie, because I don't like to remind you of your illness," Madame began with considerable diffidence, "but it seems to me that you have completely recovered from it." There was a pause in which Shirley waited with bated breath for what might be coming next. "I am so pleased by the improvement in your dancing. It has always been impressive technically, but now you have mastered that intangible quality, expression. You have absorbed the emotional content of the music and you really seem to be part of the music, heart and soul."

"Thank you, Madame!" Shirley exclaimed in pleasure, her fears allayed.

"Wait, I haven't finished yet," Madame said, raising an index finger. "So it seems to me that it is time for you to apply again to Sadler's Wells! In my opinion your talents are wasted here."

Shirley was taken off guard; she took a deep breath while she contemplated a tactful answer. "Thank you for suggesting that, Madame, I am flattered," she replied. "I haven't thought about Sadler's Wells for ages, but give me time to collect my thoughts, please."

This was not quite true, because there had been the occasion when Violet had suggested that Shirley should apply for her place, and of course there had often been times when she had mulled over the possibility of approaching the famous Ninette de Valois at Sadler's Wells once again, but had rejected the idea for several reasons. However, if Madame Belinskaya honestly believed that she now stood a chance of taking up her rightful place after a lapse of more than two years, the thought was tempting and certainly worth considering.

Sadler's Wells was rapidly growing in renown, establishing ballet as an art form in Britain and performing in a style that blended the best of Russian and Continental techniques of dancing, while adapting them to compositions by British composers and choreographers, which meant that the concept of a truly British ballet was at last being established. The possibility of joining the company was very beguiling, so Shirley rehearsed her arguments for reluctantly rejecting that possibility once more that evening to see if they were still valid. She put them to her pa over supper before he went out to the pub.

He did his best to look interested and concerned, but at first found it difficult to participate in an informed discussion. Nevertheless, once he realized how important the issue was to his daughter, he tried his best to produce a few worthwhile observations. "Of course, I know you were doing very well before you fell ill, and it was a terrible disappointment not to be able to take up that place they offered you," he began, "and I know it's what you always wanted to do. Do you still feel the same about dancing?"

"Yes, I think I do," Shirley replied.

"Do you suppose your leg is strong enough now?" was his next question. This was above all the problem that troubled her and for which she did not have a definitive answer.

"I can't really tell. It seems much better until I get too tired or very upset about something, and then it starts to ache; sometimes it goes into a cramp and just sometimes, after my patrol for instance, it feels limp."

"Hmm," said Pa, "that tells me you're not ready for the strain of dancing all day every day, late into the night. I've read about that woman – Madam what's her name – in the papers, and I gather that although she's very well respected, she drives them very hard. And she wouldn't make an exception for you. There will be other companies you can join, you wait and see. I'm sure of that."

Shirley nodded. "Mm, thanks, Pa, I think you may be right."

This was the major reason that she repeated to Madame Belinskaya the following week for not renewing her application to Sadler's Wells, yet adding that she wouldn't like to find herself on the receiving end of the sharp edge of Ninette de Valois's tongue. Madame nodded understandingly. Shirley went on, "Anyhow, I think I'm too old: they're taking in very young dancers, fifteen-year-old teenagers, even younger, and I've just had my twentieth birthday! I'd feel ancient in amongst them. What's more, I don't expect I'd be taken on as a principal; I'd have to put up with the *corps de ballet*, and that's not what I want, not in that company anyway. To tell the truth, I'm happier here choreographing the shows and dancing the principal roles, even if it's only a couple of times a year."

"I see," Madame replied. "I wanted you to know that if you should think of applying to the Wells again I wouldn't hold you back, but I have to say I am delighted that you want to stay here with us. You are such a good teacher as well as a dancer and choreographer. You may be sure I will give you a good reference whenever you ask for one, though

I should be very sorry to lose you." Shirley smiled in gratitude. "Oh, and by the way," Madame continued, "sometimes I read advertisements for front-of-house staff and occasionally they advertise for ushers at the Wells. Would you like to do that sometimes, so that you can get the feel of the place and see what's happening there before applying to dance on the stage?"

"Yes, I would! That is a nice idea; then I could see what they're doing, providing it doesn't conflict with my ARP duties," Shirley replied, grateful for yet another opening. In fact, although reasonably content with her current arrangements, the drabness and the smoke-laden atmosphere of life beside a railway line, not to mention the tiredness caused by the late nights devoted to ARP duties, were starting to weigh her down a little, so she welcomed the chance to escape to work in the theatre from time to time.

"I'll ask Mees Smeet to find out if they need staff," Madame promised, "though it won't be for a little while. The company is out in the provinces at present, you know."

These days Shirley's visits to central London were less frequent than they once were. She and Cynthia kept in touch by phone, but they met less frequently because Cynthia went from job to job, from musical to musical, without a break, and never had any spare time between rehearsals and performances. As for Violet, Shirley could not quite summon the courage to pay her another visit in her reduced circumstances, where damp nappies were strewn all over the miserable one-room flat, and her ne'er-do-well husband was conspicuous by his lengthy absences. Cynthia had given graphic accounts of Violet's worsening situation and her treatment by the adored Henry, who turned up about once a month, stayed for one night and then disappeared again, leaving a handful of loose change on the table. Violet's parents had relented and given their daughter a small allowance, but only enough to keep her and the baby alive. According to Cynthia, Violet was quite happy, but Shirley found that hard to believe. How could she be happy living in such a dismal place with sole responsibility for a baby and scarcely enough to live on? "Oh, but she has her little Harry and she loves him to bits," Cynthia said.

"Yes, maybe," Shirley replied, unconvinced that any bawling infant could ever make up for what Violet had lost, "but think about the sacrifice she made for that cad! She had a career in the top ballet company in the country, so she must have been mad!"

There was bitterness in Shirley's appraisal of Violet's circumstances. It seemed to her that Violet had had everything offered to her on a plate, but had thrown it all away: she came from a wealthy background, her parents used to dote on her and probably still did at heart, she had talent, she had won a place at Sadler's Wells and had a career stretching before her that Shirley would have died for, and moreover she enjoyed reasonably good health. "It's not quite as you suppose," said Cynthia, sounding a note of caution, "you see, Violet always maintained that her mother pushed her into the ballet regardless of whether she wanted to dance or not; she didn't give her any choice, so I suppose Henry and Harry were a way to rebel against her parents."

"Well," Shirley replied, "I think she has been stupid, and that makes me very annoyed."

Cynthia laughed. "You have strong opinions, Shirl," she remarked, "everyone knows that, but often people don't do what you want them to. You might think that's stupid, but you must remember what's right for you might not be right for them."

Shirley kept quiet, despite her irritation. "I'm sorry. I've been insensitive, and I do understand how you feel," Cynthia added after a moment or two. Shirley brushed the matter aside because she did not want to fall out with Cynthia, yet she was still put out and held to her opinion that Violet, who had always been scatty, had been stupid into the bargain. She decided that she definitely would not go to see her, in case she was tempted to speak her mind. There was no question: she would not be inviting Violet to join her belated birthday outing, even were Violet able to persuade her mother to babysit.

In February, there was a small celebration in the shop for Shirley's twentieth birthday. Eileen had come round during the afternoon, armed with a chicken for supper. Parcels had arrived from America, which Shirley could not resist opening. Nestling inside an empty chocolate box were several pairs of stockings that had the feel and the appearance of silk, but which, according to Maman's accompanying card, were actually made of a new synthetic fabric called Nylon. "That's clever," Cousin Archie remarked that evening when Shirley was showing Eileen the precious gifts. "Your mother must have put those silk stockings in a chocolate box to fool customs!"

Eileen then held out a delicately wrapped present, saying apologetically, "Shirley, dear, I hope you will like these. They're not new. I've had them since I was your age, and I think it's time I started giving them away." Shirley took the box, which she set carefully down on the table before opening it. Inside were four small china ornaments.

"Oh, they are so pretty!" she exclaimed, as she lifted them out one by one. The first was a shepherdess with a sheepdog at her feet, the second a boy playing a flute, the third a kitten and the fourth a china flower basket.

"I began collecting those more than fifty years ago," Eileen sighed, "when the old queen was on the throne. There are lots more of them; I expect you've seen them in our sitting room. I thought you might like to start with four. In case they're not to your taste, that is." Shirley gave Eileen a beaming smile and a hug that left her in no doubt that her present had been well received.

Pa's present was unexpected in more ways than one. He waited until supper time to announce it. "Shirl," he said, raising his glass of beer to her, "twenty is not as significant as twenty-one – that's for next year – but I want to wish you a very happy birthday, and I want to thank you for all your help with the business by giving you this surprise." Cousin Archie cheered. "Here," said Pa, patting his trouser pocket, "I have something for you." He was enjoying the sight of the expectant faces round the table, for it gave him an unprecedented sensation of power. "Let me get them out," he said, prolonging the suspense. He pulled out an envelope and handed it to Shirley. "Here you are, Shirl: you can open it and see what's inside!" She took the envelope gingerly, as if there were something very delicate inside that might break.

"What can it be, Pa?" she asked. "Have you bought tickets for the ballet?"

"No, open the envelope and you'll see," he replied, savouring the moment. She drew out a birthday card with six tickets inside it, and scrutinized them.

"Oh, wonderful!" she exclaimed. "Tickets for *Gone with the Wind*! You knew I wanted to see that, didn't you?" Flinging her arms round her father's neck, she kissed him on the cheek. "But all these tickets, who are they for?" she asked a moment later in puzzlement.

"Well, I thought we would invite Archie and Eileen," Pa replied.

"Suits me nicely, thank you, Reggie," Archie said, jumping at the invitation, while Eileen was more cautious:

"I haven't been to the pictures in years," she said, "but it would be nice to have an evening out. Thank you very much, Reggie."

"Who are the other two tickets for, Pa?" Shirley demanded.

"Um, I thought you might like to invite your friend Cynthia," he said, shifting from foot to foot.

"And the other one, who's that for?" she persisted, hoping against hope that perhaps Pa had received news that Ted would be coming home. Pa's change of expression did not suggest that he was the bearer of such good tidings, quite the contrary.

"Well, that's a bit awkward. I hope you won't mind," he began apprehensively and then blurted out, "but I had to ask Bert because he got the tickets for me through his friend the projectionist."

Shirley was aghast. She jumped to her feet, her face reddening in anger. "How could you, Pa? For my birthday treat! And you know how I hate the sight of him! Don't let him sit next to me!" she shouted, and then ran out of the room in tears. Eileen followed her into the kitchen. She put her arm round the weeping girl.

"Shirley, Shirley, don't cry," she said gently. "If your father has made a silly mistake, I know he's sorry for it. He meant well. Archie and I will make sure you don't have to sit next to this Bert person you dislike so much." Shirley rushed into her room, where she fell onto her bed, sobbing at her father's extraordinary insensitivity.

Before the visit to the cinema, there were however other more major concerns that overshadowed the treat in store. The French army was being pushed back into France, hotly pursued by the Germans who had made threatening incursions into French territory; the Russians had succeeded in occupying Finland, and Norway and Denmark had been invaded by Hitler's forces. Reggie was in no doubt that the conflict, which was breaking out on all fronts, was coming closer, and the Phoney War was now fast becoming a real one, and an ugly one at that. His main concern, of course, was for his son. "Shirl, please would you try phoning Louise to ask how Ted is?" he asked plaintively.

Shirley did so, but it was hard to hear what Louise was saying because of the hubbub from the bar in the *estaminet*. All that she could grasp was, "*Ma Chérie*, you must not worry! He's fine. There's no war here, but I am very busy. *Au revoir!*" Louise then quickly put the phone down.

"Hm, I don't believe that. They're living in cloud-cuckoo-land" was Pa's reaction. Shirley was worried by Louise's abruptness, which was not like her at all.

The showing of *Gone with the Wind* was timed to begin early, at six o'clock one evening in late April, because of the inordinate length of the film. Nonetheless, at a quarter to six, the queue outside the cinema was still a hundred yards long. Only then did Shirley begin to understand why her father had been forced to resort to methods he regarded as underhand to acquire tickets. Consequently, she forgave him his perceived insensitivity by inviting Bert to join the party. In the event, Bert, with an unlikely display of chivalry designed no doubt to impress Shirley, gave up his seat to a hopeful elderly lady in the queue, who paid Reggie for the ticket, and, to Shirley's relief, he went off to sit in the projectionist's box. Shirley allowed herself to bestow a faint smile and a regal nod of the head in his vague direction.

As a result, there was no embarrassment about the seating and, comfortably wedged in between Cynthia and Eileen, she was able to relax and enjoy nearly four hours of thwarted passion and tragedy against the background of the American Civil War. It was certainly a beautiful, sumptuous film, and the acting was superb, but she came away from the cinema shocked at the portrayal of warfare. She had always imagined that wars happened on battlefields somewhere else, but in this film towns and homes were destroyed and the inhabitants themselves either fled or remained behind to be killed. She told herself that was in the old days when war was conducted on horseback, so perhaps it would be different now.

Only a couple of days after the film, a letter addressed in Maman's handwriting to both Reggie and Shirley arrived. It initially raised Pa's hopes that his wife might be back in the country. That soon proved not to be the case: mysteriously the letter had not come either by post or in the diplomatic bag and had apparently been delivered by hand during the night, presumably by a friend or at least someone whom Jacqueline could trust. It was little more than a short note enclosing a wad of cards and tickets. "My dear Reggie and Shirley," it read. "It seems that the intelligence reports in January were correct. The Nazis are going to invade Holland and Belgium and then France very soon. Please bring Ted home from France! His life will be in danger. I enclose passes that will enable Shirley to take a ferry from Dover to Calais and home again with Ted. Please do this as soon as you can. You must wear drab, unremarkable clothes, Shirley, and definitely not nylon stockings, as you must pass unnoticed."

Silence fell. It was broken after a long pause by Reggie, who remarked with a deep sigh, "I certainly don't want you to go to France, Shirl, but you are the only person who can persuade your obstinate brother to leave the farm. If you're prepared to go, I can take over your air-raid patrol and I'll let your ballet lady know that you have had to go away."

46

On a fine, bright day in May 1940, Shirley crossed the Channel alone, despite her father's repeated misgivings. In spite of his assurances about taking over her patrol duties, he was keen to accompany her to France, fearful of what she might encounter both on the journey and while she was there. "No, Pa, you're far too English. Anyone would know that you are not French as soon as you open your mouth, whereas, if I hide my hair under a beret, I can pass for French." It was true. Pa was reasonably fluent in French, but his accent was appalling; everywhere he went, he was recognized as English, even when he said only "*Merci*". She won the argument and promised that she would return as soon as she could and that she would definitely bring Ted with her. He insisted on taking her to Dover in the Lanchester, but of course was not allowed to drive into the militarized port, which was a relief to his daughter, who was dreading the fond and inevitably tearful farewells. Having hugged him briefly, she ran off, pausing only once to wave back at him as he stood, a forlorn figure, by the parked car. He shouted words of warning after her in a final attempt to avoid breaking the fine thread of contact before she disappeared from view.

"Remember to be very careful: there are bound to be spies about," he called. The travel pass and tickets sent by her mother had proved valid and so effective that, with scarcely any delay, she found herself being ushered aboard a troop carrier laden with soldiers on their way to war.

Whereas under normal circumstances she might well have smiled at the lads and taken it upon herself to entertain them with idle chatter, she kept herself to herself, sitting out on deck, enjoying the spring sunshine and eating her sandwiches, but feeling unaccountably lonely. Eileen had quickly fitted her out in an old two-piece that smelt of mothballs and needed shortening; her headgear, a beret, she found discarded at the bottom of Maman's wardrobe. Dressed as she was in brown from head to foot, her modest appearance did not attract any attention, which was so unusual that she was tempted to take off the beret, but her father's warning as they parted company rang in her ears.

On board, as the cliffs of Dover receded to the west, some of the men sat thoughtfully watching the calm green ripples on an otherwise glassy sea. For many of them it was probably the first time that they had left home, certainly the first time they had gone abroad. Others were noisier, but their laughter and bravado sounded forced: by speaking loudly and joking coarsely they sought to create a pretence that this extraordinary situation was no more than an everyday occurrence. She had no more idea than they what to expect on the other side, but so far she had encountered no problems. In the same packet as the travel passes, there had been French identity papers both for her and for Ted. "Do not show your British passports anywhere in France," Maman had written in her letter. "Keep them hidden and only produce your French identity papers if asked for them."

In mid-Channel, she leant over the rail and dropped a handful of the remaining English coins in her purse into the sea as instructed by her father. "Even one or two English coins will give you away if they come to light," he had warned her.

When the ferry docked in Calais at the Gare Maritime, the troops, no longer joking but soberly apprehensive, disembarked in orderly file, while Shirley, with her French identity papers, was waved through with a cheerful "*Bonjour, madame!*" from the immigration officer. She followed the soldiers into the station, but there she parted company with them. They boarded the waiting trains, which were destined for Belgium, while she crossed the line to where the Paris express was on the point of departure.

"You'll have to run, Mademoiselle," the guard warned her as he raised his whistle to his mouth.

The agility of this frumpish, dowdy passenger must have surprised him, for she climbed aboard in no time after sprinting down the platform. The Paris-bound train was full of men in suits and impressive uniforms, a far cry from those of the ordinary foot soldiers on the boat. She supposed that these august figures must be diplomats, generals and brigadiers and made her way along the train to the restaurant car ahead of them to find an empty table where she could sit alone and watch the green fields as they sped past the window. *La France!* How happy she was to be again in the country she loved so much! To reactivate the French side of her character, she allowed herself to indulge in a typically delicious example of French cuisine, painstakingly prepared and elegantly served.

As the train pulled into the station at Arras, where she was to change trains, she was disconcerted to see small groups of tall, fair-skinned men waiting silently on the platform; they appeared to be neither French nor British. She speculated that they might be spies, but then reasoned that spies would not make themselves so conspicuous. In the booking hall she found a phone booth from which she tried to call Louise, but there was no reply from the *estaminet*, which was worrying, because she had hoped that Charlot might come down to the station to pick her up or, if he couldn't do that, maybe a message could be taken to Ted, who of course had no idea that she was coming, for it had all happened so quickly. After half an hour's wait she caught the slow local train that ran westwards along the river to the coast. Three-quarters of an hour later it stopped at Séringy, the station down in the valley nearest to Trémaincourt.

The sun was low in the sky when she stepped off the train into the darkened, deserted village, which already seemed to have shut down for the night. Although she was weary after the long journey from London, she felt in need of exercise so set off on foot up the long hill out of the valley, but soon regretted that there been no telephone booth on that rural station platform from which to ring Louise. It took her a half an hour to climb the hill and another half-hour to reach Trémaincourt. From there to Pépé's farm there remained a good kilometre. Her left leg was dragging behind her and she was thirsty and tired, so instead of turning right at the crossroads, she turned left on impulse and headed down the short slope to the *estaminet* in the middle of the village, hoping to see Louise and take some refreshment before the final stretch of her journey.

The *estaminet* was still open. In fact, in contrast to the deathly silence everywhere else, the sounds from inside were of a party in full swing. Raucous voices tore into the night air, laughing and singing loudly. She pushed the door open and went in to the brightly lit interior. At one end of the bar, where Charlot was serving beer, there stood four or five men, looking not unlike those she had seen at the station in Arras. The noise had evidently originated with them, as there were scarcely any other customers present, and those regulars who were there sat quietly at corner tables, saying little, just watching the goings-on at the bar. The tall, blond men glanced in her direction as the door opened, but then turned swiftly back to their drinks, since clearly the newcomer was of no interest to them. Indeed, so successful was Shirley's disguise of brown woollen skirt and jacket, with the brown beret hiding her blond curls, that even Louise did not recognize her. It was only when she spoke that Louise looked up at her. "*Bonsoir, Louise,*" Shirley said quietly.

"*Mon Dieu!*" Louise exclaimed, then lowered her voice. "What are you doing here, *ma petite*? Careful! Those are Germans at the end of the bar over there; they insist on having all the lights on despite the blackout."

Exhausted and now scared as well, Shirley spoke in a despondent whisper that was not much more than a sigh. "I've walked all the way up from the station and I was hoping that Charlot might be able to take me the rest of the way to the farm."

"Of course, but first you must have a drink," Louise said, pouring water onto a spoonful of a red syrup at the bottom of a glass and handing it to her. The strawberry drink quenched her thirst, although she did not like it much: it was too sweet and sugary. Louise did not call out to Charlot, but went to the end of the bar where he was washing glasses. He looked up in Shirley's direction when his mother prodded him, and gave a wry smile at the sight of her drab outfit. Wiping his hands he came to greet her discreetly. "I must say, your disguise is unbelievable! You'll need it here," Louise remarked *sotto voce*, and, head down, went back to washing glasses. Meanwhile, grinning to himself, Charlot went off to fetch his van. With a slight nod of the head, Louise gestured in the direction of the revellers and murmured, "You must keep away from here. It's too dangerous for you and for your brother."

When she had finished the glasses, Louise wiped her hands and followed Shirley outside to wait for Charlot's van. "*Ma petite*, you must take care," she said. "I've told your brother not to come down here because those noisy brutes in the bar are Germans – Nazis no doubt – believe it or not, and they are living in the *château*. Poor old Claude was packed off to an asylum when they arrived last autumn after the outbreak of war: they looked like holidaymakers, and after a couple of weeks they went away again. Here they are again. I don't know why they were let in, though apparently it is perfectly legal for Germans to come into the country as individuals. I don't like having to serve them – they used to come in every evening when they were here before, and drink the place dry. My regulars don't like them either, but what can we do?"

Just then, as Charlot drew up, his mother gave a wan smile. "Charlot here is a wonderful spy," she said. "They all think he's stupid so they don't take any notice of him, but he keeps us all informed of what's going on. We don't know whether they broke into the *château* or whether they were invited to come here. I strongly suspect they are friends of Jean-Luc's, but we haven't seen any of the de la Croix family since they left last year. Anyhow, you and your brother must keep well out of their way. Have you come to take him back to England?" Horrified by Louise's account, Shirley nodded. "I was hoping you would come for him," Louise said in an undertone. "Who knows what will happen next? Today on the news we heard that they are already advancing through Belgium and Holland. Goodness knows what that means for us."

With dimmed headlamps, Charlot drove slowly past the *château*, where lights shone from every window, shedding bright shafts out over the lawns, nearly reaching the unremarkable old shed in the grounds where Claude used to live. Charlot vigorously jabbed the forefinger of his left hand towards the shed; then he put it to his temple and pulled into a passing place for tractors and horses and carts by the wood down in the dip, a hundred metres or so beyond the *château*. There he stopped the engine. Getting out of the van and taking care not to make a noise, he beckoned Shirley to join him by the petrol cap. He pointed to it, then waved in the direction of the *château* and then again pointed at his petrol cap.

At first she was mystified, but when she recalled how he had insistently indicated the old shed, she began to grasp his meaning. In the light of the waning moon he persevered with his attempts to communicate by opening the back of the van and shining a torch on two petrol cans. Again he put his finger to his temple, presumably indicating that he had discovered something. Her mouth fell open in amazement: he was telling her that he had found petrol cans in that shed and had helped himself to a supply of them! "Charlot, how brave you are!" she muttered. He counted out ten on his fingers. She smiled broadly at him. "You are amazing, Charlot," she said, and he bathed in the warmth of her admiration.

Shirley's heart sank on finding the gates to the farmyard closed after her long and wearying journey. Undaunted, Charlot turned the car to face the house and flashed the headlamps. At the same time he gave four sharp taps on the horn followed by a piercing whistle, which he made by putting the first two fingers of each hand into his mouth. A dim light went on in the yard and, a couple of minutes later, Céline, carrying a torch, came nervously round the corner of the building and up to the gate. "Who is that?" she called out cautiously.

"Don't worry, Céline, it's me with Charlot!" Shirley cried.

"*Oh, ma Chérie*," Céline stammered, putting her hand to her heart, "how you made me jump! Come in, come in! I thought I heard Charlot's whistle and the taps on his horn, but at this time of night you just don't know what to expect!"

She opened the gates for Charlot to drive into the yard. "Where's Pépé?" Shirley asked, surprised not to see her grandfather.

"Oh, he is so tired after a day's work these days, he goes to bed early," Céline replied.

"And Édouard. Where is he?" Shirley said, even more surprised that her brother was nowhere to be seen.

"Ah, I'll call him in a minute," Céline answered cagily. Charlot did not drive off until after he had unloaded not only his passenger and her small travel bag, but also a can from the back of his van. "You are such a treasure, Charlot," Céline said. "How much do I owe you?" He wrote the amount on a scrap of paper and handed it to her, and while she went to fetch the money Shirley gave him a hug. In the light from the kitchen she could see him blushing from ear to ear and was glad to have rewarded his kindness and loyalty.

"*Ma Chérie!* You must have something to eat!" Céline exclaimed when she came back indoors after closing the gates and all the shutters. "You must be so tired!" Shirley yawned, kissed her and summoned a feeble smile. It was so like Céline to welcome a visitor with the offer of food. She probably thought that Shirley had not eaten properly since she left France last September. "Look," she said, "there is still some supper left in the big pot on the stove. Let me give you a bowl of that and you can be eating it while I go to fetch Édouard."

"Where is he?" Shirley asked. "Can I come too?"

"*Non, non, ma Chérie*, he is in hiding. When we heard Charlot's van, Édouard ran off to his hideout, because we thought it might be the Germans invading us. You know they've invaded Holland and Belgium?" Céline continued. "Your grandfather and I have decided that no one else should know where the hideout is."

"I understand," Shirley said and sat down to eat her dinner. She was too tired to indulge in games of hide-and-seek; so as long as Ted was safe, she was content to let Céline go to fetch him. She heard her steps on the rickety wooden ladder that led up into the loft.

Some ten minutes later, Céline reappeared followed by Ted, who looked distinctly bleary-eyed. "Here he is. He was asleep!" Céline exclaimed.

"Well, it's so dark up there, and when I lay down on those cushions you had put down for me, I was so comfortable I just dozed off," he said, rubbing his eyes and peering through the haze of sleep at the person sitting at the kitchen table. "Shirl! Is it you?" he cried in astonishment. She stood up and they ran into each other's arms. "What are you doing here?" he asked. "I never thought that it would be you when Céline said there was a visitor for me!" Shirley told him why she had come. She showed him the letter from their mother and brought out the travel passes and identity documents for him to see. "Identity papers! Just what I need!" Ted exclaimed in delight. "So now, if anyone asks for them, I have them. And look, Maman has given me her family name Pruvost, which of course is Pépé's name, so there will be no question that I belong here!"

The exchange was not going at all as Shirley had intended. She had expected that Ted would be delighted to have the passes and the papers so that he could travel back home to England, but that was by no means his interpretation of her visit. In his excitement at seeing her, perhaps he didn't hear that she had said that she had come to take him home, or perhaps he deliberately misinterpreted it. "No, Ted, listen: I've brought you those papers so that you and I can get home to England as soon as possible," she protested, tired, confused and hardly knowing what she was saying, except that her innate determination forced its way to the surface and told her that she was going to have to fight to make her brother see sense.

Already he was saying, "But I don't need to now. I can prove that I'm French; I can throw my British passport away and no one will ever know. I can stay here and fight!" Céline had been watching the siblings and, although she did not understand a word of what was passing between them, realized that tempers were rising.

"*Mes enfants*," she said, intervening, "it's too late for this discussion tonight. We will talk about it in the morning."

It was late the following morning when Shirley woke. Her legs ached, her feet were sore, her head throbbed and she felt dizzy. Her face was also burning. Her first reaction, which was to wonder in a panic whether the infantile paralysis could have returned, was a worrying one, but since her right leg felt as bad as the left and the left leg was not numb, she decided that she was safe in that respect. She struggled to clamber out of bed to pull her clothes on, but had to fall back onto the mattress and close her eyes again. She dozed intermittently for half an hour or so, before remembering with a shock that she was in France, not in London, and she had a very special mission to fulfil. With a shudder, she reached out for her watch and saw with relief that it was only eight o'clock. However, her relief was short-lived when she reminded herself that in France it was really nine o'clock. She never remembered whether she had to put her watch forward or backward when crossing the Channel, and yesterday, to her shame, she had forgotten even that minor precaution. She would be a useless spy. She jumped out of bed in haste, fearing that Ted might already have gone down to the recruiting office in Saint-Pierre and signed up to join the French forces fighting losing battles in the east and in the north.

"*Ma Chérie*, you look terrible!" was Céline's greeting when she stumbled into the kitchen. "Back to bed with you at once!" she commanded. Shirley had no choice but to do as she was told. She asked Céline to send Ted in to talk to her, but whether he came or not she had no idea, because she slept for the rest of the day. Much later, she woke when Céline peeped round the door. "Chérie, you have had a bad day!" she said. "I have brought you some chicken soup. You must eat it all: it will help you recover. You have been very feverish. I did not let Ted come near you."

"What's the time?" Shirley asked, sitting up. Although her head swam, she was feeling better than she had that morning."

"It is nearly seven o'clock. I am cooking dinner. Will you have some?"

"Oh, no!" Shirley cried out, not in reference to Céline's offer of dinner, but because a whole day had gone by. She ate her soup and then eased herself out of bed. She had to talk to Ted, but Céline would not let her leave her bedroom.

"You don't want Ted to catch your germs, do you?" she said. She was adamant: "No, Chérie, you must stay there until you are better; then I am sure you will be well enough to leave your room and talk to Ted. What difference will one day make?" Shirley could have wept. One day might make the difference between safety and capture, between crossing the Channel back to England or being arrested here in France. She resolved to get up very early the next morning and set out with Ted to the coast straight away. But the next morning she was covered in red, itchy, blistery spots.

"Ah, Chérie!" Céline exclaimed. "You have the chickenpox! You must stay in bed and I will make you a poultice to relieve he itching!" With a splitting headache Shirley sank back onto the pillows. How long would this wretched illness at the worst of times take? she asked herself in despair.

When finally the doctor, called in by Céline, pronounced her fit to travel after a frustratingly longer stay than she had intended, and she felt strong enough to leave, the foreseeable problem was that Ted could not be persuaded to pack up and go. Firstly he said he could not drop everything and leave the farm, because Pépé was not as strong as he used to be, and secondly he was not persuaded that there was any pressing need for him to leave anyhow. Shirley grew more and more exasperated. She wished that she had listened more closely to her father's daily reports of Nazi advances and atrocities, for then she would have the necessary ammunition to hand. As it was, she had to rely on the wireless reports to convince Ted that the situation was extremely serious, and she insisted that the longer they stayed in France, the greater the danger they would face. She repeated Louise's words when she had told her to be very careful and avoid the *estaminet*. "If that's what Louise thinks, and she listens to the wireless all the time, then it must be dangerous. If the Boche invade France and find us here, what do you think they'll do? Some of them are here already – you must know that, at least." Ted shrugged his shoulders. "Well, I'll tell you," she went on. "Either they'll shoot us outright when they discover that we're English, or they'll ship us off to labour camps or something of the sort in Germany. And if we survive that it will be a miracle."

In desperation she brought Pépé into the argument after lunch, not expecting much help from that quarter, but his clear thinking surprised her. He drew on his pipe while considering what to say. "I don't know what's going to happen," he began slowly, "but I do know that our forces have been having a hard time on the front line for months now, and that the Germans are breaking through. Well, more than that, they have advanced into Belgium and Holland, so it will be only a matter of time before they arrive here in their tanks. You could say that we are surrounded already." He paused. "I gather they are here already, some of them, living down in the *château* and in some of the houses they've bought up in the towns. They've been coming here in twos and threes since last year when the war broke out in fact. It's so easy to spot them. So don't worry about me and the farm, Édouard. There will be jobbing workers needing the money, so we will manage. I think you should go back to England as fast as you can." He puffed on his pipe, having given his opinion, and fell asleep in his armchair.

"You see, Ted? Even Pépé thinks you ought to leave," Shirley whispered.

Ted drew her out of the kitchen into the passage which housed the piano and his bed. "You don't understand, Shirl," he said. "Hélène and I are planning to meet quite soon. I'm going to catch a train down to Switzerland for a day or two, possibly three, and stay with a friend of hers; I think she's a waitress in a café. Anyhow, this friend has been posting Hélène's letters to me and at last we're going to see each other! Just imagine, for the first time in twenty months!" In other circumstances Shirley would have been touched and saddened, but not in the present situation. However, before she could respond as sharply as she intended, the sound of explosions ricocheted off the house.

They ran to the door and out to the gate from where they scanned the eastern horizon. In the distance, plumes of smoke were rising, darkening the clear blue sky, while from the same direction there came the menacing drone of aircraft engines. Shapes like small crosses, black against the blue, were circling and diving, weaving in and out of the clouds of smoke. They emitted tiny black dots that dropped down to the ground and burst in more explosions, giving off more clouds of dense smoke. Before long the sky in the east had darkened as the smoke blotted out the enemy aircraft, deadening the sound of the planes and the explosions. "Oh, goodness, that's the airfield they've bombed!" Ted exclaimed in horror.

"Yes, that's just a taste of what's to come, and it won't be long now!" Shirley cried. "Come on, Ted, we must collect up our things and be on our way," she urged him. "Don't worry about Hélène. You know she will be safe in Switzerland – it's a neutral country – and she'll be relieved to know that you're safe in England. You'll be able to write to her from there."

47

Shirley ran back indoors. "Céline, Pépé!" she shouted. "Come quickly! We must leave now!" Céline was not in the kitchen but came running from the meadow as fast as her plump legs would carry her.

"Chérie, what is happening?" she cried in alarm.

"Didn't you hear the bangs and see the smoke?" Shirley asked. By now Pépé had roused himself from his afternoon nap and had come to see what the fuss was about.

"What's going on?" he asked as the four of them congregated in the yard.

"Come and see," Ted urged him, taking his arm and pulling him towards the gate. "Look over there!" The expressions on the faces of the old people registered terror and despair, indicating such sights were not new to them in the full knowledge of what they implied.

"It's coming our way again," Pépé remarked stoically. "The Boche are on the march and their tanks have broken through again; there's nothing we can do to stop them."

He turned to Shirley and Ted. "And," he announced sternly, "it's time you two were leaving, but not until dark. It's too dangerous to leave by daylight if they are already dropping bombs over there." He gestured to the east and soberly they walked back into the house.

Shirley disappeared into her room to pack her belongings, while Ted went to milk the cows and say his goodbyes to them. "Who knows when I shall be doing this again," he murmured softly, trying to resign himself to a sudden departure that night.

Céline served a delicious dinner, saying as she did so, "You young things need to have plenty of good food inside you before you set off." Each absorbed in his or her own thoughts, no one spoke while they ate, until Pépé declared that he had been thinking, in itself a remarkable occurrence.

"The question is: where do you think you are going to?" he asked, looking round the table at the astonished faces of his grandchildren.

"We're going to England, of course, Pépé!" Shirley and Ted chorused in amazement that their grandfather could have posed such an obvious question. However, Céline had a better understanding of what he meant.

"No, no, children, your grandfather knows that you are returning to England, but what he is asking is this: which port are you going to and how are you going to get there?" The smile disappeared from the faces of the younger generation. After a moment's consideration, Shirley spoke up for herself and her brother.

"I suppose, if you would drive us in the pony and trap, Pépé, we'll go down to Séringy or Saint-Pierre to catch a train to Arras, and from there to Calais." She waited expectantly for her grandfather's reply.

Eventually he shook his head. "You would be lucky to find a train late at night. In any case, hasn't it occurred to you that they'll be bombing the railway lines at the same time as the airfields? I know what they're doing: they're trying to put us out of action before they send the troops in. Who knows, they might have bombed the ports already. These Boche, they are always one step ahead of us."

Silence fell. Their grandfather's pessimistic assessment had given his grandchildren pause for serious thought. Neither of them had expected anything so drastic so quickly, nor had they anticipated such frightening consequences. "So, what do you think we should do?" Ted enquired, sounding him out, now helpless in the face of a crisis he had expected to avoid, so confident had he been that he would never have to return to England.

"If you want my opinion," Pépé began, "I think you should go by car – there is enough petrol in your car, isn't there, Édouard?" Ted nodded and Pépé went on, probably addressing a rapt audience for the first time in his life. "Go by the valley road," he said, "the hill road may be more direct, but it is too exposed. Cross the river down in Freslan-la-Tour, and take the road up to the forest. Then take the dirt tracks through the forest until you come to a sign to Namiers. From there you will have to follow the main road but, with any luck, you will be well ahead of any invaders, and it will be very dark by then."

Shirley butted in: "Pépé, you don't understand, the passes Maman sent us are for Calais not Boulogne!"

"*Non, ma petite*, I am not sending you to Boulogne," Pépé explained patiently. "I am sending you to my brother-in-law François at Beauport. You remember him, don't you, Édouard?"

"Oh, yes, of course I do," Ted replied and, turning to his sister, he said apologetically, "I forgot to tell you, Shirl: I drove Pépé and Céline over to Beauport to visit Aunt Suzanne, his sister, and her husband François last October. We've visited them in the summer holidays. You remember them, don't you? He's a fisherman."

"Ah, yes," said Shirley uncertainly, "Aunt Suzanne never seems at all pleased to see us. She's worse than Madame de la Croix."

"That's not important; François will take you across the Channel," Pépé said without looking at his grandchildren, but picking up his pipe and tapping it on the side of his plate before restoring it to its rightful place in his mouth.

Céline stood up to clear the plates and then started preparing and wrapping baguettes, which at any other time could have been ample fare for a picnic in the fields, but were in fact the rations for the pair for the length of the journey ahead. "It's nearly dark," she commented nervously, glancing out of the window into the yard. "It's time you two were going. By the way, Édouard, take that can of petrol with you that Charlot brought, and give it to François, because he will need it if he's going to take you across the Channel and return to France the same night. Charlot has already brought us several cans, so your grandfather will still have plenty. And I suppose if he runs out we shall just have to use the old horses again."

Céline's musings were interrupted by a sharp whistle from somewhere outside. "Ah! That must be Charlot! I recognize his calling signal; I knew he would come!" she exclaimed, and hurried off to open the gate. Charlot drove his van into the yard and fairly jumped out of it. Wide-eyed, he gesticulated wildly, clutching their arms, and then pulled out his notebook and pencil. He scribbled his message on a blank page. Open-mouthed they watched as his pencil continued to scrawl across the white sheet. He looked up in the hope that his audience would be able to read his scarcely intelligible hieroglyphs. Shirley was quick off the mark. "I know what he's telling us!" she declared. "He says, 'Germans bombing Arras!' and wait, he also says" – here she paused to study Charlot's scrawl – "Oh! He says, '*Château* preparing for action. Leave at once!' That's terrible! Oh and look! He's drawn a picture of a tank!" Although the shock took her breath away, she kept her head. Charlot nodded vigorously and pointed to his van. "You are so kind," she said, putting her arms round him in a bear hug, "but it's all right. Don't worry. We are going in Édouard's car and are just about to leave. He ran out to his van and fetched a can of petrol that he forced into Ted's hands, despite his protestations that they already had plenty. Charlot would not take no for an answer. He beckoned to them to follow and climbed into his van.

Ted was already in his driving seat when, at the last minute, Shirley exclaimed, "Hold on, we ought to cover the headlamps like we have to do at home!" She sent Ted indoors for some cardboard and scissors. Céline went with him, saying, "There's something I've forgotten."

Then Pépé, who had been hovering in the gloaming, said, "Well, *ma petite*, it's time I was going to bed, but there is just one more thing. He put his arms round his granddaughter, then his grandson and hugged each of them as he never had before. "And," he added awkwardly, "if you write to your mother, send her my love." Shirley gently put her hand in his and squeezed it.

Céline came out of the kitchen carrying a large cardboard box. "Here are some provisions for Suzanne and François," she said, handing the box to Shirley. "There's half a ham, some butter and some eggs." Ted by now had pierced holes in the cardboard and cut it to stick on the headlamps of both the car and the van. Although Charlot was becoming more and more agitated at the delay, Ted was impressed by this precaution, which had not yet universally been adopted in France. The leave-taking was swift and deliberately unemotional on all sides; it was as if Ted and Shirley, following Charlot, were simply going out for the evening and would be returning soon.

Ted was perplexed when the latter turned left out of the gate instead of right. "But he's taking us in the wrong direction!" Ted exclaimed.

"No, wait and see. Follow him: he knows where he's going," Shirley said in the firm belief that she could read Charlot's intentions. "I think he's avoiding the main road and the *château*; he might be taking us a long way round, but trust him: he knows what he's doing." Ted persevered, driving very slowly in the murky light from the headlamps along the rough track that led out into the fields, the scene in happier times of so many glorious harvest days. The memory of them brought a lump to Shirley's throat, while Ted could be heard to sniff as if clearing his nose, but equally he was also probably fighting back the tears and remarked plaintively:

"I wonder if we shall ever have those wonderful harvest suppers again." Shirley sensed that he was really wondering whether he would ever meet Hélène again and would have tried to comfort him, but decided that this was not the moment for indulging in sentimental memories.

The car windows were open, admitting the warmth of the evening, which brought out the rich smell of the earth in the field where Ted had, that very day, been applying a top dressing to the soil, before planting cabbages. They also let in an unfamiliar hubbub coming from the main road, the hill road. "What's that noise over there?" Shirley asked.

Ted shrugged, keeping his eyes on the twists and turns in the track. "No idea," he said.

"It's so odd," Shirley remarked. "It sounds as if a lot of people are tramping along the road, pushing prams and carts. It doesn't sound like lorries, though I can hear cars hooting. What's going on, I wonder?"

With the village and the *château* safely behind them, Charlot, who now drove faster, led the way down to Séringy and along the valley road in the direction of Freslan-la-Tour, but he turned off before reaching the edge of the town. "It's a shame," Shirley grumbled quietly as she looked out of the window attempting to identify landmarks on Charlot's route, but it was too dark to see anything. "I haven't even had time to go down to the market in Freslan. Catching that chill was such a nuisance. I suppose, though, it wouldn't have been a good idea to go out, even in these awful clothes – with all those Germans wandering about, I mean. I think they must have been spies, don't you?" She took off the brown beret and shook out her curls. "There, that's better," she said. Ted was concentrating too hard on following Charlot to be able to take much notice of her chatter. He crossed the river, headed up the hill on the other side and took a turning into the forest. Tall trees, but nothing worse, loomed out of the darkness as he veered onto another bumpy track, along which the van and the car bounced for kilometre after kilometre.

"Hmm, this is not doing my suspension much good," Ted groaned. Shirley refrained from saying what was on her mind, which was that maybe that would not matter, because in all likelihood Ted would never see his car again if, as she suspected, the Nazis commandeered it after its present occupants had disappeared across the water.

All she did say was: "Where will you leave your car when we reach Beauport?"

"I expect I'll be able to leave it at Aunt Suzanne's, and then I can come back to collect it after the war," he replied, ever hopeful. Shirley raised a mental eyebrow and bit her tongue.

Charlot stopped his van at a turning onto a narrow road when they emerged from the forest. The same strange hubbub was still audible, though fainter, from the main road far across the river. "But what *is* that noise over there?" Shirley asked as they stood huddled in a small group. In the dim light from the headlamps of the two vehicles, Charlot ran on the spot, bent double as if he were struggling to carry a heavy load and push a heavy cart. Shirley watched him. "He's telling us that that sound comes from people trying to escape and pushing carts along the road. Poor things! I wonder where they come from?" she said, interpreting the actions for her brother. Charlot then did an extraordinary thing. He rolled up his sleeve to indicate his watch and pointed to the number five on the face; then he ran round in circles, his arms outstretched, imitating an aeroplane and making shooting movements with his fingers towards the ground. "Oh, no! He's saying that the Boche come over with their planes in the early morning and they shoot at the people fleeing!" Shirley cried. Charlot nodded and then put his fingers behind his ear, clearly listening for tanks. He made the shape of a tank with his outstretched arms, put his head in his hands in a show of despair and then waved frenetically at the open landscape ahead of them, urging them to drive on as fast as possible to arrive at the coast before dawn. He took two more cans of petrol out of his boot and gave them to Ted, before kissing them both and swiftly getting back into his car. In no time he had disappeared into the depths of the forest.

The siblings set off, less sure of their tortuous route without Charlot's guidance, and unable to see the way ahead at all clearly; they took several wrong turnings before emerging onto one of the roads to the coast, still in the valley. Although it was the dead of night, the narrow road was blocked on one side by a long queue of slow-moving cars, buses, bicycles, lorries and motorbikes, all of which were crammed with passengers and driving with just their sidelights on. Many of the cars and buses had luggage strapped to the roof, the lorries were piled high with furniture, mattresses and all sorts of personal belongings, and the motorbikes pulled sidecars with hastily attached carts and wagons that slewed dangerously out of control across the road. "Oh my goodness, what do we do now?" Ted said, shaking his head in bewilderment.

"Isn't there any other way?" Shirley asked, equally nonplussed by this unforeseen obstacle to their best-laid plans and terrified of being mown down at first light by a tank.

"No, I don't think there is," Ted replied, the tension evident in his voice, as he extracted his feeble torch from his pocket and shone it on a map. "Without Charlot I wouldn't have a clue how to negotiate the farm tracks and side roads. We shall have to join the queue – if, that is, they will let us in."

After several minutes' wait, he boldly edged out of the turning onto the road in front of a heavily laden lorry that was advancing at walking pace. "Glad we're in front of that one!" he announced with satisfaction, but when, shortly afterwards, the column came to a complete standstill, his relief was short-lived. The drivers showed considerable restraint in honking their horns, but there was a chorus of exasperated shouts when they got out of their cars to see what was happening ahead. Ted went to join a huddle of men assembling by the roadside. He returned to his car some minutes later. "We might as well have some of Céline's coffee in that flask," he stammered, betraying the nerves that he was trying so hard to suppress. "It seems we might be here for some time. They say a lorry has broken down with an overheated engine several kilometres down the road, and we shall have to wait for it to cool down." Shirley poured the coffee in the light of Ted's torch and handed him a cup.

In between taking sips of his drink, he told her the upshot of the news he had heard from the other travellers, which confirmed Charlot's graphic depiction. "Most of these people on the road have come from Arras. The Germans are bombing the city and, what's more, in the daytime their Junkers and Stukas are firing indiscriminately on the people trying to escape," he said, grim-faced. "They say it's terrible. Mothers pushing babies in prams, old people in wheelbarrows, fathers carrying children, the Stukas are shooting them all as they struggle along the roads out of the city." His voice trembling with emotion, he continued, "The wounded and dead are lying in the roadside ditches with nobody to help them. The big problem is that no one seems to know where the Germans are coming from. Some say that they are coming in from the north through Belgium and the Ardennes, others say they're coming from the south-east, where they've broken through the lines, so nobody knows which direction is the safest to go. As for the tanks, they are advancing from everywhere," he took another sip of his coffee. "These people here are lucky: they have transport and managed to flee by night when the Stukas don't seem to be flying. But you never know, they say. Would you believe it, they started bombing Arras at four o'clock the other morning! And the longer we have to wait here the more dangerous it is, because the tanks start moving at daybreak and they'll soon catch us up."

Shirley listened thoughtfully. "Dreadful," she sighed, "but I don't want to be a sitting target for a Stuka or fodder for a tank, so let's be on the move."

"Shirl! What are you talking about? Have you gone mad?" Ted exploded, for now he was tired as well as tense, and at the end of his tether.

"No, not at all," she answered quite calmly, "but if you look, you will see that this is almost as good as a two-lane road, not for lorries perhaps, but your little car could manage it all right and, in all the time I have been sitting here, not one car or anything else has come in the opposite direction. Anyhow, why would they want to run into the arms of the Germans? So instead of waiting for the lorry to cool down while the cars pass it, one by one, why don't we drive straight down the other side of the road? It would be a bit dicey and you'd have to watch out for ditches, but we'd have to take a chance on that. It's better than waiting for the Stukas to come at daybreak and shoot us to smithereens or being ground to pieces by a tank."

"I suppose we could give it a try, but I'd have to take some of the cardboard off the headlamps first: I can't do that without being able to see," he replied. With his headlamps partially operational, he proceeded at first cautiously then faster along the wrong side of the road until they reached the breakdown, where they met with a certain amount of indignation from the drivers who had been patiently queuing in line for their turn to overtake. Beyond the lorry the road was clear. Shirley was right: there had not been a single car, bus, lorry or motorbike coming towards them.

There was light in the sky by the time they reached the coast at Beauport. "Don't forget, I've only been here once by car," Ted said, sounding a word of caution, lest his sister think that they were going to drive straight to Uncle François and Aunt Suzanne's door. "You remember, don't you? It's in a narrow street off the main road, on a hillside, a small white cottage with blue-painted windows and door," he said, racking his brains to recall the geography of the little port.

"So look out for something like that, will you?" It was still too dark to distinguish the colours of the windows and doors, though every cottage seemed to have whitewashed walls. "Well, it's here somewhere. We can't be far away now…" Ted was saying when he stopped suddenly in mid-sentence. He turned off the headlamps and drew into a side street, so narrow that it could have been simply an alley, pulled into the kerb and turned the engine off, saying as he did so, "Shh, keep your head down!" Shirley did as she was told and stayed motionless, listening to the sound of hobnailed boots striking the cobblestones as they passed the end of the lane. "Phew, it's all right now. I happened to glimpse that shape walking up the hill towards us, so that's why I turned off and told you to lie low," Ted explained. "It seems that the Jerries already have an advance party here."

He got out of the car and, looking around, exclaimed, "That's funny! I think we may be in exactly the right place, and if I'm not mistaken we've parked outside their front door!"

"We can't knock at this hour of the morning!" said Shirley. "We might as well stay in the car and try and sleep – now that that German has gone past."

"No, I don't think we need to!" Ted cried out. "Look who's coming!"

A cheerful, burly man with a beard came into view in the dawn light. "I was wondering who had parked outside my house!" he said on seeing Ted. "What are you doing here, young man? Oh, and you have your lovely sister with you!" He shook hands with both of them warmly and kissed them. "Come in! Come in!" he said as he opened his front door and bent low to avoid hitting his head on the lintel.

He called his wife Suzanne, who, although day had scarcely dawned, appeared from a small kitchen at the back of the house, bearing a large jug of coffee. Evidently she was not nearly as thrilled as her husband to have visitors so early in the morning. She was taller than her husband, with an unsmiling face, tight lips and a pinched expression. "Who is that?" she asked sharply.

"It's your great-nephew Édouard, and Chérie, your great-niece," her husband replied, showing the new arrivals into the room. "Come in and have some coffee and tell me what you are doing here," the fisherman said with a beaming smile, as he offered them chairs at the table. Sensing that her aunt was not pleased to see them, Shirley went straight over to her, shook her hand and kissed her on both cheeks.

"We are very sorry to have arrived so early and disturbed you, Aunt, but Pépé insisted that we should travel by night. He said you might be able to help us." Aunt Suzanne's thin lips wordlessly spoke of resentment at the disruption and of reluctant recognition.

"If my brother wants us to help you, then I suppose we must," she replied grudgingly. "I am just about to leave for the fish market, so you will have to make do as best you can. I suppose you have brought your food with you? You can eat it here." She pointed to the table, before taking a blue-and-white striped apron off a hook on the kitchen door and tying it round her middle. Her working outfit was completed by a scarf, which she tied tightly round her head. She left the house without a word.

Uncle François, on the other hand, genially ignored his wife's indifference. He sat himself at the table and poured more coffee for the three of them. "Have a bite of bread, my children," he said, inviting them to tear a chunk of bread from the baguette that he had picked up from the baker's: it was still warm from the oven. "I've just come into port and I've unloaded my catch, so now the wife has to go and sell it in the market. She hates fish, but she does a good job and she'll be more cheerful after the market at lunchtime. But after breakfast, we'll all have a sleep. You two look as if you've been out all night. Tell me why you've come here, though I can make a good guess why." He shook his head. "Bad times are on their way, and I suppose you two want to get back to England, isn't that right?" They nodded, afraid that François was going refuse to take them. "Well," he said, as if it were simply a matter of going for an afternoon's fishing trip, "we'll see what we can do. But it won't be before tonight and until then you'll have to stay indoors." They sighed and thanked him.

"Wait a minute, though," he said, struck by another thought, "that car out there, is it yours?"

"Yes, it's Édouard's. He did it up himself," Shirley said, pouring out information that was of little interest to Uncle François.

"Yes, yes, very clever of you, young man, but what I was going to say was that you can't leave it out here. If the Boche see it, they'll be interested in it and will come calling, asking awkward questions. We must hide it round the back of the house. If you give me the keys, I'll drive it round to our back entrance. Then we'll put a tarpaulin over it and no one will be any the wiser. But bring your belongings indoors first." Weak with tiredness, they brought in their few pieces of luggage from the car and were settling down for their sleep when Shirley remembered Céline's provisions on the back seat.

"I think I should bring those in; perhaps they'll help cheer Aunt Suzanne up; what a misery she is!" she said, but Ted was already asleep.

48

Shirley had lain down on an old sofa from which the cushions had been taken to make up a bed for Ted, allowing him some relief from the hardness of the stone floor in the front room of the cottage. Both were so exhausted that they slept soundly, oblivious to the extreme discomfort of their circumstances. Aunt Suzanne returned home in the late morning. She made no concessions to the sleepers in her living room, but came in huffing and puffing and generally making a great deal of noise. Her eagle eye saw the box on the table the moment she came through the door. "Who put that box on my table? What is it?" she called out loudly and accusatorily, waking Ted and Shirley, and probably her husband in the one bedroom as well. Shirley sat up rubbing her eyes. "We brought that box for you, Aunt. Céline sent you all those provisions from the farm."

Aunt Suzanne strode over Ted's somnolent body on her way to the table to inspect the contents of the cardboard box. "Good Lord!" she exclaimed. "Half a ham! And eggs and cheese! No more fish for now, thank goodness! I never would have believed that that Céline could be so thoughtful! She seemed to me to be far too much of a busybody." Like a bird of prey she swooped down upon the contents of the box, which she carried into the kitchen, where it became her private property to be kept under lock and key; then she went into the bedroom to change out of her working clothes, which indeed smelt to high heaven of fish.

At lunchtime she cooked fish for her husband, because he would eat nothing else, but she generously offered her great-niece and nephew a choice of food. They both considered it politic to opt for fish, since obviously that was in plentiful, possibly excessive supply in that household, whereas the farm produce was Suzanne's private treat. Her mood softened as she devoured a plate of ham and eggs, and she began to show more interest in and sympathy towards her young visitors. "So you are hoping that your Uncle François will take you to England, are you?" she enquired in less peevish a tone than that of her previous communications.

"If that's possible," Shirley replied with some hesitation, not sure how Suzanne would react to what seemed a preposterous request in the circumstances, but Suzanne did not answer immediately.

Instead, she went into the kitchen to fetch a jug of water and returned, saying, "I heard down at the market that the panzers are advancing on Boulogne already, so it's just as well you've come here. We are too small for them to bother about us at the moment, so we are safe here, but only for the time being."

Ted joined in the conversation, glad to find that his seemingly impervious great-aunt was unexpectedly concerned about the situation. "Last night we were told that the Germans had captured Arras," he told her, "and that their tanks were advancing from all directions. And you should have heard the noise of the long lines of people heading south and west, trying to escape! We were lucky, but they say that the Stukas start bombing them from the crack of dawn as they struggle along the road with all their possessions."

"Terrible! Poor things!" Aunt Suzanne agreed with some show of sympathy. "But in fact the Boche have been filtering in here too for some time. It's not difficult to recognize them, though so far they've spent most of their time drinking down in the White Horse. In the past few days we've discovered who they are, because they've started dressing up in their uniforms and those dreadful jackboots, and are out in the streets in ones and twos. Who knows when they'll start picking our boys up and carting them off to heaven knows where!" When she stopped to draw breath, her features softened, "It's my boys I'm worried about, what with all these invaders about. And there's not much we can do to stop them. There are too many of them for the gendarmes to be able to round them up, and if they did, more would come in to take their place. We're wondering what will happen next." She was about to attack the remaining slice of ham on her plate with vehemence, as if she were personally spearing a German invader on her fork, when a distant booming sound spread through the air, rattling the windows. Aunt Suzanne sat frozen to her chair, her fork poised above the ham. "*Oh, mon Dieu!* Listen to that! We've heard that before, haven't we, François?"

Having finished his fish pie, Uncle François was leaning back in his chair, contentedly puffing on his pipe until the grim interruption. "Yes, my dear," he said, blowing out his cheeks in an extended sigh, "that's gunfire: they've arrived at Boulogne and they're forcing their way in."

More booming explosions resounded from the north, rattling the windows again and again for the rest of the afternoon. When darkness fell, the detonations stopped. Both Ted and Shirley had expected François to say that the Channel crossing was off, that it would be too dangerous and that he was not prepared to undertake it. Quite the contrary, he had quietly ignored the unremitting bursts of shellfire and the deeply sonorous, man-made thunder, giving the impression that, as far as he was concerned, the matter of the trip across the Channel was already settled. "If they're busy at Boulogne, they won't arrive en masse just yet, so we have time to get you young things out of here."

He continued to puff on his pipe, appearing to be philosophical about the latest unnerving development, and dozed off. But when he woke only five minutes later, he picked up the thread of his thoughts as if he had never let it go. "I know it's rather cramped in our little house, but you must stay indoors until late this evening," he said gravely, "then we will sneak out the back way and hurry down to the port. You must follow a couple of metres behind me. At least with those jackboots the Germans are a dead giveaway, because you can hear them coming a kilometre off. But if we do hear them, you must make yourselves scarce in yards or alleyways. Above all they mustn't see you. Once on board the boat, you must lie low and keep very quiet until we leave port with all the other fishing boats. Nobody must know that you are with us. Only when we are out at sea can you raise your heads and sit up. Is that understood?" Both Shirley and Ted nodded. "Now you must rest as much as you can, because you won't be doing that when we are at sea."

He took another puff of his pipe and then said, "Oh and, by the way, Ted, you've met my son Hervé, haven't you?"

"Yes, of course!" Ted replied.

"Well, he's coming with us tonight, but when you see him, don't say a word, don't greet him or hug him in recognition. We don't want him carted off to a German prison camp."

"Of course, we understand that," Ted said. A second or two later, he struck himself on the forehead and exclaimed, "Oh, Uncle François, how silly of me! I forgot to tell you that I have two cans of petrol for you in the boot of my car; but how can we take them down to the port?"

"Excellent!" François replied, rubbing his hands. "We'll have plenty of fuel for the round trip, and if you bring them down to the port on the handcart I keep out in the yard, no one will be any the wiser, especially if you wear some old overalls. There are always chaps pushing handcarts about with petrol cans on them down in the harbour.

"Suzanne!" he called out to his wife. "Find some old overalls for these two, will you? They need to look as if they're part of the fishing fleet!" In contrast to her earlier resentment at the intrusion, nothing seemed to be too much trouble for Aunt Suzanne as far as her great-niece and -nephew were concerned. She hurried into the bedroom from where she could be heard opening and closing drawers and cupboards. Minutes later she came out carrying a large, untidy armful of clothes, which seemed to consist more of rags than garments. She also insisted on arming her great-niece and nephew with provisions to last the night, which they stuffed into their bags. That evening a passer-by, German or otherwise, might have mistaken Shirley and Ted for walking scarecrows, she in overalls inherited from Aunt Suzanne that were much too long, despite the legs being cut to size, and he in dungarees belonging to Uncle François that were much too baggy. He wore a fisherman's cap while her hair was hidden under a tightly tied scarf. Pulling the cart down the hill over the cobbles, laden with its cans of petrol, was easier said than done, but it was certainly easier than pushing it, for then, as Ted found out, either the wheels stuck on the jutting stones or, where the way was smoother, it ran away with him. Shirley helped him keep it under control.

Their uncle strolled along jauntily ahead of them apparently with not a care in the world, while they tried to assume the same carefree pose, but the struggle with the cart and their hearts pounding inside their chests made that impossible. François had almost reached the bottom of the hill when the sound of jackboots came out of a side street and marched uphill in their direction. They felt trapped, for there was no way they could push the cumbersome cart into one of the parallel rows of side alleys without tipping out its load onto the cobbles. Shirley nearly died of fright. "*Allons, ma chérie*," Ted said jovially and loudly. "*J'aimerais boire un verre au Cheval Blanc avant d'aller à la pêche!*" She could not tell whether he was serious in his suggestion of a drink in a bar or whether this was just a ruse to put the German off the scent. Sensing it was the latter, but still clutching the handle of the cart more for comfort than to impede its motion since the slope of the hill was less steep now, she responded as boldly as her nerves would let her.

"*Oui, pourquoi pas, mon cher?*"

Uncle François had disappeared round a corner, unaware of their predicament, and she had no idea where the White Horse was, although Ted seemed to know what he was doing. The German strode past without taking any notice of them, except to say *"Bonsoir!"* most courteously. They acknowledged his greeting, held their breath for a split second and then carried on down the hill, appalled and scared that they had been seen. The road had flattened out altogether, so Ted was able to control the cart with one hand as they advanced arm in arm, hugging each other close for comfort, for all the world like a couple out for a stroll before the man went to sea, walking at as steady a pace as the adrenalin pumping through their veins would allow. The urge to run was all but irresistible. The German was well out of earshot when they calmly walked past the White Horse, from where raucous sounds of rowdy behaviour rent apart the unnatural calm in which the harbour lay.

François was waiting for them round the corner by the harbour. He cast a watchful eye over his shoulder before speaking. "So that German saw you? I heard him and thought he would. Well, there's not much we can do about that. The *Sainte Marie de la Mer* is over there, the fourth boat along at the end of that wooden jetty. Do you see? We're all dimming our lights to a minimum, given what's happening up the coast there," he said, gesturing to the north in the direction of Boulogne.

They strained their eyes in the darkness, relieved only by a pale lantern hanging over the porch of the inn, until at last Ted declared, "Yes, I think I know where she is. You took me out in her once, years ago, do you remember?"

"You'll know when you find her," François replied. "I have seen Hervé, and he is already on board."

With that he disappeared into the White Horse. Unlike his father, Hervé showed no restraint about greeting his passengers in an effusive fashion, except that he reduced his naturally booming voice to a whisper. "Édouard! How good to see you!" he exclaimed quietly, as he embraced his cousin. "And here's my lovely young cousin too!" he whispered, gallantly assessing Shirley in the glow emanating from the White Horse which reflected in the still water, but Ted dismissed the Gallic charm with an impatient brush of the hand.

"You've already met my sister, haven't you?" he said in a hushed, matter-of-fact tone. "She came to fetch me back to England, so here we are." Shirley was somewhat affronted at Ted's disregard of Hervé's fulsome greeting, which was helping to restore her confidence, and she was not averse to a little encouraging flattery, especially in the present circumstances, which demanded the concealment of all her best features. Perhaps she looked better in the overalls and headscarf than in the brown woollen outfit and beret. She certainly hoped so.

Hervé took them on board and helped Ted unload the cans of petrol. "That will certainly come in useful: we have a long voyage tonight; my father has told me that we are crossing the Channel. I've never been to the other side," he remarked. Although he had volunteered this much information, Shirley noticed that neither he nor his father had asked how they had come by the petrol. She had circulated very little in the past few days, but she had nonetheless noticed that the French, even on the farm, had become very guarded about requesting or passing on information. She was reminded of the poster in England that proclaimed, "Careless talk costs lives", and whereas in the past it would have been quite normal to share her admiration for Charlot with Hervé, she and Ted avoided talking about him altogether; indeed, they had scarcely mentioned Pépé and Céline, except to point out the provisions that Céline had sent. It was as if people were training themselves to keep their mouths shut for fear of incriminating others. The rest of the fishermen were preparing their boats, but there was little communication between them; at most they worked by the dimmed lights on their boats and by torches held low and out of sight of the shore. In any case, Shirley and Ted had remembered Uncle François's warning that they must take care to avoid being seen.

Ted produced his torch from his pocket. "Can I use this?" he asked his cousin.

"Yes, but shield it and keep it pointing down," Hervé replied. "The less anyone on shore can see, or hear, the better. You never know who might be watching or listening." By the light of Ted's torch, they saw a very small boat with only a small wheelhouse for shelter. There was nowhere to sit. "Where would you like us to, to, um, stand?" Shirley asked, uncertain where to place herself on such a small fishing vessel. She wondered if it were capable of putting out to sea, let alone of crossing the Channel and reaching the other side. Hervé unrolled a length of hessian matting and spread it out at Shirley's feet. "You can sit or lie here, on top of the hatches," he said. "We won't need to open those until we catch our fish on the journey home. In fact, it would be better if you were to lie down, then nobody would see you at all." Cautiously, she sat down on the hatch. The rank smell of fish was overpowering and nauseous; queasiness attacked her before they had even put to sea. It was all too obvious why Aunt Suzanne refused to eat fish; Shirley swore that she too would never eat fish ever again in all her life. She lay back and looked up at the stars, so distant and so impervious to the drama being enacted on earth, the tiny planet among many others that encircled the sun. How insignificant it was and how pointless the violent human activity on it seemed!

Uncle François came on board in an aura of beer and cigarette smoke. "I went into the White Horse, as you know, and bought them all a round of drinks. They were dead drunk already, so I don't think there'll be any trouble from them tonight," he announced, but nonetheless he told Ted to lie low. "Once we are out on the open sea, you can sit up," he said, "but, until I tell you, I want you both to lie down." There was no sound from the land, no more gunfire from Boulogne, as the boat cast off, and after that there was only the swish of the water against the hull as the small craft glided out of the harbour into open water. "You can sit up, now," Uncle François called out quietly. His voice was the only part of him detectable in the blackness.

It was a relief to be able to sit up, although that was uncomfortable enough, but it was definitely preferable to lying on the hard, smelly surface of the hatch. Shirley peeped overboard. She saw that some boats had faint lanterns strung from ropes stretching from the stern to the roof of the wheelhouse, whereas the *Sainte Marie de la Mer* showed no lights at all: Uncle François was navigating his way in the dark. Moreover, there was very little noise from the engine as the boat gradually slipped away from the fleet and headed out to sea. Then Uncle François shone a tiny light onto the waters ahead and checked the boat's position on a chart.

A chill breeze blew down the Channel from the north. Shirley made herself as small as possible, clutching her knees up against her chest, in an attempt to conserve heat and shut out the nausea that threatened to overwhelm her. Then she remembered the woollen suit that she had crammed into her bag, intending to give it back to Eileen on their return home. She reached into the bag, pulled the suit out and put it on over the dungarees and the thin cotton blouse that Aunt Suzanne had provided. She resumed her former position, hugging her knees, and once a little warmth had begun to percolate through her body she allowed herself to raise her head.

The fishing fleet was nothing more than a collection of fairy lights bobbing on the water in the far distance. Ahead there was only blackness, apart from the light of a single torch in the wheelhouse, where Ted, Uncle François and Hervé were standing poring over charts. François was running a finger over the charts, evidently explaining their route to Ted, who was concentrating intently. The breeze carried the sound of their voices away to the south, so that Shirley could catch only an occasional word when the wind dropped. She thought she heard Ted say "Ah, can we dock there?", but Uncle François's reply was carried off by the wind. Shirley caught a word here and there: "Going south-west means we'll be carried south by the current!" – "It will help with the tide." – "It'll take us longer to get back, but we can always say a surge carried us off our course." – "Better to get our passengers onto their own dry land as quick as we can."

Shirley gazed into the darkness, twisting round to scan in all directions. "Oh! Look at that!" she exclaimed. They all turned to look northwards and saw a crimson glow spreading across the black sky.

"That must be Boulogne; that's what those guns we heard this afternoon have done. It's probably all that's left, one big bonfire," Uncle François could be heard to sigh in a lull between the gusts of wind.

"If only we had brought my Claudine and my little Amélie with us to England," Hervé said mournfully.

"Don't you worry, my boy! Your mother will see that they're all right. I pity the German who tries to mess with her!" said Uncle François, his joking attempt at encouragement clearly audible on the breeze. Shirley stood up unsteadily and tentatively edged her way along to the wheelhouse.

"We are making for the south coast, Shirl: Uncle François thinks the narrow part of the Channel is too dangerous and we will be safer if we head further south and west," Ted told her.

"That's right," Uncle François explained, "those U-boats, you never know where they are, and there might be warships, and now with Boulogne in their hands, as it surely is, we'll be better off keeping well out of the way. It will be a longer crossing, so just go and make yourself comfortable."

Comfort was out of the question. Indeed, Shirley would have felt guilty at being able to make herself comfortable. She sat staring out into the blackness in numbed shock at the discovery of what war really meant.

There was much more to it, she realized, than rationing, blackout, patrolling the streets at night and delivering leaflets. This really was war, not the phoney war that England had grown accustomed to, or the *drôle de guerre* as it had come to be called in France. Real war was invasion, murder, massacre, bombing, shelling, destruction and violence. Why should one country invade another and destroy its towns, cities, inhabitants and even its churches and cathedrals? Lives were being shattered indiscriminately, mercilessly, for no apparent reason. What was to be gained by it? It did not make sense, but it did shed some light on her father's anguish and his terrors if this ever so slightly resembled what he had experienced in the Great War.

What about the people they had left behind? Not just Uncle François's family in Beauport, but Pépé and Céline, Charlot and Louise and all their other friends and acquaintances in northern France. What would happen to them? She was ashamed to remember how lightly she and Ted had parted from Pépé and Céline, without a thought for their safety, concerned only to escape to England before the Germans arrived. Were they already suffering or going to suffer the terrible fate of so many of the travellers whom she and Ted had met on the road to Beauport? Then she wondered if she or Ted would ever go to the farm again. Would Ted ever see Hélène again? She concluded that he probably would not. One thing was certain: never again would she dance or choreograph a frivolous ballet. In future her ballets would always have a single dark theme: the brutality of man to man.

Lost in this dismal reverie, she was scarcely aware of the flickering glimmer that appeared on the port side, approaching the boat from the west. She was no sailor, yet even she could see that it was advancing so quickly through the night that it would soon cross their bow. She yelled at Uncle François, "Look out! There's something coming towards us!" He came out of the wheelhouse just in time to see a massive ship looming out of the darkness and rushed back inside to grab the wheel, hoping to steer his little boat out of its path. The ship, however, slowed its pace, and from somewhere on deck a beam of blinding light shone down at them. Through a loudhailer, a stentorian voice barked at them in English:

"Ahoy, there! You are in British territorial waters! Who are you? Friend or foe?"

Poor Uncle François panicked: this was not the reception he had expected on the other side of the Channel and, of course, he could not distinguish the English language from the German. He was on the point of turning about when Hervé pushed him aside and seized the wheel, while, with a cool head, Ted took charge of the negotiations. "We are English, escaping from France!" he shouted back as loudly as he could.

There was a pause in which the crew on the other vessel must have been conferring among themselves. "Why are you in a French fishing boat?" came the next question, less brusquely delivered, through the loud speaker.

Ted replied calmly, "My uncle has brought my sister and me across the Channel from Beauport in his fishing boat. We are heading for the south coast."

This was the cue for another question to be fired at him. "Do you have permission to dock?"

Ted consulted Uncle François, who shrugged: "No, I expected to be able to enter a harbour and dock for just as long as it took you to disembark." Ted relayed this response to the vessel – in fact a naval trawler – and waited for the reply, which came in the form of yet another question, after more conferring:

"Do you have British passports?" the disembodied voice enquired.

"Yes!" Ted shouted into the glaring beam and then turned hastily to Shirley. "You do have my passport, don't you?" he asked hopefully.

She shook her head. "No, you said you were going to throw it away, so I only have my own. But don't worry, I do have papers. Just keep quiet!"

"Draw alongside," the loudspeaker on the naval ship instructed, "and we will pick you up, but only the British passport holders. You will climb the rope ladder we shall let down for you." Neither Uncle François nor Hervé seemed disappointed to be excluded from the boarding party: quite the contrary, they were pleased not to be arrested, as had seemed likely, and to be allowed to return to the French coast much sooner than they had feared, with luck before daylight, from a trip into unknown waters that was becoming more and more fraught. They might even arrive in time to join the fishing fleet, make a sufficient catch and enter their home port without their absence being observed.

The goodbyes and expressions of thanks were hasty. Shirley wished that she and her brother had brought more than a couple of cans of fuel to give their relatives in return for their kindness, then glanced up at the rope ladder, swaying as it was unfurled above the fishing boat, which had pulled alongside the larger vessel. A light shone over the ladder and the fishing boat. Then she realized that her brown skirt was much too tight for her to be able to climb the ladder with ease, so, in full view of both boats and to the accompaniment of many a wolf whistle, she peeled it off, only to reveal Aunt Suzanne's dungarees underneath. There was a brief round of applause from above, which was quickly extinguished by a brusque command from an officer. Undaunted, she picked up her bag, leapt at the ladder and shinned up it in a flash. Ted found it more difficult, as he was not only carrying his own bag but also one containing Celine's and Aunt Suzanne's provisions, so that more than once he grazed his knuckles against the side of the ship.

The reception at the top of the ladder was not of the most welcoming kind. The person behind the loudspeaker was a gruff disciplinarian who did not waste time in niceties. "Where are your passports?" he growled, as if he were ready to throw them into the sea if the said passports were not produced at once or not found to be in good order. Shirley asked for a pair of scissors so that she could cut hers out of the inner lining of her bag, while Ted stood on the deck shifting uneasily as if the surface were burning his feet. Shirley had reconciled herself to the fact that Ted had disposed of his British passport and quickly she searched in her bag for the rather tattered papers and passes that her mother had sent from Washington, which she had used so effectively for her outward journey.

She bestowed one of her most inveigling smiles onto the surly man as she handed him her passport, together with the wad of papers. "I'm sorry to say," she began, appearing to hold back tears, "my brother had to abandon his passport when it looked as if the Germans were going to catch up with us. Mine was sewn into the inner pocket of my handbag, so I have it here, and I also have these papers, which are passes for us to travel on the troop ships returning to England, but because Calais and Boulogne are in German hands we couldn't catch a boat from the ports and had to go to our uncle's at Beauport. He was bringing us across the Channel when you stopped us."

Cowed, the man snorted as if he were not sure whether to believe the story, but when he saw that the travel passes were genuine, issued in the French Embassy in the United States but authenticated in London, he simply said, "Right, well, you will have to go below for an interrogation. My men will show you where, and I will join you in a minute."

If the passenger ferries could be uncomfortable at times, and the fishing boat was very basic in its facilities, this ship was spartan in the extreme, lacking all creature comforts. Shirley and Ted descended a ladder into the bowels and were then ushered into a cabin and told to await the captain, for that was who the unpleasant man was. The next hurdle consisted of an in-depth interrogation as to why the two of them were in France, what their movements had been over the past weeks and months and so on, until Shirley felt her head nodding over the table. Ted had sunk into the same posture, but no one seemed to care, certainly not the ship's captain, who was conducting the interrogation. Identifiable by his voice, he was the same man who had shouted at them through the loud speaker. Unable to evince any damning information out of either of them, in spite of the harshness of his manner, he finally gave up. "If you can find a bare patch of deck to sit on, you are welcome," he said with a hostile glare, "but remember, this is not a pleasure boat and we have better things to do than pick up teenagers illegally crossing the Channel in wartime. You are not only putting yourselves at risk but my sailors as well." Shirley thought better of arguing: she was simply glad that after this final reprimand the Captain stormed out.

"Well done, Shirl," Ted whispered. "At least we are nearly home, although I haven't a clue where we're going. I wish I could have sent a message to Hélène though."

"Don't worry," Shirley reassured him, "you can write to her when we are back in London. You do have the address in Switzerland, don't you?"

"Yes, of course, I picked it up before we left the farm," he replied, plunging his hand to the bottom of his pocket. Shirley just nodded; it would have been so much easier if Ted had picked up his passport as well as Hélène's address.

49

A couple of hours later, a small boat, which had all the appearance of a fishing boat painted grey, drew alongside the naval vessel, and Shirley and Ted were ordered to descend the rope ladder down onto its deck. Day had dawned, but they had no idea where they were, because a thick mist had descended while they were below deck on the frigate. Land might have been a few miles away or a hundred. They both shivered in the cold fresh air, but for the first time since leaving France they received a friendly, humane reception from the crew, who, though dressed as fishermen, did not look or sound the part with their clipped accents and martial bearing. Moreover, the boat smelt only of fresh paint, with not a trace of the sickly, fishy odour that had been redolent of Uncle François's craft. They were given rugs to wrap round their shoulders and were each handed a cup of hot chocolate. On board, no one asked who they were or where they had come from, although they were warned that the earlier ordeal of interrogation would be repeated on arrival in port after a further hour of chugging over still waters. "Can you tell us where we are going?" Shirley asked of one of the crew.

"No, sorry, miss, we're not allowed to reveal our destination, and in any case, only the ship's master knows that.

The harbour was crammed with small boats that appeared to be awaiting some sort of seagoing festival. More interrogations conducted by customs officials and then by the military police were followed by a full body search to ascertain whether these two young ragamuffins were bringing messages for German spies concealed about their persons. Ted proved to be an especial target because of his missing passport, but when Shirley produced the travel passes that should have allowed them to travel through Calais or Boulogne, and after a series of phone calls, he was released. A long time later, though still very early in the morning, they were escorted out of the port and ejected onto the streets, hungry, thirsty and tired, not having eaten anything since leaving their Aunt Suzanne's the previous evening in Beauport.

"Frankly, I think I would rather have stayed in France if this is what England is like!" Ted observed dejectedly. "Let's find something to eat and then catch a train to London."

"That would be a nice idea, but do you have any money?" Shirley asked.

"Of course not," her brother replied irritably, "why would I have English money on me when I've been living in France for nearly a year?"

"I wondered because I don't have any either," Shirley announced.

"*Comment?* You mean you didn't bring any with you? How could you be so silly?" Ted exploded, mixing French and English in his confusion and frustration.

Shirley had a ready answer, which she delivered with quiet but unmistakable indignation. "It's all very well for you. If it hadn't been for your obstinacy, I shouldn't have had to come to France at all. As it was, I had no idea what to expect. Pa said I had to be very careful in case the Germans had already invaded, because if they caught me with English money in my purse I would be in deep trouble. So he gave me just enough for the journey and told me to ditch any leftover change which might look suspicious." She added, with a grin, "I threw it in the sea at Calais."

A tense hiatus hung in the air. "Pa expected we would be returning to Dover and he said he would meet us there if we rang him from the *estaminet*, but it was too dangerous for us to go in there to use the phone, and we can't get in touch with him now because we haven't even any loose change for a phone call, so he won't have any idea where we are or that we've arrived. He doesn't know any more than we did that we were going to end up here. We'll probably have to walk home," she declared defiantly after a mental review of their circumstances, and then fell silent.

"What's the name of this place anyhow?" Ted asked angrily, but Shirley did not reply. "So you don't even have enough money to telephone Pa?" he asked again.

"No, I've already told you I don't!" came the terse response.

A chill, grey mist wafted in from the sea as they sat forlornly on a bench racking their brains for a solution to the predicament. "There is one thing we've forgotten," Shirley ventured tentatively.

"Oh, yes, what's that?" Ted snapped.

"Aunt Suzanne wrapped up some baguettes for us for the journey; they're in that bag you were carrying. I expect they'll be squashed by now, but to tell the truth I don't care what they're like – I need something to eat. And, don't you remember, Céline gave us some supplies too?"

"Ah," said Ted, "I didn't like to tell you this, but Céline's picnic is either still in the car or in Aunt Suzanne's cottage!"

Deliberately ignoring this latest piece of bad news, Shirley bent down to pick up the bag and let out a yell. "Hey, look at this!" She bent double, reaching under the seat. When she sat up, she was holding the provisions in one hand and in the other a threepenny piece. "This must have fallen out of someone's pocket as they sat here, and you had the provisions all the time, so things aren't quite as bad as they seemed!" she said, anxious to break the angry silence that still lingered between them in the cold air.

Ted's eyes popped out of his head. "I say, that's a stroke of luck," he remarked with a broad smile. "That's just what we need to telephone Pa! We can change it into pennies in that shop over there. And look! There's a phone box down the road!" They ran over to the shop, but it was not yet open.

"Oh, well, let's eat our baguettes. Anyhow, perhaps it's too early to ring Pa," Shirley said.

They sat down on the bench again, happily convinced that in a matter of hours they could expect to see their father arriving in his car. The squashed baguettes, which to their surprise contained thin slices of the precious ham and slivers of cheese, brought Céline, Pépé and the farm to mind, and gave them such a sense of well-being that they were able talk calmly about their adventures of the night, safe in the knowledge that the fear of capture was behind them. "There's one thing I have to say," Ted declared in a genuine attempt to cool their frayed tempers, "when I heard those explosions yesterday afternoon and saw the red glow in the sky over Boulogne, I was jolly glad and grateful that you had come to persuade me to come back here, Shirl. It's all much worse than I expected."

"That's all right: it was quite exciting really, wasn't it?" she rejoined, glad that the tension between them had been dispelled.

In her heart there lurked a pang of guilt at the inexplicable exhilaration that had come upon her during the uncertain course of their escape. It was a sensation that she had only previously experienced when performing on the stage, and consisted of a combination of excitement and fear. Indeed, the fear enhanced the excitement. The guilt arose from the awareness that while she and Ted were making their getaway, other people were suffering a terrible calamity. She asked him whether he felt the same and was comforted to hear that he did. "It was strange, wasn't it? We were in great danger but it all seemed like an adventure. I wasn't at all scared – were you?" he said.

"Not at all," she agreed, but added, "I do hope Pépé and Céline are safe."

"And I hope Hélène is too," Ted whispered more to himself than to his sister, but she heard and reprimanded him gently:

"Ted, don't be so silly! Hélène is in Switzerland and Switzerland is a neutral country. She's much safer there than in northern France. Possibly," she concluded, speculating on the future, "she's even safer there than we are here in England."

When the keeper of the shop across the road came out of his door, they stood up, brushing the crumbs off their clothes for the seagulls whirling through the mist and screeching overhead. They watched as the man brought out his rather scant greengrocer's wares, among which there was a marked shortage of fruit and an abundance of unappetizing root vegetables; the greengrocer himself was as unappealing as his produce. "I don't think he's going to help us," Ted said. "Perhaps he might, but only if you do the talking." Shirley walked across a patch of grass, fully aware that in her woebegone state there was no hope of exerting any charm over that man. Her hair was lank and matted from the damp, salty air, her complexion was grey from tiredness and the brown woollen suit, into which she had changed in the ladies' room at the port, smelt horrendously of rotting fish.

The greengrocer eyed her suspiciously as she crossed the road and asked harshly, "What do you want?"

"We wondered if you could kindly change this thripp'ny bit into small change so that we can use the phone, please?" she asked.

"No, I don't do that," he replied. "I'd have people in here all day demanding change for the phone box, so the answer is no, unless, that is, you are prepared to change your threepence for tuppence ha'penny." Outraged at this blatant profiteering, Shirley turned her back on him and walked away.

They sat down once more, contemplating their next move. "Let's go over to the phone box," Shirley suggested, "maybe there's a post office nearby, or a bank, or somewhere we can change this threepence." They wandered over to the phone box, which was on a street corner, and indeed only a couple yards round the corner they found a post office where they easily changed their brass coin for pennies and ha'pennies.

However, when Shirley dialled home, the call was answered by Tilly, not their father. "Oh, Shirley! It's so nice to hear you! Where are you? We were so worried about you with the Germans taking over so much of northern France! Your Pa will be so pleased to know that you are safe!" She exclaimed.

There was no chance of interrupting Tilly's flow until finally, unable to stand it any longer, Shirley butted in, almost shouting down the phone, "Tilly, I would like to speak to my father at once please!"

"Oh, didn't you know, Shirley? He's not here. Oh just a minute! My little Albert's climbing up the ladder to the top shelf!" She dropped the phone while she went to lift her small son down. "Sorry about that," she said, resuming the one-sided conversation. "He's such an active baby, but I had to bring him to work with me this morning because Mother has a bad cold and Archie has gone to help your father."

"Help him do what?" Shirley interrupted her, screaming with impatience.

"They've gone to help move your grandmother up to Birmingham. It's such a big job. First they have to supervise the removal men and then they are going to bring her piano round here for Ted. After that they are going to drive her all the way there, to your Aunt Winnie's, and they'll be staying there the night."

The money was running out when Shirley slammed the phone onto its cradle. "Now what are we going to do?" she asked despondently. "And I'm desperate for a cup of tea, or even a glass of water."

They returned to their seat and sat in silence, neither of them daring to make any suggestions for fear of appearing stupid. At last Ted spoke, "I can see a drinking fountain over there, Shirl. Do you see it? Why don't you go and have a drink." Grateful for this most minimal of mercies, she stumbled across to the fountain, from which she drank in gulps of cold water. They quenched her thirst but did nothing to raise her spirits. Ted sat deep in thought, apparently racking his brain for a faint memory that lay buried in its depths. "Wait a minute!" he exclaimed eventually. "Didn't you go to the wedding of one of your ballet people somewhere near Brighton?" Shirley's immediate reaction was to bristle at being reminded of an occasion that had left her confused and unhappy, and which she had wanted to erase from her mind.

"Yes, it was Nora Patience's wedding to Dr Ellison. What of it?"

"Well, there you are! The crossing was so long, I think we can't be far from Brighton. We'll go back to the phone box and look them up, unless you have their address with you?"

"I have it at home, but I don't remember what it is."

There were no directories in the telephone box; they had all been removed in the interests of national security, and once more the trouble was that they had no money: their searches under all the benches in the park revealed no more threepenny pieces, only discarded paper bags and dirty scraps of newspaper. "We could walk to Brighton, I suppose," Ted suggested.

"I don't think my leg would carry me that far and I'm too exhausted," Shirley moaned. "I just want to sleep." She stretched out along the bench and put her bag under her head. "Wake me up when you've had a good idea," she told her brother.

"Mm, I think I have one already," he said.

She sat up at once. "Really, go on then: tell me what it is before my head drops off," she said drowsily.

"Do you remember that Clark Gable film we saw when it came round the second time?" he asked.

"Which one?" she demanded.

"The one where the girl is supposed to marry a chap, but runs off with someone else. I can't remember what it's called," he said.

"Oh, I know, it's *It Happened One Night*. It was a hit at the time, but I thought it was rather silly. What about it?" Shirley replied.

"Well, it showed what they do in America when they haven't got any money or any transport: they stand in the middle of the road and put their thumbs out to stop the traffic. It's called hitch-hiking. Why don't we do that? Just to Brighton."

Shirley laughed. "We could give it a try," she said, now fully awake, "but I'm not going to pull my skirt up to attract the drivers like the girl in the film did."

"I don't see why not," Ted retorted. "You wear silly little skirts for your ballet, so what's the difference?"

Ted made some enquiries, which enabled them to find the way out onto the Brighton road. Once clear of the town, he started raising his thumb at the passing traffic. They were beginning to despair of any vehicle ever stopping for them when a truck laden with squealing piglets pulled into the side of the road. By his worn, dirty clothing they judged that the driver was so obviously a farmer that his truck seemed the ideal form of transport: the smell of the piglets would quell the smell of fish, and he would probably not be put off by their bedraggled appearance. He explained that he was on his way home from collecting the piglets and asked where they wanted to go. "To Brighton, please!" Shirley cried with such pleading in her voice that he could not refuse.

"Jump on board!" he said. "But tell me what are two nice young people like you doing thumbing lifts along the road to Brighton?" Shirley expected him to say "looking like scarecrows", but he was too polite for that. Ted briefly explained the circumstances, at which the farmer raised his eyebrows. "That's quite some story!" he remarked. "So you're a farmer too, young man. I'm happy to help one of my own kind, so climb in and I'll drive you as far as I can, that is until I have to turn off. Ted climbed into the truck first and then gave his sister a hand getting up. Squeezed on the front seat between Ted and the door, Shirley disregarded the farmer's propensity to chat about all his main concerns, from pig farming and the price of bacon to his preferred tipple in the local pub, and fell asleep leaning on the rattling door frame.

When the lorry stopped with a jolt, she woke up to hear the farmer saying to Ted, "This is my turning; it's a short cut for me and I'm afraid this is as far as I can take you, because I need to unload these piglets before lunchtime. The wife doesn't like it if I come in late. But here, take this loose change: it will pay your bus fare to Brighton," he dug into his pocket and handed Ted a handful of coins. He then addressed himself to Shirley. "I gather from your brother," he said, "that you are looking for Dr Ellison. He's well known round here, and I rather think you'll find his house is somewhere near the town centre," he said. "Everyone knows him, so you only have to ask and you'll be directed to his house straight away." He glanced at his watch. "I reckon the bus will be along soon and will take you right into the centre."

Bleary-eyed, Shirley climbed out of the truck and stood waiting while Ted and the farmer finished off the animated conversation about agricultural matters that must have developed while she was asleep, and Ted showered the man with thanks. She noticed that he had stopped by a signpost, one arm of which pointed along the coast and the other to the turning on the opposite side of the road. Although the destinations on both had been erased, the one pointing inland had not been treated to such vigorous scrubbing. Shirley rubbed her sleepy eyes to be able to read it more clearly and could make out a capital "H", an "m" and a "y" at the end of the word. "It must be 'Hambley'," she thought, the scene of Nora Patience's wedding and of her sighting of Alan's father; the very name made her feel weak at the knees and made her head swim. She leant against the post, trying to steady herself. Mixed reactions raced through her brain.

She was struck by horror that a memory she had successfully, or so she believed, obliterated could so easily be revived. She told herself that in all the time she had been in France, Alan's image, and dreams of him, had not crossed her mind at all. She scolded herself for being so stupid as to let a mere signpost bring back that confusing aberration with such force, because that simply was what it was: it was nothing more than a teenage aberration that had encouraged her to fall in love with someone whom she had met for two minutes at most and who had now faded to a fleeting image. At the same time, a compelling curiosity to return to Hambley swelled up inside her. There might be just a chance that this farmer could take her back to the village, and on the way there he could tell her more about its inhabitants. He probably knew Alan's family because it was such a small village. There might even be a chance that Alan would appear from around a corner. She was on the point of asking the farmer if he would take them with him, but he was already back in his cab and was starting his engine, so it was too late. No sooner had he gone than she realized what a fool she would have made of herself had she so much as opened her mouth.

In contrast to their earlier experiences, the rest of the day passed like a dream. Mrs Ellison was delighted on the one hand and appalled on the other to find her best pupil and her brother on the doorstep, dressed as ragamuffins and smelling of pigs and fish. Without asking any questions, she herded them into her kitchen and quickly gave the two of them food and drinks, and then ran a hot bath, first of all for Shirley and then for Ted. After which she ushered them into delightful guest rooms, where the beds were already made, and told them to sleep for as long as possible. "You can tell me where you have been and we can make arrangements for you later, but for now you must rest and you must stay here tonight. While you sleep, I am going to go down to the Scout hut, where they are having a jumble sale today, and I hope to find you some decent clothes there! Oh, and I have to call on my mother: she's in an old people's home now. But I won't be long."

Dr Ellison had come home by the time they awoke. His wife brought him to Shirley's door. "Shirley, dear, I hope you don't mind, but I thought my husband should examine you, as you looked so ill when you arrived. Goodness knows where you and your brother have been, but I'm sure it was nowhere very pleasant."

Dr Ellison followed his wife into the room and checked Shirley's heartbeat, her lungs and her blood pressure. He stood back, paused and then asked, "Now young lady, I suspect you've had chicken-pox. Is that right?"

For the first time since leaving Tremaincourt, Shirley looked in the mirror and was appalled to see her face covered in fading, purplish blotches. "Oh, dear, yes! And it still shows!" she groaned. "And," Dr Ellison went on, "I would say that you and your brother have been through some sort of hair-raising adventure and you need to rest. Is that right?" he pronounced.

"Yes, I suppose you could say that," Shirley admitted.

"Well then, get yourself dressed in these clothes my wife found for you, then come down to dinner. She said the meal would be on the table in half an hour." On a chair by the bed a neat pile of clothes had appeared while she had been asleep: it was plain that neither the pretty blue-and-white cotton dress nor the blue cardigan had been bought in a jumble sale. She put them on and went down to dinner.

Ted was also smartly dressed, though possibly *his* clothes, a shirt and tweed trousers, had been purchased second hand at the sale rather than new in a department store. He did all the talking at supper time because his sister was still very subdued. Her hosts put this down to the strain of the chickenpox and her experiences over the past forty-eight hours, though she knew that the cause of her silence was a multitude of additional factors: the tension of the escape, the sound of the guns, the tiredness, the Channel crossing and then to cap it all, that wretched signpost which had reawakened the old obsession. She tried to focus on the conversation. Dr Ellison was talking about the bad news of the British Expeditionary Force that was filtering through to Britain. The soldiers were all trapped on the beaches at Dunkirk, the only major port that the Germans had not yet taken.

Listening to Dr Ellison, Shirley saw how lucky she and Ted had been. That they had been in extreme danger was undeniable, for they had teetered on the edge of war yet were never totally immersed in it, whereas these hundreds of thousands of soldiers, some of them no older than Ted, were on the edge and immersed at one and the same time. Inevitably, she began to wonder whether Alan was caught up in the Dunkirk emergency and to fear that, had he been mobilized, her chances of ever seeing him again were absolutely zero. She vaguely heard Dr Ellison asking Ted if they had seen lots of small boats when they came into port. On hearing that the harbour was full, he shook his head wisely and remarked that the rescue mission was sure to be on its way very soon.

After a good night's sleep in comfortable beds, Shirley and Ted were treated to a cooked breakfast and then invited to stay for lunch. "We have worked it all out for you," Nora Ellison declared. "You must stay for lunch, then we shall give you the money for the train back to London. Perhaps you father will be kind enough to reimburse us when it suits him." She would admit no argument.

Late that Sunday evening they arrived home to find that their father was awaiting them, greatly relieved that both his son and daughter were no longer in France. "I was so worried about you!" he said, the furrows in his brow appearing even deeper than usual, and I am heartily relieved that you are home!" He too was tired after the ordeal of removing his mother to Birmingham. Evidently she had put every possible obstacle in his way, even questioning whether she really wanted to let Ted, her favourite grandson, have the piano which she herself never played, probably because she did not know how to. Ted was delighted with it, and charmed his father and sister that evening with tunes from the shows.

Throughout the neighbourhood Ted and Shirley became heroes: unlike anyone else they had actually been in France during the German invasion and had seen at first hand the brutality that was being inflicted on the population. Customers in the shop were eager to hear the story of their escape, and they were stopped in the street by people they had never met before and congratulated on their bravery, when in fact they would have preferred to be able to consign the experience to the past as quickly as possible.

There was no time to recover from the ordeal of the escape from France, yet it was hard for Shirley, who felt that she had been away in another world for years, not simply a few days, to readjust to the way of life that had become normal over the past eight months, since the outbreak of war. She was also trying to come to terms with the confusing shock of seeing that signpost outside Brighton, although other more urgent matters competed for her attention, because both she and her father were gravely concerned about Ted, who, despite the joy of having his own piano, was having even greater difficulty in settling down than his sister. Although he had taken the journey in his stride with far fewer complaints than she, he had become morose and restive at discovering that London, the destination of that arduous journey, was most definitely where he did not want to be. He hated the noise, the bustle, the smoke and the traffic and pined for the green fields, hills and forests of northern France. Standing at the window and looking out at the stream of buses, lorries and cars, he kept saying with a sigh, "I wonder how Pépé is getting on with the silage," or, "If only Céline could send us some fresh eggs!"

Added to which, he, a strapping lad, used as he was to a plentiful supply of wholesome fresh food grown on the farm, could not reconcile himself to the meagre rations available in his temporary ration book. Even when his full ration book came through, the situation did not improve, because it required him to adjust to a very different culinary experience. "You're in England now, remember," Shirley remarked curtly when he groaned at her valiant attempts to concoct a proper meal out of baked beans, tiny morsels of bacon, sliced spam and mashed swede, combined with a huge quantity of potato. For an hour or two at a time he gave a hand in the shop, where in truth there was little for him to do, for with both him and Shirley at home it was certainly overstaffed, but he soon became dejected in there, and would regularly have to go out for a walk. Even that did little to lighten his mood, since he would come back even more discontented at the lack of fresh air and open spaces, as well as at the abundance of restrictions imposed by the wartime regulations.

Reggie found an outlet for some of his son's excess energy by sending him out on the paper rounds in the evening, when there was always a shortage of paper boys, and at night Ted willingly took over the two ARP shifts from his father and his sister. "As there's nothing much for me here, I might as well do the night shifts and sleep in the morning," he declared with resignation. In the afternoons, up on the top floor which his father had converted into a makeshift bedroom for him during his absence, he spent hours engaged in writing long letters to Hélène, after which he would play increasingly morbid pieces on the piano.

Naturally he would scan the post for a reply from Switzerland, and only when a letter came would he cheer up for a day or two. Generally he would feed Shirley titbits of information, telling her for instance that Hélène was fine and was untouched by the conflict. On one occasion he told her that Hélène had written that her mother, who was living with her sister in the south of France, was concerned by the German occupation of the *château* in Trémaincourt in case the invaders were wrecking it. In the same letter Hélène vaguely gave Ted to suppose that Jean-Luc had somehow been involved in making the *château* available to the enemy. In another she mentioned that her mother was openly claiming that her son, Jean-Luc had taken the petrol from the cans stored in a shed at the *château*, filled the cans with water and distributed the petrol to the villagers of Trémaincourt. Of Hélène's brother and father there was no news: no one, least of all Hélène, seemed to know where they were. Some of this news brought a smile, either of indignation or glee, to Shirley's lips, but, on hearing about Jean-Luc, she thanked her lucky stars that at least her obsession with Alan had saved her from his clutches.

Ted went to the cinema with his father to see the Pathé newsreels three times a week, then he would go down to the pub for a drink with his pa's friends before setting out on his night-time patrol, which, given the time of year, was inevitably rather late. Otherwise, he followed the news closely in the papers and was particularly absorbed by the Pathé film of the evacuation of hundreds of thousands of British and French soldiers from Dunkirk. The news on the wireless and the film in the cinema revealed why there had been so many small boats assembling in that harbour on the south coast where he and Shirley had been dumped by the naval "trawler". The discovery that he and his sister had had such a narrow escape only days earlier from the horrors of the Nazi invasion of his beloved France struck him to the core, so he decided there and then that he would sign up to defend and avenge his two homelands, Britain and France. Gone was the happy-go-lucky young farmer, and in his place there appeared a determined fighter, ashamed of being idle while others bore the brunt of war. Such was the sum total of Ted's life in Britain, at least for the first ten days or so.

In no doubt that the authorities would know of his return to London, despite his lack of a passport, his hope was that his call-up papers would come through at any time since he was ready and willing to go into battle. Meanwhile, however, a much more attractive proposition fell into his lap when, on 18th June, he heard, over the wireless, the exiled General de Gaulle insisting that the war for France was only then beginning, unlike Marshal Pétain who had the previous day had told his country-men that the war was over for them. De Gaulle appealed to Frenchmen via the BBC to respond to his call to arms and join him in London. His eyes moist with joy, Ted packed a bag and told his father and sister that the moment had come. He would have walked out immediately, had not his startled family compelled him to eat something before leaving. Reggie was heard to joke ruefully that Ted was going in search of better food on the other side of the Channel, but this half-hearted attempt to lighten the atmosphere was lost on Ted. Then he was gone, on his way to the Olympia Exhibition Halls, one of the first of many recruits to the cause of the Resistance.

The abrupt separation from his only son, with whom he had so recently been reunited, was almost more than Reggie could bear. He sank into the depths of despair, the like of which Shirley had witnessed so often in the past and which might herald a recurrence of the symptoms of shell shock. She too was taken aback at the speed of Ted's departure, though unlike her father she understood his sudden decision to leave at the first opportunity, an opportunity that would restore his self-respect and fulfil his urge to participate in the conflict, for she had no doubt that he had felt guilty at abandoning France at her lowest ebb and in her hour of greatest need.

Ted's departure was in fact only temporary. The next evening he reappeared, bursting with excitement and full of news. He told them that Olympia had been packed with volunteers, with scarcely standing room, let alone space to lie down for the night. There had been rousing speeches from the General and his colleagues, much cheering and singing and a great deal of recruiting, for which he had been the first in one of the queues. Using the identity papers that his mother had sent, he had signed up as a French citizen, but was frustrated then to be told to go home to his London address and there await further developments. He was, however, confident that his fluency in both languages would qualify him for a job on the General's staff at first, then active service in the field later. He did not specify what this active service meant, and neither Shirley nor their father were very inclined to find out too much detail, so great was their relief at having him home for a little longer.

Like most of the population they were forced to grasp at small straws, since there was little else to celebrate. It was bad enough that the days of the phoney war had come to an abrupt end with the German invasion of France, but with the enemy in sight of Britain across the Channel, tensions were mounting steadily. The withdrawal – no one liked to talk of "defeat" – of British and French troops from Dunkirk, leaving thousands of bodies on the beaches, brought home to the population at large the enormity of the danger facing the country. Although Ted and Reggie continued to go to the cinema for the news, and they all read the daily papers, a tacit understanding prevailed that, in the home, talk of the war was kept to a minimum to preserve the sanity of the occupants.

The lack of discussion meant that Shirley found herself isolated as she tussled with the question of her own contribution to the war effort. She did not feel the same urge as Ted to fight, but, on the other hand, she wanted above all to contribute in a useful way. The ballet, which to date had been such a fundamental part of her existence and, in effect, her only talent, now appeared to be frivolous and even futile. What could a troop of dancers do to aid the battle against the monstrous evils of Nazism? While her ballet shoes and her leotard lay untouched in her wardrobe for days on end, her records and her gramophone gathered dust and the paper for choreographing new dances faded as it lay in the in the sunlight on her table, she agonized over the options open to her. She was not ready to let Madame Belinskaya know that she had returned from France, so she studiously avoided the dance school. Instead she took herself off to the council offices to look at the posters and enquire whether there might be some useful occupation that she could take up.

Her searches in the local library and the recruiting office revealed that she could apply to join various voluntary services: for instance the girls in the Women's Land Army were digging the soil and planting vegetables to feed the nation, but the trouble with that was that there was no land to dig in her area, apart from the allotments already established in parks and gardens. As for entering the armed services, she was well aware that her unreliable left leg made it highly unlikely that she would pass the medical to join the WAAF or become a Wren, the glamour of either of which might well have held some appeal. As for the ATS, the Auxiliary Territorial Service, the hideous khaki uniform was so unflattering she simply could not see herself wearing that.

While she was surveying the posters and studying the leaflets, a pleasant young woman of about her own age came up to her to ask if she needed help. "I'm wondering what on earth I could do," she replied, explaining that over the past two and a half years she had been recovering from infantile paralysis, and although her left leg, which had been paralysed, was much stronger, it could still give her trouble when she was tired or overworked. "Oh, poor you!" the girl said with genuine sympathy and stopped to consider Shirley's problem. "I don't think the armed services are for you, but you might like to try the WVS, the Women's Voluntary Service," she suggested. "They do all sorts of work: they have helped evacuate children from the cities, they've set up canteens and soup kitchens to feed the soldiers returning from Dunkirk, they help the ARP patrols and so on."

"I am an ARP warden," Shirley said, to the woman's surprise.

"Well, in that case you are involved in the war effort already!" she declared with a smile. "But may I ask what are your qualifications?"

"I don't have any really, only the Higher Certificate at school and lots of ballet diplomas."

"Goodness!" the woman explained. "It sounds to me as if you have plenty of qualifications. Are you able to dance at all?"

"Yes," she replied, "it's fine if I can dance to a set schedule, even non-stop for a few hours and then have a rest, but I couldn't go on long marches or be on duty all day in the services. That's the problem."

The young woman then made a suggestion that astonished Shirley. "Why don't you carry on dancing, then?" she asked.

"It's simply that it seems too trivial in these circumstances," Shirley replied once she had recovered from the surprise. "I would like to be doing something more useful."

"But dancing is useful!" the woman cried out. "Don't you realize that entertainment is a great contribution to keeping the nation's spirits up? It's very necessary, even more so now that the Germans are so close. You should join a dance company and dance for the troops! Don't you know that last year the government set up an organisation called ENSA, the Entertainment National Service Association actually, especially for that reason? Take some of these leaflets about the ENSA. You'll probably find something that you can do."

Much cheered by this revelation, Shirley decided that she would pay Madame Belinskaya a visit after all. "Ah, *ma petite*! Welcome back!" Madame exclaimed on seeing her. "We were so anxious; we did not know what had happened to you! Thank goodness you have come back to us. And what about your brother, is he safe too?"

Shirley reassured her on Ted's account, making light of their escape from France and feeling rather ashamed that she had not returned to the dance school sooner. "How is the new ballet progressing?" she asked.

"Without you it has been difficult, but we have done our best," Madame replied regretfully. "No one really knew how to proceed without our prima ballerina, and the classes are missing you so much. So they will all be so happy to see you, and I hope you will find that they have made some progress." Shirley could hardly believe that the pleading old woman standing before her was that same Madame Belinskaya who had cut such an imposing figure at their first meeting. Taking pity on her, she felt her enthusiasm for the ballet returning, welling up irresistibly inside her, even if ballet seemed so inappropriate to the times.

"Let's get to work on the new ballet, shall we?" she said.

There was comfort in the old routine of giving a helping hand in the shop, teaching her classes, rehearsing and directing her ballet and conducting her patrol through the neighbourhood in the dead of night. The hours of patrol began late, allowing her to stay at home practising until nine fifteen, and by half-past midnight she was back again, having handed over to Ted, who, for the time being, until he received a summons from the General, acted as her relay. He regarded night exercises, as he called them, as useful practice for the future. Sometimes he and Reggie arranged practice sessions for getting people out of burning buildings or rescuing them from under rubble, and then Shirley had to be present to maintain law and order among the onlookers. Generally there was no trouble, because, with the threat of warfare coming so much closer, the local residents were scared and consequently much more obliging. They recognized her almost with gratitude for her dedication to duty; these days, when darkness fell and she called to them to extinguish their lights, they obeyed instantly.

Ballet came easily to her, against her expectations, because it was inherent within her being; the intense concentration it required allowed no time for dwelling on current events, so that, in the run-up to the two performances in a local community hall where there was a suitable stage, Shirley once again gave the dance her full attention. Her major role demanded a balletic form of flamenco, for which she wore a shiny wig, the black hair of which was scraped back into a bun, and a beautiful red tiered dress assembled from scraps of material by the mothers of her pupils. Gravy browning tanned her skin, and she assumed a disdainful pout. She held castanets in both hands, though their sound came from the gramophone record, and turned, stamped and swirled in a manner that brought gasps of wonder from the full house on both nights.

Madame Belinskaya was overwhelmed by the attention the production was receiving, since it seemed as if the whole borough had turned out to watch the show, which several ARP wardens had advertised by putting leaflets through the doors on their rounds. The audience was rewarded by a sense of elation lifting each and every person out of their dread and foreboding, and transporting them into the colour, light and rhythms of an exotic foreign country. Shirley thought she spotted the young woman from the council offices in the audience and was grateful for her encouragement, which had inspired her to take up the ballet again. This was proof, if proof were needed, of the effect of such entertainments on an anxious and fearful populace.

The scent of success was thrilling, but only for the short amount of time that Shirley was fêted in the community hall. As she left, in the company of her proud father and brother, the unwelcome figure of Bert appeared from among the departing crowd. "That was quite a show, Shirl! Wasn't it, Mr Marlow?" he exclaimed, attaching himself to the family and appealing to Reggie to corroborate his uninformed opinion. Shirley grabbed Ted by his good arm and, without introducing him, swiftly marched ahead of her father and Bert. She hoped that Bert would infer that Ted was her boyfriend, but that hope was quickly dispelled. He did indeed ask who the young man walking with Shirley was, and

Reggie, being a paragon of honesty, told him that Ted was his son and Shirley's brother. By the time they arrived at home, Shirley was fuming: at her back, she could hear that her father and Bert were engaged in conversation, and she was angry with her pa for his disloyalty. As Reggie unlocked the door, Shirley turned on Bert and hissed, "Why aren't you in the services?"

"I work on the railways. That's a reserved occupation – you know that! See you on patrol!" he answered with a cheerful smile. Shirley followed Ted indoors and slammed the door in Bert's face.

"Really, Pa, you know I can't stand Bert, and all you do is to encourage him," she fairly shouted.

"Oh, we were just having a chat about the railways," her father replied mildly. She stormed off up the stairs to the flat to nurse her fury and console herself at the way Bert had managed to spoil yet another special occasion for her.

The following day, which was a Sunday, she explained to Ted why she disliked Bert so much and why she was afraid of meeting him, especially on the air-raid patrol. He came to the rescue. "Don't worry," he said, "I'll take over your patrol again, then if Bert strays onto our patch he will have a surprise. He'll have me to deal with." Shirley smiled at the thought of burly, squat Bert expecting to meet her, but instead stumbling into tall, athletic Ted on the rounds, and she felt happier. There remained the outstanding problem with Pa, who seemed not to grasp how odious she found Bert's attitude to women. She brought the matter up more gently than on the previous day.

"I'm sorry, Shirl," he said apologetically, "but Bert is my only contact with the railway these days, and a chat with him helps me keep in touch. He's changed from being a signalman to a fireman, and I reckon in a year's time he'll be a driver. He knows his job back to front and he'll be earning a good wage before long. You should bear that in mind." There was no point in continuing the conversation.

Shirley took herself off to the ballet school for the whole day on the Monday after that exchange. There she was treated with the respect due to her after her performance, which helped her forget about Bert and her disagreement with her father. "You were wonderful, Shirley!" everyone from Madame down to the shy little girls in her class said, heaping the longed-for praise upon her. Madame, however, took her praise a stage further. "I hear that the Wells are back in Islington and I think you should go over there and investigate, Shirley," she said. "I happen to know that they are urgently advertising for front-of-house staff to man the theatre. You will have to usher, sell programmes, serve ice creams and so on at first, but you will also be able to watch the ballets and find out about the company's style, which could be very useful preparation for when you actually put in an application." This was exactly what Shirley wanted to hear. Madame rang the Wells and arranged for her to visit, find out what was required and probably join the staff, which would enable her to attend a performance. "It's very short notice, only next Thursday, three days from now, but I hope you can go. They were very pleased," she said, "and would love to have you." Shirley took a deep breath. At last her dream was beginning to come true. "Go prepared to work," Madame added. "They are very short of staff and it's the first night of a new ballet by Madam. I think they said it's called *The Prospect before Us*. It begins at eight o'clock."

51

With trepidation, Shirley crossed the threshold of Sadler's Wells Theatre that afternoon, Thursday, 4th July 1940. Inside, people were rushing about in all directions. Some were probably issuing instructions, others fulfilling them, but the general impression was one of chaos. Shirley hesitated before approaching a tall man who was standing holding a board in the middle of the foyer. "Excuse me, I've come to do front-of-house duties," she said. He looked down at her as if to say, "Don't bother me now!' but in fact directed her over to the ticket office, where a couple of women were anxiously studying a chart. When they saw Shirley, their mouths opened wide and both spoke at once. "Have you come to help out?" they asked. "We do hope so: we are so short of staff!" She nodded, and, before she had time to speak, one of them said, "Ah, that's good, we'll put you down to check tickets and sell sandwiches or ice creams in the interval. Collect your uniform from Gladys over there and she will show you what to do." There was little chance of finding out anything else. Clearly she would be learning on the job.

Gladys proved to be efficient and helpful, if somewhat authoritarian. She began by saying, "I can't take you into the theatre because there's a rehearsal in progress," before launching into a litany of Shirley's duties. Without appearing to draw breath, she went on, "But all you have to do is stand at one of the doors into the auditorium and check the tickets. I don't know which door yet, because there are several, but that won't be difficult. You then stand inside the door and you can watch the performance if you like, but you have to keep an eye on the audience in case someone falls ill, or there's an air-raid alarm. If there is, you have to usher the audience out in good order and take them to the shelter across the road. When the all-clear sounds, you lead them to their seats and the show goes on. Do you understand?"

"Yes, I am actually an ARP warden, so I do know what to do," Shirley replied coolly.

"Ah, that's good!" Gladys's exclaimed, and her attitude mellowed, but she carried on with her list of duties nonetheless. "Just before the interval you have to come out here to collect the sandwich tray. Can you manage money? There's a little pouch in your apron to put it in." Although the information came in a torrent, Shirley saw nothing in it that she could not manage. It certainly could not be worse than working in the shop, especially in fraught situations with a long queue of impatient customers. Selling sandwiches at threepence a packet should be easy enough. Gladys fitted her out in clean overalls and a white cap, showed her where to find the sandwiches and then told her to have a look round to familiarize herself with the layout of the theatre.

She slipped silently along the corridors, not as an intruder, but as an inhabitant of a dream world in which she felt completely at home. This was where she had wanted to be for years, since before her mother had brought her to see *Giselle* in 1934; this was where she had come with Ted for her audition, as a result of which the theatre had offered to open its doors and all its opportunities to her. Now that she had returned, she promised herself that she would eventually assume her rightful place, not selling sandwiches front of house, but dancing on the stage. She allowed herself to open a door to the auditorium a crack and to peep through. A male dancer on the stage in a baggy costume was performing a solo. Unlike his clothes, there was nothing untidy about his spellbinding but very funny performance. His lightness of touch and the insouciance with which he played his part were beguiling, but she closed the door again for fear of being detected and sacked before her job had even begun. That glimpse told her that the evening held a treat in store. She made her way down a long passage that led to the stage door. There old Tom was still at his post. Leaning against the wall, his stick dangling from one hand, he seemed not to have moved in nearly three years.

"Hello, Tom," she said cautiously. "I don't think you will remember me."

He surveyed her. "Now let me see," he pondered, scratching his head with his free hand. "Your face is familiar, little miss." He searched his memory for no more than a couple of seconds. "I do remember you," he declared. "Your name's Shirley, isn't it? You came for an audition – oh, more than two, perhaps three years ago, I'd say – with a young man, your brother, I think he was: I tell you, your dancing made such an impression on Madam that you were the talk of this theatre for days." He sighed and added: "When we heard that you'd gone down with that terrible illness, we were all very sorry. Madam, bless her heart, was very upset; she said, 'We've lost a great dancer, there.' I've often wondered what had become of you, and here you are at last, so you must be better!"

He cocked his head on one side as though he hoped that the answer might be "Yes" but was not completely sure. Shirley smiled at him, grateful to be recognized and welcomed. "Yes, I'm here again, though not as a dancer yet, but I hope to be one day. For the present I'm an usher, so that's a start."

"It's good to see you, little Miss Shirley, and to have you here again," he said, "but, tell me, have you had anything to eat? If you are going to be an usher this evening, you ought to be eating something now. Have you brought anything?"

"No," she said, "in all the excitement I didn't think of that."

Tom went into his cubbyhole and came out carrying a plate laden with sandwiches. "They always bring me this plate of sandwiches before they start selling them," he said. "Far too many for me, so why don't you have some of them? Sit yourself down in my cubbyhole – there are two stools in there – and tell me what has been happening to you." He poured out some tea for her from his thermos flask and listened while she told him everything, except for her obsession with Alan.

He watched her as she spoke, but he also kept an eye on the huge clock that was disproportionately large for the size of his cubbyhole. "I think it's time you were taking up your position at the front of the house, miss, not that I want to break up our chat. It's not often that people come to talk to me like this, but you are welcome any time." He stood up and showed her the way along the corridor to the foyer, which had filled up with smartly dressed people milling about and talking loudly. For a moment Shirley feared that she had arrived too late, but when she rushed to take up her position by one of the double doors to the auditorium, she was reassured to find that they had not yet been opened. Another usher came to join her, and together they waited for Gladys to arrive. As soon as Gladys flung the doors wide, the crowds swarmed through, scarcely giving Shirley time to check their tickets.

A hush of expectancy descended on the theatre as the orchestra began to play. The first item was Act Two from *Le Lac des cygnes*, as it was advertised, or *Swan Lake* as it had become more commonly known. Shirley was enthralled. This was the music that she had danced to so often at home! Here on stage the story that she had imagined in her mind's eye came to life in the court scene, where the queen was urging her son Prince Siegfried to choose a bride. He could not make up his mind and was distracted when Odile, the black swan, appeared before him. She was the image of his beloved Princess Odette, the white swan, so he chose Odile, mistaking her for Odette. The disastrous case of mistaken identity would have tragic consequences both for the Prince and for Odette, but the curtain came down on their fate, and rose again to reveal an entirely different set of circumstances as the company launched into the new ballet, *The Prospect before Us*. It was enchanting and extraordinary, so unlike anything that Shirley had ever seen. It was light and airy, full of charm and humour, incorporating traditional techniques in a fresh and humorous vision of life in a theatre in the eighteenth century, where the two warring parties rivalled each other for ownership.

She was spellbound particularly by Robert Helpmann's rendering of Mr O'Reilly, the hapless clown, and was astounded that this ballet was a product of Madam's imagination. How could such a severe, unsmiling person produce such a delightful, lively entertainment? The dancing was superb and graceful, easy and seamless in its coordination, arousing the niggling doubt in her mind that she could ever attain that astronomical standard of performance. Utterly absorbed in the action on the stage, she was startled when Gladys tugged her sleeve and whispered, "Time to fetch your sandwiches." Unable to take her eyes off the action on the stage, Shirley reluctantly followed her out into the foyer to pick up her tray.

A dauntingly long line had formed for sandwiches in the foyer, while other balletomanes queued in the stalls bar for drinks. The only way to deal with the demand was to concentrate hard, keep her head down and not panic. She worked methodically, dishing out cheese, tomato and cucumber sandwiches wrapped in brown paper bags, taking the money, always hoping that it would be the correct amount and, when it was not, quickly working out the correct change. The worst situation arose when someone gave her a ten-shilling note in payment for five bags, because that reduced her supply of change rapidly. Otherwise, it was rare for anyone to buy more than two or three packs at sixpence or ninepence respectively, so the calculations were not very demanding, but even so, Shirley hardly had time to look at her customers, let alone smile at them, and had no idea by how much the length of the queue was diminishing. It felt as if the whole audience was queuing up to buy their refreshments from her.

Towards the end of the interval, when the queue was much reduced, she began to sell her wares at a more leisurely pace, but then the remaining customers became agitated, wondering if they would be served before the second act started. "Hurry up, young lady!" an elderly man exclaimed. "We'll still be queuing here at the end of the performance at this rate!" She winced under the criticism, but carried on without responding. She served him and then pushed the remaining packages into a group in the centre of her tray so that it would be easier to pick them up.

While she was doing this, she heard a male voice a little way off say, "*Bonsoir, mademoiselle!*" She supposed that the voice must be addressing someone else, so she did not take her eyes off her tray. The greeting in French was repeated, closer to her: "*Bonsoir, mademoiselle!*" This time she did look up. There, standing right in front of her was an apparition, a vision of that someone who for so long had filled her dreams and almost every waking moment, and whose memory she, fearing for her sanity, had tried to suppress. At first she thought she was hallucinating, but when she discovered that she wasn't, her reaction was one of embarrassment that he had found her – of all things – selling sandwiches, dressed in overalls, as an usherette!

Her head swam and her legs threatened to give way beneath her as she stared at her last customer in disbelief. "You are French, aren't you?" he asked gently.

The words stuck in her throat as she tried to articulate them. "I… I'm half French. My mother is French," was all she could say.

"Of course! Do you remember that we met on a ferry nearly three years ago?"

"Yes, I do remember," she whispered, as hot and cold flushes swept over her at one and the same time. He picked up three packs of sandwiches. "I think this is the right money," he said, handing her several coins. She did not bother to count them. "I… er, I mustn't hold you up, but I do so much want to see you again," he pleaded without moving away. "After the end of the performance I shall have to hail a taxi for my mother and my sister; they're sitting in the front of the stalls. Can I see you outside the theatre as soon as I've sent them off home, please?"

Her heart thumped in her chest. Their eyes met. Time stood still and their surroundings, the general hubbub, the crowds of people, the raising of the safety curtain ceased to exist. They stood in a vacuum of time and space with eyes and ears only for each other. She had difficulty finding her tongue and at last, with a dry mouth, murmured, "Oh, yes, yes, please! I would love that!"

He closed his eyes, picked up his purchases and said with a smile, "Oh, good, I'm so happy to have found you at last!" He lingered before making his way into the auditorium. She watched him go through the door and stood on tiptoe to see where he sat down. He joined two women sitting in about the fourth row of the stalls. She could see only their backs: one was grey-haired and the other had brown curls.

Gladys appeared suddenly. "Come on, Shirley," she said, shaking her abruptly out of her dream world. "It's time to clear the trays away and count up the money. Off you go. You'll see the other girls out in the foyer. Oh and, by the way, you do know, don't you, that you have to stay behind to clear up afterwards?"

"No, I didn't know that," she stammered aghast, "and I have to meet someone straight after the performance."

"It won't take long; the quicker you work, the sooner you can go," Gladys announced briskly, making no concessions to her new employee's patent anxiety.

Shirley put her tray down on a table, where a group of ushers were already cleaning theirs and counting their money into piles. "Bad luck!" said the girl who had been checking tickets in the doorway with her and must have witnessed the encounter in the interval. "Did the Gladeyes catch you?"

Shirley nodded. "Yes," she replied, restraining her tears, "and she said I have to clean up the auditorium before I can leave."

"That's right," the girl said, "but don't worry: it only takes a few minutes. Look, I've finished piling up my money; I'll help you with yours. The problem is the more sandwiches you sell, the longer it is before you can get back inside, and you don't want to miss the second half. It's the Fonteyn, you know, that young girl who danced the black swan? She dances again as the poor girl in *Nocturne*. She must be about your age, or even younger." She gave her a cloth with which to wipe her tray, and began counting the cash for her. Although she missed only the beginning of the second half of the programme, Shirley's mind was no longer fixed on the ballet about night-time in Paris, which in the normal course of events she would have found absorbing, but which that evening wafted before her unseeing eyes as in a dream. The sudden encounter with Alan, who was sitting in the same theatre only yards away, had left her trembling uncontrollably, just as she had trembled on seeing his father in Hambley. She leant against the wall, scarcely able to stand upright and unable to revel in the joy of that unexpected meeting. She tried to pick out his outline down there in the stalls near the front, but to no avail, and the fleeting joy of meeting him had disappeared under the dull weight of dread that she might lose him once more if she could not find a way to let him know that she had to stay in the theatre after the end of the performance. What was she to do?

In a distant fog the ballet had come to an end, and the company were taking endless curtain calls. When the last strains of applause had faded away, the audience rose to its feet for the national anthem and then in an unruly mass made for the exits. Shirley debated whether to stand guard in the doorway in the hope of being able to exchange a word with him, but as she had not noticed him entering, it was unlikely that she would see him leaving, given the surging crowds squeezing through the exits. Anyhow, he and his mother and sister might have taken another way out. She ran ahead of the advancing army to collect a paper sack for the rubbish and stood impatiently waiting for the theatre to empty.

The ushers all appeared to be of one mind: as soon as the last member of the audience had left, they raced into the auditorium to fill their sacks with paper bags, cigarette packets and other detritus, including a number of forgotten items. Shirley went along the fourth row of the stalls and picked up three empty sandwich bags. She knew whose they were and was tempted to take them home with her, but was deterred by the messy remains of tomato, cheese and cucumber, so dropped them into her sack. Then she scoured the other rows, picking up all the packages that she had sold and more. The work stained her hands and left her feeling so dirty, untidy and dishevelled that after hanging up her overall and her cap, she had to pay a hasty visit to the ladies' room to smarten herself up. The doorman was just about to lock the main doors as she came out. In a panic she called out to him to stop, and pleaded with him to let her through. He said he would oblige just once.

There was no one standing outside the theatre, so rather than wait forlornly, she suppressed the rising panic and kept her wits about her. She supposed, because it seemed sensible, that Alan would have walked towards the Tube station after hailing a taxi for his mother and sister, so she ran to the corner and then, straining her eyes, scanned the road to the left in the direction of the Underground. The crowds had dispersed and it was still light enough to distinguish individuals walking away from her. There were two or three couples, a smartly dressed woman and several men ahead of her. She began to walk briskly up the slight hill towards the station and then to run again when she spied a tall figure with sloping shoulders and an erect bearing gradually increasing the distance between her and himself. She ran faster, but he disappeared into the station. It would be impossible to catch him up or to know which line, north or south, he would take. He was lost to her again. She stood stock still, with the tears rolling down her cheeks.

Overcome with misery, she stood rooted to the spot. Passers-by stared briefly at her, some perhaps wondering whether they should stop to offer help, though, nervous of interfering and thinking better of it, they carried on their way. "What should I do?" she asked herself. The only calming, positive idea that came to mind was the hope that possibly, if he really wanted to see her, he might return to the theatre tomorrow, but how could she wait that long? Cold reason, however, insisted that he had probably taken her non-appearance to mean that she did not want to see him, so it would be useless for him to return the next day. Another idea came to mind, which would involve taking her courage in both hands. She would take the train to Brighton and somehow find a bus, or even at vast expense a taxi, to take her to Hambley to call at the house where she had seen his father. Perhaps Mrs Ellison would help her if she told her the story; indeed, either she or Dr Ellison might possibly be acquainted with Alan's family. All these and many more ideas, some more improbable, impractical and stupid than others, raced through her brain in a desperate flood. Finally, head drooping and hands falling limply by her side, she resorted to prayer. "Please, please, dear God, bring him to me!"

From behind her there came the sound of running footsteps. She glanced over her shoulder and turned round. Incredulously, she watched the approaching figure, then spread her arms wide in absolute joy. He ran towards her and swung her off the ground in a long, tight hug. "I thought I had lost you again!" he sobbed.

"I thought I had lost you too," she stuttered, their tears blending on their wet cheeks. When at last he lowered her gently onto the pavement, they stood gazing into each other's eyes, bewitched by the magic of that longed-for encounter.

In an impulsive movement, she took a step backwards, still holding his hands and looking into his eyes. "This is crazy," she said with a laugh. "I know your name. It's Alan, but you don't even know mine."

He laughed too. "Oh yes I do!" he said. "Your name is Shirley!" She was taken by surprise.

"But how do you know that?"

With a mischievous grin, he said, "Oh, I have a good memory."

Puzzled, she frowned slightly. "But we've only just met again, and the first time, on that ferry, there was no chance of introductions. It was only because your father called you that I heard your name."

Unable to keep her in suspense any longer, he soon cleared up the mystery. "Ah yes, but on that ferry you told me your name, don't you remember? And in any case, I've had it confirmed today. I waited outside the theatre, hoping that you would come out, and when you didn't I went round to the stage door to ask for you there. A very old man came out to talk to me – I think his name was Tom. He immediately recognized the person I was waiting for when I asked if he knew of a very pretty blonde usherette. 'You mean little Miss Shirley, sir,' he said. "She's very special, should be on the stage, she should, not selling sandwiches. She was here having tea with me this very afternoon. She'll be out soon, but the usherettes have to clean up after the show.' So I came to the front of the theatre and then to the street corner, only to see you running up the road towards Angel station!"

"Thank goodness for dear old Tom!" she said. "I thought you might have gone to the Underground station!"

"Do you have to go straight home? Could we go out together for a little while first? We have so much caching up to do, don't we?" he asked anxiously.

She did a quick assessment of what she was wearing. "Yes, that would be lovely," she agreed, glad that, not knowing what to expect, she had chosen to wear her second-best summer clothes for her first session at the Wells. "Perhaps if we could find a phone box I should ring home to let my pa know that I shall be late."

"Take my arm, will you?" he begged. "We're going in the wrong direction. We need to go back to the stage door where my car's parked, and there's a phone box right beside it."

She eagerly took his arm, for that was the most natural thing in the world to do. But this was not the first time she had done so, she recalled, when memories of being guided by him through the crowds during those precious seconds on the ferry recurred as if it were yesterday. They turned round and strolled slowly back in the direction from which they had come. Old Tom was locking up the stage door as they passed him. He smiled and waved. "Found her, have you, sir? Look after her, won't you? And make sure she has something to eat; a puff of wind will blow her away if you don't," he called out.

"Don't worry, Tom," Alan replied. "I'll guard her with my life!" Shirley blew Tom a kiss. She went into the phone box from where, all the while endeavouring to keep her excitement under control, she rang her father to tell him that she had met a friend and would not be home till late. In the meantime, Alan had unlocked his car, a low-slung yellow sports car, and when she emerged from the phone box he stood with the door open for her.

"Oh, my goodness! That's a wonderful car!" she exclaimed. "My Pa would love that! What make is it?"

"It's a Jaguar, but it's not new," Alan said modestly, hastening to correct any misunderstanding. "It was my twenty-first birthday present from the whole family. But I'm glad you like it."

"When was your birthday?" she asked.

"Oh, my twenty-first was in April last year," he replied nonchalantly.

"I wish I had known that," she remarked sadly, aware of how much must have happened to each of them without the other one knowing.

"I wish you had too," he said equally sadly, "because then you could have come to the party." He started the engine, and they drove off into the night.

Although they ate in one of the smartest restaurants in the West End, neither of them took much notice of the menu, the food, the wine or the service, for they had eyes only for each other and preferred to talk rather than eat. They laughed, reminiscing about the dreadfully rough ferry crossing that had first brought them together: that fleeting encounter that had been so decisive, had by all accounts led to much heartache, uncertainty and frustration for both of them ever since.

More soberly, and with many a sigh, they exchanged tales of their individual efforts to find each other. Shirley told him of her hopes that her dancing career would eventually bring him to her side, while he said that he had been sure that with her lithe figure, her erect posture and her light springing step, she was most certainly a dancer, so had searched through programmes and scanned posters for her picture but without success. "You wouldn't think it, but I have become quite an expert in the ballet," he observed with a genial smile. "That's why I brought my mother to Sadler's Wells for her birthday treat. Thank goodness I did!"

"You didn't expect to see me selling sandwiches, though, did you? I hope you weren't disappointed," she countered, and then explained why he had not seen her name in lights but found her working as an usherette. She recounted the sorry tale of her bout of infantile paralysis, at which he turned pale, so, to reassure him, she glossed over the agony of that period, saying blithely, "I'm fine now and I had begun to consider applying to Sadler's Wells to dance again, but, having found you, I'm not sure that I want to do that after all."

He laughed. "You are funny as well as brave. I was sure you would be!"

It was his turn to tell her how, in his efforts to find her, he had searched the crowds everywhere he went. Just once, he said, he reckoned there might have been a chance of seeing her, because he recognized her mother by her red coat as she walked arm in arm with a man whom he supposed to be her father, somewhere in the region of Piccadilly, but they had disappeared into the crowds and there was no sign of her. When Shirley's face clouded over, he quickly apologized. "Have I said something to upset you?" he asked.

"No, don't worry," she replied, shaking her head.

Rather than elaborate on that incident, she told him how she had looked for him everywhere – in London wherever she went, on ferries to and from France – and was sure that she had seen his father in a little village near Brighton. "Oh, where was that?" he asked.

"Hambley," she replied, anticipating instant recognition of the name, but he screwed up his face and said:

"Hambley... Hambley, now where exactly is that?"

Astonished that he did not instantly recognize the name, she pretended that it was of no importance, mumbling, "I don't really know, somewhere outside Brighton. My ballet teacher was married there a couple of years ago."

"Ah, now I remember, my father has an old friend who lives there and is not very well. He goes over to visit him from time to time," he said. Hambley had proved to be such a red herring that Shirley was annoyed with herself for having spent so much time thinking about it.

After dinner, he looked at his watch. "I say, it's past midnight!" he exclaimed. "I ought to be taking you home and I have to..." He did not specify what he had to do, but finished the sentence by saying awkwardly, "I'm expected: I have to work tomorrow." Shirley was unnerved by this hesitation on his part. Surely, she thought, he was too young to have a wife waiting for him at home, especially because she knew that his twenty-first birthday had been only a year and three months or so ago, but of course there might well be a girlfriend. She was even more unnerved to discover that he intended to drive her home. Had her destination been the old family home, small though that was, she would not have minded, but she could not imagine a handsome, well-spoken, well-educated young gentleman taking kindly to her situation in a flat over a newsagent's shop in one of the most depressed areas of south London.

"No, no, please, just drop me at a Tube station and I can easily find my way home," she begged.

"Certainly not," he rejoined very firmly. "I've only just found the love of my life again and I'm not going to abandon her at a Tube station."

Taking a deep breath, she decided that the only way to deal with this problem was to launch into an explanation of her pa's reduced circumstances, which had entailed their moving to the shop. All he said in reply was, "Well, I look forward to meeting your parents one day very soon. I'm sure they must be lovely people, though I'm sorry they've been through such difficulties."

Only partially reassured, she fiddled with her latchkey all the way home. Alan, however, seemed completely unfazed by the gloomy, soot-blackened area through which they passed and which led to her front door. She comforted herself with the notion that, possibly, in the dark and with his headlamps blacked out, not much detail was visible. He pulled onto the pavement, stopped the engine and put his arm round her shoulders. "Can I see you again tomorrow, please, miss?" he asked with a teasing laugh.

"Yes, of course you can. I have signed up for theatre duties tomorrow evening, but I could cancel that if you like," she replied.

"No, that's all right," he said. "Let's have a repeat of today, shall we? In fact, let's repeat today every day!"

She laughed, "Yes, let's!"

"Would you like to go dancing?" he asked.

"Oh, yes!" Shirley said, nestling into his shoulder and breathing in the intoxicating smell of him. He bent down to her level and gently kissed her on the forehead.

52

When Shirley locked the front door behind her and tiptoed up the stairs, there was a trace of sadness in the realization that the most astonishing, fantastic and unbelievable day of her life was drawing to an end. How she wished that she could hang on to every second of it and preserve it in amber for ever! It had been a day, or rather an evening of suspense and surprise that would never in a million years be repeated. All sorrow, uncertainty and anguish had been firmly consigned to the past, while before her lay golden fields of happiness, stretching as far as her imagination could see, whatever the war might bring. She skipped quietly round her room, pretending that she was dancing with Alan in a whirling Viennese waltz. Shutting her eyes, she saw his lovely face through their closed lids; she breathed in the fresh, clean, slightly perfumed, manly smell of him; under her left hand she felt the warmth and strength of his arm through the light cloth of his summer jacket and the firm clasp of his hand in her right hand. She sank onto her bed, casting her mind over every tiny second, every minute, from their meeting when he had come to buy sandwiches, through the frustration of having to work after the performance and the fear that she had missed him, losing all hope of ever see him again, to the sheer joy when he came running after her and picked her up in his arms, followed by the ecstatic evening spent in his company.

She rehearsed to herself every word, every sentence, every question, every answer that Alan had spoken to her and she to him. She could hear his voice close to her ear and his laugh that compelled her to laugh with him. "I love you, Shirley," he had said before he left her. "And I love you, Alan," she had replied as they hugged in a long embrace. This deeply intense avowal was pronounced with no hint of frivolity and left Shirley in no doubt that he would return, not just the next day, but every day for evermore. There was so much to recall, so much delight and pleasure at the fulfilment at last of her greatest dream, however hard she had tried to suppress it, that sleep eluded her until dawn. Then, when she woke, she seemed still to be dreaming a beautiful dream in which Alan had danced a *pas de deux* with her out in the fields in open country, where the sky was blue and larks sang overhead. She breathed deeply, unable to comprehend her sudden change in fortune. She remembered her surprised, perhaps rather stupid relief that he had not been disappointed to find her selling sandwiches when he had expected at some time or other to see her dancing on the stage.

Nor had he shown any distaste when she told him about the paralysis and its occasional lingering effects, but had reached out and taken her hand, saying, "Oh, if only I had known, I would have visited you every day and sent you flowers..." The sadness in his eyes was so unbearable that she had to lighten the atmosphere by abruptly changing the subject and asking him with mock indignation where he had disappeared to after their first meeting on the ferry in September 1937. Where had he and his father gone after they had wheeled their bikes down the gangway, she asked, as freely as if she were addressing an old friend or a member of the family, Ted for example, not someone she had met for the second time only yesterday. She even allowed herself to tell him that she had reserved seats for him and his father on the train, hoping that they would be travelling to London. He listened open-mouthed and exclaimed, "Oh really? Is that so? I can't believe it! We should have been on that train, but when we came off the ship, my father found he had a puncture in his front tyre, so we had to walk to the station and missed several trains while we tried to patch it up."

Memories of the previous day gradually gave way to impatience at the long hours, probably as many as twelve of them, between the present time and their planned meeting after that evening's performance. She had no idea how to fill the hours in between. She stretched, tightened all her muscles then relaxed them before going over to the gramophone. The record of *Swan Lake* was disastrously worn and sometimes the needle jumped from its groove, but she put it on the turntable anyway, and began to dance to it barefoot, her joy pervading every step that she took.

The hands on the clock moved very slowly while she dressed and had breakfast. As she went down the gloomy staircase to the shop, she also recalled how grateful she had been that Alan had not shown any contempt for her circumstances. Only then did it occur to her that she had no idea where he lived, nor indeed what he did for a living. All she knew was that his family did not reside in Hambley. What a silly misconception that had been on her part!

Her father glanced up when she came into the shop. "Ah, Shirley, I need you this morning" was his first greeting to her. "Tilly's baby is not well so she can't come to work, and it's Cousin Archie's morning off." As there was a mid-morning lull in business at that moment, he asked with a sly innocence, "Had a good time last night, did you?"

Her shining face gave her away. "Oh, yes, Pa! It was the best ever."

"Go on, tell me more!" he said.

"I've met someone!" she answered with a radiant smile. It was impossible to conceal the reason for her obvious happiness and she was pleased to share it with him, but he had other things on his mind.

"I'm so pleased," he replied perfunctorily, adding with a good measure of parental concern, "I hope he's good enough for you."

"Better than that, Pa: he's perfect!"

"That's good. Now let's get down to sorting out these papers. I've been hard-pressed trying to keep them in neat piles," he said.

The morning dragged on, the tedium starkly broken by the shocking headlines announcing the sinking of the French fleet by the Royal Navy with the loss of a thousand lives off the coast of Algeria. "Why on earth has our navy done that, Pa?" Shirley asked in astonishment.

"I'm not sure, but it seems that the old man was afraid of the French navy falling into German hands. They were given an ultimatum according to which they could have come here or gone to America, but they ignored it, so that's what happened," he explained.

"Well, I'm glad Ted's not in the navy, French or English" was her spoken comment, though that comment hid her deeper reaction, because she was wondering whether Alan had been called up, or whether he was already in the services and only on leave at present. It was strange that he did not appear to be in the forces. She would have to ask him about it in the evening. Nevertheless, the question worried her all day.

In the afternoon she went to the dance school, uncertain of what to do there, except idly pass the time. "So tell me about the new ballet at the Wells!" Madame enquired excitedly.

"It was good," Shirley told her, "but I missed most of the second half because I had to count out the takings from the sandwiches."

"Did you see Ninette de Valois?" Madame Belinskaya asked, anxious for any news that would heighten the reputation of her school.

"They said she was in a box somewhere, but there were so many people: the theatre was packed so it was impossible to see anyone in particular. Her ballet was wonderful, though!" Shirley replied.

In truth, the first half had been exhilarating, but in the second, after counting out the takings, she had been too overwhelmed by her encounter with Alan to think of anything else. "Oh, I'm sorry you didn't see her," Madame remarked, "but are you going again tonight?" Shirley couldn't have cared less about not seeing Ninette de Valois, because the person she had met was so much more important to her.

"Yes, I think I'm on duty tonight," she said casually, anxious not to give too much away or to sound too keen. "I would like to dance a couple of routines before I have to go if that's all right."

"Of course, *ma Chérie*, you can use the big studio. Would you like me to watch? I don't have anything else to do at present," Madame asked, seemingly volunteering to give up her free time for Shirley's benefit, but the latter wanted to be alone.

"No, don't worry," she said, endeavouring to conceal her irritation. "I only want to try something out." In fact, there was absolutely nothing that she wanted to try out. The only thing that she wanted to do was set out for Sadler's Wells as soon as possible, but that was pointless because Alan would not be there to collect her until after the performance and the ballet did not begin until half-past seven, so she whiled away the time, working at the *barre*, after which she practised some movements in the centre of the studio, especially, arm movements, *porte de bras*, imagining herself to be reaching out to Alan and beckoning him to come to her. An hour later, she gave up and slipped out of the building without saying farewell to Madame Belinskaya.

At home she laid out her very best dress on the bed, the French outfit that her Maman had bought in Paris for Cousin Edith's wedding, took a bath, washed her hair, applied some discreet make-up, pulled on a pair of the silk stockings her mother had sent from America and applied a dab of the perfume from a dark-blue glass bottle that Maman had left behind. "Soir de Paris" it was called. She enjoyed the luxury of pampering herself, beautifying herself and dressing up in her best clothes. Before leaving she searched around the kitchen for something to eat, because she would have felt guilty about sharing Tom's sandwiches again, for she intended to call on him to thank him from the bottom of her heart for talking to Alan the previous evening.

Gladys looked her up and down with a critical eye when she arrived at the theatre. "My dear," she said, "you appear to be rather overdressed for an usherette."

"I'm going out with my boyfriend afterwards," Shirley announced, swelling with pride at the magic words, "my boyfriend".

"Oh, well, if you must," Gladys remarked, "go and put your uniform on and give me your dress. It's very pretty. I'll hang it up in my office to make sure it doesn't get spoilt. By the way, would you like to serve the coffees in the interval this evening?"

"No, thank you, I'm quite happy with sandwiches," Shirley answered: promotion to coffee did not attract her, for she had been looking forward all afternoon to standing in the same place, selling the same wares and reliving that incredible moment when Alan had appeared before her the previous evening.

"As you like, but you will have to learn how to serve coffee at some stage," Gladys announced, and walked off.

Shirley changed into her uniform, left her dress hanging in Gladys's office and headed off to the stage door. Tom was sitting on his stool in his cubbyhole. "Miss Shirley! I was hoping you would come to pay me a visit!" he said. "Look here: they've given me a couple of extra sandwiches today and the wife has made an extra-large flask of tea!" She was embarrassed to think of Tom's wife taking so much trouble for her and was on the point of declining when she saw that Tom was expecting her to share his sandwich feast, so although she was not hungry, having already eaten enough to tide her over till a late dinner, she took one sandwich and drank a large mug of tea.

"I really came to thank you for helping Alan find me yesterday evening," she said.

"You mean your boyfriend?" Tom said with a grin. "He's a fine fellow, I must say. You make a lovely couple. When's the wedding?"

She turned crimson, then laughed. "Not just yet, Tom, but I promise you you and your wife will be invited."

Tom looked at the clock. "Time for you to go, young lady, but I'll keep an eye open for that young man and that yellow car of his this evening," he promised, "and I'll make sure you meet each other!"

Pink-cheeked and smiling at Tom's concern for her and her "boyfriend", she ran along the corridor to the foyer to take her place at the door of the auditorium and check the entry tickets. Tonight it was not ballet on the stage but opera, *Don Giovanni*, with which she was completely unfamiliar. The music was sensational, but the plot of a nobleman in Spain who spent his time seducing then abandoning women was more disturbing than she would have wished, and she was not at all sure that she liked it. This was very different from the image of Spain that she and Madame Belinskaya had projected in their recent ballet. The singing went on and on, and that, together with the plot, had the effect of quelling her mounting excitement: it would be, she told herself, hours before this bellowing from the men and shrill screeching from the women on the stage came to an end and she would be free.

Gladys tugged at her sleeve as the curtain fell. "I expected that you would have learnt by now when to come out for your tray," she said, issuing a stern reprimand, which annoyed Shirley, because she had had no idea when to expect the interval. Disgruntled, she stationed herself in the same position as the night before in the foyer and waited for the applause to end. The houselights went up, and a queue began to form for sandwiches. Again the theatre was packed and the queue was end-less. It had already been a long day, her head ached and she began to wish that she were not doing this job. Once had proved to be enough, because, although that once might not have won her a place on the stage, it had quite by chance reunited her with her long-lost love, which was even better. There seemed no point in continuing with the job any more, because she had met Alan, and opera, she decided, was not to her taste. If only she could just come on the nights when there was ballet!

There remained only half a dozen paper bags of sandwiches, which she was pushing to the middle of the tray, when she heard that voice; it made her heart leap high like a rocket emitting bright sparks of joy. She would never forget it. "*Bonsoir, mademoiselle*," it said.

She looked up. At first she cried tears of pure pleasure and excitement, and then she laughed. "What *are you* doing here?" she exclaimed.

"Same as you, miss. Don't forget I am a fan of this theatre and, what's more, it's opera tonight. *Don Giovanni*, it has to be one of Mozart's best. I couldn't miss the opportunity to hear it, so I've come to see it – that is, if you have no objection? I have the recording at home. It's wonderful, isn't it?"

"You're the one that's funny!" she exclaimed, evading his question and echoing his assessment of her from last night. "I didn't expect you would be here so soon!"

"I can't keep away. Can you be surprised?" he replied. "Now can you tell me when you will be free, miss, please? Promise you won't run off to the Tube station like you did last night, will you? I have my fiery chariot outside waiting to whisk you away to wherever you would like to go! Indeed, my coachman, whose name is Tom by the way, is keeping an eye on it for me." This evening she did not feel faint or weak at the knees. She simply basked in the thrill of his presence and the teasing banter of their talk, all thoughts of *Don Giovanni* cast from her mind; indeed she had to be grateful that it had brought Alan to her once again. Perhaps henceforth she ought to find out more about the opera.

She noticed that her supervisor was watching them out of the corner of her eye. As soon as Alan had returned to his seat, Gladys came over to join her. "If you want to leave early tonight, don't worry, dear, I'll do your clearing up for you," she said. "But only for tonight, mark you." Shirley thanked her, touched by her unexpected kindness, especially in view of the earlier reproach. Counting out the takings spared her the early scenes of the second half, and then, with a swiftly acquired enthusiasm for the opera, she tried to concentrate harder on the action, still agitated by the outrageous behaviour of the principal character: it also disturbed her that Alan should like this opera so much. Did he applaud the behaviour of that sort of man? Could she trust him, or was he going to deceive her? However, when the don was dragged down into hell in a fury of flames and resounding chords, and received his just deserts, she felt better about it and decided in Alan's favour after all.

He was standing on the pavement with his back to her when she emerged from the stage door. Tom, who was admiring the Jaguar from the other side, was facing her, but Alan was distractedly scanning the road to right and left. It was beginning to rain. Pointing to the stage door, Tom said something to him, whereupon he quickly spun round and saw her. "Oh, thank goodness!" he exclaimed, rushing towards her and lifting her off the ground, just as he had the previous evening. "I'm so afraid of losing you. Whenever you're out of my sight, I fear I might never see you again," he cried. His heart was beating against her chest, revealing the extent of his extreme anxiety. Tom discreetly hobbled into the theatre, leaving the two of them, oblivious of the rain, to embrace on the pavement outside. Alan set her down. "You look enchanting," he murmured, surveying her green French silk dress, "and you are as light as a fairy. I will put you in my pocket and take you everywhere I go!"

"You might find that rather uncomfortable if I start doing my pirouettes in your pocket!" she retorted.

He laughed. "Where shall we go?" he asked, but did not wait for an answer. "I thought we might have a meal somewhere and then go dancing. What would you say to The Dorchester?"

Whereas yesterday she had fairly run into his arms and walked arm in arm with him, today shyness overcame her in a delayed reaction, leaving her tongue-tied. How could she say that really she didn't mind where they went, and that she was as happy as could be simply standing so close to him on the pavement? "Really," she stammered when she found her tongue, "we don't have to go anywhere special: I'm so happy being with you!"

He smiled. "I know you would like to dance, so let's talk over a meal and after that we can waltz!"

"Yes, lovely, but it doesn't have to be expensive. I don't want to bankrupt you," she said anxiously.

"Don't worry: there's nobody else and nothing else I would like to spend my money on, and when we're very old and it runs out, then we can simply go for walks in the park," he said, holding the car door open for her. When he had settled himself in the driving seat, he turned to embrace her, but without kissing her. She longed to kiss him, but restrained herself for fear of appearing forward. He started the engine and they sped away to the West End.

Their talk over their late dinner was more down to earth than it had been on the previous evening, when they had spent almost all their time laughing about the terrible Channel crossing and comparing notes about their attempts to trace each other. They had talked about the pain, frustration and longing that they had both felt and about the coincidence of their meeting at Sadler's Wells when neither of them had expected it and had begun to give up hope. It was true that they had not exchanged any information of substance that evening, apart from Shirley's account of infantile paralysis, which explained why she was not dancing on the stage, and her brief explanation of her family's present reduced circumstances.

As she had realized earlier in the day, he knew much more about her than she about him: having driven her home, he knew where to find her and where she lived, while she knew nothing about him and had been afraid that he had disappeared into the night, leaving no clues of where to find him. She was still afraid that the gaunt, grey building in which she lived and in which her father conducted his humdrum business might put him off. It would be so much more difficult to forget him a second time, not that her attempts the first time had been very successful. In addition, the loathsome but beguiling figure of Don Giovanni had begun to arouse a whole new range of fears in her young mind. She decided to challenge him at dinner.

"So," she enquired with a hint of determination in her voice once the food had been served, "you've seen the awful place where I live. Now tell me where do you live?"

"Oh, you think you live in an awful place, do you?" he replied. "That's nothing to where my parents live! You should see it. Well, I expect you will one day and you won't be at all impressed!" This was perplexing, because she had expected him to say that he lived in a fine country house somewhere just south of London. "It's just as forbidding as your home, and it's cold and draughty as well. I expect your flat is nice and warm and comfortable inside, but grey, gloomy and grim is the way I'd describe our house," he added with a grin.

"Where is it, then?" she persisted.

"It's in Camberwell, very close to you actually," he replied, "so there are some advantages to it after all!"

"Why do you live there?" she blurted out, struck by the incongruity.

He shrugged. "Oh, it's because of my father. You see, he is a clergyman and he has a deeply held belief that he should be administering to the poor and needy, so when the bishop asked him to move to this parish he agreed. My mother supported him of course; she always does. So that's where we ended up when I was about fifteen – not that I have lived there very much, because I was away at boarding school and in the holidays we always went to stay with my grandparents in Shropshire."

"But you live there now?" she enquired after a pause, sensing that there was more to come.

"I've just come down from Ox... er, I've just finished my university course and am trying to decide what to do next," he replied warily.

"So what did you study?" she asked.

"Even that's rather complicated," he joked, and then in a single breath he launched into a brief description of his course. "It's called 'Greats', and it's actually a detailed study of Greek and Roman language, history and philosophy. It was very long – it took four years – but I suppose I enjoyed it. There, now you have it!"

"Oh, I see," said Shirley, who didn't see at all because, although she had learnt Latin in school, the rest of Alan's studies as he described them were a closed book to her. "So what does it qualify you to do?" she persevered, trying to make some sense of it.

"Not much, to be honest," he said airily, "a job in the civil service or Parliament, perhaps, or maybe training for the ministry with a view to becoming a bishop one day. But frankly none of those appeal to me at all. I want to get out into the world and find something more practical to do. As a child I built lots of models out of balsa wood – cars, planes, boats, that sort of thing – and that's more my style. Well, I suppose you can see that from my car."

She laughed; then for the first time there was a lull in the conversation. "You see," he exclaimed, "the mere mention of Greats has put you off! Imagine how you would feel about it if you'd had to study it for four years and then take all those exams!" His manner was very endearing; one could not help but like him, love him, sympathize with him. "Now," he went on, "if I could get into the Foreign Office and travel the world when this war is over, that would be different." He studied her reaction. "Would you like that too, do you think?"

She stopped short and put her fork down as slowly it dawned on her that this was a tentative proposal of marriage. "Yes, that would appeal to me a lot," she replied quietly.

"That's good," he replied, "but of course you already travel a lot because you're half French and you speak French too, isn't that right? Tell me about where you go in France. I suppose you have grandparents there?"

Her eyes lit up as she told him about Trémaincourt and the summer holidays there on the farm, about the harvests and about Saint-Pierre and Freslan-la-Tour and the markets and the food, and almost everything she could think of. "That, of course, is where we had been when I met you!" she told him with a broad smile. "But where had you and your father been?"

"Hmm, well, we had been cycling in Germany, believe it or not. It was the most sobering holiday I've ever had: swastikas on all the buildings, the Nazi anthem, the 'Horst Wessel Song' blaring from loudspeakers out in the streets, people shouting 'Heil Hitler' everywhere, and in the cinemas films of the Hitler Youth in training, doing their press-ups, cross-country runs and all that, girls as well. Beautiful scenery, but it was a relief when we crossed back into France. We knew it was the build-up to something dreadful and now we know what that is." There was a lull until he said, "Oh, I'm sorry, I shouldn't have talked about the war. It's spoiling our evening…"

"Don't worry," Shirley said. "It's always there and it creeps into everything; we can't avoid it." They finished the meal in silence, but watched each other all the time, never taking their eyes off each other. Neither of them had any idea what they had eaten.

After dinner he announced in a more jovial tone, "Time to go dancing!"

"Yes, let's do that," she said thoughtfully. "Where shall we go?"

"I know a nice little place in Park Lane," he said, as he started the engine and headed off through another downpour. When at last he pulled over to the side of the road, he said, "Here we are, but we don't have to rush in: it's raining too hard out there." He turned the engine off, but did not open the door. Instead he put his arm round her, bent over towards her until their faces and then their lips touched, and they kissed long and deeply, lost in an embrace that would have held them in its electric power for ages but for a discreet tap on the driver's window.

Alan groaned, but opened the window nonetheless. A smartly dressed commissionaire was standing by the door. "Excuse me, sir," he said both deferentially and peremptorily, "you can't park here. This is reserved space for the hotel."

"We are just about to go into the hotel, my man," Alan said politely, but with a degree of irritation.

"Ah, well, sir, in that case, will you let me park your car for you? A very nice car, if I may say so." They left the commissionaire in charge of the car and ran through the rain into The Dorchester. "Nothing to worry about here," Alan remarked. "This hotel is reinforced with steel and concrete, so if the Jerries start dropping their bombs on us tonight, we shall be safe."

"Do you think they might do that?" Shirley asked in alarm.

"They're attacking ships in the Channel now, so it won't be long before they start bombing us," he replied. "But don't you worry: I'll look after you."

"I'm not worried for myself," she said. "I'm thinking about my pa and my brother out on patrol."

"They're more likely to get soaked than to be bombed by Jerries," he reassured her. "They're not very good at flying in the rain."

"How did he know that?" she wondered, her brow furrowing in puzzlement.

53

Although they still clung to each other in an attempt to prolong the effects of that first real kiss, the serious turn that their conversation had taken in the restaurant, when Alan seemed to be proposing marriage, disappeared in the burst of dazzling light that greeted them inside the hotel, where chandeliers glistened with rainbow reflections and gleamed in the mirrored walls of the ballroom. Catching a glimpse of herself, Shirley was horrified to see that her cheeks, wet from the rain, were smudged with make-up. While Alan waved cheerily to various groups of friends, she made a dash for the nearest ladies' room to wash away the stains and powder her nose. She stationed herself at the end of a row of washbasins and dabbed at the discolouration with her handkerchief, before applying more powder. She was adding the finishing touches when the door opened and in came a noisy troop of girls. They were laughing and talking loudly amongst themselves in cut-glass accents. "I say, did you see that tart gorgeous Alan brought in?" one of them asked loudly for all to hear. "He said she's French and a dancer, but I don't believe that. More likely she's from Soho, and you know what they do there!" They all sniggered. "She's certainly not from Oxford," another joined in.

Shirley froze when she recognized herself in their chatter. They too stood still in their tracks when they saw her. In less than a second she assessed the situation and was ready with a counter-attack. She slipped off her shoes, picked them up and threw them and her evening bag to the other end of the room. She waved her adversaries out of the way, and then executed a series of perfect *posé* turns along the length of the cold tiled floor, concluding with a *pirouette*. When she reached the door, she dropped to the floor in a deep curtsy, saying, "*Voilà, mesdemoiselles, voyez-vous, c'est vrai. Je suis française et je suis danseuse!*"

There was a gasp, then silence. Shaking, she picked up her shoes and her bag, and went out through the swing doors only to find that Alan was surrounded by a group of friends, mostly girls, presumably belonging to the same crowd as those she had just encountered. They were busy draping themselves about his all-too-attractive person. She hung back out of sight, trembling with mortification for a couple of seconds while she contemplated what to do next. If one thing was certain, it was that her earlier suspicions about his expressed admiration for *Don Giovanni*, whether for the opera or for the character, had been well and truly justified.

While he, facing away from her, was absorbed in the convivial atmosphere, she edged along the wall and rushed for the main door. The doorman opened it for her deferentially, "Can I help you, young lady?" he enquired sympathetically.

"Yes, please, can you tell me where the nearest Tube station is?" she asked.

He glanced doubtfully at his watch. "If you run, miss, you might just catch the last train."

"Thanks," she called over her shoulder as she set off at an olympic pace in the pelting rain, her shoes still in her hand, up the road to Marble Arch, where she leapt through the closing doors of a train that was about to pull out of the station and flung herself panting into a seat. Stunned and with closed eyes, she sat motionless, counting the stations to Liverpool Street, where she got off and changed trains for the short journey to Whitechapel; from there another change at length brought her home. She stumbled up the station steps, ran along the road, fumbled with her key in the lock and quickly closed the door behind her. She sat down at the bottom of the stairs and wept. This was how it felt to be Giselle or Odette in *Swan Lake*, or any of those women whose lives had been ruined by Don Giovanni. Eventually she heaved herself up the stairs, feeling as numb and stiff as she had after the paralysis, and lay down fully clothed on her bed and cried herself to sleep.

She slept a fitful sleep until late the next morning, when she heard her pa tapping gently on her door. "Shirl," he called, "are you there?" She turned over and reached out for her watch. It was eleven o'clock.

"Yes, Pa, I'm here. Come in." As the door handle turned, she wiped her face and slid down the bed so that he would not see that she was still in her dress.

"Oh, good, there you are!" he announced. "I've brought you your tea. Did you have a good time last night?"

Summoning every ounce of equanimity, she said in a matter-of-fact tone, "It wasn't too bad."

"I'm sorry to disturb you," he continued, "but Ted and I are rather worried. He came in after the patrol last night and saw this chap parked on the pavement outside, and he's still there this morning. We are wondering if he's all right."

Shirley sat bolt upright, revealing yesterday's clothes. "Why don't you go and ask him then? Do you know who he is?" she said, as she tried to shake off the lethargy that had invaded all her limbs and her brain overnight. The tears had dried, leaving an aching emptiness in their place.

"No, all we know is that he's sitting out there in a yellow Jaguar. We wondered if you might know who he is." At the mention of the yellow Jaguar, Shirley slipped swiftly down under the covers again. The stranger sitting in his car on the pavement could only be Alan: half of her wanted to see him more than anything in the world, the other half never wanted to see him again.

"Well, Pa," her muffled voice came from under the sheets, "if you're so concerned about him, I suggest you go out and ask him what he's doing there."

"Yes, maybe that would be a good idea," her pa agreed.

"I think I'll stay here a bit longer," she said, making a show of yawning and settling down after drinking her tea. "I'm so tired. The show last night was some opera that went on and on so I didn't get home till late and I had a rotten journey. I had to run for every single train and each one was the last; I fell into bed and that's why I'm still wearing my best clothes."

"Oh, are you?" said her father. "I hadn't noticed."

Shirley did not stay in bed for long. As soon as she heard her father and Ted descending the long flight of stairs, she hurried into the bathroom with a pile of clean clothes. She doused her face in cold water, washed her hair and dressed. The overall effect was not too bad, considering that she had spent half the night crying and even now she knew that at the slightest provocation she would burst into tears again. She reckoned that her pa and Ted would be unlikely to invite the mystery driver into the house, because they would suspect him of being up to no good. However, a voice inside her insisted, "But you want him to come into the house, don't you? You can't let him go now. Think how wretched you will be if he disappears again, especially if you send him away! You ought to give him the chance to explain himself."

Another voice countered all these arguments, saying, "Let him go. Remember how worried you were last night when he said how much he enjoyed that opera? Remember those dreadful people who must have been his friends and who upset you so badly? Remember those girls falling all over him? He's dangerous; he won't make you happy. Even if his parents live in a run-down vicarage, his upbringing was quite different from yours. They might be like those girls, snobbish and haughty. His education has been at a much higher level than yours – Oxford, he said, didn't he? And you won't have any idea of half the things he is talking about." The conflict raging in her head was beginning to drive her mad. To put a stop to it, she came out of the bathroom and crept back to her bedroom, from where, with the door slightly ajar, she could hear the gist of a conversation coming up from below.

"Come on in, old chap," her father was saying to someone as they mounted the stairs to the living room. She could hear Ted banging about in the kitchen, where presumably he was putting the kettle on.

The familiar voice of someone who seemed to have a catch in his throat was saying, "I'm so very sorry. I think Shirley was terribly upset by my stupid friends last night. I hope she got home safely. I tried to catch her up, but my car was stuck in that wretched car park and she had disappeared by the time I managed to leave."

"It's all right, old chap," Pa was saying soothingly. "She's here, but she's taken to her bed this morning. Something about a long, boring show at the theatre and having a rotten journey home afterwards." Pa ushered the guest into the living room and closed the door. He and Ted then went down the stairs.

Trembling from head to foot, Shirley went into the bathroom again and surveyed herself in the mirror. She decided that she looked far too composed and collected for someone who had suffered the torment that she had undergone the previous evening, so she washed off the make-up, rubbed her eyes, which in any case were still swollen, and tousled her hair. The final effect was of a very distraught, very unhappy girl, which was after all a much more accurate reflection of her true state than the tidier more disciplined image that she had tried to create so as not to disturb her father and brother.

Taking her courage in both hands, she opened the living-room door. Alan was sitting on the sofa: he looked a wreck. Ted had given him a cup of tea, but his hand was shaking so badly he could barely hold it. "Hello, Shirley," he said, trying to muster a smile.

"Hello, Alan, my father told me that you were sitting out on the pavement in your car," she answered with a display of seeming indifference.

"Yes, I've been there all night because I was so worried about you. I didn't know where you were, and I hoped you were safe at home, but I couldn't ring the bell at that time of night, so I waited out there till this morning. Your father and your brother have been very kind to me and have brought me some breakfast. I suppose I ought to be going. I don't want to be a nuisance and interrupt their business. Please won't you come and sit down beside me for a minute or two before I leave?" he begged.

She would have gladly rushed to sit down beside him, because it was agony for her to see him in such a dejected state, but the harsher of the two voices in her ear told her to stand her ground. "Wait for him to grovel," it said. She did not move. Before she knew what was happening, he was on the ground at her feet, crying, "I'm so sorry! I'm so sorry! I should have been much more careful last night. I simply had no idea of how badly you were being treated! Please forgive me!"

Still standing, she stroked his hair, running her fingers through the waves. "I'm sorry too," she said, "I couldn't cope with it. There was too much happening all at once. The girls in the ladies' room were so insulting, and then, when I came out, there were those other girls pawing you all over. So I ran away."

"I do know what happened," he said. "One of the other girls, not in that crowd, was in the ladies' room at the same time as you, and she told me how awful it was and how magnificently you coped with it. And as for those girls you saw around me, I've been trying to shake them off for a long time, but they always seem to turn up everywhere I go, and I find them so irritating. I was only waiting for you to reappear so they would see that I was not in the slightest bit interested in them. There's not a brain cell between them – why any of them were admitted to Oxford beats me. Somebody pulling strings, I shouldn't wonder."

He gazed at her with longing and contrition. "Please say you'll forgive me," he pleaded.

"There's nothing to forgive," she said. "It was not your fault and I'm sorry I ran away. I was desperately upset because I truly thought you didn't care about me but were playing around like that don in the opera."

"I would never do that!" he exclaimed. "Please say that you believe me!"

"Of course I do," she replied. "I suppose it was an unfortunate combination of circumstances. It was my fault too; I should never have doubted you. Maybe we have to learn to trust each other. This is all so new to me, I have no idea what to expect, so perhaps it's not surprising if I jump to the wrong conclusions sometimes."

He heaved a deep sigh. "Let's make sure it doesn't happen again, shall we?" he said. Then he asked shyly, "Am I forgiven?"

"Of course you are. Rise, Sir Alan," she said, tapping him on the shoulder, "and please forgive me too." He leapt to his feet and whisked her off hers, swinging her round and round in circles. Finally they collapsed laughing onto the sofa and resumed the passionate kiss that had been so rudely interrupted outside the Dorchester the night before.

The kiss was interrupted again when someone coughed delicately outside the living room door before cautiously turning the handle. "May I come in?" Ted asked, grinning knowingly at Shirley. "I thought I should warn you that Pa is ready for lunch and will be coming up soon."

"Gracious," she exclaimed, "I think the cupboard is bare! Wait a minute, though – we could open a couple of those tins of stew I bought to stock up for the winter and there are some potatoes and carrots in the rack. Stay for lunch, Alan, won't you?"

"I don't like to use up your rations, but if there's enough to go round, I should be delighted," he replied. Ted, however, sniffed disapprovingly at the prospect of tinned stew.

"Now then, Ted, be grateful for small mercies," she reproved him. "It will be a square meal, I promise you, even if it's not up to your gourmet French standards."

Meanwhile Alan had gone over to the piano. "I say, this is a nice piano you have here!" he remarked, running his fingers over the keys. Ted joined him, explaining that the piano had come to him from his grandmother, but that he only played by ear, never having had any lessons. "That's very clever of you," Alan said admiringly. "Would you like to play something?"

"Oh, not at the moment; I'm rather out of practice," Ted replied, "but do play something yourself if you would like to." Alan seated himself on the piano stool, tried out a few chords and then rolled up his sleeves.

"This is the slow movement of a piano concerto by Beethoven that I had to play in my last term at school," he said, turning round on the stool to face Shirley, who was watching him through the open kitchen door. "I don't remember the first and third movements very well because it was so long ago and they are so complicated," he went on, "but the slow movement is much easier – well, that is to say, if I give you the simplified version, by joining up the piano parts and leaving out the orchestra."

He began to play. Shirley stood entranced in the doorway. This was sublime, more sublime even than the music of *Swan Lake*. It was both calming and disturbing, transporting her to an unattainable realm of peace and beauty that was not of this world. When the principal theme reappeared, she hummed it quietly to herself so that she could repeat its heavenly melody at will, especially when Alan was not at her side. The music compelled her to find some natural way of expressing the feelings evoked not only by the music, but by the extraordinary situation, a situation that a week ago she would have deemed impossible. There, in the flat before her eyes, was her beloved Alan, playing her brother's piano. Forgetting the lunch, which was bubbling in saucepans on the stove, she raised her arms in a *porte de bras*, turned them and her head slowly and sinuously in time to the music, and then reached out to the piano first with one beseeching hand and then with the other. The smell of burning from the kitchen brought her to her senses.

Given the inauspicious circumstances that had brought Alan to the flat, lunch was a surprisingly pleasant and friendly affair. Both Reggie and Ted were on their best behaviour and made the newcomer very welcome. He, for his part, was helpful and charming without being obsequious. Not much of substance was discussed over the dinner table, given the injunction against talk of the war in the home, with which Alan thoroughly agreed. Ted however was allowed to tell him about his enrolment on General de Gaulle's staff, whereupon the conversation turned to France, Ted's work on the farm and his ambitions for it in the future. Alan displayed a keen interest, which suggested that he had some experience of farming himself. When asked whether he had, he said simply that he had "done the rounds" of his grandfather's property – he did not say "farm" – in Shropshire.

Ted enquired what make of tractor his grandfather used, but at this Alan had to confess his ignorance. "I'm sorry to say I can't tell you that. There are other people who drive the tractors," he said. Shirley noticed the plural.

"Don't let that worry you," Reggie chipped in. "Ted's tractor-mad. In fact he's mad about anything on wheels and anything that goes. He was always building models as a small boy."

"Oh, is that so?" Alan responded quickly, glad to be able to cover up his ignorance of tractors. "So was I, and I still am. I didn't really enjoy all that studying, but it's behind me now, so maybe I'll find something more practical to do, at least for the time being."

"So you haven't been called up yet, then?" Pa asked.

"No, not exactly. I've only just come down from Oxford," was Alan's clearly evasive reply. He swiftly changed the subject. "I was wondering if you would all like to come out for a drive in the Jaguar this afternoon," he suggested. Shirley was none too thrilled by this generous invitation, for she was ardently hoping to have Alan to herself. Fortunately for her, both Ted and her pa were extremely diplomatic in their response, saying that they would love to go out for a short trial run, but had things – which they left unspecified – to do for the rest of the day. Shirley said that she would do the washing-up while they went out in the car together.

She hastily splashed lukewarm water over the crockery and cutlery, stacked them, dried them and put them away, then she filled a thermos flask with tea and put it and Bakelite cups into a basket, after which she surveyed her wardrobe, searching for suitable clothing for a warm afternoon's drive out into the country, for that was what Alan had hinted that they might do on his return from the demonstration drive. Impatiently, she stood at the window waiting for the return of the Jaguar. She watched from the upstairs window as the car drew up on the pavement and the three men got out. They did not come straight into the building, but stood talking and surveying the vehicle. Pa and Ted walked round it inspecting the bodywork and the wheel hubs and then, when Alan lifted the bonnet, the engine. She kept her impatience in check by telling herself how infinitely preferable it was that the three of them should enjoy each other's company than any of the alternatives. Eventually they all came upstairs. "It's a wonderful car," Pa said.

Ted nodded. "Yes, maybe I'll have one like that one day," he announced.

"I don't see why not," Alan remarked encouragingly. "Second-hand they're not too dear."

Shirley waited for their interminable discussion to end, then pointed to the picnic basket. "It's my turn for a ride now," she announced firmly.

"I've made some tea and found a few rather boring biscuits, so shall we go?"

Alan smiled warmly and said, "I've promised her a ride so, if it's all right with you, Mr Marlow, we'll be going." Reggie gave them his blessing, while, to her indignation, Ted winked at her.

They drove south out of London. "Where are we going?" she asked.

"I've no idea. Wherever you like: I don't care so long as I'm with you" Alan said.

"I don't care either," she replied. "Let's find a nice place out in the country where we can stop for tea." Several miles further on, he took a turning into a lane that led to the top of a hill where wild roses in the hedgerows sweetened the air with their scent.

"How about this?" he asked, pulling off the road onto a stretch of grassland.

"Suits me," she said. While she poured out the tea and tried to arrange the biscuits in a tempting display, he spread out a rug on the grass.

"I keep this in the car for my mother. She complains how cold it is in the winter," he explained, anxious for there to be no more misapprehensions.

Having drunk the tea, they lay down on the rug. He put his arm round her and they kissed. With each electric spark that passed between them, her body compelled her to move closer and closer to him: she had no idea why, nor what was supposed to happen next. In films they never showed you the sequel to the kisses, and she had no mother to ask. In suspense, she shut her eyes and, as she did so, she heard the hum of planes approaching and then circling above their heads. He pulled away and turned onto his back, as she opened her eyes. "I hope those are not Germans," she said.

"No, no, those are ours, Spitfires," he said, pointing up at one of them as it glinted in the sunlight. "They're from Biggin Hill down the road. It's a training session," he explained. For someone who had professed not to know where they were going, he seemed remarkably well informed, and it reminded Shirley of his knowledge of German flight procedures when he had let slip the previous evening that they didn't fly in the rain. Aware that he had said more than he intended, he tried to cover it up: "Or that's what I suspect," he said, but she was not fooled.

She sat up. "How do you know all this?" she asked with a frown, certain that he was hiding something from her.

He let out a profound sigh. "I suppose I ought to tell you; I've been putting it off," he said, "but I joined the RAF." Quickly, before she could protest, he went on to explain, "You see, I had given up all hope of finding you, so I thought I would sign up to do something important for the war effort before they got round to calling me up; I didn't care what I did, so I signed on as... um..." Here he took a deep breath before blurting out "...as a fighter pilot when I came down from Oxford, and I did the training course almost straight away." There was a pause before he added unconvincingly, "I've always loved flying, you see. Some of my friends have their own planes and they taught me to fly. Then I joined a club in London, so the training to be a Spitfire pilot was a joy."

Her blood ran cold as she hung her head and her hands drooped by her side. "I'm sure it will be fine," he was saying. "The Spitfire is a terrific little plane. You'd be amazed at what she does with only the slightest touch of the controls. The Merlin engine is so powerful you can get out of difficulties in a split second..." His voice tailed off. "But don't let's think of that this afternoon. Let's lie here a bit longer. I promise you, though, I'll teach you to fly after the war's over, then you'll see how wonderful it is." She lay down again. He plucked a stalk of grass and tickled her nose with it, but she did not react. He lay down beside her and closed his eyes. She moved closer to him with her eyes wide open. While he slept she scrutinized his handsome face, the broad, high forehead, the straight line of his nose, the high cheekbones, the dimples at the corners of his mouth, his well-shaped chin, attempting to imprint every detail on her memory.

She did not blame him for not telling her sooner; how could he have done so? After all, it was less than two days since they first met. Perhaps his fate would be no worse than that awaiting her or anyone else. She stroked his wavy hair and kissed him lightly on the mouth. He woke up, looked her straight in the eye and said very seriously. "There's something I forgot to say. I have training exercises all next week, so it might be tricky for me to escape, but I'll phone you as soon as I am free." He glanced at his watch. "Hey," he said more light-heartedly, "we must be going! You'll be late for the theatre and I have my ticket again for this evening. It's *Aida* and it will be magnificent!"

54

The two-day-old relationship, already so unpredictable in its ups and downs, altered dramatically after the Saturday picnic in the country. The glorious joy at unexpected meetings and the black despair at misunderstandings rapidly evolved into equally powerful but more muted reactions and emotions, dictated on Shirley's part by fear rather than confidence in the future. Endless happiness no longer stretched before her like the golden cornfields that had so entranced her in France in the summers of her childhood, because a huge cloud had suddenly appeared out of a blue sky; it hung over those golden fields of the future, casting long, dark shadows and threatening to drown them in floods, not of rain but of tears.

Alan, for his part, became more pensive since the mere fact of admitting to his chosen course of action as a fighter pilot had brought him face to face with the possible, even probable outcome of that choice, which until a few days ago he had disregarded. He possessed the presence of mind and strength of character never to permit himself to show the slightest regret, although from his reticence and subdued expression Shirley saw that he had been silently agonizing over that fateful decision since the encounter at Sadler's Wells that had dramatically changed their lives, their outlook and their expectations. What had seemed the right thing for him to do for king and country before 4th July, at a time when his future held out little promise of fulfilment, suddenly appeared very wrong, but the stark truth was that he no longer had any say in the matter. Withdrawal from the RAF at this stage would be branded an act of despicable cowardice, an act that would bring down such shame on his head that even Shirley would not allow herself to contemplate it.

She remembered all too well how she and the rest of the country had witnessed the abdication of Edward VIII and had shared the national horror at his dereliction of duty. She loved Alan too much to consider taking away his self-respect and made up her mind, albeit with a leaden heart, to accept what could not be altered and to support her beloved throughout all the challenges facing him, even though that would be extremely hard, much harder than coping with infantile paralysis and its consequences, much harder than keeping the home going for her father and brother, much harder than trying to reconcile herself to her mother's departure, much harder than anything she had ever had to do, because this situation demanded a superhuman strength of mind, character and endurance, even, perhaps, of faith. There was no option other than to believe that he would survive the war and would return alive. Turning her back on the black cloud, she resisted the tendency to weep, and in her imagination gazed wistfully only over the fields where the sun, though fitful, still shone.

Aida on the Saturday at Sadler's Wells was as magnificent as Alan had predicted, yet for Shirley the fate of the lovers was immeasurably tragic. He queued for a packet of sandwiches in the interval and waited for her after the performance, just as he had for the past two nights, and although the pleasure at seeing each other and the longing to be with each other were still poignantly apparent in the looks they exchanged, there was none of the elation and excitement of those earlier occasions. "Is everything all right, Shirley dear?" Gladys, who had been watching them in the interval, asked with measured concern.

Shirley replied impassively, "It's this war: he'll have to go away soon."

"Ah, yes," Gladys responded sadly, "that's hard; there are lots of other young couples in the same situation." Then she walked off. Tom too sensed that all was not well when they met by the car outside his door.

"You two look as if you need cheering up," he observed, quite accurately. "Why don't you go dancing?"

"Shall we go dancing tonight?" Alan asked, taking his cue from Tom. "I don't mean to the Dorchester," he hurriedly specified, "but just to a local dance hall where no one will know us." She agreed readily; she did not want to have to share him with anyone, let alone with his Oxford friends and those spiteful girls, although she might well have enjoyed dancing cheek to cheek with him in full view of all her rivals.

They danced far into the night, holding each other tight and kissing fervently. She was already familiar with the feel of his hand in hers, and the feel of his arm under his jacket was as reassuringly muscular as it had been that first night. He danced expertly, holding her close and leading her with a firm hand against her spine. There, in among the throng of dancers, they were alone and anonymous. Often they closed their eyes, willing the dance to last for eternity.

As the band played the last waltz, he whispered in her ear, "I love you and I can't live without you, Shirley."

"There's no one else and there will never be anyone else in my life; I can't live without you either because I love you so much," she answered quickly. They walked arm in arm from the dance hall to the car. He unlocked it and then put his arm round her shoulder.

"When this war is over, will you marry me?" he asked.

She did not hesitate for a second. "Yes, yes! Most certainly I will!"

He laughed. "Well, now I know that I shall have to come back, because I have so much to look forward to!" The tears rolled down his cheeks in defiance of his stoical patriotism and his courageous commitment to the war effort.

She reached up, pulled his head down to her level and wiped his eyes and face, which she then covered with kisses. "You had better come back. I shall never forgive you if you don't," she said jokingly, but no sooner were the words out of her mouth than she regretted saying them. "No, no, that's not what I mean," she added clumsily. "I mean…" But words failed her, because she really did not know what she meant to say, except that now that she had found him life was unthinkable without him.

Aware of how brave she was trying to be, he changed the subject. "What would you like to do tomorrow? I would love to take you to meet my parents, but my sister is getting married in two weeks' time so at present the vicarage is in chaos and my mother is running round like a mad thing, trying to find enough rations for the reception. So this is definitely not the best time for you to meet them. But soon, when that wedding is over and I have time off, I shall introduce you to them. I know they will love you and then there'll be another wedding, ours!"

She smiled, hoping that his confidence was not misplaced. "Anyhow," he went on, "I've met your father and your brother, so it's time you met my parents." He paused for a second or two. "Oh, by the way," he went on, "I'm sorry not to have met your mother. Is she away? I hope she's not in France."

Until that moment Shirley had studiously avoided any reference to her mother, and it came as a shock to have the matter of her absence brought up so unexpectedly. "No, she's not in France. She worked for the French Embassy in London and has been transferred to Washington," she replied bluntly and as dispassionately as she could manage. For a split second she wished that she could say that her mother was dead. All of a sudden the words came tumbling out: "She has left us!" she exclaimed, leaving Alan speechless. This revelation had taken him by surprise, leaving him in confusion.

"Oh, I am so sorry," he mumbled, and fell silent. Then he put his arm round her and drew her to him in an all-enveloping embrace. "That is very sad news. Your poor father! How brave he is!"

"I don't really think I should be talking about my own family at this moment," he went on, "but what I was about to say was that next time I have leave I shall have to attend my sister's wedding, but after that I will take you to the vicarage and you can meet my parents. Then maybe we could drive over to Shropshire. Granny died two years ago and Grandfather died last year, but the house hasn't been sold yet, and I would love you to see it. I think you would like it."

"Oh how nice!" Shirley exclaimed at this welcome distraction from the subject of her mother's absence from her life. Her pleasure at Alan's suggestion was nevertheless tempered with sadness that she did not have anything comparable to offer him, certainly not a visit to France at the present time. A visit to Aunt Winnie and Uncle Horace was not on the cards, not even in passing on the way to Shropshire, especially now that Granny Marlow was in residence and by all accounts was driving her daughter and son-in-law, and anyone else who crossed her path, crazy.

"Anyhow, what about tomorrow?" Alan asked, interrupting her thoughts.

"I'd love to go out into the country again, perhaps further if we can set out early and it doesn't rain too much," she answered eagerly. "I'll try to conjure up a picnic, shall I?"

"No," he said firmly, "it's my turn tomorrow."

"Oh, but you are paying for the petrol and using your rations!" she protested. "That's nothing," he insisted, "so let's not argue about it. Anyhow, I'll let you into a secret: I've inherited some money from my grandfather, which is how I can afford to come to Sadler's Wells every night and take you out, even buying us lunch in a nice hotel if that would suit you?"

"At least let me bring a flask of tea," she demanded.

Reggie was down in the shop instructing the paper boys when Alan arrived on the Sunday morning. "I expect they're both asleep," he said as he directed the visitor up the stairs. Ted, who had been out on ARP duties the previous night, was still in a deep sleep and Shirley was only just waking up when she heard the voice calling her gently from the staircase. She jumped out of bed, pulled on her dressing gown and went down to the landing.

"Oh, my darling! You are early!" she exclaimed, throwing herself into his arms and nearly knocking him down the staircase.

"It's a lovely day, so I thought we should make the most of it," he explained, "and maybe, if you like," here he paused nervously, "we could stay a night in a hotel – in single rooms, of course? I'd have to bring you home very early tomorrow morning to be sure of getting to the base on time, but what do you think?"

"You had better go and ask Pa what he thinks, not what I think!" she replied mischievously. He ran down the stairs and into the shop, where there was only a handful of customers, while she grabbed some clothes and disappeared into the bathroom. He came upstairs again a couple of minutes later.

"Your father wants to talk to you," he said, standing outside the closed bathroom door.

"What does he want?" she called out.

"I don't know – you'll have to ask him," Alan said.

The shop was empty both of customers and paper boys when Shirley went down to talk to her father. "Shirl, I wanted to have a word with you," he began awkwardly.

"Yes, Pa, what is it?" she asked.

"I don't know how to say this to you. Really your mother should be here – it's her job and she could do it better than me, but as she's not," – there was a touch of bitterness in his tone when he referred to his absent wife – "there are a few things I should like to say to you before you go out." Shirley waited for him to explain. "This may sound very unconventional," he said, "but I am very pleased that you and Alan have found one another. You seem so right for each other. You could make each other so happy. Well, it seems to me that you do that already." He stopped for breath in the middle of his long, serious speech. "Alan told me that he has trained to be a fighter pilot; you do know that, don't you?"

Shirley nodded. "Yes, Pa, and I don't like to think about it," she responded with a heartfelt sigh.

"I understand," he said, "because it is a very dangerous occupation and it may be that he will have to go into battle very soon. So the point of what I am trying to say is this: you have my blessing to go away together tonight, and if you want to share a room, that's not a problem as far as I am concerned. I have seen too many lives destroyed by war in the course of my life to allow other people to dictate the moral standards that we should live by." Hurriedly picking up a pile of newspapers, he went over to the shelves and began to arrange them. Shirley followed him and put her arms around his neck.

"Thank you, Pa," she whispered.

They drove out to the grassland where they had picnicked the previous day. Shirley said little during the drive. "You're very thoughtful, my love; what's on your mind?" Alan enquired.

"It's just that I would rather go somewhere further away from Biggin Hill, please," she answered, giving voice to another perfectly valid reason for her reserve.

"Yes, of course, I understand. I should have thought of that earlier," he said apologetically, "although I have to say I'm not stationed at Biggin Hill, but let's not go into that now. Let's go into Kent and see what we can find there." He drove on until they came to a small town nestling in the foothills of the North Downs. "Do you like the look of this?" he asked. "Maybe we should stop for lunch and look for somewhere to stay before we head off into the Downs."

"No, let's go on for a bit; it's still early, it's not raining, and I've brought a flask of coffee and a flask of tea, so we can stop for elevenses and for tea," she said.

They followed a road that climbed up onto the Downs and eventually petered out. He parked the car on the grass and got out. "How about this for a coffee stop?" he asked, stretching out his arms and breathing in the fresh air. Although the ground was damp underfoot, he spread out the rug in the shelter of a low hedge. There was no sign of habitation for miles, only the peaceful green landscape blending into distant purple, with sheep grazing for miles all around them.

"Who would have thought there is a war on?" she mused, leaning on his shoulder. He lay down and she lay beside him. They drew closer together and kissed. "What about the coffee?" she said, jumping up.

"Oh, that can wait a minute or two, can't it?" he said. "The thermos will keep it hot." He pulled her towards him. Their eyes met and closed and their lips touched under the blue sky, caressed by the sun, obscured by only the occasional fluffy white cloud.

Wrapped in the cocoon of ecstasy, all thoughts of war forgotten, they failed to notice when the sky clouded over; droplets suspended in a fine mist wafting high over the Downs settled on their skin and cooled the air around them. Shirley shivered and opened her eyes. "Look! The sun has gone and it's raining over there!" she exclaimed, pointing to a misty haze approaching them from the valley beneath. Slowly they sat up and began to collect their belongings. Scarcely knowing where she was or what she was doing, she moved in a daze, overwhelmed by the wonder of the physical reality of their love. Alan appeared to be in a similar state. He poured another cup of coffee from the flask for each of them, and then sat beside her in the car out of the rain, which was streaming down the windscreen.

"Shirley, my darling," he said quietly after a long silence, during which they nestled up against each other, "I take you for my wedded wife, to have and to hold, for richer, for poorer, in sickness and in health, from this day forward, for evermore, until death do us part." Tears welled up in her eyes. Less familiar than a vicar's son with the words of the marriage service, she stumbled in her attempt to repeat them correctly, though there was no doubting the sincerity and the fervour of her intention. "Shall I ask my father to marry us in a simple ceremony in his church as soon as these exercises are over? Would that suit you, my darling?"

"I would like that more than anything," she replied.

"I'm sorry that I don't have an engagement ring to give you," he said. "There hasn't been time since last Thursday to go out and buy one."

"It doesn't matter," she reassured him. "You are more important to me than a ring."

They found a hotel, where they had lunch, without noticing what they were eating, and booked in as a married couple for a one-night stay. As it was still raining hard, they repaired to their room after lunch and stayed there for the rest of the afternoon, emerging only to come down for dinner, after which the skies cleared and Alan suggested taking a walk through the village. In the course of their leisurely stroll, arm in arm like an old married couple, they stopped to admire the profusion of summer blooms in the gardens, where yellow and red roses tumbled over pergolas and tall, deep-blue delphiniums stood sentinel over the smaller border plants and flowers. "I would love to live somewhere like this!" Shirley cried, marvelling at such rural perfection. "It's so pretty and peaceful!"

"If you like it, then so do I," said Alan, squeezing her arm. "Let's keep an eye open for 'For Sale' signs and buy somewhere in this area. It should be quite possible. I suppose I shall have to find a job though; maybe the Foreign Office is not such a good idea if we're going to settle down here. I'll apply to take the civil-service exams anyhow and see what comes up." He stopped to consider the possibilities. "But of course," he added, "if you want to dance, you won't want to live out here, miles away from central London, will you?"

"Dance?" she said. "I won't want to dance if I'm married to you! I shall want to be here with our children or maybe away in foreign parts with you!" They both laughed and kissed and ambled back to the hotel.

They woke in each other's arms much later than they had intended the next morning. "Goodness!" Alan exclaimed when he looked at his watch. He jumped out of bed, saying, "I shall be late at the base! I'm sorry about this, but we must leave in about ten minutes if I'm going to take you home and be there in time for manoeuvres."

Shirley frowned at the intrusion of warfare into their idyll, but understood his urgency. "You don't have to take me home!" she said, trying to be helpful. "I can catch a train. I saw a sign to the station last night when we were out on our walk; if you drop me there, I'm sure there'll be trains to London. That will give us much more time."

"Are you sure?" he asked. "I don't like to leave you like that."

"Don't worry," Shirley said. "Come on, get back into bed for a bit longer." He succumbed to her wheedling and took advantage of another half-hour in bed with her.

All too soon he was dropping her off at the station. "I'll try to phone you as soon as I can," he promised, "though how I shall survive without seeing you I don't know."

"It will be the same for me," she said, suppressing the knot in her throat, "but so long as you take care of yourself and I can expect to see you when you have leave, then there will be something to look forward to." They hugged and kissed until the train arrived. She climbed into a compartment and lowered the window. The guard was blowing his whistle, but she hung on to Alan's hand until she had to let go; then she leant out of the window blowing tearful kisses. He ran along the platform trying to keep pace, waving and calling out to her until the train speeded up and he lost the battle.

She sat gazing out of the window with empty eyes, as though she had walked right through a paradise garden and had come out on the other side into the same old world where little had changed and full-scale war was an ever-present anxiety. Alan existed in the dream world that she had left behind. She had nothing tangible to cling to, only memories of their idyllic time together during the past four days, especially the past twenty-four hours, which had established their relationship on a profoundly intimate and committed footing. She leant against the rough upholstery and closed her eyes, attempting to recall every detail of those past four days and consign them all to memory, so that she would never forget them. She promised herself that, although they had parted, that parting was only going to be temporary.

What a blessing that job as usherette at Sadler's Wells had been! The coincidence of their meeting had been a long time in coming, but perhaps that was for the best. If they had met while he was a student in Oxford and she was recovering from infantile paralysis, the outcome might have been less auspicious: he would have been too preoccupied with his studies, and also perhaps with the demands of his friends, while she, with her limp, would have felt clumsy, inferior and out of place. This had been in fact the perfect time to meet. How miraculously lucky it was that he had felt the same way about her as she had about him ever since that fleeting encounter on the ferry, and that while she had been searching for him, he had searched for her everywhere.

He had said that life for him was incomplete without her, just as she could not live without him, and they were both old enough and mature enough to be able to fulfil all their longings and realize those cherished dreams that each had harboured for so long. There remained, of course, the question of the war, but Alan was cautiously sure that it would be over in a few months, not that he gave any compelling reason for his conviction, but because he had a much firmer grasp of what was happening than she did; she believed him. In London, she floated along the smoke-filled platform, through the grimy passages of the Underground and finally up the steps out into the familiar street only a short walk from home. In that short walk she became prey to an intrusive, disturbing reflection: if only he hadn't joined up as a fighter pilot!

Pa, Cousin Archie and Tilly were all in the shop. She could hear them talking as she pushed the door open. Without calling out a greeting, she went straight up the stairs to the flat. Alan was the last person she had spoken to, his was the last voice that she had heard and she wanted to hang on to that precious exchange as long as she could. She certainly did not want to become involved in the idle chatter that accompanied a morning's work in the shop. Soon after her return, however, her father came upstairs for his mid-morning drink, which meant that she had to break her resolve. "Pa," she said, "I'm so grateful to you for those few words of advice you gave me before we left. Thank you, very much."

He was embarrassed by the mention of his moment of emotional expansion, and said gruffly, "Your Alan is a very special young man; I should be very happy to see you married to him, Shirl."

"We are going to be married, Pa!" she announced quietly. "As soon as it can be arranged. He proposed to me while we were away, but of course he hadn't had time to buy a ring. He's wonderful, and I'm so glad you like him!"

"Yes, yes, very good, very good!" her pa responded in his absent-mindedly restrained fashion.

55

Although he certainly was concerned for his daughter's well-being and happiness, it was obvious that Pa was preoccupied with other things: it was not long before Shirley discovered the essence of them. Ted, who had been working for General de Gaulle since June, was becoming restive. His office job did not suit him, even though he was working in French with the French. "There are so many different departments and factions, and none of them can agree," he grumbled one Monday evening over supper. Shirley was at home, since the theatre was closed on Mondays, and in any case she felt very reluctant to work there any more because there would be no chance of seeing Alan. "I'm fed up with sorting out the post, being a messenger boy and making the coffee, and I honestly don't want to sit in an office listening to a list of complaints from people who should know better and who ought to be working together to free France. Anyhow," Ted went on, "it's top secret, but I gather that some chaps are going to be airlifted into France to help whip up some support. I wish I could go too."

Pa's face dropped. Shirley racked her brains for something helpful to say, although she could not concentrate on anything other than Alan, always wondering where he was and what he was doing. "I'm sure your turn will come," she said at last, as soothingly as she could, "but it's early days yet and there are probably lots of arrangements to make. I expect that half the people who have come over here don't know each other and will have to learn to work together before they can do anything positive."

"That's true," Ted replied. "There are people from all sorts of different branches of the military all squeezed into three rooms in St Stephen's House; they all seem to think that they know best. It'll be better when we move to Carlton Gardens and have proper offices."

"Be patient," his father advised him. "I doubt that many of them are as bilingual as you are; you may be sure you'll be needed for more than making the coffee."

"Perhaps you're right," Ted conceded, "but I do quite a lot of the interpreting for them already. The problem is that Hélène says she's heard that the situation is desperate in the north; whole villages are being razed to the ground, she says. They are trying to get some resistance going, but it's only piecemeal; they need someone to come in and take charge."

"But aren't you involved in the 14th July parade past the Cenotaph? I gather General de Gaulle is leading it?" Pa enquired, tactfully veering the talk away from contentious issues.

"Well, that *is* quite exciting," Ted conceded. "I'm working on the arrangements for it in the office. It's one of my jobs at the moment. There are lots of soldiers, sailors and airmen who have come over to join the Volunteer Legion. You could come and watch if you like. I might be in it, dressed up as a soldier. It will end up at the statue of Marshal Foch in Grosvenor Gardens. The General is going to lay a wreath there." He looked from his father to his sister to see if there was any interest.

"I'll come," his father said. "What about you, Shirl?"

"Yes, I'll be there too," she promised, if only to keep Ted happy, although she desperately hoped that since 14th July would be a Sunday, she might be going out with Alan.

Reggie yawned. "I am a little weary. I was wondering if either of you would be kind enough to do my ARP rounds tonight?" he asked.

"All right," Ted answered rather reluctantly, but cheered up when Shirley volunteered to accompany him.

"I don't have to work this evening and Pa has done so many of my rounds for me; I'd be happy to come with you," she said.

"That's nice of you, Shirl. I'd be glad of the company," he replied.

"We can have a chat while we walk," she said. "It seems like ages since we landed on the south coast, and we haven't talked much since then."

They set out together as darkness fell and at first their conversation consisted of speculation about the war: how long it would last, whether Pépé and Céline – whom not surprisingly they had not heard from – were all right and other such matters. As night enveloped them, Shirley grew bolder. "There's something I want to say, Ted, which is I'm sorry I haven't been more sympathetic to your worries about Hélène," she said, thankful for the cover of night, as the blood rose to her cheeks and her face became uncomfortably hot.

"There's nothing to apologize for," he replied calmly. "Anyhow, you were quite right. She's fine in Switzerland, and although we miss each other we can write. It's not as if she were in Trémaincourt, because then we wouldn't have any contact at all." Ted's nonchalance caught Shirley unawares, making it awkward for her to pursue her train of thought.

"Quite, quite," she said, wondering how to reintroduce her topic. Eventually, having reordered her thoughts, she began again, "All I wanted to say was that I do understand how you feel about Hélène, because, well, I'm in a similar situation."

A long silence ensued. "Um, do you mean that you have fallen for a Frenchman and he's in France?" Ted asked in evident confusion. "I thought that chap who sat all night in his car, that yellow Jaguar, out on the pavement was your boyfriend."

Now Shirley had her chance to explain. "Yes, he is and that's what I mean," she said. "Alan is my boyfriend, or rather, my fiancé!"

Ted whistled between his teeth. "I say, that's quick, isn't it? Does Pa know this?"

His sister was beginning to wish that she had never broached the subject. "Yes, he does, and all I wanted to say," she asserted in some irritation, "was that I understand how you feel about Hélène because I feel the same about Alan."

"Ah, I see," Ted replied, lingering on the *see*. "Well, good. He's a nice chap. What does he do?"

At last Shirley was given the opening she was hoping for and began to talk about Alan. "He's in the RAF and flies a Spitfire," she began tentatively, trusting that that much information would satisfy Ted, but his next question floored her:

"Where is he based?" he enquired.

"I don't exactly know – somewhere not far from Biggin Hill, I think," she replied, abashed at her own ignorance.

"Could it be Hornchurch? That's where Group Eleven fly from. Is he in that group?" he persevered.

"Yes, I think so – maybe, I don't know. We don't talk about the war much," Shirley mumbled. This conversation was proving much more painful than she had anticipated, because it brought to the fore an aspect of her relationship with Alan – his role in the war effort – which she and he had tacitly agreed to try not to talk about. After confessing that he had signed up for the RAF because he despaired of ever finding her again, Alan had been unwilling to go into too much detail, and she had thought better of pressing him. In any case, they had far better things to do and to talk about. "I think, if you don't mind, I'll go home now. My leg is aching," she said, keen to quell her rising anxiety.

"That's fine. I'll carry on until daylight," Ted answered.

It was unfortunate that Bert should cross Shirley's path on her way home. He loomed silently out of the darkness before she realized that there was anyone other than herself and Ted out in the streets that night. "Oh, it's little Shirley, is it?" he gloated menacingly, shining his tiny torch in her eyes. "What would you be doing out here without your father or your brother for protection? I've come along just at the right moment, haven't I? You need me to look after you, don't you, dearie?" She ducked as he reached out to put his arm round her, and aimed a high kick in his direction. As his glasses fell clattering onto the pavement, she started to run, certain that his lumbering form would never be able to catch up with her. Indeed, he would not have stood a chance, had it not been for an uneven paving stone that tripped her up, flinging her headlong onto the ground. In no time, Bert was upon her. "Thought you'd get away, my pretty one, did you? We'll see about that," he said, tearing at her clothing. She screamed and fought as he tried to put his hand over her mouth.

Then all of a sudden a torch shone over Bert's head, and she could see that he was being yanked away from her by an unseen hand. One minute he had been grabbing her, the next he had vanished and she was free. Trembling and breathing a sigh of relief, she sat up, adjusted her helmet, which in the fall and the tussle had gone askew, and straightened her uniform, from which only one button was missing. Somewhere very close by she heard a thud and sounds of a scuffle. Judging by the yelps and groans, Bert was receiving a good drubbing at the hands of his assailant, her unknown, invisible saviour. Finally he let out a long yell, at which windows opened and various indignant voices called out, "Stop that noise. It's one o'clock!" In spite of her distress, a flicker of a smile came to her lips.

Footsteps approached. Expecting that they were Ted's, because he might well have heard her screams and come to her rescue, she stood up and exclaimed, "Oh, Ted, well done! That was a nasty surprise! I'm quite shaken." Then she heard that slight laugh that she knew was not Ted's and which made her heart leap. "Alan! No, it can't be you, can it?" she called.

"My darling!" he replied. "Are you all right?" He ran to her, picked her up, held her tight and covered her with kisses. "If I ever see that rogue anywhere near you again, he'll end up in a worse place than a rose bush!"

"How did you know where to find me?" she asked. He explained that her father had told him her whereabouts when he called at the flat.

"Your poor father was getting ready for bed. I'm sorry it's so late," he said, "but I've only just been able to get away from the base. We've had manoeuvres all day and I can't stay long." She did not ask what those manoeuvres were. "The car is on the pavement outside your shop," he said. "Would you like to go for a drive?"

"In my ARP uniform?" she queried.

"Yes, why not?" he said. "You can take your helmet off and nobody's going to see you. It's not as if we're going dancing. I thought perhaps a little drive into the country, if you like. I have the rug in the back of the car. We can sleep under the stars. It's a warm night."

She agreed, trying to cast all thoughts of the ghastly Bert aside, though she was still aware of the loathsome smell of his sweat on her clothing. She dashed upstairs while Alan unlocked the car, had a quick wash and changed out of her uniform.

The night under the stars was romantic and passionate, though much too short, and at five in the morning, when they arrived back outside the front door, Shirley was fighting a losing battle to keep her eyes open. As she swung her legs out of the car, concern that he had not had much sleep jolted her out of her stupor, prompting her to ask, "What will you do now? Where are you going?"

Instead of replying, he pulled her back into the passenger seat. "Just a moment, my darling; I have been meaning to tell you that I had hoped to buy a ring for you, but I haven't had a chance. I'm so sorry and I don't know when I shall be able to get away again, not this week anyway. Kiss me once more, please!" There was a pleading urgency in his request. They kissed.

"Don't bother about the ring," she said when at last parting had become unavoidable. "Take great care of yourself: you are so much more important to me than any ring."

"Don't worry about me," he replied. "I shall be fine. You take care. Keep out of that lout's way. Don't forget your helmet!" He reached into the back of the car and handed it to her, saying, "I'll see you just as soon as I can!" She leant into the car and kissed him again; then she ran to the door without looking back for fear of bursting into undignified tears.

She did linger on the doorstep, but by then the engine was in gear and he had his foot on the accelerator. She was not sure that he had seen her nervous wave as he sped away.

As he had anticipated, Alan was not able to escape from his duties at all the next week. For Shirley time stood still. She went about her usual business like an automaton: she helped in the shop, took her classes at the dance school and went back to work at the Wells, but her mind was constantly elsewhere as the hours dragged by. In the shop, although her father tried to conceal the headlines from her, she was distracted by the reports of dogfights over the Channel, where the *Luftwaffe* were bombing shipping convoys and the RAF were flying out to counter-attack and send the marauders back to France.

Cousin Archie, of course, dwelt on every item of news, despite Reggie's attempts to stop him. "This looks bad," Archie said, shaking his head, having read the headlines out loud, "they're trying to put a stop to our shipping and draw the RAF out at one and the same time. Once they've demolished our supply lines and our fighters, they'll have free access to our ports and our beaches." Reggie tried to ignore his cousin's remarks, but Archie persevered. "I always said we should have sent our planes to bomb them out of existence as soon as they crossed into France."

"Maybe. I said that too, but we don't know all the reasons," Reggie countered, trying to put a stop to Archie's speculation, for although he did not admit as much to his daughter, he too was very anxious on Alan's account. He had been most impressed with him on first meeting and not only considered him a very suitable match for Shirley but also a delightful prospective son-in-law. There was no doubt that the two of them were passionate about each other, just as he and Jacqueline had been so long ago. He fervently hoped that no evil forces would interfere with their love for each other. Above all, he hoped that this war, the second – even the third, if one counted the Second Boer War – in his lifetime, would not leave Alan scarred, as he himself had been after the Great War, and forced to live with the strain that it subsequently wrought on his marriage.

At the ballet school, a listless lethargy immobilized Shirley's limbs and brain, so that her classes, the last before the school closed for the summer holidays, became little more than a mechanical repetition of practice exercises with few innovative ideas for dances. The ballet, which until last week had been her great passion, had to yield pride of place to a yet more powerful emotion, that of her boundless love for her future husband. The irony that this was in fact the stuff of most ballets was not lost on Shirley, who found that even *Swan Lake*, however much she listened to her records of it, was not adequate to express her feelings for Alan. Madame Belinskaya watched her anxiously, but wisely refrained from making any comment. She knew her protégée well enough to realize that she was suffering from the terrible coincidental combination of war and a major affair of the heart. Indeed, as she would eventually confess, she too had suffered similarly in the Great War and the outcome had been disastrous. Hers was not a tale that she thought appropriate for Shirley in her present circumstances.

At the Wells, Shirley had no interest in any of the performances, despite her best efforts to concentrate. Each evening in the first half she would hope against hope that Alan would appear in her queue in the interval, ostensibly to buy a bag of sandwiches, and in the second she waited impatiently both for the performance to finish, scarcely noticing what was happening on the stage, and for the moment to arrive for her to dash home to sit by the telephone in the expectation of a call. Nonetheless, she still went to visit Tom every afternoon, because he had witnessed the lightning development of the relationship from its birth, only the previous Thursday, and she knew that he would be quick to notice not only Alan's absence but also her state of mind. It seemed that last Thursday was a whole lifetime ago, a lifetime in which she had passed through almost every known emotion, from surprise and elation, through sorrow and humiliation to the peaks of joy and ecstasy. She did not believe that anyone else could understand her feelings, so although she desperately needed to be able to confide in someone, her lips were sealed. What had happened to her in the past week was very intense and very private; the only person with whom she ever wanted to share it was Alan. To talk about it to anyone else would be tantamount to diluting it, diminishing it, even tainting it. Tom, however, was different, because with him no explanations were required: he already knew or could guess everything. He was careful not to make sympathetic noises, but talked in his usual style over their tea and ventured a joke or two about the Jaguar. "Must drink the petrol, that car, I'd say," he observed. Then with a wink remarked, "Not much room in there for a cuddle, is there?"

Going home on the Underground was the most dismal experience after those jaunts in the Jaguar. It was so lonely, sitting there avoiding the eyes of the other passengers. The only two consolations were that, firstly, it was anonymous: she was not required to chat with anyone; and, secondly, her spirits began to rise in anticipation of that phone call, even though she often sat by the phone waiting for it from the second she returned from the Wells until late into the night. Although she seated herself right by the phone, it always caught her off guard and made her jump when its shrill tones sounded in her ear. Shivers would run down her spine as her whole body quaked, quivering in nervous excitement. She was annoyed at having to waste precious time pulling herself together before picking up the receiver.

As the week wore on, Alan's voice at the other end increasingly betrayed his exhaustion, although he told her very little about what he had been doing, but insisted on asking how she was, what she had been doing and so on. There was not much to tell, because her routine followed its usual course, which in the telling sounded more and more boring. When he asked about the performances at the Wells she was at a loss because she had paid them so little attention. On one occasion she summoned the courage to ask him how the manoeuvres were progressing. "Oh, fine, fine," was all he said. It seemed that, instead of bringing them closer, the phone line was beginning to accentuate the distance between them. He did not give her the information she wanted, probably, she suspected, because he was trying to protect her, and she tried hard to sound positive, cheerful and confident to encourage him; sometimes, though, a sob crept into her voice and the words "I miss you so much!" would creep out. A pause would follow, and then he would say, "Wait until the end of the week! I might be able to wangle a day off!"

The Saturday performance at Sadler's Wells came and went with no sign of him in the auditorium or in the queue for sandwiches. Like Madame Belinskaya, Gladys kept a watchful eye on her without actually saying anything pertinent, except "You can go early this evening if you like, Shirley; I have plenty of helpers tonight". Rather than leave by the main doors of the theatre, Shirley left by the stage door, convinced that she would find the yellow Jaguar waiting for her, but it was not there. Her heart missed a beat and she felt all the more foolish because she had allowed herself to confide in Tom at teatime that Alan would probably be coming to the performance that evening. Tom perceived at once how downcast she was and put his arm round her. "Don't you worry, young lady, I expect he was held up. Nobody knows where they are these days," he said. "I am sure he'll turn up tomorrow and then you can have a day out."

"I hope you're right, Tom," she said, and, with drooping shoulders, turned left to walk up the road to the Tube station.

The phone call came through very late that evening. "I'm so sorry. I just couldn't leave the base," he said, sounding as if every drop of energy had been drained out of him. "I had wanted to come to tonight's performance and surprise you. Failing that, I would have waited for you at the stage door, but I'm afraid it was impossible."

"That's all right," she replied, falsely cheerful. Then she told him about Tom and tried to repeat some of his jokes, but they fell rather flat. The call was not a long one.

"I hope I might be able to escape tomorrow evening. How would that suit you?" he said. "We could go into town for dinner and maybe stay a night in a hotel, if you'd like that?"

"I can't wait!" she answered in huge relief.

"Right, tomorrow evening it is. I'll come for you as soon as I can, so be ready!" They blew kisses down the phone line, both heartened to think that the week's ordeal was nearly at an end.

That Sunday morning Shirley rose early enough to reverse the roles and take her father a cup of tea. He was amazed at the change in her mood. "You're bright and cheerful today, Shirl," he remarked.

She smiled. "Yes, I'm fine, Pa. Alan thinks he might be able to have time off this evening!" she said.

"Good, good," her pa replied, "don't forget that it's the 14th July today and we have to go into Whitehall to watch Ted on parade.

"Oh, I had completely forgotten!" she exclaimed. "I'll take him some tea and cook breakfast for him. There must be something in the larder." She bustled about in the kitchen, rustling up a square meal out of minimal rations for her brother. He came in dressed as a French soldier, clearly very proud of his uniform.

"At last, I feel as if I'm involved," he declared, and I can hold my head high. Nobody can accuse me of shirking." He left home briskly as soon as he had finished his breakfast.

Shirley and her father set out at a more leisurely pace to join the crowds of French expatriates assembling on a warm, sunny day in Whitehall. The atmosphere of excitement and optimism was infectious: at last, under the leadership of the General, France was once again going to be a power to be reckoned with in the fight against Nazi Germany. Already before the procession began there was a hubbub among the crowd: "We're going back into battle!", "The battle of France is not over!", "We'll show the Boche what we think of them!", "My son's in the Volunteer Legion. He signed up as soon as we arrived!", "I have nightmares every night about our escape, it was so scary!" and "I've never been so terrified in my life: those Stukas fired on anyone and anything!" were the snatches of conversation that Shirley heard and joined in. Her father listened, making the occasional comment and nodding, and then became involved in a discussion with an old soldier about the misuse of tanks in the Great War.

A wave of sound – cheers, shouts of "*Vive la France!*" and "*Vive le Général!*" and beating drums – came flooding down Whitehall, engulfing the crowd in its exuberance. Defeat, invasion and repression were all forgotten in that one glorious moment when the towering, unmistakable form of General de Gaulle appeared at the head of the march. His figure, tall and commanding, was as distinctive as Mr Churchill's, although in an entirely different manner. De Gaulle certainly had the appearance and the bearing of an inspiring leader of men. His presence made Shirley proud of her French ancestry. The Marlows, father and daughter, joined in the cheering and scanned the columns of marching soldiers, airmen and sailors for a glimpse of Ted. "*Le voilà! Le voilà!*" Shirley shouted to her father, pointing out the young soldier in battle fatigues in the middle of the procession that he had helped to organize.

The mass of exhilarated French men, women and children fell into line behind the march-past and followed the troops to Grosvenor Gardens, where the General laid a wreath at the foot of the statue commemorating Marshal Foch. The crowds dispersed to seek refreshment in true French style, some spreading out their glasses and bottles on the grass while others went in an often fruitless search for food and drink elsewhere, which doubtless brought them back to earth with the reminder that they were in London on a Sunday and not in Paris.

On the way home, Shirley asked, "Who was Marshal Foch, Pa?"

"He was the greatest French general of the Great War," Reggie replied, stroking his chin thoughtfully. "He negotiated the armistice in 1918 and he was honoured here as well as in France. And as well as being a great and brave soldier, he had extraordinary foresight. After the Treaty of Versailles, which allowed Germany to remain intact as one nation, he said, 'This is not a peace. It's an armistice for twenty years.' How right he was!" This accurate if disturbing prediction of the present reality plunged Shirley into thought. She was appalled that her generation was paying the price because no one had respected the opinion of that honourable old man at whose statue they had just assembled. That thought threw her back into the slough of despond from which she had so briefly escaped.

At home she smartened herself up, ready to go out again as soon as Alan phoned or, even better, when he arrived at the door. She made tea for herself and her father and then cooked him some supper. She did not eat with him, because she was certain that Alan would suggest going to one of those little hotels in the country. She sat waiting while her father ate, then retired to her room where she idly flicked through her records and put one on the turntable. In the background she could hear that her pa was listening to the six-o'clock news. She closed the door to avoid hearing the reports. The music played, but she felt no urge to dance, although she had tied the laces of her ballet shoes round her ankles. The long wait was becoming more intolerable by the minute. She stretched languidly, but, as that was of no use, she stood up and, resting her arms on the window sill, gazed out of the window. Trains rumbled in both directions along the tracks, but there was little to see apart from the blank windows of houses on the other side of the line. She felt like those windows: utterly blank and unseeing. She went to join her father in the living room. He reached out to turn the radio off hastily when she came in, and remained sitting in his armchair with his eyes closed and a grim expression on his face, as if he had good reasons for not wishing to be disturbed. The phone was silent; there was no ring at the doorbell.

56

Those days and weeks following 14th July 1940 were a complete blank for Shirley, as blank as those unseeing window panes on the other side of the railway line. She dressed and attended to her personal care in a perfunctory manner; she breathed and she walked and occasionally she was persuaded to eat a minute amount of food, but whatever she was doing, she had no idea what it was. In fact, she had no awareness of anything at all. Her father's anguish at her state made no impression on her, nor did Ted's well-meaning attempts to rouse her with his mimicry of the General, his accounts of the goings-on in the Volunteer Legion, where former chiefs of staff jockeyed for position, or his jokes both in English and in French which usually would send her into fits of laughter. The bright summer sky and the warm sun left her cold. Her gramophone and her collection of records lay untouched. She did not try on her ballet shoes or her leotard and she seemed to have forgotten all about Sadler's Wells, Madame Belinskaya and the ballet school. She wept outwardly and mourned internally, crying without tears and wailing without sound. She never spoke. Only a few words circulated in her brain and, however much she might have wanted to say them aloud, shout them, scream them, her vocal chords could not produce them. Those words that repeated themselves endlessly, spiralling in her mind, were "Alan, Alan, Alan! My darling, my darling! Please come back to me!" Her existence had been sucked into a vacuum from which there was no exit.

When Cousin Archie reported back to Eileen how dire the situation was and how worrying it was for Reggie, she offered without hesitation to care for Shirley, for whom she had developed a grandmotherly interest and fondness. Eileen was unobtrusive and tactful. She well knew what Shirley was suffering and waited for the appropriate opening to confide her own grief. One afternoon towards the end of July, she sat down opposite Shirley, who had sunk into her father's old armchair. Taking out a handkerchief, Eileen wiped her eyes before speaking. "I have something to tell you, Shirley, dear," she said slowly and quietly.

Her words produced no reaction as her charge sat blankly, impassively, staring out of the window without speaking. Eileen waited a little longer. "You may not believe this; you may not want to believe it, but I have suffered in much the same way as you are suffering now." Again Shirley's pale, drawn face revealed no reaction, as if she had not heard a word. "I lost someone very dear to me," Eileen went on, then paused to see if her little speech was having any effect. Maybe she detected a slight movement of the girl's head.

"Archie and I had a son, our only son. His name was Lionel. He was about the same age as you are now, although at that time he and your father were the same age," she said. Shirley shifted in the chair. Trying hard to restrain her tears, Eileen stammered, "He went off to war, to the Great War. We took him to the station to board the train with the other troops." Shirley stared at her as she carried on. "We never knew where he was, and in those days news was slow in coming." It was impossible for her to contain her own emotions, and she broke into a sob. "We never saw him again. He died on the last day of the Battle of the Somme, 18th November 1916. We did not find out about it for a long time. They sent us a letter saying that he had fought bravely for his king and country and that he was missing, presumed dead." Shirley turned in the chair and sat up straight. She watched Eileen as she spoke. "I was just like you, dear. Life had no meaning for me. All I could do was to scream, 'Lionel, Lionel, Lionel!'" She paused. "It was very hard for Archie, because he was suffering too, but he had to be strong for me. That's why he still insists on working all the time; he needs something to occupy his mind." The old lady's handkerchief dropped to the floor as she let the tears fall. Shirley blinked. She stood up and limped over to Eileen's chair. Quivering, she put her arm around her elderly relative's shoulders and then went to put the kettle on in the kitchen.

These first tentative signs of recovery were soon to be obliterated when a week later a letter arrived; it was addressed to Shirley in an unknown hand. Her father brought it with him when he came upstairs at lunchtime. Eileen had done some shopping and was cooking the meal for all of them – that is, for Reggie, Shirley, Archie and herself; Shirley was helping her. "Here's a letter for you, Shirl," her pa announced light-heartedly. "Let's hope it contains some good news!" Shirley turned the communication over in her hand. It was more than a mere letter: it was a package.

She studied the handwriting, frowned, then went into her room and closed the door. The postmark was illegible. With a beating heart she opened the envelope; the blue writing paper inside bore a trace of lavender perfume. She unfolded the letter and let that single sheet of paper fall, because enclosed inside that was another envelope addressed in a hand that she did recognize. It was Alan's handwriting. She laughed in relief, reached down for her handbag, which was on the floor, and pulled out a couple of the many little love letters that he had written to her during their outings. He must have scribbled them in the car when she was not looking and slipped them into her handbag for her to find the next day. Each was hardly more than a short sentence, saying "I love you!" or "I can't wait to be with you again!" or "Stay with me always!", but those short sentences were sufficient for her to be able to recognize his clear, firm hand, and indeed those billets-doux were in the same script as that on this envelope, which was simply addressed to "Shirley". She opened it, took out the letter inside and began to read:

My beloved darling Shirley,
The past few days have been the most extraordinary and the most amazing of my life. To have met you again only on Thursday and to have found that you feel for me, and have felt for me, as I do for you – that is to say, with the greatest, deepest passion possible for a human being to experience has transformed my life in the most humbling, ecstatic and wonderful way. I love you and always will and the sooner we can become husband and wife, the happier I shall be – and I hope that you will too.

Before reading on, Shirley clutched the letter to her heart, closed her eyes and breathed in deeply. Perhaps she had been stupid to be cast down in such sorrow, such dejection and despair. Perhaps Alan was so busy that he had had to ask someone else to post the letter for him. Perhaps everything was going to be all right. Then she continued her perusal, tracing every flourish of the pen with her finger as she read:

My darling, I am writing this to you in a quiet moment, fully deter-mined and expecting that I shall return from this terrible conflict and that you and I will spend the rest of our lives together until we are very old and are surrounded by a large family of beautiful children and grandchildren. This is my great wish for us. But I am going to send this letter to my sister Elizabeth, so that, if for some reason I do not return, she will post it to you and you will know what has happened.

With dread her eyes followed the flowing script down the page:

If the worst should happen to me, my beloved Shirley, I insist that you do not waste the rest of your life thinking of me and dwelling on the past. Please make the most of your time on earth. You could have a splendid career dancing for the troops and you would be so good at it! I wish I could have seen you dancing. Ballet would help you to forget the past, and in performing it you would be making a real and important contribution to the war effort. Then, maybe when the war is over, you will meet someone good and kind and you and he will have a family and will live happily ever after. I wish that for you with all my heart.

Do not let the memory of me to ruin the rest of your life. You are too precious to me for that.

Cry a little for me, if you must, but then allow yourself to dream again.

And I do firmly believe that we shall meet again one day.

Your devoted, adoring

Alan

Shirley read the letter over and over again until she had soaked it with her tears. She was not inclined to read the covering letter from Elizabeth, because she could already anticipate what it was going to say. Instead she lay down with Alan's letter close to her skin and dreamt of him. She recalled every second, every minute and every hour that they had spent together since that day, Thursday, 4th July, when all those cherished dreams that she had harboured for well-nigh three years had come to fulfilment, an even greater fulfilment than dancing on the stage at the Wells. She dwelt on every hug, every kiss, every embrace, every dance, every conversation and every joke that he had told her, but glossed over the painful, unfortunate episode at the Dorchester. It was of course quite impossible, quite unthinkable for her ever to forget Alan, which meant that in this she could not obey him. Only when she had fully indulged and mentally documented all her memories did she reach for the covering letter. It was cold and formal by comparison, lacking the warmth and the passion of Alan's, and bore neither date nor address:

Dear Miss Marlow,

My brother Alan wrote to tell me that you are a friend of his.

I am therefore enclosing herewith the letter that he asked me to send to you in the event of his not returning from combat exercises.

It is with great sadness that I have to inform you that my brother was shot down over the Channel on Sunday 14th July when he was fighting enemy aircraft to protect a convoy of British ships.

We have been told that he is missing, presumed dead.

I apologize for not informing you sooner of this tragedy in our family. You will understand that this news has come as a terrible blow to us.

Yours sincerely,

Elizabeth Robinson

This letter jogged Shirley's brain into startling lucidity, waking it from its long stupor with a confusing mixture of questions and emotions as it transported her back to the 14th July, the day of the Free French parade, a day when she had been so happy in the sunshine in Whitehall, watching Ted marching past and joining in the celebrations. She had allowed herself to be excitedly happy at the time, because she believed that she could expect to see Alan that very evening. But when later he neither appeared nor telephoned, the nerve-racking intimation stole upon her that she would never see or hear from him again, especially when she noticed the grim expression on her father's face after he had listened to the BBC news on the wireless. She had not dared to ask why he looked so serious. At that instant, the state of torment in which without a doubt she would live for the rest of her life truly began. It was infinitely worse than having infantile paralysis. She would prefer it that way in any case because to lead a happy life would signify an unbelievably profound disloyalty to Alan and his memory. She hoped that the return to her senses was not equally a sign of disloyalty. It seemed that Elizabeth's letter had brought clarity to the situation, so that instead of worrying and wondering, she could mourn deeply and eternally.

She read the covering letter again. By comparison with Alan's letter, the one from his sister was so strange that she could not believe that the two missives had come in the same envelope from people in the same family. Alan's was alive and vibrant, conjuring up an overwhelming image of the glorious person who had written the letter, whereas his sister's might have been a bureaucratic composition penned by an official in the Ministry of War. Why could the said Elizabeth not have come the three or four miles across from the family vicarage in Camberwell to impart the heart-rending news in person? Why not give a date and an address, as everyone else did when writing a letter, so that at the very least she could have written to express her condolences to Alan's parents? Possibly they might have invited her to go over to Camberwell to the vicarage in person. By Alan's account they were good, kind people and would have welcomed her. If only he had had time to introduce her to them!

Then she recalled that his mother was preparing a wedding for the weekend after 14th July, and reasoned that Elizabeth, the bride, must have found herself in an appalling situation and had in all likelihood written her letter as speedily as possible, without being aware of the depth of her brother's commitment. Her surname, Robinson, which was not her maiden name, suggested that the wedding had gone ahead, probably, in the circumstances, on a much reduced scale. Shirley also sadly realized that her address in such a depressed corner of south London might have given Elizabeth the impression that this Miss Marlow was not of the sort of class to be an appropriate girlfriend, fiancée or wife for her cherished brother, with his Oxford education and the promise of a high-flying career. She might even have thought that Miss Marlow was up to no good. This much depressing speculation, combined with the actual effects of the waking nightmare, exhausted Shirley, causing her to fall into a fitful sleep, punctuated only by distant thunderclap explosions.

She was surprised to find Eileen sitting at the end of her bed when she woke up. "I hope you don't mind, dear, but I knew that something was wrong, so I tiptoed in when you were asleep," she said apologetically. "I want you to know that I am here whenever you need me. I don't have to tell you that I can cook and shop and sew, but if you need someone to talk to, I should be more than willing to listen."

Shirley stifled a sob. She pushed Elizabeth's letter towards her, saying between the sobs, which welled to the surface despite her efforts, "Read this then you'll know for sure what has happened."

Eileen scrutinized the letter. "Yes, I see: I suspected as much after your father had brought that package up for you at lunchtime," she said. There followed a long silence. "Had you ever met Alan's family?" Eileen asked eventually.

"No," Shirley replied bluntly.

"Ah," Eileen replied, that single syllable implying that she was not therefore surprised at the tone of the letter.

In the absence both of a living grandmother worthy of the name and of her mother, who had, in her opinion, deserted her family so callously, Shirley was comforted by Eileen's discreet and watchful presence, and began to regard her as a surrogate grandmother. Her insubstantial form flitted from room to room, tidying, cleaning, performing all the household chores and speaking only when she sensed that Shirley was ready to talk. "I have made a decision," Shirley announced to Eileen one afternoon in early September. "I shall join the WAAF."

Eileen stood stock still in the centre of the room, raising only one eyebrow. She did not express any surprise, shock or negative reaction. "What makes you want to do that, Shirley?" she asked innocently, although of course she already knew the answer.

"If I could fly, I would go straight into battle in a Spitfire and knock out those Messerschmitts one by one, but as women aren't allowed to fly, I'll have to shoot them from the ground with anti-aircraft guns. I think the WAAF are trained to do that." Shirley's answer came forcibly, relaying the unmistakable message that the WAAF would enable her to exact revenge on the enemy in active service.

"I understand," Eileen said with characteristic calmness. "I've heard they are calling up all women between the ages of eighteen and forty-three, so I suppose you might as well join up now while you have the choice. Otherwise you might find yourself working in an armaments factory. Shall I come with you to the recruiting office?"

Early the next day, for the first time since 14th July, Shirley, in company with Eileen, left the flat. Reggie was mystified both by his daughter's sudden decision to go out of doors and by her air of defiance, which was in such contrast to her grief-stricken appearance of the previous weeks. Eileen gestured to him to keep quiet. Half an hour later the two women were sitting waiting to be seen in the recruitment office. A couple of young men had stood up and offered them their seats, undoubtedly on account of Eileen's age, but Shirley was pleased to be able to sit down. Weeks of inactivity had left all her muscles taut, except for her left leg, which was limp. Not only that, she was also feeling somewhat indigestive. This she ascribed to her recent irregular eating habits. When her turn came, she impassively answered all the questions put to her and signed the necessary documents. The fact that she had already acted as an ARP warden helped her case. She was told to return for a medical examination later in the week.

For that appointment, Shirley told Eileen that she was capable of going alone. Eileen did not try to gainsay her, but let her do as she wished. In the doctor's waiting room she gathered from the conversation of the other would-be recruits that in the long period of her torpor since 14th July, the war had come much closer: the *Luftwaffe* had taken to bombing airfields in the south-east of England with the intention of putting the RAF out of existence while its planes were still on the ground, and then had moved on to armaments factories and ironworks elsewhere. Though why on 22nd August bombs should have fallen on Harrow, nobody had a clue. "I think they were offloading their bombs anywhere they could," a man said with some authority. Apparently they had dropped bombs on cities on the south coast and Birmingham, Bradford, Liverpool and many other places. "They reckon a thousand of them are coming over every day," one man reported. "Good for Mr Churchill for sending our lot out to bomb Berlin. That'll show 'em!" Shirley listened open-mouthed. This indeed was a clarion call to wake up to the current reality. Her determination was fired: she would fight to the last drop of her blood to honour and avenge her fiancé's memory. Had she been a man she would have been prepared to take the *Luftwaffe* on single-handedly.

It was her turn to be examined. "Are you in good health, Miss Marlow?" the doctor asked.

"I think so," she replied. "I had infantile paralysis in 1937, but I've recovered well and the sooner I can get to work in the WAAF, the happier I shall be!" Here she was proudly conscious of echoing a phrase in Alan's letter. The doctor revealed himself to be understanding almost to the point of intuition.

"Have you lost someone dear to you in this war, Miss Marlow?" he enquired while she lay on his couch and he conducted his examination.

"Yes. My fiancé," she confided.

"I'm sorry," he said, adding, "I've lost one of my brothers. We must fight in every way we can, mustn't we?" She wholeheartedly agreed with him. "Right," he said, "you can put your clothes on again, then come and sit down. I've finished my examination, but I must ask you a few more questions first." His questions were searching and concentrated on personal matters to which Shirley, in her ignorance of human biology, had not given much attention, considering them insignificant by comparison with everything that was happening around her.

Once dressed, she sat down on a chair by his desk expecting him to give her a clean bill of health, but watched anxiously as he thumbed through some papers and made notes. "Well," he said, taking a deep breath in, "I would say that the shock of your fiancé's death has put a great strain on you and you have not been eating properly, although of course that is difficult in the present circumstances. Otherwise, you are in good health. Are you a games teacher by the way? You have a very strong heart and seem quite robust." She told him that she was a dancer. "Good, good," he said, "but I'm afraid I cannot pass you for entry to the WAAF."

Shirley was dumbstruck. "Oh, but that's what I want more than anything! I don't care if I'm not fully fit. I don't care about anything except fighting!" she said when she had caught her breath.

"That's not the point," the doctor said. "You haven't asked me why I can't pass you."

"Why not, then?" she asked.

"Because," he replied, "you are expecting a baby."

Startled, she stared at the doctor. "Surely not?" she exclaimed. "We didn't have time to be together very much."

"That makes no difference," he said, "but now after so much weeping you can begin to dream again!"

57

Shirley dawdled home reflecting on the doctor's prognosis, but, lighter of heart than she had been for weeks, a lilt began to creep into her step. The news of the pregnancy had taken her completely unawares since, in her hazy understanding of biological matters and without a mother to advise her, she had never expected that a baby might so quickly be the outcome of her passionate encounters with Alan. When the truth of what the doctor had said started to sink in, she had laughed, and the doctor, a white-haired man who must have been too old for military service, had laughed with her. "Yet another nicely brought-up young lady who has never been told the facts of life! I've seen plenty of girls like you, but they are not all as pleased as you are at the news. How will your parents react, do you think?"

Shirley had no qualms. "I don't think it will be a problem at all," she replied with a confident smile. "My father had met my fiancé and liked him." The confident smile disappeared as a catch in her throat interrupted her words in mid-flow. Faltering, she eventually continued, "Of course he knows what happened to him." She dabbed her eyes and her nose. "My brother won't be bothered and my mother is away: in fact she has left us, but I have an old aunt at home who will be really pleased," she stuttered in a vain attempt to regain her confidence.

The doctor nodded. "Well, Miss Marlow, I understand how you have suffered and I am sorry, but I have to say you are a very lucky young lady. It sounds as if your baby will have a good home. Of course you will not be able to join the armed forces, although I see here that you are an ARP warden; I suppose you can carry on working at that for the time being, if you are careful." He glanced at her notes. "Let's see, I reckon you are about seven or eight weeks pregnant. I'll write a letter for you to take to your own doctor and then he'll be able to keep an eye on you. You can expect to feel sick in the mornings until about the twelfth week; that's to be expected. You should be fit and well for the rest of the pregnancy, but do take care of yourself." With that the medical came to a close.

The lilt in her step turned into a dance when an extraordinary revelation flashed into her mind: she had not lost Alan entirely after all, for he would live again! He was already living, in the miracle child she was carrying! She had cried and cried, as Alan, and the doctor, had predicted, but this was her chance to dream again. The baby would be a boy and he would have the same wavy hair and bright eyes as his father. He would indeed be the image of his father and would inherit his intelligence and his winning personality. She would cherish him and would want nothing more from life than to see him grow up healthy and strong in a world where, thanks in part to his father's courage, peace would be restored. She would continue with her ARP commitments, but having this baby was so much more fulfilling than seeking revenge on the Germans by joining the WAAF. She would teach him French and might take him to France after the war.

In a flight of fancy she imagined that one day she might even take him to meet his grandparents in their Victorian vicarage over in Camberwell. They would be astonished, naturally, but the similarity between the baby and their lost son would leave them in no doubt that he was their grandchild. He would gladden their sorrowing hearts and they would be certain to take her and the child into the bosom of their family, doubtless regretting that they had not met her sooner. She would have to explain gently why Alan had not introduced her to them, but that was well within her powers. Her brain racing with plans for the future, she arrived at her door. No sound came from the shop, where Cousin Archie and Tilly were bent over some papers, probably the week's accounts.

"Hello!" she called out as she climbed the stairs to the kitchen, where Eileen was taking a cake out of the oven; its warm, delectable aroma filled the flat. She was startled when Shirley burst in, making more noise than she had in the whole of the past several weeks. "You will be the first person to hear my good news, Eileen," she cried out. "I'm going to have a baby!" Eileen turned from the stove and leant against the kitchen cupboard, overwhelmed by the whirlwind that had blown in.

"Ah, I am thrilled for you, my dear!" she stammered. Wiping her hands on a tea towel, she said, "A baby will help ease the pain of your loss, dear, and, er, I can start knitting!" Warming to her subject, she continued, "I shall so much enjoy having someone other than Archie to knit for. Baby clothes and baby blankets will be so much nicer than pullovers and socks. If that's all right with you?" She looked at Shirley, unsure of her response. "Perhaps you would prefer your grandmother to make these things for you?" she enquired nervously.

"Granny Marlow?" Shirley exclaimed in disbelief. "She's never made anything in her life! She wouldn't know how. Anyhow, you are much more of a grandmother to me than she ever was, and I don't think she ought to be told about this. She wouldn't understand. And please don't say anything until I've told Pa!"

Eileen beamed a delighted smile that quickly became more guarded. "I should send you to lie down dear," she said, "but I was in the shop about half an hour ago when a visitor for your father arrived, so I came upstairs to make a cake for their tea. The door's closed, so you probably didn't hear their voices." She returned to her preparations adding, "This cake's rather short of margarine, but I put more eggs in it because I have plenty of them, from the farm, you know. I've brought you half a dozen," she laughed, and added, "and just in time it seems, because you will have to eat as well as possible, but now you had better go and meet the visitor; I'll bring the tea through in a minute!"

"Who is it?" Shirley asked. Eileen answered rather cagily that it was someone she had never seen before, but that it was obviously someone important, because Reggie had left the shop immediately to take that person upstairs.

Shirley was baffled. Visitors were few and far between these days, except for the customers who assembled in the shop for a chat. Even Granny Marlow phoned much less frequently. She went quietly to listen at the door; she could hear a hum of conversation from within, and detected her father's voice, but the visitor's voice was too quiet to hear. Her gentle tap produced no result, and she was going to knock more loudly when Ted came bounding up the stairs. "Shh!" she whispered, motioning towards him with a finger on her lips. "Eileen says there's a visitor in there, but she's not sure who it is. I forgot to ask if it was a man or a woman. Will you come in with me?"

She tapped again, but still there was no response from within, so Ted opened the door. He stood motionless on the threshold, barring Shirley's way into the room and obscuring her view. Eileen came out of the kitchen, carrying a laden tea tray. "Well, well, you two," said she, "are you going to let me pass? Why don't you go in?" Ted had no choice but to advance into the room, and Shirley followed him, allowing Eileen to enter and put the tray down on the table. Only then did

Shirley look up: at first, as expected, she saw her father slumped in his armchair; then she saw a small, elegantly dressed woman with permed hair standing by the window.

"Maman!" she exclaimed. That word, uttered harshly, resounded with a joyless reproach. Her mother came towards her with her arms out-stretched, but Shirley shrank away, so Jacqueline turned to Ted instead. "*You* are pleased to see me, aren't you, Édouard?" she asked in French.

"*Oui, Maman*," he said dutifully, before turning his back on her and going across to the table to pour the tea into the delicate china cups, a chore at which he was not very practised. Shirley joined him at the table and took charge of the teapot. She poured four cups and gave two of them to Ted to distribute, one to each parent.

"Your mother flew over in the diplomatic bag!" their father said in a half-hearted attempt at a joke, which was enough to arouse Ted's interest.

"Ah, Maman, so you came on one of those flying boats?" he asked agog. "They say it's a long journey but very luxurious! Pa and I have seen them in the newsreels. They land at Southampton, don't they?" Gratified to have found an opening, at least with her son, Jacqueline proceeded to describe her flight across the Atlantic, without elaborat-ing on the contents of the diplomatic bag. Ted was captivated by her account of the unpredictable and hazardous journey over the vast extent of the Atlantic Ocean by day and by night, so she took advantage of his fascination to expand on it at length and dispel the gloom that her presence had so clearly generated.

Meanwhile, Shirley still hovered by the table, impervious to and unim-pressed by the traveller's tale of huge distances across the seas covered in a matter of hours in the extraordinary, gravity-defying new form of transport. Instead, in the empty space inside her where otherwise there would have arisen a bubbling excitement and admiration, there grew a welling sense of anger and resentment, fuelled by the memory of all those times when she had missed her mother, all those times when she had longed for her companionship, help and advice, all those times when she had wondered where she was and when she would come home to her family. Her mother had been her best friend, but that best friend had cruelly abandoned her until of late she had begun to fade from view, eclipsed by the more urgent considerations of wartime, of love found and lost, leaving only the bittersweet trace of a domestic happi-ness destroyed in favour of a gilded, peaceful existence thousands of miles away. Jacqueline was no better than a traitor who had no right to come, oh so casually, back into the family home and expect a warm welcome. Prodigal mothers were not prodigal sons and could not expect the same treatment.

Shirley struggled against the mounting swell of conflicting emotions: on the one hand she wanted to run into her lost mother's arms and hug her; on the other there had been too much deceit and distance between them for her ever to find it in herself to love her mother again. Jacqueline turned to her with a pleading smile. "Please, Chérie, come and give me a hug," she begged, then plunged her hand into her coat pocket and produced a small box. "Look, I have brought you something special." She opened the box and held it out to Shirley, who gasped in amazement. "This is your pendant," her mother said, "I have bought it back from the pawnshop for you. You see, when you were so very ill I was desperate about the huge bills for your treatment and the doctor's bills for your father's treatment that we couldn't pay, so I pawned the pendant and bought you a cheap replacement instead. It was the closest thing the jeweller could find. I always meant to pay you back for the real one, but I couldn't tell you about it at the time because you were still not at all well, and I didn't want to upset you." She paused to see if her words were having any positive effect, which they were not. Although near to tears, she continued regardless. "Now I have money to buy you whatever you want, real diamond pendants, dresses, fur coats, whatever you like. So please take this and show me you love me!"

While Reggie, searching in some remote corner of his memory for the subject in question, subsided deeper into his armchair, and Ted looked on with confusion written all over his face, Shirley, staring her mother straight in the eye, took the box and flung it on the floor. "So you think you can buy me, do you? Why should I be at all surprised at that!" she screamed, red in the face as her anger burst out, overcoming her gentler emotions. "You treated me like a child, taking my pendant without telling me, although I suspected that what you brought home wasn't the real one, and then you left us, doubtless for that Monsieur Lavasseur! Now you think you can waltz in here back from your cushy life in America and pretend that we are all one happy family again! Well, I tell you, we're not! Go away! I don't ever want to see you again!" She dashed out in floods of angry tears.

58

ENTR'ACTE

In the seclusion of her bedroom, Shirley's rage boiled over in hot, angry tears at her mother's presumption and her insensitivity. How could she simply turn up without warning to visit the family she had abandoned years ago, and expect to be welcomed with open arms? Clearly, after all the glamour of her life in Washington, DC, the tailored clothes – the shiny shoes, the crocodile handbag – she was not intending to take up residence in the small flat above a newsagent's shop in grimy south London. What's more, she had flown over in a luxury aeroplane, which abruptly introduced images of other types of aircraft into Shirley's fevered brain: not comfortable passenger planes but fragile, small, exposed war planes, Spitfires and the like, so that at once and inevitably she was plunged into searing recollections of Alan's terrible fate. What a shocking contrast that was with her mother's relatively secure and easy mode of travel!

In the United States, thousands of miles away from the theatre of war, she could have no idea of the pressures of life in wartime London, no awareness of the privations, the shortages, the lack of good food or of the blackout, no understanding of the constant peril of bombardment, the mounting death toll, the sacrifice of so many, above all the loss of Alan, whom she, Shirley's own mother, had met fleetingly, only that once on the Channel crossing in rough weather. True, she had sent the passes to allow Shirley to travel to France and bring Ted home, but she hadn't bothered to ask about their return, which had been so perilous. As far as Shirley was aware, she also knew nothing of Ted's work for General de Gaulle and the dangers that that involved. And had she been there to accompany her daughter to the doctor for her medical that very day, she, not Eileen, would have been the first to learn of her daughter's pregnancy, which in a matter of months would make her a grandmother. This last was news that Shirley vowed she would never tell her.

Had Maman even taken the trouble to write regularly to ask about the many circumstances affecting her family, let alone ask for news of her father and the farm, rather than relying on packages of silk stockings sent through the post at Christmas and on birthdays, the outcome of her visit might have been very different. Communication had at the best of times been difficult on account of the distance and the time change between them, and today the remaining tenuous links had been broken by her attempt to buy her daughter's affection. Her admission that she had pawned the diamond pendant and replaced it with a cheap copy without telling her daughter was bad enough, but then, after a long absence, coolly and unashamedly to arrive bringing that diamond as a sort of peace offering was unbelievably insulting. Almost worse was the embarrassing recollection, revived by the reappearance of the gemstone, of the suspicions that Shirley herself had cast on Francesca and her subsequent treatment of that innocent, friendly, hard-working Italian girl who, by rights, being a close relative of the Salvatores, should in any case have inherited the pendant.

Shirley pummelled her pillow in frustration: why was it that whenever she had wonderful news to tell, as she had today, something bad always intervened to cut short her excitement and her pleasure? Why did these bolts from the blue always fall on her head? Life was hard enough in the wider world, so why should her own mother make it even harder for her? The only way to cope with the present, she decided, was to keep one's own counsel and not share her private life, her thoughts, her hopes or her decisions with anyone else.

Gradually, as her fury subsided and the floods of tears abated, she closed her eyes and sobbed quietly at the loss of the mother who truly had been so dear to her, who had been her constant companion, with whom she had shared so many good times throughout her childhood and her adolescence, who had given her so much encouragement, who had found life so difficult in England and who had cared devotedly and uncomplainingly for their father for years. Perhaps there was still time for a reconciliation, perhaps just a hug would be enough to bring them closer. She opened her bedroom door and heard heavy steps descending the lower staircase, which meant that Pa must be on his way down to the shop. Moments later she detected voices on the landing, which then grew fainter as her mother and Ted also went downstairs and out of the building.

She tiptoed into the living room. The door was ajar; there was no one inside. Ted had definitely gone out, their father was still down in the shop to judge by the hubbub of customers coming up from below, and Maman had most certainly left. The jewel box with the diamond in it lay on the table. Shirley picked it up and took it back to her room, where she pushed it to the bottom of her underwear drawer to join its fake substitute. On second thoughts she took it out again and opened the lid. The pendant was breathtakingly beautiful, glistening and glowing in the early-evening light. She pulled out the fake pendant and put the two side by side. There was no comparison between them.

Father, son and daughter ate supper in gloomy silence that evening until Ted spoke. "I was very surprised to find Maman here," he said. "What was that business with a pendant about? I didn't understand what was going on at all. I thought that was finished with ages ago…" Turning enquiringly to Shirley, he met with an angry glare, which spoke louder than words. "Be quiet, you idiot!" it said. "Ah, of course, I had forgotten," he muttered. Only then did Shirley remember with relief that she had told her father that the pendant was a fake a while ago, and anyhow that afternoon he had hardly seemed to notice anything, so preoccupied was he with his own thoughts, so she hoped he hadn't really registered what was happening.

She shrugged and whispered to Ted, "I'll tell you about it one day."

He took the hint and, changing the subject, announced, "Well, I have to say Maman was very helpful to me; she brought me the addresses of some contacts of hers and I went to call on them after she'd gone." If Reggie had shown no interest in the drama of the diamond pendant, his glum features sank into a veritable slough of despond on hearing Ted's announcement.

"What do you mean by that?" he asked his son wearily. "What can these contacts do for you?"

"I don't know yet," Ted replied, tempering his excitement. "I shall have to see. Maybe I'll be coming and going a bit, but I expect I'll be here quite often. And anyway, as Maman is back, she'll be here to keep you company."

"No, she's not back!" their father roared, fully aroused from his piti-ful state. "She flew over with a diplomatic delegation and simply came here to ask for a divorce before returning to America!"

CHAPTER 58

That night, the blood-curling wailings of a haunted spirit recoiling before the horrors and spectres of a past war rent the air as they teemed out of Reggie's bedroom and echoed through the darkened flat with their ghoulish sounds. Shirley stuffed cotton wool in her ears and turned her face to the wall.

TO BE CONTINUED

Acknowledgements

I am extremely grateful to the following kind people who have spared the time to give me help and advice in the writing of *Cry to Dream Again*.
To:

Simon Fielding for sharing his compendious knowledge of the First and the Second World War,

Simon Palmer for his advice on the challenges and circumstances facing a "little boat" crossing the Channel in wartime,

Jon Iveson, the curator of the fascinating and excellent Dover Museum, for useful information about the Port of Dover in the years up to and including the Second World War,

Jane Muntz of Umberslade Children's Farm in Tanworth-in-Arden in Warwickshire, for sharing her expertise in farming methods and machinery in the 1930s,

Jane Hands, ballet dancer and teacher, for vetting and advising on the text, and the standards required of an aspiring ballerina,

Tina Pilgrim, the director of King Slocombe School of Dance, Cambridge, for taking time from her very busy schedule to read a part of the text, and for her encouraging reaction to it,

Dame Beryl Grey for sharing an invaluable piece of information about life as a young dancer at Sadler's Wells in the 1930s

And to the staff both of Sadler's Wells and Islington Public Library for their help in allowing me to examine the Sadler's Wells archive.

Un grand merci to my dear friends and consultants in northern France, especially Jean-Pierre and Béatrice Degand, and Monsieur François Masse, who have given freely of their time, their memories and their knowledge to help me create a tableau of life in France in the period covered by this novel.

Alessandro Gallenzi of Alma Books, my publisher, and all his highly reliable and helpful team, especially my excellent editor, Alex Gingell, Alma's publicist, Elisabetta Minervini, Will Dady and Christian Müller.

Jonathan for his endless support for my projects generally and extraordinary patience in sorting out my day-to-day computing problems.

My lovely family for encouraging me in my writing.

ALSO BY JANE HAWKING
SILENT MUSIC
FIRST IN THE 'IMMORTAL SOULS' SERIES

ISBN 978-1-84688-412-2 • £9.99

Growing up in London in the aftermath of the Second
World War, Ruth is an observant and thoughtful child who
finds herself in a confusing and mysterious adult world.
She seeks refuge in her memories of her idyllic stays with
her grandparents in the picturesque East Anglian countryside – which provide comforting visions of a simpler life.
As she comes to terms with her surroundings and her own
adolescence, Ruth finds the motivation to pursue the tantalizing dream which has governed her childhood, and dis-
covers some family secrets along the way.

A coming-of-age novel about the unpredictable nature of
human behaviour and about taking control of one's destiny,
Silent Music is a timeless portrait of post-war Britain, as
well as a lyrical paean to hope and aspiration.

TRAVELLING TO INFINITY

THE TRUE STORY BEHIND THE AWARD-WINNING FILM

THE THEORY OF EVERYTHING

Jane Hawking

THE NUMBER ONE BESTSELLER
ISBN 978-1-84688-366-8 • £7.99

THE INCREDIBLE STORY OF
JANE AND STEPHEN HAWKING

His Mind Changed Our World. Her Love Changed His.

"Stephen Hawking may think in 11 dimensions, but his
first wife has learnt to love in several."
The Sunday Times

"What becomes of time when a marriage unravels?
And what becomes of the woman who has located her
whole self within its sphere? For Jane Hawking, the physics
of love and loss are set in a private universe."
The Guardian

"Jane writes about her former husband with
tenderness, respect and protectiveness."
Sunday Express

 eBook: 978-1-84688-373-6